THE PROFESSIONALS

BOB ROCCA

A BearManor Media Publication

The Professionals

CI5: Criminal Intelligence 5. A team specially formed by the Home Office to combat an increasing wave of terrorism. Special men - experts from all branches of the army, the SAS, the police. It offers tough, hard men to deal with tough, hard situations. Their brief? To keep Britain clean, keep it safe. Protect it from anarchy, from acts of terror, crimes against the public.

Lewis Collins and Martin Shaw are Bodie, ex-paratrooper, ex-mercenary, and Doyle, ex-CID detective, two of the deadliest special agents on the block...deadly spirited, often abrasive but always tempered by mutual respect...and they always get results.

Gordon Jackson portrays George Cowley, the straight-talking chief of CI5 in a series that takes an intriguing look at the loyalties, treacheries, perils and dramas of a government department battling against the real world of espionage, organised crime and terrorism.

THE PROFESSIONALS
Copyright © 2009 (revised 2010) Bob Rocca. All rights reserved.

All photographs used are from the author's private collection and reproduced herewith with the kind permission of the copyright owners **Mark I Productions**. Others are courtesy of David Cherrill, Shirley Harris, Ted Hawes, Simon Hume, and Stephen Snow.
The photographs featured in this book are reproduced in the spirit of publicity and are copyright to the respective copyright holders. No attempt is made to supersede any of these copyrights.

All rights reserved. No part of this publication may be reproduced in any form or by means, electronic, mechanical, digital, photocopying, or recording, except for the inclusion in a review, without permission in writing from either the publisher or author.

Published by **BearManor Media**.

ISBN-10 1-59393-331-2
ISBN-13 978-1-59393-331-9

Book and cover design by Bob Rocca.

CONTENTS

ACKNOWLEDGMENTS..................................page 7

FOREWORD..page 9

PREFACE..page 11

INTRODUCTION..page 13

SERIES I..page 15

SERIES II..page 151

SERIES III..page 281

SERIES IV..page 423

SERIES V..page 553

THE ACTORS..page 607

MERCHANDISE..page 623

Martin Shaw filming the first series Title sequence during production on THE FEMALE FACTOR.

ACKNOWLEDGMENTS

I WOULD like to thank the following people for their help and contribution to this book:

JAN HOLLOWAY for her continued support and invaluable help.

From the Mark I Production personnel:
Brian Clemens, Laurie Johnson and **Albert Fennell** for making it all happen.

Dennis Abey (who recalled each episode with great accuracy), William Alexander (who allowed me access to all the production schedules from series 3. Sometimes it's worth being a magpie?), Rufus Andrews, Geoff Austin, Del Baker, Howard Baker, David Barron, Sue Black, Gavin Bocquet, William Brayne, Peter Brayham, Chris Brock, Al Burgess, Peter Carter (who pointed me in the right direction with location information after viewing various stills), David Cherrill (who allowed me to view various call sheets, stills and scripts), Mike Collins, Fraser Copp, Ray Corbett, Peter Cotton (a fantastic memory with reference to locations from some 30 years ago), John Crome (for his comments on *You'll Be All Right*), Ken Court, Peter Crowhurst, Colin Dandridge (who viewed ten episodes in the space of a week. Your information was greatly appreciated, thanks), Gregory Dark, Nick Daubeny, Brian Elvin, Willie Fonfe, Stuart Freeman, Ron Fry, Mervyn Gerrard, Shirley Harris, Ted Hawes, Frank Henson (thanks for the stills), Jo Hidderley, Simon Hinkly, Chris Howard, Simon Hume (huge thanks for the stills), Tony Imi, Peter Joyce, John Keen, Norman Langley (who took time to view all the episodes he worked on), Vernon Layton, Cheryl Leigh, Denis Lewiston, Sue Love, John Maskall, Robin McDonald, Phil Meheux, Raymond Menmuir (for clearing up the loose ends!), Malcolm Middleton, Chris Munro, Barry Myall, Gerry O'Hara, Gladys Pearce, Trevor Puckle, Pat Rambaut, Ron Purdie (who viewed various tapes and without whose help I would have been lost. It took a few years to get the book published Ron, but got there in the end), Guido Reidy, Pennant Roberts, Nigel Seal, Ken Shane, Anthony Simmons, Malcolm Smith, Stephen Snow (for all the location info, and stills from *The Untouchables*), John S. Smith, Dennis Spooner (whom I was lucky enough to speak with some years back), Chris Streeter, Roy P. Stevens, Roy Stevens, Robin Tarsnane (for viewing hundreds of stills), Gerry Toomey, Malcolm Vinson, Kenneth Ware, Andrew Warren, Chris Webb (who allowed me access to various production notes), Bill Westley, Derek Whitehurst (who took time out to view the episodes he worked on), Jeff Woodbridge and Terry Yorke.

Thanks are also due to Werner Schmitz who allowed to me to use various extracts from his German publication, *Die Profis*

Also, all the help I received at the BT Archive, Tony Buller, Leon Cerri, Sarah Christmas (Granada Media), Maria St. Clare, Colonna Press, a huge thanks to Alan Field, Harry Fielder, Des Glass, Dacre Holloway, Cheryl Kennedy, Les Martin, Dave Matthews, Ben Ohmart (for having faith in the project), Queen Anne Press, Christian Ray (Granada Media), Barry Reynolds (Ford Motor Company), my brother Daniel Rocca (who navigated as we searched London for the filming locations), Dave Rogers, Stephen Snow, Carla Wansey, Anja Wanka, and Alun Webb.

THE PROFESSIONALS: *Lewis Collins, Gordon Jackson, Martin Shaw.*

FOREWORD

IF good books are like wine, demanding care, dedication and most of all, time, then this book should be a rare vintage! Bob started his research as far back as 1986, just when the series had finished on a crest of devotion, so it is apt that it now reaches fruitition when *The Professionals* is again reappearing, delighting old fans and making new ones.

As a writer myself I appreciate the long and lonely hours he must have spent pouring over his subject. The result is, undoubtedly, a work to be savoured, packed with detail, meticulously ferreted out information and best of all, love.

When I created *The Professionals* way back in the late 70's, the best I could hope for was a reasonable run on TV, and perhaps make a few friends along the way. It is a constant source of pleasure that I made so very many, and even more so that so many remain loyal to the series today, enabling it to run and run again. I am told that our dyed in the wool fans never tire of watching Bodie & Doyle leap from their Capri to tackle yet another villain, and along the way find time to argue, disagree, but always 'cover' each other when the chips are down. Of such teams are legends made; I hope the team I dreamed up will continue to entertain, and that such devoted scholars as Bob Rocca will continue to document their exploits. Thanks Bob and, for a long arduous research completed so immaculately - congratulations!

Brian Clemens
November 2007

Actors Martin Shaw and Lewis Collins on the set of NO STONE in May 1981.

PREFACE

TRANSMISSION *and production order:* The stories listed in this book are all presented in their production order. This differs wildly from the chronological order of transmission. Each section, therefore, contains a transmitted order, which intermixes episodes from various series - to avoid any confusion, these episodes are indicated where necessary.

Shooting/Location Schedules and dates: The information contained in this book, on both the location sites and dates when filming occurred, has been compiled, wherever possible, from the official production documentation.

The primary documents used for sourcing the location details have been the official location/shooting schedules provided by the location managers. However, even this provides limited information with TBA (To Be Advised) inserted on numerous occasions when a filming site had not been found within the time allocated to the production of the said document. All other information has been gleaned from other production documentation, scripts, actor and crew recollections, etc.

All locations, wherever possible, have been referred to under their original designation at the time the relevant filming for the programme occurred. All locations have been verified personally, however, some sites have been significantly altered over the years or even been demolished completely, but the details given should be adequate to find the locations with the least amount of investigation.

Martin Shaw, Lewis Collins, and Gordon Jackson: THE PROFESSIONALS. Pictured here on location in Black Park, Fulmer, Buckinghamshire, during filming on the story A HIDING TO NOTHING in June 1979.

INTRODUCTION

FOR a programme like *The Professionals*, the production initially revolved around two permanent figures answerable to the production company, the producer and the script editor. The producer assumed responsibility for the series, artistically, editorially and financially and, as such, he was in overall control of the finished product. Working closely with him was the script editor, who bore the responsibility for commissioning and editing of the series' scripts, and for ensuring that what they contained could effectively be realised within the budget assigned to the programme. Thereafter, the conditions closely followed those for film production.

The Screenplay: for 'ideas', which were then discussed with the producer and script editor. The most promising being written up into an outline up to around fifteen pages. If accepted, the writer would go to a first draft screenplay which, following input from the producer and script editor would go to a second draft, usually with the script editor contributing major revisions.

Pre-Production: Directors would then be assigned those screenplays, which, the producer felt would best be suited to. They would be invited to make suggestions, criticisms and ask for rewrites around the first or second draft stage. Each episode had two weeks pre-production, casting, finding locations, making screenplay changes and two weeks shooting.

One episode alone would produce mountains of paperwork, with one of the first documents produced at the beginning of each series being the unit list, which was issued to all the personnel working on that particular batch of episodes, ranging from the art director to the unit doctors. This document provided contact addresses and phone numbers for all involved in that particular series and would be updated during filming as, and when, a member of a particular department left the production.

Once a story had been commissioned, and a suitable director appointed, a location manager would be assigned to track down suitable locations appropriate to that script. He would negotiate for their use, get the relevant permissions to film from the police and any other interested parties, sort out the parking for the unit vehicles, catering vans, make travel arrangements, etc. He would seek out the most prominent requirement after reviewing the script, and once this primary site like a mansion house or gas works has been found, efforts would be made to find any secondary locations within the same area, thus keeping any necessary travelling time down to a minimum.

Once a set of locations had been found, the director would then assess their suitability, either by examining photographs taken by the location manager during the recce or, on occasion, by visiting the suggested location with the first assistant director.

Following the confirmation of the locations by the production manager, who would determine the costs involved in travelling, and setting up a production unit at each site, one of the next tasks by the location manager would be to assemble a movement order: a document detailing the scenes to be shot at each different location, with thorough directions, and maps if deemed necessary, on how the production unit could travel to each area with the minimum of fuss.

The production manager would then decide which scenes had to be filmed first and in the main, would choose the primary shots from the story, with minor sequences like car run-bys or establishing shots, being left towards the end of the shoot, or even allocated to a second unit, whose prime objective was to complete such scenes, which were usually achieved using stand-ins or doubles.

A location schedule would then be prepared stating the date of filming, the set name, site address with contacts, and a police contact at each. This was accompanied by a shooting schedule, which detailed the scene numbers and characters required, special requirements needed, such as animals or weaponry, and details of any 'extended days', which required extra filming.

A cast list was then added, which included details of all the characters to be portrayed by the artistes listed on the same document. The information on this document included the artistes' address and agent's name, coupled with any special stipulations such as photo shoots, for which extra negotiation in terms of reimbursement would be needed. As this document contained personal information it was only made available to the various heads of each department.

The first assistant director would then assemble, in conjunction with the director, a call sheet, which would indicate details of a days filming together with information on which artistes would be required on various sets and what scenes were scheduled to be completed. The purpose of this document, coupled with the movement order, was to ensure that everyone in the production unit, which could include anything up to sixty people, would know where and when they should be at any given moment. Once completed, this document would be circulated not only to all the members of the production team, but also to the various heads of production at the finance companies, insurance agents, transportation co-ordinators, publicity department, caterers, etc.

Production: As the series went into production, there could be four or five screenplays in a more or less completed state. The first episode then went into its four-week cycle, and the next episode, started pre-production two-weeks later with a different director, lighting cameraman and crew, though this would apply more from the third series. Thus there were effectively two units working in parallel on a ten-day turn around.

Post Production: With shooting finished, the director would work for a week with the editor, then the producer and the editor spend another two weeks in the cutting rooms. The music composer would then write and record the score before the episode was dubbed and sent for negative cutting and printing at the processing laboratory.

SERIES I

"Anarchy. Acts of terror. Crimes against the public. To combat it I've got special men, experts from the army, the police, from every service. These are THE PROFESSIONALS!"

THE PROFESSIONALS: Martin Shaw, Gordon Jackson, and Lewis Collins filming for the first series 'original' Title sequence.

THE PROFESSIONALS arrived on British television screens on 30th December 1977, from the creative force behind the filmed episodes of *The Avengers*, and *The New Avengers*. Not only was creator Brian Clemens the leading stylist on these shows, but he had also contributed to the development and direction of *The Champions*, *The Persuaders!* and some of the earliest episodes of *Danger Man*.

Born 1931 in Croydon, Surrey, Clemens did National Service at Aldershot and then worked his way up from messenger boy to copywriter at the J. Walter Thompson advertising agency. It was while he was a copywriter that he submitted a play to the BBC, *Valid for Single Journey Only* (1955) that brought him to the attention of independent producers the Danziger brothers, where he scripted numerous B-movies and episodes of *Mark Sabre, Sabre Of London* and *The Man From Interpol*. Moving on he penned episodes of *Armchair Theatre, Sir Francis Drake, Man Of The World, The Sentimental*

Agent, The Avengers, ITC's *Danger Man, Intrigue* and *The Protectors*. Along the way he also provided scripts under his Tony O'Grady pseudonym for both *HG Wells Invisible Man* and *The Baron*. He also found time to return to the BBC to act as a scribe on *Adam Adamant Lives!*

In 1972 he created the domestic sitcom series *My Wife Next Door* for the BBC, a BAFTA winning show about a divorced young couple that buy cottages in the country and find themselves unwitting neighbours. Back in his stride, Clemens developed the chilling twist-in-the-tale anthology series *Thriller* (*Menace* in the US). He also worked on the features, *And Soon The Darkness, Dr. Jekyll and Sister Hyde, See No Evil (aka: Blind Terror)* and, in 1972, the Hammer fantasy horror *Captain Kronos, Vampire Hunter* as producer, writer and director. The following year he scripted the movie, incidentally with Martin Shaw in a guest role, *The Golden Voyage Of Sinbad*.

Clemens' partners in the Avengers (Film and Television) Enterprises production company, which had been set up in 1975 to produce *The New Avengers*, were long-time associates - producer Albert Fennell, and composer Laurie Johnson, whose production assistant, Trisha Robinson, became the company's production co-ordinator. Linda Matthews (later Pearson), who had been producer Monty Berman's (*Randall & Hopkirk (Deceased), Jason King* and *Department S*) long time associate, became the production secretary.

Albert Fennell, born in Chiswick, London, on 29th March 1920, had been in the industry since the 1940's initially as a designer on *Root Of All Evil* (1947), progressing to production supervisor on the 1946 swashbuckler *Caravan* and the atmospheric horror *The Innocents* (1961). Two years later he worked on the Oscar nominated *This Sporting Life*, starring Richard Harris. Throughout the Sixties, he was working on films such as the road-to-ruin melodrama *Bitter Harvest*, the Oscar nominated World War II drama *Tunes Of Glory*, starring Alec Guiness and John Mills, and the black magic horror *Night Of The Eagle (Burn Witch, Burn!)*, directed by Sidney Hayers and starring a pre-*Jason King*, Peter Wyngarde. Later, joining Brian Clemens to produce *The Avengers*. In the next decade he continued his partnership with Brian Clemens and co-produced *And Soon The Darkness, Dr. Jekyll and Sister Hyde,* and *Captain Kronos, Vampire Hunter*.

Born in Hampstead, London, on 7th February 1927, Laurence Reginald Ward Johnson (Laurie Johnson) studied at the Royal College of Music and later taught there. He spent four years in the Coldstream Guards for his National Service. At the age of twenty-one he began composing and arranging for the Ted Heath Band and went on to write for Geraldo, Jack Parnell, Ambrose and others. He entered the film industry in 1955 and, considered very much of the old school, composed for over four hundred films. He broke into television by constructing the hard-hitting theme to the police series, *No Hiding Place*, and it's spin-off *Echo Four-Two*.

Over the next few years he created TV themes for ABC Television's *The Persuers* and the instrumental piece *Las Vegas,* which was used as the theme to the BBC children's series, *Animal Magic*. In 1963, he did some recordings for Pye Records including a version of the Latin-styled *Sucu Sucu*, written by Tarateno Rosa, the theme to the espionage series *Top Secret,* and scored a well-deserved top ten hit single. Showing off his considerable talents, he continued writing themes like the exotic sounding *Latin Quarter*, for Redifussion's national crime series *Riviera Police* and *West End*, the themes to *Whickers World*, *Shirley's World*, and *Thriller*.

In *The Professionals*, Brian Clemens devised a fast-moving buddy show, with two often conflicting lead characters, and plenty of action, shot in a method made popular in the UK by Euston Films, with *The Sweeney*. Set against the background of late 1970's/early 1980's Britain, under the threat of terrorist action and civil unrest, *The Professionals* was a series in touch with the times.

The Professionals was the result of a commission from Brian Tesler, the Managing Director of London Weekend Television (LWT), who was clearly looking to emulate the success of *The Sweeney*. In February 1977, Tesler put out the word that he was looking for a similar series and indicated that he wanted to make a new fast-moving show that related to the seventies. Brian Clemens approached Tesler offering to do a series. Taking into account Clemens' track record, as both a writer and producer, Tesler was equally interested in commissioning an idea from Brian, who was informed that, if the format was good, LWT would sanction it. In the event, Brian came up with two formats, one about undercover cops and another about an anti-terrorist unit initially called *The A-Squad*. They liked the second one and asked Clemens to develop a script, which, if Tesler thought was good enough, would result in a commission for a thirteen episode series.

At the time, funding for *The New Avengers* was static. Inflation at this time was pushing up the cost of producing episodes, with the second batch of the series only being saved by an influx of foreign finance. Both French and Canadian TV money was forthcoming as long as episodes were made in their respective countries. The writing was on the wall regarding *The New Avengers*, and after the second series no more episodes would be made, leaving Clemens, co-producer Albert Fennell and composer Laurie Johnson, free to move on to the new project. Ironically, Tesler was also looking for ideas towards a Brian Clemens produced modern thriller anthology series, part-financed by Canadian money. Tesler suggested the umbrella title *Where Danger Lives*, with the title being expressive of the wide-ranging scope the series was intended to have. The idea came to nothing and was dropped.

Clemens' first script for *The Professionals* was *Old Dogs With New Tricks* and took two weeks to complete. Ultimately it would be the first to be filmed.

Brian Clemens: "The writing doesn't take long, but it takes a lot of thinking time. In the first script, you are setting down the basic principles and rules that then have to be obeyed. You are stuck with it from there on. You might think it quite interesting, for instance, to have the head of the bureau with a stutter and it would make one very funny episode. But after fifty-seven episodes, it gets very boring. You have to be very careful about what characteristics you give them, which areas they live and even what sort of home they live in. Decisions taken at that time had to last me through five years of the series."

Clemens agreed to change the show's title to *The Professionals*, because Tesler argued it would be impossible to sell a series with 'A' in the title.

Veering away from the traditional cops and robbers format which had been amply covered by *The Sweeney*, he developed something with an internationally acceptable format, yet surprisingly in terms of series concept something that was not transatlantic.

Brian Clemens: "The pilot story did not pose any special problems, because I pinched things directly from the original working format, so all the hard work, the exploratory work, was already done."

To illustrate Clemens' original theme, that working format is reproduced in its entirety:

The A Squad

Background: In November 1971 a meeting was called by the Home Secretary; also present were prominent members of the Police and the Armed Forces; while MI5 was represented by George Cowley.

The subject under discussion was the increased use of violence, coercion techniques and sophisticated weapons in the country; a trend spear - headed by terrorist movements, but rapidly emulated by criminal factions. Cases were cited of hijackings, bomb threats, hostage kidnappings, and snipers - all representing a threat not only to law and order in Great Britain - but also to the general populace.

One point became clear; often the antagonist was better organised than the authority that had to combat him; often the police had to request specialised services of the military (and vice versa); frequently these demarcations and divisions of responsibility resulted in confusion and dangerous delays.

The meeting came to one important decision; to form some very special men into a very special squad, with a very special brief:

1: To elevate criminal intelligence to the very sophisticated levels already existing in military intelligence, and thus attempt to defuse these situations before they had a chance to escalate.

2: To deal with these situations if or when they did get out of hand.

Thus CI5. Criminal Intelligence 5. A select body controlled from a small suite of offices actually within the Home Office and presented to the public as, Home Affairs (S). The S is for Security.

CI5. Although those in the know have rapidly come to call it 'the action squad'; 'the A squad', or merely 'the big A'.

But it isn't that big. It's total strength is probably no more than forty men - specialists drawn from all the forces available, SAS, marines, paras, police and....although it could never be admitted....at least two men drawn from the wrong side of the law - including a safe cracker who served eleven years at Dartmoor.

CI5 is a properly formed and functioning Government department - but there any bureaucratic resemblance ends. CI5 is unique. And that unique quality springs directly from its controller, George Cowley, himself a unique personality.

Cowley - sometimes affectionately, and safely out of his earshot, referred to as 'The Cow' - was for some years MI5's most unpopular, and ultimately, most respected, administrator.

Joining MI5 in the wake of the Philby and Blake debacles, Cowley was quick to realise that MI5 was hopelessly outmoded in concept. It didn't stand a prayer against the sheer professionalism of security forces in Israel, South Africa,

France, Germany or Russia; the age of the talented amateur, the time of the Oxford don asked to 'keep an eye out while you're doing that dig in Syria, old chap' was over.

Cowley realised that 'who you know' had to be replaced by 'know how', and he set about it, weeding out the languid dross and replacing them with tough, hard men to deal with tough hard situations. At first Cowley's burr of Northern accent was a positive demerit; but it soon became associated with very plain speaking indeed. And getting the job done. Even his jealous rivals had to admit that, 'I don't like the man, but if I'm going to be sent to risk my neck, I'd rather he set up the job!'

'Never send a boy on a man's errand - they'll pinch his bike'.

Saddled with the occasional awful pain (and a very slight limp) from an old wound in his left leg, Cowley's days of scrambling over the wall were over - and so he eagerly accepted the challenge of forming and controlling CI5. He was delighted because, for the very first time, he could choose absolutely the right men for the job. The mandate for CI5 does not extend beyond the shores of Britain (within which they can be omnipotent), and so a man's ability to speak a French dialect, or to merge with the diplomatic protocol of a Berlin junket, becomes secondary to his ability to climb a tall building, or fire a Smith and Wesson .38 accurately.

Cowley may be getting on a bit (and he's knocking 55) and he may have that slight limp and the occasional bouts of debilitating pain, but he still has the ability to fire his men with enthusiasm and loyalty. Cowley's philosophy has become that of the entire squad.

'Our job is to see that no one craps on our doorstep, and that means preventive detection, preventive action. It's no good the girl taking The Pill after the boozy weekend...(polite laughter) ....and the same applies to us. You're the Bisto Kids - you get the slightest whiff of anything and you move in - shake 'em down, crush 'em before they even start to grow. All right, so once in a while you'll turn one law-abiding citizen into an authority hating anarchist, but it's worth it if we get in first! Like an alley fight, that's what it is, an alley fight. Hit him in the goolies first, do unto others now what they're only thinking about. Oh there'll be squeals occasionally, and letters to MP's but that's the price they have to pay - and we have to pay to keep this island clean and smelling, even if ever so faintly, of roses and lavender. You make a mistake like that, and I'll back you to the hilt. But make the other kind of mistake, the one that ends up with innocents bleeding all over the high street, and the only backing you'll get is with my boot!'

Plain speaking Cowley. Commanding, controlling CI5. The action squad. The big A. CI5; the office suite is small because, as Cowley says, 'Their office, their place of work is out there, in the back streets and the mean streets. As far as I'm concerned, if a man's standing around his office, then he isn't doing his job.'

CI5, Police, Paras, marksmen, cliff climbers....a motley crew welded together into one squad. Their brief is clear; their methods startling. That's Cowley again, 'Fight violence with violence, and save innocents from violence.'

Amoral? Quite definitely. Cowley discourages full action reports (save for intelligence purposes), so how they get around a situation is not often recorded. Which is just as well, because CI5 are not averse to kidnapping a kidnapper; or chaining a bomber to his own bomb - and let him defuse it.

Amoral - yes - but let's get it into perspective. They're up against dangerous, violent men, and frequently against the clock too. If you have sixty seconds to question a man and get an answer that may save many lives, you can't afford to be too subtle in your interrogation methods. And again, many of the men they come up against deal in fear and coercion - so maybe fear is all they understand.

CI5. The A Squad. The big A.

It's total strength probably no more than forty, and yes, we will meet the different specialists from time to time – and when necessary.

But in the main we are concerned with Cowley and the 'Bisto Kids'. Two young men who work as a team in the action squad.

They're not kids.

Ray Doyle is nearly 30. Doyle? Well, maybe way back there is a touch of the Gaelic about him (and that would explain two aspects of his character), but he certainly doesn't look it; his hair is fair, his eyes are blue, and his handsome face has a deceptively gentle look to it. It's those blue eyes really; they have a lazy, dreamy way of looking at you. Just before he hits you! In the girl/bed stakes, his eyes are his biggest ammunition. Nor does he sound Gaelic; Ray's a Londoner - not a Bow Bells Cockney, south of the river, but on a clear day, with the wind in the right direction, he might just have heard them.

Ray's a copper. Detective. CID. Mind you, he didn't start out for the police; no, he worked in a shop and studies art in the evening (his stories about those nude models often enliven a stake-out) - then he realised he had no talent, except for appreciation. So he joined the force. He was out of uniform and into CID plain clothes in record time - because of the special way he has with him, that deceptively gentle way. Some tough postings around the East End, then into the Yard proper on special duties. He's the finest shot with a handgun in the entire Met Division.

Those touches of Gaelic? Well, he can be a bit of a dreamer, an idealist verging on the romantic; funny the job hasn't knocked it out of him, but it hasn't. And, Gaelic style, side by side, with the dreamer is a terrible temper. Oh, it takes something huge to arouse it - but when he does flare...!

Girls? Well, a man who looks like that, girls would have to figure in his life, wouldn't they? Two have, to the point of getting engaged (both gave him the ring back, and he wears it on a chain under his shirt). The job and permanent relationships don't mix - so now he plays the field. And he works for CI5; and if anyone in that amoral organization has leanings towards a morality, it's Ray Doyle.

His partner is Bodie. William Andrew Philip Bodie. But he answers only to Bodie. He's maybe two years younger than Ray, though you'd never know it. In fact, you might take him for older than Ray. See him downing a pint in a King's Road pub and you might mistake him for a Chelsea player. Certainly he has the powerful, pugnacious build of a goal scorer; and the confidence of a man who knows he can handle himself. From his dark hair to his balanced stance, he exudes the kind of aggression that seems to go hand in hand with success these days. He likes to dress well too - not a dandy, but he takes care over his appearance.

Bodie's a soldier. Sergeant. 19th Airborne. Bodie's formative years are open to conjecture, because each time he tells it, it gets bigger! Certainly he joined the Merchant Navy when he was seventeen. Certainly he jumped ship in East Africa some two years later. Maybe he made his way into the interior and joined a mercenary force. Probably lived with - and off - an older woman in Cape Town. Undeniably he joined HM Forces when he was 23. It was a matter of record that he served in Northern Ireland at the height of the troubles, and a matter of conjecture that he took part in several undocumented raids in Jordan. His particular skills are rifle shooting, climbing and girls. Usually girls who are socially above him - but that doesn't concern Bodie, give him an audience and he's away. If Ray is a romantic, Bodie is a romancer (except there is usually more than a grain of truth in his stories).

If CI5 is amoral, then Bodie is its star turn. The job is all that matters, and if people get in the way, then hard luck. He's not a bigot per se, but he's apt to call a spade a spade - and up fighting a room full of them!

So there you have them - Doyle and Bodie. The Bisto Kids. The Terrible Two. The Team. Black and Decker. Marks & Spencer. Nitro & Glycerine. Chalk and Cheese? Well, perhaps on the surface, and yet, not quite. If they were that diametrically opposed they wouldn't function efficiently as they do. Some say that teaming them up was Cowley's little joke. But actually it was Cowley's little stroke of genius - Cowley's incisive knowledge of human nature because Ray and Bodie are the blade and the steel, the flint and the wheel, each complementary and indispensable to the other.

Flint and wheel, complementary certainly, but let's not forget that, bring them together, and sparks fly!

Ray and Bodie's relationship is an abrasive one, often expressed in a verbal shorthand, and always tempered by a mutual respect (and more important a mutual reliance), a relationship highlighted by the differences between them that usually manifest themselves in humorous exchange - with a bite to it.

Neither is senior to the other. This again is Cowley's deliberate policy:

'Two fellers on a roof top, arguing about who's in charge – they'll both get shot! You're a team. Like footballers are a team - they don't have a conference in front of goal, do they? Too bloody right they don't. The first one there kicks the ball! Have anything to discuss, do it before or after the game. Preferably after!'

Most CI5 assignments start with Intelligence; an overheard remark, a stranger in town, something that doesn't add up. If they're lucky - definite information. 'Intelligence begins in the field. And usually ends there too.' Cowley again, and he's right. Which is why Ray and Bodie are in with the most likely - and sometimes the most unlikely places, foraging, watching, listening.

It can start small - some kids, waste land, an empty ammunition box....and quickly escalates to a square mile of city, and you know that somewhere up there is a sniper - where is he? Who is the target?

The arrested terrorist - and the innocent hostage snatched and held in retaliation - to be exchanged. But the terrorist dies accidentally. CI5 have to fake that he is still alive, and desperately try to find and release the hostage.

The joy-riders who steal a car - not knowing about the powerful bomb in the boot. And all the while they are driving deeper into congested urban areas. Kids playing in the street, mothers wheeling babies...

Panic used as a weapon to extort money - pay up or I'll explode a device in the stadium - and start a human stampede.

The trouble maker we can't deny entry to the country - and his own organization are planning to assassinate him to start bigger trouble!

For it's the public that CI5 are ultimately responsible to. They don't pull their punches. Fight violence with violence. But, and there is a big but, never let those methods endanger so much as a hair of an innocent bystander.

Beyond that prime directive CI5 agents have a free hand to use whichever methods will get the job done. Because Cowley wants the end result right and morality and ethics might play but a small part in how they get there.

There are no filing cabinets bulging with neatly typed reports. When danger is averted the only people who know are those that matter.

The Writing Brief:

Any political motivations must be subjugated to the ordinary human involvement.

Set up the story, set up the problem CI5 have to deal with - and then let's see how they solve the apparently insoluble.

Keep the relationship of Ray and Bodie - with Cowley - firmly in the foreground.

Steal the situations from the headlines. No situation must suspend belief.
Keep it moving, Fast.

Brian Clemens: "The basis of any duo relationship is that it has to have an element of conflict. You would end up with a dull 'marriage' if the characters liked each other all the time. There is no drama unless there is some conflict. Let's say you have a story about a man under siege in a house and Bodie and Doyle say 'Come out!' and he does then you've got no story, have you?

"You can't have them kicking doors in all the time. There has to be parts where they are simply going from A to B and on the way, they have to have something to talk about. They might, for instance, be investigating a crime about aquariums and one of them will say that he used to keep goldfish when he was younger. The other one will probably say that the only way he likes fish is with batter round it!

"The way I saw it was that Bodie was a swine and Doyle was the one with the conscience. I gave Cowley a limp, because I wanted him to be an irascible man. That sort of thing comes out of being a man of action, shot in the leg and chair bound. He would like to be out with the boys but due to his injury was limited in what he could do."

The interplay between Bodie and Doyle (and their collective interplay with Cowley) was central to the series and one of the things that London Weekend Television and Brian Tesler was looking for, perhaps trying to emulate the American import *Starsky & Hutch*, which was doing well on the BBC at the time.

Brian Clemens: "It wasn't a conscious steal from that kind of show. It's just in television the most leading characters you can have is three and the twosome is something that has been successful in all sorts of forms for many years. I suppose Laurel and Hardy started it all off."

Avengers (Film & TV) Enterprises were finishing off the second series of *The New Avengers*, filming both the French and Canadian episodes. These were the last to be made and overlapped with the start of production on *The Professionals*. Together with director Ray Austin, associate producer Ron Fry and Albert Fennell travelled to Canada, while Clemens continued to develop the new show. This suited their well-established working patterns.

Brian Clemens: "It really wasn't a problem because *The New Avengers* had reached the stage at which the episodes set in France and Canada were due to be filmed, so Albert went overseas with that unit, while I remained here to set up *The Professionals*. Albert and I always had shared a good working relationship. My input has always been one of pre-production and finance, while the filming, dubbing and editing, which takes much longer, and the bit in the middle, that of actually being on the studio floor to ensure that everything runs smoothly, was more Albert's thing. He was the person who employed the right cameraman, the right set designer and so on, while I get all the colourful balloon ideas and wild thoughts about casting. I looked after the scripts, the creative look and design, and at the end Albert would sit down with the editor and cut the finished film. I then added my two-pennyworth, and he would then go away and dub the soundtrack. My idea of doing any series, is not to stay with it for too long, but to set it up, make certain the rules are clearly understood, set the production rolling and then let someone else fill in the gaps!"

To fill this void left by Fennell, director Sidney Hayers was approached to act as on-line producer, on the first series, on the understanding that it would only be for these thirteen episodes. The two men had first worked together back in 1962 on the feature, *Night Of The Eagle*, and having been hired to direct eight episodes of *The Avengers* and four episodes of *The New Avengers*, Hayers was the perfect choice for the position.

Born in Edinburgh, Scotland, on the 24th August 1921, Hayers began his film career in 1942 working in the sound department, as a focus puller, and in the cutting room, before graduating to editing such features as *Romeo and Juliet* (1954) and *A Night to Remember* (1958). He broke into directing with 1958's *Violent Moment* and kept busy with such features as *Circus of Horrors* (1960) and *Night of the Eagle* (1962). With *The Avengers*, he established himself as a bankable TV director, as well. Hayers' penchant for tension and the macabre often found him stepping behind the camera for such horror-flavoured thrillers as *Assault* (1970), *Revenge* (1971), *Deadly Strangers* (1974), and *Diagnosis: Murder* (1974). He continued his career with filmed TV work, including *The Human Jungle*, *The Persuaders!*, and *The Zoo Gang*. Prior to his engagement on *The Professionals* he worked as a second unit director in the Netherlands on Richard Attenborough's *A Bridge Too Far*.

Moving over from *The New Avengers*, associate producer Ron Fry assumed the same role on *The Professionals* and assisted Hayers in setting up the new show. Fry's career dated back to the early 1960's where he served as a production manager on *The Edgar Wallace Mystery Theatre*, followed by work on *Z Cars*, *The Avengers* (1968-69) and *Space:1999* (1975-76).

Ron Fry: "My role as associate producer encompassed many aspects of the production from initial development, raising production finance where needed, supervising the production design team (sets, costumes, etc.), supervising post-production, directing the second unit, and co-ordinating the work of the various visual effects employed. I would carry out any production work that the producer was too busy to supervise personally, and which was not covered by one of the other production roles.

"I was on good terms with our *New Avengers* location manager, Nick Gillott, and made him production manager for the new show. He was instrumental in setting up the rest of the crew and found Harefield Grove for our unit base. Second assistant director Peter Cotton was promoted to location manager and a close friend from my *Z Cars* days, Ken Ware, became our script editor. *The Professionals* was set up as a secondary series to our main production of *The New Avengers*, which we were shooting at Pinewood. The filming of the new series ran for a good part of the time concurrently with the making of *The New Avengers* French and Canadian episodes. This meant that having set-up *The Professionals* and seen them started I was not on set as much as I would have liked to have been as I was away a lot of the time, mostly in Toronto."

Nicholas Gillott, born (27th March 1945) in Sheffield, Yorkshire, had worked as a production manager on *The Sweeney*; Peter Cotton had just completed the film *Jabberwocky*, and had worked on *Alfie Darling* (1975), and *The Great McGonagall* (1974); and Kenneth Ware had worked extensively on the long-running BBC series *Compact* (1962-65) and *The Troubleshooters* (1965-72), *Van Der Valk* (1972), and co-wrote the 1969 film *The Last Grenade*.

Kenneth Ware (script editor, interviewed at the time): "In British television drama the writer is honoured, the success of any series is determined by the script. It all begins with the writers; without quality scripts you might as well go out and sell double-glazing. The television medium favours the spoken word; the size of the television screen inhibits the impact of the visual image. The television screen is small, and the picture doesn't overpower the viewer as in the cinema; the sound doesn't come washing round the living-room in stereophonic waves......people listen to television. It's more like radio with pictures than it is like movies. In modern films, the words are usually, and often intentionally muffled; the director wants to tell his story with pictures and sound, not pictures and dialogue. He is interested in large-scale dramatic effects. On the small screen large-scale effects simply don't work; the screen won't take them. What the screen will take is people talking intelligibly to each other.

"I was accountable for turning the writer's manuscripts into the shooting script, as well as foresee and counter any potential legal problems created by specific references in the script. It was important to avoid causing any offence and embarrassment by referring unintentionally to the names and addresses of real people and organisations. A series of 'negative checks' was carried out to avoid this. With the scripts finalised and checked out, the production script was given a programme number and typed up by the Producer's Secretary to await duplication and distribution. All the consequent rewritten scenes, as they became available, would be typed up and distributed as the production continued."

Other senior crew members who had worked on *The New Avengers* also assumed similar roles on *The Professionals*, including post production supervisor Paul Clay (who had been composer Laurie Johnson's music supervisor for several years), and fight arranger Joe Dunne, whose career had started back in the 1960's working on the original *Avengers* series. He progressed onto shows such as *Randall & Hopkirk (Deceased)* and *The Persuaders!*. Lighting cameraman Ernie Steward, born on the 8th January 1914, had worked on various Norman Wisdom comedies and several Carry On films, and was approaching retirement at his appointment to the show.

Standing in an estate of two hundred acres of farm and woodland, Harefield Grove is a three-storey grade II listed building built in 1810, situated off Rickmansworth Road on the outskirts of the village of Harefield in Middlesex. The estate was hired for a £100 per day, which also included stables, a farmhouse and various outbuildings. These premises had already been used as a TV location in *The Adventures Of Black Beauty*, *Spy Trap*, *Thursday's Child*, *Dial M For Murder*, *Clayhanger* and *The Seven Faces Of Woman*, plus the comedy sketch shows *The Two Ronnies* and *Dave Allen At Large*. The building and surrounding grounds were also used in the films *The Hireling*, the rock opera *Tommy*, and the BBC documentary series *Omnibus*.

With the format, crew, and base of operations to *The Professionals* now established, the next stage was casting. Clive Revill, who had just completed *The New Avengers* episode *Dead Men Are Dangerous*, was interested in playing Cowley. Born (18th April 1930), in Wellington, New Zealand, Revill was educated at Rongotal College and Victoria University. After appearing on Broadway in the 1952 musical *Mr. Pickwick*, he spent three years with Britain's Ipswich Repertory and studied with the Old Vic School in London. His films include *Fathom*, *Modesty Blaise* and *The Assassination Bureau*, while on TV he had a guest-slot in *Jason King*. However, he would not commit himself to *The Professionals* because he had just completed a pilot in America and was hoping it would be picked up as a series. Shortly afterwards he provided the voice of the Emperor in *The Empire Strikes Back*.

Ron Fry (associate producer): "For the part of Cowley we had hoped to get Clive and I spent a lot of time, on behalf of Brian (Clemens) and Albert (Fennell), trying to persuade him to take the part. I had done two pictures with Clive previously, including *The Legend Of Hell House*, which had been produced by Albert, and we got on quite well. He was tempted but in the end felt he had to have another go at The States and so turned us down. It was a great shame because I felt he was very suited to the part; he would have been wonderful in the role. In the end I think whatever he wanted to do in The States never came off."

Executive producer Albert Fennell then suggested Gordon Jackson who had just finished a long-running role as Hudson the butler in *Upstairs Downstairs*. Gordon Cameron Jackson was born in Glasgow, Scotland on 19th December 1923. Leaving school aged fifteen he gained employment as a draughtsman for Rolls-Royce.

Jackson's film career began when Ealing producers were looking for a young Scot to take part in the film *The Foreman Went to France* (1942). This was the beginning of a fruitful association with Ealing Studios, which saw Jackson appear in such films as *San Demetrio, London* (1943), *Pink String and Sealing Wax* (1945) and *Whisky Galore!* (1949). As he aged, Jackson went from playing the youthful innocent to the weathered yet weak adult, notably in *Tunes of Glory* (1960), *The Great Escape* (1963) and *The Ipcress File* (1965).

Harefield Grove,
Harefield,
Middlesex.

TO HEADS OF TV PRODUCTION/PRODUCERS   April 1976

HAREFIELD GROVE

You may never have heard of Harefield Grove and Estate, but if you have seen the film Tommy or The Hireling, or episodes of Spy Trap, or the ITV series Clayhanger, or a number of other TV and feature films - then you have probably seen the location we want to tell you about.

Harefield Grove is an 1810 Grade II listed property, situated in Harefield, Middlesex, about 19 miles from London and a handy 2 miles from the Denham film labs. Both the house and grounds are available to you and your clients for filming commercials.

You can hire the entire property or any part of it from as little as £100 a day, with reductions for long term shoots.

The attached sheet gives details of the house.

As you can see, it has three storeys and a gravel drive leading up to the front door. There are several main rooms on the ground floor, the largest being over 1,200 square feet. Amongst the great variety of different rooms and room settings, there is a billiard room, Edwardian kitchens and wine cellars. The house is partly furnished and kept in good condition.

The Harefield estate covers over 200 acres of farmland and woodland. There are stables, a farmhouse, and many other outbuildings. Large areas of varied woodland, a lake with an ornamental bridge, and dozens of delightful spots for outdoor work.

In fact, it is the variety of setting and moods both inside the house and out that make Harefield such an attractive location.

If you'd like to come out and have a look, get in touch with John Cox on Harefield 2245. We look forward to showing you Harefield.

The original letter used to publicise Harefield Grove, Middlesex, which was already on file at Pinewood Studios, hence picked up by the producers as a likely candidate for use in filming.

Gordon Jackson as Cowley, Martin Shaw as Doyle and Lewis Collins as Bodie - THE PROFESSIONALS. During a break in filming of the first series 'original' Title sequence.

Gordon Jackson: "I had not long finished my part as Hudson and had done some live theatre when the script was offered to me. I don't know why they picked me, but Albert Fennell and I had worked together some years before on the film *Tunes Of Glory*. I read the script and liked it. I thought the part was right for me."

Brian Clemens: "When I first devised the show, I simply made Cowley a Northerner. It was a way of saying that I didn't see him as a public school boy. I wanted him to have a roughness factor. Of course, I didn't know who would be playing the part when I first started writing the scripts but when Gordon became Cowley we simply adjusted the screenplays. Gordon was the perfect professional. He was never temperamental, always reliable and beneath that rather haggis-like exterior, there was a lively imagination."

Gordon Jackson: "Neither Hudson nor Cowley were written as Scots, but I was invited to play both parts and quite naturally played both parts with a Scottish accent as I always do. I think you can get away with an accent providing it's not too heavy and that the part doesn't specifically reveal that the person comes from a particular country or part of the country. I worked with Orson Welles and did an American play once. I told him I didn't think I could do an American accent. He told me it didn't matter, merely to give a suggestion of it. He said that if you played a part sincerely and fully, people wouldn't notice the accent and I think that's true."

Ron Fry (associate producer): "Gordon was a fine actor and a lovely man, but I always felt he wasn't quite right for the part. Nevertheless, he had a great talent and soon made George Cowley his own. This became the least of our worries, as we still had to cast the parts of Bodie and Doyle."

The new production company set up on 20th April 1977 to produce *The Professionals*, Mark II Productions, arranged a set of screen tests (a method of determining the suitability of an actor in a particular role in front of a camera to see if they are suitable) on Tuesday 10th May to be held at both the new unit base of Harefield Grove and Pinewood Studios' sound stages J & K. Directed by producer Sidney Hayers, a small crew gathered to film a number of actors being put through their paces as Bodie and Doyle.

Executive producers Brian Clemens and Albert Fennell were quietly confident that actor Jon Finch was the perfect candidate to portray Doyle on the screen, and the part of Bodie would be the order of the day. That said, the first test saw Martin Shaw in the role, coupled with Simon Oates as Bodie. In the remaining tests Finch took over and Peter Finlay, Ken Hutchison and Oliver Tobias filled the shoes occupied by Oates. Still not entirely convinced that Bodie had been found, Hayers arranged for Finch in the part alongside Tommy Boyle as Doyle.

The screening of the 'rushes' (the processed film negative) were held the following day at Anvil Post Production, Denham, Middlesex, where both Brian Clemens and Albert Fennell were suitably bowled over with Finch's performance that he was offered the part of Doyle that same afternoon. The casting of the Bodie character remained undecided at this stage and would prove to be more difficult than had ever been envisaged.

Jon Finch was born on 2nd March 1941 in Caterham, Surrey. The son of a merchant banker, his first stage role was in elementary school at the age of 13 playing a Roman nobleman.

```
                    MARK II PRODUCTIONS LTD

                    C A L L      S H E E T


ARTIST TESTS                        DATE:  TUESDAY 10th. May 1977

LOCATION:    HAREFIELD GROVE        CALL:  8.30 a.m.
             RICKMANSWORTH ROAD,
             HAREFIELD, MIDDX.

                                    DIRECTOR:  SIDNEY HAYERS


ARTISTE                  CHARACTER              CALL


TEST NO. 1.

SIMON OATES              BODIE                  8.30 @ Harefield Grove
MARTIN SHAW              DOYLE                  8.30         "

TEST NO. 2.

PETER FINDLAY            BODIE                  10.30 @ Harefield Grove
JON FINCH                DOYLE                  10.30        "

TEST NO. 3.

KEN HUTCHINSON           BODIE                  12.00 Pinewood J & K
JON FINCH                DOYLE                  From above

TEST NO. 4.

JON FINCH                BODIE                  From above
TOMMY BOYLE              DOYLE                  2.00 Pinewood J & K
OLIVER TOBIAS            BODIE                  2.00 Pinewood J & K


PROPS:       FIELD GLASSES, COMMANDO KNIFE, SPECTACLES, HAND GUN, PLAYING
             CARDS AS ARRANGED.

CAMERA:      16 BL, 10:1 zoom, Arri head, T. and S. legs as per
             Grahame Edgar. Elemac, wheels (2), 30 ft. track and
             Minilock to be delivered by 8.30 a.m. from Cine Europe
             (01-402-8385) Collection from 5.30 p.m.

ELECTRICAL:  12½ KVA Alternator. 3 Blondes. 4 Redheads etc. to be
             delivered by 8.30 a.m. from GBS Lighting (01-748-0316)

SOUND:       Nagra Kit etc. as per Robin Gregory.

TRANSPORT:   Unit Car (Brian Boreham) to work to instructions.

RUSHES:      Executive Rushes screening 10.00 a.m. Wednesday 11th. May
             At Anvil, Denham Studios (Ken Sommerville - Denham 3522).

CREW:        Asst. Director - Bill Westley
             Cameraman - Grahame Edgar
             Operator - Kelvin Pike
             Follow Focus - David Litchfield
             Loader - Beaumont Alexander
             Grip - Brian Osborne
             Sound Recordist - Robin Gregory
             Boom - Terry Sharratt
             Sound Assistant - T.B.A.
             Make-up Artist - Basil Newall
             2 Electricians - Via GBS.          NICHOLAS GILLOTT
```

The original call sheet for the 'Artist Tests' on Tuesday 10th May 1977.

After gaining experience in amateur theatre groups and following a short stint with a folk singing group, he suddenly left for military service at the age of eighteen, serving in a parachute regiment. He returned to acting a few years later and delved seriously into classical theatre with several different repertory companies, appearing in over sixty plays, including *Night Of The Iguana* and *She Stoops To Conquer*, and serving as stage manager or assistant director for several of these companies.

His first television break came in 1967 and shortly thereafter won supporting roles in a couple of Hammer Studio film productions. *The Vampire Lovers* and *The Horror Of Frankenstein* were both made in 1970. This was a sign as to the direction his cinematic career would take. His Gothic-edged film career peaked in the early 1970's with such classy fare as Roman Polanski's *Macbeth* (1971), in which he played the tormented title role, in a particularly gory and controversial presentation. Alfred Hitchcock's macabre serial-killer thriller *Frenzy* (1972), in which he is a suspect in the dastardly crimes. *The Final Programme* in 1973, an end-of-the-world sci-fi adventure that has since earned cult status.

Prior to his engagement on *The Professionals*, he had completed *The New Avengers* episode *Medium Rare*. Despite knowing Doyle's background, Finch had no sooner made an agreement to be in the show when he stated that he could never play an ex-policeman.

Brian Clemens: "He tested, read the script and said, 'Yes, it's lovely, I'll do it'. Then almost immediately afterwards he said, 'Of course, I can't possibly play an ex-policeman', even though the role of Doyle had been made very clear before the test. So he was giving us trouble even before we made a start and I thought an actor who is trying to change the character this early...no, it can't be. So Finch was asked to leave, and we went back to the drawing board."

As a consequence, the production still only had one of its three lead characters. Meanwhile, in production at Pinewood Studios at this time was *The New Avengers* episode *Obsession*, in which actor Martin Shaw had a guest part. During the sequences filmed on Wednesday 25th May, Brian Clemens and Albert Fennell were suitably impressed with the acting skills of Shaw that they reviewed the first screen test he'd performed as Doyle and decided he was indeed suited for the part.

Born in Birmingham on 21st January 1945, Martin Shaw had started his small screen career by doing instalments of anthology series like *Play Of The Week* and *Summer Playhouse* in 1967, followed by a short stint in *Coronation Street*. After appearing in episodes of *Strange Report* and *Fraud Squad*, he went on to do *Helen: A Woman Of Today* in 1973, which led to *The New Avengers* episode, *Obsession*.

A new set of screen tests were hastily arranged for the following Monday (30th May) under the renamed company of Warmwood Productions to find a partner to co-star alongside Shaw (Mark II Productions had came under fire from the hierarchy at LWT, who deemed it sounded like a second-rate company; so it was dropped in favour of Warmwood Productions). Sidney Hayers again directed; this time six tests were held with the Bodie character portrayed by Anthony Andrews, John McEnery, Peter Armitage, Jack

MacKenzie, Nick Tate and Stephan Chase. At Anvil Post Production the following day, Brian Clemens and Albert Fennell were witness to the new set of 'rushes', and cast Anthony Andrews as Bodie.

CALL SHEET

EPISODE NO. 18. "OBSESSION"   DATE: Wednesday 25th. May 1977

SETS: 1). EXT. ROAD TO SITE
2). EXT. ROCKY/SANDY GROUND
3). EXT. BASE
4). INT. DOOMERS PLACE

UNIT CALL: 8.00 JK Car Park
8.30 on Location

SC. NOS: 1). 102. 103. 105. Day
2). 61. 64. Day
3). 22. Night. 34 Day
4). 75. 78. 80. Day.

LOCATIONS: 1). Sevenhills Road
2). Ivor
3). Studio Lot
4). J Stage

DIRECTOR: ERNIE DAY

FOR FURTHER DETAILS SEE MOVEMENT ORDER

ARTISTE	CHARACTER	DR. ROOM	MAKE UP	ON LOCN.
PATRICK MACNEE	STEED	JK 275	11.30	12.00
GARETH HUNT	GAMBIT	JK 277	8.00	8.30
MARTIN SHAW	DOOMER	JK 278	9.30	10.00
LEWIS COLLINS	KILNER	JK 280	8.00	8.30
ANTHONY HEATON	MORGAN	JK 280	8.00	8.30
MARK KINGSTON	CANVEY	JK 279	S/BY at Home	
TOMMY BOYLE	WOLACH	JK 278	11.30	12.00

Standins:

John Clifford for	Mr. Macnee		11.30	12.00
Gerry Paris for	Mr. Hunt		8.00	8.30
Bill Rimley for	Mr. Shaw		9.30	10.00

Stunt Doubles:

Dicky Graydon	PURDEY	JK 281	8.00	8.30
Bill Weston	GAMBIT	JK 281	7.30	8.30
Eddie Stacey	KILNER	JK 284	7.30	8.30
Graham Kronver	MORGAN	JK 284	7.30	8.30

Action Vehicles:

Honda 125 Motorbike - PURDEY'S BIKE (via Production Office)   8.00 JK Car Park
Bedford Truck - KILNER'S TRUCK (via 99 Cars)   8.00 JK Car Park

Props: As per script to include: STEED'S CARNATION. GAMBIT'S GUN AND SHOULDER HOLSTER. HANDCUFFS. ROCKETS. CANVAS SHEET. "DANGER" SIGN. FIRE FIGHTING EQUIPMENT. LOCK BREAKING EQUIPMENT. NEWSPAPER CLIPPINGS. BOTTLE OF LIQUER.

SFX: Crashed truck to be steaming (Locn. 1.)

Stunt Arranger: JOE DUNNE - to be on set from 8.30 a.m.

Lighting: Red Light FX - Sc. 22.

Catering: A.M. break to be collected from Studio. Lunch at Studio. P.M. break to be advised.

Rushes: 5.30 p.m. Theatre 7.

Transport: Car to pick up Mr. Hunt from his home at 7.00 to be at the Studio for 8.00 a.m.

AL BURGESS

The call sheet from THE NEW AVENGERS episode OBSESSION where Martin Shaw and Lewis Collins met for the first time! Their work here would eventually lead to both stars being cast in THE PROFESSIONALS. However, at this stage, only Martin Shaw had attracted the attention of the producers.

WARNWOOD PRODUCTIONS LTD

CALL SHEET

ARTIST TESTS:
LOCATION: Harefield Grove, Rickmansworth Road, Harefield, Middx.

DATE: Monday, 30th May, 197
CALL: 8.00am
DIRECTOR: Sidney Hayers

ARTISTE:	CHARACTER:	CALL:
TEST NO:1		
MARTIN SHAW	DOYLE	8.00am at H. Grove
ANTHONY ANDREWS	BODIE	8.00am at H. Grove
TEST NO:2		
MARTIN SHAW	DOYLE	From above
JOHN McENERY	BODIE	9.30am at H. Grove
TEST NO:3		
MARTIN SHAW	DOYLE	From above
PETER ARMITAGE	BODIE	11.30am at H. Grove
TEST NO:4		
MARTIN SHAW	DOYLE	From above
JACK MACKENZIE	BODIE	2.00pm at H. Grove
TEST NO:5		
MARTIN SHAW	DOYLE	From above
NICK TATE	BODIE	3.00pm at H. Grove
TEST NO:6		
MARTIN SHAW	DOYLE	From above
STEPHAN CHASE	BODIE	4.00pm at H. Grove

PROPS: Binoculars, 2 Hand guns, 2 Doctor's coats, spectacles, playing cards, newspaper.

CAMERA: 16BL with 12:120 Zoom, Minilock, Ronford Fluid 15 Head, tall & short legs, Elemack, 30ft track, Unit box - from Cine Europe 7.45am at Harefield Grove

ELECTRICAL: Alternator & lamps as arranged with Elstree Lighting Ltd., 7.45am at Harefield Grove.

SOUND: As per Delta Sound

CREW:		
BILL WESTLEY	-	ASSISTANT DIRECTOR
NORMAN LANGLEY	-	CAMERAMAN
BRIAN ELVIN	-	OPERATOR
TONY WOODCOCK	-	FOCUS
DAVID BUDD	-	C/LOADER
BRIAN OSBORNE	-	GRIP
DEREK BALL	-	SOUND RECORDIST
-	-	BOOM OPERATOR
JANE ROYAL	-	MAKE/UP

2 ELECTRICIANS via Elstree Lighting Ltd.

RUSHES: Denlabs processing - screening at Anvil 10.30am Tuesday, 31st May.

NICHOLAS GILLOTT
PRODUCTION MANAGER

The original call sheet for the second set of 'Artist Tests' filmed on Monday 30th May 1977. This time to determine the actor to play the part of Bodie.

Anthony Andrews was born in London on 12th January 1948 and started his acting career in 1968 on the *Wednesday Play* instalment, *A Beast with Two Backs*. His first bit part in a movie was playing Hugo Flaxman in 1973's *Take Me High*, followed by a part in the 1974 production *Percy's Progress*. His career continued in television with notable appearances in the TV series, *QB VII*, *The Pallisers* and *David Copperfield*. In 1976 he portrayed Sergeant Jozef Gabcik in *Operation Daybreak*. It was in this production that he struck up a close friendship with his *Professionals* co-star Martin Shaw. Three more instalments of *Play Of The Month* including *London Assurance* in October 1976, and *The Country Wife* in February 1977 were produced prior to his engagement on *The Professionals*.

Actress Bridget Brice would portray Cowley's secretary, Betty. She had starred in the West End, worked in all major repertory theatres and performed in countless television programmes. These included guest slots in *Department S*, *Public Eye*, *Doctor In Charge*, *Doctor At Sea* and *The Sweeney*. She also had a part in the feature film *No Blades Of Grass* and the Mel Brooks movie *The Twelve Chairs*.

Also cast around this time were the three leads' 'Stand-Ins'. These were the people who, when the actors were learning their lines or were in make up or similar activity, would go through the scenes with the director. This way the director was assured all the lighting and camera positions were correct and, therefore, waste no valuable shooting time. Stand-ins would normally be the same height and roughly the same build as the star.

Bill Risley took on the character of Doyle, Gerry Paris was Bodie and Ron Watkins was Cowley. They remained with the production until the end of the show in 1981.

Ron Watkins (Gordon Jackson's stand-in): "A good stand-in will be in demand because of his forethought and readiness to do more than just stand here, say that, and go there. For example, a good stand-in will think to wear similar clothes to those his star is wearing in the scene. This helps the lighting cameraman. It is essential for a stand-in to watch all rehearsals so he knows the moves his star has to make. If any changes are made when I am standing-in for him, I will go and tell him what they are.

"Although a stand-in is never in front of the camera during a take, he will sometimes stand behind and read the other character's lines when only one actor's half of a scene is being filmed. Having been on the stage for many years, I like to think I read the lines well enough to help the actor with his reactions. *The Professionals* was a tough set to work on as we were nearly always on location and not studio bound, which at the time was unheard of."

Initially, British Leyland supplied vehicles for the series on a contract left over from *The New Avengers* and the 'Bisto Kids', as Cowley sometimes referred to his best men, were seen driving a variety of Triumphs and Rovers. The extra cars were initially hired through a mechanic, Bernard Barnsley. He had worked on *The Sweeney*, but had proved to be unreliable on several occasions; cars would often turn up late, or not as requested. Consequently, many vehicles, like the army lorry from *Old Dog With New Tricks*, were hired from Tony Johnson and Freddie Wilmington at Kingsbury Motors, Kingsbury Road, North West London.

One of the cars used by Doyle in first two episodes (*Old Dog With New Tricks* and *Long Shot)*, was a Rio brown 1970 Rover P6 2000 automatic, EMK 760J. This car can also be seen briefly in the film, *Sweeney 2*. The main Bodie car in the early stories was a white Triumph Dolomite Sprint, registration POK 79R. The Rover SD1 3500, in Turmeric yellow, driven by Cowley, sported false number plates, MOO 229R (apt for the Cow). This vehicle was a pre-production model, having previously been driven by Steed in *The New Avengers* (when it had the plates MOC 229P) and it also appeared in the *Return Of The Saint* episode, *Yesterday's Hero*.

In terms of communications, and used on the first episode *Old Dog With New Tricks*, the CI5 team favoured the Pye Pocketfone PF1. Introduced in 1965 it was the first ever Police personal radio used in the United Kingdom. The UHF PF1 was a two set unit consisting of a transmitter and receiver.

For this series, both Bodie and Doyle would wear Ollech & Wajs Caribbean 1000 wristwatches. In the 1970's, they were highly desirable military items, with stainless steel bracelets, and were capable of hitting depths of 1000m (in comparison to the Rolex Submariner which could only manage 200m). They had a unique feature that allowed the owner to easily replace the glass should it suffer damage in 'battle'. Cowley wore a Longines manual with second hand and date indication.

Firearms were courtesy of Peter Dinley's company Bapty. Responsibility for supplying all weaponry fell to 'Major' Drew, who had not only supplied artillery for numerous James Bond films since *Dr. No*, but also varying equipment to *The Sweeney* television series. Cowley carried the American made Smith & Wesson .38 calibre weapon with a snub-nosed two-inch barrel. Bodie and Doyle's main choice was the Browning Hi-Power automatic pistol. Designed by J.M Browning in 1926, it has been in constant use since its introduction in 1935 and was used extensively during World War II by combatants of both sides. The Hi-Power became the standard firearm of the British Army and NATO.

Warmwood Productions (Mark II Productions) also had staff at Pinewood Studios, Buckinghamshire in rent-free offices provided against profits from *The New Avengers*. However, with an allocated budget of £115,000 per episode, Mark II did not use any of the on-site soundstages, only the editing and sound dubbing facilities. Here, at Pinewood, the company was still editing and dubbing the last of *The New Avengers* and post-production supervisor Paul Clay was gearing up to cope with both post-production on *The New Avengers* and pre-production on *The Professionals*.

It was decided that with *The New Avengers* nearing completion that he would join producer Sidney Hayers and *The Professionals* crew at Harefield Grove, where the stable block was converted into cutting rooms and post-production facilities. With Pinewood Studios only being a short drive away; the Warmwood team worked comfortably between the two. With both shows in production, Laurie Johnson's composing became somewhat strained and during a session scoring a *The New Avengers* instalment he unexpectedly conjured up what was to be *The Professionals* theme; quickly jotting it down on a sheet of manuscript paper, before returning to the episode in hand.

Old Dog With New Tricks: *An escaped prisoner decides to kidnap the Home Secretary as a hostage in exchange for his imprisoned brother. But he gets more than he bargains for when he takes Cowley instead*

Contracts for the three leads went out late-May 1977 and, by the middle of the following month, the crew were ready to film interiors at Harefield Grove. Production began here on Monday 13th June, followed by work on location at Amersham General Hospital, Buckinghamshire, on Brian Clemens' pilot story, *Old Dog With New Tricks*, directed by Sidney Hayers.

WARMWOOD PRODUCTIONS LTD.
HAREFIELD GROVE.

"THE PROFESSIONALS"
T.V. SERIES:

CALL SHEET NO. 1

EPISODE NO. 1. DATE: Mon. 13th June, 1977

LOCATION: Harefield Grove UNIT CALL: 8.00 - 8.30 on se

SETS: INT. CELLAR
      INT. BACK ROOM
      INT. SQUAD CORRIDOR
      INT. BODIE'S APARTMENT

SC. NOS: 13,15,28 Day
      33 Night
      34 Night
      31 Night
      36,37,38 Day

DIRECTOR: Sid Hayers

ARTISTE:	CHARACTER:	M/UP:	ON SET
MARTIN SHAW	DOYLE	09.00	09.45
ANTHONY ANDREWS	BODIE	09.00	09.45
PHILIP DAVIS	BILLY	07.45	08.30
JOHNNY SHANNON	CHARLEY	08.30	09.15
RICHARD HAMPTON	MORGAN	08.30	09.15
HOWARD BELL	C.I.D. SGT.	09.15	09.45
STEPHAN CHASE	DAPPER	08.30	09.15
FIONA CURZON	CLAIRE	14.00	15.00

STAND INS:

Bill Risley	for Mr. Shaw		09.00
Gerry Paaris	for Mr. Andrews		09.00

CROWD:

2 Men	Toughs		09.00

PROPS: As per script

WARDROBE: Police button Sc. 33, Bodie's Army Uniform Sc. 38

CATERING: Tea on arrival, A.M. & P.M. Breaks, Lunch for 60 please.

TRANSPORT: Brian Boreham to pick up Martin Shaw at 08.00
          Steve Smith to pick up Anthony Andrews at 08.00

BILL WESTLEY
ASSISTANT DIRECTOR:

The first days call sheet for filming on OLD DOG WITH NEW TRICKS, with Anthony Andrews as Bodie!

Gordon Jackson as George Cowley, controller of CI5; on the set of OLD DOG WITH NEW TRICKS.

The shooting of a show such as *The Professionals* involved a large number of people and required a large-scale backup in the engineering and craft areas. To enable the director to concentrate on the artistic aspects of the production, the organisation and co-ordination of actors and crew was largely delegated to Nicholas Gillott, the production manager, and Ernie Steward, the lighting cameraman.

Nicholas Gillott (production manager): "Planning an efficient production schedule requires the balancing of aesthetic and financial priorities. The task is a significant responsibility in view of the inevitable repercussions on the budget if the series falls behind schedule. From the actors point of view it is without doubt preferable to shoot the script in a narrative sequence. However, the idea of a production unit continually on the move is both impractical and uneconomic. More time would be spent setting up and in shifting locations than in shooting. Therefore, it is standard practice to break down the script according to locations and to shoot all the scenes that occur at one particular location before proceeding to the next. Inevitably this often requires scenes to be shot out of order, presenting problems for actors, wardrobe and make-up."

Ernie Steward (lighting cameraman): "Seldom was anything discussed in terms of style or anything else, it was basically up to me or the camera operator to sort out what it ought to look like. Most of the shots were discussed on the day, more often than not immediately prior to shooting. Admittedly recces were made by the crew to each of the locations some days before shooting to discuss lighting, sound and camerawork in general terms, but that was it. Sid Hayers, was not only a wonderful producer, but also an exceptional director. Normally it's rush, rush, rush, 'We've got to get this scene done before lunch!' Whereas Sid would say, 'We're going to get this done full stop! Whether we finish before lunch or tonight'. That's the difference, the money and schedule was there and Sid wouldn't accept it if it wasn't right."

Four days footage was filmed before production ground to a halt. It was decided that Anthony Andrews and Martin Shaw looked too alike and were too chummy to create the necessary spark for the abrasive relationship Clemens was looking for.

Brian Clemens: "All they did was sit around and giggle at each other - we wanted something with a little more friction and rivalry. There was no magic, so reluctantly, very reluctantly, we told Anthony it wasn't going to work, and we paid him off and started looking again."

Albert Fennell: "It was bland and boring. No chemistry. No real character interplay. Nothing was working. They were friends, no sense of rivalry between them at all. We wanted to keep Martin Shaw, he had such a marvelous look and presence about him, but we needed to spark it off. Andrews was the one who was asked to leave the production and later achieved fame as Sebastian Flyte in *Brideshead Revisited*."

Despite keeping Martin Shaw, the producers weren't happy at the way he had adopted his new look.

Martin Shaw: "I was told by the producers they (Bodie and Doyle) were going to wear suits and have short hair. I thought that was so stupid. I said 'No, no, what's much cooler these days is jeans and long hair.' They told me that if I turned up to the shoot wearing jeans, they'd send me home. I had my hair permed, so that they couldn't do anything about it, apart from shave my head. I do seem to recall that the crew did laugh quite a lot when I turned up on the set. It was just a search for a disguise. I arrived in jeans and a leather jacket. I can't stand things around my throat. I hate wearing suits. Sid Hayers, the director, didn't know that I'd been issued with this threat. He just said 'nice' and we started shooting, and that was it.

"Everything you saw in Doyle was drawn from myself. The character's nature, pain and experience were all derived from my own. But it was just the physical things I adopted; his voice and attitudes were not matched to mine. Every person has the fake inside him, and desires to be self sufficient, and has the element of the mass murderer inside him. Frank Finlay played Adolf Hitler and became him, yet he is one of the kindest people you could meet."

In recasting the Bodie character, the producers remembered an actor called Lewis Collins, who had appeared with Martin Shaw in *The New Avengers* episode *Obsession*. Although the two had not shared much screen time, there was clearly something in their on-screen chemistry that prompted the decision to cast the two actors together.

Brian Clemens: "I remembered the rapport he had shared with Martin, so we tested him. He seemed perfect for the role and was hired at very short notice as we needed to get back on schedule."

Gareth Hunt, who played Gambit in *The New Avengers*, has said that he was considered for one of the leads in *The Professionals*, but his ongoing commitment to that production prevented him from being considered seriously.

Lewis Collins in one of his first scenes in OLD DOG WITH NEW TRICKS, since taking over the role of Bodie from Anthony Andrews.

Lewis Collins: "I actually did a three minute test for the part of Gambit in *The New Avengers* with Gabrielle Drake as the female lead. I don't think I missed the part by much. Probably got a bronze medal. I later appeared in an episode with Martin. When they started production on *The Professionals* they remembered me and asked me to play Bodie. Actually they tricked me, they got me down to Pinewood Studios (screen tests were held here and not the Harefield unit base), saying, 'We want you to play this Sergeant, you know, come on for a week and do this Sergeant'. And I thought, 'You know, great!' But all these producers were sat around me, like laying into me, going, 'Yes I think he's got the look'. And I thought, 'I'm only playing a Sergeant for Christ-sakes', you know, and they said, 'OK you've got it'. And that was on the Friday and by the Wednesday I was filming as Bodie.

"Originally, I saw myself as a Hutch clone from *Starsky And Hutch* and I didn't want to play Hutch. Bodie looked lifeless. No depth. A bit of a show-off; but also very weak. I thought he had to be toughened up. This guy was meant to be an ex-SAS Sergeant so he better look like he could handle himself."

Born in Birkenhead, Liverpool, on 27th May 1946, Collins first found fame as *The Mojos* bass guitarist, before spending a few years at the London Academy of Music and Dramatic Art (LAMDA). After several more years in repertory companies visiting both Canada and America, he got his first break on the small screen, playing a retarded teenage recluse in *Z Cars*. Prior to his engagement on *The Professionals* he achieved fame as Gavin, the lodger, in *The Cuckoo Waltz*. He then toured the UK playing Leonard Brazil in *City Sugar* with the Prospect Theatre Company. Following this, in January 1977, Prospect offered him a year's contract and a world tour in classical plays with Derek Jacobi and Timothy West. He declined the offer, leaving himself free to take any opportunities that came along that would lead to feature film-making. A wise decision, for five months later he was on the set as Bodie.

The same three days footage, shot with Anthony Andrews at Amersham General Hospital, was then filmed with Lewis Collins, who recalled it was quite a nervous experience when, on his first day, he had to retrieve a grenade from guest star Pamela Stephenson's bra. He jokingly admits to getting it right after several takes!

Martin Shaw: "I remember poor old Lew being very nervous about the scene where we were hidden behind the car."

A 'nervous' Lewis Collins on location at Amersham General Hospital, Buckinghamshire. A scene from OLD DOG WITH NEW TRICKS.

Lewis Collins: "It was a very special thing for me because another actor (Anthony Andrews) had been shooting on it for over a week. So all the crew were sort of watching me, see the new guy on the block, you know, how's he going to do and this particular shot, which was the opening scene, was me retrieving a grenade from the bra, or cleavage rather, of Pamela Stephenson (fresh from Australia and a year before her star-making role as a member of the *Not The Nine O'Clock News* team).

"So, not only am I nervous on the first take of the day, I have to get this grenade and, all in one take, throw it into this bin, which was about 25-feet away. The other actor did it on take two, and I took five, six, seven, takes! I seemed to pass the test and carry on with the series."

Martin Shaw: "Lew and I had originally met for the first time on *The New Avengers* and we didn't particularly get on. We didn't have much interaction anyway in that episode, but when we did it was fairly abrasive."

Unlike *Starsky And Hutch*, where the lead characters were open about their friendship and respect, the pairing of Bodie and Doyle was much more ready to argue and even fight each other. The casting of Collins alongside Shaw created the tense working relationship the producers wanted.

In *Old Dog With New Tricks*, the main themes and characters are introduced and there is a long monologue from George Cowley (to a group of new recruits) that virtually repeats whole sections from the writer's brief that had been produced in the months prior to filming by Clemens.

On Wednesday 22nd June, the scenes of the weapons being stolen from the army base, were set up at the goods inwards entrance of Harefield Hospital and referred to as 'the old barracks' on the shooting script.

Peter Cotton (location manager): "We had lots of help from the hospital and used it simply because it wasn't far from the production base."

Chris Webb (stunt man): "I appeared as the army base security guard in the scene. It was Del Baker driving the truck and in rehearsals the swine nearly hit me for real. I seem to recall that the stunt arranger, Joe Dunne, did very little on the show, with Peter Brayham taking an uncredited arranger's job. I moaned to production manager, Nick Gillott about it and I think, in the end, Peter took the job full-time, even though he wouldn't be credited until series two.

The police station seen in the episode was the old Windsor Police & Fire Station in St. Leonards Road, Berkshire, which is no longer used by the emergency services, having been converted into offices, and it is now called Admiral House.

Peter Cotton (location manager): "It wasn't being used at the time, but we had a nightmare trying to close the street off for filming. It's on a busy part of town, in fact, it's on the main drag, past the main shopping area. I remember that it was difficult to stop the general public from wandering on the set. We also used the coach car park off Arthur Road, by the gas works, for the meeting place of Bodie, Doyle and Cowley. The reason was simple; it's where we arranged for the crew's trucks to be parked. Footage of a police car was also filmed here at the junction with Alma Road.

"I was told that my main priority was to find exterior shots and all interiors would be achieved within the production base at Harefield Grove. I personally found that very repetitive, but our producer Sid Hayers was adamant that the art department could recreate any set, that's what they were being paid to do! Therefore, the interiors for CI5 HQ, Cowley's office (which became a 'standing set' and would feature throughout), and Bodie's flat, were all shot at Harefield Grove, together with the prison interiors that were created in the large indoor squash courts. The interrogation room scene was executed in the large Edwardian kitchen. This room would later be redressed to provide other interiors in later episodes.

"I seem to recall we shot the sequence with Bodie's girlfriend twice, once with Anthony Andrews and once with Lewis. However, our first had a different actress to the one eventually seen on the final print (Felicity

Devonshire), the original actress (Fiona Curzon) being unavailable when re-shooting the said scene."

Visual aspects of many drama series are taken completely for granted by the viewer, and the role of the art department is seldom consciously noticed.

Michael Sierton (assistant art director): "Meticulous preparations on a huge scale are needed to ensure that the environment is always suitable in terms of setting, properties, costumes and make-up. The show ranged over one-hundred separate locations, any one of which might contain several different rooms with each requiring dressing with lots of property items. It also required the costumes, 'action props', make-up and hairdressing for artists and extras. In such a large scale procedure, planning and co-ordination feature significantly and a large team of people are involved: the scenic designer, the costume designer and make-up artist, each with an assistant; the production manager, the assistant directors, the property buyer, the dressers and numerous other location operatives.

"When a designer does an historical-period series he really puts himself on the line; research is paramount and cross-checking is phenomenal on the simplest of things. You do a programme that's 1950's and put a 1960 radio set in and there's somebody going to tell you about it in a very loud voice. If you do it dead right they won't even notice! Design is best left unobserved in a contemporary show like *The Professionals*; this is where a lot of young designers go wrong. They become infatuated with 'ego-tripping'. Their contribution is their 'design' and what it 'looks like'. And it's not there for that! Design is there only to improve and create an environment for people to work in and, as long as you do that well, it shouldn't be noticed. Because, after all, television is about people; scenery and costumes are all second-best to the people. In drama it's a guy's face that you look at."

On Friday 25th June, *The Professionals* was announced in *Screen International*, which described it as coming from *The New Avengers* team of Sidney Hayers, Brian Clemens and Albert Fennell and being funded by a major independent backer, though not revealed as London Weekend Television at this point.

Over the course of the next few episodes it was decided that, in order to tie-in with *Screen International* and various other press announcements, to rename the company yet again by introducing *The New Avengers* logo (the Union Jack lion seen in the opening credits of that show) to the title, hence Warmwood Productions was incorporated into Avengers Mark I Productions - as LWT thought Avengers Warmwood Productions didn't quite sound right.

Long Shot: *Cowley and his team know that Ramos is in town. They know he's a top assassin. They know he holds an innocent girl captive. The only thing they don't know is - who's his target?*

Anthony Read's *Long Shot* commenced filming on Monday 4th July. Born (21st April 1935) in Cannock, Staffordshire, England, he had early writing success as a freelance writer for the BBC on series such as *Z-Cars*, before sometime later becoming the script editor on *Doctor Who*, providing two scripts, *The Invasion Of Time* and *The Horns Of Nimon* between 1978-79. He would later adapt John Wyndham's novel *Chocky* for television in 1984.

THE PROFESSIONALS: Cowley (Gordon Jackson), Doyle (Martin Shaw) and Bodie (Lewis Collins) in this scene from LONG SHOT filmed on location at Stoke Park House, Stoke Poges, Buckinghamshire.

Anthony Read: "My memories, such as they are, are mainly happy. I was originally hired by Ken Ware, whom I knew well from our days at the BBC, when he was in the next-door office to me, working as script editor. He had taken over from the great John Hopkins. I was editing and then producing a series called *The Troubleshooters*, a big-business series about the fictional Mogul Oil company, which ran for seven years and won lots of awards. I also knew Brian Clemens pretty well, largely from involvement in the Writers' Guild.

"Ken invited me over to Pinewood Studios, where they were first based, and asked me if I'd be interested in a new show called something like the 'A Squad', which was in its very early stages of development. I remember having long conversations with him and Brian Clemens about the concept. It was to be action-adventure, fast and with lots of very tongue-in-cheek humour - a show like *The Sweeney*, but not a carbon copy. Although it was a new area for me, I fancied having a go, sketched out a few ideas, and was commissioned."

The action was commanded by 50-year-old Ernest Day (born 15th April 1927), who had entered the British film industry as a camera operator in the mid 1950's, before becoming a director of photography in 1968. He later became the second unit director on the James Bond feature, *The Spy Who Loved Me* a few months before arriving on *The Professionals* set.

Boom operator Ken Nightingall. Behind-the-scenes on LONG SHOT.

Minor revisions were made to the original script, when Ramos makes his second attempt on Cowley at CI5 HQ. His attack being staved off by Bodie and Doyle, they chase Ramos to a deserted aircraft hanger and apprehend him. In the finished product Ramos is simply captured in Cowley's office at CI5 HQ.

The properties, furniture and furnishings chosen by the set dresser to dress a set are extremely important both in shaping the environment and defining the characters using it. This can be said of Cowley's office, which would be used throughout the series as a standing set. Although the designer is responsible for the visual appearance of the room, ultimately all decisions about the way it will be finally presented on the screen rest with the director. In keeping with the approach usually adopted by designers in contemporary location work, assistant art director Michael Sierton made no attempt to draw up elaborate sketches and plans in advance. The design was negotiated through discussion, where necessary trying out ideas in rough by sketching hypothetical furniture arrangements on a photograph of a bare room with a chinagraph pencil.

Michael Sierton (assistant art director): "The person who actually decides what is the focus point of the room and where the principle characters are going to be positioned when Cowley's behind the desk, and the relationship between where he sits, the door, and various other equipment is, of course, the director. He's going to shoot it; only he knows how. But on the basis that we've both read the script, and there are certain basic mechanics in filming which with experience everyone acquires, you very easily latch onto the same lines. You invariably follow how a director is thinking.

"With a director like Ernest Day you could see it 'ticking around' even if he wasn't committing himself an awful lot. With another director, who was less sure, you could decide on that room and say, 'I've decided if we put that desk there, with the door there, we can pan people this way and that'. And they'd say, 'That looks fine, thank you very much!' However, with Ernest you couldn't do that. You can offer it up, but with almost the certain knowledge that it would be rejected. The rejection though was a positive step, in the sense that you knew that it wasn't what it was going to be. So you could start thinking again.

"It's a bit like playing mental hide and seek with someone. He wasn't forthcoming in the sense that a designer could say, 'That's what he wants!' He'd say, 'I think he's the sort of person who'll have numerous phones on his desk'. He'd talk background and character any time you wanted, but when it came to the procedure of actually shooting it he became very non-committal, and a lot of the time I didn't think he'd made up his mind until the last minute. I think he was a very spur-of-the-moment person in an image sense."

The crew used the large club house at Stoke Poges Golf Club, near Slough, Berkshire, for establishing shots of the conference building, where footage for both *The New Avengers* episode *The Eagle's Nest* and *The Saint* adventure *The Man Who Liked Lions* had previously been shot, as well as sequences for the James Bond film *Goldfinger*.

Ed Bishop (Dr. Harbinger): "They were on their ass, they did not have any money, so they were reduced to bringing in film crews which is the kiss of death. There were a whole bunch of these old codgers sitting on a porch while we were filming. I said to Nadim Sawalha, who was dressed as an Arab, 'Come on, let's walk around', and I had my briefcase with me. So these guys couldn't hear us, but they could see us. I'm there in my suit, with this Arab, looking like I was pointing things out to him. It looked like the place was being flogged."

Ed Bishop was born (11th June 1932) in Bay Ridge, Brooklyn, New York as George Victor Bishop, but changed his name to Edward Bishop when he realised an actor named George Bishop already existed. He came to England in 1959 and studied at LAMDA - and quickly made a career as an American actor in England. He is best known for his television roles working with producer Gerry Anderson, most notably as Commander Ed Straker in *UFO*.

Although *The Professionals* made use of as many real-life structures as possible, sometimes this was not always possible, and a construction team was hired to build a suitable set. Responsibility for this fell to Fred Walker, who as construction manager co-ordinated the entire process of set building, from initial planning through to the final coat of paint on the finished sets.

Lewis Collins and Martin Shaw (above) on location at Stoke Poges Golf Club for LONG SHOT. And behind-the-scenes with clapper/loader Simon Hume (below).

Fred Walker (construction manager): "The script required that at the conference centre we had to have an 'army-type' watch-tower built for the two leads to keep guard from. The first problem we encountered was that although we'd been given the go-ahead to erect the structure by the land owners, they stipulated exactly where we had to set up our team and build it. They put us up out of the way of the main house, and we had terrible trouble getting the crew down there. When we eventually got all our materials together it was nearly a day wasted, leaving the producers none too happy that we were so far behind. Then we had to build it; and that took some doing as at first the material supplied kept causing the structure to sink due to the soft ground. In the end we had to re-enforce the base with timber, and eventually the director achieved the desired shots/scenes very late in the afternoon/early evening.

An American diplomat requires protection, but are Doyle (Martin Shaw) and Bodie (Lewis Collins) protecting the correct target? A scene from LONG SHOT.

"I also remember that during the filming of the sequence when Martin and Lewis had to clamber over the wall at the mansion house, we had problems with actor Robert Gillespie (Sammy); because he just didn't feel he could jump down the other end saying it was too high and he might injure himself. Finally the two leads helped him out, but it caused us much frustration, because there was no other way we could have shot the scene. He wasn't keen on the next shot either where he had to grab the branch and shimmy along. In order to stop the branch swinging back, out of shot, we had a couple of guys weighing it down."

Undoubtedly the most problematic location to find for this episode was the demolition site where Ramos has hidden Mitchell's daughter, Mandy. Location manager Peter Cotton was still searching for a suitable location well into the first week's filming, and time was running out. Unfortunately no demolition company was prepared to hold up work on a commercial site for a few days, for fear of penalty clauses being exacted. For this reason Peter had been forced to search housing development sites where the developers were not under the same pressure. Sadly no site could be found that, even with a use of restricted camera angles, looked appropriate to the filming requirements.

The site that was eventually adopted for the production was found completely by accident as Peter Cotton drove the director, Ernest Day, back to the unit base after a fruitless recce to a housing estate in Central Watford, Hertfordshire.

Peter Cotton: "Everywhere I found wasn't really suitable, or we couldn't get permission to film. Finally we compromised on this place that we passed on the way back to Harefield, an old factory that was already partly demolished. We had a meeting with the site foreman and, at first, he was in two minds as to whether it was safe enough to mount camera crews around the structure. Finally, he agreed providing the actors and crew would be covered by our insurance, and should anything untoward happen it wouldn't come back on him. Ernest agreed that we would cause the minimum of disruption, and filming would be wrapped up in a day. Come the filming all seemed to run to plan."

Where The Jungle Ends: *Mercenaries, jungle fighters; parachuting in to wage bloody war...in Britain! These are the real pros, the real killers. Can Cowley match them?*

Where The Jungle Ends went before the cameras on Monday 18th July. This was the second script written by Brian Clemens and directed by future producer Raymond Menmuir, who had previously directed videotaped episodes of *The Avengers*, *Redcap*, *Upstairs Downstairs* and *The Duchess Of Duke Street*.

Martin Shaw as Ray Doyle takes aim in a un-used scene from WHERE THE JUNGLE ENDS.

The work of the actors and director is paramount, but even simple sequences were not without problems:

Ernie Steward (lighting cameraman): "I recall that director Ray Menmuir had terrible trouble trying to get any sort of 'character' out of actor David Suchet (who subsequently won popular acclaim for his definitive portrayal of Hercule Poirot). Many scenes had to be re-shot because David was either lacking in vocal delivery, or would forget his lines, usually accompanied by a long pause between sentences. At one point, Ray said something like, 'David, why are you such hard work?'

"On a funnier note is the scene when Lewis's character is getting told off by Cowley in the office; it took several takes because Gordon Jackson was such a wonderful man, who rarely lost his temper, that I think Lew saw the funny side of it. Every time Gordon raised his voice, Lew would start to giggle, and he found it very difficult to keep a straight face throughout the shoot. The only person who wasn't laughing was Ray, when this simple scene ended up taking much longer that it should have done."

A bank raid is carried out military style! Bodie knows the group responsible, but they seem to have got the better of CI5 boss George Cowley (Gordon Jackson) in this scene from WHERE THE JUNGLE ENDS.

Benny's wife, Cynthia, lived at Hazlewood Tower, Golborne Gardens, Kensal Town, West London, and this site got location manager Peter Cotton on the wrong side of the producers.

Peter Cotton: "Selecting sites for the director and designer to view and obtaining permission for their use from the owners is a time-consuming activity. It was necessary to choose sites that could accommodate the considerable number of vehicles associated with a production unit and, especially in the case of houses or flats, to choose locations in quiet roads where shooting would not be constantly interrupted by disruptive background sound. Based out of Harefield, it was difficult to get suitable locations like this. I was told we only had a fifteen-mile radius of the unit base. The series was supposed to be set in London, yet we were not allowed to film near the capital. Director Ray Menmuir insisted on the location and it was used. We also used the old Air Terminal on Kensington High Street in London.

"The old barracks at Harefield Hospital were utilised again as 'The Barrowsby Nuclear Plant', with the large house situated nearby in the grounds, the Park Mansion, doubling as the school, attended by Sinclair's daughter. The police/truck chases we did just behind Slough's High Street (some footage of a blue Police car, filmed at the St. Laurence Way roundabout, was even inserted into the shows first episode, *Old Dog With New Tricks*, which was in the editing rooms at the same time). The bank was on Eton's High Street and we had a nightmare closing off the street. Other footage was filmed at Croxley Hall Wood, near Croxley Green, which was where Bodie, Doyle and Cowley pursue Krivas and his gang. We then continued the pursuit through the gravel pits back at Harefield."

These scenes climaxed in an unarmed fight between Bodie and Krivas.

Lewis Collins: "I remember it as being one of my first unarmed fights in the series. The actor, who was in fact a stunt man, worked out a few movements beforehand, but as the cameras started 'rolling' he hit me, hard, and almost without thinking I punched him back. We got a bit carried away and both ended up tearing each other to shreds. At the end of it all we emerged with two black eyes and very bruised faces! The best part of it was that we remained firm friends and later enjoyed a pint at the local!"

A group of former comrades from Bodie's mercenary days reappear in England; can Doyle (Martin Shaw) catch up with Krivas, the ring leader? A scene from WHERE THE JUNGLE ENDS.

After a disagreement with Ray Menmuir, assistant director Bill Westley, who had once been Diana Rigg's stunt double in *The Avengers*, broke his collarbone and was unable to continue filming which forced the crew to bring in Bert Batt to take over for the remainder of the episode. Westley's response to the incident was short and sweet: "The man (Menmuir) was a 'robber'!"

Bill Westley: "Well, I suppose it was my fault really! We'd got Lew, who was a nuisance at the best of times and actually not that great at the action stuff, so Ray told me to take him out and show him the ropes. We headed off into the grounds of Harefield Grove and I was showing him how to go from one tree to another while holding a gun at the same time. After a couple of swoops I got my foot caught in a root and fell badly, and then I heard the crack, I'd broken my collarbone. I was laid off for a few weeks, and my old colleague Bert Batt came in to help out. What annoyed me was that Ray had told the producers I had done the damage off my own back, and was, therefore, not covered by the company insurance. Bert actually finished the episode off when Ray couldn't wrap it up in the ten days allocated to the episode. Bert wasn't over keen on the production, did me the favour, and left."

However, that wasn't the only time Bill Westley had a problem that day!

Robin McDonald (focus puller): "I had been called in to take over for a few days and we were in a room at Harefield Grove. David Suchet was giving orders to his gang and we were doing the head and shoulder shots, the close ups. Westley called it a wrap, when I said to Menmuir, 'Hang on, we haven't done a close up on David yet'. Westley argued blind we had. Of course, we hadn't, and Menmuir came over and thanked me with a firm handshake. When I got the full time job the following year, that's how Menmuir told me he'd remembered me."

Original location 'recce' shots of the cellars at Harefield Grove, which served as Cusak's gun store in WHERE THE JUNGLE ENDS.

Although associate producer Ron Fry was not as hands-on as he would have liked at this stage due to his commitment in Toronto with *The New Avengers*, he did however make return visits to the production.

Ron Fry: "I remember on one occasion arranging for Martin and Lewis to have some combat tuition from the Special Air Services, SAS, which I fixed through my, then, contact at Scotland Yard. They were trained in self-defence and unarmed combat by an SAS major and spent time at a training establishment where they were taught how to use guns and explosives. A further day was spent at a police driver finishing school in London, learning how to control a car safely on the skidpan."

Martin Shaw: "We had a regimental sergeant from the SAS to give us advice on the martial arts for the series. And it's frightening what you could do with your hands. But I would never use those kind of skills if I got into trouble."

Lewis Collins: "I particularly looked forward to meeting him in my efforts to toughen up the Bodie character. But afterwards I wasn't so sure. He terrified me. Martin had been trained in karate and knew a lot of people capable of killing with their bare hands, but as he said, the difference was this guy had done it! We tried to explain that we were only a pair of actors, but he wouldn't have any of it. He dragged me off to a wood and ordered me to empty the magazine of a 9mm Browning pistol at him, roll over, reload and then get off two more shots...as he came blasting with a machine gun. He took it all for real and even though we had been firing blanks, he frightened the life out of me. I was running wild-eyed and trying to re-load as he hit me. 'You're dead!' he screamed, wrenched my arm back, kicked the pistol away and slammed his boot into my back. I couldn't stand for days."

Post-production is the concluding stage in the process of finishing an episode; from the mass of material recorded, what will finally be transmitted is selected, ordered and refined. Film editor Barry Peters recalled that the bank robbery scenes had to be extended.

Barry Peters: "When we came to edit these shots, both producer Sid Hayers and myself decided they needed more in the way of police cars chasing the truck. A small second unit was immediately dispatched and shot sequences of several police cars in pursuit. We didn't have the truck at the production office, so we carefully intermixed the new footage to give the indication that they were indeed behind the truck."

Killer With A Long Arm: *The CI5 team become aware of an assassination plot involving a rifle with a range of over two miles. But where is the gunman and who is his target?*

Another Brian Clemens script, *Killer With A Long Arm* came next, starting on Monday 1st August and showed the wide-ranging remit of CI5. This was the first episode to showcase the series international flavour. David Wickes directed the episode with a good degree of tension that included stock footage from that year's Wimbledon finals featuring Bjorn Borg.

David Wickes was born in 1940 into a show business family and spent several years in the army before moving into television and becoming the first director on *World Of Sport*. He later crossed over to drama and worked extensively on *Public Eye*. After directing episodes of *Special Branch* and several commercials, he went on to direct on *The Sweeney* as well as the *Sweeney!* feature film.

David Wickes (director): "It always helps to work with people with whom one has a rapport (Michael Latimer and Diane Keen). What I liked best about *Killer With A Long Arm* was the idea behind it, that death can come silently, out of nowhere, and end the life of a leading figure like King Constantin in full view of the world, 9/11 in microcosm."

Martin Shaw as Doyle on the set of KILLER WITH A LONG ARM.

CI5 become aware of an assassination plot involving a rifle with a range of over two miles. But where is the gunman, and who is the target? Can Bodie (Lewis Collins) find out in this scene from KILLER WITH A LONG ARM.

Michael Latimer (Georgi): "I have played a role in two *Professionals* episodes, once the corrupt copper boss (Willis in *Fall Girl*) and once the killer. Like in all British series the episodes were shot in ten days, therefore there was no time for discussions on action and motivation. I had to speak with a Greek accent in this episode, and that was fun. Georgi was invented as a character role, in my opinion, really to play-act and have fun. David Wickes was in my eyes the best director of TV films in those times, and I was exhilarated to be able to work with him. Directors have the tendency to work with people they like and whose skills they appreciate, this makes life easier. David and I get on well together and even if I had not got the hang of the play-acting, I would, surely have worked with him again.

"I believe that I have worked with Gordon Jackson at least five times (naturally two of which in *The Professionals*). He was such a kind man, that one would wonder, how does he do it? He was polite and patient from morning till evening and had a nice word left for each and everyone. In *The Professionals* Martin and Lewis were all the time flying all over the country, masculine and dynamic, intervening then Gordon, always cheerful and calm all through the day."

CI5 become aware that an assassination plot on a group of visiting Greek Royals is being planned using a long range rifle. But Doyle (Martin Shaw) must first find out who the gunman is before it's too late in this unused scene from KILLER WITH A LONG ARM.

David Wickes: "Sidney Hayers was older than later series producer Raymond Menmuir and far more experienced. He had also been a fighter pilot, so he knew a thing or two about danger and tension. Sidney was highly knowledgeable about all aspects of filmmaking (he had once been an outstanding editor) and had made some very successful feature films, not least among which was the famous *Payroll* starring Stanley Baker, which set the tone for many later icons such as Mike Hodges' *Get Carter*. As a consequence, working with Sidney Hayers was a privilege and a pleasure. I brought him in to direct some of the HBO series *Marlowe Private Eye* and also *The New Professionals*."

Well over a thousand design properties were required for *The Professionals*. A proportion of these were already available at the location and Peter Cotton, the location manager, negotiated their use separately with the owners. Responsibility for the acquisition of the rest was in the hands of Gordon Billings, the property buyer. The series required a substantial number of 'action' props (properties handled by the actor in the course of the action), about thirty motor vehicles, and additional 'out-of-vision' items used to maintain and clean the locations.

Gordon Billings (property buyer): "We had some very odd ones for this episode, and one which I particularly remember is the scarecrow in the middle of the field. You'd think finding an item such as this would have been easy; but scarecrows weren't as widely used as you may have thought. In the end, after a fruitless time asking, and searching, the local farms, we made our own in the production office with help from the wardrobe department.

"Another odd requirement was the purchase of several dozen plates, to be smashed by 'the boys' during the Greek restaurant scenes. The restaurant owner didn't want to supply crockery from his own stock for obvious reasons, so it necessitated a visit to a local manufacturer in West London."

Doyle is seen driving Bodie's car (Triumph Dolomite) during the episode, and Gordon Billings also has some clear recollections about this.

Gordon Billings: "The car Martin Shaw had used (the Rover) had broken down, or been damaged, or something like that. I was told to obtain a replacement as soon as. Dealing with British Leyland was not a happy experience; the only car we had on a 'permanent' contract was the white Dolomite, the others, including Cowley's Rover and various other Austins, could be recalled whenever they (British Leyland) felt like it. I told their Press office, we needed another 'permanent' car, which we could keep until the end of production. They kept telling me they didn't have anything, and after much deliberation I eventually managed to secure a TR7. I told producer Sid Hayers everything was in hand and Martin would have a TR7 to drive in a few days, which was good because it was needed for this episode. Guess what? It never showed, and British Leyland's press officer told me they'd had problems getting it from whoever it was with, but I was to be confident this was only a minor delay, and things would be resolved in matter of days. I had that excuse for weeks, and I seem to recall it was a few months before it was finally delivered."

Lighting cameraman Ernie Steward recalls his own problems associated with the filming of this episode.

Ernie Steward: "We were filming at a house in a busy part of Windsor, and director David Wickes wanted a panning shot of Martin and Lewis chasing the young lad (Jonathan Hyde) from the house into the alley. We had two problems here: First, in order to get the shot we had to reposition the camera to the opposite side of the road and this was plagued by the onslaught of traffic. Second, David didn't like the back of the house for the fight sequence, so we had to pack up and move to a similar bit of waste ground, and an alleyway, further up the road in order to obtain the type of sequence David was after.

"Another scene we did was when actress Diane Keen gets knocked over outside the shopping centre in Watford. Although the Supermarket had agreed we could use the inside of the shop, they wouldn't close to the public in order for us to get our shots, so we had to bide our time, and wait for a non-busy period when crowds were at a minimum, and that took several takes; people kept waving, or looking, at the camera and crew. In the end we did it very quickly and with the camera positioned out of the way behind a display cabinet so as not to attract the attention of any shoppers. We got there in the end, but it took a lot longer than it should have."

Bodie (Lewis Collins) springs into action during the pursuit of a wanted gang member in KILLER WITH A LONG ARM.

In terms of communications, and seen for the first time in this episode, Bodie, Doyle, and Cowley favour the Pye Pocketfone PF8 radio (replacing the PF1 seen in *Old Dog With New Tricks*), a unit commonly used by the police at the time. However, although a very strong, rugged design, they weren't particularly powerful. Generating only 0.5 watts of power and operating on the UHF band between 450-470 MHz, they would only achieve a reach of just over a mile! The units would be used right up to the end of the show in 1981.

A sequence set at Doyle's flat was trimmed from the story for timing reasons; scheduled to be filmed immediately before Cowley briefs the two agents following the shooting of the policeman by Costa. The scene was laid out in the shooting schedule as follows:

Ext: Doyle's flat

Bodie knocks on his partner's flat door.
BODIE: *Mornin', Doyle - let me in. Big news...*

In KILLER WITH A LONG ARM a golfer has been killed by a top Greek assassin. Doyle (Martin Shaw), forensic expert Mervin (Anthony Carrick), and Bodie (Lewis Collins) must find out why?

Location manager Peter Cotton called upon the services of Flackwell Heath Golf Club, near High Wycombe, Buckinghamshire, for these scenes: "No other golf clubs, like the ones near the Harefield Grove unit base - Moor Park (Rickmansworth), and Denham (Middlesex) - were able to accommodate our tight schedules. I found this one while on a location recce trip along the M40 to Amersham."

DOYLE: *You, Bodie* (keeps the chain firmly on the door) *can wait three minutes. Then I'll be out.*
BODIE: *Is this the way to treat a pal?*
DOYLE: *It is when there's a Betty involved.*
BODIE: (trying to peer around the door) *You don't have - in there?*
DOYLE: *You wouldn't know, would you, Bodie? Or are they all Betty's to you?*
BODIE: *They had a way of treating people like you in the jungle. Stake 'em out with a trickle of honey up their legs, and...*
DOYLE: *Yeah, I've heard all about those ants in your pants. Now let me say a sweet good-bye and I'll be with you* (closes door).
Emerging Doyle wiped his mouth very ostentatiously and smirked. That convinced Bodie that Doyle had been alone in the apartment - hadn't he?

Peter Cotton (location manager): "The apartment block that the Greek terrorists use as their base was Minster Court, just off Hanger Lane, in Ealing, London, which again was quite a way out from the unit base, but it was the only suitable location we could find. High-rise flats like that were virtually non-existent near Harefield, the unit base."

Heroes: *A protection job for Bodie and Doyle - innocent people are in jeopardy and the assignment gets out of hand. The CI5 team fight a race against time...*

The next episode, *Heroes*, which sees a protection job for Bodie and Doyle - where innocent people are in jeopardy, went into production on Monday 15th August. It was credited to James McAteer, a pen-name for Peter John Hammond (born 1934), who was unhappy with rewrites enacted by Brian Clemens and asked for his name to be removed. Hammond was a well-established writer by the mid-1970's acting as script editor on *Z-Cars* and submitting ideas to *Dixon Of Dock Green*, *Hunter's Walk*, *Special Branch*, *Target*, *New Scotland Yard* and *Spy Trap*. He also worked on telefantasy serials such as *Ace Of Wands* and later created *Sapphire And Steel*.

Peter John Hammond (writer): "I've always preferred writing character-led stories that relied on atmosphere and, if you like, dealt with areas on the edge of crime. I never liked writing about guns and fast cars. That's why programmes like *Z-Cars*, *The Gentle Touch* or episodes of *The Bill*, suited me. I was less happy working on shows that depended upon action for action's sake, and my ideas suffered because of this.

"Having worked on many crime shows, I like to think that I would never allow myself to write clichéd scenes that involved criminals sitting around a table with a map and toy cars, saying, 'This is the way we do it.' I've always preferred to use hidden menace. In my original draft of *Heroes*, the criminals were never seen and I felt that this added to the build up of menace. It was ordinary people being threatened by the unknown. So what did I find when I received my production copy of the script? You've guessed it, crooks sitting around a table with maps and toy cars, etc. Without consultation, my script was 'written over' by the producers and ended up being just another run-of-the-mill cop show.

"I was told by the then script editor (Ken Ware) that this was nothing new as far as production scripts were concerned. I therefore decided to withdraw my name from the script; this was the first and only time I've ever been inclined to do this, but was advised by the script editor to use a pseudonym in order to protect my right to royalties. Therefore Jim McAteer was born.

"It was a sad experience, especially as I'd delivered a second episode, which was of course rejected when I decided I wanted nothing more to do with that particular company. The episode called *Victims* was about a political extremists' failed raid on a diplomatic vehicle. In order to escape from the trap, they capture a bus, which was on its way to the airport. The passengers are families of illegal immigrants who would be deported. These people regretfully are taken hostage by the extremists, and it is Bodie and Doyle's task to follow the bus and kind of ensure that they would capture the villains and that the immigrants suffered no harm. I thought that was a very moving story, and I was very proud of it. It is regrettable that, due to the many quarrels, they never filmed it."

When a newspaper irresponsibly publish a list of witnesses' names to an assassination, it is left to C15 to not only protect them but, at the same time, apprehend the killers before they strike again. Bodie (Lewis Collins) in a scene from HEROES.

The producers wanted Bill Bain to direct the episode, but the production secretary became confused, or misheard the name, and Canadian director William Brayne was contacted and offered the work. Graduate of Euston Films, Brayne, born 10th October 1935, had worked on film series such as *Special Branch*, *Van Der Valk* and *The Sweeney* and had been jokingly given the comical nickname of 'The Brain Of Britain' as he never got things right the first time (and wasn't even British)! He would become the shows most prolific director.

Bill Westley (first assistant director): "We had to set up the traffic jam where the security van is ambushed on the Tring by-pass, but the production wouldn't stretch to many more than eight cars. I remember that during the pre-production talks director Bill Brayne had requested to the producers that we'd need at least fifty cars to set it up properly. I turned to Bill and said that they wouldn't give us that many, we'd be lucky to get a dozen, never mind fifty. I promised him that with the eight cars we'd been given, and some clever editing, I'd show him how to give the impression that we had more, and when Bill eventually saw the rushes, he was pretty impressed with what we'd achieved."

Director Bill Brayne encountered other issues during the filming of this episode - the shoot was plagued by constant heavy rain, which held up filming on several occasions.

Bill Brayne (director): "Despite the rain, this was not one of my favourite episodes. I liked the use of the masks and the only good shot is when the car turns over and you see the actors in the same frame. I don't even think we had a second camera on that one. It was something I would have tried to do often had the budget allowed - but sadly on shows like *The Professionals* this wasn't the case and we had to make do with what we had."

Director William Brayne on the set of HEROES set with Lewis Collins and Martin Shaw. The shoot was plagued by substantial rainfall, which caused a disruption in filming.

Peter Cotton (location manager): "Location work for the shoot-out with the raiders was done at the Benskins brewery complex on the High Street, Watford - then deserted and now demolished. The hi-jack, and subsequent killing of Patterson, occurred on the A41M, which was the recently built Tring by-pass - some construction work was still taking place, which is why we managed to make use of the complete stretch of road. Additional footage was executed at Jock's Cafe on the A4 Colnbrook by-pass, which was a favourite stopping point on many productions including *The Sweeney*."

John Castle was born (14th January 1940) in Croydon, Surrey and studied English and German at Trinity College, Dublin, before training for the stage at RADA. Prior to his role as CI5 agent Tommy McKay in HEROES, he took on the role of Postumus in the 1976 BBC television adaptation of I, CLAUDIUS.

According to the script, the newly weds, Mr. and Mrs. Bilston are allegedly staying at The Ship Hotel in Dorking, Surrey.

Peter Cotton (location manager): "Actually it's the Compleat Angler Hotel, near Marlow Bridge, Buckinghamshire, which was a late replacement when my original location of the Monkey Island Hotel, near Bray, became unavailable due to the production falling behind schedule. The shooting of the couple takes place on the nearby riverbanks. I went past the Compleat Angler when I was on a recce of Maidenhead for the next episode *Private Madness, Public Danger*. This episode (*Heroes*) was the turning point in the show, as we seriously fell behind in filming, which didn't go down too well with the hierarchy - and it's not as if I hadn't told them that it was heading this way!"

In the climatic shoot-out on the banks of the River Thames, near Datchett, Berkshire, the script required that in order to protect Mr. Sumner, Bodie must tackle him to the ground thus preventing him from getting shot. However, in reality, Lewis Collins and actor David Baron, didn't see eye-to-eye over the scene and the two actors nearly ended up in what can only be described as a 'pub brawl'.

Martin Shaw and Lewis Collins behind-the-scenes on the set of HEROES.

Things came to a head while *Heroes* was in production and the script editor, Kenneth Ware, departed before principle shooting on the episode was complete.

Ron Fry (associate producer): "I had just returned from Canada, after finishing *The New Avengers*, to find Dennis Spooner had reluctantly agreed to take over. Apparently Ken was not having much success with the scripts, especially this one by P J Hammond, which over ran by six weeks. The second unit worked for another couple of weeks to complete it."

Dennis Spooner, born in Tottenham, North London on 1st December 1932, had written jokes for Harry Worth, scripts for *Coronation Street* and played football for Leyton Orient's third team. By 1961 he was also working on the Gerry Anderson puppet series *Fireball XL5*. This was followed with work on *The Avengers, No Hiding Place, Stingray, Hancock* and *Doctor Who*. He then returned to the Gerry Anderson fold for *Thunderbirds*, and would later script edit *Doctor Who*, write on *The Baron*, co-create *Man In A Suitcase*, create *Randall & Hopkirk (Deceased)*, write on *Thriller, The Adventurer*, and *The*

New Avengers. He only took the position on *The Professionals* as favour to Brian Clemens, as in his opinion, it wasn't the kind of show he preferred to work on.

Brian Clemens: "When I created the series, it was my intention to write only one or two episodes and, having employed a script editor, I went on holiday and left him to commission further stories. In the end, however, I had to write the majority of the stories because they weren't moving fast enough...it really was a crisis situation because they didn't know what to do. Ken Ware became a little of a disappointment actually because he was one of the old school script editors who, if the script wasn't any good he couldn't, like Terry Nation or Dennis Spooner could do, sit down and write the damm thing himself. What we'd have is a poor script added to which Ken, who was a nice man, but didn't seem to have much of a sense of humour in real life and I think that appeared in the work he was associated with."

Several additional scenes were added and filmed over the course of the coming months: The opening scene with Patterson at the hotel; Doyle buying the newspaper from the newsagent and informing Cowley of its content regarding the witnesses (originally scripted to occur within Cowley's office); and the attempted drive-by killing of Ralph May (estate car owner) had to be re-filmed.

Cast as John Gerry Patterson was Bruce Boa; born (10th July 1930) in Calgary, Alberta, Canada, he played for the Calgary Stampeders (Canadian Football League) in 1952 before he decided to settle in England around 1959 with his wife where he found himself cast in many roles (generally as an American) on British television and in films. On television, his most notable role is probably the belligerent American guest, Mr. Hamilton, in the *Waldorf Salad* episode of the BBC hotel sitcom *Fawlty Towers*.

Bruce Boa: "Despite being hired for the duration of the episode the production fell behind in filming and I can only recall doing the office (CI5 HQ) scenes at Harefield on the initial shoot. I didn't do the motorway hijack scenes as they used a stunt double in my place and then did a close-up back in the studio. I then remember getting a call from my agent some time later telling me they wanted me for some more footage as the episode needed extra scenes doing. We did these at the Hotel ('Holiday Inn') near Heathrow Airport late in the afternoon, or early evening, and involved me in some shots with Gordon Jackson, who was a stickler for learning his lines, and was always spot on with his delivery. A sequence outside where I get shot at from the Hotel roof also had to be filmed. This bit took a few goes, as the explosive charge used to smash the glass on the cars wing mirror didn't go off with the cameras rolling. Three, or four, goes later the director was happy with the shot."

Private Madness, Public Danger: Take a dangerous drug, add a killing or three, an addict and a crazy man. Stir well, and you have big, big trouble for Cowley and his men.

Writer Anthony Read provided the script for *Private Madness, Public Danger*, which began filming on Tuesday 30th August.

Anthony Read: "Brian Clemens was so pleased with the script *Private Madness, Public Danger*, which had an original working title of *Timebomb*, that he said he wanted to use it as the opening episode (first to be broadcast), rather than one of his own. That was quite a privilege to have the writer and producer of a show say that."

The threat to release a deadly chemical into London's water system was allegedly based on real incidents inspired by the IRA.

Another *Doctor Who* director, the late Douglas (Gaston Sydney) Camfield (born 8th May 1931), who had also worked on *Paul Temple, Van Der Valk, Blake's 7, The Nightmare Man, Special Branch, The Sweeney* and a well-received BBC adaptation of *Beau Geste*, commanded the action. His work is fondly remembered by many of the crew that worked with him:

Ernie Steward (lighting cameraman): "Doug Camfield was an excellent director. He was always thinking several shots ahead. In a sense, he was not only the director, but also served as the first assistant. Most directors can only think of the shot in hand, but Doug was already discussing the next one before we'd even set it up - watching him work was mind-blowing. He brought his time as a Second Lieutenant in the British Army to the set and was very regimental in his outlook; he'd get the crew doing as he wanted with the click of his fingers. He was a genius and a pleasure to work with and seemed to know more about camerawork than I did!"

Bill Westley (assistant director): "Doug had a reputation for being a very visual director. He was brilliant at taking pictures. You could see a Doug Camfield shot a mile off, like the one where the guy (Ian Fairbairn) jumps from the window of the office block in a dreamy-drug induced state. The way he incorporates the clever use of effects lens and distortion techniques. That is a Doug Camfield shot, and he'd say there weren't many of those."

In PRIVATE MADNESS, PUBLIC DANGER Bodie (Lewis Collins) and Cowley (Gordon Jackson) investigate the effects of ADX?

Bodie (Lewis Collins) gets 'wet' in PRIVATE MADNESS, PUBLIC DANGER.

The sequence where Cowley orders Bodie and Doyle to investigate the deaths at World Chemical Products underwent a number of changes from what was initially planned in both the script and the filming schedule. The following scene was not filmed and the character of Tony Bastable was dropped:

Ext: CI5 Training Grounds
Bodie and Doyle are in a remote area being put through their paces: Target practice, obstacle courses, etc.
Bodie and Doyle are shooting at man-shape targets. New recruit Tony Bastable has joined them.
BODIE: *Not bad. If the target had been smiling lately he'd have missed with a couple.*
DOYLE: *You were slow opening up, Tony.* (Doyle taking the mickey) *It don't always pay to go into the stance, no matter what regulations say. Like we told you...*
BODIE: (nodding) *Regulations say a police marksman with a rifle must always fire from the shoulder and use the sights. Well, Tony, we're not police. We're CI5. Sometimes you have to cut corners.*
DOYLE: *Not, Bodie, whilst I am within earshot!*
Cowley's voice cuts them short...
COWLEY: *Bodie, Doyle...*

Making one of three appearances in the show was Trevor Adams as CI5 agent Benny, later seen in *Stake Out* and the second series story *The Rack*. He attended the former Harold Hill Grammar School, in Romford, Essex, from 1957 to 1964 and played leading roles in a number of school plays. Later he trained at RADA and was a member of the National Youth Threatre. He spent a year at Stratford-Upon-Avon before turning to television, where he was often cast as a criminal.

He appeared in a variety of programmes such the 1971 TV play *Private Road, Public Eye* (1972), and in *The Wedding Party* episode of *Fawlty Towers* (1975). He is fondly remembered as Tony Webster in *The Fall and Rise Of Reginald Perrin.* Prior to his engagement on *The Professionals*, he was cast as Sandy, a filing clerk, in *The New Avengers* episode *Dead Men Are Dangerous.*

Nesbitt meets Susan Fenton at Thorpe Park Ski Lakes, Chertsey, Surrey, and the later sequence, when he is finally hunted down in the vicinity of the reservoir, was also filmed there. Location manager Peter Cotton admitted that it was the only location available at the time of filming. Filming scenes here proved problematic for actors and crew alike.

Bill Westly (assistant director): "A majority of the scenes we shot from a small boat positioned by the ski ramp. We had problems, firstly, because we only had room on the boat for a small crew, and secondly, because it proved very difficult to keep the cameras steady while filming. In the end, most of the guys close-up 'head-shots' we achieved by being positioned away from the ramp on the bank-side. Filming Keith Barron's scene where he rows up to the barrel and positions the target explosive did not go according to plan either. Every time Keith pulled up near the barrel, and tried to put the target on, he kept pushing himself away from it. If you watch the sequence you will see how much difficulty he has keeping the boat steady, and near the barrel - in the end we had to settle with what we could get because there was no way the boat was going to keep still for long enough."

Keith Barron, born (8th August 1936) in Mexborough, Yorkshire, is well known from numerous appearances on British television from the 1960's to the present day. One of his best-loved and most-remembered roles was in the 1980's British sitcom *Duty Free*.

In PRIVATE MADNESS, PUBLIC DANGER, CI5's Doyle (Martin Shaw) and Bodie (Lewis Collins) investigate a number of mysterious deaths at a chemicals company, and discover a plot to contaminate London's water supplies.

Joe Dunne (fight arranger): "The fight sequences we did at the farmhouse (Love Hill House, Iver, Buckinghamshire) were executed military style by director Douglas Camfield, and beautifully edited together under his guidance in post-production. One of the stunt guys lost control of the bronze Ford Cortina when he hit one of the outbuildings. The car proved fairly unusable thereafter. Lewis Collins also managed to damage the underside of the Triumph Dolomite on its arrival at Thorpe Park; he took the hump in the field way too fast, necessitating some damage to the front suspension. Luckily the shots we needed the car for had been done, and it was 'carted' back to the unit base for inspection."

John Brackstone (owner of Love Hill House): "My first recollections of the two days *The Professionals* arrived at our farm house for filming was when a young man (Peter Cotton) wandered on to the farm and introduced himself as the location scout for a new series being made called *The Professionals*, and asked if they could do a bit of filming on the farm; making full use of the land for parking the crew trucks. We hadn't heard of the show at the time, so we agreed a fee and a few weeks later they arrived. It was amazing to see that the first thing that turned up, at around seven in the morning, was the food wagon, which promptly set up and starting making breakfast. From then on masses of large lorries, trucks, and cars arrived, parked up, and about a hundred people made their way to be fed; that was before anybody had even set a camera up! Shortly afterwards, they began setting up the generators for the lighting and cameras. I think the actors arrived early morning, and started to be put through their paces by a very flamboyant director. In the background the stunt guys were rehearsing the fight scenes and car sequences over and over again.

"My mother had fond memories of the shoot, as she was a huge fan of Gordon Jackson, who in the scene where they first use the house entrance, kept poking his head around the door and asking her to put the kettle on. He joked around with her most of the day, whereas Martin Shaw and Lewis Collins spent a lot of time with the stunt guys getting their scenes right. When it came to filming the car chase, one of the stunt guys badly damaged not only the car he was driving, but also the wall and out-building he had hit, which was concealed behind some bushes. We were told not to worry, and that the filming was insured and we would be paid for any damages. They also damaged some of the house brickwork when they used some small explosives to simulate bullets hitting the house. Not only did we never see any money for the damages, but also my father had terrible trouble getting any form of payment out of the production company for the days filming. Nevertheless, it was a day I shall never forget."

Record-keeping during shooting falls to the production assistant, or as is customary in filmed drama, the continuity person. Cheryl Leigh helped the director with casting, and assisted with the formulation of the cash budget and the planning of the schedule. This was followed with keeping a careful record of the shooting as production continued.

Cheryl Leigh (continuity): "The 'tram-line' script, as this record of shooting-coverage is known, gets its name from the series of vertical lines drawn in different colours alongside the dialogue and used to mark the dimensions of particular shots. I compiled both the 'tram-line' script and separate continuity notes which, comment on the particular shots and indicate the preferred takes. The director and editor are thus provided with easy access to the considerable quantity of film generated. Without such a record, editing would be almost impossible.

"I left at the end of this episode to work on the feature *Force 10 From Navarone*, but one thing I can remember was that when I went Gordon Jackson gave me a bottle of champagne and a card stating how nice it was to work with me. We had become quite close and he would rehearse his lines with me before each scene was to be filmed. He was so word perfect he hated to get his lines wrong. I did return the following year and he was so pleased to see me."

Gordon Jackson (interviewed at the time): "Saturday means work. I learn my lines then relax. I must be the slowest learner of lines in the world, I really do have to work at it, so while I'm in the thick of making *The Professionals*, Saturday means work, learning my script from morning till night. It means death to my social life but I have to do it: I have a terror of arriving on location and not knowing every word of my part inside out and back to front.

I like to feel that if the Atom bomb fell while we were filming I'd still deliver my next line. So I read my script, in the garden if it's warm, or in a comfortable chair indoors. I am the most unathletic person you could imagine, so Saturday has never been a day to exert myself. I'm no walker, I'm not keen on gardening, and when I played football with my teenage son a couple of years ago he astutely pointed out that it was the first time I'd ever kicked a ball about with him. When I'm satisfied I know my script, music is my main interest. I'll sit down and listen to my favourites: Mozart, Wagner, Debussy and Liszt. And later I'll pick up a book; I'm just enjoying the last volume of Proust's *Remembrance of Things Past*."

Fight arranger Joe Dunne also departed the production at this stage to be replaced by Peter Brayham, who first became a stunt man when he was thirteen. A movie mogul spotted him in a swimming pool.

Peter Brayham (stunt man): "This guy came up to me and asked me to do a fall for him in a film. He'd seen me swimming and diving and reckoned I wasn't scared of heights. At the time I was doing aqua shows every night so I went off and did this fall off a gasometer, a bit like diving, and it earned me as much from that one jump, fifty quid, as I did from one week in the aqua shows. That made my mind up and I've been doing stunts ever since."

Brayham, born 12th July 1936, began his career in 1950, working on some of the early James Bond films, including *From Russia With Love*, doubled for John Wayne in *Brannigan*, when he jumped a Ford Capri over an open Tower Bridge, and had also been in charge of stunts on *The Sweeney, Target, The Racing Game, The Strangers* and *Minder*.

Doyle's new mode of transport was a Triumph TR7 (OOM 734R) in Pageant Blue and, upon its arrival, Lewis Collins took it for a test drive and in his own words: "I was stopped for speeding by a police car."

The Female Factor: *A lady of the night is looking for Doyle, and ends up wet, naked and very dead. And there's a sexy nymphet, a porno film and a blackmail plot. The KGB are in there too!*

The Female Factor was next in production, with the cameras rolling on Monday 12th September. Written by Brian Clemens and directed by David Wickes, this featured a standard plot where an attractive young woman is used to get secrets from a shadow government minister (and potential future Prime Minister).

Thanks, in part, to director David Wickes, *The Professionals* made its third major visit to central London in order to undertake location shooting. Simon Culver and Sara set up Milvern's accident on Prince Consort Road, Kensington, with exteriors for Culver's apartment being shot at Albert Court, near the Royal Albert Hall, but with interiors invariably done back at Harefield Grove.

Ron Fry (associate producer): "When the car hits actress Felicity Dean in the opening scenes, the art department had to make sure the bag of shopping she is carrying contained only soft items, as during the stunt the contents had to fall on top of her. In reality the car was stationary and one of the crew pushed the bag off the bonnet onto her. On the first take they pushed the bag too hard and it missed her all together. The director insisted that he wanted the shot with her covered in the groceries, so we had to set it up again; this time, most of the things stayed in bag. On the third take, we pre-split the bag. Watching it back, the bag of flour just misses her chest! Not sure who put that in there?"

An Iron Curtain agent is using a young girl to extort secrets from, and ultimately destroy, the career of Sir Charles Milvern, the future British Prime Minister, unaware that the girl is the long-lost daughter of a well-known local prostitute. British actress Felicity Dean (born 24th January 1959) played the young girl, Sara Seaford, in THE FEMALE FACTOR. A relative newcomer to the world of acting she had previously appeared in the ITV Playhouse (Short Back And Sides), BBC2's Play Of The Week (Shooting The Chandelier), and alongside Oliver Reed and Raquel Welch on the movie CROSSED SWORDS.

A future British Prime Minister is being blackmailed by KGB agents in THE FEMALE FACTOR: Lewis Collins as Bodie on location in Hammersmith, London.

Ann Seaford runs across Hammersmith Bridge, West London, to Doyle's old flat on the corner of Lower Mall and Mall Road on the north bank of the River Thames. These scenes had to be filmed quickly as Ron Fry recounts:

Ron Fry (associate producer): "Actress Pamela Salem was really naked under the fur coat during the take, or as close to being naked as you can get! It wasn't a very warm day, so when the coat got pulled off, we had to rush to get the shot done quickly; rehearsals hadn't posed any problems as we did it with Pam fully clothed. Due to the nature of the scenes being filmed, and the exposure of Pam, we had crew-members stopping any curious onlookers on the bridge from seeing what we were doing as by now quite a crowd had gathered. There was a lot of publicity for these shots, and the press were everywhere."

On their way back after filming these scenes, David Wickes, Peter Brayham and the crew stopped at the derelict Rockware Glass Works complex near Greenford, Middlesex, to film the first series opening title sequence. Footage for *Old Dog With New Tricks* had already been filmed here, so the location was no stranger to the film crew.

Every television programme has its opening title and closing credits sequences to identify, and differentiate, it from others. The titles sequence, frequently adopting striking visual images and normally accomplished by 'catchy' theme music, offers a powerful inducement to watch the programme. The images in the titles sequence are intended to arouse viewer interest and at the same time to help signpost dramatic content. *The Professionals* would be no exception....

The original Title sequences shot for Series 1. Left: Main Title sequence. Top Right: The caption used before, and after, commercial advertisement breaks. Middle Right: The filmed caption used for the end credits originally intended for overseas use. Bottom Right: The revised caption used for the end credits. Cast and production crew details would be drafted on over these end sequences.

Martin Shaw and Lewis Collins during the filming of the main Title sequence, complete with guitars!

Lewis Collins: "Martin and I didn't mix much socially outside of the series, but he used to come to my place in Golders Green, where we tried writing a few songs in my recording room, a left-over from my pop days. When that news got out, the record companies were highly intrigued. They remarked that a musical Bodie and Doyle would sell even better than a singing Hutch (David Soul from the hit American show STARSKY & HUTCH). But we were only doing it for a bit of fun!"

Peter Brayham (stunt man): "When I got the call if I could do the title sequence I asked who was directing it. They told me they weren't sure, but David Wickes had been lined up. I told them that if David came onboard, he'd probably ask for me anyway. That's how I started full-time on the show. They asked me to stay, as Joe Dunne wasn't coming back. I don't think it had worked out with him. Then they pulled all *The Sweeney* guys over as and when they could. We'd done it already on that show, so they thought it would be easier to get the guys who'd done it first."

The title action showed Bodie and Doyle screaming up in a Rolls Royce. Bodie and Doyle then do an assault course with two other men, abseil from a great height, dive through a plate glass window (in slow motion), then get back in the car and drive off.

In order to maintain series continuity for repeat showings and foreign sales, LWT later replaced these with the series two titles that start with a Ford Granada smashing through a large plate glass window. The logo used before, and after, the advertisement breaks was also slightly different from subsequent series (no silhouettes).

In an attempt to let viewers know who these people are, over the opening credits Cowley gets a short voice-over: 'Anarchy. Acts of Terror. Crimes against the public. To combat it I've got special men. Experts from the army, the police, from every service: These are *The Professionals*'. It was only heard on the original titles. It was not transferred to subsequent repeat showings featuring the new second series titles. Two closing credit sequences were filmed; one used for UK prints showed a CI5 logo (as per the advert breaks), while the other, for foreign sales, showed a London skyline across the River Thames.

With the main crew filming at Mount Fidget, the second unit was still busy working on pick-up shots for *Heroes*; as production was now well behind schedule on this instalment. It had only just entered post-production and the producers decided that action should be taken to prevent any further delays. Besides losing Ware, the entire art department under the control of Ken Court left the series, as presumably set design was being done too slowly, and a new team under the control of Tony Curtis was brought in.

Peter Cotton (location manager): "I'd just about had enough by this stage. I was getting no help, despite constant demands. So enough was enough, I sorted out the next episode and left. Coaxed out of retirement, they hired Peter Crowhurst and Roger Lyons and so now they had two locations men!"

In another effort to move episodes along quicker four assistant directors, Gordon Gilbert, Sean Redmayne (incorrectly credited as Shaun in the closing credits), David Bracknell and Ken Baker, were appointed to replace Bill Westley and Al Burgess who also left the production around this time.

Bill Westley: "They had fallen behind schedule quite badly, and although I'd liked to have stayed on, I had been offered a contract to work on the second *Sweeney* feature film, which I couldn't turn down. I think Al decided he'd had enough too."

Everest Was Also Conquered: *1953 was a good year...for some. But it turns out to be a very dangerous one for CI5, with a shotgun killer on the loose, and Bodie gets it in the face!*

Everest Was Also Conquered, the eighth episode to be made commenced filming on Monday 26th September, was directed by Francis Megahy from yet another Brian Clemens script. Manchester born Megahy (1937) had started his career as a writer with partner Bernie Cooper, where they scripted episodes of *Man In A Suitcase*, and the film, *Freelance* (1971), which Megahy produced and directed. Prior to his engagement on *The Professionals*, he had directed the *Target* episode *Vandraggers*. Later, in the 1980's, he wrote on *Hammer House Of Horror*, and would go onto direct episodes of *Minder* and *C.A.T.S Eyes*.

Megahy had a curious way of working, which was not always welcomed:

Francis Megahy: "The more an actor gives his all in rehearsals, the more emotionally exhausted he becomes, and I had this practice of rehearsing little and taking scenes while they were 'hot'. I found this very effective. This caused a few arguments between the producer, Sid Hayers, and myself. There wasn't any tantrums and jumping up and down; it was creative dispute. Sid was the sort of producer you were glad to have around, very solid; a great contributor personally and a lovely producer with whom to kick ideas to and fro. However, he was a man steeped in logic. I'm a strong believer in the illogical. His rational reasoning at a time of crisis I sometimes found finicky, but always something good came out of it. It produced a friction that was very creative."

In EVEREST WAS ALSO CONQUERED a dying man's confession triggers the re-opening of 25-year old police corruption case. Lewis Collins and Martin Shaw prepare to film scenes at the Harefield unit base in Middlesex.

Actor Peter Blake was born (8th December 1948) in Selkirk, Scotland and prior to his being cast in this story as CI5 agent Tony Miller was in the public eye through his portrayal of a 'Fonz'-type character in the cult Pepsi-Cola TV commercial, which later led to a hit record, 'Lipsmackin' Rock'n'Rollin', entering the charts w/e 15th October 1977.

Peter Blake (Tony Miller): "I seem to remember having one day on the shoot; as things were very different then, I'd have been collected by car and driven to the unit base; given breakfast, frocked, made up and then put somewhere to wait until required. The interiors were shot late morning, I think, and then we waited for twilight as I remember. My only memory is those exploding condom thingies filled with stage blood actually hurt quite a bit when they go off come the 'take'."

Gordon Gilbert (first assistant director): "The scene that took a long time to get right was the sequence where Richard (Greene) throws the drink over Lew. The first time we shot it, poor old Richard missed altogether and more drink went over Lew's shoulder than on his face. After we'd set up again, Lew kept getting the giggles every time Richard was about to throw the drink. A couple of goes later, after Lew then pretended to dodge the drink; we got it in the can. It had been a long day, and add this to the fact that Richard just couldn't get his lines right in any of his scenes, meant we were all fairly exhausted at the end of this particular day.

Actor Richard Greene on the set of EVEREST WAS ALSO CONQUERED.

"Back at the Harefield unit base, in the scene where actor Michael Denison meets with Gordon (Jackson) in the office, someone, probably Lew, had rigged the office door so that the outer handle was loose. That's why there was a lag between him coming in the office; then Bridget Brice (Betty) had to control herself from going into hysterics. Michael was such a serious actor that he played the scene as if it was just a minor mishap, in reality the rest of us were dying not to laugh throughout the take, we only shot this scene once!

"In another scene where the boys visit CI5 Records, one of them, again almost likely Lew, had arranged that a half-eaten sandwich be left in one of the filing cabinets, and you should have seen the look on the face of actor Robert Booth when he pulled open the drawer to retrieve the files; well, you can imagine the fits of laughter on the set."

In keeping with the script requirements location manager Peter Cotton recced Southall, Middlesex, for the scenes involving Frank Goodman. The shooting draft stated that Frank would be followed to a betting shop and taken for a cruise around the mean streets of London before arriving at a pub near a gas works.

Peter Cotton (location manager): "Filming included some material shot outside The White Lion Pub on White Street, Southall, near the gas works. It is here, that the guy is chained to the railings, by the subway, after being picked-up on The Broadway. There was another trip to Lockwell House near Northwood. Cowley's office was the only interior used at Harefield Grove, with the exterior of the building suitably dirtied-down to become the Star Hotel.

"Ann Berry's kennels were part of Pynesfield Manor, at the end of Coppermill Lane in Harefield. This location included a scene where the front tyre on Bodie's Capri is shot."

Peter Brayham (stunt man) : "The Capri was meant to come charging out of the gates onto the main road. However, there was a blow-out and it was very difficult to control the car and I nearly lost it, but with the cameras rolling they simply amended the script and had the villain shoot the tyre out so they could use the footage."

Executive producers Brian Clemens and Albert Fennell had been unhappy with both the reliability and lack of duplicate vehicles provided by British Leyland on *The New Avengers;* deciding early on in the production of *The Professionals* that a change to another manufacturer was essential.

Peter Brayham: "I suggested the Ford Capri (Bodie and Doyle pictured above inside the car) to the producers after using one to jump Tower Bridge in the John Wayne film *Brannigan*. Sid Hayers said if it was good enough for John Wayne, then it was good enough for us."

As a consequence a deal with Ford Motor Company was made to provide vehicles for the LWT series. Brayham's contact on *Brannigan*, Brian West, was consulted and having tasted success with providing cars for *The Sweeney*, a deal with department chief, Harry Calton, and Barry Reynolds of the Ford Press Office was agreed. As a result, the Ford Press garage in Brentford, Middlesex, issued Mark 1 with a selection of vehicles. Doyle is seen driving a Strato silver Ford Capri Mk II 3.0S (SOO 636R), fitted with an X-pack body kit. Ford had used this vehicle in its 1977 publicity shoots and various car magazine advertisements. Meanwhile, Bodie drove an Arizona gold Ford Capri Mk II 3.0 Ghia automatic (PNO 580R), and Cowley's transport was a Ford Granada MK II 2.0L in Sahara beige (VHK 456S).

Bodie and Doyle in EVEREST WAS ALSO CONQUERED.

Close Quarters: Bodie's main interest is in making time with his girlfriend. But suddenly he is running out of time - when he finds himself holding a dangerous terrorist, besieged in a vicarage with gunmen moving in.

Next in production was *Close Quarters*, which came before the cameras in early October. Brian Clemens, had submitted the script in August, and the completed revised draft was ready by 28th September.

Directed by William Brayne, who cast both Gabrielle Drake and Hildegarde Neil to headline the guest list, Drake went on record saying that she did not enjoy making the episode due to the violence, nor did she consider the story, or the show, to have much in the way of morality.

Writer Brian Clemens seems to have based the Myer-Helmut group in his script on the activities of the West German group The Red Army Faction led by Andreas Baader and Ulrike Meinhof. Their motto was, 'Don't argue, destroy'.

This was the highest-rated episode of the first series (and the second-highest of all time), getting 17.4 million viewers and fifth place in the weekly viewing charts.

With schedules still not being met, producer Sidney Hayers and script editor Dennis Spooner commissioned scripts that would only contain one or two main locations, thus being quicker to complete. Their plan worked as this episode would get things back on track. Many of the early scenes were filmed in and around Maidenhead, Berkshire, including material on the river around Maidenhead Bridge and Boulter's Lock. The car park where Bodie steals a Cortina was part of Bushnel's Boat Yard on Ray Mead Road, now replaced by apartments.

Lewis Collins: "I remember the scenes (filmed at Maidenhead) where actress Gabrielle Drake was rowing me in a boat. It was a very dramatic scene or supposed to be, with no dialogue just background music. I don't know why, but I suddenly saw the funny side to the situation and starting teasing her by shouting orders, just like an Oxford rowing coach.

"She was desperately trying to keep a serious face at the same time as guiding our boat in a straight line. Suddenly we hit the bank, the boat rocked and she fell in. By this time I was almost hysterical with laughter and stood up to help her, then I fell in the water too with a loud splash. Director Bill Brayne eventually saw the funny side, even though we held up shooting for the rest of the day as we dried off."

Actress Gabrielle Drake in CLOSE QUARTERS.

On leave from CI5 with a hand injury, Bodie takes a day trip with his girlfriend and finds himself face-to-face with the leader of a terrorist group. He captures him but then the rest of the gang arrive and he finds himself hiding in a vicarage from Inge Helmut, the gang leader, portrayed by actress Madlena Nedeva. A scene from CLOSE QUARTERS.

With the help of the British Airports Authority, the location work around Heathrow Airport, London, progressed without any major problem.

Peter Crowhurst (location manager): "The opening scenes we did inside the old Terminal 3 lounge at Heathrow Airport, which back then was being used in all sorts of shows, like *The New Avengers* and *Return Of The Saint*, so it wasn't an issue to get permission for filming. We used the car park of the Nag's Head pub between Great Missenden and Little Missenden on the A413 London Road, simply because it was on the way to Hundridge Manor, the house doubling as the vicarage."

Alun Webb (British Telecom engineer): "If you see the bit where they stop the Cortina at the pub to phone in for help, across the road is an old British Telecom van. The engineers inside were told to keep out of sight as the production team filmed the sequences. Getting the shot right for the Audi turning round took many attempts; the crew had the Audi thrashing up and down the road until they got a good take (if you look at the shots of these scenes the skid marks on the road would seem to bear this out). Also when Lewis opens the door of the phone box (not a genuine one), they had to shoot this a couple of times as on the first take Lewis either broke a nail on the door, or got a splinter off it, hence the take was lost with a lot of expletives. The BT guys shared a drink with Lewis (cup of tea) during a break in shooting, they said he was extremely pleasant and came over to them during the break rather than them approach him."

During the car chase scene, the red Audi very briefly becomes left-hand drive! This was a deliberate move in the editing rooms; the film is reversed to portray the car turning round in the road in two different directions. This was the only option rather than film the sequence again.

Sean Redmayne (first assistant director): "The bit we did inside the airport lounge took a little bit of setting up because we were using real members of the public for most of the scenes; which wasn't the norm, but our budget was quite strict; we'd only managed to get an agreement to shut off a small part of the lounge. For the most part things went as planned, but one guy was so transfixed by the film crew that he went head-first into a pillar and almost knocked himself out.

"The stunt we did with the dinghy falling of the car roof at Springwell lock didn't go as planned to start with: we'd originally intended that one of the stunt drivers would push the thing off the roof on the director's prompt. But when we came to shoot that, he couldn't get enough force behind his push and the thing barely moved. We then carefully placed the dinghy at an angle, and wetted the underside with washing-up liquid, so as the car took the corner it flew off. We were a little concerned it would fall before he went over the canal bridge, but luckily it didn't and fell off as planned leaving the director happy.

"At Hundridge Manor, we had to arrange for the construction team to build the exterior doorway, which had to be trashed by the (Inge's) car. They carefully constructed the doorway like an extension to the main doorway, and, I think, they matched it in beautifully. It was made mostly of plywood and light plasterboard. So much so, that when we filmed the car crashing into it, the doorway collapsed and the car survived mostly unscathed."

Making one of two appearances in the show was Joseph Charles, a CI5 agent named Jax. He would reprise the role again in *Klansmen*. The young black actor had previously been seen in the 1974 film *Antony & Cleopatra* and also appeared in *The Sweeney, Angels,* and *Casualty.*

In CLOSE QUARTERS Bodie (Lewis Collins) is hiding from a terrorist gang.

Look After Annie: *Cowley in love, his judgment clouded by a woman? But the woman is Annie Irvine - beautiful, successful and in deadly danger! Bodie plays Cupid...with a gun!*

Look After Annie was directed by Charles Crichton from another Brian Clemens script, and started filming on Monday 24th October. Born in Wallasey, Cheshire on the 6th August 1910, Crichton started in the industry as an editor, before becoming involved with the Ealing comedies, directing films such as *The Lavender Hill Mob* in 1951. He also had a wealth of TV film series experience including *The Saint, Danger Man, Dick Turpin, The Protectors, The Avengers, Man In A Suitcase* and *Space: 1999*.

Annie Irvine, an extreme left-wing preacher, and former flame of Cowley's, becomes the target of a hit man when one of her meetings comes to London. Cowley (Gordon Jackson) tries his utmost to protect her in LOOK AFTER ANNIE.

Charles Crichton (director): "Can't say things ran smoothly on this one! They (the production company) were in such a mess, way behind schedules, that I had little time to prep anything. I can't even recall a recce to the chosen locations. The shooting script was only given to me a matter of days before we commenced production, and in this time I was expected to return a completed episode in ten days. This was just not the case.

"I remember problems with the casting and was given a choice of Diana Fairfax and a couple of unknowns to feature as Annie and that was it? Casting director Maggie Cartier had nothing else on offer in such a short space of time. Not a sterling performance as I remember. We were based at Harefield, and the place was a mess; people running round like headless chickens and I reckon around three or four episodes getting near a completed stage, when it should really have been only mine! There were different units (main and second) coming and going and for the best part I had to work around them, with the two leads, Martin and Lewis, constantly getting whisked away to complete shots for other episodes at the expense of mine."

Peter Crowhurst (location manager): "To try and keep on schedule we used the Uxbridge trading estate (Highbridge Industrial Estate) for most of our shots. Footage showing Bodie's Capri was filmed on the Uxbridge High Street by the second unit during a non-busy period, I think on a Sunday."

Actress Patricia Quinn took on the role of Isla in LOOK AFTER ANNIE. But has Doyle (Martin Shaw) grounds to be suspicious when he is assigned to look after an old flame of C15 boss George Cowley.

David Bracknell (first assistant director): "In the scene where actor Derek Francis is showing his henchmen the 'Annie Irvine' posters, the extras who'd been hired to act as his men found the posters rather comical. Admittedly the art department had not done a good job on them, and they looked really awful, so in hindsight, you can see why they keep sniggering throughout the take. It took a few takes, and even David Mallinson (Frank) got the giggles in the end. Derek, the professional that he was, barely flinched as we kept shouting 'Cut!'

"The fight scenes we did near the end proved a little problematic to shoot. They involved the use of a chain, which the stunt arranger, Peter Brayham, was not happy with, as it was difficult to control when it was swinging in the air, in a sequence involving several actors. In the scene when Martin's arm takes a blow from the rifle butt being used by actor Nick Brimble, things did not go according to the rehearsed stunt; either Martin or Nick went in too early and Martin's arm took a bigger blow the it should have done, leaving him in 'real' pain for quite a while. I don't think Nick realised how hard he'd hit Martin until after the take, even though Martin's arm had been suitably padded to absorb the impact."

An error occurred during post production: while Bodie is driving along in the Capri there is a long shot of Cowley's Granada taken from the previous episode *Close Quarters*! Both episodes were in the editing suites simultaneously and was a result of the pressures being felt by the production team to get episodes completed on time, and within budget.

The stock footage of the rioting was culled from newsreels and the film *All Coppers Are...*, incidentally, directed by producer Sidney Hayers. The stock footage of the ecstatic audience used in the opening shot came from the same stock footage as that used in the legendary video for Sid Vicious's version of 'My Way'.

When The Heat Cools Off*: Can a copper be wrong? Could he arrest the wrong man and send him down for thirty years? Doyle thinks so - and he was the copper that made the arrest.*

The next episode, *When the Heat Cools Off*, provided some background for Doyle, allowing viewers to see him in his previous role with the Metropolitan police force.

From Monday 7th November, Ray Austin took up the director's reins on yet another Brian Clemens script, casting Lalla Ward who later became a companion to *Doctor Who*. Ray Austin, born in London on the 5th December 1932, established himself as a second unit director/stunt arranger in 1960's on shows such as *The Avengers*, before becoming a fully fledged director in both the UK, on *The Saint*, *Department S*, and *Return Of The Saint*, and the US, on *Hawaii Five-O*, *Quincy*, and *The Love Boat*.

The dialogue for *The Professionals* was normally recorded directly onto audiotape during shooting so picking up a true sound picture of the location. This method undoubtedly accounted for the greater realism of the sound image compared to other TV series at the time, where more usually the dialogue was dubbed over later by the actors in the studio. For, Ken Scrivener, the sound recordist, a number of problems that arose were never totally resolved. Although there was a degree of compromise, Ken felt that in the production process the sound always came last.

Ken Scrivener (sound recordist): "No-one works in the media if they are not prepared to compromise. It's the amount you compromise your particular work as opposed to someone else's! If you think someone else is getting away with it at your expense then you fight the little war and in the end you come to an agreement that is in itself a compromise. Regrettably sound is the last compromise, which has to be made because we seem last always, whether it's in the studio or outside, sound is always last and it's just a function of the way we did the show. We recorded live, and as long as everything else went well, we were expected to go along with it, even if I thought we could do better our end, for instance when the Capri hits the pillar at the (Lockwell) house, most editors would have taken that out so as not to distract the viewer, but not in our case, that was what we'd recorded, and that's what went out with the print - there was this kind of constant frustration throughout the series."

Top and right: Scenes from WHEN THE HEAT COOLS OFF.

In WHEN THE HEAT COOLS OFF Lalla Ward plays Jill Haydon, the daughter of a man imprisoned by Doyle six years ago when he was a policeman. She claims to have new evidence, which will exonerate her father!

Actor Michael Sheard, born the son of a minister in Aberdeen, caught the acting bug in 1950 and trained at RADA. He was well-liked by casting directors as a dependable, versatile character actor; he gained the nickname 'One Take Mike' through his sheer professionalism. However, this wasn't the case on *The Professionals*?

Michael Sheard (Merton): "I'd been employed to play a small role set in Cowley's office, with the three leads, as a gun expert. The director, Ray Austin, had the clever idea that we could throw the gun to each other rather than just pass it. Martin and Lewis were a riot; each time I threw it they'd drop it, and burst into fits of laughter. They kept apologising to Ray and telling him the gun was slippery, but it was obvious they were letting it drop on purpose. It took quite a few takes to complete the scene, and in the end even Gordon Jackson was pleased when Ray was content with the final sequence and called it a wrap. I read somewhere later that Martin and Lewis didn't see eye-to-eye during the production; that I find hard to believe on what I witnessed during my day on the show!"

Peter Crowhurst (location manager): "Filming was executed at Oxhey Park near Watford, which is where the police diver finds the gun in the lake. We'd originally intended to use Springwell lakes, nearer the studio, but it was nigh impossible to get a filming crew permission to film there. We also had to consider that in the script they were supposed to be looking for a hidden gun amongst grassland, and then a police diving team would search the canal, so the lakes would have looked too industrial and way to deep to get a film crew and police divers into. Hayden's home was Lockwell House making another, albeit, brief appearance, and the car dealership where the Jaguar was being sold was Datsun dealer J R Inwards, located on the High Street in Ruislip. Finding a car dealership that would agree to our needs was quite a task. 'Inwards' agreed, but on condition that any signage displaying their name would be blacked out. If you look closely, during filming, they removed a few bulbs from the illuminated sign at the front of the shop. The interior to Ambury Mansions where Doyle's partner, P C Syd Parker, is killed was the usual stairs and lift at Harefield Grove. Doyle's mews flat was the old converted stables, with the squash courts becoming the interior of the prison where Haydon is serving his sentence."

Lewis Collins discusses a scene with WHEN THE HEAT COOLS OFF director Ray Austin (above left). Bernard Kay portrayed barman Harry Scott; born (23rd February 1928) in Bolton, Lancashire, he appeared four times in the DOCTOR WHO series in various roles, most notably as Saladin in the classic story THE CRUSADE, alongside William Hartnell and Julian Glover. He also made appearances in Z-CARS, CORONATION STREET, FOYLE'S WAR, and as the Bolshevik leader in the 1965 DOCTOR ZHIVAGO film.

Costume design on the series was appointed to Jim Smith, and later, as on this episode, Jackie Cummins. Complete wardrobes of dress were built up for each of the major characters following discussion with the actors and especially 'the Boys', who were the main source of information on their own roles.

Jackie Cummins: "You get the script and you break down the idiosyncrasies or anything the author writes that gives you clues to the character and you try to build these into the clothes. You try to piece together the social background and piece together what he would wear. You probably begin by using a lot of clichés, but then you get your clichés and break it down into acceptable dress for the character."

The importance of the designer's availability during shooting to coordinate the final effect created by the costumes was particularly important in the scenes involving extras, both in the pub shots and the sequences filmed at Oxhey Park, Hertfordshire. Because it was a contemporary series they were required to attend in their own clothes, matching them up themselves as nearly as possible to the requirements of the action. Jackie Cummins was able to make adjustments to the appearance of the extras by substituting costume from three additional rails she carried with her:

Jackie Cummins: "A lot of extras didn't have the right costume and if they're going to be featured you like to have control of it. So you've always got to be around the camera to spot things such as two coming up in identical costume, for instance. So you always carry a lot of costume and you try to get as much humour or realism into characters just visually. And you were allowed to do that. Once you'd got the confidence of the director, they'd leave you to do that."

One scene planned, and scheduled to be filmed, but subsequently removed during editing was a scene set in Bodie's car outside the prison after, in the final moments of the story, Doyle has informed Bill Haydon that his plan has been thwarted.

Ext: Prison - Bodie's car
Cowley and Bodie wait for Doyle in the car. Doyle gets in and Bodie pulls away.
COWLEY: (looking at Doyle) *Well. Cheer up, Doyle. You can't win 'em all! Especially those you already won seven years ago!*

Stake Out: *Stake out a bowling alley and observe. Yes, this one starts small but soon escalates into the biggest threat London will ever face - a nuclear bomb that's primed and ready to blow. Only Bodie and Doyle can defuse it...if there's time.*

In order to bring the next episode in on time, Dennis Spooner wrote *Stake Out* so it had just one main setting - a bowling alley; but even that caused location manager Peter Crowhurst certain issues.

Peter Crowhurst: "I travelled for miles to find the bowling alley. I had a hell of a job! Basically we needed it for most of the ten days schedule, which meant they would effectively be closed for much of that time. We eventually came to a compromise with the owners and agreed to do the filming after hours in the early part of the week; Monday to Wednesday or something like that. Behind schedule, we also used Highbridge Industrial Estate in Uxbridge again for Fraser's car crash. We did that quite late in the evening and I remember it was absolutely freezing. Thomas 'Fat Man' Blackey's Bedford home was really Harefield Grove - the unit base. We had so much filming to do at the bowling alley, I wanted to keep the others simple and close-by."

Peter Joyce (assistant art director): "I'd just joined the crew and I remember they needed a bowling alley for the story. Our location guy, Peter Crowhurst, was finding it difficult to find one that could spare us filming time, and eventually the bulk of the action took place at an alley in Hemel Hempstead. I understand these premises were, some years later, demolished and it's now a car park."

Newcomer Benjamin Wickers directed proceeding but ran into issues with the conclusion to writer Dennis Spooner's story which appeared in the shooting script as follows:

Int: Bowling alley
As Frank is left to disarm the bomb, Bob appears with two heavies. Doyle throws a bowling ball and hits Bob over and Bodie apprehends him. Meanwhile, Doyle handles one of the thugs while Cowley gets the other with another ball. Frank continues on the bomb as Cowley grabs his gun and watches until the man has disarmed the bomb.
Doyle and Bodie, still holding the bowling ball, join Cowley.
COWLEY: *Good work. You can take the rest of the night off.*
He notices the ball in Bodie's hands and takes it, hurling it towards the pins, clearing them all. Bodie and Doyle look at each other, exchanging disgusted glances and as one:
BODIE / DOYLE: *He'd play for money!*

The desired shots with the bowling balls proved so problematic to achieve that Spooner duly amended the story's finale.

In STAKE OUT a CI5 agent is murdered, leading to the discovery of a man who is dying as a result of plutonium poisoning linking CI5 to the imminent explosion of an A-bomb at the same bowling alley. It's left to Doyle (Martin Shaw) and Bodie (Lewis Collins) to try and de-activate the fuse… …

Gordon Gilbert (first assistant director): "The night we came to shoot the first part of the car crash, filmed on the streets outside the bowling alley, it was raining quite hard, so on-street run-bys proved very difficult to achieve. It was also early evening and pretty dark, so in the end we rigged up a camera inside the car and deliberately shot much of it out of focus and 'wobbly' to highlight the plight of the character. It seemed to work quite well, especially as the car was not driving very fast at all.

"As far as I recall, all the people in the bowling complex were extras, and while shooting one of the scenes one of them fell flat on their backside, necessitating the need for the unit nurse to attend to their injuries. I'm not too sure if Tony Osoba and Martin were really 'acting' in their squabble scene, it looked to me like the two actors had really fallen out over something, there was definitely some friction between the two on set, and Tony tended to be more chummy with Lewis during the shoot."

Klansmen: *Cowley and his men confront racism when Bodie and Doyle are called upon to investigate violence against the black community.*

Klansmen (Some production notes refer to the episode as *Klansman*) was the final episode to be made, entering production in early December. It was scripted by Brian Clemens, from a story by 29-year old Simon Masters, whose career dates back to 1971, when he submitted scripts for *The Onedin Line*. He continued to write on shows such as *Emmerdale Farm*, *Blake's 7*, *Dallas* and *Juliet Bravo*.

Brought in as director was Pat Jackson. Born in Eltham, London in 1916, Jackson had previously worked on the TV shows *The Prisoner*, *Man In A Suitcase* and *Arthur Of The Britons* and the features, *Shadow On The Wall* (1950), *Encore* (1952) and *King Arthur, The Young Warlord* (1975).

Members of a Klansmen group go on the rampage in London, attacking the local black residents in an attempt at forcing them to leave the area. Lewis Collins, Gordon Jackson and Martin Shaw on the set of KLANSMEN.

Gordon Jackson, Lewis Collins and Martin Shaw pose for a publicity photograph during a break in filming KLANSMEN.

Pat Jackson (director): "Thanks to location manager Roger Lyons, we managed to create a good overall look, filming mainly amongst the very helpful, and understanding, black community in Southall. It added realism to a rather dull script, which we played as written. Still, despite the racist overtones, the crew didn't really seem that bothered. They were at the end of the series and the feeling, especially from Martin Shaw, was that this would be the end of the show. He wasn't planning to do anymore and didn't see the show being a success based on this script. For me, personally, I was in my early sixties at the time and glad of the two weeks work."

In KLANSMEN, CI5 are sent into the black community in order to investigate a series of racial attacks and an undercover Doyle is badly injured. Martin Shaw finds time to pose for a publicity shot complete with facial plasters!

Gordon Gilbert (first assistant director): "We were tackling a very controversial subject matter on *Klansmen* and I had to make sure all relevant authorities were informed well in advance of any filming. However, the white hooded outfits caused concern when the guy is pushed from the rooftops. The building was on a main road through Southall, whereas a good percentage of the other scenes were shot around the streets looking out to Southall gas works, which only had one way in, and our crew had sealed this off with help from the police. Although we'd shot our scenes on the rooftop successfully, the street below couldn't be closed to traffic or pedestrians, and therefore, we had to shoot the street scenes back at the gas works.

"When we had to set light to the burning cross on the lawns of the house, we had problems getting the wood to light because it was a damp December evening, and in the end one of the props guys poured petrol over it, and that's why on screen the flames are so vivid. It didn't however stop a drunken passer-by from the pub, which was literally a few doors up, from wondering what the hell was going and calling both the police and fire brigade. Luckily I had already informed both services of the filming, and a quick phone-call put an end to that. In the same sequence we had to throw black paint over actress Sheila Ruskin. Although we'd told her it was not real paint, but thickened up food dye, she was still none too pleased at the idea, but in the end was persuaded to continue after chatting to her co-star Trevor Thomas who had to have a liberal dosing of white paint thrown over him!

"The same evening we shot the scene where the Klansmen are spraying 'Nigger' on the garage door, the street was just around the corner from the house where we'd light to the cross, but we had to literally try and inform all the local residents what we were doing, so as not to cause anybody any unnecessary anger."

Actor Anthony Booth (born in Liverpool, Merseyside, 9th October 1931) was best known at the time for his role as Mike Rawlins in the BBC series *Till Death Us Do Part* and as Sidney Noggett in the *Confessions of....*series of films with Robin Askwith. He was looking forward to guest starring as Dinny on the episode, but equally ran into issues during filming.

Anthony Booth (Dinny): "As a long standing socialist and anti-racist I thought the script was a very good example of how a popular series could make a very serious critique of racism - I couldn't wait to do it.

"With filming underway, a great personal friend of mine Louis Mahoney (who played the Doctor) pulled me to one side and said to me, 'the brothers want a word with you because they believe that you are a racist.' With that six guys came in - really big guys - and they asked me the question and I answered, 'this is what I have to do, don't you understand that. I'm exposing these people for what they are - absolute utter racists!' And they said, 'yeah, but we still believe you are a racist.' And I thought that's the point of it, surely to God, when you are living the part, this is what it is."

The predominance of male leads and the contemporary setting ensured that make-up and hair dressing requirements for *The Professionals* were small-scale in terms of a drama series. Only on the days when large numbers of extras were needed was additional help required. Nevertheless for make-up artist John Webber the work needed on this episode proved a little more satisfying.

John Webber: "Both lead characters in this story took a considerable beating. I decided that we'd had so many little injuries on Martin's forehead, and indeed Lewis's, that we'd got to be a lot more extreme after the fight. It helped that the state he'd been in would have given him stubble. Then I gave him a split lip with special plastic stuff, then the beginnings of a black eye, and various other bits and pieces. It's amazing how a face can be destroyed with make-up! We so rarely see injuries. Most people have got a plaster on and they're covered up. If you're lucky you get a reference from the hospital, but most of the time you have to just imagine and make it up. I mean I've never seen anybody that's just banged his or her head against a lamp post. You just do some sort of scar work and it's got to be believable."

The various injury effects and make-up transitions required for Martin Shaw and Lewis Collins were frequently complicated by the need to create and develop them out of narrative order. The need to maintain continuity in a schedule often shot out of sequence is a crucial feature of the work in both make-up and costume. To help ensure absolute continuity, both departments, as usual, compiled continuity books noting all the relevant details and containing Polaroid photographs of the actors at the end of each sequence shot.

A series of racist attacks involves Cowley and his CI5 agents Bodie and Doyle in a deadly case, where all is not as it seems? Martin Shaw and Gordon Jackson during a break in filming KLANSMEN.

This episode was pulled by LWT prior to transmission. Despite being screened in many foreign countries, it has never been broadcast in the UK. Made as a well-meaning piece of anti-racism, the episode was seen by television executives as reinforcing racial stereotypes and, therefore, unsuitable for transmission. The only way to have salvaged the episode would have been to heavily cut it, which at best, would have rendered the episode too short, and at worst, made it incomprehensible.

The 1978 press release issued by London Weekend Television about *Klansmen* stated:

The 'Klansmen' script was very powerful, very challenging, and very good. But it did not fall into the pattern of the rest of the series. We felt that if we had shown it, we would have upset many regular fans because the story and content were very different from regular Professionals fare. We were also concerned - in the light of events in the real world - that some viewers would have been disturbed by characters in the programme expressing extreme points of view. While we often tackle controversial and sensitive subjects in our drama programmes, we felt that 'The Professionals', as an action-adventure series, was not the vehicle for this particular storyline. It was a very good script, but it was, in our opinion, not right for the series.

LWT's stance seemed strange when all shooting scripts were submitted for their approval and amended as requested. However, at least five days filming had already taken place before a copy of the *Klansmen* script arrived at London Weekend Television's South Bank offices for vetting. Brian Clemens was unhappy with the ban, as he considered his script to have tackled the issues and headlines of the day and he obviously wanted to reflect events in the real world, which had always been a part of the original brief for *The Professionals*. He also firmly believed that Mark 1 could have re-shot the offending scenes possibly in the second series production run, but this idea was a non-starter as by that time the episode had already been sold to foreign markets.

Brian Clemens (writer and co-executive producer): "It wasn't transmitted because LWT felt it was racist, when, in fact, it was anti-racist. It was about CI5 sorting out a gang that was racist, but along the way we had to use, though not in a negative sense, 'forbidden' words like 'nigger' and so on because you can't portray a racist without using those words. That offended some people and I think it particularly offended Brian Tesler at LWT, who was very sensitive about race and indeed many years before had banned an *Armchair Theatre* episode, which again, was a highly-charged racial subject.

"We tackled tough subjects on the show and 'race' should have been no exception. We were making an episode that was going to change attitudes not reinforce them. And anyway, if it had been controversial, if there had been complaints and letters, so much the better because all these racist things, you have to bring them out from under the stone and air them."

The fact that, 'Some viewers would have been disturbed by the characters expressing extreme points of view' seems to be levelled at the characterisation of Bodie, and Lewis Collins remembers there being heated words about this, as well as that of Dinny played by Anthony Booth.

Lewis Collins: "I wasn't a big fan of that show. My character was definitely racialist. There were some strong words over that with the producers and eventually it was axed."

Brian Clemens: "Well, he never expressed them to me! I tried to make the point that it's bad and yet one can change - it's much better if somebody you know, through long viewing the series, changes visibly. I think that's the height of morality, it's the basis of a lot of scripture really - you take the wicked man and you change him."

Martin Shaw: "Brian has to be credited for the original idea, and his storylines were sensational, but I didn't like his dialogue. I don't think it wasn't screened not because of the violence, but the treatment of the racial thing. People in the business whom I respect say it was right not to show it. I am totally against groups like the National Front."

Production wrapped up on 22nd December with the story *Heroes* being the final episode in the cutting rooms. It should be noted that from this point on, many of the episodes filmed would be in a 'print-ready' stage as near to production order as possible. The scheduling problems associated with this first series would mean that stories were completed by additional filming units and assembled in a very haphazard order, with *Heroes* highlighting this fact. The episodes were 'print-ready' in the following order:

Killer With A Long Arm, Old Dog With New Tricks, Close Quarters, Look After Annie, The Female Factor, Long Shot, Private Madness, Public Danger, Stake Out, When The Heat Cools Off, Everest Was Also Conquered, Where The Jungle Ends, Klansmen, Heroes

LWT had a winner, with the first series, screening from 30th December 1977, averaging ratings of just over sixteen million viewers. *Close Quarters*, the seventh episode screened on 10th February 1978, was the highest-rated episode of the first series (and the second highest of all time), getting 17.4 million viewers and fifth place in the weekly viewing charts. LWT were quick to commission a second series at this point.

In January 1978, Martin Shaw and Lewis Collins recorded a comedy sketch for *The Freddie Starr Experience*. Broadcast some months later on Sunday 10th September, the *World Of Sport* golf segment, introduced by Dickie Davies, also featured *Hazell* star Nicholas Ball, Frank Windsor from *Z Cars* and *Softly, Softly*, and from the Gerry Anderson series *The Secret Service*, Stanley Unwin. Lewis and Freddie Starr were old friends from the stars days back in Liverpool, and they immediately struck up an off-screen relationship.

But the rigorous task of working non-stop since June 1977 had taken its toll on the two stars.

Martin Shaw: "When I read Paul Michael Glaser's (Starsky from *Starsky & Hutch*) interview about the emotional stress experienced at the end of a series, I thought, 'Yeah, yeah, you must be crying all the way to the bank, you poor devil'. But that was before I realised that the industry is run by accountants not artists, who deal with cash flow and not people. When they decide it should be possible to shoot two episodes, they simply don't account for the mental change of gear needed to cope with a second run.

"You begin to realise why the old Hollywood stars were pampered so much, it was to keep them alive and fresh for the next scene. You can't say to an actor: 'Sorry, you can't have a coffee break or a light-bulb in your dressing-room' and expect him to be as fresh at the end of a seven-month series as he was at the beginning.

"It took a phone-call from my co-star Lewis Collins to make me realise he too was feeling 'out of his tree'. I felt a hell of a lot better and slept for about five weeks, then spent a few very quiet days with friends in the country. I'd never expended so much mental and physical energy as I did on *The Professionals*, even working for directors as demanding as Roman Polanski."

Lewis Collins maintained a characteristically down-to-earth approach to the period between series.

Lewis Collins (interviewed in March 1978): "It sounds good, doesn't it? Eight months on and four months off, but my God, you need it! The big money scene is a myth, it's peanuts really. You could earn more as a member of a good theatre company, and what's more they wouldn't tell you what to do with your spare time! In many ways it's comforting to know there's work to go back to, but it's also very restricting, not being able to tackle any of the offers that seem to be pouring in, and I know that Martin feels the same."

Actor Lewis Collins takes a break from filming on THE PROFESSIONALS.

On Thursday 23rd March, Lewis Collins made one of his first public appearances at the Ideal Home Exhibition (an annual event run by the Daily

Mail newspaper in London). It was a real family outing as the Collins family turned out in full force, including Lewis's father Bill, and fan club secretary Amelia. Collins spent two hours meeting his fans and signing over 2000 autographs.

Lewis Collins: "I had no idea how many fans would turn up; it would have been awful if just one had come to see me! I was a bit nervous at first, because to be honest, I hadn't had much experience of meeting huge crowds. But when I discovered how friendly everyone was, it really helped me relax, and I ended up having a great time and met lots of nice people. I never expected that kind of response. I'd only gone as a favour to one of my dad's old friends."

The same month, Lewis Collins recorded a special appearance singing and dancing on the *Cilla Black Show* (broadcast on Monday 29th May), as part of some comedy sketches that included Frankie Howerd (as a punk rocker), Irene Handl, Joan Simms, and Nicholas Parsons.

This was followed by the lavish Thames Television musical production *Must Wear Tights* (broadcast Wednesday 27th September). It told the story of a famous television star, played by Collins, and an unknown young actress, played by Gemma Craven. Their paths cross, they fall in love, and it all ends happily ever after. Produced by Keith Buckett the guest cast included Eamonn Andrews, Lionel Blair, Tommy Cooper, and The Dougie Squires Dancers.

Lewis Collins: "I wasn't very good and to make matters worse, I didn't get any rehearsal and we shot it all in one take! So it's a bit rough to say the least....that's what happens when a show runs out of studio time."

Collins made further appearances during late April; firstly, on the panel of judges for the *Miss A.T.V Beauty Contest*, and then, as a guest, on *Celebrity Squares*.

During the Summer months, Martin Shaw, who lists horse-riding as one of his favourite hobbies, next to rock-climbing, was invited by Mark 1's unit publicist Paul McNicholls and FAB 208 magazine to try riding, but with a difference - at a western-style ranch! And the Hunters Moon Ranch in the New Forest, Dorset, provided the setting.

Martin Shaw at the Hunters Moon Ranch in the New Forest, Dorset.

Owned and run by Freda Williams, a well-known western-style riding judge and author, this unique ranch was opened in the late 1960's. Western riding is quite different from traditional styles, for instance, the saddles are different, more like bucket seats, and you ride with one hand instead of two.

Martin Shaw (interviewed at the time): "I've never done this kind of riding before. I suppose the nearest thing to it was when I rode in my part as Banquo in Ken Russell's *Macbeth*. We had a very tough riding instructor there, I think he was ex-army, but he taught me most of the riding I know on medieval saddles, which are pretty similar to these.

"I've never actually had proper riding lessons. I've always liked horses and wanted to learn to ride, so when some friends suggested I come with them, I jumped at the chance. Once I did ask a riding instructor to give me a few pointers as to where I was going wrong. The list must have been endless because he just summed it up in a word - 'untidy'!"

Martin Shaw had also been a rock-climber for seven years at the time, and was first hauled up by a life long friend, and brilliant climber.

Martin Shaw: "I don't like heights. In fact, I hate them. I climb rocks because I love the wild countryside, fresh air, beautiful views and solitude. The most satisfying way of indulging this love of mine is on the rock face. The Llanberis Pass climb is a classic one. Don't make it sound too glamorous. A lot of people go climbing these days and they would know it isn't that difficult."

The Llanberis Pass in North Wales is around 600-feet above the road. His favourite target: the Flying Buttress, the 300-feet Dinas-Y-Gromlech, high above the narrow stone bridge carrying the road down to Llanberis.

Martin Shaw: "People who are top-class experts, like Joe Brown, still go and climb the Flying Buttress because it's an absolute classic. It's got everything on it. It's a relatively simple climb; the actual grading for it is 'very difficult'. It is mainly a psychological climb, and classic in that it involves nearly all the techniques of rock-climbing at once. There are some rocks in Tunbridge Wells, Kent called 'Harrison's Rocks'. They are popular because they present a huge variety of climbs. I have a friend who is a first-rate climber and I rely on him totally. If you climb as second man to an expert, and you observe the rules and ceremonies, it's a pretty safe sport. The worst that can happen is that you slip off a ledge and are left dangling in space."

Meanwhile, The English Tourist Board, hearing that Martin was just as active off screen as he was on, suggested something just as demanding, but a little less hairy: as an 'Able Seaman'. Four glorious days were spent at the Newton Ferrers Sailing School, Yealm Road, near Plymouth, Devon with *The Professionals* unit publicist, Paul McNicholls. Martin confessed he was a beginner and feared the worst.

Martin Shaw (interviewed at the time): "I was in the Sea Scouts, but given that my branch was in Birmingham we didn't see very much of the wet stuff. Our boat had the bottom sawn off and was firmly berthed in the local park. In fact one of the punishments was to weed the grass from between the boards! Even with the greatest imagination it was difficult to pretend to be at sea, unless you could conjure the gasworks into resembling an iceberg; I was dishonourably discharged for giggling. It's so rewarding; with even the most basic skills under your belt you find yourself harnessing the wind and cutting along the bay. I almost wish I hadn't started this though, I think that I've been bitten by the sailing bug!"

Indeed, Martin confessed he spent every spare moment discussing boats with the locals, most of whom, incidentally, hadn't seen him on television. They took him for just another tourist, but with a little more skill and enthusiasm than normal. Martin, still hiding behind the beard he'd cultivated whilst 'resting' between series, didn't mind this a bit.

Unit publicist Paul McNicholls and Martin Shaw boating at Newton Ferrers Sailing School, near Plymouth, Devon.

FAB 208 then invited Martin Shaw and Lewis Collins to feature in their 1979 annual as 'Stars In Costume'. Publicist Phil McNicholls arranged the photo shoot and interviews to be conducted at IPC Magazines, King's Reach Tower, Stamford Street, London, not too many miles from LWT's Headquarters. Shaw became a Cossack and Collins a Cavalier.

Martin Shaw: "I've always fancied being a Cossack. I've got faintly Slavonic features, and I suppose when you're a kid you try and imagine possible roles you could play, and no one kicks sand in a Cossack's face, do they? The clothes definitely appeal, long flowing baggy shirts and pants. They're excellent horsemen too, and I've always been a show-jumping fanatic. Cossacks are health freaks and vegetarians too and that appeals. They say that there are Cossacks who've lived to 140 and had over thirty children on a diet of yoghourt and milk."

Lewis Collins: "When I was first asked to think of a period in history that I would have wanted to live in; I immediately had visions of peacocks for some reason. In many ways costume is like plumage isn't it? I chose this period in history because like the Stuart era, it was full of romance and chivalry, but it was also very much a man's world. It was amazing how easy it was to slip into the character and role, I felt a bit uneasy at first, because I kept thinking that the wig would fall off!"

This was only the beginning to the popularity of Lewis Collins and Martin Shaw, as Bodie and Doyle would return in more action-packed adventures later in 1978. However, for the second series of *The Professionals*, Mark I would move their base of operations and, in the main, be made by a different production team.

SERIES I EPISODE GUIDE

Lewis Collins takes aim in PRIVATE MADNESS, PUBLIC DANGER.

OLD DOG WITH NEW TRICKS

by **Brian Clemens**
© Copyright Mark 1 Productions Ltd MCMLXXVII

Charley Turkel	Johnny Shannon
Dapper	Stephan Chase
Billy Turner	Philip Davies
Morgan	Richard Hampton
Nurse Emma Bolding	Pamela Stephenson
Henry Turkel	Anthony Morton
Police Inspector	John Judd
Dr. Brook	Basil Hoskins
High-ranking police officer	Edward Dentith
CID Sergeant	Howard Bell
Betty	Bridget Brice
Young Lady	Sammie Winmill
Uncredited	
Murphy (Irish Terrorist)	Ken Kitson
Camp Guard	Chris Webb
Irish Terrorist	Bobby Ramsey
Irish Terrorist	Dave Cooper
Claire	Felicity Devonshire
Police Station Desk Sergeant	Guy Standeven
Police Station Officer	Dennis Plenty
Police Station Radio Operator	Alan Harris
CI5 Man	Jerry Baker
Turkel's Aide	Gerry Paris

Director: **Sidney Hayers**

BODIE and Doyle, CI5's top agents, are alerted to the theft of a large number of rifles and hand grenades from an army base and later discover the bodies of the Irish terrorists who stole them, but the arms have disappeared. A well-known criminal, Charley Turkel and his men have taken the arms from the terrorists. Turkel is planning to use new terrorist methods to rescue his brother Henry from long-term imprisonment. He intends to snatch an important hostage and then exchange him for his brother. The arms are stored in the cellar of Turkel's house but one of the gang, an unbalanced youth named Billy, secretly removes a gun and a hand grenade which he intends to use to settle a grudge against a psychiatrist, Doctor Brook. At the hospital where Brook works, Billy takes Emma Bolding, young blonde nurse, hostage, inserts the grenade into her bra, and threatens to blow her up unless the doctor comes to meet him. Bodie and Doyle are alerted and Bodie springs a trap on Billy by wearing the Doctor Brook's white coat.

In OLD DOG WITH NEW TRICKS, CI5 agent Ray Doyle sets out to stop a gangster called Turkel who devises a plot to free his brother from jail by taking hostage an important figure in authority. Martin Shaw poses for a publicity shot on location at Amersham General Hospital, Buckinghamshire in June 1977.

The nurse is rescued safely and Billy is taken in for questioning. When they discover that the hand grenade used by Billy comes from the cache of arms stolen from the army base, he is cross-examined by Cowley. Billy admits that Charley Turkel has the arms, but Billy has no idea what his boss intends to do with them. He only knows that a big operation is planned for Friday, and that a 'top cop' is involved. When the squad searches Turkel's home, he has already escaped with the arms. The situation looks desperate until Cowley reasons that the 'top cop', who Turkel intends to use as hostage in order to secure his brother Henry's release, must be the Home Secretary who is due to visit a small police station on Friday. All the Home Secretary's engagements for that day are changed, but Bodie suspects that Turkel and his men have probably already taken over the police station and now lie in wait to seize the Home Secretary during his planned visit.

Taking a gamble, Cowley himself arrives at the police station and enters the building expecting to be mistaken for the government official. His deception works, and he is immediately seized by Turkel who then puts out a radio message that the Home Secretary will be shot unless his brother Henry is released from prison and a plane is made ready for their escape. Henry Turkel arrives as ordered, but beside him in the street is Ray Doyle, a sawn-off shotgun pressed firmly into Henry's neck! Cowley explains to Turkel that if one single shot is fired, his brother will be killed instantly! Faced with the inevitable, Turkel and his gang lay down their arms and surrender.

Production Unit

Created by	Brian Clemens
Executive Producers	Albert Fennell, Brian Clemens
Music	Laurie Johnson
Producer	Sidney Hayers
Associate Producer	Ron Fry
Script Editor	Kenneth Ware
Production Manager	Nicholas Gillott
Assistant Director	Bill Westley
Location Manager	Peter Cotton
Continuity	Cheryl Leigh
Casting	Maggie Cartier
Art Director	Ken Court
Assistant Art Director	Michael Sierton
Construction Manager	Fred Walker
Wardrobe Master	Jim Smith
Lighting Cameraman	Ernie Steward
Camera Operator	Brian Elvin
Make Up	Alan Brownie
Hairdresser	Barbara Ritchie
Fight Arranger	Joe Dunne
Editor	Barry Peters
Sound Recordists	Derek Ball, Paul Carr
Dubbing Editors	Peter Keen, Graham Harris
Music Editor	Alan Willis

Post Production Supervisor   Paul Clay

An Avengers MARK 1 Production For LONDON WEEKEND TELEVISION

Shooting / Location Schedule

Production Dates: Monday 13th June to Friday 1st July, 1977, Wednesday 27th July; Monday 24th October, 1977. Production Number: 9D11181

13 June	***Int: Cellar / Squad corridor / Bodie's flat***: Harefield Grove, Rickmansworth Road, Harefield, Middlesex
14-16 June	***Ext: Hospital & car park***: Amersham General Hospital, Whieldon Street, Amersham, Buckinghamshire
20-21 June	***Charley Turkel's Farmhouse***: White Gates (Three Acres Farm), Harefield Road, Harefield, Middlesex
22 June	***Military Base***: Harefield Hospital, Hill End Road, Harefield, Middlesex
	Warehouse / Doyle's car: Rockware Glass Limited, East Side Warehouse (West Entrance), Rockware Avenue, Greenford, Middlesex
23-24 June	***Ext: Hospital & car park***: Amersham General Hospital, Whieldon Street, Amersham, Buckinghamshire
24 June	***Int: Doyle's car (Rover)***: Rickmansworth Road, Harefield, Middlesex
	Int's: Bodie's flat / Prison / Interrogation room: Harefield Grove, Rickmansworth Road, Harefield, Middlesex
27 June-1 July	***Ext: Prison***: Eton College, Natural History Museum, Keats Lane, Windsor, Berkshire
	Police Station: Windsor Police Station, St. Leonard's Road, Windsor, Berkshire
	Side street: Doyle's look-out to Police Station: Keppel Street, Windsor, Berkshire
	Doyle's car run-by: Alma Road, Windsor, Berkshire
	Car Park (meeting with Cowley): Coach & Lorry Park, off Arthur Road, Windsor, Berkshire
	'White' Police car run-by: Arthur Road (junction Alma Road), Windsor, Berkshire
27 July	***Ext: Bodie's flat; Doyle's car***: Holland Road (near Napier Road), Kensington, London, W14
	'Blue' Police car run-by: Merton Road / St. Laurence Way roundabout, Slough, Berkshire (n.b: filmed for *Where The Jungle Ends* and inserted here at a later stage)
24 October	***Side street: Doyle's 'look-out' to Police Station***: Keppel Street, Windsor, Berkshire

LONG SHOT

by **Anthony Read**
© Copyright Mark 1 Productions Ltd MCMLXXVII

Ramos	Roger Lloyd Pack
Villa	Martin Benson
Sammy	Robert Gillespie
Walton	Peter Cellier
Sheikh Achmeia	Nadim Sawalha
Dr. Harbinger	Ed Bishop
Mitchell	John Horsley
SAS Sergeant	Shaun Curry
Detective Sergeant	Tony Caunter
Agent	Brian Haines
Mandy	Judy Matheson
Corporal	Max Mason
Driver	George Mallaby
1st Security Guard	Archie Tew
2nd Security Guard	John Hamill
Girl in Gym	Gillian Duxbury

Director: **Ernest Day**

AN international anti-terrorist conference is to be held at a top security camp in England, and Bodie and Doyle are assigned to protect a former US Secretary of State, Harbinger, who is to be one of the principal delegates. Cowley, also a delegate, meets Sheikh Achmeia of Murani, who frankly tells him that any terrorist caught in Murani is immediately shot. Despite all the extra security measures taken at the conference, Ramos, a notorious terrorist, manages to infiltrate the grounds and, as Harbinger is returning from an early morning run with Bodie and Doyle in attendance, Cowley, wandering over to meet them, spies a gun barrel gleaming in the early morning sunlight. Throwing Harbinger to the ground, Cowley shouts to his men and the three shots from Ramos' rifle narrowly miss them and lodge in a nearby building. Ramos escapes, and Cowley calls for a countryside search.

Later, a petty criminal named Sammy Martin is arrested while trying to run away from the grounds of a large house owned by millionaire Willard Mitchell. Sammy had tried to break into the house but found Mitchell at home. Cowley's interest is aroused when the police inform him that Sammy has told them that he saw Ramos with the millionaire, and Bodie and Doyle are sent to investigate. They find that Ramos has already left for an unknown destination and Mitchell explains that he harboured the terrorist only because Ramos has kidnapped his daughter and threatened to kill her if Mitchell did not co-operate. When no further attempts are made on Harbinger's life and he leaves the country safely, Cowley studies the photographs of the marks made by Ramos' bullets on the wall of te army building, and comes to the conclusion that the shots were not aimed at Harbinger, but at himself, the Head of CI5!

Ramos soon makes a second attempt on Cowley's life, but Bodie and Doyle manage to stave off the attack and Ramos is captured. However, he does not seem bothered about the arrest and explains that Mitchell's daughter is still being held captive and will certainly die if he is not released the following morning; only if he is put safely on a plane to Aden will he tell CI5 where she is being held so that she may be rescued. Against his better judgement, Cowley is forced to agree to the terrorists' terms, and the following morning Ramos is put aboard a plane and tells Bodie and Doyle where the girl is hidden, in a derelict building that is due to be demolished that very morning.

They race to her rescue, and find her unhurt but gagged and bound. Cowley, however, seems unconcerned about Ramos' escape; in fact he has played one last winning card. He has sent one of his agents on board Ramos' plane and, as the plane nears the Middle East, the CI5 man swallows a pill, which causes him to show all the symptoms of a heart attack. The plane is immediately diverted to the nearest airfield, Murani, and the CI5 chief soon receives word from Sheikh Achmeia that Ramos has been shot while attempting to escape.

Production Unit

Created by	Brian Clemens
Executive Producer	Albert Fennell, Brian Clemens
Music	Laurie Johnson
Producer	Sidney Hayers
Associate Producer	Ron Fry
Script Editor	Kenneth Ware
Production Manager	Nicholas Gillott
Assistant Director	Al Burgess
Location Manager	Peter Cotton
Continuity	Cheryl Leigh
Casting	Maggie Cartier
Art Director	Ken Court
Assistant Art Director	Michael Sierton
Construction Manager	Fred Walker
Wardrobe Master	Jim Smith
Lighting Cameraman	Ernie Steward
Camera Operator	Brian Elvin
Make Up	Alan Brownie
Hairdresser	Barbara Ritchie
Fight Arranger	Joe Dunne
Editor	Mike Campbell
Sound Recordists	Derek Ball, Paul Carr
Dubbing Editor	Peter Lennard, Graham Harris
Music Editor	Alan Willis
Post Production Supervisor	Paul Clay

An Avengers MARK 1 Production For LONDON WEEKEND TELEVISION

Ex-Glamour model Gillian Duxbury played CI5 agent Susie, the 'Girl in the Gym' in LONG SHOT.

Gordon Jackson as George Cowley, Commander of CI5, in LONG SHOT.

Shooting / Location Schedule

Production Dates: Monday 4th to Friday 15th July, Monday 19th September, 1977. Production Number: 9D11190

4-5 July	***Mitchell's country house (interiors / grounds)***: Black Firs, Fulmer Common Road, Fulmer, Buckinghamshire ***Mitchell's country house (gates / wall / lane)***: South View Lodge, 60 Hedgerley Lane, Gerrards Cross, Bucks ***Mandy's car run-bys / driveway***: Hedgerley Lane, Gerrards Cross, Buckinghamshire
6-8 July	***Conference***: Stoke Park House, Stoke Park Golf Club, Park Road, Stoke Poges, Buckinghamshire ***Ext: Doyle's car (on route to derelict building)***: Church Lane, Stoke Poges, Buckinghamshire ***Int: Doyle's car (on route to derelict building)***: Wexham Park Lane, Wexham, Slough, Berkshire ***Int: Doyle's car (on route to derelict building)***: Uxbridge Road (A412) (near The Frithe), Slough, Berkshire
11 July	***Ext: CI5 HQ & reception / Police Station***: Horlicks factory, Stoke Poges Lane, Slough, Berkshire
12-14 July	***Doyle's car run-by***: Harefield Road, Woodcock Hill, Batchworth, Hertfordshire ***Int's: Airport Lounge / Ramos' office / Gym / Aeroplane / Cowley's office***: Harefield Grove, Rickmansworth Road, Harefield, Middlesex
15 July	***Derelict building (Demolition Site)***: British Moulded Hose Company Limited, Sandown Road, North Watford, Hertfordshire
19 September	***Mitchell's country house (Ramos scenes only)***: Fulmer Rise Manor, Fulmer Rise Estate, Fulmer, Bucks

WHERE THE JUNGLE ENDS

by **Brian Clemens**
© Copyright Mark 1 Productions Ltd MCMLXXVII

Krivas	David Suchet
Benny	Del Henney
Simon Sinclair	Geoffrey Palmer
Franky	Christopher Reich
Tub	Paul Humpoletz
Pole	Leon Lissek
Denver	Jeremy Bulloch
Betty	Bridget Brice
Cusak	Robert James
Cynthia	Georgina Kean
Butler	Arthur Blake
Bank Manager	Desmond Jones

Uncredited

Air Terminal Desk Clerk	Dave Church
Bank Clerk	Les Conrad
Bank Customer	James Charlton

Director: **Raymond Menmuir**

A GROUP of hardened and highly-trained professional fighters plan to rob a London bank. The leader of the group, Enrico Krivas, enters the bank with Franky, and the robbery is carried out easily, although the bank manager manages to press the alarm bell and is felled by a blow from Krivas' gun butt. In answer to the alarm, police cars converge on the street outside, and immediately come under fire as two paratroopers, Tub Weston and Benny Marsh, sweep them down with machine-gun fire. Krivas and Franky fill their sacks with cash; race outside to a waiting truck, and speed away towards a nearby airport. The police give chase, but their car tyres are raked by machine-gun fire. One car, which is still giving chase, is forced to crash when the gang's bullets smash its windscreen. The fifth man in the group, Pole, has commandeered a small aircraft and the gang get on board and take off.

At CI5, the Squad listens to the police radio messages. The air force is alerted to follow the plane and force it down, but as Bodie predicts, the gang parachute to safety and leave the plane to crash. To Bodie, also a trained fighter, everything about the robbery marks it as the work of professionals. By chance, he has seen Benny in London the day before the robbery, and instantly connects his presence in London with the raid. He is also sure that Benny will be working with Krivas, Bodie's particular enemy from the past, and from descriptions given of the others in the gang, he decides that the men are Tub and Franky.

Martin Shaw as Ray Doyle on location for WHERE THE JUNGLE ENDS.

Cowley is puzzled that no trace of the gang is found, but Bodie tells him that the men are probably following their military training and taking cover in the countryside. Meanwhile, Krivas has left his men in a wooded area and gone to the home of Simon Sinclair, a criminal boss whose territory Krivas has deliberately chosen to invade. As proof of the competence of his men, the terrorist offers Sinclair the entire proceeds of the robbery if he will give them a task, which will truly reward their professionalism. Impressed, Sinclair instructs Krivas to carry out the robbery of plutonium from a nuclear waste disposal plant. Sinclair has a client waiting and an agreed sum of money will be deposited in a Swiss bank under Krivas' name.

Cowley's (Gordon Jackson) 'standing-office' set at the Harefield Grove unit base in Middlesex. Pictured here during WHERE THE JUNGLE ENDS.

Anticipating that Benny will probably want to visit his girlfriend, whom he has not seen for four years, Bodie is waiting when Benny arrives at his girlfriend's flat. Benny is seized and taken to Cowley and it is only when the CI5 chief threatens to release him and send him back to join the losing side overseas that Benny tells him of Krivas' involvement with Sinclair. Knowing that Sinclair is unassailable by normal police methods, Cowley tells Bodie and Doyle that he is suspending them from duty while he investigates 'complaints' about them; meanwhile they are not his responsibility.

Free from the usual restrictions, the two men kidnap Sinclair's daughter and Bodie, pretending to be one of Krivas' criminal rivals, threatens to injure her if Sinclair does not reveal the nature of the deal he made with Krivas. Sinclair tells them of the plutonium raid planned for the following night. When the Squad arrives at the nuclear plant, Krivas and his gang have already staged the robbery. The lorry used for the robbery is found nearby, but the gang has fled across country on motorbikes. Cowley, Bodie and Doyle set off after the men on foot, but unable to keep up with his younger colleagues, Cowley stops to rest. The two agents soon discover an abandoned police car and the bodies of two dead policemen. Bodie is surprised that the gang, have left such an obvious clue; then realises that the gang have deliberately left a false trail and are now heading back up country, to the very spot where

Cowley is resting! The CI5 chief has taken on Franky, but during the struggle has been injured. Bodie and Doyle arrive as Tub and the Pole move in for the kill. Tub is wounded and the Pole is killed in the crossfire, while Bodie takes his revenge on Krivas with his fists.

Production Unit

Created by	Brian Clemens
Executive Producers	Albert Fennell, Brian Clemens
Music	Laurie Johnson
Producer	Sidney Hayers
Associate Producer	Ron Fry
Script Editor	Kenneth Ware
Production Manager	Nicholas Gillott
Assistant Director	Bill Westley
Location Manager	Peter Cotton
Continuity	Cheryl Leigh
Casting	Maggie Cartier
Art Director	Ken Court
Assistant Art Director	Michael Sierton
Construction Manager	Fred Walker
Wardrobe Master	Jim Smith
Lighting Cameraman	Ernie Steward
Camera Operator	Brian Elvin
Make Up	Alan Brownie
Hairdresser	Barbara Ritchie
Fight Arranger	Joe Dunne
Editor	Barry Peters
Sound Recordists	Derek Ball, Paul Carr
Dubbing Editors	Peter Lennard, Graham Harris
Music Editor	Alan Willis
Post Production Supervisor	Paul Clay

An Avengers MARK 1 Production For LONDON WEEKEND TELEVISION

Shooting / Location Schedule

Production Dates: Monday 18th to Friday 29th July, 1977; 2nd Unit: Thursday 18th August, 1977. Production Number: 9D11113

18-19 July	***Blue Police car run-by / truck run-by***: Merton Road / St. Laurence Way (roundabout), Slough, Berkshire
	Police cars: chase with truck / crash: Alpha Street / Grove Close / Albert Street, Slough, Berkshire
	Ext / Int: Bank & robbery: 54 High Street, Eton, Windsor, Berkshire
	Airfield: Denham Aerodrome, Tilehouse Lane, Denham, Buckinghamshire
19-20 July	***Simon Sinclair's House / Woods***: Lockwell House, White Hill, near Batchworth Heath, Hertfordshire

21 July	***Truck run-by (Krivas jumps, hides in bushes)***: White Hill (Lockwell Estate), Batchworth Heath, Hertfordshire ***Range Rover Police car (Krivas watches)***: Mount Vernon Cottages, White Hill, Batchworth Heath, Hertfordshire ***Cowley's car run-by - truck stunt***: Harefield Road, near Woodcock Hill Cemetery, Batchworth, Hertfordshire ***Barrowsby Nuclear Plant***: Harefield Hospital, Hill End Road, Harefield, Middlesex ***Sinclair's daughters school***: Park Mansion, Harefield Hospital, Hill End Road, Harefield, Middlesex
22-26 July	***Woods: Krivas & gang landing***: Croxley Hall Wood, Croxley Green, Hertfordshire ***Gang's hide-out / Fields / fight / bikes***: Harefield Gravel pits, Moorhall Road, Harefield, Middlesex & Harefield Lime Works, Springwell Lane, Rickmansworth, Hertfordshire ***Hi-jacked Police car***: Rickmansworth Road, Harefield, Middlesex ***Cowley's car run-by***: Springwell Lane, Harefield, Middlesex
27 July	***Air Terminal***: TWA Air Terminal, 380 Kensington High Street, Kensington, London, W14 ***Int / Ext: Bodie's car (on route to Benny's)***: Russell Road, Kensington, London, W14 ***Ext: Cynthia / Benny's house***: Hazlewood Tower, off Golborne Gardens, Kensal Town, London, W10
28-29 July	***CI5 Interrogation room / Int's: Krivas & gang's office***: Harefield Grove, Rickmansworth Road, Harefield, Middlesex
2nd Unit: 18 August	***Ext: CI5 HQ: Bodie's car run-by***: 33 High Street, Harefield, Middlesex ***Ext: CI5 HQ (not car run-by)***: Harefield Grove (stables / mews), Rickmansworth Road, Harefield, Middlesex ***Cusak's gun store***: Harefield Grove, Rickmansworth Road, Harefield, Middlesex ***Police cars chase: 'Blue' Police car only***: Park Lane (near Colney Farm), Harefield, Middlesex ***Blue 'Allegro' Police car run-by***: Newdigate Road East (near Northwood Way), Harefield, Middlesex ***Blockade street: Blue 'Allegro' Police car only***: Newdigate Road, Harefield, Middlesex

KILLER WITH A LONG ARM

by **Brian Clemens**
© Copyright Mark 1 Productions Ltd MCMLXXVII

Georgi	Michael Latimer
Hilda	Diane Keen
Costa	Milos Kirek
Tarkos	Alan Tilvern
Tommy	Jonathan Hyde
Betty	Bridget Brice
Mervin	Antony Carrick
Barbara	Mitzi Rogers
CID Sergeant	Howard Bell
Carter	James Leith
Poacher	Hal Jeayes
Pretty Girl	Suzanne Danielle
Uncredited	
Golfer	Pat Gorman
Golfer	Chris Bunn
CI5 Man	Walter Henry
CI5 Man	Eric Kent
Wimbledon Security Officer	Les Conrad

Director: **David Wickes**

THE passenger of a car speeding from Dover to London shoots a policeman dead after the officer makes a routine motorway check. The CI5 forensic team, who discover a niche where an unusual rifle has been carried, checks the abandoned car. Suspecting that the weapon has been smuggled into the country for a particular criminal purpose, Cowley alerts the police force. CI5 soon receives a report that a man has been seen firing a powerful rifle in a rural area near London and the Squad are sent to investigate. They find evidence which points to a gun capable of firing at two miles distance and, when the stub of a special brand of Greek cigarette is found on the ground nearby, Cowley orders Bodie and Doyle to interview a well-informed Greek restaurant owner about any planned killings in the Greek community. The man gives them the name of a wealthy young Greek, Tommy.

Tommy meanwhile is harbouring two men in his flat: Georgi, a professional assassin, and Costa, the man who has hired Georgi to kill someone. Bodie and Doyle raid Tommy's home, but the two men escape via a back entrance. Tommy is taken to Cowley for questioning and, after cross-examination, reveals that Costa is planning a political assassination. Georgi and Costa have now met Hilda, one of Costa's accomplices, and she drives them to a secluded spot in the country where Georgi can get more practice with the rifle; he tests his marksmanship by shooting a golfer two miles away! All three then travel to a flat in Wimbledon from which Georgi plans to carry out the killing: the target will be shot as he sits watching the tennis championships on the Centre Court of the All England Club, two miles away. The occupants of the flat are terrorised into silence. Hilda leaves to buy a stock of food, but runs into the road when she sees two policemen and is knocked down by a Taxi. Bodie and Doyle are sent to the scene when two packets of the special Greek cigarettes are found in her shopping bag.

Guest starring as Tarkos is Alan Tilvern in KILLER WITH A LONG ARM.

Cowley and his men drive to Wimbledon on the day of the championships, after establishing that the drawings found show the Centre Court and the trajectory to it from a high block of flats almost two miles away. Costa's car is soon discovered near a high-rise and the team begins to check out the rooms. The situation looks hopeless, and then Cowley spots a rifle barrel positioned in a window high above them. Bodie takes a daring gamble and swings down from the balcony immediately above the flat. As Bodie deflects the rifle wide of its target, a major Greek official, Doyle races up the stairs to burst into the flat and help his colleague.

Production Unit

Created by	Brian Clemens
Executive Producers	Albert Fennell, Brian Clemens
Music	Laurie Johnson
Producer	Sidney Hayers
Associate Producer	Ron Fry
Script Editor	Kenneth Ware
Production Manager	Nicholas Gillott
Assistant Director	Al Burgess
Location Manager	Peter Cotton
Continuity	Cheryl Leigh
Casting	Maggie Cartier
Art Director	Ken Court
Assistant Art Director	Michael Sierton
Construction Manager	Fred Walker
Wardrobe Master	Jim Smith
Lighting Cameraman	Ernie Steward
Camera Operator	Brian Elvin

Make Up	Alan Brownie
Hairdresser	Joan Carpenter
Fight Arranger	Joe Dunne
Editor	Mike Campbell
Sound Recordists	Derek Ball, Paul Carr
Dubbing Editors	Peter Lennard, Graham Harris
Music Editor	Alan Willis
Post Production Supervisor	Paul Clay

An Avengers MARK 1 Production For LONDON WEEKEND TELEVISION

CI5 become aware that an assassination plot on a group of visiting Greek Royals is being planned using a rifle that has a range of over two miles. A scene from KILLER WITH A LONG ARM featuring Bodie (Lewis Collins) on location at some 'waste-ground' off Alma Road, Windsor, Berkshire in August 1977.

Shooting / Location Schedule

Production Dates: Monday 1st to Friday 12th August, 1977. Production Number: 9D11187

1-2 August   ***Georgi's car run-by: A2 Dover sign***: Old Amersham Road / Amersham Road (A413), Tatling End, Buckinghamshire
Int: Cowley's car (titles): Amersham Road (A413), near Woodhill Avenue, Gerrards Cross, Buckinghamshire
Town Centre and Road Sign: London End / Windsor End, Beaconsfield, Buckinghamshire
Motorway bridge (Costa kills policeman): Hedgerley Lane (over M40), Hedgerley, Buckinghamshire

	Int: Cowley's car (on route to high rise): Packhorse Road, Gerrards Cross, Buckinghamshire *Golf Club*: Flackwell Heath Golf Club, Treadaway Road, Flackwell Heath, near High Wycombe, Buckinghamshire *Forensics garage*: Amersham Motors Limited, Chesham Road, Amersham, Buckinghamshire
3 August	*Int: Doyle's car (route to Restaurant / Tommy's)*: Watford Road (A412), junctions between New Road / Baldwins Lane, Croxley Green, Hertfordshire *Shopping Centre / Supermarket*: Caters Fresh Food Stores, The Parade, Watford, Hertfordshire *Int: Hospital*: AGF House, 3-5 Rickmansworth Road, Watford, Hertfordshire
4 August	*Cowley's car run-by*: Harefield Road / Woodcock Hill, Batchworth, near Rickmansworth, Hertfordshire *Rifle testing fields*: Jacks Lane, off Park Lane, near Colney Farm, Harefield, Middlesex *Scarecrow field*: Chalfont Lane, off Denham Way (A412), Chalfont St. Peter, Buckinghamshire *Car run-by (route to Restaurant)*: Breakspear Road North (near The Swan pub), Harefield, Middlesex
5 August	*Tarkos' Greek Restaurant*: P. R Parada, 10 Station Parade, Denham Way, Denham, Middlesex
8 August	*Int / Ext: Hilda's flat / Tommy's place*: 33 Osborne Road, Windsor, Berkshire *Waste 'walled' ground (Tommy)*: rear of Frogmore Hotel, 71 Alma Road, Windsor, Berkshire *Alleyway-lane: Tommy captured by Bodie & Doyle*: off Alma Road (between Clarence Road / Bexley Street), Windsor, Berkshire *Hilda's car (by alleyway)*: Alma Road / Clarence Crescent, Windsor, Berkshire *Int's: Hilda's car*: St. Marks Road (near Windsor Fire Station), Windsor, Berkshire / Alma Road (near Clarence Road), Windsor, Berkshire *Royal's car run-by*: Castle Hill, Windsor, Berkshire *Royal's car run-by*: M4 Motorway Junction 6 / Windsor & Eton relief Road (A332), near Maidenhead Road (A308), Berkshire
9-12 August	*High Rise flats*: Minster Court, 28 Hillcrest Road, Ealing, London, W5 *Ext: Georgi, Costa, & Hilda from escape Tommy's place*: Alvechurch, Hillcrest Road, Ealing, London, W5 *Street: Cowley's car pulls over*: Hillcrest Road / Park View Road, Ealing, London, W5
12 August	*Int's: CI5 HQ / Interrogation room*: Harefield Grove, Rickmansworth Road, Harefield, Middlesex

HEROES

by **James McAteer**
© Copyright Mark 1 Productions Ltd MCMLXXVII

Tommy	John Castle
Tin Can	Rufus Collins
Estate Car Driver	Ralph Michael
Mrs. Lewis	Dorothy White
Huntley	Thomas Baptiste
Raider	Damien Thomas
Mr. Lewis	Robert McBain
Lorry Driver's mate	Jim McManus
Mr. Sumner	David Baron
Raider	Chris Dillinger
Raider	Neil Kennedy
Lady in Sports Car	Luan Peters
Bride	Gay Close
Bridegroom	Christopher Neil
Raider	Jonathan David
Lorry Driver	Peter Davidson
Security Man	Peter Craze
News Reporter	Valentine Palmer
Uncredited	
John Gerry Patterson	Bruce Boa
Latymer	Anthony Bailey
The American	Kenneth Nelson
CI5 Man (Hotel 1 & 2)	Don McClean
CI5 Man (Hotel 2)	Alan Bennett
Loading Bay worker	Patrick Connor

Director: **William Brayne**

CI5 hears that an assassination attempt is to be made on the life of John Gerry Patterson, an important American politician, when he pays a visit to Britain. Cowley manages to save the man from one such attempt at the Hotel where he is staying, and then decides that, for his own safety, the politician must leave the UK immediately.

Arrangements are made for Patterson to be transported to the airport disguised as a security guard protecting a large load of silver bullion, but the men paid to assassinate Patterson discover the plan in advance. As the security van slowly edges its way through a traffic jam on the approach to an underpass, four armed and masked raiders block its way, blow open the door and kill Patterson.

Drivers of other vehicles watch these events with horror, but they are held back by one of the raiders at gunpoint. However, when Patterson is killed, a bystander rushes up to one of the raiders and manages to pull his mask off;

this encourages other bystanders to follow suit and the raiders, threatened by the harassment, drive away at speed in a waiting car, leaving the silver bullion behind.

One of the witnesses has managed to take a cine film of these events and the face of the unmasked raider is briefly shown, so Cowley decides to panic the gang further by announcing that the man has been positively identified and there are plenty of witnesses willing to identify the killer in court. To his dismay, however, the newspapers print the names and addresses of every witness and Cowley, alarmed that the gang will attempt to silence everyone named, hastily assigns armed guards to every witness. Nonetheless, one witness, a lorry driver, is murdered before Tommy McKay, a CI5 operative can reach him and a second, a young bridegroom on his honeymoon, is shot dead as the CI5 guards arrive. Meanwhile, Bode and Doyle manage to save the life of Ralph May (the estate car driver) at his home.

CI5 agents Bodie (Lewis Collins) and Doyle (Martin Shaw) apprehend one of the raiders in HEROES after fellow agent Tommy McKay has been killed.

Cowley decides to gamble on the desperation of the gang and set a trap by letting it be known that he has taken his guards off one of the witnesses, Tom Sumner, a man who lives in an isolated house by the river. As expected, the raiders attack, but CI5 are waiting for them. During the battle, Tommy is killed, as are three of the raiders. The fourth, who is badly wounded, leads CI5 to Latymer, the wealthy nightclub owner who organised the robbery, and subsequent killing of Patterson.

Production Unit

Created by	Brian Clemens
Executive Producers	Albert Fennell, Brian Clemens
Music	Laurie Johnson
Producer	Sidney Hayers
Associate Producer	Ron Fry
Script Editor	Kenneth Ware
Production Manager	Nicholas Gillott
Assistant Director	Bill Westley
Location Manager	Peter Cotton
Continuity	Cheryl Leigh
Casting	Maggie Cartier
Art Director	Ken Court
Assistant Art Director	Michael Sierton
Construction Manager	Fred Walker
Wardrobe Master	Jim Smith
Lighting Cameraman	Ernie Steward
Camera Operator	Brian Elvin
Make Up	Alan Brownie
Hairdresser	Annie McFadyen
Editor	Barry Peters
Sound Recordists	Gordon Everett, Ken Scrivener
Dubbing Editors	Mike Hopkins, Jeanne Henderson
Music Editor	Alan Willis
Post Production Supervisor	Paul Clay

An Avengers MARK 1 Production For LONDON WEEKEND TELEVISION

CI5 agent Tommy (John Castle) saves the day in explosive style in HEROES.

Shooting / Location Schedule

Production Dates: Monday 15th to Friday 26th August, 1977, 2nd Unit: September - October, 1977. Production Number: 9D11184. Locations in *italics* were originally scheduled but ultimately not used.

15 August	***Hijack road***: A41M Tring By-pass / A4251 Tring Road, near Wiggington, Hertfordshire
16-17 August	***Brewery hide-out***: Ind Coope Limited, Benskins Brewery, 194 High Street, Watford, Hertfordshire
	Int: Bodie's car: Watford brewery: streets around Watford High Street, Hertfordshire
18 August	***Café***: Jock's Café, A4 Colnbrook By-pass, Brands Hill, Colnbrook, Berkshire
	Int: Lewis' house: The Cedars, High Street, Colnbrook, Berkshire
	Warehouse loading-bay: Lakeside Road, Colnbrook By-pass, Colnbrook, Berkshire
	Int: Tommy's car: A4 Colnbrook By-pass, Colnbrook, Berkshire
19-25 August	***Sumner's riverside house***: Sandlea Court, Southlea Road, Datchett, Berkshire
	Gang's hide-out / Riverbank: Weir Bank, Old Mill Lane, Bray, Berkshire
	Approach road-canal bridge: Monkey Island Lane, Bray, Berkshire
	The Ship Hotel & riverbank: *Monkey Island Hotel, Old Mill Lane, Bray, Berkshire*
26 August	***Hospital & CI5 HQ***: Harefield Grove, Rickmansworth Road, Harefield, Middlesex
	Ext: Bodie's car run-by: on route to brewery: High Street, Harefield, Middlesex
	Int: Cowley's car: radio: Springwell Lane, Harefield, Middlesex
26 August	***The Ship Hotel & riverbank***: Compleat Angler Hotel, Bisham Road, Marlow Bridge, Marlow, Buckinghamshire
	Huntley's snooker club: Gatsbys, 57 High Street, Chesham, Buckinghamshire
2nd Unit:	
22 September	***Paper shop***: The Newspaper Shop, 12 Station Parade, North Orbital Road, Denham, Middlesex
	Int: Bodie's car (after paper shop): Moorhall Road, South Harefield, Middlesex
28 September	***Estate car owners house & street***: 12 Walkwood Rise, Beaconsfield, Buckinghamshire
7 October	***Street: Estate car owners house (departure only)***: 57 Warren Road, Ickenham, near Uxbridge, Middlesex
	Holiday Inn Hotel / Int: Latymer's club: Holiday Inn, Stockley Road, West Drayton, Middlesex
10 October	***Int: Cowley's car (Granada): POV of pub***: Kings Head, 41 High Street, Harefield, Middlesex
	Int: Cowley's car (Granada): after pub: Breakspear Road North (near Gilbert Road), Harefield, Middlesex

PRIVATE MADNESS, PUBLIC DANGER

(originally *Timebomb*)
by **Anthony Read**
© Copyright Mark 1 Productions Ltd MCMLXXVII

Nesbitt	Keith Barron
Sutton	Donald Douglas
Susan Fenton	Di Trevis
Gerald Harvey	Angus Mackay
Benny	Trevor Adams
Biggs	Christopher Ellison
Cummings	Peter Penry-Jones
Pam	Penny Irving
Pretty Nurse	Gloria Walker
Betty	Bridget Brice
Hoskins	Donald MacIver
Barmaid	Melanie Peck
Miller	Ian Fairbairn
Secretary	Malou Cartwright
Uncredited	
Pub Drunk	Eddie Stacey
Lady in Pub	Pat Astley
Man in Pub car park	Joe Dunne
Man in Pub car park	Stuart Gregory
Dazed Man in car (at pub)	Mike Leader
Ambulance man	Vic Gallucci
Man in club	Maxwell Craig

Director: **Douglas Camfield**

WHEN an executive and a young secretary at the offices of World Chemical Products die suddenly in unusual circumstances, CI5 are asked to investigate. Bodie and Doyle discover that some strong poison, ADX, has been inserted into the office-dispensing machine and the two dead people were unlucky enough to drink it. They go to interview Susan Fenton, who controls the dispensing machines, but find her at home heavily drugged. Doyle believes that she has taken a massive dose of pure drugs and she is rushed to hospital.

Cowley meanwhile hears that an anonymous ultimatum has been received by the Prime Minister, if Britain does not guarantee to cease all manufacture of chemicals for biological warfare, thousands of people will be poisoned by the discreet use of ADX; the executive and his secretary were killed as a warning, and a further warning is given when several customers at a local pub die after drinking poisoned beer. Meanwhile, Bodie waits at the bedside of

Susan to question her when she regains consciousness; she is obviously a drug addict, and almost certainly handed over the keys to the dispensing machines in return for drugs. The overdose afterwards may have been intended to silence her.

Charles Nesbitt, an expert on chemical weapons, threatens to contaminate the water sources of London with a lethal hallucogenic drug. Lewis Collins poses for a publicity shot on the set of PRIVATE MADNESS, PUBLIC DANGER.

With the help of fellow agent, Benny, Doyle arrests a well-known drug dealer, Eric Sutton, and arranges for him to be brought in for questioning. The man remains silent until Cowley threatens to forcibly inject him with drugs and turn him into a hopeless drug addict, after which Sutton is so terrified that he confesses to the CI5 chief that a man named Charles Nesbitt told him to give Susan the overdose. Nesbitt, a man who lives alone and is obsessed with the conviction that biological warfare must be stopped, intends to use his own skills as a chemist to achieve that aim and manages to escape when Cowley and Doyle raid his home. Bodie, who has been given Nesbitt's name by Susan, joins them and they trace the man to a secluded reservoir where he has planted enough ADX to poison the entire population of London, if the Prime Minister's announcement is not made by 5.30 that afternoon.

Anticipating Nesbitt's next move, the CI5 men arrive too late to stop the man firing a well-aimed shot which sets off a poison device he has put in the water. Bodie and Doyle race over, seize Nesbitt and force him into the reservoir to help them disarm device. Aware that his own life is now threatened, Nesbitt helps them to stop the device. Cowley radios the Prime Minister to cancel the announcement.

CI5's Benny (Trevor Adams) in PRIVATE MADNESS, PUBLIC DANGER. This scene was filmed in a first-floor night club called Gatsby's in Chesham High Street, Buckinghamshire.

Production Unit

Created by	Brian Clemens
Executive Producers	Albert Fennell, Brian Clemens
Music	Laurie Johnson
Producer	Sidney Hayers
Associate Producer	Ron Fry
Script Editor	Dennis Spooner
Production Manager	Nicholas Gillott
Assistant Director	Bill Westley
Location Manager	Peter Cotton
Continuity	Cheryl Leigh
Casting	Maggie Cartier
Art Director	Ken Court
Assistant Art Director	Michael Sierton
Construction Manager	Fred Walker
Wardrobe Master	Jim Smith
Lighting Cameraman	Ernie Steward
Camera Operator	Brian Elvin
Make Up	Alan Brownie
Hairdresser	Annie McFadyen

Fight Arranger	Joe Dunne
Editor	Mike Campbell
Sound Recordists	Gordon Everett, Ken Scrivener
Dubbing Editors	Peter Lennard, Graham Harris
Music Editor	Alan Willis
Post Production Supervisor	Paul Clay

An Avengers MARK 1 Production For LONDON WEEKEND TELEVISION

Shooting / Location Schedule

Production Dates: Tuesday 30th August to Friday 9th September, 1977; 2nd Unit: Monday 12th September, 1977. Production Number: 9D11180. Locations in *italics* were originally scheduled but ultimately not used.

30-31 August	**Office: World Chemical Product's / Int: Hospital**: Costain House, Nicholson's Walk, The Broadway, Maidenhead, Berkshire
	Doyle's car / Ambulance: Nicholson's Shopping Centre: Service deck ramp, The Broadway, Maidenhead, Berkshire
1 September	**Pub**: The Red Cow, 140 Albert Street, Slough, Berkshire
	Street: Pub car crash / Cowley's car: Castle Street / Mere Road, Slough, Berkshire
	Doyle's car run-by (roundabout): St. Laurence Way roundabout, Slough, Berkshire
2 September	**Rex Theatre (stage door)**: The Palace Theatre, 20 Clarendon Road, Watford, Hertfordshire
	Int's: Interrogation room / Sutton's home: Harefield Grove, Rickmansworth Road, Harefield, Middlesex
5 September	**Ext / Int: Susan's flat & street**: Bedford House, The Farmlands, Northolt, Middlesex
2nd Unit:	**Ext: Susan's flat street (ambulance)**: Victoria Road / Franchise Street, Chesham, Buckinghamshire
	Bar & Night Club: Gatsbys, 57 High Street, Chesham, Buckinghamshire
6-8 September	**Sports Club / Reservoir**: Thorpe Park Ski Lakes, Thorpe Road, Chertsey, Surrey
9-12 September	**Nesbitt's country house**: *Breakspear House, Breakspear Road North, Harefield, Middlesex*
	Love Hill House, Love Hill Lane, Iver, Buckinghamshire
	Doyle's car run-by: Moorhall Road, South Harefield, Middlesex
	Ext: Walled gardens (CI5 HQ): Harefield Grove, Rickmansworth Road, Harefield, Middlesex
12 September	**Pub car park and crash**: The Red Cow, 140 Albert Street, Slough, Berkshire

THE FEMALE FACTOR

by **Brian Clemens**
© Copyright Mark 1 Productions Ltd MCMLXXVII

Sir Charles Milvern	Anthony Steel
Baker	Walter Gotell
Sara	Felicity Dean
Ann	Pamela Salem
Simon Culver	Barry Justice
Paula	Maggie Wright
Terkoff	Patrick Durkin
Big Man	Fredric Abbott
Wences	Stefan Kalipha
Reeve	Michael Burrell
Jo	Sally Harrison
Tilson	Kenneth Watson
Betty	Bridget Brice

Director: **David Wickes**

DOYLE suspects that Ann Seaford, a girl he had met several years previously and whose body is now dragged from the River Thames, may have been murdered to stop her from speaking to him. He and Bodie go to Ann's flat to search for clues to her death, but Cowley arrives and tells them that the case is not CI5's business. He soon changes his mind however, when the Prime Minister's private telephone number is discovered doodled on a message pad in Ann's flat. Bodie and Doyle's interest is further aroused when they arrest the pimp who looked after the girl's affairs. He tells them that Ann's daughter, another pimp, Simon Culver, is using Sara, in a blackmail attempt; it was because Ann wanted to talk to Doyle that she was killed.

Sara herself is also a drug addict and is being supplied by Culver in return for her seduction of the Opposition Shadow Minister, Sir Charles Milvern. The blackmail threat is being organised by Sam Baker, an agent, and Terkoff, a Russian. Milvern has been shown photographs of him making love to Sara, and the men threaten to make them public unless the Minister steals a secret file for them. The file is actually unimportant, but the men know that once Milvern has stolen it, he will be in their power. Sara and her pimp have been told that once Milvern is hooked, their involvement is ended, but the Russian intends to kill them to ensure that Milvern's treachery remains secret. That night, Culver is strangled, but Sara overhears the murderer and escapes to Culver's flat where she knows the man keeps a large supply of drugs.

The squad arrives shortly afterwards but remain outside to watch, and when Baker arrives with the Russian, Cowley is astounded that Terkoff, a top Russian KGB man, is involved. When the two men leave, Bodie and Doyle pursue them, and Baker and the Russian are killed in the shooting match that follows. Sara confirms Milvern's involvement, and when Cowley discovers that the Minister was the person who doodled the Prime Minister's number on the message pad, Milvern is confronted with the evidence and obliged to retire from public life.

The apparent suicide of a high-class prostitute known to Doyle (Martin Shaw) leads CI5 into THE FEMALE FACTOR. Actor Martin Shaw on location in Hammersmith, West London.

Production Unit

Created By	Brian Clemens
Executive Producers	Albert Fennell, Brian Clemens
Music	Laurie Johnson
Producer	Sidney Hayers
Associate Producer	Ron Fry
Script Editor	Dennis Spooner
Production Manager	Nicholas Gillott
Assistant Director	Al Burgess
Location Manager	Peter Cotton
Continuity	Pamela Mann
Casting	Maggie Cartier
Art Director	Ken Court
Assistant Art Director	Michael Sierton
Construction Manager	Fred Walker
Wardrobe Master	Jim Smith
Lighting Cameraman	Ernie Steward

Camera Operator	Cece Cooney
Make Up	Alan Brownie
Hairdresser	Annie McFadyen
Editor	Alan Killick
Sound Recordists	Michael Sale, Ken Scrivener
Dubbing Editors	Peter Lennard, Graham Harris
Music Editor	Alan Willis
Post Production Supervisor	Paul Clay

An Avengers MARK 1 Production For LONDON WEEKEND TELEVISION

Shooting / Location Schedule

Production Dates: Monday 12th to Friday 23rd September, 1977. Production Number: 9D11183

12-13 Sept	***Ann's house***: 11 Claremont Road, Windsor, Berkshire ***Doyle's car run-bys (on way to Ann's house)***: streets around Claremont Road, Windsor, Berkshire
14-15 Sept	***London bridge***: Hammersmith Bridge, Hammersmith, London, W6 ***Doyle's old flat***: Digby Mansions, Hammersmith Bridge Road, Hammersmith, London, W6 ***'Series 1 Title sequence'***: Rockware Glass Works, Rockware Avenue, Greenford, Middlesex
16-19 Sept	***Sam Baker's house***: Mount Fidget, Fulmer Rise estate, Fulmer Common Road, Fulmer, Buckinghamshire ***Int: Culver's car***: Fulmer Road, Gerrards Cross/Fulmer, Buckinghamshire
20 September	***London car accident***: Prince Consort Road, Kensington, London, SW7 ***Ext: Simon Culver's flat / car park***: Albert Court, off Prince Consort Road, Kensington, London, SW7
21-23 Sept	***Tobacconist shop***: 78 High Street, Watford, Hertfordshire ***Cemetery***: Woodcock Hill Cemetery, Harefield Road, near Batchworth, Hertfordshire ***Culver's car run-bys***: Rickmansworth Road (Birch Court), Northwood, Middlesex ***Int: Doyle's place / CI5 HQ / Phone Box / Int & Ext: Sir Charles' house / Jo's mews flat / Culver's flat***: Harefield Grove, Rickmansworth Road, Harefield, Middlesex ***Int: Dancing Club***: Gatsbys, 57 High Street, Chesham, Buckinghamshire

EVEREST WAS ALSO CONQUERED

by **Brian Clemens**
© Copyright Mark 1 Productions Ltd MCMLXXVII

Lord Derrington	Michael Denison
Neil Turvey	Richard Greene
Ann Berry	Ann Lynn
Mrs. Turner	Kathleen Byron
Sammy (Frank) Goodman	Charles Keating
Turner	Gary Waldhorn
Sally	Helen Cotterill
Hamer	Roy Boyd
Sir Arden French	Llewellyn Rees
Betty	Bridget Brice
Sir Frederick Tallen	Jeremy Hawk
McKay	Andrew Downie
Angus	Graham Padden
Julia Turvey	Caroline Argyle
Tony Miller	Peter Blake
Bremer	Robert Booth
Mark	Mark Colleano
Priest	Dick Sullivan

Director: **Francis Megahy**

IN 1953, on the night of the Coronation, Suzy Carter, a girl who is the principal witness in a corruption trial, falls to her death from a window while under police protection. The corruption case, against a property dealer, Neil Turvey, cannot proceed and is dropped. Press interest is focused on the Coronation, and the incident receives little press coverage. Many years later, as a senior security chief, named Sir Arden French is dying, he confesses that he was involved in the girl's death. Several bystanders, including Lord Derrington, an important politician, overhear his confession. Derrington invites Cowley to re-examine the circumstances in which Suzy Carter died.

When he discovers that the files on the case are missing from police records, Cowley orders a young member of CI5, Tony Miller, to bring in for questioning the policeman, Eddie Turner, who was guarding Suzy Carter when she died. Before the agent can speak to Turner, the policeman is shot dead. Miller is then killed as he tries to arrest the murderers. Bodie and Doyle are sent to interview Ellie Turner and learn that her husband received a large sum of money from an unspecified source in 1953.

A further lead takes them to the home of Ann Berry, a WPC who had guarded Suzy Carter in 1953, but the girl is killed before they can question her. They discover that she acquired 20,000 valuable shares in Neil Turvey's property company, and that Sir Arden French was also working for Turvey in 1953. Bodie and Doyle are convinced that with French's help, Turvey must have bribed Turner and Berry to kill Suzy Carter and halt the corruption trial; Turvey probably also arranged to have Turner and Berry killed to silence them. When the CI5 men go to confront Turvey with their accusations, they are forced to admit that they have no proof to support their theory. Turvey simply laughs at the charge.

The deathbed confession of Sir Arden French opens up a 25-year old crime. Bodie (Lewis Collins) in a scene from EVEREST WAS ALSO CONQUERED.

Cowley is discussing the case with Lord Derrington when the two men arrive and tell their boss that they are going to interview a third policeman who was near the scene of Carter's death. The man, Hamer, is also killed before they arrive. By chance, however, Hamer was holding a camera and had taken a photograph of the killer. The developed photograph shows a well-known criminal, Sammy (Frank) Goodman.

Goodman is arrested and admits that he killed Turner, Berry and Hamer on Neil Turvey's orders, so Cowley orders Turvey to be arrested. Cowley discovers that there was a corrupt politician, who accepted bribes prior to 1953 and awarded valuable Government building contracts in return. This politician, who also arranged Suzy Carter's death, was Lord Derrington. Cowley now realises that when Derrington overheard Sir Arden French's deathbed confession, he was panicked into calling CI5 to allay any suspicion from himself.

Bodie (Lewis Collins) and Doyle (Martin Shaw) apprehend gamekeeper McKay (Andrew Downie) in this scene from EVEREST WAS ALSO CONQUERED filmed in Black Park, Fulmer, Buckinghamshire in late September 1977.

Production Unit

Created by	Brian Clemens
Executive Producers	Albert Fennell, Brian Clemens
Music	Laurie Johnson
Producer	Sidney Hayers
Associate Producer	Ron Fry
Script Editor	Dennis Spooner
Production Manager	Nicholas Gillott
Assistant Director	Gordon Gilbert
Location Manager	Peter Cotton
Continuity	Pamela Mann
Casting	Maggie Cartier
Production Designer	Tony Curtis
Assistant Art Director	Michael Pittel
Wardrobe Supervisor	Jackie Cummins
Lighting Cameraman	Ernie Steward

Camera Operator	Cece Cooney
Make Up	Alan Brownie
Hairdresser	Annie McFadyen
Editor	Barry Peters
Sound Recordists	Michael Sale, Ken Scrivener
Dubbing Editors	Peter Lennard, Graham Harris
Music Editor	Alan Willis
Post Production Supervisor	Paul Clay

An Avengers MARK 1 Production For LONDON WEEKEND TELEVISION

Shooting / Location Schedule

Production Dates: Monday 26th September to Friday 7th October; Wednesday 12th October, 1977. Production Number: 9D11186

26 September	**Sir Arden French's house**: Lockwell House, White Hill Batchworth Heath, Hertfordshire
27 September	**Woods & deer hunting**: Black Park, Black Park Road, Fulmer, Buckinghamshire
28-29 September	**Int: Neil Turvey's house**: Hall Barn, Windsor End, Beaconsfield, Buckinghamshire
30 September	**Turner's house**: Magnolia House, 74 Rickmansworth Lane, Chalfont St. Peter, Buckinghamshire
	Int: Bodie's car (Capri; route to Turvey's house): Shrubs Road / Woodcock Hill, Batchworth Heath, Hertfordshire
3 October	**Ann Berry's kennels**: Pynesfield Manor, Old Uxbridge Road, Harefield, Middlesex
4-6 October	**Int: Bodie's car (Cortina)**: Park Lane, Harefield, Middlesex
	Bodie's car (Capri) run-by 1 (day; route to Turvey's): Rickmansworth Road, Harefield, Middlesex
	Bodie's car (Capri) run-by 2 (night): Harefield Road (near High Lodge), Harefield, Middlesex
	Int / Ext: Doyle's car (run-by): Harefield Road (junction with Frogmoor Lane), Batchworth, Rickmansworth, Hertfordshire
	Int / Ext: Star Hotel / Int: CI5 offices / H/Q Staircase / Police station records: Harefield Grove, Rickmansworth Road, Harefield, Middlesex
7 October	**Street: Frank (Sammy in credits) picked up**: The Broadway (junction Lancaster Road), Southall, Middlesex
	Ext: Pub / Railings / Gas Works street: White Lion Pub, White Street / The Straight, Southall, Middlesex
12 October	**Int: Ann Berry's kennels**: Pynesfield Manor, Old Uxbridge Road, Harefield, Middlesex

CLOSE QUARTERS

by **Brian Clemens**
© Copyright Mark 1 Productions Ltd MCMLXXVII

Sara	Hildegard Neil
Julia	Gabrielle Drake
Myer	Clive Arrindell
Inge	Madlena Nedeva
Vicar	Allan Surtees
Kristo	David Bradley
Jax	Joseph Charles
Hans	Barney James
Doctor	Rowland Davies
Betty	Bridget Brice

Uncredited

Sir Derek Forbes	Pat Ryan
CI5 Agent	Pat Gorman
CI5 Agent	Roy Everson
CI5 Agent	Alan Harris
CI5 Agent	Barry Holland
CI5 Agent	Ken Lawrie
Estate car owner (boat yard)	Val Musetti

Director: **William Brayne**

FOUR German terrorists who are being hunted by police all over Europe come to Britain. They murder Sir Derek Forbes, a prominent businessman, and Cowley warns his men that they must be caught before they can commit any further outrages. Bodie, off duty because of an injured hand, is not present for Cowley's briefing, and when he arrives at HQ and notices the photographs of the terrorists on the wall, Cowley tells him that until his hand heals sufficiently to be strong enough to hold a gun, he must remain off duty. The agent uses his free time to take his girlfriend, Julia, boating on the Thames, but as they pass a small island in the river, he is startled to recognise the face of one of the terrorists, Franz Myer, peering out of the undergrowth.

With Julia's help, Myer is seized from the terrorist camp but Inge Helmut, the terrorist leader who gives chase with her group, sees Bodie and his girlfriend. Bodie manages to get Myer away from the river by stealing a car, but the terrorists do likewise and follow in hot pursuit. With no chance to stop and telephone HQ and the gang closing in behind them, Bodie seeks refuge in a lonely country house, inhabited by an elderly vicar and his housekeeper. Bodie immediately telephones Cowley and tells him that he is holding Myer, but before he can say where he is, the terrorists arrive at the house and cut the telephone wires, leaving Cowley desperately trying to work out where his colleague may be.

Bodie secures all the doors and shutters and waits for the attack. The terrorists appeal to him to release Myer, or at least talk terms, but the vicar insists on trying to talk to them and is immediately shot dead. With great difficulty, Bodie holds his gun in his injured hand and manages to shoot one terrorist as he enters the house via the cellar door. Inge makes a determined attempt to gain entrance by crashing her car through the front door, but Bodie manages to hustle Myer and the two women into a locked attic at the top of the house. While Inge positions herself outside the room with a machine-gun, the fourth terrorist tries to break into the room from the roof but is shot by Bodie. During the shootout, Myer spies his chance for freedom and attacks Bodie as Inge breaks into the room, her machine-gun trained on the agent's heart. Before she has the chance to fire, she is shot from behind by Doyle as he comes running up the stairs. Cowley and his men have traced Bodie's progress from his roof gun shot, aimed at their car, to the hideout, and Myer is taken away under guard. Bodie, whose hand is further damaged by its enforced use, is given a further two weeks leave.

Production Unit

Created by	Brian Clemens
Executive Producers	Albert Fennell, Brian Clemens
Music	Laurie Johnson
Producer	Sidney Hayers
Associate Producer	Ron Fry
Script Editor	Dennis Spooner
Production Manager	Nicholas Gillott
Assistant Director	Shaun Redmayne
Location Manager	Peter Crowhurst
Continuity	Pamela Mann
Casting	Maggie Cartier
Production Designer	Tony Curtis
Assistant Art Director	Michael Pittel
Effects Supervisor	Allan Bryce
Wardrobe Mistress	Jackie Cummins
Lighting Cameraman	Ernie Steward
Camera Operator	Cece Cooney
Make Up	Alan Brownie
Hairdresser	Annie McFadyen
Editor	Mike Campbell
Sound Recordists	Michael Sale, Ken Scrivener
Dubbing Editors	Mike Hopkins, Jeanne Henderson
Music Editor	Alan Willis
Post Production Supervisor	Paul Clay

An Avengers MARK 1 Production For LONDON WEEKEND TELEVISION

Shooting / Location Schedule

Production Dates: Monday 10th to Friday 21st October, 1977. Production Number: 9D11185

On leave from CI5 with a hand injury, Bodie (Lewis Collins) finds himself face-to-face with the leader of a terrorist group in CLOSE QUARTERS.

10 October	***Airport & assassination***: Heathrow Airport (Terminal 3), Bath Road, Hayes, Middlesex
11 October	***Boat yard / river / boats***: Bushnell's Boat yard, Ray Mead Road / Boulters Lock, Maidenhead, Berkshire
12-13 October	***Boat stunt (over canal bridge)***: Springwell Lane, Rickmansworth, Hertfordshire
	Cowley's car run-by: Moorhall Road, South Harefield, Middlesex
	Int: CI5 HQ & office: Harefield Grove, Rickmansworth Road, Harefield, Middlesex
14-21 October	***Pub car park & phone booth***: Nags Head, London Road (A413), Little Missenden, Buckinghamshire
	Vicarage & farmhouse: Hundridge Manor, Hyde End, Chesham Road, Great Missenden, Buckinghamshire
	Cowley's car run-by (turn in road): Chesham Road / Little Hundridge Lane, Great Missenden, Buckinghamshire

LOOK AFTER ANNIE
by **Brian Clemens**
© Copyright Mark 1 Productions Ltd MCMLXXVII

Annie	Diana Fairfax
Stanley	Clifton Jones
Isla	Patricia Quinn
John Howard	Derek Francis
Ben Hymer	Keith Buckley
Big Billy	Nick Brimble
Patterson	Frank Jervis
Turner	Michael Walker
Police Officer	John Golightly
Thug	John Sarbutt
Frank	David Mallinson
Thug	Jonathan Bergman

Director: **Charles Crichton**

ANNIE IRVINE draws large audiences wherever she preaches in the United States with her combination of left-wing political dogma and Christian gospel. One night, as she is addressing a meeting in New York, a man tries to shoot her. Annie is only slightly wounded, but the incident gives her wide publicity and increases her following enormously.

Two years later, when Annie is an influential figure in America, she comes to England, and Cowley insists that CI5 should be responsible for her welfare while she is in the UK. Bodie and Doyle cannot understand Cowley's special interest, until they discover that Cowley had once wanted to marry her. Annie herself has been married twice, and the CI5 chief is disappointed to find that at present she is living with her black business manager, Stanley Langdon. Langdon has been secretly making money out of Annie's popularity for some years, and has now decided that the appeal would be greatly heightened if she were to be martyred; he tells another girl working in Annie's organisation, that with Annie dead, she would be a money-making legend; they could make a fortune by exploiting her memory.

A meeting of Annie's followers is arranged at a city hall in London, and Langdon meets secretly with a criminal named Ben Hymer and pays him to arrange Annie's death that night. Hymer is to hire some thugs and wait in an alley for Langdon's signal that Annie is leaving. Cowley receives a warning from an old friend that thugs are being recruited to kill Annie, but the woman flatly refuses to cancel the meeting and Cowley is forced to double the protection around the hall.

Police blocks are placed on all the roads leading to the venue, and further policemen are on patrol when the public arrives. Various right-wing demonstrators and groups of Annie's followers clash outside the hall and the barricades are torn down as police and the opposing sides meet in an angry fight. At the very moment that the mob breaks through, Langdon urges Annie to leave the hall via a back exit, and signals to Hymer and his thugs to be ready.

As the thugs try to attack Annie, a CI5 man on the roof fires at them, but is shot by Hymer. Annie tries to run away, but is held back by two of the thugs, and CI5 are soon involved in a vicious fight for her safety. Cowley is badly beaten in his attempt to save and it is down to Bodie to save Doyle who manages to shoot Hymer before shepherding the remaining thugs into the back of a van. As Annie is led to safety, Stanley Langdon aims his gun at her and is shot dead by a recovering Cowley. Though distressed by Langdon's death, Annie refuses to believe that he planned to have her shot, and blames Cowley for 'murdering' him.

Stanley (Clifton Jones) prepares to take a shot at Annie (Diana Fairfax), but is about to be felled by Cowley (Gordon Jackson)....a scene from LOOK AFTER ANNIE.

Production Unit

Created by	Brian Clemens
Executive Producers	Albert Fennell, Brian Clemens
Music	Laurie Johnson
Producer	Sidney Hayers
Associate Producer	Ron Fry
Script Editor	Dennis Spooner
Production Manager	Nicholas Gillott
Assistant Director	David Bracknell
Location Manager	Peter Crowhurst
Continuity	Pamela Mann
Casting	Maggie Cartier
Production Designer	Tony Curtis
Assistant Art Director	Michael Pittel
Effects Supervisor	Allan Bryce
Wardrobe Supervisor	Jackie Cummins
Lighting Cameraman	Ernie Steward
Camera Operator	Cece Cooney
Make Up	Alan Brownie
Hairdresser	Annie McFadyen
Editor	Barry Peters
Sound Recordists	Michael Sale, Ken Scrivener
Dubbing Editors	Peter Lennard, Graham Harris

Music Editor   Alan Willis
Post Production Supervisor   Paul Clay

An Avengers MARK 1 Production For LONDON WEEKEND TELEVISION

Shooting / Location Schedule
Production Dates: Monday 24th October to Friday 4th November, 2nd Unit: December, 1977. Production Number: 9D11188

24 Oct-2 Nov	***Conference hall***: Odeon Buildings, 223 High Street, off Park Road, Uxbridge, Middlesex ***Bodie's car run-by (over bridge)***: Oxford Road (near the Swan & Bottle pub), Uxbridge, Middlesex ***Pub car park / John Howard's office***: Crown & Treaty Pub, 90 Oxford Road, Uxbridge, Middlesex ***Street: Biker gang 'night' meeting***: Gordon & Eve's café, 200 Oxford Road, Uxbridge, Middlesex ***Industrial estate***: Highbridge Industrial Estate, Oxford Road, Uxbridge, Middlesex ***Airport car park: Bodie's car (close-up)***: Highbridge Industrial Estate, Uxbridge, Middlesex. n.b: *see 2nd unit insert* ***Rioting / Police road blocks***: Keppel Street / Helena Road / Dagmar Road, Windsor, Berkshire ***Hotel***: Skyline Hotel, Bath Road, Harlington, Middlesex
2nd Unit:	***Airport: Bodie's car run-by (insert for close-up)***: Heathrow Airport, (Terminal 3: Camberley Road), Bath Road, Hayes, Middlesex ***Bodie's car run-by (past poster)***: 215-218 High Street (near Chippendale Alley), Uxbridge, Middlesex ***Bodie's car run-by (airport route) / Ambulance***: Park Road (junction Chippendale Waye), Uxbridge, Middlesex
3-4 November	***Bodie's car run-by (near houses - Hotel route)***: Harefield Road (junction Heron Close), Batchworth, Rickmansworth, Hertfordshire ***Int: Bodie's car (Hotel route)***: Harefield Road (near Harefield Road Industrial Estate), Batchworth, near Rickmansworth, Hertfordshire ***Int: CI5 rest room / CI5 HQ / Hospital***: Harefield Grove, Rickmansworth Road, Harefield, Middlesex
2nd Unit: 16 December	***Cowley's Office***: Harefield Grove, Rickmansworth Road, Harefield, Middlesex

WHEN THE HEAT COOLS OFF

by **Brian Clemens**
© Copyright Mark 1 Productions Ltd MCMLXXVII

Bill Haydon	Peter Hughes
Jill	Lalla Ward
Harry Scott	Bernard Kay
Minister	Gerald Sim
Syd Parker	Graham Weston
Mrs. Wilson	Shelagh Fraser
Freddy	Arthur White
Car Salesman	Alistair Cameron
Merton	Michael Sheard
Sergeant	Geoffrey Hinsliff
Fitch	Robert Mill
Betty	Bridget Brice
Uncredited	
1st Man in Pub	Dave Cooper
2nd Man in Pub	Bobby Ramsey
Man in Pub	Ronnie Wood
Man in Pub	Ron Tarr
Lady in Pub	Pat Astley
Waiter	Andrew Andreas
Uniformed Policeman	Kenny Wymark

Director: **Ray Austin**

IN 1971, when Doyle was a police constable, a police informer named Fitch was shot dead by an intruder at his home. Doyle's partner, Police Constable Syd Parker, was also shot dead as he arrived on the scene, and Doyle arrested Bill Haydon, a known criminal, for the crime. Haydon had threatened Fitch earlier that day, and when his car was seen leaving the scene of the crime, the evidence against him seemed conclusive. Apart from Doyle, the principal witness at Haydon's trial was an elderly caretaker who saw him emerge from Fitch's flat with a gun in his hand. Some years later, when Doyle is with CI5, Haydon's attractive daughter Jill comes to Doyle's home and begs him to re-examine the case. Her father has served seven years of a 30-year sentence and still protests that he was framed; and that he did not kill Fitch or Parker. He received an anonymous phone call to go to Fitch's flat, saw the dead bodies and fled; the caretaker was bribed to say he saw him with a gun, a gun that has never been found.

Doyle and Bodie go to interview the caretaker, but are told by a neighbour, Mrs. Wilson, that the man has died recently of bronchitis. She also tells them that he possessed a large amount of money obtained from an unspecified source. This would seem to suggest that the caretaker might have been bribed; it would have been possible for another man to have telephoned Haydon, entered Fitch's flat and killed the two men, then waited for Haydon to arrive before making good his escape. Doyle sets out to find the gun that such a man must have thrown away shortly after the killings, and orders the grounds outside Fitch's flat to be searched. At Jill Haydon's suggestion, a nearby pond is also searched, and when the gun is found there, Doyle makes a statement that his original evidence may have been biased, and the case should be officially re-opened.

Cowley is unhappy and arranges for the caretaker's body to be exhumed. The autopsy reveals that the man died of suffocation. Cowley, suspecting Jill Haydon of murdering the only witness to her father's crimes, sets out to accuse her of the caretaker's death. Doyle, too, is not entirely happy about the evidence he has found in Haydon's favour and searches out the car, which Haydon used on the day of the murder. The car is located, and Bodie and Doyle discover a gun compartment under the dashboard; it is obvious that Haydon hid his gun there after killing the two men and that Jill threw it into the pond so that it would be found and clear her father's name. Cowley arrests Jill Haydon, as Bodie and Doyle arrive at her house. Doyle visits her father in prison, where Haydon is appalled to hear that his daughter is being charged with murder and that the case will not now be re-examined.

Production Unit

Created by	Brian Clemens
Executive Producers	Albert Fennell, Brian Clemens
Music	Laurie Johnson
Producer	Sidney Hayers
Associate Producer	Ron Fry
Script Editor	Dennis Spooner
Production Manager	Nicholas Gillott
Assistant Director	Ken Baker
Location Manager	Peter Crowhurst
Continuity	Kay Mander
Casting	Maggie Cartier
Production Designer	Tony Curtis
Assistant Art Director	Michael Pittel
Effects Supervisor	Allan Bryce
Wardrobe Supervisor	Jackie Cummins
Lighting Cameraman	Ernie Steward
Camera Operator	Cece Cooney
Make Up	Alan Brownie
Hairdresser	Annie McFadyen
Editor	Bob Dearberg
Sound Recordists	Michael Sale, Ken Scrivener
Dubbing Editors	Mike Hopkins, Jeanne Henderson
Music Editor	Alan Willis
Post Production Supervisor	Paul Clay

An Avengers MARK 1 Production For LONDON WEEKEND TELEVISION

CI5's number one agents: Bodie (Lewis Collins) and Doyle (Martin Shaw), in WHEN THE HEAT COOLS OFF.

Shooting / Location Schedule

Production Dates: Monday 7th to Friday 18th November, 1977. Production Number: 9D11191

7 November	***Kings Arms pub***: The Buccaneer (The Bellhouse Hotel), Oxford Road, Beaconsfield, Buckinghamshire
8-9 November	***Police car run-bys (Doyle & PC Parker)***: Breakspear Road North / Park Lane, Harefield, Middlesex
	Police car run-by: High Street (junction Merle Avenue), Harefield, Middlesex
	Int: Doyle's Police car (after Parker's death): High Street (junction Merle Avenue), Harefield, Middlesex
	Ext: Ambury Mansions (Fitch's flat): Montrose, 95 Langley Road, Watford, Hertfordshire
	Haydon's house: Lockwell House, White Hill, Batchworth Heath, Hertfordshire
10 November	***Park and river***: Oxhey Park, Eastbury Road, Oxhey, Hertfordshire
11 November	***Used car dealer***: J.R Inwards, 53-59 High Street, Ruislip, Middlesex
14-18 November	***Int: Bodie's car: routes to Haydon's / car dealer***: High Street / Rickmansworth Road, Harefield, Middlesex
	Int / Ext: Doyle's mews flat / Int's: Restaurant / Ambury Mansions / 1971 Police station / Court / Prison: Harefield Grove, Rickmansworth Road, Harefield, Middlesex

STAKE OUT
by **Dennis Spooner**
© Copyright Mark 1 Productions Ltd MCMLXXVII

Frank	David Collings
Bob	Barry Jackson
Attractive Blonde	Pamela Stephenson
Fat Man	Jack Lynn
Peanut Eater	Peter Armitage
Handsome Negro	Tony Osoba
Doctor	Ronald Leigh-Hunt
Hunter	Gerald James
Man in Raincoat	Brian Hawksley
Jack	Malcolm Hayes
Major	Barry Stokes
Benny	Trevor Adams
Fraser	Andrew Bradford
Sarah	Sarah Grazebrook
Young girls	Fiona Reid, Brigitte Fry

Director: **Benjamin Wickers**

COWLEY receives a telephone call from John Fraser, a CI5 agent watching a bowling alley for suspected criminals. Fraser says that he has discovered that a major crime is about to be committed, but before he can give Cowley the details, he is murdered. Bodie and Doyle are sent to the bowling alley on 'stake out'. Their job is to observe anything suspicious and report back to HQ. The two men play bowls; watch the customers and staff, but everything appears normal until suddenly, a man who has recently entered the building collapses and dies. Bodie and Doyle have the body examined by a CI5 doctor, and the examination proves that the man has been poisoned.

Later, the two CI5 men notice a man taking photographs with a miniature camera and they take him in for questioning. The man pleads his innocence and says that he was simply taking photographs of the young girls in the bowling alley. Cowley's interest is aroused, however, when some of the snaps the man has taken show Ray Kerrigan, a Special Branch operative lurking in the background. Hunter of Special Branch tells Cowley that their man was at the bowling alley to keep an eye on Thomas 'Fat Man' Black, the leader of a 'Keep South Africa White' movement. Black is suspected of planning a retaliatory coup because the British Government has recently refused to lift sanctions against South Africa. However, when a second man dies at the bowling alley and it is discovered that he was an employee at a nearby nuclear waste recycling establishment and was suffering from plutonium poisoning, Cowley realises that the fact that the two dead men and Black were together at a place where a crime was known to have been planned points to

The 'Attractive Blonde' in STAKE OUT was played by actress Pamela Stephenson. Born (12th April 1949) in Takapuna, Auckland, New Zealand, she is best remembered for her comedy roles in shows such as NOT THE NINE O'CLOCK NEWS.

one staggering conclusion: someone is going to use some kind of nuclear device to bring pressure on the British Government.

The authorities are warned that a nuclear attack may be imminent, and Cowley and a nuclear bomb specialist set off for Black's Bedford home. Fraser, the CI5 agent, had mentioned Bedford before he died. He had also mentioned swallows, and Bodie and Doyle are startled to see a man enter the bowling alley with the word 'Swallows' on his T-shirt. They arrest the man, Frank Turner, and take him in for questioning. When they reach HQ and are told that Cowley and a bomb expert have left to search Black's home, Bodie suddenly remembers that Frank arrived at the bowling alley with a large holdall, capable of carrying a bomb! They take Frank and head back for the building. The bomb has been activated and Bodie and Doyle discover that it has a 25-minute timing device. Frank, terrified he will not be able to escape from the five square mile detonation area, decides to help.

Production Unit

Created by	Brian Clemens
Executive Producers	Albert Fennell, Brian Clemens
Music	Laurie Johnson
Producer	Sidney Hayers
Associate Producer	Ron Fry
Script Editor	Dennis Spooner
Production Manager	Nicholas Gillott
Assistant Director	Gordon Gilbert
Location Manager	Peter Crowhurst
Continuity	Kay Mander
Casting	Maggie Cartier
Production Designer	Tony Curtis
Assistant Art Director	Peter Joyce
Effects Supervisor	Allan Bryce
Wardrobe Supervisor	Jackie Cummins
Lighting Cameraman	Graham Edgar
Camera Operator	Malcolm Vinson
Make Up	John Webber
Hairdresser	Helene Bevan
Editor	Mike Campbell
Sound Recordists	Paul Le Mare, Ken Scrivener
Dubbing Editors	Peter Lennard, Graham Harris
Music Editor	Alan Willis
Post Production Supervisor	Paul Clay

An Avengers MARK 1 Production For LONDON WEEKEND TELEVISION

Shooting / Location Schedule

Production Dates: Monday 21st November to Friday 2nd December, 1977.
Production Number: 9D11189

21-29 November	**Bowling Alley / Car park / Rooftop**: Humber Bowling Ltd, King Harry Street, Hemel Hempstead, Hertfordshire **Street (Fraser loses control of car)**: The Marlowes, Hemel Hempstead, Hertfordshire
30 Nov-2 Dec	**Cowley's meeting place (Fraser's car crash)**: Highbridge Industrial Estate, Oxford Road, Uxbridge, Middlesex **Black's car run-bys**: Oxford Road, Denham, Middlesex **Police car 'night' run-bys (route to bowling alley)**: High Street / Breakspear Road North, Harefield, Middlesex **Int: Hospital / Hunter's office / Black's house**: Harefield Grove, Rickmansworth Road, Harefield, Middlesex
2nd Unit: 20 September	**Doyle's car run-by (night shot insert)**: Prince Consort Road, Kensington, London, SW7 (filmed on the set of *The Female Factor* as stock footage)

British actor Peter Armitage guest starred as Special Branch operative Ray Kerrigan - the peanut eater. Although best known as Bill Webster in the long-running British soap opera CORONATION STREET, things may have been different had his original 'screen-test' for THE PROFESSIONALS paid off? He could have graced our screens as Bodie!

KLANSMEN
by **Brian Clemens**
based on a story by **Simon Masters**
© Copyright Mark 1 Productions Ltd MCMLXXVII

Hulton	Edward Judd
Zadie	Trevor Thomas
Helen	Sheila Ruskin
Dinny	Anthony Booth
Tommy	Lawrie Mark
Jax	Joseph Charles
Topaz	Oscar James
Doctor	Louis Mahoney
Arty	George Harris
Merv	James Coyle
Miss Pearce	Madeleine Newbury
Mr. Miller	Jules Walter
Ben	Trevor Ward
Lenny	Stephen Lawrence
Mr. Culver	Allister Bain
Carter	Willie Payne
Uncredited	
Empire Society member	Chris Flannigan
Empire Society member	Brian Gregory

Director: **Pat Jackson**

AN astute black lawyer, Zadie, is helping the largely black tenants of a slum area to resist eviction threats made by Miller, head of the Miller Trust, the company who owns the properties. Late one night, Zadie's home comes under attack from a group of Klansmen; men wearing white cloaks and hoods. Cowley, who detests any form of racial prejudice, sends Bodie and Doyle to investigate the incident. A black man, Arty, tries to telephone Zadie, but is murdered as he tries to get through, and Doyle returns to HQ to report this latest development to Cowley while Bodie, hoping to pick up some information about the murder, moves around the black area on his own. While he is talking to a group of black youths, he is knifed and is taken to hospital in danger of his life.

Doyle is watching Zadie's house when a group of white-hooded Klansmen make a second attack on the property. He follows the Klansmen's car to the headquarters of the racialist Empire Society and, seeking further clues, joins the sect. Doyle discovers that Hulton, its head, is very anxious not to let the society become involved in serious violence or killings; the member's apparently only dress up as Klansmen to harass the black community. One night, when Doyle and several other members are out on just such a mission, Zadie's partner, a black lawyer named Carter, is murdered at his home by a man wearing Klansman dress. Doyle returns to the Empire Society HQ alone and secretly searches Hulton's office to see if there is another branch of the organisation, which could have organised the killing. He is discovered by Hulton and his men, then badly beaten, and thrown in the water tower.

Gordon Jackson poses for a publicity shot during filming on KLANSMEN.

One of Arty's friends, a young black boy named Tommy, finds Doyle. After attending to Doyle's injuries, Tommy tells him that Arty had burgled the headquarters of the Miller Trust shortly before he was murdered; he had stolen some papers, and was trying to tell Zadie what they contained when he was killed. Doyle relays this information to CI5 HQ, and asks Cowley to meet him there. Arriving before his boss he forces Dinny, one of Miller's men, to admit his involvement. Miller wants to evict the tenants of the area to make it available for redevelopment and thereby make a fortune for his firm.

Zadie is about to be attacked by a group of Klansmen, when Doyle, discovering the group's next move arrives in the nick of time to save the lawyer. Stripped of their hoods, Zadie is astounded to see that all the men are from the black community and Cowley arrests Miller, who is also black. Later, Doyle visits his colleague in hospital to see he has made a full recovery.

Production Unit

Created by	Brian Clemens
Executive Producers	Albert Fennell, Brian Clemens
Music	Laurie Johnson
Producer	Sidney Hayers
Associate Producer	Ron Fry
Script Editor	Dennis Spooner
Production Manager	Nicholas Gillott
Assistant Director	Gordon Gilbert
Location Manager	Roger Lyons
Continuity	Kay Mander
Casting	Maggie Cartier
Production Designer	Tony Curtis
Assistant Art Director	Peter Joyce
Effects Supervisor	Allan Bryce
Wardrobe Supervisor	Jackie Cummins
Lighting Cameraman	Graham Edgar
Camera Operator	Malcolm Vinson
Make Up	John Webber
Hairdresser	Helene Bevan
Editor	Bob Dearberg
Sound Recordists	Paul Le Mare, Ken Scrivener
Dubbing Editors	Peter Lennard, Graham Harris
Music Editor	Alan Willis
Post Production Supervisor	Paul Clay

An Avengers MARK 1 Production For LONDON WEEKEND TELEVISION

Shooting / Location Schedule

Production Dates: Monday 5th to Friday 16th December, 1977, 2nd Unit: Monday 19th December. Production Number: 9D11182

5 December   ***Zadie's house***: 3 Wood Lane, Iver Heath, Buckinghamshire
Int / Ext: Doyle's car & run-by: Wood Lane (roundabout Junction with A4007 Slough Road), Iver Heath, Bucks
Ext: House & garage door / Phone Box: 28 Wood Lane Close, Iver Heath, Buckinghamshire

6-14 December	**Street: Culver's house / Arty's body**: 28 White Street, Southall, Middlesex **Miller Trust Offices (Dinny's office)**: Southall Gas Works, White Street, Middlesex **Roof Tops (Arty pushed)**: 45 The Green, Southall, Middlesex **Water Tower**: The Water Tower, The Straight, Southall, Middlesex **The Empire Society (Hulton's office)**: Rear of 68 The Green, Dilloway Lane Trading Estate, Southall, Middlesex **Empire Society car park**: St. Anselm's Church, The Green, Southall, Middlesex **Int / Ext: Pub**: White Hart, 49 High Street, Southall, Middlesex **Int: Hulton's car**: Norwood Road, Norwood Green, Middlesex **Car run-bys: Ben's car / Zadie's car**: Randolph Road / The Straight, Southall, Middlesex **Streets: Phone Box: Doyle, Tommy & Jax**: The Green / South Road, Southall, Middlesex
15-16 December	**Ext: CI5 HQ (Doyle jogs with Jax) / Int: Royal Court flats**: Harefield Grove, Rickmansworth Road, Harefield, Middlesex
16-19 December	**Int: Hospital**: Harefield Hospital, Hill End Road, Harefield, Middlesex

Series I Production Unit: uncredited

Production Co-ordinator	Trisha Robinson
Production Secretary	Linda Matthews
1st / 2nd Assistant Directors	Bert Batt, Steve Harding
3rd Assistant Directors	Michael Zimbrick, Jerry Daly
Unit Runner	Jeremy Kelly
Focus Pullers	Peter Hazel, Robin McDonald, Tony Woodcock
Clapper / Loader	Simon Hume, Peter Rees, Beamount Alexander, David Budd
Camera Grips	Brian Osborne
Production Buyer	Michele Howell
Boom Operator	Ken Nightingall, Terry Sharratt
Casting Secretary	Debra Kane
Unit Publicist	Paul McNicholls
Publicity Secretary	Lucinda Pugh
Wardrobe Assistants	Iris Richens, Susan Wain
Production Accountant	Ron Garrett
Assistant Accountant	Gill Andersson
Accounts Assistant	Peter Garrett
Property Masters	John Chisholm, Gordon Billings
Dressing Props	Stanley Cook, Alan Adams

Stand-by Props	William Stark, Paul Hedges
Construction Manager	Jeff Woodbridge, Bill Harman
Carpenter	John Keen
Painter	John Enwright
Stagehand	Tom Buckley
Stand-by Carpenter	Dennis Bovington, Laurence Burns
Stand-by Painter	Dixie Dean
Stand-by Stagehand	Eddie Burke
Stand-by Rigger	Paul Mitchell
Sound Transfer	Delta Sound
Lighting by	Elstree Lighting / GBS Lighting
Chargehand Electrician	Nobby Cross, Hickery Brown
Electricians	Alan Barry, Stephen Swannell, Ron Lyons
Generator Driver	Peter Casey, Michael Rowsome
Assistant Editors	Noel Rogers, Michael R. Sloan
Assistant Dubbing Editor	Chris Kennedy, Brian Trenerry
Unit Drivers	Steve Smith, Brian Boreham
Action Cars/Mechanic	Bernard Barnsley
Action Cars Driver	Peter Ingram
Unit Minibus Driver	Ron Jones
Wardrobe Truck Driver	Mike Mulally
Make Up Bus Driver	Michael Devetta
Construction /Prop Driver	Dave Bruyea
Props Return Van Driver	Larry Williams
Catering Vehicle Driver	John Breen
Dining Bus Driver	Tony Leport
Various Trucks	Kingsbury Motors, Kingsbury Road, London, NW9
	Nine-Nine Cars, Power House, Elstree Studios, Borehamwood, Hertfordshire
2nd Unit Cameraman	Ricky Briggs
Stunt Arranger	Peter Brayham
Executive Producers / Music offices	Harefield Grove, Rickmansworth Road, Harefield, Middlesex

SERIES I ACTION CARS

Bodie: **Triumph Dolomite Sprint**: POK 79R - *Long Shot, Where The Jungle Ends, Killer With A Long Arm, Heroes, Private Madness, Public Danger, The Female Factor.*
Ford Capri 3.0 Ghia: PNO 580R - *Everest Was Also Conquered, Close Quarters, Look After Annie, When The Heat Cools Off.*
Ford Cortina 1.6 GL: PNO 542R - *Everest Was Also Conquered.*

Cowley: **Rover SD1 3500**: MOO 229R (Real index: MOC 229P) - *Old Dog With New Tricks, Where The Jungle Ends, Killer With A Long Arm.*
Austin Princess 1800 HL: VLO 60S - *Private Madness, Public Danger.*
Austin Princess 2200 HLS: RLF 1R - *The Female Factor.*

Doyle:	**Ford Granada 2.0 L**: VHK 456S - *Heroes, Close Quarters, Look After Annie, Stake Out.* **Rover 2000 P6**: EMK 760J - *Old Dog With New Tricks, Long Shot.* **Triumph Dolomite**: POK 79R - *Killer With A Long Arm.* **Triumph TR7**: OOM 734R - *Private Madness, Public Danger, The Female Factor.* **Ford Capri 3.0 S X-Pack**: SOO 636R - *Everest Was Also Conquered, When The Heat Cools Off, Stake Out, Klansmen.*
CI5:	**Austin Princess 2200 HLS**: RLF 1R - *Old Dog With New Tricks.*
CI5:	**Ford Cortina 1.6 GL**: PNO 542R - *Heroes, Everest Was Also Conquered, Look After Annie, Stake Out.*
Misc:	**Ford Cortina 1.6 GL**: PNO 542R - *Klansmen.*

TRANSMISSION DATES

1: PRIVATE MADNESS, PUBLIC DANGER
30th December 1977
2: THE FEMALE FACTOR
6th January 1978
3: OLD DOG WITH NEW TRICKS
13th January 1978
4: KILLER WITH A LONG ARM
21st January 1978
5: HEROES
27th January 1978
6: WHERE THE JUNGLE ENDS
3rd February 1978
7: CLOSE QUARTERS
10th February 1978
8: EVEREST WAS ALSO CONQUERED
17th February 1978
9: WHEN THE HEAT COOLS OFF
24th February 1978
10: STAKE OUT
3rd March 1978
11: LONG SHOT
10th March 1978
12: LOOK AFTER ANNIE
17th March 1978
13: KLANSMEN
Not Broadcast in UK

SERIES II

HUNTER/HUNTED

WITH an average viewing figure in the region of sixteen million, the first series of *The Professionals* had been a spectacular success for ITV. However, with both the show's producer and script editor moving on to pastures new, the show's backer, London Weekend Television, implemented plans to assume much more control over the series from the production company, Mark I.

Series one producer Sidney Hayers had departed to become the producer of Southern Television's *Famous Five*, before moving to the USA where he worked on various different series for over a decade. Having already directed *Where The Jungle Ends*, Australian, Raymond Menmuir (who was already on LWT's payroll), was appointed as the new producer.

After his interest in drama was fostered at public school and university in Australia, he gained experience in TV and theatre there before arriving in Britain in 1961, unknown but with a few contacts, a pregnant wife, and a flat in Kilburn. In England he worked mainly as a director on series such as *Top Secret*, *The Avengers*, *Crane*, *The Protectors*, *Redcap*, *Undermind*, *Out Of The Unknown*, *Fraud Squad*, *Upstairs Downstairs*, *Zodiac*, *Lord Peter Wimsey: The Nine Tailors*, *The Duchess Of Duke Street*, *Corridors Of Power*, *London Belongs To Me* and *Armchair Theatre*.

Following work on the BBC's *Headmaster* series, he was asked by LWT to take over as producer on *The Professionals*. Menmuir made two stipulations before he accepted LWT's offer.

Ray Menmuir: "I would have total creative and budgetary control and be paid by LWT and not Mark I. I cannot speak for LWT, but I was led to believe that in their view series one was not as successful as it should have been."

Mark I and Brian Clemens did not seem entirely happy at the appointment, "...he took the series into areas where I wouldn't have."

London Weekend Television chiefs had their reasons according to outgoing associate producer Ron Fry.

Ron Fry: "LWT were pretty happy with the viewing figures on the first batch, but decided they did not want 'a fields and barns' show anymore, hence Menmuir's appointment. The comments that they fed back were that the show was not featuring real London areas. Everything we were doing seemed to happen in the open countryside or in woodland areas. There needed to be more derelict warehouses and dockland work. Explosions and car chases around real London streets, like *The Sweeney*. They were basically taking control of the show from Mark I. I don't think they expected it to be as successful as it was and, therefore, wanted to make improvements - but their way!"

Ray Menmuir replaced Fry with Chris Burt (born in Hong Kong on 1st May 1942), who had experience with Euston Films as editor on *The Sweeney* and *Van Der Valk*. His main task would be to direct the second unit after a decision was taken during the second episode *Hunter/Hunted* that the production could not meet the necessary deadlines without one.

The second unit traditionally filmed footage that was of lesser importance in the script, as opposed to the first unit, who shot all the scenes involving the main actors. Second unit scenes typically included minor shots, such as establishing shots, scenery, close-ups of objects, car run-bys, and other inserts or cutaways. The editor would take charge of the second unit to film an insert, as he would know what footage he was missing. More often than not, Chris Burt would direct more important sequences, which often featured many shots with car chases, explosions, and special effects, but little, or no, dialogue.

Chris Burt: "Having directed on *The Sweeney* I took the job on *The Professionals*, as a challenge, so when I became a producer, I would know if directors were giving me what I wanted."

Martin Shaw, Gordon Jackson, and Lewis Collins pose for a publicity photograph to promote the second series of THE PROFESSIONALS.

Ray Menmuir: "You have to take those kind of balls that come out of left field. I'd always thought that the difference between British and American film series was that the British, like British TV drama overall, is word orientated and that in America they write screenplays not scripts, and I make a very strong distinction between the two. When I was a callow youth in the 50's I got the published TV work of those *Playhouse 90* writers, Tad Mosel and Chayefsky and Reginald Rose and the other people from that fantastic period; and though they may have been live, or done on tape, they were films. You read some of Mosel and you get the first line of dialogue eight pages in. On the other hand, we'd always persevered with out literary heritage. There's nothing wrong with that, of course, except when we're making moving pictures, when you should tell your story, create your mood with pictures, and only verbalise when there's nothing else you can do.

"Television seems to spend a lot of time in what I call flip-flop close ups of people talking. It tends to make a character explain himself, or has two of his friends talking about him. But people illustrate what they are by what they do, not by what they say. We have to deal with this problem, sort of 'back at the ranch'. To tell a story by linking four scenes of pictures, and create a mood, an atmosphere and also showing something about the people who are moving within those scenes is what screen writing is all about.

"Because I wasn't actually there at the formative period, I initially regarded the show as a challenge. In very broad terms, it's an action series. The challenge for me was to put together a film in a well, then, 1978 way. To use the film shorthand that I believed the audience understood, and was bored to tears if you didn't use because they're always four jumps ahead and waiting for you. Using really modern film grammar, cutting time and space, doesn't faze an audience at all.

"So in order to execute some of this, on *The Professionals*, one of the first things I did was to get rid of the standing set, but it's also a marvellous excuse when a writer can't solve his plot problems to cut back to the office and have it all talked out. So there was no standing set, as a matter of principle.

"When you are producing a series, thirteen hours of film, that's a mountain of work. You've got to have a story department, a story editor. But I didn't want a writer in this role; I wanted a director who could write. Everybody thought I was mad, but that's how I came to get Gerry O'Hara. I'd seen some of his films; read some of his scripts, screenplays, excuse me! and I felt he was the guy I needed. I'm a director, he's a director, he'll know what I mean, what I'm trying to do. And he did it superbly well. Being a director, he puts things into pictures and I think he was an enormous help to writers, in guiding them into screenplays and away from scripts."

Gerry O'Hara, born 1925 in Boston, Lincolnshire, worked as an assistant director before picking up the megaphone on his own account and, unusually for Britain, is a writer too. His credits don't make a stir with movie buffs *(The Pleasure Girls, Leopard In The Snow, The Bitch)* though critics from *Time Out* to *The Telegraph* enthusiastically received *All The Right Noises*.

Gerry O'Hara: "I'd been interested in expanding my writing and my agent said had I ever thought of being a story editor? I hadn't, but saw it as a potentially interesting idea. Ray and I had four or five meetings and eventually we decided to go ahead.

"Ray had directed one of the first series episodes, and I'd been lined up as possible director but didn't get one, so we'd seen all or most of the first series. We both felt that they were a bit parochial, a bit 'highways and byways of Ruislip'. And Ray also had the feeling that the thing to do was keep the show on the move. So he created the first rule, which was the most difficult of all for me to cope with as a story editor, in getting rid of Cowley's office and Briefing Room. That automatically put the whole show on the move. All the plot expositions, all instructions, all tensions, were created hurrying to, or from, or within cars, or getting in and out of helicopters, or riding in the back of ambulances.

"So the first year laid down the characters, was extremely successful, and established the parameters of the kind of work that CI5 could get involved with. And we put it on the streets of London and Ray gave it a kind of buzz. He's got an instinctive film head. He doesn't let shots hang about. And it's that buzz which is one of its big hooks with the audience."

Ray Menmuir: "We got out on the streets. We were mobile. Flexible to a degree, and it was a matter of continual surprise to me that such freedom alarmed every writer. They seemed to want to have walls put up, even though they were given a maximum inventive capability. Maybe this was so unusual...!"

Gerry O'Hara: "My view of a lot of series in the past was that they had been very pedestrian, very explanatory, the scenes hung about until the climaxes at the end of each act. What I thought I could do as story editor was to bring more depth of character into the various stories. I found that I couldn't do it so much with the regular characters, more with Cowley than with Bodie or Doyle. I think Cowley's a glorious character and that Gordon Jackson was such a glorious actor. It's that old, hackneyed phrase; he could play the phone book and make it sound interesting.

"Bodie and Doyle had degrees of depth, but the secret of the two characters was that the audience saw them in different ways, as they wanted to see them. Regrettably, perhaps, on paper, they hadn't been allowed to get the depth that Martin Shaw or Lewis Collins would have wanted, but they were pipped by their own popularity.

"I'm convinced that the audience saw them in special ways. Little girls saw them one way, as the fellers they long to have for themselves; young boys in another way, as heroes they wanted to be; I've got a strong suspicion that mothers and fathers saw them as the sons that they would liked to have had. Now that sounds absurd, because they whip out guns and shoot people to pieces, but I think they're 'turn-ons', they're adrenalin-releasers, for all the different kinds of people in the audience. This was where Brian Clemens was so clever. He sketched out the background for them but that was all, just sketches, so that they could be changed, pulled around, turned, sent in different directions. It was pure genius on his part."

Ray Menmuir: "Martin and Lew used to say 'we want more character...!.' With due respect what they meant was they wanted scenes where they could toss off, sackcloth and ashes-time, 'Act' with a capital 'A.' But I believe that

Lewis Collins was William Andrew Philip Bodie, one of CI5's top agents, in THE PROFESSIONALS

the audience is really clued in. They pick up on behaviour and actions. We're not really about Freudian analysis. And home psychiatry is the most boring thing on earth. Over-define a running character and you force him to be predictable.

"People in general are constantly surprising. So I always resisted 'motivation'. It has never been questioned by the audience, but it was questioned by just about everyone working on the series. 'Is he moving flat again?' for instance. Audiences don't care about things like that. It's a floating crap game. So he's got twenty-eight different apartments, they accept that and we never once explained why. You can make up your own reasons, you can participate.

"If I talk to five or six different writers, I expect to have five or six different aspects of that character, which I don't find incompatible, the paradox that behaves this way this week, but next week he doesn't do this he does that. We have to fight a terrible rigidity that's been imposed on our thinking from I don't know where, well I do, from Freud and bloody Stanislavski.

"As it is, ask anybody in the audience and they'll give you a fairly particular view of the characters. In fact, Bodie and Doyle had become part of our 'social vernacular'. Which was quite fascinating? If we had defined them more, would this still have happened in the sane way? I don't think so."

The removal of standing sets also resulted in the production as a whole moving away from studio-built interiors. With an increase of over £5,000, the budget per episode stood at £120,000, filming now took place within actual buildings, and *The Professionals* adopted the total film on the street approach of the Euston Films' series such as *The Sweeney*.

Rather than relying on time-consuming post-production dubbing, the soundtrack was now recorded live using newly developed radio microphones and redefined recording equipment adapted by the unit's sound engineer Dave Crozier.

As executive producer, Brian Clemens could have as little, or as much, input into the production as he wanted, and he settled into an advisory position vetting scripts.

Brian Clemens: "That was okay, Ray Menmuir called it as he saw it. If you give it into the hands of someone else then you can't start bickering and say this and that...although I did pull them back whenever I thought that they were going off course."

London Weekend Television insisted that the production be moved closer to London and while Brian Clemens, Albert Fennell and Laurie Johnson remained at Harefield Grove, the new Mark 1 crew reassembled at the smaller Lee International Studios, on the corner of Wembley Park Drive and Empire Way, Wembley, and due to the reduced distance this now made location shooting in central London possible. However, members of the art department, Malcolm Middleton, Peter Joyce and Ian Watson, had offices at Colet Court, on Hammersmith Road, West London, which at the time was also home to Euston Films.

Malcolm Middleton had worked in television on *Doctor Who*, *Chelsea Reach* and *Special Branch*, before doing features such as Alan Parker's *Bugsy Malone* in 1976, and prior to the show, *Valentino*.

Malcolm Middleton: "For some odd reason we were in Colet Court for a few weeks before moving to Lee Studios. Lee, at the time, I seem to recall was still having building work done. They hadn't been there that long having moved from Kensal Road in Kensal Town, West London."

MARK I PRODUCTIONS LIMITED

Please reply to:
Wembley Park Drive
Empire Way
Wembley
Middx

Harefield Grove
Rickmansworth Road
Harefield, Middlesex
Telephone: Harefield 3986/7/8

28 April 1978

Malcolm Middleton Esq
Red Woods
The Ridgeway
Horsell
Woking
Surrey

Dear Malcolm

This is to confirm your engagement with this company as Art Director on "The Professionals" at a salary of £ per week commencing on Monday, 15th May, 1978.

This engagement is subject in all respects to the conditions of the current FPA/ACTT Agreement and any amendments thereto agreed between the parties to that Agreement.

During and throughout the continuance of this engagement we shall be entitled to the exclusive rights of your services.

If you are in agreement with the above, will you please kindly sign the enclosed copy of this letter and send it back to this office.

Yours sincerely
For and on behalf of
MARK I PRODUCTIONS LIMITED

PETER PRICE
Production Manager

Signed........................
Date ....

Enc:

Production designer Malcolm Middleton's contract for his appointment to the second series of THE PROFESSIONALS in May 1978.

The responsibility of finding suitable places to film was down to location managers, Cecil Ford and Stuart Freeman, whose brief was to consider anywhere within a thirty mile radius of Wembley.

Dublin born Cecil Ford was aged 67 by this time, having been born on 24th October 1911, and had vast experience in films working for MGM in the 1950's and 60's, including *Captain Boycott, Odd Man Out*, and *The Bridge on the River Kwai*. In 1961, he was an associate producer on the classic, *The Guns Of Navarone*. In the 1970's he worked on *It Shouldn't Happen To A Vet* and *All Creatures Great And Small*. Prior to his engagement on the show he was the location manager on *The Squeeze*, starring Stacey Keach. He settled into an advisory position and being of ill health died on the 27th May 1980 in Reading, Berkshire.

Stuart Freeman had entered the British Film Industry in 1956 under the guidance of the Boulting Brothers, and worked on Cubby Broccoli's *No Time To Die* as a second assistant director. In 1962 he became a first assistant and by his appointment to *The Professionals* had worked on over forty features and rival show *The Sweeney*.

Sensitive to criticism regarding violence in the first series it was decided to tone this element down and replace it with a gritty realism.

Brian Clemens: "It had been the decade of the anti-hero, we've had the man in the cloth cap, the loser. I didn't think it was excessively violent, sure people are fascinated by violence, your newspapers tell you that; if there is a street accident people gather round. But we tried to do things with a modicum of taste. We portrayed things realistically, otherwise we would have been left with the absurd storylines coming out of *Starsky & Hutch* at the time."

Martin Shaw: "I hate violence. I'm really a very passive person. If the networks wanted to create crime series like *The Professionals* and *The Sweeney*, then it should be the job of the actor to portray them as realistically as possible, otherwise we'd have been left with the absurd situation where in the USA, they couldn't frisk people on the screen because it was supposed to look undignified. What happened was the scripts became insulting to the audience because of the lies they were telling. Unfortunately violence exists and even on *The Professionals* we became more serious about depicting it. The Bodies and Doyles existed too, but they were not heroes or anti-heroes for that matter, they were just a necessary evil which was our job to portray as grittily as possible."

Martin Shaw had a reason to hate violence. He was once brutally mugged on a London street. He suffered a fractured skull. Other facial injuries necessitated a plastic cheek-bone being inserted in his face, which tended to give him the tough guy image, almost boxer's look to his right-hand cheek.

Martin Shaw: "One night after getting a good role, I got so plastered with a friend that we were both beaten up almost without realising it. I woke up in hospital with teeth missing, a fractured skull and my right cheek smashed in. I took a long hard look at my life and packed in the booze."

Ray Menmuir: "We gave the audiences what they wanted, fast moving action! There is a difference between that and violence. The almost documentary style of shooting used had a lot to do with it. You were right there, involved with the action.

Martin Shaw was CI5's Ray Doyle and Lewis Collins was William Andrew Philip Bodie - THE PROFESSIONALS. Pictured here in a publicity shoot at St. Katharine's Dock, East London.

"Likewise, the outlandish storylines featuring doomsday scenarios of poisoning the water supply and Plutonium bombs was also left behind. LWT didn't want that rubbish anymore; they wanted realistic outlines - and that's what we planned to give them."

Other changes included Cowley's limp, so noticeable in the first series, where he had constantly complained about the pain from his injuries, was gradually forgotten about at the request of Gordon Jackson, who expressed that his character be allowed to become more mobile and involved in the field.

Brian Clemens: "Gordon losing the limp was a good thing too. You know, 'Didn't he have a limp? Okay, so it's got better!' It just became acceptable by the viewer."

Pleasing Lewis Collins, Bodie's attire became more casual, while Martin Shaw was ordered to shave!

Martin Shaw: "The beard was basically a way to camouflage my identity. Television had turned me into a master of disguises. I'd tried all kind of things like changing my hairstyle, but it never worked. People were always coming up to me to say hello, which I sometimes found a bit disturbing because I don't like people intruding on my private life, hence the beard! Doyle wasn't allowed to keep his beard in the scripts. It wouldn't have looked right, I suppose, but I grew so fond of it that I constantly grew it back between series."

Bridget Brice who had played Cowley's secretary Betty, in five first series episodes left the show and was replaced in this batch by Diana Weston, credited as 'CI5 Girl' in two episodes and as 'Ruth Pettifer' in another. However, Cowley refers to her as 'Miss Pettifer' throughout.

Born (13th November 1955) in Toronto, Canada, Diana's acting career started with the part of Helen Wiles in the 1975 Brian Clemens *Thriller* TV movie, *Death In Deep Water*, followed by a small role as an air hostess in *Sweeney 2*. On television she appeared in *The Sweeney, Raffles, Star Maidens* and the comedy series *Bless Me Father*. She is best remembered for her comedy role in 1990's British sitcom *The Upper Hand*.

Bodie, Doyle and Cowley continued to use a number of weapons and other equipment, supplied courtesy of Bapty & Company Limited. Cowley continued to use a Smith & Wesson .38 calibre revolver, with both Bodie and Doyle using thirteen round 9mm Browning Hi-Power automatic pistols and Doyle occasionally packing a German 9mm Walther P38 automatic. The gun, used extensively in the Second World War, has an eight round capacity, though an additional round can be loaded in the chamber as the safety design can be relied upon.

Brian Clemens himself was an excellent shot and had fired every weapon in the army, as a weapons training officer, during his national service.

Brian Clemens: "British policemen unfortunately look slightly comical with guns. We all know that firearms are in use but I would say that the crimes where they are involved are quite small when dealing with the ordinary criminal. That led me on when creating the series to think of extraordinary criminals and terrorists. It was only one step away to produce an elite squad.

"I don't think this attitude to the weaponry seen in the show made it excessively violent, I think it was successful because it 'was' wild and violent. It had two very modern heroes that fellas wanted to be like, and that girls wanted to get into bed with. I think it was as simple as that. That was the appeal of the *Dirty Harry* films; I didn't want to write about failures but about people who pulled themselves up. I wanted to be Clint Eastwood, and not a failure. I wanted to kick in doors!"

Diana Weston appeared as 'CI5 Girl' Ruth Pettifer. Pictured here on the set of HUNTER/HUNTED.

Ford Motor Company supplied a Strato silver Capri Mk. III 3.0S for Bodie and a decision was made to camouflage the car should it be seen in central London by having false registration plates, UOO 303T, fitted for shooting. This car was originally a press vehicle, registered as VHK 495S, for the use of motoring journalists to assist in promoting the launch of the updated Capri in March 1978.

Doyle's transport was now a Diamond white Ford Escort Mk. II RS2000, complete with index PNO 641T to hide the real identity of PNO 672R. Cowley drives a Jupiter red Ford Granada Mk. II 2.8i Ghia automatic, VHK 518S, with the Ford Press office once again providing a false registration number, YHJ 766T.

Also supplied, as a courtesy vehicle, was a beige Ford Cortina Mk. IV 2.0GL, VHK 536S. This car was driven by unit driver Alan Lind, whose job entailed collecting the two leads from their homes each morning and conveying them to each location. It did, however, also get coverage as an on-screen car in several episodes. The other Cortinas seen before the cameras, a red Mk. IV 2.3GL, VHK 537S, and a blue Mk. IV 2.0GL, VHK 534S, were also supplied on similar terms. As on the first series, Kingsbury Motors and Nine-Nine Cars continued to supply the other 'Action' vehicles.

Frank Henson (s*tunt man)*: "I remember an incident involving the 'false' number plates. I got stopped by the police late one night. They decided they wanted to look in the boot and found a selection of plates we were using on the show. I tried to explain, but I swear they thought I was going to use them in some robbery. I eventually convinced them when they checked the numbers against the show's allocated numbers."

In terms of communications Bodie, Doyle and Cowley continued with the Pye PF8 radios, while their vehicles were fitted with Dymar Lynx radios, which at the time was a favourable unit among Taxi companies. For this second batch of episodes both agents wore the Orfina Porsche Design chronograph wristwatches. They were originally designed for the Swiss Secret Service and were later adopted by the USA's top-secret Delta Force and certain motor racing teams. A super-tough design but the black anodized coating tended to peel off quite readily. In fact, both Martin and Lewis kept theirs for several years after the show had finished. Cowley stuck to his Longines manual watch, which he would keep until the end of the show.

The production crew's contracts were drawn up on 28th April 1978 and stated that pre-production work was to commence at Lee International Studios on Monday 15th May. However, problems were already afoot before production had commenced. Hired as production manager, Peter Price had dispatched the relevant contracts to the new members of the crew. This included first assistant director Ray Corbett. Starting his career in 1967, he later worked on *The Sweeney* and the feature *Bugsy Malone (*with Malcolm Middleton, the show's production designer).

Ray Corbett (first assistant director): "I received my contract at the end of April and almost immediately contacted Peter and told him I couldn't do the show as I'd been offered a feature film, which in those days paid much more. Peter went mad to say the least. He made me feel so guilty that I declined the film and said okay to the series. I then went on holiday and came back fresh to do *The Professionals*. I turned up on the Monday and found Peter was not there. Instead Donald Toms, who introduced himself as the new production manager, greeted me. Peter had left to do a feature film!"

Rogue: *Two key witnesses to the trial of a long suspected spy and drug smuggler are found murdered. A founder member of CI5 falls under suspicion and finds himself the quarry of two former pupils, Bodie and Doyle.*

The production Unit List was issued to relevant personnel on 30th May and filming got underway on *Rogue*, the first episode of the new batch, on Monday 5th June. Written by outgoing script editor Dennis Spooner for the previous series and revised in April control of the story was given to director Ray Austin. Lighting cameraman, Tony Imi, who had been drafted in to give the new series a 'feature film look', recalled that Austin directed the whole show wearing monogrammed slippers: "...delusions of grandeur."

Tony Imi, was born in London on the 27th March 1937, and arrived on the show, following filming of *International Velvet*, based on his relationship with Ray Menmuir.

Tony Imi: "We had worked together at the BBC and got on pretty well. However, no sooner had I accepted the position that I was offered another feature *Brass Target*, which was to commence filming in Germany in the next few weeks. Menmuir asked if I could recommend anyone, so I suggested Phil Meheux."

CI5 agents Doyle (Martin Shaw) and Bodie (Lewis Collins) in ROGUE.

A filming location, making one of many appearances in the show, was Cadby Hall on Blythe Road, Hammersmith, West London. A vast complex of offices and warehouses it had a great deal of unused space. The huge empty rooms with tall pillars, old doorways, and staircases, made it the ideal choice for any location manager. This huge factory unit was the headquarters of J H Lyons and Company, and during its final years, as they wound up food manufacture, it was used in series such as *The Sweeney* and *Minder*. A ring of five and six storey buildings, 10,000 people worked there, before it was demolished in May 1983.

Cadby Hall (viewed from Brook Green), Hammersmith, West London - Head Office of J H Lyons & Company.

Long before international stardom beckoned, Art Malik (billed as Athar Malik) appeared in this episode credited simply as Doctor in Hospital. He would have to wait another six years before making a name for himself in the Granada series *The Jewel In The Crown*. Later appearing in films such as *True Lies* and *The Living Daylights*. The hospital in question was Wexham Park, near Slough, Berkshire.

Colin Dandridge (boom operator): "I was truly amazed that they had got permission to film in the main A & E wards. They were so busy and it took ages for us to get set up and get past the on-looking patients."

The conversations Bodie and Doyle had, while travelling to and from jobs, were built on during this series with both Martin Shaw and Lewis Collins saying that they improvised or wrote their own dialogue for these scenes.

Lewis Collins: "Well, a lot of the writing, rewriting, was Martin and I in a car. We spent a lot of time sitting in cars and we used to muck around quite a lot."

Martin Shaw: "Feedback would come back from the rushes the following day, 'Hey, those car scenes. Absolutely wonderful! More of that boys'. And we thought are you really this stupid, don't they know that this is not the script that had been given to us; we're making this up?"

Brian Clemens: "No, they played everything as written. The only changes that were made were sometimes they'd say 'can we use this word instead of that word', or the changes that can only happen when you're on location where it says go through that door and there isn't one. So you have to change it to get up that ladder or whatever. That can be amended in cahoots with the director."

The dark coloured interior in Doyle's RS2000 made it difficult to film sequences in the Escort and so it was arranged that for the next episode, Ford would fit a clear sunroof into the car to allow more light into the interior.

Robin McDonald (focus puller): "Martin loved the car, but for the camera crew it was terrible to work with. We just couldn't get enough light into it. We had a bad time doing the interiors on *Rogue*, so they decided on the sunroof, which itself was an oversize item from some American Ford, and even that was only a slight improvement."

Lewis Collins: "When you saw those cars belting down the streets it was Martin and I at the wheel, not doubles. And in all the really heavy shots, it was us. But whilst we were doing all the car stunts, the studio wouldn't let me drive home. One minute they'd be happy to have me rolling a car over and getting bruised as hell, yet I was forbidden to leave without a chauffeur. Sort that one out."

Howard Baker (camera clapper/loader): "Yeah, but that didn't last long! Within a matter of weeks Martin Shaw was driving to the first location of the day, sometimes as early as 7.15am, on a 1000cc BMW motorbike. Not to be outdone, Lewis Collins followed suit. The producers used to give them a right telling off, but it didn't seem to stop them for long."

Both Martin Shaw and Lewis Collins were bike enthusiasts. Martin, for instance, has very fond memories of a BSA A7 Combo, which he picked up in Birmingham in 1964 for £15 and which saw him through his earlier days as a struggling actor.

Martin Shaw: "It took me a whole year to get into mint condition. I must have visited every breakers yard in Brum. It was a beautiful bike, bloody beautiful. I went out to Hampton Court one day with a girlfriend and it was incredibly hot weather. I was showing off and really thrashing it (the bike)! One of the nuts came loose on the carb through vibration. It dripped petrol on to the exhaust, which was already overheating and, whoosh! The bike went up like a torch. We just got off in time! A bus stopped and the conductor rushed over with a fire extinguisher to put it out. I pushed it back to my flat in Fulham and went out and got drunk. Of course, that was in the days when I drunk, but I haven't touched a drop since the early seventies. Anyway, I came back in the early hours of the morning and saw my poor bike outside the flat and, because I was tight I thought I would kick it over and see if it would start.

"I switched on the ignition and it all came on, so I thought 'great'! I turned on the petrol and kicked it over, but the fire had burnt all the insulation off the HT leas. Whoomph....the whole lot went up in flames again! I ran into the house and did the worst possible thing, I got a bucket of water and threw that over it, a petrol fire! It spread worse than ever! Luckily, a nightwatchman came out with a fire extinguisher, a very big one and he turned it into a wedding cake! It was horrible and it stayed outside looking really bad for about two months. Finally, this guy came to the door and asked if I was interested in selling it? He offered me £15 for it, then saw the rust and dropped it to £13. I'd had all that pleasure for just two quid……..".

Since then, he's had a 250 Matchless, a 125 Honda, a 250 Kawasaki and a BMW R100RS.

On Friday 16th June, while the cast and crew assembled at West India Docks, on the Isle Of Dogs, to film the scenes involving Barry Martin's attempted escape by ship at London Docks, Lewis Collins and Martin Shaw shared a few 'lighter' moments with reporters.

Lewis Collins (interviewed at the time): "Since I took on Bodie, I've had stacks of mail from girls. When I played Gavin (*Cuckoo Waltz*) I was good-looking, but a bit of a wet sponge. But now that I'm more aggressive, bitter and concerned, it seems to have a greater effect on girls. Can't say I object though!

"At this precise moment every muscle in my body feels like it's been jumped on by a kangaroo in football boots! I just want to go home, have a good soak and get across the road to my local for a pint. They don't bother me in there and I can just sink into a corner with my beer!

"The schedule, since we started shooting, has been so demanding. I've been running backwards and forwards across a bombsite and diving into piles of rubble. It only takes a little inaccuracy to land on a brick and give myself a hefty bruise. Just like being a kid again!

"It was a case of having to look after yourself with these (fists) if necessary. But I'd sooner have avoided a punch-up anyway. It's one thing doing it on television, but quite another having to use it to survive in real life.

"Luckily I got interested in girls at an early age. We went to the cinema a lot, especially on Sunday afternoons when the new film came round. It was great to have been the first one to see it and then tell all your mates about it. Later, of course, when all the Liverpool groups were starting...including some outfit called 'The Beatles'... my girlfriends and I started going to the clubs."

Martin Shaw: "Has he been shouting off about how many girls are after him again? It'll drive a wedge between us, mate! Really we're not bad together at all. Which is just as well when we have to spend so much time in each other's company. One thing we do have to do is keep on top of ourselves fitness-wise, and so we try to get in plenty of games or strenuous exercise.

"It's amazing how many girls write to say that they fancy me for a brother. I find that really flattering. We all know what they're after with flash boy, here....but it takes more than sex appeal to become someone's brother!"

Martin reckoned as a kid, he was too puny to pull a trolley let alone the girls. He puts part of his sexiness down to being a vegetarian.

"Think about stallions and prize bulls, they don't eat meat and they're renowned for potency. I won't eat meat because I feel it is wrong to eat dead animals. To me it's like cannibalism. I won't condemn other people for eating meat, though. I don't drink either, because it takes away the sense of discrimination. If you lose that, you can't tell which things are good and which are bad. I used to drink a lot, about a bottle of the hard stuff a day. Then I changed my outlook on life and I stopped. Some people sneer at me. They think it's apart of the tough image to swill beer. That's all so silly and unnecessary that I just laugh. Most of my friends understand, but friendships that depended on alcohol alone have gone, it's no real loss though."

Hired on the strength of his five years experience with *The Sweeney*, was supervising (post-production) editor John S. Smith. Post-production is the final stage in the process of realising a television text on the screen. From the mass of material recorded, what will finally be transmitted is selected, ordered and refined. The laborious task of 'synch-ing the rushes' begins: with reference to the slate number and clapperboard, each shot is matched and synchronised with its respective soundtrack. When this is completed the editor starts cutting. Identifying the required frames as they are run through the viewing machine, and splicing these in the desired order assemble each scene. From this the edited scenes are then assembled in order to establish the rough cut. The rough cut includes all the scenes that have been shot and tends to leave the beginning and end of scenes deliberately over-long and loose. It provides the producer and director with the first opportunity to view the film in narrative sequence and assess its effect and pace. Further alterations and refinements will be made and whole sequences omitted before the final version, or fine cut, is achieved.

Actors Lewis Collins and Martin Shaw during a break in filming ROGUE.

John S. Smith immediately ran into problems with Mark I co-executive producer Albert Fennell.

John S. Smith (supervising editor): "Albert, well, he was a tough cookie, from the old school of film making. We'd just done the rough cut on the opening episode when I was called into the producer's (Raymond Menmuir) office. Ray said I'd been summoned to see Albert at the Harefield office and that, although he (Menmuir) was in charge, I should really go and see him.

So off I went, at the height of the rush-hour, to show Albert our first edit. An hour later, I arrived at his plush offices, and after about ten minutes of running the episode he stood up shouted at me to 'Stop the machine. No book-ends!' I wasn't sure what he was talking about, as I'd never come across this terminology before. What he actually meant is that there were no establishing shots; when they (the characters) were in a house, we had to show a long shot of the exterior of the house to verify the location. The same before they were going to leave the house and so on. To me this was very old fashioned and we hadn't employed it much in *The Sweeney*, but he was the boss, and he sent me on my way with pages, and pages, of notes on what we should, and shouldn't, edit in, or out. When I returned to the office (Lee Studios, Wembley) and told Ray, he said well at least we'd showed willing. Ray phoned Albert up the following day and assured him we'd stick to the notes, but after a few more episodes that all fell by the wayside, and we went back to doing it our way."

Hunter/Hunted: *The theft of a lethal laser-sighted rifle, placed in Doyle's hands for testing, proves to be no coincidence. CI5 follow Doyle through a sadistic death-stalk by an old 'friend' with a vendetta.*

Second episode to go before the cameras, on Monday 19th June, was *Hunter/Hunted* by Anthony Read. Directed by 55-year old Anthony Simmons (born in West Ham, London on 16th December 1922), who, up to this point, had only dabbled in film direction having worked on four films (*Your Money Or Your Wife*, *Four In The Morning* with Judi Dench, *The Optimists* with Peter Sellers, and *Black Joy*) since 1960.

Anthony Simmons (director): "Script editor Gerry O'Hara was an old friend of mine and during an evening out he asked why I'd never done much in the way of directing on a tv show. I told him I'd never been asked and did he have anything in mind. The question was of course deliberate on his part, as I had no knowledge that he had already been planning pre-production on *The Professionals*. Gerry went back to producer Ray Menmuir and explained how I'd achieved the 'street' look on *Black Joy*; a look that they really wanted on *The Professionals*. Within a matter of days I got the call that they wanted me to direct what would be the second episode, even though it was the first script purchased, and bring across that experienced 'on the move' look; it was exactly what Ray wanted to get his version of the show off the ground."

The replica of the sinister American 180 laser sub-machine gun used in the episode, according to the FBI, accounted for a number of unsolved gangland killings in the USA. All the victims were slain with the type of .22 calibre bullet fired by the 180. Developed by a Mormon company in Salt Lake City, Utah, the weapon, capable of firing 900-rounds a minute, uses a laser beam to lock onto its victim and provide unerring aim.

In 1977, a man called Charles Goff, head of the company that made the rifle, was arrested at Heathrow as he sauntered through customs with five of them in his suitcase. He claimed that he had an appointment to demonstrate them to Scotland Yard. The 180's have very little recoil and firing sound. The Israeli commandos used the gun in their celebrated raid on Entebbe Airport, in Uganda, when they stormed in and released skyjack hostages held by terrorists.

George Cowley (Gordon Jackson) assigns Ray Doyle (Martin Shaw) to test a brand new high-tech laser beam rifle in HUNTER/HUNTED. Seen here on location at The Palace of Engineering, Wembley, Middlesex.

Ray Menmuir: "The gun was used extensively in America. We did not focus on weaponry in every episode, but it did add a certain authenticity to the show."

Anthony Simmons (director): "During my first meeting in pre-production with Ray, I remember he kept saying, all the while wagging his finger at me, that I had to stay on budget and complete the episode in the allocated ten-day period, he didn't want any 'over-running' and wasn't prepared to authorise any overtime payments under any circumstances. I told him I therefore would need a small second unit (which is one of the reasons they brought in Chris Burt) to work alongside me. I chose Martin Campbell to direct that unit and he completed a few short sequences including the Rotherhithe tunnel sequence with the Jaguar and the Porsche, and the scene where Maurice Richards is killed in the pub by Preston from across the Thames. As our leading guest lady we had Cheryl Kennedy, whom I'd cast as Doyle's old flame Kathie Mason, because I thought she had tremendous potential as an actress, and never put a foot wrong."

Cheryl Kennedy was born (29th April 1947) in Enfield, Middlesex, and educated at a convent before appearing, at the age of fifteen, at Stratford East Threatre Workshop in *What A Crazy World*. She enjoyed success as a stage actress, notably in West End musicals such as the 1967 revival of *The Boy Friend*. During the 1970's, she appeared in several British films, including the Lust segment of *The Magnificent Seven Deadly Sins* and as Jo Mason in the Dick Emery film *Ooh... You Are Awful*.

Cheryl Kennedy (Kathie Mason): "I recall my time on the show very fondly; both Martin and Lewis were perfect gentlemen throughout the two-week shoot; they were always there to lend a helping hand! Filming at the flats near Hampstead Heath the scene called for the 180 rifle to be aimed at me through the window. I had been informed that the laser and gun were the real 'McCoy' and I was a little concerned if it was safe; I kept thinking if the laser would burn my neck or leave any marks on my skin. They assured me it was a very safe and I had nothing to fear. But I must admit it was still a little un-nerving as the scene was being shot."

After an impressive car chase in the early stages filmed on the A40M-Westway, passing 'The White City Stadium', first assistant director Derek Whitehurst, who had worked on *The Sweeney* and several Hammer features since 1957, recalled how they nearly got on the 'wrong side of the law' while filming the sequences.

Derek Whitehurst: "We shot the scene late afternoon, and despite my protests against filming it, director Tony Simmons and lighting cameraman Phil Meheux (who had taken over from Tony Imi), thought it would look good and it was too good an opportunity to miss. We did a few rehearsal runs but it was difficult not to disrupt the traffic by setting up camera crews on the fly-over and in run-by vehicles. The first take was a bit of nightmare as the sound guys hadn't rigged their equipment right so we never had any sound to go with the footage, but luckily, come the second take we got the shots that were needed in what was, in reality, a short space of time. The stunt flowed well and due to the fact there was no major disruption, the police turned a blind eye."

Actress Cheryl Kennedy in her role as Kathie Mason in HUNTER/HUNTED.

Cheryl Kennedy: "When we did those car scenes on the A40 there was no room for the cameraman; we did a quite a few runs, and I recall having to hold, and operate, the clapperboard, while either Martin or Lewis operated the camera which the crew had mounted on the side of the car by means of a cradle. In one run Martin put his foot down and due to the speed involved we nearly lost the camera, which was shaking pretty badly by this time, and poor old Lew was getting really wind-swept sat in the back. That really was a fun days shooting. You hear so much that Martin and Lew never got on, but they must have 'really' been good actors, because they seemed to get on so well to me."

Phil Meheux, born in Sidcup, Kent, on the 17th September 1941, had started his career as a projectionist for the BBC, where he became a documentary cameraman, and remained there for a dozen years working on the *Play For Today* instalments, *The Elephants Graveyard* and *Spend, Spend, Spend*, eventually leaving to make the film *Black Joy*, which was the official British Entry at the Cannes Film Festival in 1977.

Phil Meheux: "I had just finished the mini-series *Out* and accepted the position on *The Professionals* as a favour to Tony Imi. It was the least I could do after he had recommended me. I didn't really want to do episodic television, especially another twelve episodes, so they contracted me to do four. Despite the speed in which we had to work I did enjoy myself, especially working with *Black Joy* director Tony Simmons again. Ray Menmuir was very pleased with the work I had done for him, so much so, that he would ask me to return and do some directing for him..."

CI5's Ray Doyle (Martin Shaw) tests the American 180 laser sub-machine gun in HUNTER/HUNTED.

The Pub used to film the Music Hall scenes was the 'Waterman's Arms' on the Isle of Dogs, East London. A pub made famous by the photographer and TV documentary maker Dan Farson, who took over the pub in 1962 and used it as a venue for old-time Music Hall performances. A script requirement for these scenes depicted that 'on the stage a girl, brassy and busty and attired in top hat and tails but still attractive for all that, sang an old time song.' The part went to Maria St. Clare, who started her career as a cabaret dancer, and then went on to be Chief Hostess of the 'Blue Coats' at a 'Pontins' holiday camp. Her acting took her into farce, working with John Inman at Wyndham's Theatre. She became involved with Victorian Music Hall in 1976, notably as a male impersonator, and performed at the Leeds Palace of Varieties in the long-running TV show *The Good Old Days*, as well as at the London Players' Theatre.

Maria St. Clare: "I was married to the show's director (Anthony Simmons) at the time and when he had to cast the part he looked no further. I was renowned for doing male impersonations at the time, so was quite nervous as to how the actors, and crew, would take to me. It turned out that both Martin and Lewis were extremely pleasant on set and very easy to get along with, and guest actress Cheryl Kennedy drove me to the location that day from the studio.

"It took a while to complete the scenes, with my singing sequence being re-shot. A few of the close-ups had to be re-done back in the studio against a blacked-out background. Our pianist that day was Betty Lawrence who arranged the score and the choreography; something she had no problems with being the resident accompanist at London's Players' Theatre."

Anthony Read's script required Doyle to take part in another car chase, and his vehicle to be completely destroyed. Doyle loses control of his E-type Jaguar on East Heath Road, Hampstead Heath, North West London, and is in involved in a well-executed explosive crash filmed at Hippodrome Mews, Notting Hill, West London.

Martin Shaw: "We had a brilliant effects man, Peter Graham, who set it up. He co-ordinated it so both my feet were off the ground when the blast, which was directed upwards, hit me. The really dangerous part was before we actually shot the scene because I had to go and stand right next to the car. Inside it was high explosive, TNT and gunpowder and consequently a risk of a short circuit in the wiring, which would trigger it off. If there had I wouldn't be here today. Peter's cue to press the switch for the explosion was as I jumped and crouched at the same time, so the blast would go over and under me, and not send me head over heels.

"It took at least half an hour to set something like that up, so I would spend half an hour knowing that I had to do it and not a double. That gave me a feeling of exhilaration, and when everyone used to keep coming up and saying 'Good Luck, Martin', gradually the tension would build and I started thinking that there was always a possibility that something could go wrong. I do mediation, so if I'm really worried then there's always that private place within myself...and that usually works quite well for me. And I always have a cigarette after!"

Lewis Collins: "It looked fantastic. It was a safe stunt, well reasonably safe. The only thing that could have gone wrong was if some idiot had pressed the plunger before he was away from the car. He wasn't actually in the car, of course, just standing next to it. It was shot in such a way that it looked like he had just got out of the car. They shot him jumping out of another car and then cut to this scene of him leaping from the exploding car and running to safety. Good stunt, he could have been hit by a fragment of car."

Martin Shaw rehearses his leap from what will become an exploding car in HUNTER/HUNTED.

    Martin Shaw: "We probably did around 98% of the stunts. Lewis and I insisted, and there was a certain amount of rivalry that inspired us on. We never refused to do anything. They would have stopped me doing the car stunt, had I not insisted I wanted to do it."

The remains of Doyle's E-type Jaguar after the explosion on the set of HUNTER/HUNTED.

    Derek Whitehurst (first assistant director): "The bit where we shot the exploding car was another dangerous area to film in! The place where Stuart Freeman had chosen to explode the car was right next to a school. At one point, one of the children seemed like he was going to run out, but he was coaxed by my second assistant, 'Big' Roy (Roy P. Stevens), to stay where he was until the car was exploded."

Anthony Simmons (director): "We did that explosion on a bit of waste land that was actually well used for other productions as a location before being redeveloped. We couldn't do it on East Heath Road, by Hampstead Heath, where we did the run up to it, because it had to be carried out in a controlled environment, so we weren't allowed to do it here.

"I had a hand in the decision on where to film the interiors (and exteriors) for Doyle's flat. It was decided that Doyle's flat was not to be a permanent fixture as Menmuir wanted his 'agents' to always be on the move, rarely using the same house twice. With that in mind I suggested the Cliff Road flat in Camden as it belonged to a friend of mine at the time, I remembered it because of the odd multi-level aspect, which made shooting far easier from the top of the stairs. This would not have been achieved so well and 'tight' in a usual staired flat or house."

Actor Martin Shaw behind-the-scenes in East London's Poplar Dock during filming on HUNTER/HUNTED.

Brownie's houseboat scenes and Doyle's final confrontation with Preston were executed at Poplar and East India Docks, off East India Dock Road, near Poplar Power Station, East London. The docks had closed in 1967 and by the time the crew arrived to film here, like much of the London dockland area, it was deserted and unused. One of the sequences to be filmed required Bodie to follow Doyle off Brownie's houseboat and catch him up. What looked like a simple scene ended up taking five consecutive takes, until director Anthony Simmons decided to 'cut and print.'

Martin Shaw: "We relied on the director's experienced eye for detail. It never bothered us how many times we had to go through a scene. Sometimes we'd get it absolutely right, only to be told that they'd had an electrical fault!"

Derek Whitehurst (first assistant director): "I feared the worst while filming at the docks when Martin Shaw rolled under a steel girder and hit his head. Slightly concussed, Shaw was fine, and filming continued. I do remember Maurice Richards's pub was 'The Gun', Cold Harbour, on the Isle Of Dogs, where the crew shared a drink or two!"

"For the scenes involving the gunman we positioned one of the stunt guys across the water (Drawdock Road, North Greenwich). It was here that a member of the public saw the sniper and called the police. Remember, it was a time when IRA activity was at its peak and understandably people were concerned. It was also impossible to let everyone know where filming was to take place. So when the police arrived, they realised what had happened and explained to the elderly gentlemen what was going on."

Howard Baker (camera clapper/loader): "I remembered an interesting conversation with one of the policeman that day. The guy came up to me and said: 'We know that most of the terrorists and criminals live in the area, but I can tell you this, the crime-rate is almost non-existent here!' So what he was saying was the East End mobs looked after their own and never shit on their own doorstep."

By this time, it was late afternoon and a small crowd of fans had formed nearby. Second assistant director Roy P Stevens had briefed them to be silent, or they would be removed from the set. The four girls: Mandy Frost, Sandra Swarray, Jackie Blondell and Jackie Wollen had rushed over after school when they discovered that the Mark I unit was filming nearby.

Martin Shaw: "I do have some fond memories from filming the scenes in East London. There were these other three girls: Julie, Liz and Ruth, who followed us all over the place. They were so nice and sweet and well behaved they became a sort of official group of fans. They turned up at the docks and then the following day when we were filming on the Woolwich ferry they turned up again. They stood outside in the pouring rain all day just waiting for us."

This kind of attention usually worried actor Martin Shaw, but as he explained he had a means of escape:

"Fortunately our wardrobe bus had an emergency exit. If there was a crowd of 'wild' girls outside I would just wait until somebody opened the main door and they would all charge in like the Light Brigade, and I'd jump out the side door, leap into a waiting car and drive off."

Filming on the Woolwich Ferry caused sound recording problems due to the high engine noise, and Bodie, Doyle and Martell had to be re-dubbed by the dubbing team, of Hugh Strain and Peter Lennard, under the guidance of John S. Smith, all fresh from similar positions on *The Sweeney*.

Anthony Simmons (director): "I'd used the Woolwich Ferry in 1965 on the Judi Dench film *Four In The Morning*, so I knew how to tackle that scene, which, in pre-production talks, was feared to be too problematic to mount, and would have to be replaced with another location. In the event, due to my previous experience, we achieved the desired shots with a small crew, as space on the ferry was very tight. I had control on the re-dubbing as I always insisted on staying on with the editor to put all my filmed segments together. After all, I wanted the show to be assembled the way I had envisaged it, so I spent about a week with the post production team putting the final cut together. Martin Campbell's handywork added the final touches."

This is the first episode in which Bodie and Doyle have radio call signs. Bodie's call sign is 3-7, Doyle's 3-6 (although mention is made of '4-5's place'), HQ is 2-4. In subsequent episodes, the call signs, and agent numbers, stabilise as 4-5 for Doyle, 3-7 for Bodie, and Alpha One, or occasionally Charlie, for Cowley.

First Night: *A visiting Israeli Minister is abducted from a first night performance. The resulting hover-craft and helicopter pursuit carries Bodie and Doyle into a suburban siege.*

Filming on *First Night* began on Monday 3rd July, directed by David Wickes from a Gerry O'Hara script, and in some ways became a blueprint for what Menmuir was trying to do with the series.

CI5 are left to dig deep in FIRST NIGHT when an Israeli Minister is kidnapped by hovercraft, and the only clues to his whereabouts are a shadowy photograph and a coded tape message. Gordon Jackson and Martin Shaw are taken for a ride on the River Thames, near Royal Festival Hall, South East London, in the 'Surface Craft' used for this episode by the kidnappers.

In Gerry O'Hara's original script, certain scenes were depicted somewhat differently then were ultimately visualized by director David Wickes. On Wednesday 5th July, both the script and shooting schedule stated that Cowley receives the news about the Biebermann snatch while purchasing a bunch of flowers! The scene appeared in the schedule as follows:

Ext: Flower Stall

Cowley selects red roses from the street vendor (tonight was going to be a big night, and long stemmed roses fitted the bill admirably). The flower vendor smiles at Cowley, who in turn walks back to his waiting car. Cowley signals to his driver, Doug Walters, to drive on. The radio telephone buzz's...

Martin Shaw, Gordon Jackson, and Lewis Collins, during a break in filming FIRST NIGHT.

Despite location manager Stuart Freeman gaining police permission from Leman Street Police Station (Chief Inspector Stevens) for filming, the flower vendor being hired, and the scene set up in Trinity Square/Coopers Row, East Central London, the sequence was not filmed. The scene was dropped in favour of Cowley simply buying a newspaper from the paper stand next to where the flower vendor had been set up.

An incredible action-packed pre-title sequence was filmed both inside, and outside, the Royal Festival Hall, and on the River Thames. However, the original script indicates that these sequences were originally planned to have taken place at the nearby National Theatre.

The kidnappers use the 'Surface Craft' high-speed mini hovercraft for their escape. A 2-cylinder 650cc engine gave the hovercraft a top speed of 50mph and consumed two gallons of petrol an hour. A single 'joy-stick' grip, controlled lift, steering, and speed. The machine could lift up to 2,000-lb and carried a maximum of three people.

Chris Howard (focus puller): "That blinking hovercraft! When the kidnappers leap in, the tide wasn't in and the thing went nowhere. It wasn't powerful enough to make a speedy escape with the amount of people getting in it. The props department found a foam dummy to take the place of one of the people, but the thing had orange hands and they kept getting in the shot. A crowd had gathered and was watching the filming. They began to see the funny side of things and we were plagued by laughter. It became very embarrassing."

The 'Surface Craft' plays guest to actors Martin Shaw and Gordon Jackson.

From Wednesday 12th to Friday 14th July the crew filmed the exteriors and interiors to the kidnapper's house. Utilised for these scenes was South West India Dock Entrance, on the Isle Of Dogs, East London. For these scenes Lewis Collins found himself in the cab of a crane used as a battering ram, which smashes through a window.

An Israeli diplomat is kidnapped, and its down to CI5 to find him fast! Martin Shaw as CI5 agent Ray Doyle on the set of FIRST NIGHT. Seen here on location in the gardens of the houses being used at South West India Dock Entrance, on the Isle of Dogs, East London.

Lewis Collins: "I wanted to do the stunt myself, but director David Wickes decided it was too dangerous, and refused to let me do it. The battering ram missed the window and smashed against the wall, and stuntman Del Baker only just managed to save himself by a desperate jump sideways. What you have to remember, when you see us doing a fight scene, is that it has probably taken anything up to five or six takes for the director to be satisfied."

In FIRST NIGHT stunt man Del Baker was lucky to escape being crushed?
"The crane was supposed to be used for cleaning and changing street lights. It was very unstable when it moved. It hit the pavement and set about a pendulum action, which made it miss the window. It was a narrow escape for me."

Ray Corbett (first assistant director): "The crane was rubbish (on hire from EPL International). The thing was terrible. It just kept breaking down, so Ray Menmuir's spectacular element was somewhat lost, much to my amusement."

Playing a small part as a tennis partner to Bodie's on-screen girlfriend (Sara Walkden) was actress Carla Wansey.

Carla Wansey: "I was originally spotted doing a video for Genesis which led to five happy years on the *Benny Hill show*, moving on to *Alas Smith and Jones* then onwards and upwards to all sorts of other comedies.

"On *The Professionals* we (with actress Sara Walkden) were dressed in tennis gear and larking around with Bodie and Doyle (the scenes with Martin Shaw were not used) on some tennis courts; I think we always get credited with 1st and 2nd 'pretty girl'. Lewis was extremely pleasant and, yes, he had an eye for the girlies but not at all in an offensive way. I seem to remember it was a grim wet rainy day and cold when we shot the exteriors and we had to pretend it was sunny and warm and Lewis during a break for a hot cup of tea put his jacket over my shoulders to keep me warm!

"Martin was very quiet and kept to himself and even brought his own sandwiches to the set as he is a strict veggie I think, so we did not get much chance to talk to him, all the rest of the cast and crew were very jolly. We were both typical blonde girlies. I do remember being taken to the location by car and then we came back to main HQ to do some close up stuff (scenes not used). I also remember Gordon Jackson and our director being really funny and we all had lunch together minus Martin who went somewhere quietly to read I think."

The Rack: CI5 is placed on trial after 'busting' a long suspected narcotics gang. A suspect dies in his cell and the very existence of the elite crime squad is called into question.

Next episode, in production, was *An Enquiry Into Violence*, which began shooting on Monday 17th July. It was later retitled *The Rack* as still sensitive from the *Klansman* situation; Mark I feared a negative reaction towards an episode title containing the word violence.

Written by Brian Clemens, this marked the arrival of Hungarian director Peter Medak (born 23rd December 1937, in Budapest) to the production, having already worked on numerous gothic horror movies, and the TV series *Ghost Squad, Out Of The Unknown, Journey To The Unknown, The Gold Robbers, Shirley's World* and *The Persuaders!*.

CI5's Doyle (Martin Shaw) and Bodie (Lewis Collins) are put on THE RACK.

On submitting his first draft scriptwriter Brian Clemens had envisaged the story's conclusion somewhat differently from what was ultimately filmed. After Bodie and Doyle have found Parker nailed to a wall above the table in the club, the final scenes were written as follows:

Int: Court Room

Bodie and Doyle push Parker into the room.
MISS MATHER (outraged at the intrusion): *Mr. President!*

DOYLE (wheeling Parker to the centre): *You wanted the informer. Well, you've got him?*
COWLEY: *Bodie! Doyle!*
BODIE: *The spirit of the law, sir. She demanded Henry Parker. And she's got him!*
DOYLE: *We found him nailed. Nailed! Nailed to a wall, by - person or persons unknown.*
BODIE: *But. As his identity was unknown until announced in this court, we must assume that it was a direct result!*
(looking at Miss Mather) *How does it feel to play Pontius Pilate?*

The sequence was abandoned as script editor Gerry O'Hara felt the scenes were too graphic and would be difficult to film.

Bodie (Lewis Collins) comes under a barrage of questions in this scene from THE RACK.

Michael Billington (John Coogan): "About the time of doing *The Professionals* I had just come back from Paris, where I had been doing some tests, at the time of *Moonraker*, for Lewis Gilbert who I think wanted me to do the next picture, which was *For Your Eyes Only*. I can remember that *The Professionals* was a good set and very fast, and I recall getting on pretty well with Lewis Collins who had a good sense of humour. I plucked my eyebrows completely to play the role of the ex-Boxer Coogan because it made me look a bit insane. It was a bit of a nuisance afterwards because it took them years to grow back completely. I also had a difference of opinion with Mr. Medak, the director; over the way I played the courtroom scene. To show Coogan's deviousness, I played him as though he was innocent and sincere. Peter wanted me to play him callous and hard. Maybe he was right. I think it came out somewhere in the middle."

A death in custody puts CI5 on THE RACK. Doyle (Martin Shaw) and Bodie (Lewis Collins) must act quickly before CI5 meets its demise!

New Zealand born Lisa Harrow (25th August 1943) shed her country girl image to play the part of a shrewd woman barrister. At home in New Zealand, she used to give her brother a hand on his sheep farm, riding out for miles to bring the animals in for shearing. It certainly helped her win the Variety Club's award for Most Promising Artist in 1976 for her performance in the film *All Creatures Great And Small*, from the novel by James Herriott.

She was born in Auckland and attended her home-town's University. After graduating from RADA in 1968, she joined the BBC Radio Repertory Company.

"I had a tough time on *The Professionals.* I had just come back from a whistle stop tour of the States publicising the film. I had terrible jet lag, which made me very slow learning my lines. As I was playing a 'legal eagle' I hoped to be able to cheat a little. Actress friends of mine had been in the series *Crown Court* and told me I would be holding a sheaf of notes and be able to glance down at them now and again to remind me of the difficult bits. But we were in a huge empty warehouse (Cadby Hall) in Hammersmith. There was not any cover. It was agony. So I had to slog away on my own. The last straw came when my boyfriend, who is a lawyer, was away in Canada. He could have helped."

A couple of weeks later, Lisa's reputation for solemnity caught up with her. Her parents were over from New Zealand and out sightseeing. In a cafe they happened to sit next to two young men:

"I could hardly believe it when they told me, but these boys had been the drivers (Chris Streeter, Benny Wright) on the show. My parents mentioned me. Their faces fell, 'What a serious young woman', they said, 'not a lot of laughs in that department!' My mother thought they were talking about someone else."

As the storyline featured extensive use of CI5 headquarters, location filming was minimal with Cadby Hall, Hammersmith, West London, being utilised for both interior and exterior shots, and Binfield Manor, Binfield, Berkshire, doubled as the Coogan's residence.

Derek Whitehurst (first assistant director): "Cadby Hall? What can I say? It looked like an easy episode to shoot, but due to bad lighting, damp, holes in the roof, and poor facilities, there were problems. The warehouses were huge and empty. Some had not been used for years and setting up proved difficult.

"Binfield Manor proved hard work also, especially for stuntman Del Baker. He was supposed to fall from one of the windows. With filming ready to take place I was supposed to shout 'Turn Over', to queue the cameras to start, then 'Action', to get the actors to start. I got it back to front and Del's fall was not filmed, the cameras were not rolling. I got it wrong the second time too. Del was more than pleased when the third take was in the can.

Binfield Manor in Berkshire. First assistant director Derek Whitehurst's original 'recce' shots prior to filming on THE RACK. The house was built in 1754 for Sir William Pitt (a distant cousin of Pitt the Elder, Earl of Chatham) at a cost of £36,000. He became Prime Minister in 1756.

"I left the production at the end of this episode to do the feature, *Dracula*, but one of the final things Gordon Jackson said to me was, 'How come all the nice guys end up leaving?' and I thought that was so nice."

Man Without A Past: *Bodie is suspended from duty and takes a solo trail of revenge when a restaurant bomb leaves his girlfriend critically injured and Doyle a prisoner of the Mafia.*

Filming started on the next instalment, *Man Without A Past*, on Monday 31st July. Michael Armstrong born (24th July 1944) in Bolton, Lancashire, started his career in the late Sixties as a director of horror movies, and provided this script from an original storyline by Jeremy Burnham, who had penned episodes of *The Avengers*, *Paul Temple* and *Shirley's World*.

Having only directed three obscure films in the early to Mid-Seventies, New Zealander, Martin Campbell (born 24th October 1940), was given the director's chair (after some second unit work on *Hunter/Hunted*), and would carve out a career in film series before becoming a James Bond director, starting with *Goldeneye*.

Martin Campbell (director): "I left New Zealand in the late 1960's to work in Britain as a video cameraman at Lew Grade's ATV Studios in Elstree. During this time I worked with a few directors that I felt were quite useless and I thought I could in reality do the job much better. It was really the only reason I got into directing, and my first big TV production was *The Professionals*, and it provided me with a great training ground to eventually take onto the Bond films."

"On *The Professionals* set there was definitely friction to be felt... because Martin is from the theatre, he's a professional actor...Lewis wasn't. They were different animals so to speak!"

Bodie is out at a restaurant with his girlfriend when a bomb goes off at their table, leaving her critically injured and several other diners dead. Martin Shaw and Lewis Collins during MAN WITHOUT A PAST.

Martin Shaw: "My relationship with Lewis was strictly business and often abrasive. Because of the natural strain and stress entailed during filming, we needed a break from each other. You couldn't expect people to spend all their working and social hours together. We didn't, except for our dedication to the work and a similar sense of humour, have much in common."

Shaw then recalled how he once threatened to kill Lewis during a violent on-set row.

Martin Shaw: "I think I was uncomfortably close to doing it, too. It was one of the three or four occasions in my life when I really lost my temper. Pressure builds up until it is like having a pressure cooker with the lid firmly on. Lew and I often had disagreements, but that one was different. It was a terribly bad day, we were really wound up, and he said something about one of the takes that I took offence to.

"I shrugged and walked away, as I usually did when we got in a situation like that. But I suddenly noticed that my heart was pounding and my stomach was red hot. I thought: 'What the hell is going on?' Then, I found myself walking back and saying: 'If you ever say anything like that to me again, I'll kill you'. I heard the words coming out, but it did not feel as though it was me saying them. He backed off, there was a silence, and nothing else that we could have said to each other. Afterwards, I felt ashamed. Not only was it a stupid thing to say; I thought my self-control was better than that."

"Sometime later I was on the receiving end: I had made a few cutting remarks in Lew's direction and he went mad. I was terrified, because he's built like a brick outhouse and I thought he was going to kill me. By that time I had realised more about my honesty and I told him later, 'I want you to know that when you were angry I was really frightened'. It brought us much closer together. Both of us had been so out of control in our own ways, we had been willing to kill. It showed what could happen when you were working at a frantic pace from dawn to dusk."

Lewis Collins: "Martin and I respected each other, but we were basically different types of people. Our relationship was very much as portrayed in the series. We were both honest enough to admit it. There was a rivalry between us and we spurred each other on, sometimes getting aggressive with each other, which the whole crew felt."

One of the biggest problems faced by the production team was finding a suitable building to double for the restaurant, as most properties within the location brief proved unsuitable to withstand the explosion that needed to be employed. Location manager Cecil Ford secured the services of Michel et Valerie in Maidenhead, Berkshire. Not only was he acquainted with the restaurant owners, but there was also an empty unit next door.

Colin Dandridge (boom operator): "We used the restaurant, Michel et Valerie for the meal, but the post explosion scenes were filmed in an empty unit in the same block. The owners of the restaurant understandably didn't want their premises involved in such an explosion, so the location guys searched extensively to find this location. It made shooting the scene much easier, because as we were filming the meal scenes, the special effects guys and art department were preparing the unit next door to be blown up. As ever, the explosion was over the top, and none of us were spared a shower of debris and dust."

Lewis Collins: "I caught part of the blast from the explosion and Martin had to pull the bits out of my head, that was pretty nasty. I think it hurt more afterwards than at the time. The problem was the stunt guys used to go over the top, much more than they would be able to get away with today - and you sometimes felt uneasy when you'd see them standing so far back when the explosion was primed to go off. You could sort of see them smiling away to themselves. That said, we both always seemed to escape without serious injury."

A uniformed policeman (Les Conrad) keeps watch as Doyle (Martin Shaw) arrives at the scene of an explosion in MAN WITHOUT A PAST. These scenes were filmed at Michel et Valerie in Maidenhead, Berkshire. The restaurant was known to location manger Cecil Ford.

The crew filmed the car chase scenes involving Bodie and the FBI around Firth Lane/Highwood Hill/Lullington Garth and Partingdale Lane in Mill Hill, North West London. There is some light relief when Bodie skids his Capri to a halt and jumps over the bonnet only to get a round of applause from a queue of people at a nearby bus stop.

Amelia (guest on set): "The best laugh that day was the 'fake' bus stop. Lew had to drive at full speed, skid to a broadside halt, leap over the bonnet, and draw his automatic to ambush the pursuing hoods that had been chasing him. Only in the story the pursuing car has given him the slip and does not show. A bus queue across the road watches Bodie do his athletics (thinking he's a mad man) and when nothing happens they applaud him. Now, to make it realistic, two props-men brought out a bus-stop sign from their huge props-van, positioned it, and placed grass round the base, then about ten assorted 'extras' queued up as though waiting for a bus.

"The funny thing was that there was a real bus-stop 150-yards before it round the bend out-of-sight, and for two hours it was hilarious to see bus drivers, one-after-the-other stopping at our bus stop. They'd come to a halt very slowly, scratching their heads, then when nobody would get on, they'd lean out of the window, and ask what was up. Then it would dawn on them that there was a film crew there and they thought they were on *Candid Camera* as the cheers went up from everybody around."

Peter Carter (first assistant director): "And in one take, when one of the buses (the 221 to Edgware via Mill Hill) arrived, just for a laugh, the extras actually got on-board and off they went."

Amelia (guest on set): "Lew did some daring driving in his car, slithering hand-brake turns, leaping out and over the car bonnet, gun out of its holster, then, a head-first dive over a fence as the chasing car crashed through it, followed by a head-long dash through the trees (while loading his automatic) to drag the hoods from their piled-up car. This is all shot in many short sequences with many retakes in the course of the afternoon, and pieced together back in the studio.

"There were a few laughs too, like in the dash to the piled-up car! After about five energetic rehearsals and with Lew getting a bit out-of-breath, they thought they had it right, and when the director called 'Action!' the cameras rolled and Lew began his flat out 100-yard dash for the sixth (and he hoped last) time wrenching his gun from his shoulder-holster at the same time, with the other hand, cocking back the slide, when suddenly to the crews great amusement, the hammer section flew 10-feet up in the air, and the entire gun fell to bits leaving Lew, who had come to a halt, holding only the handle! The whole unit and audience (there were about sixty people) burst out laughing. To add to the fun Lew sat down and pretended to cry like a baby!"

That wasn't the only mishap that day. One more serious incident occurred while filming the sequence near Mill Hill electricity sub-station, Partingdale Lane, North West London, which nearly cost camera operator John Maskall his life!

Roy P. Stevens (second assistant director): "As the Capri charged around Partingdale Lane, followed by the Triumph (PNM 565J), being driven by stunt man Frank Henson, both cars skidded on some water that had been left behind by a dust cart. The Capri suffered only minor rear bumper damage, but the Triumph, which actually belonged to our producer, Ray Menmuir, was a car that refused to die. It was always being hit and painted. It was heading for John Maskall, who seemed oblivious to the crew trying to get his attention. I just managed to grab him away as Henson ploughed the car into the camera."

John Maskall (camera operator): "The trouble with me is that when I get my eye to a camera, I think I'm invisible. As Henson got out of the car, he ran to the camera and I said to him, 'What you lookin' for', he replied jokingly, 'You mate'."

Having decided on the use of the council flats off Swan Road and Brunel Road, Rotherhithe, South East London, for the scenes involving Doyle chasing Pendle, location manager Stuart Freeman also needed to find a suitable spot to film the shots where Doyle is mowed down by Crabbe's car. While recceing the flats, he noticed a suitable area of waste ground backing onto Rotherhithe Street and a deal was struck with the owners, who negotiated a half-days facility fee for the use of the property.

Ray Menmuir: "We arrived in the street (Brunel Road) and found it half dug up for repairs. Not a problem you might think, but the location manger had arranged for parking on the same street, which was now full up with diggers and the construction site workmen. We had problems parking our crew's vehicles and had to use the housing estate car parks, which didn't go down too well with the residents. We still managed to get set up and film our shots though."

On a different note, the fight scene, with actor Rod Culbertson (Pendle), went badly wrong. Martin Shaw was knocked out, and was kept in hospital for twenty-four hours.

Martin Shaw: "I was sent to hospital suffering from concussion! I was supposed to be struggling with Rod and he had to throw me to the floor. Unfortunately I went down too hard and cracked my head. I was supposed to break the fall with my shoulder, but I missed and my head took the impact instead. I was knocked out for a few seconds, right out, then when I came round I couldn't see or hear properly. I carried on with the scene but I didn't really know what I was doing. So they packed me off to hospital. I decided I wasn't going to stay there and be bored so I discharged myself. They said, 'You've got to stay at home in bed'. I told them, 'Actually, I'm going to work tomorrow, but I spend all day lying down tied up'. So they let me go but very reluctantly."

The very next day, Shaw was back on the set sporting an ugly bruise on his forehead. Interviewed at the time Shaw noted:

"We're continually managing to knock ourselves out. It's just part of the job. We get cut and bruised all the time, fortunately it all ties in with the image, so it isn't as disastrous as it might seem. The only thing is that it'll probably take me about two weeks to recover from this knock, but I'll just have to get on with filming in the meantime."

In The Public Interest: *Bodie and Doyle become hunted men after beginning their investigation into a city where the crime rate has fallen mysteriously.*

Monday 14th August saw the initial filming of *In The Public Interest*. An issue-based script from Brian Clemens, directed by Pennant Roberts, there are many similarities between this episode and the earlier *Klansmen* script, in terms of a minority group being threatened and assaulted. This time it was the gay community being victimised, but unlike *Klansman*, the violence is always inferred and never actually seen.

In The Public Interest was director Pennant Roberts' (born in Bristol on 15th December 1940) first work on the show, having started his career on videotaped series at the BBC, including *Doctor Who*, *Doomwatch* and *Survivors*. After being assigned the story, Roberts decided that, in order to create the right atmosphere, filming at night would be required and set up a meeting with the producer, Ray Menmuir, to discuss his requirements.

Pennant Roberts (director): "The schedules were very tight. They were getting behind in filming and the script was only given to me on the Wednesday before the Monday shoot, which gave little time to prep anything. When I did get the shooting schedule, I noticed that out of over a hundred scenes, ninety were night shots. I asked Menmuir how much night shooting I could have. His answer was short and sweet, 'None, you'll have to do day-for-night shots'.

"My first encounter with Paul Hardwick was at the Edgwarebury Club, on the Wednesday of the first shooting week. I remember having only about ten minutes to discuss characterisation with him while camera tracks were being laid for what was probably the last shot of the sequence, the club building itself not being open at seven in the morning. Later in the afternoon we moved to the Mill Hill Gas works location opposite Mill Hill East tube station to shoot the 'Cell Block C' shot.

A virtual police state has been imposed by a local Chief Constable, resulting in a supposedly almost crime-free city. But is it IN THE PUBLIC INTEREST?

"Watford Junction was chosen as the railway station, because we wanted to steer clear of any metropolitan feel. After all, the town was set away from London in some fictional Midland locale. Equally, we needed a mainline Railway Station as a film location. Not one of the London terminals, obviously, hence Watford, which was the biggest non-terminal reasonably near to base."

"The Tower Theatre and the Wembley Hotel scenes were shot on the same day. My shooting routine was affected because of the journey time from Islington to Wembley in the middle of the day had been underestimated. As a consequence the last interior hotel bedroom scene was rushed and undershot because of the shortage of time.

"Once shooting had got underway, I immediately had problems with Lewis Collins. I was told he was nicknamed 'Loo'. I didn't find that odd, until it was time to do a take. Half way through, he'd put his hand up and want to go to the toilet. To this day, I'm still not sure if it was a wind up. The man seemed a bag of nerves.

"Bodie and Doyle got pulled over in the Escort RS2000 on Watling Avenue, Burnt Oak and it was here that Lewis Collins hung out of the car window making a public nuisance of himself. In the afternoon, we shot the interior of the gambling club, with Pamela Manson, which was in a real 'hangout for villains', according to the local Head of C.I.D, and situated in a basement within the North-East quadrant of Central Circus, Hendon. The blackjack dealer was the 'Real McCoy' and came with the club. The exterior of the club, and the day-for-night scenes were filmed in the rear car park of the Paradise Cinema, off Hanger Lane. The night shots I think looked particularly bad when I saw the rushes, but we had no alternative."

Martin Shaw and Lewis Collins pose for a publicity shot during a break in filming the story IN THE PUBLIC INTEREST.

Harry Fielder (Club Manager, uncredited): "I did a few episodes and remember me, Tony Allen (Bill from *The Sweeney*), sitting round a table talking to Gordon Jackson about cockney dialogue; him being a sweaty sock used to love hearing us talk and was going on about it when Tony said to him 'Ere Gord, you're giving me GBH of the Donald (Peers).' When we translated it for him he fell about. Martin Shaw and Lewis Collins kept to themselves but Gordon was always up for a laugh."

Pennant Roberts: "On the last shooting day the Hurlingham Court (Cowley's flat) scenes preceding the shopping centre scenes in Shepherd's Bush, a location which was squeezed in on the way back to base, and was therefore un-recced. Fraser Cains, who played the policeman, seemed to have been cast that very morning, he was certainly as baffled as I was to why he was there at all, and believed he had been engaged to act in a sitcom. The last shot we managed to achieve was Doyle's car pulling out into the Friday afternoon rush hour traffic.

"The scene where Pellin follows Cowley from the National Liberal Club may be described as second unit, but I certainly directed it. I believe that it was shot by a small unit headed by Vernon Layton (lighting cameraman) in the week preceding the main shoot. We were permitted to squeeze this in because Bodie and Doyle weren't involved."

For IN THE PUBLIC INTEREST Stephen Rea, born (31st October 1946) in Belfast, Northern Ireland, played the part of Pellin. The actor was later nominated for an Academy Award for his performance in the 1992 film THE CRYING GAME.

By now the obvious leaping around and gymnastics, working fourteen to sixteen hour days for six months without a break, was taking its toll on both Lewis Collins and Martin Shaw.

Lewis Collins (interviewed at the time): "On a good 45-minute session, wearing a thick track suit, I could lose about a pound and a half! I left the rest to the vitamin pills. I have something of a reputation, not altogether undeserved, for painting the town red on a Saturday. But not before I've been to the Army shooting range at Bisley in Surrey and spent an hour with my instructor Tom Collins, firing a variety of small arms, anything up to the powerful .357 Magnum, which sounds like a bomb going off when you pull the trigger. I owe my interest in handguns to *The Professionals*.

Lewis Collins as CI5's top agent Bodie during IN THE PUBLIC INTEREST.

"I've been hooked on it ever since they sent me on a training course to lean how to use small arms. Yes, it does get rid of a certain amount of tension, but I uncoil more on Saturday night. I have no permanent girlfriend but many female acquaintances, I might take someone out for dinner and a club, or go out with a bunch of male friends: then we usually end up going back to someone's place and ripping it apart. I try to make my Saturdays last 36-hours, not 24. For me a Saturday is a precious day off."

Martin Shaw maintained that yoga was the only way to keep the whole body in trim, but had, at the time, just taken up squash with *The Professionals* producer Raymond Menmuir.

Martin Shaw: "It was a great release for the frustration of a days filming and we used to regularly have a few rounds with Lewis too ."

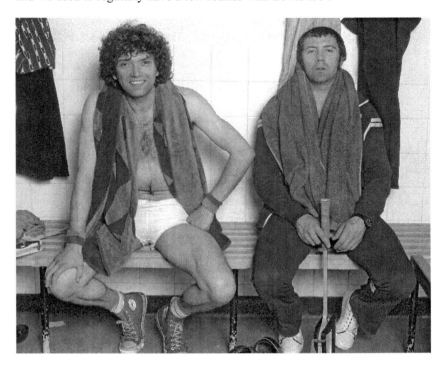

Martin Shaw and Lewis Collins (pictured above) relax after a rigorous game of squash with THE PROFESSIONALS producer Raymond Menmuir.

Martin also kept a punch ball in his study and confessed to having a ten-minute work-out before filling in his tax returns!

Coupled with the yoga, Martin Shaw's secret of keeping his cool was contained in a collection of tiny bottles, filled with special flower remedies. The 38 bottles of concentrated flower and tree essence were Martin's personal medicine chest and he had to be grateful to a gentleman by the name of Edward Bach for discovering the natural way to preserve peace of mind. One cure he admitted to taking was Impatience, which is derived from the plant Busy Lizzy, which claims to be helpful to a person who tends to be impatient, irritable, highly active and nervous. His daily routine would also include two cloves of garlic swallowed whole, fruit juice and wheat germ oil followed by tea made with linseed, fenugreek seed, peppermint and ground liquorice root.

Not A Very Civil Civil Servant: *When whole, new housing estates begin to crumble CI5 unearth corruption, even murder, in a Ministry designating 'contracts' of both varieties.*

Due to a Bank Holiday, shooting did not start on *Not A Very Civil Civil Servant* (called *Houses And Estates* in early script drafts) until Tuesday 29th August, under the control of Anthony Simmons, from a script by Edmund Ward, (born 23rd February 1928, Nottingham, England), who had previously penned episodes of *Man In A Suitcase* and *The Power Game*.

Martin Shaw taking a break during filming his scenes at The National Liberal Club, Whitehall, London, for NOT A VERY CIVIL CIVIL SERVANT.

Having vetted the script, Brian Clemens strongly advised against making the episode. Clemens always wrote, not only for the English audience, but also for Americans and the Japanese too. The action spoke louder than words, so little time was wasted with chat, and at the beginning of each script was the note: 'Cockney and pronounced accents of any kind (particularly regional) are not acceptable in this series. Should they occur, the scene will be reshot or revoiced. Expletives: "Bloodies" - "Jesus!" etc. Must only be used where scripted (and where they are scripted is for very calculated effect). Ad-libbed expletives are not acceptable.'

Brian Clemens: "I read it twice and still didn't know what it was about. So I strongly advised against making it, but LWT didn't want to buy another script and went ahead. Then when I watched the finished episode I turned it off half way through because I couldn't follow the plot and in that situation it just becomes boring. It was too complicated for it's own good. I always write for a lay audience and if you put in too much technical jargon you lose people and they won't understand or enjoy it. No matter what the subject I write it first and look up the facts later and nine times out of ten I'm right.

"How could you expect an American to understand a Geordie when most southern English people can't understand them either? Sound tracks can often deteriorate, especially at the cinema. So the story is much better told in the action itself. A film like *French Connection* for instance could be shown without the sound altogether. You would still know what was going on. Because of this philosophy I very much admire the work of Alfred Hitchcock.

"Someone once said to me 'I think that bit in *Psycho* where he sticks the knife into the girl is really frightening,' well, I've seen that film many times and you never see that happening, it is all implied. You should take violence off the screen and put it where it belongs in the mind of the audience."

The fencing scenes for NOT A VERY CIVIL CIVIL SERVANT were filmed at the National Liberal Club, Whitehall, London.

Director Anthony Simmons also had certain issues with the script but could do very little to improve proceedings.

Anthony Simmons (director): "I think they tried too hard with this story, Edmund Ward's script was way too clever in a sense and didn't meet the action criteria set out by the producers. It lost the fast-moving concept evident in the other shows and replaced it with political overtones about corruption within government offices. Even with substantial re-writing from Gerry (O'Hara) we struggled to get the end result wanted by the producers. We cast Maurice Denham against type as the villain of the piece, and I think he pulled it off pretty well as did Bill Fraser."

Guest star Bill Fraser, born (5th June 1908) in Perth, Scotland, played Claude Snudge in *The Army Game* and *Bootsie and Snudge*, and was making the film *The Corn Is Green* when, during a break in filming, he ventured into another studio where *The Professionals* was being filmed.

Martin Shaw as Doyle on the set of NOT A VERY CIVIL CIVIL SERVANT.

Bill Fraser (Colonel Summerville): "The producer saw me and asked if I had time to join them in a small role as a man from the Ministry. So I agreed. My scenes were filmed (along with Bodie and Doyle's fencing scenes) at the National Liberal Club in Whitehall, South West London."

Educated at Strathallan School, Fraser began his career in a bank before turning to acting. His first television appearance was on *The Tony Hancock Show* in 1956.

Actor Lewis Collins on the set of NOT A VERY CIVIL CIVIL SERVANT.

The script required scenes to be filmed at a construction site, and location manager Stuart Freeman again chose to use the area around Rotherhithe Street, South East London, where Surrey Commercial Docks were undergoing redevelopment.

Colin Dandridge (boom operator): "They were behind schedules by this stage and this episode had to be finished today, Friday afternoon. I didn't have time to fix Cowley's radio mike properly and in the finished print you can see it just poking out of his tie knot. It was very late in the evening by the time we'd finished and while driving home along the South Bank I had to pull over. I was exhausted and missed the next episode on the doctor's orders. Mind you, we made fun of our lighting cameraman, Vernon Layton, who'd taken over from Phil Meheux, 'You'd know we'd have a late finish if Vernon 'Late One' was on the set'. No we loved him really, listening to his stories on how he worked with *The Beatles* in the sixties."

NOT A VERY CIVIL CIVIL SERVANT: Martin Shaw, Gordon Jackson, and Lewis Collins during a break in filming.

During a break in filming Lewis Collins found time to visit the Royal Army Veterinary Training Centre near Melton Mowbray, Leicestershire, where he was given a tough time by the army's war-dogs rather than the other way round. These are big Alsatians especially trained to deal with terrorists, to sniff-out guns and ammunition, booby-traps and similar things. Equipped with a padded suit and safety cage over his head, he still managed to get bruised and a split lip when he attempted a sprint, actually covering ten yards before being dispatched by the ferocious top dog, Kingdom; who bowled him over on more than one occasion. And he also had to go into a derelict building (used for special training for house-to-house searching and fighting), where he hadn't spotted one booby-trap, and after a big thunder-flash exploded: it sent him staggering out dazed!

On Monday 11th September, at 5.15am, the 'Surface Craft' mini hovercraft used in the episode *First Night* was the target for a publicity shoot along The Mall, near Buckingham Palace, London. Unit publicist Paul McNicholls arranged for the CI5 team to test the hovercraft for themselves.

The 'Surface Craft' which originally saw service in FIRST NIGHT is photographed with THE PROFESSIONALS stars Martin Shaw, Gordon Jackson and Lewis Collins. The location was an early morning shoot along The Mall, near Buckingham Palace, London.

Martin Shaw: "It really is an incredible machine, but it does have its problems. In spite of its fourteen rudders for manoeuvring, it's rather like a helicopter and tends to move all over the place. I could only give it two-out-of-ten for directional stability. A bit like driving a car with steel wheels on ice.

If you could fit cutters underneath instead of two 14-blade lifting fans, it would make a great lawnmower. The hovercraft really is a wonderful toy, particularly over water, great fun for messing about on the river: it will turn on a lifebelt."

Lewis Collins: "It's quite powerful, but very noisy. It was almost impossible to think while I was driving. The twist grip accelerator is like a motor-bike's, quite easy to handle. It was fairly straightforward."

Gordon Jackson: "Altogether, a very smooth ride, but rather noisy. I took off my ear protectors for a while and couldn't hear for an hour or so after the ride. I think the hovercraft might be rather tricky to manoeuvre in town traffic, somewhere like Piccadilly Circus could present real problems. But it would be handy if you lived in the middle of the Serpentine."

The remainder of the day was spent filming Ray Menmuir's new title sequence, devised by designer Malcolm Middleton and assistant Peter Joyce, and edited together by John S. Smith.

John S. Smith: "Producer Ray Menmuir had been told that the titles had to be 'toned' down by the legal department at LWT. The original assault course sequence had shown Bodie and Doyle point their guns at the screen, and the IBA had received a complaint about it. Rather than trim that section out, Ray decided to update the titles completely feeling that the original was a little old fashioned and dated."

Malcolm Middleton (production designer): "I had the idea of a tunnel of black drapes over plate glass and a photo blurb of buildings reflected on it. This would be followed by a car crashing through."

Peter Joyce (art director): "I then told producer Ray Menmuir my idea of using head and shoulder silhouettes for the character captions. I took Polaroids of the stars and using a marker pen, coloured them black. A stencil was used for the logos and there you have it."

The filming of the drapes/car smash was executed on Wembley Stadium's overflow car park, which was across the road from the studio. Peter Brayham performed the stunt in his 20-minute lunch break.

Peter Brayham (stunt arranger): "The plate glass was 2-inches thick, 24-feet by 24-feet in size and set up at the top of a 6-feet ramp. It was an easy stunt, but as you can see, very effective."

Jeff Woodbridge (construction manager): "Even though it was 'sugar' glass, Brayham crashed through it with some force and when the car hit the ground it went all over the place. He won't admit it, but not only was it a dangerous stunt to be done with such little preparation work, he really struggled to keep it under control."

In the finished product, also featured, are tightly cut montages of specially filmed segments, including credit captions for Gordon Jackson, Martin Shaw and Lewis Collins.

A Stirring Of Dust: *CI5 join the Reds in a ghost hunt for a spy and defector whose sentimental return threatens the whole security network.*

On Tuesday 12th September the cameras were rolling on *A Stirring Of Dust*, from the pen of Frenchman Don Houghton. Born in Paris in 1930 he started writing in radio in 1951 before moving into film and television in 1958. In the 1970's he was a primary writer for Hammer Films (*The Satanic*

Rites of Dracula, The Legend of the Seven Golden Vampires), and also submitted scripts for both *Doctor Who* and *Ace Of Wands*.

The 'new' Titles filmed for the second series: the main Title sequence, commercial advertisement break caption, and end cast/crew credits caption. These would be drafted onto all future and previous prints to form a uniform package for sales overseas.

Direction on *A Stirring Of Dust* was by Martin Campbell and assistant director Ron Purdie, who'd started his career in the 1960's on *The Avengers*, recalled the admiration the producers had for this particular director.

Ron Purdie: "Campbell was the guy that Ray Menmuir said would go on to better things. He was the director's role model. Other director's we brought in were told to follow his lead. Of course he was right! "

A British traitor returns to his homeland and must be found before his former colleagues seek vengeance for his past betrayal. CI5's Ray Doyle (Martin Shaw) and George Cowley (Gordon Jackson) in this scene from A STIRRING OF DUST.

The storyline told of three British traitors called Furnell, MacNaught and Darby, who had long since defected to the Soviet bloc. The unknown fourth man was described as having to be rich, influential and a pillar of the establishment to have escaped detection for so long.

In *The Professionals* script, Guy Burgess, Donald Maclean and Kim Philby, the British diplomats who spied for the Soviet Union in World War II and early in the Cold War period, were called Furnell, MacNaught and Darby. The year after the episode was broadcast events in the real world followed the lead of *The Professionals* and Margaret Thatcher eventually exposed the real fourth man; the Queen's art advisor, Sir Anthony Blunt.

Both the opening and closing scenes of Bodie, Cowley and Doyle meeting the KGB's Yashinkov, were shot at the Chambers Wharf Cold Storage warehouse on Chambers Street, Bermondsey, South East London, which, at the time, was being used for storage by Courage Breweries.

Stuart Freeman (location manager): "The area was a mess. Derelict and defunct. The brewery allowed us all the time we needed to film our scenes. Although this included the warehouse, they were only using the grounds and so the emptiness called for by the director was achieved. I was familiar with the area after using it in *The Sweeney* as was the case with the park mansion (Stadden's office) at Leggatts Park, Potters Bar, Hertfordshire."

Actor Martin Shaw poses for a publicity shot during A STIRRING OF DUST.

Martin Shaw recalled a 'close shave' when Lewis Collins almost cut his finger off during a scene filmed on Friday 15th September at a house in Jesmond Avenue, Wembley, Middlesex.

Martin Shaw: "When the director, Martin Campbell, saw the blood he asked if I'd mind carrying on until they got the scene right as it was going so well, only then did they call a doctor to get it stitched. It all started while we were filming in a house in Wembley and I was being held captive. Lewis was using a knife to cut me free. The blade slipped under me as my hands were tied behind my back. I nearly lost a finger, stitches were called for, and there was blood all over the place."

The silver Ford Capri, driven by Bodie throughout this series, suffered minor damage when Lewis Collins mistimed a jump over the bonnet and, as witnessed in the final print, uses the car's bonnet as a stepping-stone! The damage that resulted was a nicely shaped imprint of Lewis Collins' sole on the bonnet.

Andrew Anderson (Ford Press Office): "It was only a minor dent. That was my claim to fame telling people that it was Bodie's footprint on the bonnet."

CI5 agent Bodie (Lewis Collins) leaps into action during scenes filmed in Wembley, Middlesex, for A STIRRING OF DUST.

Lewis Collins recalled that they were filming near two schools during these sequences in Wembley, and when those schools 'let-out' there were hundreds of children around the film crew and actors, but they behaved satisfactorily and kept 'out-of-camera' when told to. *The Professionals* stars shook a lot of hands and signed a lot of autographs that day!

Actors Martin Shaw and Lewis Collins take time out as THE PROFESSIONALS *Doyle and Bodie for a publicity shot on the set of A* STIRRING OF DUST.

Gladys Pearce (continuity): "I joined the production around this time. I was asked to do four days of second unit, which I thought would be car run-bys and double shots. It turned out to be shots with the three leads. I had only done a few days continuity on the Roger Moore feature *Escape To Athena*, in Rhodes when the continuity girl, Sue Merry, fell sick. After a day and a half on the second unit, I was asked to do a whole episode with director Martin Campbell. So I agreed and met with a friend of mine, Sally Jones, who'd worked on *The Eagle Has Landed* and *The Deep*. She gave me half a day's lesson in the basics and then I started this episode with Martin Campbell who, to this day, still finds it hard to believe that this was my first real job as continuity.

"He was a great director, and I recall he ran into a few problems while we were filming at Cadby Hall, Hammersmith. We had been set up to use one of the offices (Pulford's office), but for some unknown reason someone had forgotten to set-dress the room being used. Even the keys hadn't been left for us to get in. Valuable shooting time was lost as we waited for the key holder to arrive while desks and office furniture were drafted in courtesy of some of the workers in one of the other blocks. Martin was not happy at this set back, as he had to make sure to get the shots he wanted with very little rehearsal, which is something he was meticulous about - luckily both Martin (Shaw) and Lewis were so good in their roles by this stage, that it was achieved with the minimum of fuss."

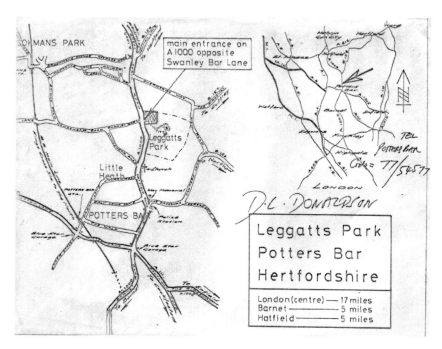

A STIRRING OF DUST: The original map attached to the movement order for filming at Leggatts Park, Hertfordshire between 18th-19th September. The Park Mansion was being used as the location for Brigadier Stadden's home.

Blind Run: *Bodie and Doyle run the gauntlet of car crashes and river shoot-outs when assigned to safeguard the enigmatic 'Mr. X' - an anonymous Arab diplomat pursued by equally anonymous assassins.*

Play Up! And Play The Game! was the next adventure in production, commencing on Tuesday 26th September. The title was taken from the English poet and historian Sir Henry Newbolt's poem, *Vitai Lampada*, but due to legal reasons on the use of the line, the script had to be changed to *Blind Run*. It was scripted by Canadian writer Ranald Graham, who had started his career writing the film *Shanks* (1974), followed by *Strange New World* (1975), on which he also served as the executive producer, before submitting storylines for *The Sweeney*.

Director Tom Clegg, born 16th October 1934, started out as an actor in the 1960's appearing in several Carry On films including the character Oddbod in *Carry On Screaming*. By the time he arrived on *The Professionals*, Clegg had already commanded the action on episodes of *Space: 1999*, *The Sweeney*, *Special Branch*, *Van Der Valk* and *Return Of The Saint*.

In BLIND RUN, Doyle (Martin Shaw) works alongside Leia played by British actress Jasmina Hilton. Born (13th February 1946) as Jasmina Hamzavi in London, she worked under her maiden name until 1969 and began her career at the Oxford Playhouse. Other theatre followed including appearances at the Dublin Drama Festival, Stratford, and the Comedy and Century Theatres in London.

Initial proceedings take place at George V Docks in North Woolwich, East London, with the Dockland streets being filmed around Kensal Town, West London. Bodie and Doyle escort Mr. X around Appleford Road, Southern Row, Hazlewood Crescent, Bosworth Road, Adair Road and Golborne Road before a dramatic tunnel shoot-out staged at Mill Hill, North West London.

Stuart Freeman (location manager): "We used the Kensal Town area a lot, simply because the area was due to be redeveloped and the streets were quite quiet. Also one of the safe houses they arrive at is Ockwells Manor in Maidenhead, which at that time was being used as the main location for the LWT series *Dick Turpin*, starring Richard O'Sullivan."

Filming the car scenes took slightly longer than anticipated due to the antics of the two stars and a mystery glove puppet, which was kept in the glove compartment of the car being used for filming.

Ann Ball (guest on set): "It is of course never seen by the camera. When they are out driving together in the car and the action is serious, they are usually alone with just a camera mounted on the door and the soundman in the boot, or back seat, screaming at them every time they hit bumps in the road! If Lew thinks Martin is over-acting, he will sneak his hand into the puppet and make fun at Martin by making the puppet pull grotesque faces at him, of course out of camera shot. Well, now, imagine such a serious scene with Gordon also in the car, stern faced, driving along, and the puppet pops up into camera-view pulling ridiculous faces. Lew says it was ludicrous, the tense spell was broken, and they have to stop laughing and start again all serious."

On Wednesday 11th October, Bodie and fellow agent Charlie lead the would-be assassins to South Lambeth Freight Yard, in the grounds of Battersea Power Station, South West London. Here a bullet ridden Austin Princess limousine (VLL 83G), driven by Bodie, smashes over a railway line and a pursuing Chrysler Valiant Cadillac (WXO 585) bursts into a ball of flames. This single scene took over a week to set up and reduced £15,000 worth of cars to scrap. Three hundred tiny explosives were fixed to the limousine to give the impression that the car was being riddled with bullets.

The scene was not written into the original script, but Menmuir's directive stipulating spectacular stunts, made script editor Gerry O'Hara insert the sequences quite late in the schedules. The original script had Bodie escaping into the forecourt of a police station and was written as follows:

Ext: Streets.
Bodie drives the Limo to the nearest Police Station. He spots a Taxi, leaps out of the Limo and runs across the road and hails it down.
Charlie gets out of the Limo, holds open the rear door and stands waiting. Then he walks up the steps into the Police Station.
The Middle Eastern gunmen walk up to the abandoned Limo - guns hidden. They look in and find nothing.
Int: Taxi.
BODIE (speaks into walkie-talkie): *This is Bodie calling C5 One. We have an emergency and I am reporting back to base.*

Although the various authorities had been informed of the recording at the freight yard, they were seemingly unaware of the size of the explosions being employed. Believing it to be an IRA attack, the fire brigade, numerous ambulances and police cars all converged at the location to discover a mass of camera and people associated with Mark 1 productions. First assistant director Peter Carter had to explain what had really happened.

Robin McDonald (focus puller): "The special effects guys broke every rule in the book with that one. In those days there wasn't as much 'red tape' as today; the production manager would simply make the call to the police, who had been pre-warned by the location manager weeks prior when scouting the area, telling them where filming was to take place, what requirements we needed, and away we went. It was that simple. No way could you do that today."

Mervyn Gerrard (sound assistant): "What an explosion that was. It really was dangerous; a passer-by called the fire brigade, thinking it was some sort of gas explosion or IRA siege. The fire engine turned up before realising we were on a film shoot. We'd usually inform the services of any filming taking place that would involve these kind of explosions - but I think everyone was so engrossed on getting the stunt right, that the first assistant had forgotten to phone the authorities. However, when the police arrived, they soon saw the funny side of the incident."

In the grounds of South Lambeth Freight Yard, London, Lewis Collins poses with the bullet ridden limousine driven by his character in BLIND RUN.

For BLIND RUN the Mark I production team set up a stunt to be filmed at South Lambeth Freight Yard, in the grounds of Battersea Power Station, South West London. Here, a bullet ridden Austin Princess limousine driven by Bodie (Lewis Collins), smashes over a railway line to a stand-still after being pursued by the enemy. This entire sequence was not part of the original script and added by script editor Gerry O' Hara to Ranald Graham's storyline.

Further publicity shots of Lewis Collins as Bodie during production of BLIND RUN.

Meanwhile, Doyle escapes to the second safe house, Stanmore Hall on Wood Lane, Stanmore, Middlesex. Only the entrance gates were used in the final print, as a fire between takes stopped any further filming. At short notice, first assistant director Peter Carter suggested Oakley Court, off Windsor Road, near Bray Film Studios as a replacement. The Grand Union Canal at Port A Bella Dock, Ladbroke Grove, West London, provides the escape from here as Bodie joins Doyle, after seconding Phillipa's canal boat. Trouble ensues as the raiders also attempt to board the vessel.

Frank Henson (stunt arranger): "We had a stunt guy, Romo Garrara (sometimes credited as Gorrara), who had to fall in the water from the boat, but he decided he didn't want to fall in or get wet. In the end I said to him, he had to do something. Del Baker fell in and he didn't complain, so in the end Romo did it.

"Problems continued as the boat then sprung a leak and it was down to the crew on board to bail out the water, before they could navigate it safely to dry land."

With the boat seaworthy again, the next shot to be filmed involved a fast escape by boat with Collins navigating. It required Martin Shaw to catch Collins and his Arab fugitives, and to do this it meant jumping onto the boat just as it drew away. Shaw rehearsed the jump several times, and then it was action! He almost missed his footing and narrowly escaped falling into the water! However, he badly skimmed his shin when leaping onto the boat and had to receive medical attention on the bank before filming could continue. The unit nurse, Susan Michael, attended to Shaw's wound, which had to be bandaged to prevent further damage, causing him to continue the days shooting with a slight limp.

Martin Shaw: "I've always done what stunts I could do myself. That comes from my drama school, one of the reasons that LAMDA was the best drama school in the country. They covered a very wide spectrum. They believe an actor is an instrument and any instrument has to be well tuned and well made. So we were taught film and stage-fighting, how to fall, how to take and throw a punch. Right from the start of my career I wanted to make the fullest use of this training and vowed to make any action scenes I had to do look better than average."

In BLIND RUN Bodie (Lewis Collins) and Doyle are assigned to protect a foreign official who is on a secret visit to Britain. But already possible enemy assassins appear to know his, and CI5's, every next move. Pictured here with her back to the camera is actress Sandra Payne who played Phillipa. Born (24th September 1944) in Royston, Hertfordshire, she is best known for her roles as Christine Harris in TRIANGLE and Marion Ballard in WAITING FOR GOD.

Both actors put the bruising down to the time spent lounging around in between shooting scenes.

Lewis Collins: "The producers always said we didn't require caravan dressing because we were working full-time and non-stop, all day. But that wasn't true. We found ourselves lying on floors all over the place, trying to get a kip, waiting for a set-up to be ready, the sun to come out, or whatever."

Martin Shaw: "Then we'd go straight into sudden bursts of activity. That was how we hurt ourselves, pulling muscles or whatever. We were both sort of languid, sitting or lying around, then we'd be off again for a minute or two..."

He used his guru meditation techniques to steel himself before he attempted any dangerous action.

"It was the waiting that could get to you. It would take hours to set up stunts and I would spend that time knowing I had to do it and not a double. That's exhilarating. With the tension building I would think of all the things that could go wrong, my meditation used to help me with those worries."

Meanwhile, the same day, the production office supplied the wrong car to the location resulting in Bodie driving Doyle's Escort RS2000. He is seen rushing to Doyle's aid at Stanmore Hall, and over the canal bridge near Ladbroke Grove, where he takes over Phillipa's canal boat.

The escape from the boat was filmed at Cadby Hall, Hammersmith, West London, where one of Lewis Collins' stunts was running across a plank between two factory roofs.

Lewis Collins: "Definitely brown bread time if I fell off. That was pretty hair-raising. Tom Clegg banned me from doing it at first. They put a stunt man, Del Baker, in my place, the plank had to fall and he had to grab for the edge. I argued a bit, well, I wanted to do it, you know. But all the directors were against us trying stunts, well it's their necks on the block if we get injured. So they shot it with Del, then set it up for me and did it all over again. I did it. I really had to move to get over that thing. No net. No wire. No nothing, just a long way down if I missed the edge. I think the end result looked pretty good."

The fight scenes along the canal, and the incident at Cadby Hall, were not part of the original script. In the first draft, when Bodie and Doyle discover that the person they are protecting is not Hanish, they safely escort him to the rendezvous. When they arrive at the docks, the place is crawling with raiders. Bodie drives the van to the water's edge and Doyle hurtles the man into the waiting launch.

An out-take from this episode (filmed at Cadby Hall) has been aired on Denis Norden's *It'll Be Alright On The Night* programmes. Doyle jumps into the back of a Ford Transit van, but loses his balance, as the vehicle rapidly accelerates away, and he falls out backwards through the back doors onto the ground. What the cameras didn't pick up were the roars of laughter and load clapping as Shaw tumbled.

Vernon Layton (lighting cameraman): "Well, it was Martin wasn't it? He did jump to his feet almost instantly and performed some karate kicks for our stills guy, Ted Hawes, just to prove he was okay. Ted was usually around to catch all the funnier antics of the stars on film."

Lewis Collins: "In reality I'd secretly bet Martin that I could get away before he could jump in. I succeeded three times, before they got it right on the fourth take."

Director Tom Clegg and the rest of the production crew were unaware of the duo's little bet, and stuntman Peter Brayham offered his view on why Martin Shaw fell out of the van:

Peter Brayham (stuntman): "It happened because by this stage they were trying to save money so they didn't want a stunt arranger on this episode. They thought they could do it themselves and that's what happens. I would have secured the doors with ropes from the inside so when Shaw entered they could be pulled shut."

The final scene, which was ultimately filmed at the docks, had originally been set in a hospital, where Leia is being treated for her arm wound. In the corridor Cowley explains that he knew Hanish was a fake.

Phillipa's phone number (485 6325), which she repeats to Bodie on two occasions was later cut from all the prints when it was discovered that the number given was indeed a real number, and the occupant began receiving calls from younger fans of the show in search of their hero Bodie.

Networked transmissions of the second series began on the 7th October with *Hunter/Hunted* (this was the first outing for Ray Menmuir's new title sequence). The ITV Network controllers moved the series to 9.00 pm Saturday nights to start before, and hopefully take viewers away from, *Starsky & Hutch* on BBC1, which had started two weeks earlier. A deliberate move on LWT's part, as the series was originally planned to be screened from January 1979, but when the BBC replaced *Starsky & Hutch* for a week with equestrian programming, the recently appointed director of programmes at LWT, Michael Grade, saw his chance and brought transmissions forward, leading to newspaper headlines like 'ITV Bring In The Big Guns'.

Fall Girl: *Bodie finds himself as a pawn in an espionage game, when following an assassination attempt, fingerprints are taken from the butt of a video game rifle and he is arrested*

The following episode in production, *Fall Girl*, originally planned as the shows only two-parter, commenced on Monday 16th October, with another Ranald Graham script. Making it a Canadian benefit, William Brayne directed, and cast Pamela Salem as the mysterious fall girl Marrika. She had already appeared as Doyle's ex-girlfriend in *The Female Factor*, the previous year.

With an immense cache of television series to her name, Pamela Salem turned to film starring in the award-winning *Shadows* by Leslie Suesser and *The Great Train Robbery*, before making *Suez Of Gold* with Ian McShane. Born (22nd January 1950) in Bombay, India, she was educated at Heidelberg University and later at the Central School of Speech and Drama in London.

Pamela Salem (Marikka): "I had to work hard at Marikka's English/German accent as Lewis Collins and I have a running dialogue when he is cornered 300-feet up, on top of a gasometer and I'm at the bottom, projection is the ultimate test of an accent. The thing was, I couldn't get rid of it for weeks! It took a trip to the United States where we all tried to be 'Super-Brits' to exorcise it."

In FALL GIRL CI5's Bodie (Lewis Collins) is re-acquainted with a former girlfriend when she shows up in London, but finds himself on the run from his own colleagues and forced to take refuge on top of a gasometer.

Colin Dandridge (boom operator): "On several occasions the actor managed to lose his footing at the top of the gasometer while he ran from side-to-side; the camera and sound crew were supplied with plenty of safety gear, but Lewis had to manage without due to the scenes being filmed."

Lewis Collins on location for FALL GIRL, where production saw filming at the top of a gasometer at Southall Gas Works, Middlesex.

Location manager Stuart Freeman had elected to use a house in Orbel Street, Battersea as Doyle's residence. But one problem that the production team hadn't foreseen was the amount of noise coming from the nearby road, carrying lorries and tankers to and from South London.

Colin Dandridge (boom operator): "Doyle's house was just off Battersea High Street and, being very close to the main road, it proved very noisy for sound. We had terrible trouble and several sequences had to be filmed over and over again."

Bodie is taken to a police station made up at Cadby Hall and escapes from here to Southall Gas Works, Middlesex, where he takes refuge on top of a

300-feet gasometer. To help Lewis Collins get used to the heights that he would be working at stunt arranger Frank Henson walked him around the top of the gasometers to acclimatise him prior to the commencement of filming. But Collins wasn't the only one who needed guiding; the sound and camera crew were also both working at great heights.

Martin Shaw poses for a rare off-duty shot during filming of the story FALL GIRL at Southall Gas Works, Middlesex.

Vernon Layton (lighting cameraman): "It was a very frightening experience working on *Fall Girl* - the camera crew were at the top of a 'Moonshot' cherry picker for much of the time and the sound crew were on the gas holder with Lewis. It took quite a while to get the equipment set up compared with the usual sequences we'd become familiar with on the show. The first few hours were spent just getting the cameras and lighting to the top of the gas holder. And then the director had to be happy with what we'd shot. We were all glad to get down after spending virtually hours in the clouds on, what was, a freezing cold day."

Howard Baker (camera clapper/loader): "Yeah, and I was the guy that had to lumber the equipment up and down the ladder to the top of the gasometer. I was knackered and we spent a fair few days filming there!"

Bodie's instinct melts with his heart when an old girlfriend from the East appears leaving Doyle to pick up the pieces. Publicity shots of Martin Shaw, as Ray Doyle, on the set of FALL GIRL.

Backtrack: *Burglar Sammy Blaydon is killed for knowing too much. Bodie and Doyle set off on a trail which leads to an embassy with a sinister secret.*

Don Houghton's screenplay *Backtrack* commenced principle filming on Monday 30th October, under the direction of 32-year old Christopher King. Born (20th June 1946) in the West Midlands town of Stafford, he had never worked in filmed television before, but would go on to a chequered career in this genre.

The leads were prevented from doing any dangerous sports or pastimes in case they were in any way injured, and production on the series had to be stopped; in fact their contracts included such a stipulation.

However, Lewis Collins had always wanted to do a parachute drop and that weekend, the same time as bonfire night, on Sunday 5th November, he did just that.

The location manager's original 'recce' shots of Warfield Hall, Forest Road, Warfield, Berkshire, used as Sir Lionel's residence in BACKTRACK.

It's just another routine house break-in for a cat burglar, until he accidentally uncovers a complex drugs smuggling operation. Martin Shaw on the set of BACKTRACK.

Lewis Collins: "Some kids want to be engine drivers, others want to be firemen. But me, I've always wanted to be a paratrooper. So as soon as I had a bit of money and some spare time, I went to Peterborough Parachute School, Cambridgeshire, to take a weekend course. And I can tell you that the reality of a parachute jump turned out far differently from anything I imagined in my fantasies.

"It's the most frightening thing I've ever done in my life. But I must add that's it's the most exhilarating experience I've ever had. The training course started on Saturday morning with all the eager pupils swinging on harnesses, learning how to roll and being lectured on techniques. The final talk was about all the things that could go wrong. That got me thinking. I had a fairly sleepless night after that one. Sunday was the big day. As I put on my kit I noticed that everyone looked a shade paler. The regular jumpers tried to cheer us up with little hints and tips, such as 'put your right foot on your left and clasp your hands together above your head and it will be easier for us to screw you out of the ground afterwards'.

"In the morning, the wind was too strong for parachuting so we all had to wait around. After lunch, I discovered that two thirds of the trainees, the sensible ones, had thought better of it and gone home. Just as we were beginning to think that the weather might force the rest of us to join them, a hole appeared in the cloud just big enough for us to drop ourselves through. It was 4.30pm by this time and getting dark. We were given a last chance of refusal, the instructors explaining that the only way out of the planes once we were in it was through a hole in the side. It was a lunatic situation and I was terrified. But I was determined to jump. Just before the jump the pilot cut the engines. Anyone who has jumped will know what I mean when I say that the most eerie feeling in the world is gliding along in silence, legs dangling in space, knowing that any second you are actually going to do something that could kill you.

"Then I pushed myself out and there I was dropping 2,500-feet like a stone. The chute opens automatically and we'd been taught to count to four seconds before looking up to check that we wouldn't need the emergency chute. I was petrified. I couldn't wait that long. I was checking at two seconds. During those first seconds, I felt completely disoriented and while I didn't black out, it's fair to say I 'greyed out'. I came to my senses only when the chute had fully opened and I was pointing straight down. Everything below me looked like coloured handkerchiefs. Then suddenly, in far less time than I had taken, and much faster than I had anticipated, the ground appeared to be rushing towards me. I landed with a thump. I remember feeling terribly shocked, then I felt the pain. I had broken my ankle.

"I was only about 100-metres off target. As I discovered later, I should have a 32-feet chute for my weight, not a 28-footer. I couldn't blame the club though; I'd picked the chute. I thought I was perfectly positioned too but can't have had my feet together. My ankle went underneath me and I jarred my spine a bit."

Unlucky Break....Lewis Collins with his leg in plaster on the set of BACKTRACK.

The Newspaper headline and blurb read: BUSTED - A TV TOUGHIE: TV tough guy Lewis Collins was feeling distinctly fragile on Tuesday (7-11-78). The seemingly indestructible star of THE PROFESSIONALS was in a plastercast with a broken ankle. Lewis, 32, came a cropper when he joined in a game of football while visiting his home in Liverpool. He will be out of action for six weeks, holding up production on the £1 million TV series.

The end result was that Collins arrived on location at Ledbury Road, Notting Hill, West London, to continue work with a very heavy limp and told producer Ray Menmuir he had done it while playing football at a friends wedding. This was not true, as it was co-star Martin Shaw who had gone to a wedding that weekend, so suspicion was already on Mark I's minds. It seemed that some of the crew also knew the truth:

Vernon Layton (lighting cameraman): "Lewis had asked me on the Friday to do the stills at the jump. I told him I'd love to, but we'd just had our first child and I wanted to be home with my wife, but told him his secret was safe with me. When I arrived on the Monday, Peter Carter, the assistant director, told me Collins had gone to hospital to get his ankle checked out and shouldn't be that long."

Roy P. Stevens (second assistant director): "Lewis was taking ages, so I went to see how he was getting on, and get him back to the set as soon as possible. When I got there his ankle was in plaster and he could hardly stand. He was so upset, he didn't know what would happen."

With one of the leads out of action, the remainder of the days filming was abandoned and guest star Michael Elphick took the cast and crew to the nearest public house, the 'Duke Of Cornwall'. The following day (Tuesday 7th November) production was suspended all together.

On Friday 10th November, the crew was given two weeks notice and production was suspended:

Donald Toms (Production Manager) to all crew members: As a result of Mr. Lewis Collins's accident, it is with very much regret that, as from today's date, we have to give you two weeks' notice of the termination of your engagement with the company, in accordance with Clause 30 (Force Majeure) of the FPA/ACTT Agreement.

On behalf of the Company, we would like to take this opportunity of thanking you for all your help and cooperation during the shooting period, and hope that we shall be able to work together again when the series is resumed.

The press wasted no time in reporting the story and the 'Sunday Mirror' newspaper devoted space to the incident that following weekend, on the 12th November.

Ron Purdie (first assistant director): "It was a silly thing to do and put us out of work up to Christmas. We could have sued him under the contract clause. We didn't of course, and Lewis Collins sent apology notes to all the crew members, stating how brainless he had been to do such a thing - which was the least he could have done!"

Lewis Collins had written the original letter to producer Raymond Menmuir on Thursday 9th, and asked that it be passed on to all the members of the crew. The letter was duly dispatched on Monday 13th.

However, the incident had not only postponed production, but also the winners of a competition held by Fab 208 magazine were disappointed that they were unable to attend a days shooting on the set.

Seventeen-year-old Hilary Jones, from Manchester, had won the Swiss Bio-facial 'Meet The Professionals' contest in a competition held in the magazine on 10th and 17th June earlier in the year.

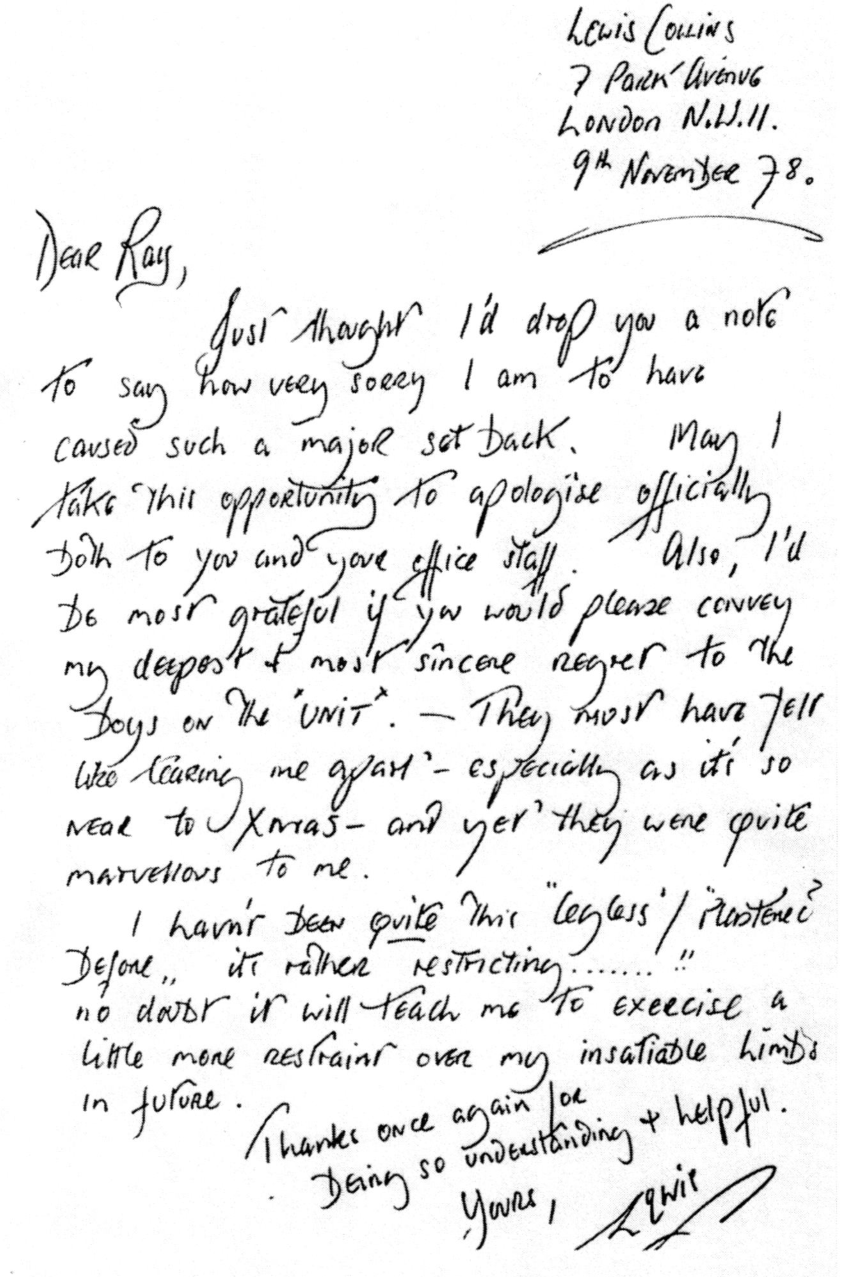

> Lewis Collins
> 7 Park Avenue
> London N.W.11.
> 9th November 78.

Dear Ray,

Just thought I'd drop you a note to say how very sorry I am to have caused such a major set back. May I take this opportunity to apologise officially both to you and your office staff. Also, I'd be most grateful if you would please convey my deepest & most sincere regret to the boys on the "UNIT". — They must have felt like tearing me apart — especially as it's so near to Xmas — and yet they were quite marvellous to me.

I havn't been quite this "legless"/plastered before,, it's rather restricting........" no doubt it will teach me to exercise a little more restraint over my insatiable limbs in future. Thanks once again for being so understanding & helpful.

Yours, Lewis

Lewis Collins original letter sent to producer Ray Menmuir after he had caused production on THE PROFESSIONALS to come to a stand-still!

Both Martin Shaw and Lewis Collins were disappointed not to be able to meet Hilary and her friend Pamela, that they put their heads together and came up with another idea: They would take the girls to lunch at their favourite haunt in London's West End. Collins hopped along, his leg encased in plaster, to meet up with his fellow co-star and the two girls.

Having only completed ten out of thirteen episodes (with the next two scripts, *Servant Of Two Masters*, scheduled for filming from November 13th and *The Madness Of Mickey Hamilton*, both at the location scheduling stage), and under pressure from LWT, Mark I considered writing Bodie out of the series temporarily.

Brian Clemens: "One of the ideas I incorporated into my original format was that it said, its got Cowley and his team, and Bodie and Doyle are the two we focus on. But always at the back of my mind was this idea that if we sold the series to the American market, and they said 'Can we put an American character in it?' or if one of the boys became difficult, or left, we could have brought in someone else within weeks. I mean, *The Professionals* was not called Bodie and Doyle; it was about the entire squad, so that idea would have worked. Again, when Lewis broke his ankle, I believe we could have worked his injury into the script. After all, this was an action series, so if one of the leads played two or three stories with his leg in plaster, it would have made an interesting and believable storyline."

However, producer Ray Menmuir and LWT decided to wait until Lewis Collins was fully fit before filming would start again. The inclusion of a new character would have caused some problems regarding sales abroad, as being a film series of the Seventies *The Professionals* was designed to be shown in any order and not affect continuity, some countries, therefore, may not have taken the 'Bodieless' episodes.

Trevor Puckle (unit runner): "We held the end of series party at Lee Studios on Stage D. Lewis turned up on crutches. Everyone had forgiven him by then; but he still seemed terribly embarrassed at putting us all out of work for the next month or so."

There was never any doubt that the show would return for another series and shooting recommenced on Monday 12th March 1979, though not on *Backtrack*. The entire third series followed, back to back. Meanwhile, the series had won the battle of the ratings with *Starsky & Hutch*, but with the audience split over the two action shows the average figure for *The Professionals* had dropped to 14.25 million.

SERIES II EPISODE GUIDE

CI5's Ray Doyle (Martin Shaw) is asked to field test a new gun, which is subsequently stolen from his flat. Explosive action in HUNTER/HUNTED.

ROGUE

by **Dennis Spooner**
© Copyright Mark 1 Productions Ltd MCMLXXVIII

Barry Martin	Glyn Owen
Maggie Briggs	Pamela Stephenson
Paul Culbertson	Tony Steedman
David Hunter	Neil Hallett
Steve Ballard	Robert Gillespie
Doctor in Mortuary	Teddy Green
CI5 Girl	Diana Weston
Old Chinaman	Andy Ho
Geronimo	Larrington Walker
Doctor in Hospital	Athar Malik
Policeman	Martyn Whitby
Uncredited	
Ticket Inspector (Train station)	John Sharp
CI5 Agent	Gerry Paris
Lady in hospital waiting room	Pat Astley
Man outside Pub	Cy Town
Ship's Captain	Guy Standeven
Crewman	Frederick Marks

Director: **Ray Austin**

COWLEY and David Hunter, Head of Special Branch, have been working closely together in conditions of the greatest secrecy to bring about the arrest and conviction of a major criminal, Paul Culbertson, who has for many years contrived to escape justice. A witness called Steve Ballard is found who is willing to testify against Culbertson, but Ballard is shot dead as he arrives to meet the two department heads. Hunter asks Cowley how the details of Ballard's arrival could have been known by his killer, but Cowley insists that only a few of his men knew about the details. The two men decide to bring in for questioning one of Ballard's associates, Alex Bolt, who is the last possible witness against Culbertson, and Bodie and Doyle are sent to bring Bolt from his home.

Barry Martin, one of the toughest men in CI5, is with them. Martin is superbly fit and an able fighter and has been a close friend of Cowley's since the war. He suggests that he should go up the fire-escape to Bolt's flat while Bodie and Doyle use the stairs. Before Bodie and Doyle reach Bolt's flat, Martin has hurled Bolt out of a window to his death, and managed to inflict a flesh wound on his own arm with a knife. Martin tells his associates that Bolt attacked him with the knife as he entered from the fire-escape and in the ensuing struggle Bolt fell to his death. Cowley is extremely displeased that his sole remaining witness against Culbertson has died, and he questions Bodie and Doyle very closely about the exact circumstances of his death.

In ROGUE, a CI5 agent murders a trial witness, and then puts Cowley in hospital...Doyle (Martin Shaw) and Bodie (Lewis Collins) find themselves pitted against a ruthless adversary as well trained as they are! The agents 'exercise' scenes with Barry Martin were filmed at Vale Farm Sports Centre, Sudbury, Harrow - not far from the production unit base of Lee International Studios.

Cowley becomes suspicious about Martin's role in the affair, particularly as Martin was present at the original briefing on Ballard and could have been responsible for his death too. After Bolt's death, Martin goes to hospital to have his wound dressed and then goes home. Culbertson is waiting for him and is angry at the precipitate action that Martin has taken in killing Ballard and Bolt. Martin explains that although his own work for Culbertson has not been extensive, he did not want his involvement brought into the open, and was forced to silence the men. Culbertson asserts that Martin's actions have laid him open to suspicion and have exposed Culbertson's entire organisation to danger and, when Martin demands money for killing Ballard and Bolt, Culbertson refuses.

Later that evening, Cowley visits Martin and accuses him of working for Culbertson. Cowley cannot understand why his friend should descend to such treachery, but Martin explains bitterly that his only chance of achieving a good living standard for himself was by working for Culbertson. Angered by his friend's treachery, Cowley attempts to arrest Martin, but the man easily overpowers Cowley and throws him down the stairs from his flat.

Martin goes to Culbertson and asks him to arrange his escape, which he does; Martin is booked to leave the country secretly the next day on a ship called the Pole Star. The CI5 men visit Maggie Briggs, Martin's girlfriend, at her flat, but Martin eludes them there and again in an underground car park. A chance remark leads them to Culbertson's home. Despite eluding their questions Bodie sees a model of a ship and realises that, as Culbertson is suspected of importing drugs and illegal immigrants, Martin will try to leave on one of Culbertson's ships. Bodie and Doyle arrive at London docks, but Martin throws a knife at Bodie, which lodges in his arm, so Doyle takes careful aim at the retreating figure of Martin. But before Doyle can fire, Martin falls dead; he has been shot from the ship under Culbertson's orders. The vessel becomes part of the enquiry and Cowley, from his hospital bed, tells Bodie and Doyle that the Captain admitted the shooting and implicated Culbertson.

Production Unit

Created by	Brian Clemens
Executive Producers	Albert Fennell, Brian Clemens
Music	Laurie Johnson
Producer	Raymond Menmuir
Associate Producer	Chris Burt
Script Editor	Gerry O'Hara
Production Manager	Donald Toms
Assistant Director	Ray Corbett
Location Managers	Stuart Freeman, Cecil Ford
Continuity	Cheryl Leigh
Casting	Maggie Cartier
Production Designer	Malcolm Middleton
Art Director	Peter Joyce
Stunt Arranger	Peter Brayham
Wardrobe Supervisor	Masada Wilmot
Lighting Cameraman	Tony Imi
Camera Operator	Tony White
Make Up	Alan Brownie
Hairdresser	Barbara Ritchie
Supervising Editor	John S. Smith
Sound Recordist	David Crozier
Music Supervisor	Christopher Palmer
Dubbing Editor	Peter Lennard
Dubbing Mixer	Hugh Strain
Music Editor	Alan Willis

An Avengers MARK 1 Production For LONDON WEEKEND TELEVISION

Shooting / Location Schedule

Production Dates: Monday 5th to Friday 16th June, 1978. Production Number: 9D11230

5 June **London Railway Terminus**: Platform 9-10, Paddington Train Station, Eastbourne Terrace, London, W2

	London Railway - British Transport Police offices: Platform 1, Paddington Train Station, London, W2
	Chinese Take-Away: Satay House Malaysian Restaurant, 13 Sale Place, Paddington, London, W2
6 June	***Sports Centre / Gym***: Vale Farm Sports Centre, Watford Road, Sudbury, Harrow, Middlesex
	Street: Doyle's car & Newsagent: Forbuoys Newsagent, 209 Watford Road, Sudbury, Harrow, Middlesex
7 June	***London Mansion Block - Alex Bolt's flat***: Hurlingham Court, Ranelagh Gardens, Hurlingham, London, SW6
8 June	***Hospital: Int / Ext: Barry Martin & Int: Cowley***: Wexham Park Hospital, Wexham Road, Stoke Green, Slough, Berkshire
9 June	***Barry Martin's Apartment***: 28 Phoenix Lodge Mansions, Shepherd's Bush Road, Brook Green, London, W6
	Pub: The Blue Anchor, 13 Lower Mall, Hammersmith, London, W6
	Sports Centre car park ('pick-up' shot): Hammersmith Club Society Limited car park, Kent House, Rutland Grove, Hammersmith, London, W6
	Int / Ext: Cowley's car: Gunnersbury Avenue / Great West Road, Gunnersbury, London, W4
12-13 June	***Int / Ext: Doyle's car (radio)***: Aynhoe Road / Blythe Road, Hammersmith, London, W14
	London street (Edge Street): Brook Green (Shepherds Bush Road junction), Hammersmith, London, W14
	Ext: Hospital: Doyle's car / GLC Mortuary: Cadby Hall, Blythe Road, Hammersmith, London, W14
	Underground Car Park / Streets: Elgin Estate car park, Chippenham Road, Maida Hill, London, W9
14 June	***Culbertson's House***: High Cannons, Buckettsland Lane, Borehamwood, Hertfordshire
	Ext: Newsagent street ('pick-up' shot): Shenley Road (near Grosvenor Road), Borehamwood, Hertfordshire
15 June	***Maggie Briggs' house & street***: Flat 5, 23 Christchurch Avenue, Brondesbury, London, NW6
	Int: Doyle's car - Newsagent ('pick-up' shot): Christchurch Avenue, Brondesbury, London, NW6
16 June	***London Docks***: West India Docks, Manchester Road, Isle Of Dogs, London, E14
	Coffee Stall-Van: Manchester Road (Marsh Wall), Isle Of Dogs, London, E14

HUNTER/HUNTED

by **Anthony Read**
© Copyright Mark 1 Productions Ltd MCMLXXVIII

Kathie	Cheryl Kennedy
Preston	Bryan Marshall
Brownie	John Stratton
Maurice Richards	Tony Caunter
Ruth	Diana Weston
Martell	Frank Barrie
Jack	Martin Wyldeck
Forensic Man	Malcolm Hayes
West Indian Woman	Jeillo Edwards
Singer	Maria St Clare
Jo	Vicki Michelle
Uncredited	
CI5 man	Del Baker
CI5 man	Romo Gorrara
CI5 man	Terry Plummer
CI5 man	Jerry Baker
CI5 recruit	Colin Skeaping
Pianist	Betty Lawrence
Man in Pub	Bobby Ramsey

Director: **Anthony Simmons**

COWLEY asks Bodie and Doyle to test a new gun, the American 180 automatic rifle, which has enormous destructive power, long range and a new type of aiming device: the gun produces a red laser beam and when the beam touches its target, the gun can be fired accurately without further checking. Doyle and Bodie try out the gun in various situations and keep it in a locked cupboard in Doyle's flat when it is not in use. One night, Doyle takes an attractive policewoman, Kathie Mason, to a riverside pub owned by a former policeman named Maurice Richards. Later, Doyle drives Kathie home and spends the night at her flat. Kathie is hoping to join CI5, and knows that Doyle and Bodie are testing the new rifle for Cowley. The following morning, as Doyle drives away, he finds that the brakes and steering of his car have been tampered with; he manages to slow the car to a halt and jump out. Seconds later, the car explodes.

The car's remains are examined by a CI5 expert who tells Doyle that whoever fixed the car and attached the bomb to it did not want to kill Doyle, but to scare him: there was a thirty-second delay fuse on the bomb to allow time for Doyle to jump clear. Concerned, Doyle returns home and finds that the 180 rifle has been stolen. Cowley is furious that Doyle allowed this to happen and suggests that whoever knew that Doyle was spending the night at Kathie's flat fixed his car and used his absence to steal the rifle. Bodie and Doyle go to see Martell, a gun dealer but he has heard nothing about the gun.

Cast in the part of Preston in HUNTER/HUNTED was Bryan Marshall. Born (19th May 1938) in London, England, he is of Irish descent and was educated at the Salesian College, Battersea, South West London. Bryan studied drama at RADA, before appearing at the Bristol Old Vic and in repertory theatre. He soon made an impression working for Hammer studios in QUATERMASS AND THE PITT, and THE WITCHES, and in 1983 emigrated to Australia where he continues to act in various film and tv projects.

As they leave to visit Brownie, an informer, a sniper's bullet narrowly misses Doyle and his partner becomes alarmed when Doyle refuses to go under cover - even though he knows that sooner or later someone will make a second attempt on his life. Brownie is unable to produce any more information than Martell. Maurice Richards tries to ring Doyle, but he is shot dead in his pub.

An autopsy reveals that a bullet from a 180 rifle killed Richards, and Cowley decides that whoever killed the former policeman was also to blame for the attempt on Doyle's life. From the CI5 files, Cowley discovers that Preston, a policeman who was convicted for corruption by Richards and Doyle, and has recently been released from prison, is the most likely suspect. They find Preston living a seemingly quiet life with no intentions for revenge. Later, Doyle gets a call from Brownie asking him to meet him at a deserted dock, claiming he has some information regarding the 180 rifle.

Actress Diana Weston played 'CI5 girl' Ruth Pettifer in HUNTER/HUNTED. Born (13th November 1955) in Toronto, Canada, she is the grandchild of the Canadian Army soldier Charles Basil Price, and is fondly remembered as Caroline Wheatley in 94 episodes of THE UPPER HAND, which ran on UK tv from 1990-1996.

Meanwhile, Bodie and Cowley have made a remarkable discovery at Preston's home in the form of Kathie Mason. She was secretly married to Preston before his conviction and has been helping him gain his revenge on Doyle by befriending him. It was the information about Kathie's marriage to Preston that Maurice Richards had tried to pass on to Doyle after seeing Doyle and Kathie in his pub on their evening out. Bodie 'convinces' Kathie to tell him where Doyle can be found. At the docks, Preston has used Brownie as bait in order to trap Doyle. Meanwhile, Bodie has borrowed a 180 from Martell and focuses the red light onto Preston. Seeing the red light and realising that he is an open target, Preston lays down his gun and surrenders.

Production Unit

Created by	Brian Clemens
Executive Producers	Albert Fennell, Brian Clemens
Music	Laurie Johnson
Producer	Raymond Menmuir
Associate Producer	Chris Burt
Script Editor	Gerry O'Hara
Production Manager	Donald Toms
Assistant Director	Derek Whitehurst
Location Managers	Stuart Freeman, Cecil Ford
Continuity	Cheryl Leigh
Casting	Maggie Cartier
Production Designer	Malcolm Middleton
Art Director	Peter Joyce
Stunt Arranger	Peter Brayham
Wardrobe Supervisor	Masada Wilmot
Lighting Cameraman	Philip Meheux
Camera Operator	Tony White
Make Up	Alan Brownie
Hairdresser	Barbara Ritchie
Supervising Editor	John S. Smith
Editor	Alan Killick
Sound Recordist	David Crozier
Music Supervisor	Christopher Palmer
Dubbing Editor	Peter Lennard
Dubbing Mixer	Hugh Strain
Music Editor	Alan Willis

An Avengers MARK 1 Production For LONDON WEEKEND TELEVISION

Shooting / Location Schedule

Production Dates: Monday 19th to Friday 30th June, 1978. Production Number: 9D11231

19 June	**CI5 training grounds & HQ**: Palace Of Engineering, Olympic Way, Wembley, Middlesex
20 June	**Car chase**: A40M: Westway (White City flyover) / Wood Lane, White City, London, W12
	Preston's House: 14 The Fairway, East Acton, London, W3
	Int: Cowley's car (route to Preston's house): Western Avenue / Old Oak Common Lane, Acton, London, W3
21 June	**Doyle's flat**: Cliff Road Studios, Cliff Road, Camden, London, NW1
22-23 June	**Tunnel: Doyle's car**: Rotherhithe tunnel, Rotherhithe, London, E1 / SE16
	Maurice Richards Pub / Bridge / Streets: The Gun, 27 Cold Harbour, Isle Of Dogs, Poplar, London, E14

26 June	***Street / footpath***: Doyle & Kathie: Preston's Road, Isle Of Dogs, London, E14 ***Gunman (pub target)***: off Tunnel Avenue / Drawdock Road, North Greenwich, London, SE10 ***Kathie's flat***: The Pryors, East Heath Road, Hampstead, London, NW3 ***Doyle loses control of car***: East Heath Road, Hampstead Heath, London, NW3
27 June	***Doyle's car explosion***: Portland Road / Hippodrome Mews, Notting Hill, London, W11 ***Int: CI5 Records***: Cadby Hall, Blythe Road, Hammersmith, London, W14
28-30 June	***Brownie's cabin cruiser / Docks***: Poplar Dock, Preston's Road, London, E14 / East India Dock, East India Dock, London, E14 ***Montgomery's house***: 4 Stewart Street, Isle Of Dogs, London, E14
30 June	***Music Hall Pub***: Waterman's Arms, 1 Glenaffric Avenue, Isle Of Dogs, London, E14 ***Ferry meeting (with Martell)***: 'James Newman' - the Woolwich Free Ferry, Pier Road, North Woolwich, London, E1 ***Streets: Doyle's car (Jaguar) - Porsche run-by (raining)***: Pier Road, North Woolwich, London, E1

Martin Shaw, Gordon Jackson, and Lewis Collins find themselves on location at the Palace of Engineering, Wembley, Middlesex in HUNTER/HUNTED.

FIRST NIGHT
by **Gerry O'Hara**
© Copyright Mark 1 Productions Ltd MCMLXXVIII

Kidnapper 1 (Frank)	Tony Vogel
Kidnapper 2 (John)	David Howey
Biebermann	Arnold Diamond
Harvey	Julian Holloway
Minister	John Nettleton
Hirschfield	George Pravda
Arab Diplomat	Nadim Sawalha
Local Police Chief	John York
CI5 Girl	Diana Weston
Kidnapper 3 (Mac)	Robert Hamilton
Divorcee	Brenda Cavendish
Blonde WPC	Pearl Ann Turner
2nd WPC	Susan Derrick
Debra	Jean Gilpin
Soldier	John Patrick
Marksman	Jack Elliott
Uncredited	
1st Plain clothes Policeman	Terry Yorke
2nd Plain clothes Policeman	Eric Kent
Uniformed Policeman	John Cannon
Uniformed Policeman	Pat Gorman
Uniformed Policeman	Reg Turner
Metropolitan Operations Policeman	Ron Gregory
Canteen Policeman	Guy Standeven
1st Pretty Girl (Jane Anderson)	Sara Walkden
2nd Pretty Girl (Tennis partner)	Carla Wansey
Boffin	Terence McGinty

Director: **David Wickes**

AN important Israeli Minister, Asher Biebermann, is visiting London under strict security. Nevertheless, a gang of kidnappers surprises him and his guards on the South Bank outside Festival Hall one evening and manage to drag him away in a mini-hovercraft. Police launches and police guarding the riverbanks pursue the hovercraft, but Biebermann is swiftly transferred to a helicopter by the kidnappers. A major air search is immediately put in motion, but before the helicopter can be followed or traced, it lands in a field near London and Biebermann is taken to an insignificant suburban house and locked away. Because of the Minister's importance, and the possible political nature of the kidnapping, CI5 are brought in, but Cowley warns his superiors that since the kidnappers have vanished with their victim, CI5 will have to await developments.

Hovercrafts, helicopters, and masked kidnappers cause problems for THE PROFESSIONALS in FIRST NIGHT.

The kidnappers telephone a national newspaper to say that a package relating to Biebermann is waiting in a telephone box. The Squad examines the package and finds a photograph of the minister in captivity, together with a tape-recording of Biebermann asking for his captors' demands to be met. From this evidence, Cowley is able to discover that the kidnappers are not Biebermann's political enemies but British criminals wanting a vast ransom, and are willing to sell him to his friends or enemies. From the photographs themselves, he is able to deduce that the kidnappers' hideaway must be on a London bus route, facing east, and with trees outside. Bodie and Doyle are sent out on a London bus to search for houses fitting this description.

All houses are discreetly checked, and one of them seems as if it might be the place they are looking for; a neighbour has seen men coming and going in the last few days. The woman and her young daughter are moved to a safe house and Cowley, Bodie and a scientific expert, with listening devices and monitors, take up residence. It becomes certain that the men they are looking for are in the house, when Doyle follows one of them to a callbox some distance away and watches the man make a phone-call. The kidnapper demands two million pounds and a safe getaway in return for Biebermann's release. As he returns to the house he notices the neighbour's little girl, who has mistakenly been allowed home from school with a young friend. The kidnapper races indoors to tell his comrades that they may have been discovered. Cowley hears the commotion on the listening device and is forced to tell his team to act immediately; Bodie, astride a makeshift 'battering ram', breaks into an upper room of the house, while Doyle smashes in through the back door. The kidnappers are overcome and Biebermann is rescued safely.

Production Unit

Created by	Brian Clemens
Executive Producers	Albert Fennell, Brian Clemens
Music	Laurie Johnson
Producer	Raymond Menmuir
Associate Producer	Chris Burt
Script Editor	Gerry O'Hara
Production Manager	Donald Toms
Assistant Director	Ray Corbett
Location Managers	Stuart Freeman, Cecil Ford
Continuity	Cheryl Leigh
Casting	Maggie Cartier
Production Designer	Malcolm Middleton
Art Director	Peter Joyce
Stunt Arranger	Peter Brayham
Wardrobe Supervisor	Masada Wilmot
Lighting Cameraman	Philip Meheux
Camera Operators	Tony White, John Maskall
Make Up	Alan Brownie
Hairdresser	Barbara Ritchie
Supervising Editor	John S. Smith
Sound Recordist	David Crozier
Music Supervisor	Christopher Palmer
Dubbing Editor	Peter Lennard
Dubbing Mixer	Hugh Strain

Music Editor   Alan Willis

An Avengers MARK 1 Production For LONDON WEEKEND TELEVISION

Martin Shaw and Lewis Collins filming on location during FIRST NIGHT.

Shooting / Location Schedule

Production Dates: Monday 3rd to Friday 14th July, 1978. Production Number: 9D11233

3 July	***Festival Hall & river bank***: Royal Festival Hall, Belvedere Road, Lambeth, London, SE1
4 July	***Festival Hall / Phone Box***: Jubilee Walk, Southbank, Lambeth, London, SE1
	Whitehall conference / staircase: National Liberal Club, 1 Whitehall Place, Westminster, London, SW1
5 July	***River Thames landing***: London Western Docks, The Highway, Wapping, London, E1
	'Blue' Police car run-bys: Shad Thames / Curlew Street, Bermondsey, London, SE1 & St. Katharines Way / Thomas More Street, Wapping, London, E1
	'White' Police car run-bys: Horsleydown Lane / Shad Thames, Bermondsey, London, SE1 & Greenmoor Wharf, Bankside, Southwark, London, SE1
	Flower Stall / Cowley's car: Trinity Square / Coopers Row, London, EC3
	Int: Cowley's car (route to Festival Hall): Victoria Embankment, Strand, London, WC2

6 July	***Metropolitan Police Operations room***: Lee Studios, Wembley Park Drive, Wembley, Middlesex ***Kidnapper's car***: Beechcroft Gardens, Wembley, Middlesex ***Int: Bodie's car (after tennis courts)***: Oakington Avenue, Wembley, Middlesex
7 July	***Police Canteen / washroom /Arab Group HQ***: Lee Studios, Wembley Park Drive, Wembley, Middlesex
10 July	***Recreation ground***: Hillingdon Ski Centre, Hillingdon House Farm, Park Road, Hillingdon, Middlesex ***Int: London Bus***: Hillingdon Road (near St. Andrews Church), Uxbridge, Middlesex
11 July	***Cinema & car park***: Paradise Cinema, Cinema Parade, Western Avenue, Ealing, London, W5 ***Int: Ruth's car (bus surveillance)***: The Ridings, Ealing, London, W5
12-14 July	***Roof Kidnap street / Kidnappers car / Shed***: 7 & 9 South West India Dock Entrance, Manchester Road, Isle Of Dogs, London, E14
2nd Unit:	***Ext: Car Park: Cowley's car (flask scene)***: Cadby Hall, Brook Green, Hammersmith, London, W14 ***Tube Station***: Willesden Green Tube Station, Walm Lane, Willesden, London, NW2 ***Street / Bus Stop 1 & 2***: Walm Lane (opposite tube station), Willesden, London, NW2 ***Bus run-by / Ruth's car***: Walm Lane (near Rutland Park Gardens), Willesden, London, NW2 ***Phone box's***: Walm Lane (near Dartmouth Lane), Willesden, London, NW2 ***Bus stop 3***: Station Parade (near Blenheim Gardens), Willesden, London, NW2 ***Bus stop 4***: Lydford Road (near St.Gabriels Road), Willesden, London, NW2 ***Int / Ext: Doyle's car (with Debra) and run-by***: King Street, Hammersmith, London, W6 & Queen Caroline Street (run-by: past flyover), London, W6
August	***Tennis courts***: Chiswick Tennis Club, Burlington Lane, London, W4 ***Ext: Bodie's car run-by (after tennis courts)***: Burlington Road, Chiswick, London, W4 ***Int / Ext: Capri run-by (sirens)***: Edgware Road / Burnt Oak Broadway / Edgware High Street, Burnt Oak, Middlesex ***Country lane (recreation ground): Bodie's car***: Montrose Avenue / Silkstream Road, Burnt Oak, Middlesex

THE RACK
(originally *An Enquiry Into Violence*)
by **Brian Clemens**
© Copyright Mark 1 Productions Ltd MCMLXXIX (should read MCMLXXVIII)

John Coogan	Michael Billington
Geraldine Mather	Lisa Harrow
Minister	Allan Surtees
Judge Hall	Cyril Luckham
David Merlin	Robert James
Benny	Trevor Adams
Parker	Ken Campbell
Frank Williams	Peter Marinker
Lorna	Jenny Lee Wright
Paul Coogan	Christopher Ellison
Reporter	Michael Mundell
McKay	James Hayes
Carter	Jonty Miller
Big Man	Charles Pemberton
Uncredited	
CI5 Agent	Mike Reynell
Doctor	Athar Malik
Vicar	Robert Lankesheer
Man at Cemetery	Robin Scott
Stenart	Walter Henry
Enquiry Panel member	Dennis Plenty
Enquiry Panel member	Charlie Gray
Enquiry Panel member	Alan Gibbs
Enquiry Panel member	Gloria Clugston
Enquiry Panel member	Melita Clarke
Jill	Dawn Rodrigues

Director: **Peter Medak**

BODIE receives information from an underworld contact that John Coogan and his younger brother Paul, two men who have been involved with every kind of criminal activity, but have avoided conviction, are to receive a large assignment of heroin at their home that night. Cowley organises a raid on the Coogans' home and the brothers are taken to CI5 HQ for interrogation. During questioning by Bodie and Doyle, Paul attacks Doyle and Doyle, in retaliation, punches Paul once in the stomach. To Cowley's disappointment, a thorough search of the Coogans' home reveals nothing, and he is ordered by his Minister to release the brothers without further questioning. As no charge has been made against them, their lawyer, David Merlin, is complaining publicly about their arrest. Bodie and Doyle are sent to release Paul Coogan from the room where he is being held, but find to their astonishment that he is dead. He is found to have died from a ruptured spleen, and Doyle is tortured by the thought that his casual blow killed the man. John Coogan is stricken by his brother's death and orders Merlin to attack and ruin CI5; with CI5 disbanded, Coogan intends to gain his own violent revenge on the man he holds responsible for Paul's fate.

Merlin is able to create a scandal in the press about the violent and lawless methods of CI5, and a Court of Enquiry is set up to investigate Merlin's claims. Merlin hires a crusading woman barrister, Geraldine Mather, to plead the case against CI5, and Cowley's minister informs him that the Squad has many powerful enemies and that its very existence will be in jeopardy if it is discredited by the inquiry. The press is present when Mather presents her evidence. She portrays CI5 as an undemocratic, violent and arrogant band of men who have attacked the home of the innocent Coogan brothers and murdered a defenceless prisoner. Bodie and Doyle meanwhile have discovered that the brothers used to have practice boxing fights together and that as John, who was once a champion boxer, injured Paul, it is possible that he was responsible for the injuries that killed his brother. While giving his evidence to the Enquiry, Bodie happens to mention that CI5 were acting on information received when they raided the Coogan's home, and Mather insists that the informer be named. The informant, Henry Parker, is named. John Coogan and Frank Williams immediately leave the proceedings. Bodie and Doyle follow the men and park outside a pool hall to see if Coogan emerges with Parker. After a while, the two agents become concerned and enter the building to find Parker brutally injured. They tend to his wounds and return with him, in a wheelchair, to the Enquiry. With this new evidence the Enquiry turns in CI5's favour and Bodie vows to see John Coogan convicted at some later date.

Production Unit

Created by	Brian Clemens
Executive Producers	Albert Fennell, Brian Clemens
Music	Laurie Johnson
Producer	Raymond Menmuir
Associate Producer	Chris Burt
Script Editor	Gerry O'Hara
Production Manager	Donald Toms
Assistant Director	Derek Whitehurst
Location Managers	Stuart Freeman, Cecil Ford
Continuity	Cheryl Leigh
Casting	Maggie Cartier
Production Designer	Malcolm Middleton
Art Director	Peter Joyce
Stunt Arranger	Peter Brayham
Wardrobe Supervisor	Donald Mothersill
Lighting Cameraman	Philip Meheux
Camera Operator	John Maskall
Make Up	Alan Brownie
Hairdresser	Barbara Ritchie

Supervising Editor	John S. Smith
Editor	Alan Killick
Sound Recordist	David Crozier
Music Supervisor	Christopher Palmer
Dubbing Editor	Peter Lennard
Dubbing Mixer	Hugh Strain
Music Editor	Alan Willis

An Avengers MARK 1 Production For LONDON WEEKEND TELEVISION

Shooting / Location Schedule

Production Dates: Monday 17th to Friday 28th July, 1978. Production Number: 9D11235

17 July	***Station yard meeting with Parker***: South Lambeth Freight Yard, Nine Elms Lane, South Lambeth, London, SW8 ***Street: Parker's rooming house***: 20 Southolm Road, Battersea, London, SW11
18 July	***John Coogan's House***: Binfield Manor, Binfield Road, Binfield, Berkshire ***CI5 Squad cars run-by***: Tilehurst Lane / Forest Road, Binfield, Berkshire
19-21 July	***CI5 HQ / Interrogation rooms***: Cadby Hall, Blythe Road, Hammersmith, London, W14
24 July	***Minister's office***: Tower Theatre, 11 Cannonbury Place, Islington, London, N1 ***Cemetery***: Highgate Cemetery, Swains Lane, Highgate, London, N6
25-26 July	***Doyle's flat***: Cliff Road Studios, Cliff Road, Camden, London, NW1 ***Prostitute's house***: 20 Cliff Villas, Camden, London, NW1 ***CI5 HQ / Interrogation rooms***: Cadby Hall, Blythe Road, Hammersmith, London, W14
27 July	***Int: Bodie's car (Bodie & Doyle)***: Homefield Road / Harrow Road, Butlers Green, Sudbury, Middlesex ***Int: Billiards Club***: Ron Gross, 289 Neasden Lane, London, NW10 ***Ext: Billiards Club***: Vale Farm Sports Centre, Watford Road, Sudbury, Harrow, Middlesex
28 July	***Hospital***: Wexham Park Hospital, Wexham Road, Stoke Green, Slough, Berkshire ***CI5 HQ***: Cadby Hall, Blythe Road, Hammersmith, London, W14

MAN WITHOUT A PAST

by **Michael Armstrong**
based on a story by **Jeremy Burnham**
© Copyright Mark 1 Productions Ltd MCMLXXVIII

Brian Forrest	John Carson
Peter Crabbe	John Castle
Madge Forrest	Rachel Herbert
Arthur	Rod Culbertson
Braddock	Ed Bishop
Haskell	John Bay
Sally Pendle	Deirdre Costello
Gino	Robert Rietty
Padgett	Robert Dorning
Carol Forrest	Hilary Ryan
Grant	James Bree
MacNeil	Alan Leith
Phipps	Anthony Bailey
Attendant	Peter Pacey
Inspector	Neville Barber
Girl	Ann Michelle
Nurse	Gloria Walker
Claire	Maya Woolfe
Uncredited	
Man in restaurant	Ron Watkins
Man in restaurant	Gerry Paris
Waiter with flowers	Phil Parks
Waiter at Police Station	Andrew Andreas
Policeman (restaurant)	Les Conrad
Policeman (Forrest's house)	Ron Gregory
Porter	Dick Sullivan
Heavy	John Morgan

Director: **Martin Campbell**

BODIE is dining out with a girlfriend when a bomb explodes near their table. Bodie is unhurt, but the girl is badly injured and two other people are killed from the explosion. Cowley decides that as Bodie is so angry and distressed by his girlfriend's injuries, he should not be involved in the case. Bodie, however, is not to be put off and discovers from the restaurant owner that Brian Forrest, apparently an ordinary prosperous accountant, had booked the table but cancelled at the last moment. Further enquiries at Forrest's office reveal nothing more sinister than the fact that Forrest is a partner of the firm. Leaving the building, Bodie goes to find Forrest's car in an underground car park, but before he can examine it, the car blows up.

An American mob informant who was given a new identity for turning state's evidence is the target in a MAN WITHOUT A PAST. Bodie (Lewis Collins) becomes involved when they injure his girlfriend in one of their attempts on his life. The scene above was filmed near Mill Hill electricity sub-station, Partingdale Lane, North London.

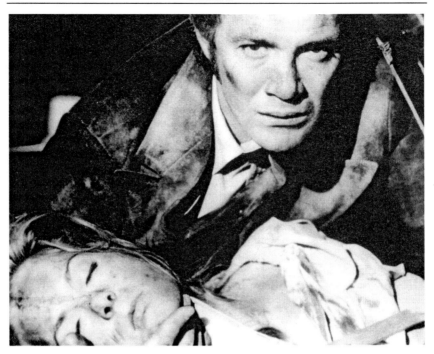

In a MAN WITHOUT A PAST Bodie's (Lewis Collins) girlfriend Claire (Maya Woolfe) suffers the blast of a bomb while dining out with the CI5 agent. Dutch actress Maya Woolfe became better known for her part in the hit BBC TV drama TENKO.

CI5's Doyle (Martin Shaw) seeks attention from the Nurse (Gloria Walker).

Doyle meanwhile has been trying to locate a young criminal, Arthur Pendle, who was seen at the restaurant moments before the bomb exploded. When Doyle finds him, Pendle runs away and Doyle, giving chase, is deliberately knocked down by a passing car, driven by Peter Crabbe, who ordered Pendle to plant the bomb in the restaurant and beneath Forrest's car. Doyle is picked up by Crabbe's heavies and taken to the man's home where he is beaten up, bound and gagged. Bodie, uninjured in the car blast, races straight to Forrest's home and demands to know why attempts are being made on his life. Forrest refuses to answer his questions, and Bodie is arrested for pestering the man. Cowley, having had Bodie released and warning him never to disobey orders again, agrees to let the agent work on the case.

Cowley later talks to Mrs. Forrest and tells her that he has checked into her husbands past life; there are no official records that support his story of his life before he got his present job in 1958. Outside in the street, Bodie stops the car that has been following him and discovers to his amazement that the occupants are FBI agents. They explain to Cowley and Bodie that Forrest was once an accountant for the Mafia in America; he was caught and gave evidence against them in return for a free pardon and a chance of a new life in England. The Mafia have discovered where he is and want him dead. The FBI have offered Forrest a new identity in another country in return for fresh evidence.

Forrest goes to Crabbe's flat and Pendle is astonished when Crabbe does not try to kill Forrest; Crabbe explains that Forrest is an old friend and Forrest's enemies did not know this when Crabbe was hired. Crabbe has taken the Mafia's hit money and the two men have made plans to escape abroad together. Doyle, meanwhile, has managed to get a message to CI5 HQ and Cowley and Bodie are racing to Crabbe's home. They arrive in time to rescue their colleague and to arrest the Mafia men who have been sent to kill Crabbe and Pendle for their failure to kill Forrest. Pendle is killed in the ensuing gunfight, and Crabbe is taken into custody. Cowley insists to the FBI that Forrest must stand trial for his role in the restaurant bombing.

Production Unit

Created by	Brian Clemens
Executive Producers	Albert Fennell, Brian Clemens
Music	Laurie Johnson
Producer	Raymond Menmuir
Associate Producer	Chris Burt
Script Editor	Gerry O'Hara
Production Manager	Donald Toms
Assistant Director	Peter Carter
Location Managers	Stuart Freeman, Cecil Ford
Continuity	Cheryl Leigh
Casting	Maggie Cartier
Production Designer	Malcolm Middleton
Art Director	Peter Joyce
Stunt Arranger	Peter Brayham
Wardrobe Supervisor	Donald Mothersill

Lighting Cameraman	Philip Meheux
Camera Operator	John Maskall
Make Up	Alan Brownie
Hairdresser	Barbara Ritchie
Supervising Editor	John S. Smith
Sound Recordist	David Crozier
Music Supervisor	Christopher Palmer
Dubbing Editor	Peter Lennard
Dubbing Mixer	Hugh Strain
Music Editor	Alan Willis

An Avengers MARK 1 Production For LONDON WEEKEND TELEVISION

Martin Shaw relaxes to pose for some publicity shots during filming on MAN WITHOUT A PAST.

Shooting / Location Schedule

Production Dates: Monday 31st July to Friday 11th August, 1978. Production Number: 9D11232

31 July	***Restaurant explosion***: Michel et Valerie, 7 Bridge Avenue, Maidenhead, Berkshire
1 August	***Hospital***: Wexham Park Hospital, Wexham Road, Stoke Green, Slough, Berkshire
2 August	***Forrest's house / Bodie's car***: The Spinney, 28 Totteridge Common, Totteridge Lane, Totteridge, London, N20
3 August	***CI5 Offices / Police Room***: Cadby Hall, Blythe Road, Hammersmith, London, W14

4 August	**Int: Cowley's car**: Blythe Road / Dewhurst Road, Hammersmith, London, W14
	Brian Forrest's office: National Theatre, Upper Ground, South Bank Centre, Lambeth, London, SE1
	Streets: Probation officer's meeting with Doyle: Stamford Street, Waterloo Road / Tenison Way roundabout, Lambeth, London, SE1
	Street: Doyle's car (Railway arch): Boyce Street tunnel, off Mepham Street, Lambeth, London, SE1
7 August	**Streets: Bodie's first car chase with FBI**: Highwood Hill / Holcombe Hill / The Ridgeway / Partingdale Lane, Mill Hill, London, NW7 / Lullington Garth, Finchley, London, N12
	Streets: Second car chase: Lullington Garth / Cissbury Ring South, Finchley, London, N12 / Partingdale Lane, Mill Hill, London, N7
8 August	**Sally Pendle's flat**: Larch House, Swan Road, Rotherhithe, London, SE16
	Housing estate: Beech House, Ainsty Estate, Canon Beck Road, Rotherhithe, London, SE16
	Streets: Doyle chases Pendle: Swan Road / Brunel Road, Rotherhithe, London, SE16
	Wasteland (Doyle run down by Crabbe): Albion Yard, off Rotherhithe Street, Rotherhithe, London, SE16
9 August	**Brian Forrest's office / car park**: National Theatre Upper Ground, South Bank Centre, Lambeth, London, SE1
10-11 August	**Int: Crabbe's flat**: 14 Thurloe Square, South Kensington, London, SW7
	MacNeil's Hotel room / Airport washroom / Crabbe's flat: Lifts & underground car park: Cunard International Hotel, 1 Shortlands, Hammersmith, London, W6
2nd Unit:	
4 September	**Streets: Phone box (Bodie phones hospital)**: 31 Bridge Street, Pinner, Middlesex
	Streets: Doyle meets 'Girl': Tops & Bottoms, 22a Bridge Street, Pinner, Middlesex
	Doyle's car run-by: High Street, Northwood, Middlesex
	Airport: Terminal 2, Heathrow Airport, Harlington, Middlesex

IN THE PUBLIC INTEREST
by **Brian Clemens**
© Copyright Mark 1 Productions Ltd MCMLXXIX (should be MCMLXXVIII)

Green	Paul Hardwick
Chives	John Judd
Pellin	Stephen Rea
Minister	Allan Surtees
Edwards	Colin McCormack
Reed	Tom Georgeson
Terry	Tony Calvin
Sally	Pamela Manson
Female Clerk	Saba Milton
Big Man	Fredric Abbott
Cop	Fraser Cains
Uncredited	
Orbit Club Manager	Harry Fielder
Paying customer (Orbit Club)	John Cannon
Blonde girl (Orbit Club)	Pearl Ann Turner
Plainclothes Policeman (Orbit Club)	Mike Reynell
Uniformed Policeman (Edwards partner)	Ron Conrad
Detective - masked attacker	Greg Eccles
Detective - masked attacker	Phil Parkes
Uniformed Policeman (Gay Youth Office)	Derek Moss
Uniformed Policeman (Gas works)	Reg Woods
Plainclothes Policeman (Gas works)	Tony O'Leary
Plainclothes Policeman (Gas works)	Tony Allen

Director: **Pennant Roberts**

A YOUNG man named Pellin comes to see Cowley privately because he thinks that the police force in a certain city is corrupt. Pellin explains that he tried to set up a Gay Youth Centre in the town, but the centre was destroyed by a band of masked men who seemed to be citizen vigilantes anxious not to have such a non-conformist element in their midst. Pellin tells the CI5 boss that he complained to the police about the raid and confided to the police that he intended to stay on at the Centre; although only the police knew about his plans, he was visited again by the masked men and badly beaten. The police force is evidently using their own gangs to enforce their personal wishes.

Worried by Pellin's story, Cowley assigns Bodie and Doyle to visit the city and take a discreet look at the way the police force operates. Later that day, Cowley's Minister warns him that nothing should be done that could upset the city's police force; since their new Chief Constable, Green, took over, the force has been amazingly efficient and crime figures have been dramatically reduced. Bodie and Doyle, however, unearth a number of disturbing incidents which seem to indicate that the police force are over zealous in their duties; innocent people are being arrested and convicted, and any person who does not happen to please the force is bullied into leaving. They report their findings to Cowley, who tells them that they will have to obtain irrefutable evidence of misconduct by the police to support their claims. Convinced that the claims require further investigation, Cowley himself visits Chief Constable Green and listens with interest as the man proudly gives his account of how effectively he runs the city.

During their visit, Bodie and Doyle have met Green's deputy, Inspector Chives. He also seems particularly tough and autocratic in his behaviour, so it is arranged for Pellin to telephone Chives and say that he intends to re-open the Gay Centre at a new address in the city. Pellin also tells Chives that two of his men will be sent on ahead to map out the centre and that they will need police protection. Bodie and Doyle arrive and, as expected, are soon under attack by a gang of masked men. Bodie and Doyle quickly overpower the men and unmask them. All the men are policemen and the CI5 men have tape-recorded and photographed the break-in. Chives is furious when he hears that CI5 have evidence against his men, and orders his gang to kill Bodie and Doyle; without their evidence, the photographs and tapes will not be enough to convict him and his men. Policemen are sent to arrest the CI5 men, and they are soon surrounded. They decide to give themselves up unarmed and, hiding the bag with the tapes and photographs, surrender to one of the policemen.

The policeman to whom they surrender, Edwards, obeys Chives' orders implicitly and approves of his methods, but he is surprised when Chives insists on bundling Bodie and Doyle into his own car and on driving them out of the city. Chives, has planned to set up a fake accident involving the death of the two agents. However, Edwards has followed his chief and disarms the police inspector before Bodie and Doyle are harmed; he admits that whilst he is prepared to help rid the city of undesirables, he will not stand back and watch his commanding officer commit murder. Cowley ensures that both Chives and Chief Constable Green are punished.

Production Unit

Created by	Brian Clemens
Executive Producers	Albert Fennell, Brian Clemens
Music	Laurie Johnson
Producer	Raymond Menmuir
Associate Producer	Chris Burt
Script Editor	Gerry O'Hara
Production Manager	Donald Toms
Assistant Director	Ron Purdie
Location Managers	Stuart Freeman, Cecil Ford
Continuity	Cheryl Leigh
Casting	Maggie Cartier

CI5 agents Bodie and Doyle become hunted men when they visit a crime-free town and begin to question the rather unorthodox methods of action taken by the local constabulary. Here, Martin Shaw takes time off as Ray Doyle to pose for a publicity shot between takes on IN THE PUBLIC INTEREST.

Production Designer	Malcolm Middleton
Art Director	Peter Joyce
Stunt Arranger	Peter Brayham
Wardrobe Supervisor	Donald Mothersill
Lighting Cameraman	Vernon Layton
Camera Operator	John Maskall
Make Up	Alan Brownie
Hairdresser	Barbara Ritchie
Supervising Editor	John S. Smith
Editor	Alan Killick
Sound Recordist	David Crozier
Music Supervisor	Christopher Palmer
Dubbing Editor	Peter Lennard
Dubbing Mixer	Hugh Strain
Music Editor	Alan Willis

An Avengers MARK 1 Production For LONDON WEEKEND TELEVISION

Bodie (Lewis Collins) and Doyle (Martin Shaw) investigate a town whose police force appears to be entirely corrupt. Can the CI5 agents flee with the incriminating evidence they have gathered on Inspector Chives before being captured? A scene from IN THE PUBLIC INTEREST.

Shooting / Location Schedule
Production Dates: Monday 14th to Friday25th August, 1978. Production Number: 9D11234

14-15 August   ***Gay Youth Organisation Offices***: 304 Kensal Road, Kensal Town, London, W10

	Street: Bodie & Doyle with camera: Village Inn, junction Middle Row / Kensal Road, Kensal Town, London, W10
	Streets: Bodie & Doyle escape with bag: Adelia Street / Kensal Road / West Row, Kensal Town, London, W10
	Street: 'Blue' Police car gives chase: Kensal Road / Middle Row, Kensal Town, London, W10
	Streets: 'White' Police car gives chase: Kensal Rd / West Row, Kensal Town, London, W10
16 August	***Green's club***: Edgwarebury Club, Edgwarebury Lane, Elstree, Hertfordshire
	Ext: Prison: Mill Hill Gas Works, Bittacy Hill, Mill Hill, London, NW7
	Int: Doyle's car (train station route): Green Lane, Hendon, London, NW4 & Hendon Lane / St. Marys Avenue, Church End, London, N3
	Train Station: Watford Junction, Station Road, Watford, Hertfordshire
17-18 August	***Chive's office / Green's office***: Lee Studios, 288 Kensal Road, Kensal Town, London, W10
21 August	***Minister's office***: Tower Theatre, 11 Cannonbury Place, Islington, London, N1
	Star Hotel: Sunset Strip, 77 Wembley Hill Road, Wembley, Middlesex
22 August	***Orbit Night Club / Int: Doyle's car***: Orbit House, 1-6 Ritz / Cinema Parade, Western Avenue, Ealing, London, W5
	Streets: PC Edwards stops Doyle: Watling Avenue / Fortescue Road, Burnt Oak, Middlesex
	Streets: Doyle's car run-bys: Goldbeaters Grove / Deansbrook Road, Burnt Oak, Middlesex
23 August	***Gasworks warehouse***: Mill Hill Gas Works, Bittacy Hill, Mill Hill, London, NW7
	Star Hotel: Sunset Strip, 77 Wembley Hill Road, Wembley, Middlesex
24 August	***Quarry / Cliff / Car interiors***: Springwell Pit / Quarry, Springwell Lane, Rickmansworth, Hertfordshire
25 August	***Cowley's home***: Hurlingham Court, Ranelagh Gardens, Hurlingham, London, SW6
	Shopping Centre: Shepherds Bush Green Shopping Centre, Shepherds Bush, London, W12
	Gas works street and entrance: The (George Cohen) 600 Group Limited, Wood Lane (opposite BBC TV Centre), Shepherd's Bush, London, W12
	Ext: street: 'White' Police car (CV5 intercept call): Bath Road (near Abinger Road), Bedford Park, Chiswick, London, W4
2nd Unit:	
31 August	***Whitehall Streets: Pellin follows Cowley***: Whitehall Court, Westminster, London, SW1

NOT A VERY CIVIL CIVIL SERVANT

(originally *Housing And Estates*)
by **Edmund Ward**
© Copyright Mark 1 Productions Ltd MCMLXXVIII

Sir James Temple	Maurice Denham
Colonel Summerville	Bill Fraser
Logan-Blake	Robert Swann
Repton	Harold Innocent
Councillor Webb	Peter Woodthorpe
Minister	Tony Church
Gillam	Lyndon Brook
Renshaw	Derek Martin
Singleton	Anthony Heaton
Halloran	David Hargreaves
Jenny Burton	Linda Goddard
Bradford	Andrew McCulloch
Musgrave	Frank Jarvis
Judge	Donald Bisset
Sam Burton	Brian Hall
Karl Drake	Duncan Preston
Uncredited	
Harry	Peter Burton
Jury member	Roy Everson
Jury member	June Everson
Jury member	Ron Gregory
Jury member	Dennis Plenty
Jury member	Ken Netsall
Uniformed Policeman (Court)	Steve Caine
Uniformed Policeman (Court)	Don Hann
CI5 Agent (Court)	James Linton
Barney	Gerry Judge
Golf Club member	Ron Watkins
Golf Club member	Alan Harris
Pub customer	Ronnie Wood
Blonde man in pub	Gus Roy

Director: **Anthony Simmons**

TWO employees of a construction firm, Temple-Blake Limited, are put on trial for corruption, along with a local housing committee chairman who is accused of taking bribes in return for housing contracts. Robert Gillam, the Temple-Blake company accountant, is to face trial too, as he authorised the payments to the councillor. An important government department has awarded contracts worth billions of pounds to Temple-Blake in the past and other valuable contracts for them are under consideration. The Minister for the department, anxious that his reputation should not be tarnished by any unpleasant repercussions from the trial, asks Cowley to keep a watching brief on the affair so that he can be kept fully informed of any developments. Cowley resents CI5 being used to protect a Minister, but he reluctantly agrees to examine the case. Sir James Temple, chairman of Temple-Blake, and his cousin, Tony Logan-Blake, director of the company, have secretly been making personal fortunes out of bribing a senior civil servant to ensure that they are awarded lucrative building contracts. The civil servant, Henry Repton, has also made a personal fortune from the deals and when he hears that CI5 have been asked to look into the case, he warns Sir James and his nephew of the threat posed by their investigation. Logan-Blake, fearing that Gillam, who is to stand trial, and who knows of the corrupt payments, may break down under cross-examination and reveal what he knows, arranges to have the accountant murdered.

CI5's Doyle (Martin Shaw), Cowley (Gordon Jackson), and Bodie (Lewis Collins) manage to uncover a series of financial blunders between a group of builders and council officials after a site of newly-built houses on a council estate are found to be crumbling. On the set of NOT A VERY CIVIL CIVIL SERVANT *at the National Liberal Club, Whitehall, South West London.*

CI5 begin their investigation by questioning the bricklayer who first exposed the Temple-Blake corruption, but he tells them that the man who might have exposed it, Gillam, is dead. Cowley meantime has been talking to George Webb, the local councillor, and makes his own assessment that the man is guilty. However, when Webb and the two men are tried in court, they are found 'not guilty' by the jury. This delights the Government Minister, and he tells Cowley that he can now call off the investigation. Cowley, however, tells the man that he is adamant that Gillam was murdered and that the trial jurors were suborned; he does not intend to abandon the case, which has now become a criminal investigation. One of Cowley's friends, a man who has long experience of the construction industry, advises Cowley that any proof of corruption would definitely show up in the company's accounts, so the CI5 man instigates an investigation into the Temple-Blake accounting books.

Bodie and Doyle talk to the jurors and find evidence that some of the jury were indeed suborned, but there is no proof to link the Temple-Blake management to the affair. Logan-Blake, however, becomes concerned when Temple points out that Gillam, a careful man, probably kept secret records of all business transactions and private accounts he handled; Gillam would have kept these hidden in case he was betrayed by those around him and needed proof of their guilt. When Cowley hears that Mrs. Gillam has been sent away for two weeks' holiday by the Temple-Blake management, he decides that they are attempting to get her out of the house to search the place. Bodie and Doyle are sent to Gillam's home to await further developments. Two men arrive and discover a package and the two CI5 men try to grab it from them; one of the men escapes with the package and takes it to Sir James. Cowley and his team are unable to prevent Sir James from incinerating the documents, but calls the man's bluff by telling him that the CI5 men found the real package a few days earlier. Sir James has now incriminated himself by accepting a package thought to contain Gillam's private accounts.

Production Unit

Created by	Brian Clemens
Executive Producers	Albert Fennell, Brian Clemens
Music	Laurie Johnson
Producer	Raymond Menmuir
Associate Producer	Chris Burt
Script Editor	Gerry O'Hara
Production Manager	Donald Toms
Assistant Director	Peter Carter
Location Managers	Stuart Freeman, Cecil Ford
Continuity	Sue Merry
Casting	Maggie Cartier
Production Designer	Malcolm Middleton
Art Director	Peter Joyce
Stunt Arranger	Peter Brayham
Wardrobe Supervisor	Donald Mothersill
Lighting Cameraman	Vernon Layton
Camera Operator	John Maskall
Make Up	Alan Brownie
Hairdresser	Barbara Ritchie
Supervising Editor	John S. Smith
Sound Recordist	David Crozier
Music Supervisor	Christopher Palmer

Dubbing Editor	Ian Toynton
Dubbing Mixer	Hugh Strain
Music Editor	Alan Willis

An Avengers MARK 1 Production For LONDON WEEKEND TELEVISION

Shooting / Location Schedule

Production Dates: Tuesday 29th August to Monday 11th September, 1978.
Production Number: 9D11237

29 August	***Repton's office***: Tower Theatre, 11 Cannonbury Place, Islington, London, N1
30 August	***Logan Blake's office / Temple-Blake HQ***: Tower Hotel, St. Katharine's Way, Wapping, London, E1
31 August	***Fencing club / Magistrates Court***: National Liberal Club, 1 Whitehall Place, Westminster, London, SW1
1 September	***Sir James Temple's house***: High Canons, Buckettsland Lane, Borehamwood, Hertfordshire
4 September	***Robert Gilliam's house***: 7 Frithwood Avenue, Northwood, Middlesex
5 September	***Pub & fight***: Willesden Junction Hotel, 47 Station Road, Harlesden, London, NW10 ***Take-Away***: 29 Station Road, Harlesden, London, NW10
6 September	***George Webb's golf club***: North Middlesex Golf Club, Friern Barnet Lane, Whetstone, London, N20
7 September	***Int: Hardware Shop***: Lee Studios, Wembley Park Drive, Wembley, Middlesex ***College***: North London College, Dudden Hill Lane (Denzil Road entrance), London, NW10
8 September	***Construction site***: Surrey Commercial Docks, Redriff Road / Rotherhithe Street, Rotherhithe, London, SE16 ***Burton's house***: 7 South West India Dock Entrance, Manchester Road, Isle Of Dogs, London, E14
11 September	***'Series Titles Sequence'***: The Barbican Centre, Silk Street / Monkwell Square, London, EC2 / 25 Old Broad Street (near the Nat West Tower), London, EC2 / Trinity House, Trinity Square, Tower Hill, London, EC1 / Rotherhithe Tunnel, Rotherhithe, London, SE16 / Southall Gas Works, White Street, Southall, Middlesex / Honeywell House, Great West Road, Brentford, Middlesex

A STIRRING OF DUST

by **Don Houghton**
© Copyright Mark 1 Productions Ltd MCMLXXVIII

Darby	Robert Urquhart
Brigadier Stadden	Andre Morell
Sorenson	Alan MacNaughtan
Helen Pierce	Carol Royle
Yashinkov	George Murcell
O'Leary	Billy Boyle
Taxi Driver	Robin Parkinson
Elsa	Shelagh Fraser
Lewis	Myles Hoyle
Callinari	Michael Petrovitch
Russian Aide 1	Chris Dillinger
Russian Aide 2	Terence Mountain
Cleric	Norman Rutherford
Uncredited	
O'Leary's Driver	Del Baker
Paul Cantwell	Walter Henry
Arthur Pulford	John Doy

Director: **Martin Campbell**

COWLEY is astonished and alarmed to receive information that the notorious spy Thomas Darby has abandoned his life of retirement in Moscow and is on his way back to England after a twenty-year absence. Darby, recruited to the Russian Secret Service while a student in the 1930s, spent many years in the British Secret Service, passing on every secret to the Russians. His true allegiance was eventually suspected and he escaped to safety in Moscow with two other spies. Bodie and Doyle cannot understand why the return of a sick and aged spy to England should be so important, until Cowley explains that Darby's reappearance could cause a major political upheaval, especially as the name of the 'Fourth Man', the powerful establishment figure who financed all the espionage arrangements, has never been discovered.

Darby knows that name and it is vital that the identity of the traitor should be discovered and discreet arrangements made for his removal. Cowley knows that the Russians will try to kill Darby before he can make any revelations, and that the Fourth Man himself will try to kill Darby. Bodie and Doyle must find Darby before his enemies. Cowley knows that foreign hit men hired to kill Darby have already started to arrive in England, and that there are also a number of ex-Secret Service agents living in London who were betrayed by Darby and will band together to try and silence him. Darby has returned to England to see his daughter Helen, the child born to him by his mistress, Eileen Pierce, who has recently died, so Cowley sends Bodie and Doyle to Helen's home to watch for Darby's arrival.

In A STIRRING OF DUST, a notorious spy Thomas Darby (Robert Urquhart), is back in England. But is he really in town to see his daughter, Helen Pierce? Actress Carol Royle was born in Blackpool, Lancashire (10th February 1954) and studied at the Central School of Speech and Drama; THE PROFESSIONALS being one of her early acting roles. Robert Urquhart was born (16th October 1921) in Ullapool, Scotland, and made his stage debut in 1947 and film debut 5-years later. He worked steadily throughout his career in spy-type shows such as DANGERMAN, THE AVENGERS, MAN IN A SUITCASE, DEPARTMENT S and countless others. He also played the lead role in JANGO, a short-lived 1961 production.

An ex-Secret Service Chief, Brigadier James Stadden, informs Cowley that Darby may try to ensure his daughter's financial security by selling the full story of how he made fools of British officials and governments for twenty years. No British publisher would dare print the story, but foreign publishers, heedless of the damage it might do to Britain, would be delighted to pay thousands for it. The manuscript of this story would have been kept in safe keeping in England during Darby's absence, and the men who are trying to kill the spy, will also want to destroy the dangerous manuscript. Two hired foreign hit-men, Liam O'Leary and Pietro Callinari, are waiting at Helen's home for Darby to appear, and when Bodie and Doyle come to the house, they knock Callinari unconscious. O'Leary escapes in a fast car with Helen Pierce held at gunpoint. Darby, approaching the house, is also seized by two of the ex-Secret Service agents he betrayed, Martin Sorenson and Elsa Coran.

Helen is forced by O'Leary to tell him the name of the solicitor who kept her mother's papers, Arthur Pulford, and O'Leary drives with her to Pulford's office, hoping to find Darby's manuscript. He bursts into the room and shoots the solicitor dead, breaking into the strong box containing Eileen Pierce's papers and finds the documents inside. As Helen stands terrified in a corner, he telephones the Fourth Man, who hired him, and arranges for the manuscript to be collected. The CI5 squad arrives and O'Leary fires at Doyle but is shot dead by Bodie. Cowley learns from Helen that O'Leary had arranged to meet his contact outside and reasons that the Fourth Man must be waiting nearby. He quickly locates a limousine carrying Paul Cantwell. Cantwell is apprehended and taken away, while Cowley goes in search of Darby. Cowley goes to Brigadier Stadden's office and finds Sorenson, Elsa and Stadden with Darby, but Darby is dead, having suffered a massive heart attack. His body is secretly shipped back to Moscow so that his death can be announced as if it took place there and his visit to the UK can remain a secret. Cowley keeps the manuscript and Cantwell is forced to leave London for Moscow.

Production Unit

Created by	Brian Clemens
Executive Producers	Albert Fennell, Brian Clemens
Music	Laurie Johnson
Producer	Raymond Menmuir
Associate Producer	Chris Burt
Script Editor	Gerry O'Hara
Production Manager	Donald Toms
Assistant Director	Ron Purdie
Location Managers	Stuart Freeman, Cecil Ford
Continuity	Gladys Pearce
Casting	Maggie Cartier
Production Designer	Malcolm Middleton
Art Director	Peter Joyce
Stunt Arranger	Frank Henson
Wardrobe Supervisor	Donald Mothersill
Lighting Cameraman	Vernon Layton

Camera Operator	John Maskall
Make Up	Bernard Brown
Hairdressers	Jan Dorman, Mibbs Parker
Supervising Editor	John S. Smith
Editor	Alan Killick
Sound Recordist	David Crozier
Music Supervisor	Christopher Palmer
Dubbing Editor	Peter Lennard
Dubbing Mixer	Hugh Strain
Music Editor	Alan Willis

An Avengers MARK 1 Production For LONDON WEEKEND TELEVISION

Shooting / Location Schedule

Production Dates: Tuesday 12th to Monday 25th September, 1978. Production Number: 9D11242

12-13 September **Int: Cowley's car**: Bermondsey Wall East / Jamaica Road, Bermondsey, London, SE16
Warehouse meeting: KGB & CI5: Chambers Wharf Cold Storage, Chambers Street, Bermondsey, London, SE16
Warehouse street: Bermondsey Wall East / Loftie Street, Bermondsey, London, SE16

14 September **Taxi stand / Coach Station / Airline offices**: Victoria Airways Terminal, Semley House, Semley Place, London, SW1
Taxi: London sites: The Mall (past Queen Victoria Memorial & The Duke Of York's Coloum), Waterloo Place; Westminster, London, SW1

15 September **Helen's house / Car chase / Int: Elsa's car**: 39 Jesmond Avenue, Wembley, Middlesex
Car stunt: Stanley Road / Clifton Avenue, Wembley, Middlesex

18-19 September **Stadden's house, projection room**: Leggatts Park, Great North Road, Potters Bar, Hertfordshire

20 September **Graveyard**: St Mary's RC Cemetery, Harrow Road, Kensal Green, London, W10

21-22 September **Int / Ext: Pulford's office**: Cadby Hall, Blythe Road, Hammersmith, London, W14

25 September **Hotel / Sorenson's place / Elsa's place / Cantwell's limousine**: 1 Montpelier Road, Ealing, London, W5

2nd Unit: **Car run-by: on route to Pulford's office**: Camden Road (near St. Pancras Way), Camden Town, London, NW1
Ferry: Dover & Ramsgate
Insert: Projector slides - stills: Carlton Avenue East / Wembley Park Drive, Wembley, Middlesex

BLIND RUN

(originally *Play Up! And Play The Game!*)
by **Ranald Graham**
© Copyright Mark 1 Productions Ltd MCMLXXVIII

Leia	Jasmina Hilton
Charlie	Tommy Boyle
Phillipa	Sandra Payne
Foreign Observer 1	Tony Jay
Minister	Kevin Brennan
Bodyguard	Ahmed El-Shenawi
Foreign Observer 2	Steve Plytas
Hanish (Mr. X)	Kevork Malikyan
Male Secretary	Rowland Davies
Georgio	Tariq Yunus
1st Official	Yashar Adem
2nd Official	Neville Rofaila
Ambassador 2	Nayef Rashed
Ambassador 1	Gabor Vernon
Security Man	Ian Liston
Uncredited	
Surveillance Expert	Ken Tracy
CI5 Agent (Safe house 1)	Ron Watkins
CI5 radio operator	Dennis Plenty
Driver Gang Car 1	Romo Garrara
Passenger Gang Car 1	Cliff Diggins
Driver Gang Car 2	Del Baker
Passenger Gang Car 2	Terry Plummer
Driver Gang Car 3	Rocky Taylor

Director: **Tom Clegg**

BODIE and Doyle undergo a period of rigorous training for a special assignment. Cowley tells them that they are to meet an important foreign politician visiting Britain in secret, escort him to two addresses for talks and then return him to the original rendezvous. There may be an assassination attempt on the politician's life, but in the event of trouble, Bodie and Doyle's link with CI5 is not to be mentioned and they will have to protect themselves as best they can. The CI5 men meet the visiting politician as he steps off a launch at the London docks. He and his large bodyguard are hurriedly shoved into a limousine driven by fellow agent, Charlie. Bodie and his partner follow the limousine at a safe distance, but after only a few miles, the politician's car comes under attack as several cars full of armed men block the road ahead of them. Bodie and Doyle ram two of the cars and jump into the limousine as Charlie accelerates away in a hail of bullets.

In BLIND RUN CI5's Bodie (Lewis Collins) and Doyle are assigned to escort a foreign official during a secret visit to Britain, but enemy assassins seem to know his every move. They quickly work out they are expendable and that a successful conclusion to their mission may be impossible.

A bullet ridden limousine spells danger for CI5's Bodie (Lewis Collins) in BLIND RUN.

The limousine reaches the first address and the politician goes into the house for talks. As he does so, Bodie and Doyle keep a careful lookout for the raiders they encountered earlier. Within minutes they appear and drive a car across the end of the driveway to block their exit. Bodie disguises Charlie as the politician, bundles him into the limousine and rams his foot on the accelerator. The limousine crashes through the barricade, and sets off at speed down the road. The armed raiders leap into their cars and set off after Bodie, firing bullets at the car's wheels and rear window. Doyle meanwhile takes the politician and his bodyguard to a second car, and drives to the second house on the agenda.

The raiders continue to follow Bodie for several miles until a series of crashes and a hail of bullets put paid to Bodie's car. A gunfight ensues, leaving Charlie badly wounded but once the raiders realise that their target is not in the car, they make quick their getaway. Bodie heads straight back for CI5 HQ to tell his boss that they are under attack and need reinforcements. To his astonishment, he finds Cowley with a group of Middle Eastern men watching a television recording of the earlier ambush and excitedly identifying the attackers as their enemies. Cowley explains that the visiting politician is an enemy of Britain's allies and Britain cannot be seen openly protecting him; at the same time, the British authorities do not want him dead, so Bodie and Doyle are to continue to protect him without official backing. Bodie races back to Doyle's aid where Doyle has already secured the help of a girl named Leia, who has recognized the politician as Hanish and wants to help protect him. They escape from the house, but the politician's bodyguard is killed. Bodie has aided their escape by seconding a boat on the nearby canal. As they board the vessel the raiders open fire and the CI5 men make their escape along the canal.

Leia, meanwhile, discovers that, on seeing the face of the politician, he is not Hanish, but an imposter. Angry, the two CI5 men plan to return Hanish back to the rendezvous before asking questions. Cowley informs them that the real Hanish will probably be visiting the country some time in the future; all his enemies have come out of hiding to attack the imposter and, having revealed themselves and been recorded on the TV monitors, they can now be safely rounded up when the politician arrives.

Production Unit

Created by	Brian Clemens
Executive Producers	Albert Fennell, Brian Clemens
Music	Laurie Johnson
Producer	Raymond Menmuir
Associate Producer	Chris Burt
Script Editor	Gerry O'Hara
Production Manager	Donald Toms
Assistant Director	Peter Carter
Location Managers	Stuart Freeman, Cecil Ford
Continuity	Majorie Lavelly
Casting	Maggie Cartier
Production Designer	Malcolm Middleton

Art Director	Peter Joyce
Stunt Arranger	Frank Henson
Wardrobe Supervisor	Donald Mothersill
Lighting Cameraman	Vernon Layton
Camera Operator	John Maskall
Make Up	Alan Brownie
Hairdressers	Mibbs Parker, Barbara Ritchie
Supervising Editor	John S. Smith
Sound Recordist	David Crozier
Music Supervisor	Christopher Palmer
Dubbing Editor	Peter Lennard
Dubbing Mixer	Ted Spooner
Music Editor	Alan Willis

An Avengers MARK 1 Production For LONDON WEEKEND TELEVISION

Shooting / Location Schedule

Production Dates: Tuesday 26th September to Friday 13th October; Wednesday 1st November, 1978. Production Number: 9D11236

26 September	***Docks***: King George V Docks, North Woolwich, London, E16
27-28 September	***Safe house 2: Gates / CI5 surveillance room***: Stanmore Hall, Wood Lane, Stanmore, Middlesex
29 Sept-2 Oct	***Ext: Dock Entrance & Exit***: Kensal Green Gasworks, Canalside House, 383 Ladbroke Grove, North Kensington, London, W10
	Dockland Streets: Kensal Road / Appleford Road / Southern Row / Bosworth Road / Golborne Road, Kensal Town, London, W10
	Dockland Streets: Porsche overtakes: Hazlewood Crescent / Adair Road, Kensal Town, London, W10
3 October	***Tunnel shoot-out***: Ellesmere Avenue, Mill Hill, London, NW7
4-5 October	***Safe house 1***: Ockwells Manor, Ockwells Road, Maidenhead, Berkshire
6-9 October	***Safe house 2: Building exterior / interior***: Oakley Court, Windsor Road, Water Oakley, Berkshire
10-11 October	***Limo Shoot-out / run-bys***: South Lambeth Freight Yard, Nine Elms Lane, South Lambeth, London, SW8 / Kirtling Street / Cringle Street, South Lambeth, London, SW8
12 October	***Safe house 2 escape / Phillipa's canal boat***: Grand Union Canal, Port A Bella Dock, Ladbroke Grove, London, W10
13 October	***Warehouse: escape from boat & streets***: Cadby Hall, Hammersmith & Blythe Road (streets), Hammersmith, London, W14
1 November	***Ext: Park - CI5 Training grounds***: Warfield Hall, Forest Road, Warfield, Berkshire

FALL GIRL
by **Ranald Graham**
© Copyright Mark 1 Productions Ltd MCMLXXVIII

Marikka	Pamela Salem
Schuman	Frederick Jaeger
Willis	Michael Latimer
Kreiber	Sandor Elés
1st Security Man	Patrick Malahide
2nd Security Man	Phillip Joseph
3rd Security Man	George Irving
Barman	Eamonn Jones
Barmaid	Christine Shaw
Julia	Lydia Lisle
Knowles	Frederick Marks
Technician	Gregory Floy
Vic	Michael Redfern
Anna	Astrid Frank
4th Security Man	John Larsen
Old PC	Lewis Wilson
Old Woman	Myrtle Devenish
WPC	Vivien Stokes

Uncredited

Hotel Porter	Jay McGarth
Man in crowd at Hotel	Derek Chafer
Man with cap (Pub)	Charlie Gray
Photographer	Roy Everson
Photographers assistant	Peter McNamara
Uniformed Policeman (Hotel)	Ron Gregory
Uniformed Policeman (Hotel)	Les Conrad
Hotel Corridor Guard	Billy Cornelius
Service Station Workman	Alan Harris
Service Station Workman	Pat Gorman
Pedestrian	Tony Allen
Bierman	Brendan Flannigan

Director: **William Brayne**

WHEN Marikka, a beautiful East German film star, pays a brief visit to London with her husband, Max Schuman, and publicity agent, Kurt Kreiber, Bodie and Marikka, who were once deeply in love, meet secretly during her visit. Schuman finds out about the meeting and decides to make the CI5 man the fall guy in a plot he is preparing. MI6 are also interested in Marikka, and photograph her with Bodie. Willis, a senior MI6 officer, warns Cowley that the woman may be a spy, and Doyle is sent to keep a watch on Bodie. Marikka has booked two adjoining hotel rooms so that she can spend some time with Bodie, and while they sit in her room and reminisce about old times, a rifle shot is fired at the Chief of the East German Secret Service, Bierman, in the street below their window. Bierman is rushed to hospital, but dies later of gunshot wounds. The security team guarding Bierman decide that the rifle shot came from Marikka and Bodie's rooms, and Bodie is arrested for the shooting. In the second room booked by the girl, the security team find a rifle which, because of a trick played on Bodie earlier, has his fingerprints on it.

The men, members of Willis' MI6 department, take the CI5 man to a police station but Marikka is released at the crime scene because she has diplomatic immunity. Doyle, who had been following his partner, witnesses these events and reports to Cowley. Having no idea how Bodie is mixed up with the East German, Cowley questions Willis about the case, but the MI6 man will only confirm Bodie's arrest and says that damning evidence has been found against him. Cowley orders Doyle to kidnap Marikka and question her about the events. Doyle does so but, after carefully questioning the girl for some time, he accepts her story that she and Bodie were only meeting as lovers and they know nothing about Bierman's assassination. When Willis discovers that Cowley has had Marikka kidnapped, he is astonished and angry, but agrees to tell the CI5 head what is happening. Schuman and Kreiber are East German spies, but they are also British double-agents; Bierman has been killed so that Schuman can take his place as Chief of the East German Secret Service. From this senior position he will be able to pass valuable information back to the British authorities. Willis tells Cowley that nothing must be done to make the East German authorities think that Schuman and Kreiber were involved in the killing. Bodie is to be the scapegoat and watertight case has been built up against him. Cowley refuses to allow this and Willis agrees to let Bodie escape. Cowley informs Bodie of the plan, but Willis immediately tells his men to kill Bodie during the attempted escape.

Despite their attempts to kill him, Bodie escapes from custody and drives to Doyle's home. As he arrives he sees Marikka being taken under escort to a CI5 safe house. Bodie follows, unaware that Willis and his men have also traced its whereabouts. Willis' men spot Bodie and begin shooting at him, but the CI5 man escapes and takes refuge at the top of a gasometer. On Cowley's orders, Doyle has tricked the policemen holding the murder weapon into passing it to him, leaving no evidence against Bodie. Cowley and Doyle arrive at the gasometer and when Willis learns that his case against Bodie won't stand up, he calls off his men. Just as things quieten down, Kreiber shoots Marikka dead, leaving no doubt that evidence will now be fabricated implicating her as Bierman's murderer.

Production Unit

Created by	Brian Clemens
Executive Producers	Albert Fennell, Brian Clemens
Music	Laurie Johnson
Producer	Raymond Menmuir
Associate Producer	Chris Burt

Script Editor	Gerry O'Hara
Production Manager	Donald Toms
Assistant Director	Ron Purdie
Location Managers	Stuart Freeman, Cecil Ford
Continuity	Majorie Lavelly
Casting	Maggie Cartier
Production Designer	Malcolm Middleton
Art Director	Peter Joyce
Stunt Arranger	Frank Henson
Wardrobe Supervisor	Donald Mothersill
Lighting Cameraman	Vernon Layton
Camera Operator	John Maskall
Make Up	Alan Brownie
Hairdresser	Barbara Ritchie
Supervising Editor	John S. Smith
Editor	Alan Killick
Sound Recordist	David Crozier
Music Supervisor	Christopher Palmer
Dubbing Editor	Peter Lennard
Dubbing Mixer	Ted Spooner
Music Editor	Alan Willis

An Avengers MARK 1 Production For LONDON WEEKEND TELEVISION

Behind-the-scenes on FALL GIRL as boom operator, Colin Dandridge, picks up actors Gordon Jackson (Cowley) and Michael Latimer (Willis) on location at Southall Gas Works, Middlesex. British actor Michael Latimer was born in 1941, is RADA trained, and has continued a chequered career in films, television, and in the West End; as an actor, writer, producer and director. He has written over 37 scripts including the BBC play THE INTERVIEW, and has directed over fifty productions in London, Sydney, Frankfurt and Florida.

Bodie (Lewis Collins) and Doyle (Martin Shaw) on the set of FALL GIRL.

Shooting / Location Schedule

Production Dates: Monday 16th to Friday 27th October, 1978. Production Number: 9D11238

16-18 October	**Int: Bodie's car (Hotel route)**: Harrington Gardens, Kensington, London, SW7 ***Marrika's Hotel (Hotel 1)***: The Gloucester Hotel (room 780), 4 Harrington Gardens, Kensington, London, SW7 ***Hotel street (Doyle buys flowers)***: Ashburn Place, Kensington, London, SW7 ***Hotel 2 (Bodie meets Marrika)***: The Forum Hotel (rooms 2013 & 2015), 97 Cromwell Road, Kensington, London, SW7
19 October	***Pub:*** Scarsdale Arms, 23a Edwardes Square, Kensington, London, SW8 ***Streets***: Edwardes Square, Kensington, London, SW8
20 October	***Parks (Bodie & Marrika / Cowley & Willis)***: Holland Park, Kensington High Street, London, W8
23 October	***Doyle's house***: 35 Orbel Street, Battersea, London, SW11 ***Int: Cowley's car***: Trott Street, Battersea, London, SW11 ***Bodie's Cortina run-by***: Shuttleworth Road, Battersea, London, SW11 ***Street: Cowley car radio***: 155 Battersea High Street, Battersea, London, SW11 ***Bodie's car run-by (Hotel route)***: Prince Of Wales Drive, Battersea, London, SW11
24 October	***CI5 HQ / Willis' office***: Honeywell Computers, Honeywell House, Great West Road, Brentford, Middlesex
25 October	***Police station***: Cadby Hall, Blythe Road, Hammersmith, London, W14
26-27 October	***Int: Pub (Willis, Kreiber & Schuman)***: White Lion Pub, White Street, Southall, Middlesex ***Petrol Service station & amusement arcade***: Granada M4 Services, Phoenix Way, Heston, Middlesex ***Safe house (gas works)***: Southall Gas Works, White Street, Southall, Middlesex

BACKTRACK

by **Don Houghton**
© Copyright Mark 1 Productions Ltd MCMLXVIII

Margery	Liz Fraser
Garbett	Michael Elphick
Truitt	John Bennett
Pulman	Brian Gwaspari
Miller	Brian McDermott
Sammy	Stacy Davies
Gunman 1	Michael Halphie
Gunman 2	Charlie Price
Sniper	Kevork Malikyan
Alf	Luke Hanson
Herbie	Rudi Patterson
Kabil Kammahmi	Antony Scott
Uncredited	
Uniformed Policeman (alley)	Mike Mungarvan
Terrorist 1	Phil Parkes
Terrorist 2	Billy Cornelius
Anson	Geoffrey Bateman
Uniformed Policeman (manor house)	Peter Roy
Metropolitan Police Agent	Ray Cronk
Metropolitan Police Uniformed Officer	Doug Stark
Metropolitan Police Uniformed Officer	Ken Lawrie

Director: **Christopher King**

CI5 are investigating terrorist activities in London and track down a large and expensive cache of arms brought by Arab terrorists, but the terrorists themselves cannot be questioned as they commit mass suicide as soon as CI5 attack their hideaway. However, it is clear from the quality and quantity of arms found that the Arabs who have come to pursue their personal and political objectives by violent means are drawing on vast financial sources, obtained in London. One night, police catch a cat burglar named Sammy Blaydon who is taken to a police station, and tells the duty officer, Sergeant Garbett, that he has important information, which he will only impart to a police officer he knows, Inspector Truitt. Meanwhile, a solicitor named Pulman arrives at the police station to represent Blaydon and Truitt telephones Cowley to arrange a secret rendezvous so that he too can hear Blaydon's story, but when the pair of them arrive to meet Cowley, a sniper kills them both.

Bodie and Doyle are with Cowley at the rendezvous and give chase to the sniper, a young Arab, who is shot while trying to escape. Cowley decides that the two CI5 men will have to backtrack on Sammy Blaydon's movements until they discover what it was that the burglar told Truitt. Bodie and Doyle first talk to Sergeant Garbett, who advises them to seek further information on Sammy from the fence, Margery Harper. 'Marge' takes an immediate liking to Doyle. She tells the agents that on the night he was arrested, Sammy had just burgled two houses in a select part of London, the home of ammunitions dealer Sir Lionel Laverton, and the home of an important Arab diplomat, Kabil Kammahmi. While Bodie and Doyle are talking to Marge, two Arab gunmen secretly plant a bomb under their car in the street outside.

Doyle (Martin Shaw) finds a stock of heroin in Kammahmi's house. A scene from BACKTRACK.

Fortunately, Doyle notices the bomb hidden under the car just as Bodie is about to drive off, and tells him to call the bomb squad. When Cowley receives their information about the burglaries Blaydon carried out, he makes checks on Laverton and Kammahmi to find out whether either might be involved with the Arab terrorists. No concrete evidence is found against them, so Cowley decides that Bodie and Doyle must burgle both houses and find out what Sammy discovered; he meanwhile, will try to find out who heard about his rendezvous with Sammy and Truitt and alerted the terrorist who shot them. Cowley discovers that Pulman was in the room when Truitt telephoned him about the meeting, and that Pulman has worked for Kammahmi in the past. Sammy obviously found something at Kammahmi's house, which he wanted to tell the authorities about, and the Arab sent Pulman to the police station to try to stop Sammy from talking. By this time, the two CI5 agents are already in Kammahmi's house, and find a large stock of heroin, neatly packaged and ready for sale. Kammahmi's guards disturb

Bodie and Doyle, and when Pulman orders the CI5 men to be killed, Kammahmi argues with the solicitor as the scandal may affect his diplomatic residence. In the confusion, Bodie and Doyle overpower the guards; Cowley and a team of CI5 men are close behind to save the two agents. Pulman tries to escape but Marge is on hand outside to help.

Production Unit

(episode not completed, personnel below apply to the six days filmed here. Episode completed in series III, and those personnel are listed there)

Created by	Brian Clemens
Executive Producers	Albert Fennell, Brian Clemens
Music	Laurie Johnson
Producer	Raymond Menmuir
Associate Producer	Chris Burt
Script Editor	Gerry O'Hara
Production Manager	Donald Toms
Assistant Director	Peter Carter
Location Managers	Stuart Freeman, Cecil Ford
Continuity	Majorie Lavelly
Casting	Maggie Cartier
Production Designer	Malcolm Middleton
Art Director	Peter Joyce
Stunt Arrangers	Peter Brayham, Frank Henson
Wardrobe Supervisor	Donald Mothersill
Lighting Cameraman	Vernon Layton
Camera Operator	John Maskall
Make Up	Alan Brownie
Hairdresser	Barbara Ritchie
Supervising Editor	John S. Smith
Sound Recordist	David Crozier
Music Supervisor	Christopher Palmer
Dubbing Editor	Peter Lennard
Dubbing Mixer	Ted Spooner
Music Editor	Alan Willis

An Avengers MARK 1 Production For LONDON WEEKEND TELEVISION

Shooting / Location Schedule

Production Dates: Monday 30th October to Friday 10th November, 1978. *Production suspended on Monday 6th November.* Production Number: 9D11239

30-31 October	**Drab Street**: Freston Road, Notting Hill, London, W11
	First Floor Room: 90 Freston Road, Notting Hill, London, W11
	Corner shop: Ear Recording Studios, 91-97 Freston Road, Notting Hill, London, W11 - *Original schedule only. Not filmed*

	Suburbs: White City / Wood Lane, Shepherd's Bush, London, W12
	Streets: Cowley's car: A40M-Westway, North Kensington, London, W12
1 November	***Sir Lionel's house***: Warfield Hall, Forest Road, Warfield, Berkshire
2-3 November	***Int: Metropolitan Police Station***: J. Lyons & Co. Ltd, Cadby Hall, Blythe Road, Hammersmith, London, W14
6-7 November	***Int: Margery's shop***: F.E.A Briggs, 83-85 Ledbury Road, Notting Hill, London, W11
	Ext: Margery's shop: F.E.A Briggs, 66-68 Ledbury Road, Notting Hill, London, W11
	Int: Margery's parlour & street: 73 Artesian Road, Notting Hill, London, W11

The following scenes were scheduled but not filmed:

2nd Unit: 31 Oct	*Fashionable Streets*: Belgrave Square / Chesham Place / Lowndes Place / Wilton Terrace / Belgrave Mews, Belgravia, London, SW7
8 November	*Kammahmi's residence*: Warfield Hall, Forest Road, Warfield, Berkshire
9-10 November	*Ext: Park - Common*: Black Park, Black Park Road, Fulmer, Buckinghamshire
9 November	*Ext: Fashionable Streets*: W.F.C Bonham & Sons, 1 Cheval Place (alleyway) / Trevor Street / Montpelier Terrace / Rutland Street, Knightsbridge, London, SW7

Series II Production Unit: uncredited

Production Assistant	Barbara Back
2nd Assistant Director	Roy P. Stevens
3rd Assistant Director	Michael Zimbrich, Jerry Daly
Unit Runners	Jeremy Kelly, Trevor Puckle
Secretary to Mr. Fennell	Sallie Beechinor, Linda Matthews
Secretary to Mr. Menmuir	Jane Dickins
Trainee Secretary	Kim Olney
Location Assistant	Jeremy Kelly
Focus Pullers	Chris Howard, Robin McDonald
Clapper / Loader	Howard Baker, Simon Hume
Camera Grip	Jimmy Gomm, Brian Osborne
Production Buyer	Michele Howell
Art Department Assistant	Ian Watson, Robin Tarsnane
Boom Operator	Colin Dandridge
Sound Assistant	Mervyn Gerrard
Casting Secretary	Debra Kane
Unit Publicist	Paul McNicholls
Publicity Secretary	Lucinda Pugh
Wardrobe Assistants	Donald Mothersill, Iris Richens, Susan Wain

Production Accountant	Ron Garrett
Assistant Accountant	Gill Andersson, George Marshall, Mary Breen-Farrelly
Accounts Assistant	Peter Garrett
Property Master	Gordon Billings
Dressing Props	Stanley Cook, Alan Adams
Stand-by Props	William Stark, Paul Hedges
Construction Manager	Jeff Woodbridge
Carpenter	John Keen
Painter	John Enwright
Stagehand	Tom Buckley
Stand-by Carpenter	Dennis Bovington, Laurence Burns
Stand-by Painter	Dixie Dean
Stand-by Stagehand	Eddie Burke
Stand-by Rigger	Paul Mitchell
Chargehand Electrician	Nobby Cross, Hickery Brown
Electricians	Alan Barry, Stephen Swannell, Ron Lyons
Generator Driver	Peter Casey, Michael Rowsome
Assistant Editors	Mark Auguste, Peter Gray
Assistant Dubbing Editor	Chris Kennedy, Brian Trenerry
Producers Driver	Steve Smith
Unit Drivers	Chris Streeter, Alan Lind, Benny Wright, Ivan Ellias
Action Cars Driver	Peter Ingram
Unit Minibus Driver	Nick Perry
Wardrobe Truck Driver	Phil Knight, John Emery, (Willies Wheels)
Make Up Bus Driver	Michael Devetta
Construction / Prop Driver	Dave Bruyea
Props Return Van Driver	Larry Williams
Catering Vehicle Driver	John Breen
Dining Bus Driver	Tony Leport
2nd Unit Cameraman	Ricky Briggs
Special Effects	Effects Associates, Peter Graham, Martin Gutteridge
Studios	Lee International, Wembley, Middlesex
Laboratories	Rank Labs, Denham, Middlesex
Insurance	Ruben Sedgwick Insurance, Pinewood Studios, Iver Heath, Buckinghamshire
Executive Producers / Music offices	Harefield Grove, Rickmansworth Road, Harefield, Middlesex

SERIES II ACTION CARS

Bodie: **Ford Capri 3.0 S**: UOO 303T (Real index: VHK 495S) - *Hunter/Hunted, First Night, The Rack, Man Without A Past, A Stirring Of Dust, Fall Girl, Backtrack.*
Morris 1800: PPK 156E - *Blind Run.*

	Ford Escort RS 2000: PNO 641T (Real index: PNO 672R) - *Blind Run*.
	Ford Cortina 2.3 GL: VHK 537S - *Fall Girl*.
Cowley:	**Ford Granada 2.8i Ghia**: YHJ 766T (Real index: VHK 518S) - *Rogue, Hunter/Hunted, First Night, The Rack, Man Without A Past, Not A Very Civil Civil Servant, A Stirring Of Dust, Blind Run, Fall Girl, Backtrack*.
	Ford Cortina 1.6 GL: VHK 534S - *Backtrack*.
Doyle:	**Ford Escort RS 2000**: PNO 641T (Real index: PNO 672R) - *Rogue, Hunter/Hunted, First Night, The Rack, In The Public Interest, Not A Very Civil Civil Servant, Fall Girl*.
	Jaguar E Type V12: LPE 7K - *Hunter/Hunted*.
	Honda Civic: XGK 598S - *First Night*.
	Ford Fiesta 1.1L van: YPU 750S - *Blind Run*.
Misc:	**Ford Fiesta 1.1L van**: YPU 750S - *Hunter/Hunted, In The Public Interest, A Stirring Of Dust*.
CI5:	**Ford Cortina 1.6 GL**: UOO 304R - *Rogue, First Night, The Rack*.
CI5:	**Ford Cortina 2.0 GL**: VHK 536S - *First Night, The Rack, Backtrack, Fall Girl*.
Misc:	**Ford Cortina 2.0 GL**: VHK 536S - *Blind Run*.
CI5:	**Ford Capri 1600 Base**: VLO 325M - *The Rack, Fall Girl*.
CI5:	**Ford Cortina 2.3 GL**: VHK 537S - *Backtrack*.
Misc:	Air Film Services (Helicopter) - *First Night*.

TRANSMISSION DATES

1: HUNTER/HUNTED
7th October 1978
2: THE RACK
14th October 1978
3: FIRST NIGHT
21st October 1978
4: MAN WITHOUT A PAST
28th October 1978
5: IN THE PUBLIC INTEREST
4th November 1978
6: ROGUE
11th November 1978
7: NOT A VERY CIVIL CIVIL SERVANT
18th November 1978
8: A STIRRING OF DUST
5th November 1978
9: BLIND RUN
2nd December 1978
10: FALL GIRL
9th December 1978

SERIES III

A HIDING TO NOTHING

AFTER production had been suspended in November 1978, a skeleton crew was kept on at Lee Studios as the space had been paid for until the end of the year.

Barry Myall (producer's driver): "I was hired on the 27th November, as they still had loose ends to tie up. One thing that sticks in my mind from those days was Ray Menmuir's call sign, 'Silver 113'. It was like being at school, various members of the crew were always chasing him. He liked the working phone he had in his car so much that he insisted to the prop guys that Cowley's car was to have a similar phone. They rigged up a dummy phone based on Menmuir's working model. Coincidently, both Menmuir and Cowley drove Ford Granada's.

"Due to the behaviour of the previous drivers, I would not be allowed to take the cars home, leaving my own vehicle at the studio, then leaving to pick up Menmuir for 6.00 am and escort him to the first location of the day. Then back to Lee Studios, before finishing the day's shift anywhere between 8-11 pm. I even bought Menmuir's old dark blue Triumph 2000TC (PNM 565J), which they'd used in filming as a police car. £395 I paid for that, putting a vinyl roof on it to cover the hole left by the police sirens."

Lewis Collins, still with his ankle in plaster after the previous years ankle incident, recalled how while he was in bed "...someone broke in and took all my gear...couldn't have done a thing about it. He was just roaming around the house, walking away with all the merchandise."

A very few hectic months followed before filming recommenced on the new batch of episodes for which producer Ray Menmuir instigated several changes.

Ray Menmuir: "The success of *The Professionals* was due to the realism of the stories and the true-to-life characters of Bodie and Doyle. All our stories could happen today, or maybe tomorrow. We sent Martin and Lewis on a special course, designed to show them how to operate the very latest anti-terrorism equipment as it came from the designer's workshop. It's amazing to find out how our real life counterparts operate. There were bugging devices that were so small you could hardly see them. Sometimes we had the latest weapons before they went into service, and we had to know how to handle them."

Lewis Collins: "It was fascinating meeting the experts who showed us how it was done, though sometimes we felt that they were using us as guinea-pigs just to make sure that they worked before giving them to the people who had to use them for real!"

In early February it was arranged by the Mark I unit publicist, Paul McNicholls, that Lewis Collins and Martin Shaw, would spend a week (12th to 18th February) as guests of the navy at Gibraltar. The day started with an early morning PT lesson before the 'Wrens' (The Women's Royal Naval Service - WRNS; popularly and officially known as the Wrens) issued a challenge for a dinghy race around the harbour. However, a dispute about whose turn it was at the tiller caused them to overturn.

Lewis Collins: "Martin had sailed before, but I hadn't. I took great delight in getting the boat over on a 45-degrees angle without capsizing, but Martin - he turned it right over!"

In February 1979 the Mark I unit publicist, Paul McNicholls, arranged a 'publicity' trip to Gibraltar for the two stars of THE PROFESSIONALS - pictured here is actor Martin Shaw.

Collins, dazed from a bump on the head, had a panic moment when he under the boat, as he caught by the rope around his waist. He was saved by the trapped air and managed to free himself and swim away safely. They were also immediately befriended by the apes, which are the main attraction of 'The Rock'.

Martin Shaw and Lewis Collins in Gibraltar. But it wasn't all plain-sailing!

Next stop was RAF Brize Norton in Oxfordshire, where Lewis Collins was hoisted on a free-fall simulator at the parachute-training centre. This was followed by a visit to an inter-services girls' rifle shooting match at Lee-on-Solent, Hampshire, where the two stars were fully kitted out in shooting outfits with telescopes, and surrounded by girl marksmen from each of the services; the Army, the Navy, and the Air Force.

More travelling was planned in connection with the series, to the South of France to the 'Mardi Gras', and to Tunisia in North Africa.

Martin Shaw was also anxious to try out the silent world of scuba-diving, so with the help of the British Sub Aqua Club's London branch, it was fixed up that Martin would have a one-day course, a very rare occurrence for beginners. In spite of the air tanks weight (28-lbs), Martin had to be weighed down with six weights, each 4-lbs, to make sure he wouldn't rise to the surface.

Meanwhile Lewis Collins was allowed to go out on night-patrol a few times in a CID 'Q' car (unmarked car dealing only in serious crimes). He admitted it was a fabulous experience, 'the real thing', and it was very helpful to him in his part in the series. He was present on four arrests, two raids, one bank robbery in Oxford Street, and a 'stake-out' involving fourteen CID men and himself until 4 am. Following a briefing they all lay in ambush; Lewis was in the lead car where he was witness to some excellent driving at over 80 mph on the wrong side of the road in busy traffic!

Another noticeable difference in the latest series was Collins' and Shaw's latest individual choice of dress and style. Complete wardrobes of dress were built up for each of the major characters following consultation with the actors and especially 'the boys', who were the major source of information on their own roles.

With the exception of the extras, Donald Morhersill obtained all artists' clothing and accessories for the production. To maintain control over the design it is not practical to have actors buying or wearing their own costume. A considerable element of the work done in costume department took place behind the scenes and remained completely invisible in the final programmes. Actors must be kept warm off set. Coats have to be made available for the thinly clad and also to cover policemen's uniforms to conform to legal requirements. If water scenes are called for, wet-suits have to be supplied to be worn under costumes.

Ray Menmuir: "Bodie and Doyle were top men in their field. They had to be ready for any occasion. One day they could meet the Prime Minister, the next they could be up to their waists in Thames mud. That meant that both guys needed a selection of clothes and a good sense of style. Martin and Lewis both had a strong sense of what was right or wrong for them and between us we managed to come up with a range of outfits which reflected their personalities and lifestyles."

Lewis Collins: "We could hardly fight terrorists, madmen and urban guerrillas in pin stripe suits and make it believable, could we? Luckily we were able to adapt our own style to the characters, and that's what made us so believable!"

Donald Mothersill (wardrobe supervisor): "Martin Shaw liked interesting fabrics, jeans, casual shirts and 'Kickers' shoes. Therefore, Martin and I made straight for Kings Road, Chelsea, choosing the wardrobe for Doyle. We stocked up with 'Newman' jeans, soft and stylish jackets and things made of tweed. Knowing his love of everything natural it was perhaps obvious that he would go for non-synthetic materials.

"It took three days to supply Martin with a wardrobe of clothes that would fit in to any type of action that might be called for in the scripts. We have to double up on costumes so that if a stunt man or double is needed, they have a set of identical clothes. Their wardrobe was worth a fortune and we had to take the lot on location with us in case something was damaged or the boys decided to change what they were wearing. But they were great guys to work with and we very rarely differed on what they wore."

Lewis Collins however, was more of a problem to fit. Because he was a broad 42-inch chest, Donald decided to have some smart leather and suede jackets made to measure by a West End tailor. He also had many of his shirts made to measure.

Donald Mothersill: "Lewis was mad on cords and had a whole range made up to go with every outfit, but it was quite a brain taxing job, not only did I do the two boys outfits but I was responsible for the rest of the cast. We did cheat on occasion, as much of the time, what people wore on the first day's shoot they could change back in on the forth. And each night all the clothes had to be cleaned or washed and pressed to keep in good condition."

Brian Clemens: "On a long-running series you always want to cast the actor that's nearest to the character you've envisioned because then he's not having to give a performance every time. In the early days of the show, the characters were as I had conceived them on the printed page. Later on they started to do things that I wasn't too happy with, but if you've got the potential of a long running series, you want your artists to be happy, so you welcome their input, and they welcomed being welcomed as it were.

"Lewis wasn't quite as smooth as I originally wanted. I wanted him to be a bit more 'Armani' and never totally ruffled, you know, after every fight he could just straighten his tie and walk away, whereas Doyle was the man of the street who'd be in jeans and leather jackets and so on. As we got deeper into it, those began to blur and sometimes Lewis was the one in the leather jacket and Martin was the one looking smart. So whereas I wanted to retain that disparity, it didn't always quite work because to do that you have to sit on the set the whole time and roust your actors, which is not conductive to a happy set, so I let it go.

"Then, after a time, the public grew to like it, so I thought why worry about it. Also, they'd been doing it for a while then and they were getting into their characters and probably knew more about Bodie and Doyle than I did, because they were playing them. That was okay, too, that's how series develop; the actor starts to take over from the actual character, and that's good because the less acting they have to do the less tiring it is for the artists and you get a better performance."

Transport was, again, provided by the Ford Motor Company, who were only too glad to loan a new Strato silver Ford Capri 3.0S, COO 251T, for use by Bodie. The original silver car, VHK 495S being past its peak. In order to maintain continuity the Ford Press office issued it with the same false index, UOO 303T, as seen in series 2. It did, however, sport it's real index in the first episode in production, *The Madness Of Mickey Hamilton*, before the Mark 1 production office realised that they had forgotten to put on the UOO 303T number plate. Martin Shaw's character would, again, use the Diamond white Ford Escort RS2000, PNO 672R, which Ford had kept 'on ice' for Mark 1. It would also keep its false identity, PNO 641T. Cowley would drive a new Jupiter red Ford Granada 2.8i Ghia, FEV 24T, again using the series 2 false index, YHJ 766T. This car too, would feature wearing its real index in *A Hiding To Nothing*, and wearing the Capri's UOO false index in *Backtrack*!

The remaining vehicles, used by CI5 agents and various villains (usually Ford Cortinas and a Rover SD1 'Police' car) were the models kept over from the previous year, with the rest hired, as and when needed, from Kingsbury Motors. The helicopter seen in *Stopover* was courtesy of Air Film Services, while in *Weekend In The Country*, Alan Mann, based at Fairoaks Airport, Chobham, Surrey, supplied one of theirs.

For personal armament Bodie and Doyle were supplied with Magnum .357's, though Doyle would also occasionally still use the 9mm Walther P38 automatic. They are very powerful and impressive firearms with the only disadvantage being that, in a crowded situation, the .357 round could over-penetrate and hit an innocent person, behind your chosen target! The .357 is basically a lengthened .38 Smith & Wesson Special round, and as such, any revolver that is chambered for the .357 can equally use the shorter, less powerful .38 Smith & Wesson Special cartridge.

Before production had even started it was announced that ITV had plans to show the entire sixteen-episode run, yet to be produced, from Saturday 8th September until the 22nd December from 9-10 pm. LWT was already gearing up to produce thirteen more episodes in 1980 and 1981 and the possibility of a feature film in 1980. By this time the series had been sold to twenty-one countries. However, due to an ITV technicians strike the proposed transmission dates would be dented.

On Sunday 4th March, Lewis Collins made an opening speech at the famous London palladium for the *Royal Variety Performance.*

The Madness Of Mickey Hamilton: *A killer without a cause tests the resources of C15 when hospitals are attacked and a medical convention is wired up for a holocaust.*

The crew was contracted from Monday 5th March to film the two postponed episodes, *The Madness of Mickey Hamilton* and *Servant Of Two Masters*, from the last batch, and to complete the partly filmed episode, *Backtrack*. The first story, *The Madness Of Mickey Hamilton*, commenced production on Monday 12th.

In THE MADNESS OF MICKEY HAMILTON C15 computer operator Julia (Lydia Lisle) comes up with the name Mickey Hamilton; Cowley (Gordon Jackson) instructs Doyle (Martin Shaw) to find the deranged killer before he can cause any more deaths.

Under the control of William Brayne 35-year old writer Christopher Wicking's script had been scheduled for filming the previous year (the completed draft being received by LWT on 10th November 1978), but had been suspended due to Lewis Collins' ankle incident.

Christopher Wicking: "I was originally contacted by Gerry O'Hara saying he and Ray Menmuir were actively seeking writers for the series who knew about movie-writing. I was intrigued. And delighted when I found that my interest in, and admiration for, the best American series, *The Defenders*, *Dragnet*, *Dick Powell Theatre* et al was shared by them. In fact, it was more than shared. Film-making was the name of the game. When I became involved in talking possible storylines, I felt inhibited by the fact that the three main characters were not 'mine', i.e: they had a life beyond the one that I might give them, and was concerned that some sort of consistency should pertain. Would I write things that they 'wouldn't do' or 'wouldn't say?' I was amazed by the fact that there was no 'Bible', the do's and don'ts of character and overall requirements. This seemed to be some sort of freedom, but it was a very worrying one and took me a long time to get used to. It seemed to me that Ray and Gerry didn't know what they wanted. How could you be running a show and not plan the kind of material you want to use? In fact, of course, they knew exactly what they wanted, and this was how they ensured they got it.

"We eventually settled on an idea that probably sprung out of *Dirty Harry*. We open with a man on a rooftop with a rifle. The 'lunatic killer' who's after random targets. There had to be an ultimate pattern to the random-ness, though, and Gerry suggested that the character should have a personal vendetta against, well, why not priests? I was amazed. Could we do a show about a priest killer? Apparently, we could. But I couldn't generate enough feeling against priests (where Gerry could, having had a miserable childhood jumping to their whims). What about doctors? Sure, doctors would be okay.

"So the character, Mickey Hamilton, hated doctors enough to want to kill them. Why? And why should CI5 get involved? So I had him miss his first target (though the audience knows who he's really after) and hit someone in a car driving across his field of vision at the moment he fired, and the someone was an African diplomat, which makes the abortive killing appear to be a political assassination attempt and therefore justifies CI5 involvement. For it was important to me that the 'real' world of the story should be more of a 'working class' one than usually appears in these kind of shows, where the villains all live out in the stockbroker belt.

"Mickey would live out in the high-rise council flat where the lift doesn't work and the 'victim' of a hospital asylum which has many cracks and flaws. His wife has had a child, the complications at birth have made the child a vegetable for all of her life, and she is now on the point of dying. His wife, blaming herself, has later taken an overdose, and has died, at the same hospital. Mickey cracks up, believing that neither tragedy need have happened, blames the doctors and wants to kill them all so they won't ruin other people's lives. Such is 'The Madness Of Mickey Hamilton'. Other characters, like his sister, never listen to what he is saying, and a priest, who doesn't know what he's talking about, says it probably is alright to 'kill with kindness', which seems like a blessing and a tacit permission to blow up a medical conference for the third act climax.

"As an admirer of Budd Boetticher movies, where his leading character never explains himself and it is left to the support cast to provide information, it became a little game to never have Mickey explain himself properly, leaving his sister, characters at hospital, etc, to do the exposition, in order that there would be a 'mystery' about him to keep people watching, which would hopefully turn to sympathy, just as Cowley, Bodie and Doyle come to understand and be moved by the various kinds of loss of life ('I think I'd go mad if I had to live here' says Cowley, looking at the crumbling high rise.)

In THE MADNESS OF MICKEY HAMILTON, actress Shelagh McLeod played Doyle's girlfriend, Toni. Born (7th May 1960) in Vancouver, Canada Shelagh was diagnosed in her teenage years as having degenerative scoliosis (a hunchback condition) for which she had to undergo two grueling operations to realign her spine. She spent five days in intensive care when her lung failed to re-inflate. To help her through drama school she once had a holiday job as an ancillary nurse in a hospital.

"So what? you may say, this is not earth-shattering dramaturgy. Even so, I was delighted to get my rocks off and find a way to satisfy the 'requirements' of the series while dealing, however tangentially, with things that concern me. I was delighted too, by the way Bill Brayne directed it, in a very 'organic' non-flashy style, confirming that he is one of the few contemporary directors with the gift of clarity, directing for 'the whole' rather than using some of 'the parts' to show off. I had quite consciously shied away, though, from dealing with the three regulars, who function as little more than investigators. As it happened, I needn't have worried, for part of the 'freedom' lay in these very areas."

Location manager Bernard Hanson had joined the Mark I personnel after both Cecil Ford and Stuart Freeman had opted not to do another series. Hanson had worked on the James Bond films, *Diamonds Are Forever* (1971) and *Live And Let Die* (1973), and *The Omen* (1976).

One of the first tasks faced by Bernard Hanson was to find a suitable location that could represent Mickey's run-down council flat as depicted in Christopher Wicking's script. Following an initial recce around Golborne Road in North Kensington, West London, he spotted the ideal location in the guise of the Erno Goldfinger designed Trellick Tower. By chance he bumped into a gentleman in the lift and the man's flat seemed to give Hanson the perfect locale.

The film crew drew up outside Trellick Tower in the early hours of 19th March to film several sequences. The first of which had Lewis Collins breaking the glass in the front door to let himself into the flat. A scene completed to perfection by Collins on the first take. Next, he had to kick the door open and search the flat. The door opened, but the noise of scraping glass on the floor was too much. Nine takes later, director Bill Brayne was happy with the sequence. However, by this time the schools had turned out and it was up to Martin Shaw to keep the crowd quiet as filming continued. By 6 pm, all the day's scenes were completed and the front door was put back on its hinges.

The conclusion to the story was filmed at Wembley Conference Centre, Middlesex, only a stones throw from Lee International Studios - and the Mark 1 unit base.

Mike Silverlock (boom operator): "We had some (police) dogs being used in some of the scenes. They turned out to be extremely misbehaved - they were constantly running off and interrupting rehearsals. Come one of the takes, as Martin and Lew come up the stairs, one of the dogs, out of camera shot, breaks free of its handler and goes bowling over the chairs heading for the boom microphone. The crew were in fits of laughter for ages as we tried to get the thing out of the dogs mouth and continue filming!"

Bone marrow transplant girl, Michelle Beckley, lived out her dream by appearing in the episode. Her starring role was a scoop for LWT. Arranged by the BBC's *Jim'll Fix It*, eleven-year-old Michelle was visited on 9th March by her heroes in hospital. They dropped in to see her at Hammersmith Hospital, when she was told that she was to be kept in for an extra day, after already spending six weeks there. The bone-marrow transplant made medical history as her donor, three-year-old sister, Martine, was the world's youngest.

Her scenes in the episode were filmed on location at St. Hubert's House, Gerrards Cross, Buckinghamshire, on the 14th March, under the watchful eye of Jimmy Saville. Michelle, from Dagenham, Essex, played the part of a little girl (Mickey's daughter) in a germ-free bubble as she had in real life.

In THE MADNESS OF MICKEY HAMILTON actor Ian McDiarmid guest stars as the deranged killer Mickey Hamilton. Born (11th August 1944) in Carnoustie, Tayside, Scotland, he studied for an M.A. in Clinical Psychology at The University of St. Andrews, but eventually found that his calling was in acting. He went to the Royal Academy in Glasgow, where he received the prestigious gold medal for his theatre work and is perhaps most famous for his chilling performance as The Emperor in the STAR WARS films.

Meanwhile, later that day, Gordon Jackson received the OBE from her Majesty the Queen. Gordon, with his wife, Rona, and their two sons Graham and Roddie, arrived for the investiture in good time, and Gordon was most surprised when one of the royal ushers asked him for his autograph! It was Gordon's second visit to the Palace, the previous year he'd been invited by her Majesty for lunch.

Minor script revisions were implemented during the episode's conclusion. Originally Bodie finds Mickey and is able to keep him talking while Doyle disconnects the explosives. Mickey tries to escape, takes a shot at Bodie, and is then shot by a police marksman. Wounded Mickey is taken away to stand trial. In the finished product, Doyle keeps Mickey talking, while Bodie finds the bomb. Doyle then persuades Mickey to hand over the detonator, but Mickey is startled by one of the guard dogs and runs into sight of Inspector Shannon, who hastily shoots him. Mickey then dies from his injuries.

Bodie's Capri wears its correct index (COO 251T) in one scene, before being exchanged to its fake one (UOO 303T) as filming continued; the false number plates had been mislaid by a member of the production crew.

Admirably, this episode achieved 14.3 million viewers, and topped the weekly ratings chart during a repeat broadcast on 10th January 1981.

Servant Of Two Masters: *Bodie and Doyle stalk their own master in disbelief, when Cowley steals a lethal nerve gas and starts sales with a foreign power.*

Servant Of Two Masters, penned by Douglas Watkinson, whose completed draft had been received by LWT on 2nd November 1978 was originally scheduled to be filmed from 13th November that year. Watkinson had started his career on the TV series *The Onedin Line* in 1971 before producing scripts for *Emmerdale Farm* from 1972.

Under the guidance of director Ferdinand Fairfax (born in London 1st August 1944), *Servant Of Two Masters* commenced principle shooting on Monday 26th March. Fairfax had been an assistant director in the late 1960's working on movies such as *The Chairman* (aka *The Most Dangerous Man In The World*) and the Irish film, *Quackser Fortune Has A Cousin In The Bronx* (aka *Fun Loving*).

Gerry O'Hara extensively amended the script. Originally, with Bodie and Doyle locked in the cellar at Hahn's farmhouse, Cowley is asked to release the gas on the two agents. But before he can, Bodie and Doyle escape from the cellar and break into the room. Hahn and his men escape and Bodie and Doyle place Cowley under arrest. As they drive away Cowley explains he is undercover. Cowley demands to see the papers Plum issued to arrest him. Doyle confesses he does not have them and arranges a meeting with Plum, who maintains he did not know Cowley was undercover. Cowley leads the raid on the farmhouse and finds CI5 arms expert, Alfred Cole, has been supplying the weapons.

In the finished print, an unconvinced Hahn, despite the CI5 chief's attempts to help his men escape, throws Cowley in the cellar with Bodie and Doyle. Hahn plans to escape at an airport (even this was originally to have been done by boat, but this proved impractical) but is stopped when Cowley and his men arrive. As per the original script, Cole is also apprehended.

When some countries broadcast this episode the title was reversed to 'Master Of Two Servants', and appears as such in certain production notes!

Martin Shaw poses for a rare off-duty shot in a SERVANT OF TWO MASTERS.

David Bracknell (first assistant director): "My instructions from producer Ray Menmuir were very clear. After the previous year's ankle incident, I was told to keep an eye on Lewis Collins when doing anything that could involve holding up the production. Basically, he wasn't allowed to do any of the dangerous stunts called for in the script. No matter what he said! We did a scene where Martin and Lewis are training in a deserted warehouse and they have to crash through some specially set up windows. Martin posed no problem and Frank (Henson) prepared to do the stunt. But Lewis said he was okay doing it himself. After some heated words we managed to get Del Baker to do it.

"Later in the episode, Lewis is being chased by a guy on horseback. After a struggle, Lewis (Bodie) had to hit the guy off using a branch. We did the close-ups with Lewis as we had no alternative, but the bit where Bodie picks up the branch and hits the guy off, we decided that Del Baker should step in. Lewis again decided that he should do it. And, again it took a lot of persuading to get him to allow Del to do the stunt. I admired him for wanting to do every little bit of action, but I had my instructions."

In a SERVANT OF TWO MASTERS Ryan Michael plays Wilf, one of Otto Hahn's henchmen.

Lewis Collins and Martin Shaw pose for the stills cameraman between takes on a SERVANT OF TWO MASTERS.

John S. Smith (supervising editor): "They brought in Ferdie Fairfax to direct this one, he was a very clever director, but also very slow. He would set up scenes and think about how they would be edited before we had even seen the rushes. He did all the establishing shots himself, rather than leave it to a second unit, wasting lots of main unit shooting time. He filmed everything that was needed in a 'Hitchcock' style that could not be done in the ten days allotted to each episode, and that caused us all a headache in the cutting rooms; he would sit in post-production and try to do our jobs for us. It took us ages to get this one out."

William Alexander (art director): "Ferdie Fairfax was murder to work with. He wanted things doing that were just impossible to do in the tight schedule and budget involved in this kind of show. It came as no surprise that the script was extensively altered to accommodate the fact they we were already struggling to keep the episode on budget and on the scheduled ten-day turnaround. Whether this was the reason that it was the only episode he worked on, was not made clear."

William Alexander had worked as an art director on episodes of *Special Branch*, *The Sweeney* and *Van Der Valk*, starting his career in the 1950's on the 1957 Boulting brothers movie *Brothers In Law*, and later as an assistant on some of the Carry On films.

"In 1973 Malcolm Middleton, the art director on *Special Branch* asked me to fill in for him for four weeks (the reason why has gone); but their operation was an eye opener. George Taylor and Lloyd Shirley in the shape of Euston Films, were blazing a trail for Thames Television: the cameras were lightweight super 16mm, Nagras recorded the sound, the colour stock was blazing fast and we shot everything on location, including interiors. Fifty screen minutes (an hour show) was shot in two weeks, five minutes every day, twice the speed of a movie with half the crew, and without overtime. Not to say that the unions were happy to accept this, but that is another story! The film was cut to the same strict time scale and in those days everything was on film. Today, even if it is still shot on film (rare), it is immediately transferred to tape, edited and delivered digitally.

"It was due to my relationship with the editor and associate producer, Chris Burt, that I got the job on *The Professionals*. We had worked together on *The Sweeney* and *Van Der Valk*. I had been hired at short notice, as the previous series production designer, Malcolm Middleton and his assistant Ian Watson had been drafted in by *The Professionals* script editor, Gerry O'Hara, to work with him on the Joan Collins film, *The Bitch*. Gerry was directing the feature and was, therefore, also absent from the production for a month or so. They obviously liked the work I was doing as they kept me on for the rest of the series.

Bodie and Doyle are shocked to discover that Cowley (Gordon Jackson) appears to be selling nerve gas to a group of East Germans in order to line his own pockets, and are assigned by his rival Plumb to track their boss's every move. Here, in an unused scene he attempts to sell PS2 to Otto Hahn (David De Keyser) in SERVANT OF TWO MASTERS.

William Alexander: "I was warned about the two leads from the outset. 'Don't get fooled by them' I was told. Lewis Collins approached me and asked me to supply two new guns, convincing me they were essential as the old ones were past their sell-by-date. I managed to get two brand new ones from the prop department. One was black and the other stainless steel (a Smith & Wesson 629). When Menmuir heard what they had done, he went mad and for continuity reasons the chrome one was painted black. But Lewis Collins, when no one was looking, would scratch bits of black paint off. It caused constant frustration for the continuity girls, much to the two guys' amusement."

Between takes at Warfield Hall, Berkshire, which was being used as the Otto Hahn's residence in the story, the three leads decided to try a spot of football - with a couple of chairs as goal posts mayhem ensued! Gordon Jackson, in his position as goalkeeper watched and commented that he was the most unathletic person you could imagine. The same day, the entertainments editor of the 'Daily Star' newspaper visited the set and found himself in the thick of the action, tied and gagged in the back of a van being used on the set *(pictured below with Martin Shaw)*.

William Alexander: "Warfield Hall was a wonderful grand white house, but a headache for any art director! We were using the farmhouse, situated in the grounds, as Hahn's residence. Warfield Hall had belonged to a Quaker family who had put it up for sale. Therefore, it wasn't furnished. So every time it was used it had to be dressed from top to bottom and obviously different sets mean different dressing. Not only that, but when we'd finished, it all had to be stripped back again."

Backtrack: The final postponed episode, *Backtrack*, was still to be finished and had over a weeks worth of footage to be made, from Monday 9th

April until Friday 20th April, with the crew and actors breaking for Easter from Wednesday 12th to Sunday 16th.

Doyle's hairstyle is different in the scene where he and Bodie are waiting outside Cowley's apartment block, due to the production hiatus encountered during the filming of this episode.

Location manager Bernard Hanson had opted to bow out of the production at this stage, which left the way open for a new scout to join the team. Peter Carter was born in Hornsey and started his career as an uncredited assistant director on the David Lean feature *Ryan's Daughter* (1970), before becoming a location manager on Gerry Anderson's *The Protectors* in 1972. He then spent some time in South Africa filming *Zulu Dawn* in 1978, before returning to England to work on Ian Ogilvy's incarnation of *Return Of The Saint*, and then as assistant director on the second series of *The Professionals*.

Peter Carter: "I had already been doing some firsting (assistant director) for them the previous year. So when Bernie left I was asked to manage the locations rather than continue as an assistant director. On top of finding the location, my job did not stop there, I had to contact the local Police, although they couldn't give permission to film by law, they were usually quite understanding as long as I told them what was happening. I then had to make sure that at least 35 vehicles had places to park. After all, it's no good finding a good location if the crew can't get all their equipment there, so this sometimes involved special agreements for the use of NCP car parks and local authority parking bays."

It's just another routine house break-in for a cat burglar in BACKTRACK, until he accidentally uncovers a complex drugs smuggling operation. When CI5's Doyle (Martin Shaw) and Bodie (Lewis Collins) step in, they realise it's not just the burglar's life that is now in danger.

CI5 discover a large and expensive cache of illegally imported weapons, a number of dead terrorists, and a cat burglar who has seen too much. Doyle (Martin Shaw) gains the help of Margery Harper (Liz Fraser) in BACKTRACK.

During the Easter break (12th to 16th April), Gordon Jackson took a trip to see the Renaissance treasures of Rome; Lewis Collins went for sunshine, exercise and action in Tunisia; and Martin Shaw sought solitude exploring England's Canal system.

By this time the National Viewers and Listeners Association, led by Mary Whitehouse, voted *The Professionals*, 'Top Of The Cops'. They claimed the show proved to be less violent and used fewer swear words than any other programmes in the same idiom.

Stopover: *Bodie and Doyle are pitted against a KGB killer team when a CI5 agent is raised from the dead.*

The first 'real' series three script was John Goldsmith's *Stopover*, which under director William Brayne's control began production on Monday 23rd April. Goldsmith's career had started in the early 1970's on Gerry Anderson's *The Protectors*, before writing *The New Avengers* story, *The Lion And The Unicorn*. Prior to *The Professionals* he had written five episodes of *Return Of The Saint*.

This episode, when broadcast on the 10th November 1979, was the highest rated of the series, achieving 15-million viewers, and number twelve in the weekly viewing charts.

The camera crew arrived early in the morning on the first day's shoot at King George V Dock, East London.

Robin McDonald (focus puller): "We'd always arrive early to get the gear set up, and besides, the guys from the catering truck (John Engleman and John Lane) used to prepare one heck of a breakfast so, at around 7.45am, as we settled down to tuck into our bacon and eggs, we looked out across the River Thames and saw what looked like a dead body floating in the water. The Police were called, who immediately stopped us from filming until they had finished their investigations. We later discovered it was the body of a tramp, who had drunk himself silly and fell in. He'd been dead for some time. What a start to the day, and our breakfast, that was!"

Photographers from 'Corgi Toys' visited the set of STOPOVER on the 26th April 1979 to shoot images for their forthcoming Ford Capri car set.

The conclusion to this episode, filmed over two days between 26th and 27th April, at Warfield Hall, Berkshire, had the three stars arriving at speed in Cowley's Granada.

Gordon Jackson: "I didn't enjoy being in the car with either of the boys. Both were very good drivers, but I found it very difficult to remember my lines and appear calm while filming along private country roads at 99mph. The boys used to drive themselves and we had to switch on the camera in the car and set off. I remember Martin was driving along and overtaking other stunt cars. I was thinking, 'Are we going to make it?'"

Martin Shaw: "I was taught to drive by Peter Brayham, and he is one of the world's best. We did 99% of the driving in the series and it's a great skill to have. Even though I did manage to hit the RS2000 into a garage at one point in the story (slightly damaging the front bumper)."

On 2nd May, during the sequences filmed at Frithwood Avenue, Northwood, Martin Shaw and Lewis Collins highlighted to director Bill Brayne the rivalry that existed between them. The shooting script required that Doyle was to escort, and protect, Meredith from Kodai inside Safe House 12. Watching from the sidelines Lewis Collins decided he would show Martin Shaw how the scenes should be acted out. Therefore, in the final print, it's Bodie inside the house with Meredith, leaving Doyle to drive the Ford Capri.

Peter Brayham (stunt arranger): "They (Martin and Lewis) were so incredibly fit and such perfectionists that it was easy to teach them to drive and fight. They were both in excellent shape, which was important, as you could easily get hurt in rehearsals. They were both terrific drivers but I taught them a few tricks for the camera. Most people look at a car chase on the television and think they could do that, but could they do it at 5.30 on a freezing Monday morning, and could they perform the moment the cameras start rolling, and stop, the instant the director yells: 'Cut'.

"When we did a car chase I would never finish with the brakes on. If the cameraman was holding the camera to his face and I put the brakes on he'd lose an eye. He would be strapped in with a harness and I made sure they locked the door, as it wasn't unknown for them to fall out along the way. I'd always talk to him on the way round, as I was nearly always the double for someone so they wouldn't be recording my voice. I'd say, 'I'm going to make a right here. I'm going to brake now, braking slightly, take your eye away', and they'd lean back."

Lewis Collins, however, managed to damage the front panel on the Ford Capri while filming, on the 3rd May, at Sherwood Street, Whetstone, North London. Attempting to do a hand brake turn at the bottom of the road, he misjudged the kerb and creased the front panel. This resulted in some heavy visible damage. It appeared in the next two episodes (*Runner* and *A Hiding To Nothing*) before the car could be spared from filming and repaired.

DEBBIE'S DREAM DAY: Friday 27th April turned out to be very a special day for Deborah Bartlett from Essex. She was the winner of the Mates magazine competition 'Meet The Professionals' run the previous year (28th October 1978) and joined the Mark One crew for a days filming at Warfield Hall, near Bracknell, Berkshire. After a morning watching Lewis Collins and Martin Shaw in action it was time for a spot of lunch!

Another sequence filmed at Sherwood Street required the stunt rider standing in for actor Morgan Sheppard, who was portraying Malenski, to fall from his motorbike. When the scene was enacted, instead of falling over, the motorbike stayed upright and ploughed straight into the camera crew, hitting both camera operator John Maskall, and focus puller Robin McDonald. The damage sustained was minimal and filming continued.

Cowley is offered the name of a highly-placed double agent from an old colleague, who in return wants to be guaranteed protection with CI5. Lewis Collins and Martin Shaw in STOPOVER.

Runner: The CI5 team explode into action when a single code word heralds total war between the authorities and a massive Mafia network.

Runner, by Michael Feeney Callan, who went onto become the story editor on *Shoestring*, started filming on Tuesday 8th May (due to the May Bank Holiday) with director Martin Campbell at the helm.

In Michael Feeney Callan's original script, certain scenes were depicted somewhat differently than were ultimately visualised by director Martin Campbell. One sequence was the scene where Duffy is killed: This underwent two rewrites; Sylvie pushing Duffy to his death and getting shot in the arm as his gun went off; and then Doyle was to have pulled the trigger killing Duffy, but in the finished product Sylvie is holding the gun having saved Doyle from Duffy.

Peter Carter (location manager): For *Runner* we needed a derelict block of flats for a shoot-out (The Highlands, Crouch Hill, North London) and possibly an explosion. We looked at different boroughs near the studios where there were big estates being renovated or demolished. We got tremendous co-operation from the Islington Borough, the publicity officer there, Keith Sargent, was so helpful that we found ourselves constantly going back during the course of the show.

"Keith was really genned up on filming and I only had to pick up the phone and tell him what sort of location we needed and he would have all the information at his fingertips. He sorted out a lot of red tape procedures for us leaving the unit free to continue filming."

"I would only receive the script seven to ten days before production would commence, sometimes even later. Bearing in mind that up to thirty locations can be required for one fifty-minute programme, locations had to be within an hour's drive of Lee Studios. They tended to be within a thirty-mile radius of Wembley. We would rarely go south of the Thames, because of the time involved travelling. The choice would be made up from sites which I knew personally, for instance, Hornsey, where we filmed dozens of car chases and second unit stuff, or areas like Islington, where I had plenty of co-operation in the past from Keith.

"Another area we used was the village of Warfield, near Ascot. There are a couple of country estates there, which we used for helicopter scenes, gunfights and special effects sequences. The open country there is ideal."

In RUNNER a former mobster who has a grudge against both the mob and Doyle (Martin Shaw) attempts to incite a war between CI5 and the mob.

Norman Langley (lighting cameraman) : "I had joined the show at the invitation of associate producer Chris Burt (David Findlay had left to pursue other projects after only one episode). I knew Chris from a few years back, when we had worked together on numerous shows of the *The Sweeney*, on which he served as a supervising editor. It was a pleasant, but very hectic, experience working on both these shows. Martin Campbell directed this one; he is a very inventive and energetic director and great fun to work with. I had no idea then he would be so successful, but I'm not surprised. Action scenes are always a team effort, director, cameraman, the script, and stunt person. I had already worked on plenty of *The Sweeney* shows that had lots of action in them so knew exactly what to expect."

In RUNNER an attempt to start up a street war is launched by a gangland breakaway opposition group...but its Bodie's (Lewis Collins) CI5 partner Doyle who becomes a target!

The scenes filmed at 'The Green Man' pub car park in Muswell Hill, North London, on the 15th May, had to be partially reshot the following week by the second unit when it was discovered that the camera negative was damaged. Problems were further compounded when the sequences in question, the conclusion to Doyle's car chase, were hampered by heavy downpours and the Datsun 180B (FLA 941T), on loan from Kingsbury Motors, was fitted with the incorrect indexes (UMD 25P). However, by the time these discrepancies had been picked up it was too late to mount another shoot.

The theft of a large consignment of arms leads CI5 to think the Organisation is active again. Martin Shaw and Lewis Collins on location as CI5 agents Doyle and Bodie on the set of RUNNER.

The original script also had a slightly different undramatic conclusion. The bomb, planted under the government building, fails to explode, when Bodie and Doyle find, in haste, Duffy has forgotten to put a detonator on it. The scene and extra dialogue was scripted thus:

Ext: Government Offices
The wires on the bomb come free - the clock moves to six. There is a dull clack-clack. No explosion.
BODIE: *Bang!*
DOYLE: *Yeah* (eases back plastic detonator sleeve). *No detonator.*
COWLEY: *I heard the call. Duffy?*
DOYLE: *Yeah. Double vendetta - get me and back at the Organisation who wouldn't take up his fight.*
COWLEY: *Clever boy, he could have brought this city down round our ears.*
BODIE: *Not clever enough to remember the detonator on a simple 1-2-3 bomb though, was he?*
DOYLE: *Situation defused.*
BODIE: *For the time being, anyway?*

To make the ending more dramatic, script editor Gerry O'Hara scripted the following:

Bodie and Doyle race against time to disconnect the bomb, planted in the Government building's car park, and in the nick of time cut the correct wires.

Martin Campbell (director): "This is why I prefer the pre-production and post process the best. I don't like the actual shooting at all; I find it very demanding and tough especially in the tight deadlines associated with a show like *The Professionals*, but I love post and the whole process of seeing the episode ultimately come together. You start ironing out all the rough spots, and the really bad ones you chuck away. So from day one of post to the last day, you see nothing but improvements."

Martin Shaw finds time to joke around during filming on RUNNER, much to the amusement of co-star Lewis Collins.

A Hiding To Nothing: *Doyle has a 'licence to love', after a ministerial secretary betrays summit talk security details to her agent lover.*

Tuesday 22nd May (due to the May Day Bank Holiday) saw work commence on Ted Childs' *A Hiding To Nothing*, with the director's reins picked up by Gerry O'Hara. Childs started his career in factual television, making documentaries for *The World At War*, before writing scripts for *Special Branch* and becoming producer on *The Sweeney*.

While filming at 'The Holiday Inn', Swiss Cottage, North West London, the production unit had a few problems with members of the public.

Jerry Daly (third assistant director): "If you ever tried clearing a London street of traffic, you'll just know how hard it was to stop all those curious on-lookers from cruising by slowly, especially when you are filming outside an hotel. Then we had to set up scenes involving the two leads, Martin and Lewis, in the Ford Capri. Even in daylight, extra lighting was needed otherwise the cameras would not pick up the faces in the car, and this again attracts unwanted attention as the lights are very bright."

On Monday 4th June, the crew assembled at Black Park, Fulmer, Buckinghamshire, to film the final scene of the story. The action called for an ambush by Palestinian freedom fighters with plenty of retaliation from CI5, including Bodie and Doyle.

Frank Henson was in charge of all the stunt action and had set himself up for one of the dangerous and difficult stunts called for in the script. He had to jump out of a Rolls Royce at 30 mph. To cushion his fall, he was wearing elbow and hip pads, but even a mere timing mistake may have left him going head first into a tree. In 35-years as a stunt man, he has had but a few injuries.

A dummy run that has been staged for the visit of a Middle Eastern official is found to have been recorded by a foreign student, subsequently leading CI5 to suspect a security leak. Gordon Jackson and Martin Shaw test the latest weaponry (seem here with a Bazooka Rocket launcher) in Black Park, Fulmer, Buckinghamshire for use in the story A HIDING TO NOTHING.

Frank Henson: "If you meet a stunt man who says he has broken every bone in his body, forget him, he can't be that good! I never was the popular image of a stuntman. I am average in height and build, not a big, burly muscle man.

"That's mainly because by the time we did *The Professionals*, the stars, at that time, were very different from previous years. The John Wayne's and Charlton Heston types had given way to smaller heroes like Paul Newman and Steve McQueen. And Martin Shaw and Lewis Collins were both under 6-feet tall."

Stunt arranger Peter Brayham took up to two weeks to decide which equipment and men were needed for the scenes to be filmed.

Peter Brayham: "Frank needed bags of soft peat for his jump, but decided that the ground was soft enough!"

Also waiting in the sidelines to do her stunt that day was Dorothy Ford, one of only ten stuntwomen in the country at the time. She was to crash a car into a tree, smashing the windscreen.

Frank Henson: "We had to cut the tree three quarters through so it would fall easily. The windscreen itself had also been specially prepared with a layer of plastic film so that the glass did not fly back and hit her in the face!"

Dorothy Ford: "I'd been in the industry ten years and worked on a Bond film at the time where I had to climb out on the roof of a cable car 3,000-feet up, so the car stunt didn't seem so bad."

Shelley (Lise Hilboldt) prepares a takeaway meal for Doyle (Martin Shaw). The two stars find time to pose for the camera on A HIDING TO NOTHING.

Ian Wingrove's special effects team was also present that day. They made up a Bazooka Rocket launcher that had to look like the real thing firing, but the 'plastic' shell made the weapon no less life-like and when it fired, sending the shell hurtling off at great speed, the noise of the small explosive charge was more than convincing.

Ian Wingrove: "The problem with 'plastic' shells is they do not explode. We used a shallow pit filled with sandbags to cushion the blast and with a detonator, sacking, cement dust and broken cork blocks, the scene was set. The camera followed the Rolls Royce, which was supposed to be minus a driver and out of control. It went into the blast site and the explosion sent earth and debris through the air. On screen, the shell misses the car, but in the open air of Black Park, none of the crew were spared a liberal coating of smoke and cement dust. However, a cue was missed for a second car to skid on the scene and we had to set it all up again. We didn't take long though."

Peter Davey was also on hand to simulate people being shot. Their wounds were already in the special effects box.

Peter Davey (special effects): "It is all done with a thing called a 'kicker board', a detonator, and 'Kensington Gore'. The gore is artificial blood. This is inside a plastic bag attached to a small metal plate. The plate is strapped to the person doomed to be shot and a foam pad protects them from bruising. From the detonator we run an electrical wire down through their clothing and away to where the gunshot would be set off. The actor can set it off, but for safety reasons we like to do it.

CI5's Ray Doyle (Martin Shaw) battles with an intruder (stunt-man Del Baker) on A HIDING TO NOTHING.

"Lewis Collins also had a slight mishap with the Bazooka. A photo shoot was called for the three stars and I told him it would give a kick similar to a shotgun. Reassured he knelt down to make a test shot and 'boom!' There were clouds of smoke and on the ground was Lewis with the beginnings of a black eye and a cut lip. He said it felt like the kick of ten shotguns. Martin Shaw and Gordon Jackson both saw the funny side of things as their co-star picked himself up from the floor!"

Martin Shaw managed to scrape the door of the Escort RS2000 on some bushes during a scene. The damage necessitated paintwork to the nearside door, which was visible on the cars next featured episode, some two months later, *The Purging of CI5*, when over-spray can be seen on the door handle.

Meanwhile, Bodie's Ford Capri suffered a nearside rear tyre blow out, when the second unit filmed the stunt involving Bodie following Luis. The wheel cap was mislaid and the production office had to order a new one from Ford Motor Company. The cap was never replaced and the car is seen in the remaining episodes minus the item.

Lewis Collins gets more than he bargained for during a publicity shoot on A HIDING TO NOTHING involving a Bazooka Rocket launcher!

David Crozier (sound recordist): "I left the production at the end of this episode - I had worked almost non-stop on the show for a few years and thought I could do with a change. I admired Ray Menmuir for giving me my big break and he knew it, so he was only too pleased to give me some time off to go and do the feature film *McVicar*. Jerry Daly, the third assistant director, with whom I got on really well, joined me. Anyway, it was nice to get away from Martin and Lewis constantly moaning and bickering, or messing about holding up production."

Actors Martin Shaw and Lewis Collins during A HIDING TO NOTHING.

Dead Reckoning: CI5 faces death and double-dealing when an exchanged British spy returns with a mixed bag of loyalties and identities.

Robin Estridge used the pen name Philip Loraine to submit *Dead Reckoning*, which was approved by LWT only seven days before filming began on Monday 11th June. Estridge, whose career dates back to 1953, had written the movie, *Northwest Frontier* (1960) and *Permission To Kill* (1975).

Former cameraman Denis Lewiston (born in London on 22nd May 1934) was invited to take up the director's reins by producer, Ray Menmuir, and script editor, Gerry O'Hara. Denis began his career at the age of sixteen, as a clapper/loader, before becoming a camera operator on films such as *Stardust*, *Doctor Zhivago*, and *The Rocky Horror Picture Show*.

Denis Lewiston (director): "The producers had witnessed my camerawork on various features and told me I had the eye for directing. They liked the hand held work I had done and reckoned it suited the show's style. Gerry O'Hara had a big say in it as we had worked together very recently on *The Bitch*, *The Brute*, and some years previously on *The Pleasure Girls*. Thanks to Gerry it was my first stab at directing.

"The ever-dependable Alan Tilvern caused us a few issues through no fault of his own; mid-way through production he contracted some kind of virus and his vocal delivery suffered as a consequence. We rushed through much of the conclusion as a consequence."

Alan Tilvern as double agent Stefan Batak in DEAD RECKONING. Alan was born (5th November 1918) in Whitechapel, London and originally worked as a barrow boy in the East End of London. He made a career out of playing foreigners and appeared in over forty movies.

A spy is extradited to Britain with an attempt to keep his arrival top-secret. However, the Bulgarians from Batak's homeland who sent him appear to be trying to make his movements as public as possible. When he is eventually murdered, CI5 suspect his music student daughter of poisoning him. Actress Carol Royle as Anna Batak in DEAD RECKONING.

Bodie makes a slanting reference to the murder of the Bulgarian dissident broadcaster Georgi Markov at Waterloo Bridge in September 1978, when telling Cowley that his 'Bulgarian mojo' is a 'cross between a force beam and a poisoned umbrella'. A member of the Bulgarian Secret Police, the Darjavna Sugurnost, killed Markov, using a poison-tipped umbrella as a murder weapon.

Wishing to expand the CI5 team, series creator, Brian Clemens introduced a female CI5 agent in this story; Sally Harrison played Susan Fischer - Cowley's female chauffeur. However, she only appeared in one further story, *The Purging Of CI5*, before being dropped. Sally, who has been acting since she was 12-years old, enjoyed the gun-toting action on the show, it was a far cry from playing the ultra-feminine Alice in *Whittington On Ice*. Her acting credits include the 1973 horror movie *And Now The Screaming Starts!*, where she met, and later married, art director Tony Curtis, who himself had worked on *The Professionals* first series. Her roles continued throughout the decade in sex comedies such as *Confessions Of A Pop Performer* and *Can You Keep It Up For A Week*.

Ray Doyle (Martin Shaw) has his gun at the ready in DEAD RECKONING, while earlier he has a meal with Anna Batak (Carol Royle) and Michael (Michael Hadley).

Gordon Jackson had played many parts, but "...asserting his authority as Cowley was definitely more difficult.

"I found Rose and Ruby much easier to cope with as Hudson in *Upstairs Downstairs* for they hung on my every word. Bodie and Doyle looked at Cowley and he knew they were saying to themselves, 'Well, we'll think about it', when he gave them an order. I like to imagine they respected Cowley, otherwise I think they would have left CI5 years ago."

Gary Weir (boom operator): "I remember the scenes we did at the square in Barnsbury (Thornhill Square, North London). The set dressers had prepped the house in the morning, while we were doing the car run-bys on the nearby roads. We shot the main sequences around midday, then someone said 'I'm sure the house number should be number 11?' On checking the script it did indeed state number 11. Not a problem you may think, but the house number had been mentioned in the dialogue, yet the house door clearly stated number 8. The director decided you couldn't have CI5 entering number 8 after they'd said they were going into number 11. So Denis Lewiston decided to shoot the offending scenes again (using number 8 in the finished result). He was none too pleased when he caught up with the art department!"

William Alexander (art director): "The problem with Denis was that he was very superstitious, and wouldn't use my green pen, perhaps that's why he didn't write down '11' at the time!"

Martin Shaw poses for a publicity shot on the set of DEAD RECKONING.

Mixed Doubles: *Assigned to protect a Middle Eastern leader, who is in England to sign a peace treaty, Bodie and Doyle have no way of knowing that Rio, the World's greatest assassin, has inside information - and has been sent to kill them.*

Dead Reckoning was still in production when Brian Clemens' *Mixed Doubles* entered production. The script was approved on the 15th June, and commenced production on Monday 25th. 34-year old director Roger Tucker (born in Bristol on 13th May 1945) had recently commanded the action on episodes of *1990, Strangers* and *Shoestring*.

Brian Clemens: "This was only my second script for the show in eighteen months. I came back because I was invited. They needed scripts in a hurry, they knew that was my forte. It (the series) had become grittier, more dour and certainly some of the scripts were too complicated for their own good. I guess that's because I wasn't at the helm."

Two assassins have targeted a Mid-Eastern leader as their victim - CI5 agent Bodie (Lewis Collins) keeps a watchful eye on proceedings in MIXED DOUBLES.

A majority of the locations needed for the script were discovered by location manager Peter Carter in, and around, Southall Gas works, Middlesex, and were recced by the key members of the production team between 20th and 22nd June, only a few days before filming was due to commence.

Peter Carter's location assistant, Geoff Austin, recounts how even a chosen location could be changed at the last minute:

In MIXED DOUBLES Ray Doyle (Martin Shaw) tackles a gang of bikers after a disturbance in a local pub. And (below) with Bodie (Lewis Collins).

Geoff Austin (location assistant): "We ended up using Brocket Hall for one of the conference houses needed in the script. It was a last minute replacement. We'd originally planned to use the gasworks for one of the houses, but the director told us we needed something better then we could get out of the Southall locations. The only place available was Lord Brocket's house."

In reality, Brocket Hall, had been used for high-level security conferences. Its bullet and sound-proof room, made of glass, prevented the planting of bugging devices. In the 1980's Lord Brocket built up a classic car museum at the Hall, but was later found guilty of fraudulent insurance claims against stolen vehicles.

Gladys Pearce (continuity): "The best part, for me personally, was having the honour of working with Gordon Jackson. He and I got on so well that I always had to read his lines off for him. What a gentleman. It was a tough job as we had a new script every ten days, which I had to breakdown, time and know it by the Monday morning, the first day of shooting. I must admit that by this stage they all merged into one, as they were basically all shot in the same way, saying the same kind of dialogue and dressing in almost the same clothes. It was a fun show to work on and very satisfying to have worked alongside such a wonderful team of people."

After a security leak Cowley (Gordon Jackson) keeps guard at the signing of a peace treaty in MIXED DOUBLES.

Need To Know: *Cowley gets word that Gorky, a senior KGB official, plans to snatch Drake, a senior M15 man suspected of being a double agent, from custody. He assigns Bodie and Doyle to take the prisoner to safety - but they come under immediate attack.*

Chris Menaul's outline for *Need To Know*, was adapted by Brian Clemens, which, under director William Brayne, began filming on Monday 9th July, having only been approved by LWT on the 4th. Chris Menaul had acted as script editor on the first four episodes of this batch, while Gerry O'Hara was away directing the film *The Bitch*, and had submitted his idea around this time. He later directed the David Lodge drama *Nice Work* and the feature film *Fatherland*, adapted from Robert Harris's story of an alternative Britain in which Hitler had won the Second World War.

Ray Menmuir (producer) : "We used an astonishing anti-riot truck which turned out to be the 'star' of the episode. It never ceased to amaze me at what the props guys would come up with."

Peter Carter (location manager): "We then did a car stunt involving the truck on the Binfield Road (B3018), which goes over the M4 motorway. That took some sorting out! The road had to be closed either side of the bridge and that caused some confusion, as the road links the villages of Binfield and Shurlock Row, Berkshire."

The stunt had to be performed several times as during rehearsals the Capri suffered a nearside rear tyre blow-out causing the crew to set the shot up again.

Agents Bodie (Lewis Collins) and Doyle (Martin Shaw) go undercover as uniformed policemen in one scene from NEED TO KNOW.

Filming by this stage had become a little routine, so Martin Shaw and Lewis Collins devised a way of livening things up. Once every few weeks, the entire crew would hold a foreign week; for instance the French day when cast and crew did their best to conduct all rehearsals with phoney French Peter Sellers accents. Other weeks included an Australian week, when everyone turned out in cowboy hats with corks hanging from them; an Irish week, where for some strange reason, no one got anything 'right first time!' and a German week which involved the crew turning up in colourful Bavarian hats!

This also highlighted that the friction between the two leads had softened by this stage.

Martin Shaw: "I said to Lewis, 'Look, you probably know, I didn't want you to do this. I was not in favour of it and absolutely fought against it, but I've changed my mind: I think you're really great in the part...and can we be friends?' I think he still thought I was an arsehole...for a while!"

Following the end of production on this episode, the crew and actors were given a three-week Summer break from Monday 23rd July to Friday 10th August. Martin Shaw chose to explore the British countryside via the canals and Lewis Collins jet-setted off to Los Angeles and a well earned break. Gordon Jackson went to the Loire Valley to visit the various châteaux as he was a great lover of architecture and art.

The Purging Of CI5: *A 'ghost' with a vendetta seems to be around as the foundations of C15 are rocked by bombings and assassinations.*

The cast and crew were reassembled for work on Monday 13th August. Joining the team was casting director Esta Charkham, who replaced Maggie Cartier. A former actress who switched to the casting side, first as a secretary, and later, as a general manager of a Broadway producer's London office, Esta would never pick an actor, or actress, just because their face fitted the part, she used to audition them personally before the director laid eyes on them.

A friendly hug for the three stars of THE PROFESSIONALS during filming on THE PURGING OF CI5.

The first episode in production was *The Purging Of CI5*, written by Stephen Lister and directed by Dennis Abey, who had previously written, produced and directed the 30-minute short film *Gollocks! There's Plenty Of Room In New Zealand*, *Never Too Young To Rock*, and commanded the action on LWT's television incarnation of *Dick Turpin* .

Stephen Lister, from Barrow-in-Furness, Cumbria, was 19-years old at the time, and submitted to the production company, a storyline, which he hoped, could be used for the show. Apparently, he enjoyed the series so much that he simply wrote the script, sent it to the production office and achieved the impossible by having it accepted. The final draft was approved as late as 31st July, and on the 16th August Stephen had an invite from the producers to witness a days filming at Southall Gas Works, where he met Martin Shaw and Lewis Collins.

Chris, one of the informers in THE PURGING OF CI5, is found dead by Doyle (Martin Shaw) in a disused railway carriage. This scene was filmed at Thorntonfield Railway sidings, Warton Road, East London.

Gerry O'Hara (script editor): "Normally all scripts were written by 'invitation' only. The primary reason stories, even though sometimes properly submitted, were not accepted boiled down to the fact the writer was not usually familiar enough with the series format, and their outlines would be lacking in the real relationship of the characters to each other. It was Brian Clemens who discovered Stephen Lister, a boy who seemed to have grown up with a TV set in his lap, and a remarkable flair for writing action. On Brian's advice we bought this episode. I had a hand in editing that script and subsequently encouraged him to supply some more storylines. He even got featured in the 'Young Observer' around the same time."

Lewis Collins during THE PURGING OF CI5.

In THE PURGING OF CI5, Doyle (Martin Shaw) and Bodie (Lewis Collins) are joined by fellow agent Lake (Norman Gregory).

Sally Harrison joined the cast as CI5 agent Susan Fischer - pictured here on the set of THE PURGING OF CI5.

Trevor Puckle (unit runner): "Dennis Abey tried to do the Hitchcock thing (and in true Hitchcock style he appears in the crowd as a workman after the explosion at the block of flats), getting his name checked on screen on the boxes...not sure why he went around with a parrot on his shoulder though!"

Dennis Abey (director): "Why not? I tried to get away with what I could. It was all one big laugh for me, hence the 'Dennis Abey Rules Okay' on the boxes at Southall Gas Works. The phone dial at Lewis Collins' flat had Gordon Jackson's picture on it. I thought it was exactly the sort of thing the Bodie character would do. By the time Ray Menmuir saw the 'rushes' the following morning it was way too late to re-shoot these scenes, as one included a car explosion, and the other a lengthy scene at the flat. He was mad, I called it the '11 o'clock bollocking'.

"The two boys were a huge laugh and I thought I always got the best out of them. We filmed everything as it happened, and I wouldn't let the odd mishap interrupt the flow of the programme; in the office when Martin pins Peter Jolley up against the cabinet slightly more than was planned fell on Peter's head! I didn't redo that because it added realism to the proceedings, and we all had a good laugh about it when the scene was done, even Peter, who didn't know what had hit him! In the final scenes at the Royal Free Hospital, a trolley had to be pushed out of the way and the original script called for the trolley to be in shot. It took eight takes, before Gordon Jackson came up to me and told me to give Martin and Lewis a close-up instead. They did that on take one!"

Geoff Austin (location assistant): "I found the hospital location. That particular wing of the Royal Free wasn't being used at the time. They were short on money and had closed it down. It was ideal; we had full use of the entrance and the large car park. We used it whenever we could few years."

Martin Shaw as Ray Doyle between filming takes on THE PURGING OF CI5.

Robin McDonald (focus puller): "With Dennis Abey on the set, it was a riot. We would usually hold up shooting over silly things and Ray Menmuir used to go mad. I would look at Lewis during a shot, he would raise his eyebrow and that was it, we'd be in fits of laughter for ages. I seem to recall that at one point Lewis was approached by a gang of kids, looking for a fight.

They actually saw him as Bodie, not as Lewis Collins, a man acting the part of Bodie. Mind you, with Lewis you never could tell?"

On the 15th August, a scene was set up at Southall Gas Works where a caravan had to be blown up, leaving the charred remains for the firemen to tackle. When the fire brigade arrived, the only evidence of the caravan was a large crater in the ground.

Ian Munro (sound assistant): "That was Doctor Death, our special effects guy, Mike Collins. He was mad with explosives. There were bits of the caravan everywhere, even in what was left of the large disused warehouse we were using. Following the stunt the producers called for a photo shoot to include the production crew.

"Photographer Ted Hawes asked if it was safe to set up near the smouldering remains of the caravan. Mike said it would be fine, as all the explosives had been removed. The chairs and tables were set up and the photos taken, and then we all got up to get our tea. No sooner had we left the area where we had been standing that another explosion occurred. Mike said he'd forgotten about that one!

"We also had another mishap that day with Mike's bag of tricks. Earlier the bullet being fired at the caravan in the same scene, had to go through the window. Using a brick to simulate the broken glass, it was thrown at the window. Not being toughened glass it went straight through and out the other side, hitting the camera operator, Mike Proudfoot, right on the head. Despite being very bruised he seemed to be fine."

Mike Collins macabre nickname, 'Doctor Death' was given to him by actress, Joanna Lumley when she was asked about explosions in *The New Avengers* series, which he had set up. She told Michael Parkinson on his chat show: "My friend Doctor Death looks after those for me!"

Mike, originally from Taplow, near Maidenhead, Berkshire, had begun his career when he followed in his uncle's footsteps and became a props man as soon as he left school.

Mike Collins (special effects): "Special effects originated from the props department. When film audiences began to demand more and more spectacular effects in films the special effects man came into his own and wasn't just a poor man's prop man any more."

He came up through the era of films at Pinewood Studios where so many famous films were made. He was involved in the making of the Hammer Horror films and his teacher was in fact the famous late Les Bowie, who won an Oscar for his work on the *Superman* film.

Mike Collins: "I was on that film for two years. I worked on the opening scene with Krypton exploding? It took over a hundred men to do the effects on that film. All the pyrotechnic work was my responsibility.

"I was physically sick when we blew up the chateau in the *Dirty Dozen*, but the elation after it's all over is so great that you suffer nearly as much as you do before it happens! You check and check again to make sure nothing can go wrong. You start to shake because you are concentrating so much. You are continuously checking the fireboard, which is the trigger point. Then it's the countdown. You hit the button and it's gone. The schedules on *The Professionals* were much tighter and you were working not on film sets but in real places. When you saw us blow up a car, we actually blew it up for real. I would see the scripts beforehand of course, but we had to move faster than the cameramen, so we could set up ahead of where the next action had to take place. I had to carry my gear around with me all the time and make up special effects on the spot, simulating them in real houses."

Fugitive: *Bodie is a walking time bomb when he crosses a gang of international gun-runners.*

Tuesday 28th August saw the first day's shooting on Anthony Read's outline for *Fugitive*, originally entitled *The Fugitive*, which had been adapted by Gerry O'Hara. It had been approved by LWT on the 14th and was directed by Denis Lewiston.

Anthony Read: "In March 1979, I submitted a script with the working title *The Fugitive*. I can't remember exactly what went wrong on this one, but I do recall agreeing that Gerry O'Hara could take it over and do a substantial rewrite, and that I would take my name off it. There was a new regime in place by then, and Brian Clemens had little to do with the series. Producer Ray Menmuir was the one who didn't like it.

"I didn't particularly want to do any more, not because I was miffed at having a script rewritten, that was a normal part of the business, but because I found the format very limiting, felt that I'd done the areas that interested me, and was ready to move on to something fresh, which I did. I was very busy at that time with other projects, including my first non-fiction book. Like so many things in life, it was fun while it lasted!"

CI5's Ray Doyle (Martin Shaw) takes aim in FUGITIVE - but who is he aiming at?

When a CIA agent is murdered in London, CI5 launch a fake arms deal with the terrorists responsible. But the gang uncovers the plot in time, taking Bodie (Lewis Collins) hostage in FUGITIVE.

Denis Lewiston (director): "I cast Brigitte Kahn in the episode, and had not realised that her husband, Ronnie, was ill. He sadly died shortly after we had finished filming. In fact, I recall she was very upset when she was called to do some post-production sequences.

"We had hired the '209: Yeading' bus for a scene where Bodie chases Karen on, and off it, outside the old Wimpy on Wembley Park Drive. It was the height of the rush evening peak hour and Lewis Collins was supposed to alight from the bus but be impeded by boarding passengers. Sadly, a number of real passengers boarded the bus too, and he found himself against the front bulkhead. Gordon Jackson was also given a larger quota of action and dialogue. He tackled it superbly, with the final freeze frame ending, only being ruined by the title music."

Hairdresser Sue Love took over from Paula Gillespie for the last six episodes of this batch. She spent twelve years in the famous Mr. Teasy-Weasy's salons before deciding to go it alone and into the film industry.

Sue Love (hairdresser): "The actor's hair has to fit the part he or she is playing and relate to what is happening in that scene. I used to get actors coming to me with lovely clean hair and I would turn them into, say, drug addicts with greasy stringy hair. If they had been in a fight, they had to look dusty and unkempt. I also used to have to change the colour of people's hair. Take a 'double' for instance who was brought in to do some stunt work. If he had blonde hair and it needed to be black, it would be sprayed with a special kind of paint.

"Martin and Lewis were not that vain. I cut Martin's hair, though he'll tell you a guy called Keith did it at 'Smile' in Knightsbridge. Lewis' hair? Well, the best thing to say was that he and I cut his hair between us! Lewis would say, 'Why not? I've been trained to do it'. As for Gordon, his hair stayed in place easily and didn't need a lot of attention."

Martin Shaw and Lewis Collins filming scenes for the story FUGITIVE in the pub car park of The Green Man, Wembley, Middlesex.

When *Fugitive* was finally broadcast on 21st September 1980, the programme became the investigation of a real Police enquiry. Detectives hunting missing Humberside girl, Gloria Bielby, were tipped off that she had appeared in the show, sipping Martini. The tip-off came from her twin sister, Carol, who had telephoned the police after watching the programme convinced she'd seen Gloria. Her sister had vanished from her home in Dawnay Road, Bilton in February 1979. The officer in charge of the inquiry, Detective Superintendent Bob Carmichael, had said: "Something serious, possibly suicide or homicide," had occurred.

The woman was seen in two shots, lasting no more than five seconds, in scenes filmed at 'The Green Man' public house in Wembley, Middlesex, some seven months after she had vanished. Gloria had last been seen getting into a car outside her home. She had left her 12-year old son, Nigel and estranged husband, Bernard, with no clues to her whereabouts. Interpol had also been called in to check on sightings in Majorca, Holland, Sweden and Germany, after she had vanished, all with no success. The Police later apologised to Ingrid Bradley, the genuine 'extra' who had appeared in the episode, for any distress that may have been caused following the incident.

Paul Dean (manager: the Green Man): "The Green Man pub was constantly used throughout the series (as a location or unit base). Peter Carter, the location guy and I became good friends and we constantly joked about the amount of money paid for using the premises. The going rate was around £250, but I recall a conversation I had with one of the sound crew while filming was underway, 'Did you enjoy watching the action?' he asked me. I replied, 'It was great and the fifty quid for the privilege was a bonus'. I swear he believed that Peter had really pocketed the difference.

"Another rumour we'd started was that Peter would leave a brown envelope in the ladies toilet. His contact from the police would come in, retrieve the envelope, and Peter would have his permission to film in certain public areas. We'd roar at that one."

Transmission had originally been set for the coming weekend (Saturday 8th September), but an ITV dispute caused no screenings at all with, at the time, no idea when normal programming would resume (The ITV Network remained shut for eleven weeks between August to October).

The Acorn Syndrome: *Bodie and Doyle are in hot pursuit of a group of East German agents who are blackmailing a government engineer whose daughter's life is being held hostage against the plans of a new jet-engine tank.*

John Kruse's *The Acorn Syndrome*, which began filming on Monday 10th September under director Martin Campbell, had been approved by LWT on the 22nd August. Kruse's career dates back to 1958 when he submitted ideas for *The Adventures Of William Tell*. He followed this up with work on *The Human Jungle, Top Secret, The Avengers, The Saint, Return of The Saint* and *Shoestring*.

Martin Shaw and Lewis Collins in THE ACORN SYNDROME.

British actress Kate Dorning played Nancy in THE ACORN SYNDROME.

Some elements of the plot are drawn from the (real-life) Balcombe Street siege in December 1975, where four IRA gunman barricaded themselves in a Marylebone flat, holding a couple hostage for four days.

Martin Campbell (director): "*The Professionals* was a very hard action piece. It was tougher than *Starsky & Hutch* and I'm really amazed at the violence we got away with. The violence was awful. It's very contentious for television and I'd never do it again. In 20/20 hindsight, what you got away with in television violence then, was much more than what you could get away with now."

With filming already underway, one of the biggest problems facing location manager Peter Carter was finding a suitable building to double for the secret weapons establishment Apex McInross. He located the ideal building during a recce in Windsor a few days later. Negotiations were immediately entered into with Combermere Barracks over the use of the heavily guarded building and suitable terms were eventually agreed. However, to comply with the area's high security, Mark I personnel were forbidden from taking any still photographs of the premises without a pass and told not to enter the building unless specific permission had been obtained. On the set, Martin Shaw and Lewis Collins found themselves taking a ride in the 'Scorpion' reconnaissance vehicle. It's a tank with the ability to roar along at 70 mph and it has the scorpion's lethal sting too, in the form of a 76mm cannon. The actors relaxed between takes with soldiers who were members of The Life Guards Regiment based there.

Martin Shaw and Lewis Collins catch a ride on a powerful Scorpion tank at Combermere Barracks, Windsor, Berkshire, which served as the setting for the weapons establishment Apex McInross in THE ACORN SYNDROME.

William Alexander (art director): "The working relationship between the art and location departments is key, up front time required for construction, painting and dressing, is as important as parking up the 'circus' on the shoot. Pete Carter was ace, even though by this stage the series had a special problem: most series has a 'Starship Enterprise' - a standing set with a couple of days work (and respite!), but CI5 had no base. It was awesomely hectic: we were running into problems with late scripts and directors running behind schedule. We had two units, or even three, keeping us on the go to catch up. But I had a great, totally reliable crew: Ken Ryan was already a qualified art director; Robin Tarsnane went on to become a very professional art director, as did Jamie Leonard. The late Terry Parr was one of the best in the business and my indispensable buyer, the late Bert Gardner, had been with me for all of my Euston Films work to date. I couldn't have done it without them."

Lewis Collins as Bodie rehearses a scene for THE ACORN SYNDROME.

On Thursday 13th September the cast and crew assembled at The Hoe, Carpenders Park, Hertfordshire, to film the siege scenes required for this story.

Robin McDonald (focus puller): "It was like a cul-de-sac with three houses on each corner. We had laid the camera track down the street and most of the residents had gathered to watch the filming. The scene involved Cowley arriving to brief Bodie and Doyle on the hostage situation. One of the residents decided he wanted to get his car out of his driveway just as filming had commenced. We asked if he could wait. But he couldn't and drove over the track, damaging it and causing us to set up again. He literally would only have had to wait a few minutes."

Gary Weir (boom operator): "The situation probably wasn't helped by director Martin Campbell! A brilliant director as he was, he was very forceful when it came to crowds. Other directors would have gone round and talked to the residents, but not Martin, he arrived, took over the street, and started ordering people about like he was in the army. Definitely not a people person!"

Chris Streeter (transportation co-ordinator): "Ford Motor Company had loaned us a batch of new MK.V Cortinas (a red 2.0GL: HPU 724T and a beige 2.0GL: HPU 725T), including a Midnight blue Ghia Estate (HPU 754T), for this episode. Lewis Collins managed to smash it into the kerb, the car had been involved in a chase with an old desk tied to the top and it became difficult to control. By the time Lewis had hit the pavement, we had already 'lost' the desk! It held up shooting for a time while I changed over the front suspension at the roadside. In the end they couldn't wait for me to finish, left me to get on with it, and moved on to film the next scene, albeit across the road in the flats. Director Martin Campbell decided that the scene of the car crashing into the kerb was to be left in the finished print!"

A scene from THE ACORN SYNDROME as Bodie (Lewis Collins) puts an end to a car chase.....on location at North Thames Gas Works, Slough, Berkshire.

The script required that the desk was to have been collected from Muswell Hill, but location manager Peter Carter had secured the services of a craftsman based in Ossian Mews, Stroud Green, North London. What had been overlooked was that the prop phone box positioned outside the yard, which was paramount to the script as the villains, Angadi and Coleman, try to use it to make a phone call, was minus an actual phone inside. With no time to find a working payphone, the café along the street provided a suitable replacement, albeit not the usual item found in telephone boxes at the time.

Slush Fund: *Bodie and Doyle investigate a Euro-consortium building a death-trap fighter plane. They have already killed 50 pilots - and mean to rub out anyone standing in their way...including the two C15 agents*

The Acorn Syndrome was behind schedule, finishing on Wednesday 26th September, when the next episode *Slush Fund*, by Roger Marshall (born in Leicester, England, March 1934), rolled before the cameras on Monday 24th September. Marshall had worked in live television, scripted the movie

Theatre Of Death (1967), and written storylines for *The Avengers* and *The Sweeney*, before being asked to write for the show at the invitation of his close colleague, Gerry O'Hara, who by this stage was in desperate need for some quality scripts. Marshall produced two scripts, this one, and *Take Away*, in record time.

Martin Shaw with SLUSH FUND co-star Victoria Burgoyne (Kookie Girl).

For this episode location manager Peter Carter ventured onto the Chalk Hill housing estate in Wembley, to find two suitable properties to serve as Hope's house (Windsor Crescent), and the empty / surveillance house (Bluebird Walk). Built between 1966 and 1970 'The Chalkhill Estate' was not a great success and quickly became a crime hot spot with reports of gangs intimidating residents, drug use, criminal damage of schools, and anti-social behaviour.

Al Greene (local resident): " I lived in the area at the time, and constantly saw them filming but was amazed when they had chosen to film on the actual estate. I'm sure they weren't aware of its reputation! When the crew set up for filming at Bluebird Walk, there was a mass of lorries and people, and it didn't take long for the word to get around what was going on and the crowds began to gather. On the estate even the milk delivery cart looked like a security van; when people had milk delivered the milkman wouldn't get out and people had to come to him to get it - that's how bad it was! The cart had iron bars on it so the milk bottles couldn't be stolen or used as weapons, and the milkman used to hand you your milk through a steel hatch - it really was like a security van delivering money to a bank.

"Most of the day the filming continued uninterrupted, but by late afternoon the gangs had gathered, and you could sense something was about to happen - even a Police presence wouldn't stop them for long. The crew must have been told to pack up their equipment quickly, because you could see them running to get all the camera and sound gear back in the lorries before making a sharp exit with a Police escort. Don't think they ever came back to film here again after that!"

In SLUSH FUND a hit-man is employed by a group of East German officials to assassinate a reporter who is planning to publish a report in which their new fighter plane is branded as a potential death-trap. Lewis Collins and Martin Shaw share a joke on location at White Waltham Airfield, Berkshire.

The 'Fohn Fighter' depicted in the script was loosely based on the real-life F104-Lockheed Starfighter initially used by the USAAF (United States Army

Forces), and later in the early 1960's by the Germans, who requested major modifications (in an attempt to make it a fighter/bomber) which in due course affected its structural integrity and stability. But political pressure forced the German government to continue with them and about forty crashed before they admitted defeat. Dubbed 'The Widowmaker' by the Luftwaffe, most losses were due to the fact that the ejector seat often failed at low altitudes.

Scheduled for a Sunday shoot (30th September), Gatwick and Redhill train stations were to be used for the arrival of Van Niekerk. This proved impractical and, at short notice, filming was relocated to White Waltham airfield, Berkshire.

Location manager Peter Carter elected to film a car stunt, where Doyle is trapped in the boot of a stolen car, which subsequently explodes at the bottom of a quarry, at Castle Lime Works, South Mimms, Hertfordshire - an area he was familiar with after putting it into service on the Gerry Anderson action-adventure series *The Protectors*.

Robin McDonald (focus puller): "We had to roll a Jaguar car down a cliff and explode it at the bottom of a quarry near South Mimms, Hertfordshire. The stunt, directed by Bill Brayne, did not go as planned! The car was lifted to the top of the quarry by a JCB as there was no road to the top of the hill. The rear wheels lifted and the throttle jammed on. A rope was tied to the front in order for the car to be pulled down. Bill called, 'Action' and the car was let down, the wheels dug into the gravel and away it went. Someone had forgotten to put the steering straight and the car went in the wrong direction making it impossible for our camera operator, John Maskall, to follow. The car was heading straight for us. We all dropped tools and legged it. Luckily the car stopped short of us anyway."

Bill Brayne (director): "It was very difficult to judge where it was going. It took three hours to set up the shot, so we did it again. This time the car rolled down the cliff at a snails pace and failed to explode at the bottom. Third time lucky and a few hours later we got it right."

Peter Brayham (stunt arranger): "They had themselves to blame for that one. They were trying to save money and didn't want to pay for a stunt arranger on the shoot. They had mannequins in the car, which, to be honest looked awful, especially on camera when one of the heads fell off. But they couldn't re-shoot it as it had cost them double what it should have done already - so they left it in."

Bill Brayne (director): "Martin Shaw had escaped the explosion but had to call Bodie from a phone box, to collect him. Back at the roadside, no one had thought about the phone box, so the one you see him propped up against in the episode was courtesy of the props department. We had to wait for that and it arrived in two halves on the back of a truck."

On Wednesday 3rd October and continuing the format of filming in unusual settings, location manager Peter Carter gained permission to film in the midst of the rolling presses of the 'Daily Express' newspaper print room, who at the time were based in Fleet Street, East Central London. The following day they ran the headline, 'Murder At The Daily Express, On our own doorstep...the television show you won't see for months', referring to the ITV dispute, which had still not been resolved.

Weekend In The Country: *Bodie and Doyle spend an idyllic weekend in the country with their girlfriends, but it isn't long before they find themselves back in business - defending a farmhouse under siege from a gang of escaped prisoners.*

Ex-cameraman James Allen (born 28th April 1930) directed Gerry O'Hara's story *Weekend In The Country* from Monday 8th October. Allen had written and directed a short film in 1971 called *Memorial*, which in May of that year won the Best Short Film Award at the Cannes Film Festival, and, in 1973, it also won a BAFTA Film Award. Prior to working on *The Professionals* he had directed the action on LWT's *Dick Turpin* series.

The first task faced by location manager Peter Carter was to find a suitable location to portray the farmhouse, and grounds, belonging to the Shaw family. One of the locations he scouted was Warfield Hall, Berkshire, which had already been used in previous episodes. However, when director James Allen conducted his recce of the area it was arranged that the majority of the episode would be shot at the nearby Scotlands Farm, a location he thought was more suited than the large mansion-type house offered by Warfield Hall.

Robin McDonald (focus puller): "Lewis became very good friends with the daughter of the couple who owned the farm at the time..."

Lewis Collins enjoys a spot of fishing on location at Warfield Hall lake, Berkshire, on the set of a WEEKEND IN THE COUNTRY.

On the 8th October, the first days shoot, the golfing scenes were set up at North Middlesex Golf Club, Friern Barnet, North London.

Gordon Jackson (interviewed at the time): "My brother used to be a keen golfer and I tried a round once as a boy in Glasgow. I didn't enjoy it though. I don't enjoy the walking; my wife, Rona, however, is a good golfer."

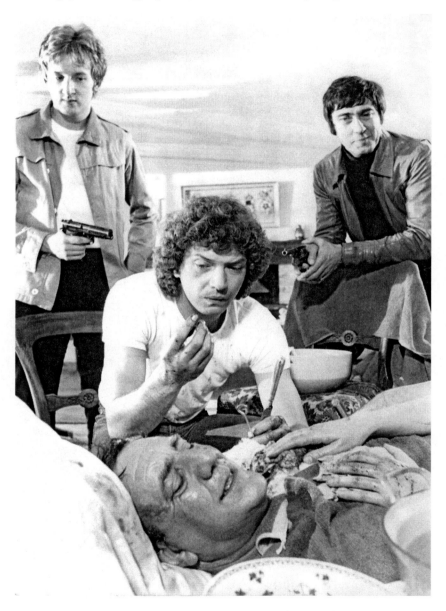

CI5's Doyle (Martin Shaw) tends to the wounds of escaped convict Bert Case (Bryan Pringle) watched by Vince (Ray Burdis) and Georgie (Brian Croucher) in WEEKEND IN THE COUNTRY.

Incidentally, the Rolls Royce being used at the golf course wore the number plate, SLE 71R, which in reality was the real index to the Ford Capri used in the first series, and opening titles, of *Minder*!

On location at Warfield Hall, Berkshire, for WEEKEND IN THE COUNTRY, Lewis Collins and Martin Shaw seem very happy to be joking around. Jacqueline Reddin and Louisa Rix played the girlfriends of Bodie and Doyle.

Playing Bodie's girlfriend, Liz, was Irish actress Jacqueline Reddin in a WEEKEND IN THE COUNTRY.

Louisa Rix, actress daughter of Brian Rix, was cast as Doyle's girlfriend Judy Shaw. She had appeared in *Coronation Street*, *Danger UXB* and with father, Brian, on television and mother, Elspet Gray on stage. She later admitted it was an episode she'd rather forget. The first part of the filming at Warfield Hall, Berkshire had to be re-shot, and she was given a different horse. He was the horse from the Lloyds Bank commercials of the late 1970's.

Louisa Rix (Judy Shaw): "He was a monster. He literally snorted and pawed at the ground when I went near him. It was suggested I took him for an introductory trot through the woods. Someone heaved me up on him and he took off at what seemed like 90 mph, only stopping when a Land Rover blocked his path. I was petrified. In an important shot on camera where Martin Shaw and I are out riding and agree to take different routes home, I hurtled through the air into a large clump of bracken on the right, while the horse followed Martin down the left-hand path. No bones were broken, but I happen to bank with the Lloyds and I still get hot under the collar when I see the sign."

Actor Bryan Pringle was cast as the wounded criminal Bert Case. He had starred in Yorkshire Television's *Good Companions*, and in the BBC's *On Giant Shoulders*, the play about a thalidomide child with Judi Dench as his wife. Continuing his career in dramas such as, *Henry IV*, *Henry V* and *When The Boat Comes In*. At the National Theatre Company he made a mark in live theatre with a limited season in a play called *The Passion*. He was also one of the stars in Jack Rosenthal's legendary sitcom *The Dustbinmen*.

Bryan Pringle: "*The Professionals* was very enjoyable to work on and we shot scenes at break-neck speed. I do recall one amusing incident in the sequence we shot in the woods where my character was stumbling around; the ground was very wet and muddy, and I kept losing my footing and falling flat on my backside much to the amusement of Martin and Lew. So each time we went for a take Lew, more so than Martin, who was much more professional, kept smiling. This wasn't what the director wanted, as my character was supposed to be holding them at gun-point! The two guys were great to work with, and the show seemed like a 'ball' for them, with Lew always after the girls!"

Actor Brian Croucher, who portrayed the villain Georgie in the story, adds that director James Allen ran into difficulties during the filming and was replaced with substantial re-shooting required. Barry Myall, who was producer Ray Menmuir's personal driver, remembers that day very well.

Barry Myall: "It was always my task to drive producer Ray Menmuir to the first location of the day so he could congratulate, or discipline, crew members based on the previous days rushes. On this one particular day he was none to pleased at what had been coming back from the director; scenes not completed, poorly lit subjects, dire acting, etc. He saw little alternative but to sadly dismiss the director in question and finish off the episode himself, it was way too late in the schedules to re-hire, and with the budget being so tight it was the only way to complete the story without hiring a second unit to take over. They only had a few episodes left to do and couldn't fall behind shooting. This was the one, and only, time that Ray had to step in and take over from a director."

Take Away: *Cowley is asked to investigate a drug-smuggling operation that could have international repercussions, and assigns Bodie and Doyle to the case. The latter goes undercover as a street-market trader, while Bodie moves in with a gang of drug addicts.*

Roger Marshall's *Take Away*, directed by Douglas Camfield, was the next episode in production, beginning on Friday 19th October, a day ahead of schedule and back to back with the last day of shooting on *Weekend In The Country*.

Chris Webb (stunt arranger): "Peter Brayham was away in Southend doing some stunt work with Eddie Kidd on the film *Hanover Street*, and asked me to do the arranging on this one. I drove all the way from the Eddie Kidd set to do it and met with Dougie (Camfield) the same night. He told me that Peter would always write/draw all the stunts, move by move, on paper before shooting them for real. So that evening I carefully worked out the moves and typed them out to present to Dougie the next day. I was knackered the following day on the shoot.

"I later found out that Peter and he had no such agreement. I told him he was a 'bloody swine'. Being a karate scene it had taken me ages to work out and Dougie knew it. Anyway, on the set doing the balcony scene, one of the guys had to go over it. One guy was Philip Tan, who wasn't on Equity's books, so was not allowed to go over. In the end we got Frank Henson to stand-in and he went over. Ray Menmuir, being a 'tight so and so' didn't want to pay Frank for doing it."

Chris Webb's original notes, given to Douglas Camfield, for the scenes filmed on Tuesday 30th October, at Walkinshaw Court, Elizabeth Avenue in Islington, North London, are as follows:

Chinese thugs kick down door. 1st thug comes into room. Doyle kicks thug in stomach. A two handed blow to side of thugs head knocking him into corner. Doyle faces 2nd thug and aims blow at him. Thug evades and moves up stairs. Doyle hit back against wall faces stairway. Two kicks from thug. Doyle evades 1st one side then the other, then Doyle moves backwards towards street door. Thug comes in, aims several blows to head and body forcing Doyle backwards onto balcony, Doyle defending as well as possible. With Doyle's back touching wall, thug aims chop to side of Doyle's head. Doyle moves aside, thug oversteps and falls over balcony.

British actress Sharon Duce, born (17th January 1950) in Sheffield, Yorkshire, played Annie, Jimmy the drug addict's sister, in TAKE AWAY. Her biggest role came in 1984 when she was cast alongside Ray Brooks in the BBC comedy drama BIG DEAL.

In the role of drug addict Jimmy was actor Gary Shail (born 10th November 1959), who recalls that there was a long discussion with the producers about whether or not Bodie would smoke dope in TAKE AWAY. They decided that, having been a mercenary in the past, he would; and would know where to get the best gear.

Chris Webb: "I remember Gordon Jackson used to rehearse his lines, over and over again. The guy was so word perfect. He once called me over and said to me, 'How the bloody hell do those two', referring to Martin and Lewis, 'just look at the script and read off their lines. It's amazing'. 'It's your age', I joked with him. What a gentleman!"

On the 25th October location manager Peter Carter had elected to film the conclusion to the story at the Master Brewer Motel in North Hillingdon. The car park outside formed the rendezvous point for director Douglas Camfield, cast and crew. One of the first problems faced by Camfield was the weather; heavy rain had started only 30-minutes after filming had began, which continually held up filming.

Mike Silverlock (boom operator): "Douglas Camfield's greatest strength was his handling of action sequences, like the ones we did outside the Master Brewer Motel at the end of the show. He would inject huge amounts of energy into getting the best out of the actors and carefully planned all the gun battles and fights with great attention to detail."

William Alexander (art director): "Dougie was known affectionately as the 'scoutmaster', he was very organised, calling the troops in the morning with the day's work all on a board (rather like Val Guest did). His early death was a great loss to the industry. He was a pleasure to work with and always knew exactly what he wanted and how to get it."

Gordon Jackson looks shocked at Lewis Collins' latest outfit in TAKE AWAY.

By this time, the ITV dispute had been resolved and transmissions had started on the Saturday 27th October with the episode, *The Purging Of CI5*, notching up an impressive 9,499,000 viewers. It did, however, mean that it would be a short run of only eight episodes concluding on the 15th December 1979. The remaining eight would be scheduled for the following autumn. But there was a dark cloud on the horizon over future production. By now, both Collins and Shaw were just as eager to leave the series and had been constantly bemoaning the fact that neither had been given the opportunity to have a say in the way the production was being made. They felt that little thought was being given to the artistic merits of the series and that the episodes were being churned out simply to make a profit for the production company.

Martin Shaw (interviewed at the time): "If I could leave in a way that was fair to all concerned, I would. When we started the first series, I simply didn't imagine it would be anything like the success it is. Now I am held to a contract that still has some two or so years to run. While it is not, in practice, part of my contract, it has resulted in my commitments to the series excluding me from other work.

"Now I feel I am doing it under sufferance. If I am held to my contract than I shall go back and do it to the best of my ability. I shall continue to dedicate myself to it as hard as I can because that's the only way I know how to work. But it doesn't alter the fact that I would be enormously relieved if I were to be released from my contract. I am not in any way criticising the people concerned with the show's production, for whom I have great respect.

However, I created the personality of Doyle, and within the limitations of this kind of show there is no way I can operate to my fullest capabilities. The series has been good to me but I don't want to remain one person for any length of time. I play hundreds of people and my career doesn't begin and end with Ray Doyle.

"I accept under sufferance, a degree of promotion for the series, as a part of my job. I hate it when I go out and people stop and stare. I find that kind of recognition a constant irritation. I'm a private person and my job doesn't extend beyond what I do in the series, it doesn't consist of signing autographs or meeting the public."

Lewis Collins (interviewed at the time): "I just feel the original spark is missing from the series now. I watched it the other night and it just isn't the same as it used to be. Sure, I'd had some success with *The Cuckoo Waltz*, but suddenly I was being offered a series, which was going to make me a TV star. I did have some misgivings about the length of time I'd be committed, but eventually I signed. I think Bodie and Doyle should get more of a chance to show what they're like as people. And I'd like the locations to be more adventurous too! Still, I'm no troublemaker. All I want is to do my job as an actor to the best of my ability."

Gordon Jackson: "If they wanted to shape the scripts, they should have gone away and been script writers. They were willing to break their contracts and leave the show. Lewis had demanded a bigger say in the scripts, criticised the locations and revealed that he was ashamed to watch the show. I had no sympathy over the locations. It was all a question of finance. Shooting on location costs money, and even going into the West End to film would be time-consuming and expensive. The interviews with them had come after nearly thirty weeks of filming. They were obviously very tired."

It was, therefore, decided that production would cease and any future shows would depend on the success of the current episodes being transmitted. No decision would be made until two months before going into production. Was this the end of *The Professionals*? Both stars, Martin Shaw and Lewis Collins, were confident that the next episode would be their last. LWT closed the official fan club, which they had opened in late 1978.

However, viewing figures were on the increase and by the show's second broadcast episode, *Backtrack*, on 3rd November, the ratings had increased to 12,676,000, with a position of 19th place in the viewing charts. *Stopover* on the 10th November saw another raise to 12th spot and viewing figures of 14,942,000. But LWT chiefs were still adamant that they would not announce filming on a new series until two months before going into production.

Involvement: *Doyle's friend Benny dies after being savagely beaten in an attempt to silence him leaving Bodie and Doyle racing against time to smash a major drug smuggling ring - led by Holly, the father of Doyle's Girlfriend.*

Brian Clemens furnished the final story, *Involvement*, with associate producer Chris Burt directing the proceedings from Monday 5th November.

Cast by Chris Burt as Doyle's love interest, Ann Holly, was British actress Patricia Hodge.

Robin McDonald (focus puller): "Patricia Hodge and Martin Shaw got on really well. They had been in the same drama school and this was the first time they had acted together. They both seemed to enjoy each other's company and the buzz around the set while filming was fantastic. They really looked forward to being on set acting together. Martin actually seemed like he wanted to do the episode!"

In INVOLVEMENT Ann Holly is played by British actress Patricia Ann Hodge, who was born (29th September 1946) in Cleethorpes, Lincolnshire and grew up in Grimsby, where her parents ran an hotel. One of her first TV roles was alongside John Hurt in THE NAKED CIVL SERVANT; she has since won the Laurence Olivier award for her theatre work.

The woods near Holly's home were realised at Black Park, Fulmer, Buckinghamshire. With the schedules becoming very tight, production manager Ron Purdie decided to film the scenes on the morning of Saturday 10th November. Located on the flight path to Heathrow Airport, filming was continually interrupted by the sound of aeroplanes flying overhead, causing the sequences to fall seriously behind schedule. Producer Ray Menmuir duly agreed over-time payments as filming continued into the afternoon.

Trevor Puckle (unit runner): "I can still recall the events of the Saturday shoot at Black Park. What a great day....Chelsea beat Orient 7-3!"

Filming on the story INVOLVEMENT, Lewis Collins, Martin Shaw, and Gordon Jackson pose for a publicity shot during a break in filming at Cadby Hall, Hammersmith, London.

Present during the car chase involving Bodie's Capri and Marli's van, filmed around Felix Avenue, Hornsey, North London, was stuntman Frank Henson - and his curly wig!

Frank Henson: "Martin did most of his own stunts and driving, so when they called for me, it was usually to climb up buildings or fall off things. They were the sort of jobs where if Martin had injured himself the whole production would have been held up. I received my fair share of knocks and bruises but the wig was the worse. They'd pin it on my own hair so tightly it made my eyes water. It came in useful though; I also used it to double for ladies..."

Gary Weir (boom operator): "At some point during this episode one of the production crew decided to take Bodie's Ford Capri for a spin around the Wembley area and promptly ran into trouble! It was wet, and they spun the back wheels on the car and hit something. The damage can be seen in the form of a deep scratch below the nearside rear 'S' stripe and a small dent in the rear quarter near the light cluster. More damage was incurred, when one of the exhausts hit a high kerb. The bosses weren't that happy, because the car was still needed for a few shots. The damage was not rectified as the car was soon to be returned to Ford Motor Company."

The dying words of an Italian informant leads to the smashing of a drug operation, run by the father of Doyle's girlfriend. THE PROFESSIONALS (Gordon Jackson, Martin Shaw and Lewis Collins) pictured between takes on the set of INVOLVEMENT.

Lewis Collins on location at CI5 HQ, realised at Cadby Hall, Hammersmith, West London. Cadby Hall was a major office and factory complex, which was the headquarters of the pioneering catering company Joseph Lyons and Company for almost a century.

In the midst of a shoot-out during a drugs smuggling investigation, Doyle meets and falls for Ann Holly, only to discover that CI5 suspect her of being closely linked to the scam herself. Lewis Collins poses for a publicity shot during filming on INVOLVEMENT.

Lighting cameraman Dusty Miller got a name-check on screen, as his name was clearly visible on the back of one of Ann's photographs.

Production ceased on Tuesday 20th November and the end-of-series party was held at Cricklewood production village on Cricklewood Lane, North West London.

Robin McDonald (focus puller): "Lewis and I had become good friends and during the evening festivities he had split his trousers and asked me to drop him home to his house in Golders Green to change. When we got there, he realised he hadn't got his keys and attempted to do a 'Bodie' and climb up the drain pipe and go in through an open upstairs window. Of course, he wasn't Bodie and this wasn't a stunt. His weight was too much and, half way up, the pipe broke. He began to fall, heading straight for the pointed garden fence. As he fell, I just managed to push him away from the fence and onto the ground. He was out cold for a few seconds. He was concussed, so I called an ambulance and he was sent to hospital. Every time I see him I remind him how I saved his life!"

At the end of the nine-month gruelling production schedule, which included 14-hour days, and several weekends to produce sixteen episodes of 50-minutes duration, Martin Shaw went to a friend's cottage in Wales to recover, by horse riding and walking. Lewis Collins contemplated a visit to San Francisco, where he'd been before while lecturing with the Theatre Workshop. He was also planning his first parachute jump with the Territorial Parachute Regiment in order to gain his Red Beret. As part of his training, he was seen running over Hampstead Heath in London carrying 40-lb packs and finally, in February 1980, he went through the fortnight's selection course at Hythe Assault Training area, Kent. He got through successfully and thus earned his Red Beret, of which he is very proud. Gordon Jackson drove through France and Southern Germany to Vienna with his wife, Rona Anderson. The object of the holiday was to visit several galleries and chateaux on the journey and to hear a Mozart concert in Southern Germany.

To aid Jimmy Saville's Spinal Unit Building Fund, at Stoke Mandeville Hospital in Buckinghamshire, Martin Shaw and Lewis Collins attempted to make the first ever crossing of the Channel in a two-man hovercraft. Teddington-based manufacturers, Pindair supplied the small two-man skima and the company's owner, Michael Pinder, proved to be very keen about the use of his hovercraft, which years earlier had seen service in the *Doctor Who* story *Planet Of the Spiders*.

Barry Myall (producer's (Ray Menmuir) driver): "It was a bitterly cold day with that horrible drizzly rain. We had an extravagant meal at the White Cliffs Dover Hotel, before Lewis and Martin prepared to depart by 8.30. They had trouble getting out, but arrived at the other end for lunch. They broke down on the way back and had to catch the last ferry back, around 11pm I think."

Sponsored by LWT for the Dover to Calais run, and despite breaking down on route, they raised £2,000. Jimmy Saville presented the cheque at the hospital, where he commented: "A tremendous effort." The fund had, at the time, only been launched in January and was half way to its £10 million target.

Lewis Collins and Martin Shaw attempt to make the first ever crossing of the Channel in a two-man hovercraft.

SERIES III EPISODE GUIDE

Gordon Jackson as George Cowley. Pictured here during INVOLVEMENT.

THE MADNESS OF MICKEY HAMILTON

by **Christopher Wicking**
© Copyright Mark 1 Productions Ltd MCMLXXVIII

Mickey Hamilton	Ian McDiarmid
Kay Costa	Marjorie Yates
Frank	Barry Stanton
Sergeant Bellager	Shaun Curry
St. Jacques	Clifton James
Captain Tepper	David Henry
Inspector Shannon	David Calder
Mr. Pagett-Munro	John Saunders
Priest	Dick Sullivan
Doctor 1	Maurice Thorogood
Sylvester	Olu Jacobs
Dr. Dyson	Kevin O'Shea
Sister Noel	Anni Domingo
Nun	Myrtle Moss
1st Doctor (Hospital washroom)	Benjamin Feitelson
Mr. Lemon	Rufus Collins
Toni	Shelagh McLeod
Pat	Lynne Ross
Nurse	Susie Jenkinson
Computer Operator	Lydia Lisle
Dr. Norris	Andrew Hawkins
Uncredited	
Uniformed Policeman	Peter Roy
Ambulance man	Tony Allen
Roof-top Agent	Charlie Price
Roof-top Agent	Chris Bunn
Kathie Hamilton	Michelle Beckley

Director: **William Brayne**

ABRAHAM St. Jacques, the Babwesi ambassador to Britain, is shot and seriously injured as he leaves hospital in his official car. CI5 are called in to investigate the shooting, and Bodie and Doyle soon discover the room in a deserted block of flats next to the hospital from which the rifle shots were fired. From the evidence they find, they decide that the shooting was not carried out by a professional assassin, so Cowley issues them with a list of names of people who might have a political motive for making an attempt on the ambassador's life. Bodie and Doyle also make their own enquiries from contacts that know Babwesi well, but they are assured that St. Jacques is not important enough to be assassinated. CI5 try to discover from the ambassador the names of any personal enemies who might want to kill him, but the man knows of no one. As Bodie and Doyle leave the hospital after talking to St. Jacques, the man who fired the shots at him, Mickey Hamilton, enters the hospital unnoticed.

Ray Doyle (Martin Shaw) and girlfriend Toni (Shelagh McLeod) pictured during THE MADNESS OF MICKEY HAMILTON.

Mickey has become mentally unbalanced following two tragedies in his life - for both of which he blames doctors, and he is determined to avenge them. Mickey did not intend to shoot St Jacques, but was aiming to kill a hospital doctor who happened to be beside the ambassador's car. Carrying a revolver, he walks down the hospital corridor and shoots three doctors dead before the alarm is raised. Mickey escapes arrest and returns to his home. As he enters, he finds a letter asking him to visit his seven-year-old daughter in the home for damaged children where she lives. During his visit, the matron warns him that the child has not long to live. Mickey tells the woman that it was the carelessness of the doctors attending his daughter's birth that brought about the damage to the child, and that he blames the hospital doctors for her sad condition. He also blames the hospital for the suffering his wife endured during his daughter's birth.

Meanwhile, after the shooting of the doctors at the hospital, CI5 suspect that St Jacques was only the accidental victim of a madman who is determined to kill doctors. The rifle and the revolver used by the killer are found abandoned near the hospital and, upon examination, are found to have come from an army base at Larchmount. Bodie visits the base and finds that a quantity of arms and explosives were stolen recently, so he asks for a list of who would have known the base well enough to steal the arms, but who left the army within the last six months. Assuming that the killer has a grudge against the particular hospital where St Jacques and the doctors were shot, Doyle also obtains a list of all deaths at the hospital in the last ten years, and both lists are fed into the CI5 computer to find any existing link between the two. Mickey Hamilton meanwhile is planning to blow up a conference hall where a medical meeting is planned.

The computer produces the name of Mickey Hamilton, an ex-soldier whose wife had died in the hospital four years before. The nurse who was in charge of Mrs. Hamilton when she was admitted tells CI5 that Mr. Hamilton was furious at the delay in the hospital treatment of his wife and blamed this on her death, after which Mickey suffered a mental breakdown. Arriving at Mickey's flat, Cowley and his men find a newspaper article there about the doctors' conference. Realising what Mickey has planned, they go to the conference hall, and start a search for Mickey and the explosives. Doyle finds Mickey and is able to keep him talking, while Bodie finds the explosives. Mickey surrenders himself to Doyle, but is startled by the police guard dogs, and in the confusion runs into the sight of Inspector Shannon, who shoots the unarmed Mickey. Mickey dies from his wounds.

Production Unit

Created by	Brian Clemens
Executive Producers	Albert Fennell, Brian Clemens
Music	Laurie Johnson
Producer	Raymond Menmuir
Associate Producer	Chris Burt
Script Editor	Chris Menaul
Production Manager	Ron Purdie
Production Accountant	Terry Connors
Assistant Director	Dominic Fulford
Location Manager	Bernard Hanson
Continuity	Gladys Pearce
Casting	Maggie Cartier
Art Director	William Alexander
Set Dresser	Ken Ryan
Wardrobe Supervisor	Donald Mothersill
Lighting Cameraman	Dusty Miller
Camera Operator	John Maskall
Focus Puller	Robin McDonald
Make Up	Eddie Knight
Hairdresser	Paula Gillespie
Supervising Editor	John S. Smith
Sound Recordist	David Crozier
Boom Operator	Mike Silverlock
Dubbing Editor	Peter Lennard
Dubbing Mixer	Hugh Strain
Music Editor	Alan Willis

An Avengers MARK 1 Production For LONDON WEEKEND TELEVISION

Shooting / Location Schedule

Production Dates: Monday 12th to Friday 23rd March, 1979. Production Number: 9D11241

12 March	*Cheap Dive*: Cobden Working Mens Club, 170 Kensal Road, Kensal Town, London, W10
	Slum Street: under White City Flyover, Latimer Road, North Kensington, London, W10
	Seedy Club: Mangrove Restaurant, 6 All Saints Road, Westbourne Park, London, W11
13 March	*Abandoned flats*: Hurley House, Cotton Gardens Estate, Kempsford Road, Kennington, London, SE11
	Church: St. Annes Church, 363 Kennington Lane, Kennington, London, SE11 / St. Mary Of The Angels, Moorhouse Road, Notting Hill, London, W2
14 March	*Institution*: St. Hubert's House, St. Hubert's Lane, Gerrards Cross, Buckinghamshire
	Int: Computer Room: Honeywell Information Systems, Honeywell House, Great West Road, Brentford, Middlesex
15 March	*Conference*: Wembley Conference Centre, Empire Way, Wembley, Middlesex
16 March	*Army Base*: Palace Of Engineering, Olympic Way, Wembley, Middlesex
19 March	*Mickey's flat*: Trellick Tower, flat 24:13, 5 Golborne Road, Kensal Town, London, W10
20 March	*Kay's flat*: Trellick Tower, flat 18:16, 5 Golborne Road, Kensal Town, W10
	Ext: Mickey's old house: Bevington Road (opposite Bevington Arms pub), North Kensington, London, W10
	Wasteland: Alderson Street (Haymills construction site), Kensal Road, Kensal Town, London, W10
21-23 March	*Ext / Int: Hospital & Rooftops*: Lambeth Hospital, Brook Drive, Lambeth, London, SE11
	Ext: Bus stop (bus 155): Kennington Park Road (near Penton Place), Kennington, London, SE11
	Ext: Bus stop (bus 159): Kennington Road (near Wincott Street), Kennington, London, SE11
	Ext: Ambulance run-by: Newington Butts, Newington, London, SE11
	Cowley's car (alley & shops): off Brook Drive, Newington, London, SE11 / 40 Kennington Lane, Kennington, London, SE11
	Int: Cowley's car: Kennington Lane (near Cottington Street), Kennington, London, SE11

SERVANT OF TWO MASTERS

by **Douglas Watkinson**
© Copyright Mark 1 Productions Ltd MCMLXXVIII

Otto Hahn	David De Keyser
Alfred Cole	Glynn Edwards
Jutta	Christina World
Robert Plumb	John Savident
Dr. Forbes	Dennis Burgess
Man 1	Tony Scannell
Karl	James Lister
Groves	Kenneth Owens
Ted	Will Stampe
Man 2	Frank Ellis
Wilf	Ryan Michael

Uncredited

CI5 Man (Interrogation room)	Jerry Baker
CI5 Man (Interrogation room)	Fritz Aardvark
Party Girl	Jackie Noble
Ammunitions Storeman	George Hillsden
CI5 Man (Ammunitions store)	David Whitely
Man 3	Terry Plummer
CI5 Man (Airfield)	Derek Chafer
CI5 Man (Airfield)	Alan Harris
CI5 Man (Airfield)	Pat Gorman

Director: **Ferdinand Fairfax**

BODIE and Doyle are off-duty one day when a Secret Service official, Robert Plumb, approaches them and explains that Cowley is suspected of using his superior position to make unlawful profits for himself. The two men are astounded by Plumb's accusation and refuse to believe that the charge has any foundation in truth, but Plumb tells them that he has official papers ordering him to investigate Cowley's activities. The next day, Cowley tells the two CI5 men that he wants them to spend all their time keeping a suspect under observation, but Bodie and Doyle find someone else for the surveillance duty and secretly follow Cowley. The CI5 Chief has already taken two lots of special arms from a CI5 firing exercise, and now he goes to the man in charge of weapons for CI5, Alfred Cole, and takes out a top-secret weapon called the PS2. Bodie follows his boss as he sets off with the weapons in his car, while Doyle questions Cole about what weapons Cowley has taken; when he discovers that Cowley has taken the PS2, he begins to take Plumb's suspicions seriously.

Bodie follows Cowley to a remote farmhouse and as Cowley enters the door, Bodie parks his car in the woods nearby, fights off a man who attacks him, and returns to watch the farmhouse. Doyle, who has also fought off two men in a nearby wood, soon joins him and through an open window they hear their boss negotiating with a foreign politician named Otto Hahn, to sell top-secret British weapons illegally.

Hahn hopes to set up a dictatorship in the country of Mata Alpa and badly needs new-sophisticated arms to achieve his aims. He tells Cowley that other suppliers of illegal arms in the UK are offering better terms for their weapons, but Cowley offers to sell him something special, the PS2.

Hahn's men attack Bodie and Doyle, and this time they are overpowered and taken prisoner. When Hahn becomes suspicious Cowley, makes up a story that the two men are mercenary fighters who want to join in the fighting at Mata Alpa. Bodie and Doyle are thrown in the cellar and Hahn suggests that Cowley should demonstrate the practical uses of the weapons he is offering on the two men. However, Cowley is thrown into the cellar with them, but the trio escape before Hahn's men can follow them.

Cowley explains that he is working under-cover with ministerial authority, and is only pretending to sell arms to find out who is behind the plot to sell top-secret arms to the would-be dictator. Plumb admits to he has no official papers that ordered Bodie and Doyle to spy on their own boss - he was acting on his own initiative. Cowley leads a raid at an airfield where Hahn keeps his private jet, where they also discover the man supplying the weapons - Alfred Cole, the CI5 arms expert. Cole explains that he was trying to ensure a prosperous and comfortable future for himself when he retired from the service.

Production Unit

Created by	Brian Clemens
Executive Producers	Albert Fennell, Brian Clemens
Music	Laurie Johnson
Producer	Raymond Menmuir
Associate Producer	Chris Burt
Script Editor	Chris Menaul
Production Manager	Ron Purdie
Production Accountant	Terry Connors
Assistant Director	David Bracknell
Location Manager	Bernard Hanson
Continuity	Gladys Pearce
Casting	Maggie Cartier
Art Director	William Alexander
Set Dresser	Ken Ryan
Stunt Arranger	Peter Brayham
Wardrobe Supervisor	Donald Mothersill
Lighting Cameraman	David Findlay
Camera Operator	John Maskall
Focus Puller	Robin McDonald
Make Up	Eddie Knight

Hairdresser	Paula Gillespie
Supervising Editor	John S. Smith
Editor	Alan Killick
Sound Recordist	David Crozier
Boom Operator	Mike Silverlock
Dubbing Editor	Peter Lennard
Dubbing Mixer	Hugh Strain
Music Editor	Alan Willis

An Avengers MARK 1 Production For LONDON WEEKEND TELEVISION

Martin Shaw is pictured having 'fun' on the set of the SERVANT OF TWO MASTERS.

Shooting / Location Schedule

Production Dates: Monday 26th March to Friday 6th April, 1979. *Originally scheduled to commence filming on 13th November, 1978 (with locations in italics below).* Production Number: 9D11240

26 March	**Cemetery**: Highgate Cemetery (Eastside, near Chester Road), Swains Lane, London, N6
27 March	**Plum's house & office**: Tower Theatre, 11 Cannonbury Place, Islington, London, N1 *6 Roman Road, Bedford Park, London, W4*
28 March	**Petrol station / phone**: Gulf Petrol Station, Marn Garage, 53-63 Wembley Hill Road, Wembley, Middlesex Texaco Petrol Station, 240 Kingsbury Road, London, NW9 **Int: Doyle's car (route to Manor End Farm)**: Church Lane (near Deanscroft Avenue), Kingsbury, London, NW9

29 March	***Int: Bodie's van (route to Manor End Farm)***: Cool Oak Lane, West Hendon, London, NW9
	Car park: *Avis, Olympic Way, Wembley, Middlesex*
	NCP car park, Queen Caroline Street, Hammersmith, London, W6
	Bodie's van run-by: Hammersmith Bridge Road, Hammersmith, London, W6
30 March	***Doctor Consultation Room***: *Vale Farm Sports Centre, Watford Road, Sudbury, Middlesex*
	Cadby Hall, Blythe Road, Hammersmith, London, W14
	Club (Cole's party): Cadby Hall, Blythe Road, Hammersmith, London, W14
	Cowley's car run-by: Shepherd's Bush Road / Brook Green, Hammersmith, London, W6
2 April	***Cowley's brief***: *Haberdashers Aske's School, Elstree, Hertfordshire*
	Warfield Hall, Forest Road, Warfield, Berkshire
3 April	***London streets / CI5 / Hostage house***: Cadby Hall, Blythe Road, Hammersmith, London, W14
	Ext: Doyle's car (traffic lights): Hammersmith Road, Hammersmith, London, W14
4 April	***Derelict buildings***: Palace Of Engineering, Olympic Way, Wembley, Middlesex
5 April	***Country roads / boat***: *Walton-On-Thames Bridge area*
	Country roads / airfield: White Waltham Airfield, Waltham Road / Cherry Garden Lane entrance, White Waltham, Berkshire
	Van run-by (under bridge): Cannon Lane, Cox Green, Berkshire
6 April	***Manor End Farm***: *Leggatts Park, Great North Road, Potters Bar, Hertfordshire*
	Warfield Hall, Forest Road, Warfield, Berkshire
2nd Unit:	***Ext: Doyle's car (route to Manor End Farm)***: Forty Avenue (near Gabriel Close), Wembley, Middlesex

BACKTRACK

Postponed from series II. Storyline & cast details in Series II. Production personnel completing the episode in this batch listed below:

Production Unit

Created by	Brian Clemens
Executive Producers	Albert Fennell, Brian Clemens
Music	Laurie Johnson
Producer	Raymond Menmuir
Associate Producer	Chris Burt
Script Editor	Gerry O'Hara
Production Manager	Ron Purdie
Production Accountant	Terry Connors
Assistant Director	Dominic Fulford
Location Manager	Peter Carter
Continuity	Gladys Pearce
Casting	Maggie Cartier
Art Director	William Alexander
Set Dresser	Robin Tarsnane
Stunt Arranger	Peter Brayham
Wardrobe Supervisor	Donald Mothersill
Lighting Cameraman	Dusty Miller
Camera Operator	John Maskall
Focus Puller	Robin McDonald
Make Up	Eddie Knight
Hairdresser	Paula Gillespie
Supervising Editor	John S. Smith
Sound Recordist	David Crozier
Boom Operator	Mike Silverlock
Dubbing Editor	Peter Lennard
Dubbing Mixer	Hugh Strain
Music Editor	Alan Willis

An Avengers MARK 1 Production For LONDON WEEKEND TELEVISION

Shooting / Location Schedule

Production Dates: Monday 9th to Friday 20th April, Wednesday 6th June, 1979. *Originally scheduled to commence filming 30th October to 10th November 1978. 6 days were completed between 30th October and 7th November.*

9-10 April   **Int: Margery's flat**: 73 Artesian Road, Notting Hill, London, W11
Ext: Truitt's car: Talbot Road, Notting Hill, London, W2
Int: Truitt's car: Westbourne Grove (Westbourne Grove Mews) / Chepstow Road, Notting Hill, London, W11
Int: Truitt's car (rear window view): Talbot Road (near Shrewsbury Road), Notting Hill, London, W2

11 April **Ext: Fashionable streets**: 2 Carlton House Terrace / Waterloo Place / Carlton Gardens / Spring Street / Cockspur Mews, St. James's, London, SW1

EASTER: no shooting

CI5 investigate terrorist activities in London. The squad track down a large and expensive cache of arms brought by Arab terrorists. Doyle (Martin Shaw) and Bodie (Lewis Collins) in a scene from BACKTRACK.

17-18 April	**Derelict ground**: Southall Gas Works, Southall, Middlesex
19 April	**Kammahmi's house**: Warfield Hall, Forest Road, Warfield, Berkshire
	Country Roads: Littlefield Green (over M4 motorway on B3024), White Waltham, Berkshire
20 April	**Truitt's office**: Cadby Hall, Blythe Road, Hammersmith, London, W14
6 June	**Ext: Cowley's flat**: Hurlingham Court, Ranelagh Gardens, Fulham, London, SW6
	Cowley's car run-by: Grimston Road, Fulham, London, SW6

STOPOVER

by **John Goldsmith**
© Copyright Mark 1 Productions Ltd MCMLXXIX

Meredith	James Laurenson
Kodai	Michael Gothard
Radouk	Morris Perry
Sir Peter Pelham	Peter Cartwright
Malenski	Morgan Sheppard
Tramp	Paul Dawkins
Dale	Frank Jarvis
Doctor	Alec Linstead
Captain	Jacob Witkin
Stevens	Robert Booth
Customs official	Godfrey Jackman
Uncredited	
Gunman	Peter Brace
Kodai's Aide	Chris Webb
CI5 Man (Airfield)	Ron Conrad
CI5 Man (Airfield)	Ray Cronk
CI5 Man (Airfield)	Paul Heasman

Director: **William Brayne**

COWLEY is urgently called to London Docks to speak to a half-starved, ragged stowaway called Colin Meredith who has just been found on a boat from Holland. The CI5 man is surprised to see Meredith, an old friend, in this condition, and the man explains that he has been held prisoner for the last two years in a Cambodian concentration camp. A man called Radouk has released him to come to England and negotiate a deal between Radouk and Cowley. Cowley knows that Radouk was once a top KGB agent, but Meredith tells him that the man has recently been working for China, and now wants to start a new life with a British passport and a large sum of money. If Cowley will agree to provide these, Radouk will give him the name of a senior British Intelligence agent, codenamed Iron Sphinx, who has secretly been working for the Russians. A deadly Russian assassin named Igor Kodai has been ordered to stop this deal and has been trying to kill Radouk and Meredith. Cowley realises that Kodai may already be in England, and Bodie and Doyle are ordered to rush Meredith to safety, but as Cowley and Meredith hurry across the docks to a waiting car, a shot rings out and Meredith is wounded. The two CI5 agents pull Meredith and their boss out of range and race off after the gunman, Kodai. But before they can reach him, he is whisked away at speed in a black limousine; Bodie recognises the driver as Yan Malenski, a top KGB agent.

In STOPOVER Cowley is offered the name of a highly-placed double-agent from an old colleague - who in return wants to be guaranteed protection with CI5. On location at Warfield Hall, Berkshire (Radouk's country house), Lewis Collins has his hair adjusted between takes by Paula Gillespie.

Meredith is taken to a CI5 safe house where a doctor treats his wounds and prescribes a complete rest, but Meredith insists that he must first visit Radouk in London and arrange the meeting between him and Cowley. When he meets Radouk, Kodai is there too; all three men are involved in an elaborate KGB plot to bring about the death of their enemy, Cowley. Kodai is furious that Meredith, having successfully lured Cowley to the docks, accidentally got in the way as Kodai tried to kill him. On his return to the safehouse, Meredith tells Cowley that the rendezvous is set; Radouk will meet him at a deserted airfield at Manley. Radouk will arrive by helicopter, so there must be tight security at the airfield perimeter to prevent Kodai breaking in, and Cowley must be quite alone. Bodie and Doyle bring in Malenski, and Cowley persuades the Russian to tell him where Kodai is hiding. The two agents are then sent to the address to find the assassin but Meredith, supposedly sedated by the doctor, is wide awake and able to warn his colleagues, who escape from Bodie and Doyle. Cowley becomes suspicious of Meredith and has him taken to another safehouse, where Bodie is told to watch him. Meredith, however, secretly contacts Kodai and requests that the man rescues him, and when Kodai and his armed men arrive, the guards hold off Bodie at gunpoint while Kodai deliberately shoots Meredith dead.

At Manley airfield, Bodie and Doyle reluctantly leave Cowley alone in an empty aircraft hanger to wait for Radouk, while they watch the airfield perimeter for Kodai. A helicopter lands and a man goes to meet Cowley. Identifying him as Kodai, Cowley is felled by a shot from Kodai's gun. As the two CI5 agents race over to Cowley's side, Kodai escapes in the helicopter. Cowley is alive and well as he was wearing a bullet-proof vest. He explains that he took the extra precaution of arranging to have the helicopter tracked as it left the airfield. The three men follow its course to a country location. Radouk and Kodai try to escape, but Kodai is killed in the ensuing battle, and Radouk surrenders. Cowley tells the man that the identity of Iron Sphinx was well known to him; he was actually a double agent working for British Intelligence, who had died a few days earlier.

Production Unit

Created by	Brian Clemens
Executive Producers	Albert Fennell, Brian Clemens
Music	Laurie Johnson
Producer	Raymond Menmuir
Associate Producer	Chris Burt
Script Editor	Chris Menaul
Production Manager	Ron Purdie
Production Accountant	Terry Connors
Assistant Director	David Bracknell
Location Manager	Peter Carter
Continuity	Gladys Pearce
Casting	Maggie Cartier
Art Director	William Alexander
Set Dresser	Robin Tarsnane
Stunt Arranger	Peter Brayham

Wardrobe Supervisor	Donald Mothersill
Lighting Cameraman	Dusty Miller
Camera Operator	John Maskall
Focus Puller	Robin McDonald
Make Up	Eddie Knight
Hairdresser	Paula Gillespie
Supervising Editor	John S. Smith
Editor	Alan Killick
Sound Recordist	David Crozier
Boom Operator	Mike Silverlock
Dubbing Editor	Peter Lennard
Dubbing Mixer	Hugh Strain
Music Editor	Alan Willis

An Avengers MARK 1 Production For LONDON WEEKEND TELEVISION

Shooting / Location Schedule

Production Dates: Monday 23rd April to Friday 4th May, Thursday 7th June, 1979. Production Number: 9D11330

23-24 April	***Docks***: King George V Dock / Victoria Dock, London, E16 ***Ship Warehouse / rooftop***: Victoria Dock, Gate 19, 4 Berth, Silvertown By Pass, London, E16
25-26 April	***RAF Manley / Hanger***: White Waltham Airfield, Waltham Road (Cherrygarden Lane entrance), Berkshire ***Country road run-by***: Church Hill, off Waltham Road, White Waltham, Berkshire ***Cowley's car run-by***: Littlefield Green (over M4 Motorway, on B3024), White Waltham, Berkshire
26-27 April	***Radouk's house***: Warfield Hall, Forest Road, Warfield, Berkshire
30 April / 1 May	***Safe House One***: The Spinney, 28 Totteridge Common, Totteridge Lane, Totteridge, London, N20
2 May	***Safe House Two***: 7 Frithwood Avenue, Northwood, Middlesex ***Bodie's car (Doyle in street)***: Rofant Road / Eastbury Road / Frithwood Avenue, Northwood, London, N20
3 May	***Radouk's London house***: 141 Friern Barnet Lane, Whetstone, London, N20 ***Bodie's car run-by***: Friern Barnet Lane (junction Myddleton Park), Whetstone, London, N20 ***Malenski's house***: 12 Sherwood Street, off Friern Barnet Lane, Whetstone, London, N20
2nd Unit:	***Ext: Church / Cemetery***: The Church Of St. Mary The Virgin, off Church Hill, Harefield, Middlesex
4 May	***Interrogation room / PLA***: Cadby Hall, Blythe Road, Hammersmith, London, W14

7 June
Int: Bodie's car: Brook Green, Hammersmith, London, W14
Int: Pub: The Great Northern Railway Tavern, 67 High Street, Hornsey, London, N8

An old colleague of Cowley's offers some vital information, but only in exchange for his safe-keeping. Bodie and Doyle are assigned to the case and are pitted against a KGB killer team in the process. On location in Frithwood Avenue, North London: Martin Shaw and Lewis Collins are in deadly pursuit - an unused sequence from STOPOVER.

RUNNER

by **Michael Feeney Callan**
© Copyright Mark 1 Productions Ltd MCMLXXIX

Duffy	Michael Kitchen
Sylvie	Barbara Kellerman
Albie	Ed Devereaux
Glover	James Cosmo
Ted	Sean Caffrey
Morgan	Billy Murray
Alice	Valerie Holliman
Old Man	Keith Marsh
Harry	Forbes Collins
Davis	Denis Bond
Girl in Betting Shop	Robyn Gurney
Bodie's Girl	Debbie Linden
Young Housewife	Samantha Brandsden
Ted's Girl	Jeh Welcome
Albie's Girl	Barbara Allen
Uncredited	
CI5 Man	Alan Harris
CI5 Man	Derek Chafer
Works Foreman	Jim Smith
Betting Shop customer	Chris Flannigan
Betting Shop customer	Alf Mangan
Heavy at Gaming Club	Billy Cornelius
Delivery Driver (Gaming Club)	Mike Vary

Director: **Martin Campbell**

WHEN a gun shop is raided, CI5 receive a tip-off but arrive on the scene too late to catch the raiders. The code used for the tip-off is recognised as one used by the Organisation, a vast and powerful criminal network, and Cowley, fearing that the raid may herald the start of a major war between the Organisation and the authorities, instructs Bodie and Doyle to make some discreet enquiries. Doyle goes to see an ex-CI5 man named Morgan, while Bodie is delegated to lead a group of CI5 agents to seize two minor Organisation criminals. Morgan, who once had contacts in the Organisation, can tell Doyle nothing about the raid but Sylvie, his girlfriend, works in a club used by top men in the Organisation and, although she says nothing to Doyle, she knows something about what is going on.

Meanwhile, Bodie and his men are compelled to use force to seize their prisoners. Cowley, however, is concerned that Bodie's unsubtle tactics may precipitate a war between the gang and CI5, and he orders Bodie to release the men immediately. Even so, Albie, the Organisation leader, decides that the arrest of two of his men cannot pass without retaliation. Albie did not organise the gun shop raid, and is very anxious to avoid any conflict with the authorities at present. He realises that a man named Duffy and his associate Glover made the raid; both men had been members of the Organisation until recently, but Duffy has a grudge against Doyle and wants to kill him. When Albie refused to help him do this, Duffy withdrew with Glover and is now trying to start a war between the gang and CI5, and kill Doyle. Albie traces Duffy's whereabouts in London, but Sylvie has met Duffy at the club and warned him that Albie is looking for him.

The stolen guns are eventually found dumped in a river, and Cowley deduces that they must have been stolen by a 'runner', a man who has split from the Organisation and is now bent on causing trouble. Duffy and Glover then set up a robbery at a casino and again alert CI5 with the Organisation code. Albie, again, assures Cowley this was nothing to with the Organisation. Morgan arranges to meet Doyle to hand over some information he has discovered. Duffy overhears the phone call and secretly awaits the two men at the meeting place. However, his shot, meant for Doyle, kills Morgan instead. Later, Glover brings Sylvie to a deserted block of flats, where Duffy has taken refuge. Doyle is lured to the flats, but when he sees Sylvie and tells her that Morgan has been killed, she warns him of the impending danger. The warning enables Doyle to evade Duffy's fire and, eventually, a shot from Sylvie sends Duffy to his death. She tells Doyle that Duffy has made one more attempt to start a war between the Organisation and the authorities; he has placed a bomb in a government-building car park. Bodie and Doyle arrive just in time to stop the explosion.

Production Unit

Created by	Brian Clemens
Executive Producers	Albert Fennell, Brian Clemens
Music	Laurie Johnson
Producer	Raymond Menmuir
Associate Producer	Chris Burt
Script Editor	Chris Menaul
Production Manager	Ron Purdie
Production Accountant	Terry Connors
Assistant Director	Dominic Fulford
Location Manager	Peter Carter
Continuity	Gladys Pearce
Casting	Maggie Cartier
Art Director	William Alexander
Set Dresser	Robin Tarsnane
Stunt Arranger	Peter Brayham
Wardrobe Supervisor	Donald Mothersill
Lighting Cameraman	Norman Langley
Camera Operator	John Maskall
Focus Puller	Robin McDonald
Make Up	Eddie Knight
Hairdresser	Paula Gillespie
Supervising Editor	John S. Smith

Sound Recordist   David Crozier
Boom Operator   Mike Silverlock
Dubbing Editor   Peter Lennard
Dubbing Mixer   Hugh Strain
Music Editor   Alan Willis

An Avengers MARK 1 Production For LONDON WEEKEND TELEVISION

On the set of RUNNER - Martin Shaw as Doyle and Lewis Collins as Bodie.

Shooting / Location Schedule
Production Dates: Tuesday 8th to Friday 18th May, Friday 8th June, 1979. Production Number: 9D11331

8 May	***Playground***: Alexandra Park, The Avenue, Muswell Hill, London, N10
	Morgan's flat / Bodies girl's flat: 26 South Villas, off Camden Square, Camden Town, London, NW1
9-10 May	***Derelict Tenement***: The Highlands, Crouch Hill (near Mount View Road), London, N4
	Rooftop: Derelict Tenement: Warltersville Mansions, Warltersville Road, London, N19
10-11 May	***Int: Duffy's flat / Glover's flat***: Flat 10, Brambledown Mansions, Heathville Road, Crouch Hill, London, N7
	Int / Ext: Ted's house: 5 Heathville Road, Crouch Hill, London, N7
	Streets: house / bus stop: Heathville Road / Ashley Road / Crouch Hill, Stroud Green, London, N4
	Ext: Doyle's car (gun shop route - segment 4): Hornsey Rise / Hornsey Lane, Upper Holloway, London, N19
	Ext: Doyle's car (route to stables / garage): Crouch Hill (near Mount View Road), London, N4
	Ext: Bodie's car (Government offices route - 1): Crouch Hill (near Mount View Road), London, N4
	Ext: Doyle's car (Government offices route): Crouch Hill (near Blythwood Road), London, N4
	Ext: Bodie's car (Government offices route - 2): Crouch Hill / Mount View Road, Upper Holloway, London, N4

13 May	*Garage & yard*: Arch 9, under railway arches, St. James's Lane, Muswell Hill, London, N10
14 May	*Drinking club*: Skindles Night Club, Mill Lane, Maidenhead Bridge, Maidenhead, Berkshire
15 May	*Gaming club / Casino*: Green Man pub car park, 56 Muswell Hill, London, N10
	Casino car chase (thru railway arch): St James's Lane, Muswell Hill, London, N10
	Casino car chase & run-bys: Hornsey Rise Gardens / Hornsey Rise, Crouch End, London, N19
	Lake / Common: Black Park, Fulmer, Buckinghamshire
16 May	*Stables & garage*: Clare Hall mental hospital, Blanche Lane, Ridge, Hertfordshire
	Government offices: Civic Centre car park (Elstree Town Hall), Shenley Road, Borehamwood, Hertfordshire
17 May	*Gun Shop / Ext: Phone Box*: The Gun Shop, 78 High Street, Shepperton, Middlesex
18 May	*Bookie's shop*: Hector MacDonalds (old shop), 32 Topsfield Parade, The Broadway, Hornsey, London, N8
	Roof / Streets / shop yard: Topsfield Parade, Tottenham Lane / Elder Avenue, Hornsey, London, N8
	Ext: Pub: The Favourite, 23 Beaumont Rise, Upper Holloway, London, N19
	Morgan's workplace (lorries): Construction site off Cromartie Road / Hornsey Rise, Crouch End, London, N8
	Ext: Cowley's car - street meeting: Wall Court, Stroud Green Road, Finsbury Park, London, N4
	Casino car chase (continued): Ashley Road / Highcroft Road / Heathville Road, Upper Holloway, London, N19
	Int: Cowley's car (meeting): Mount View Road, Stroud Green, London, N8
	Int: Cowley's car & run-by: Denton Road / Ridge Road / Oakfield Road, Stroud Green, London, N8
8 June	*Int: Doyle's car (Gun shop route - segment 1)*: Exeter Road, Willesden Green, London, NW2
	Ext: Doyle's car (Gun shop route - segment 2): Walm Lane (near Blenheim Gardens), Willesden Green, London, NW2
	Ext: Doyle's car (Gun shop route - segment 3): Cranhurst Road, Willesden Green, London, NW2
	Int: Doyle's car (on radio to Morgan): Blenheim Gardens, Willesden Green, London, NW2
	Ext: Doyle's car (route to derelict tenement): Walm Lane / Station Parade, Willesden Green, London, NW2
	Int: Doyle's car (route to derelict tenement): Lydford Road, Willesden Green, London, NW2
	Int: Doyle's car (government offices route): Cranhurst Road, Willesden Green, London, NW2

A HIDING TO NOTHING
by **Ted Childs**
© Copyright Mark 1 Productions Ltd MCMLXXIX

Frances Cottingham	Sylvia Kay
Shelley	Lise Hilboldt
Doad	Nadim Sawalha
Luis	Christopher Reich
Colonel Masterson	Gerald Sim
Mrs. Cottingham	Phillada Sewell
Hassam Alousha	Adam Hussein
Mrs. Waller	Yvonne D'Alpra
Khadi	Nicholas Amer
Pilar Hernandez	Leticia Garrido
Smith	Frederick Warner
Uncredited	
Roof-top Agent	Johnnie Clements
Burglar 1	Del Baker
Burglar 2	Nosher Powell
Doctor	Lionel De Clerc
Car Driver	Terry Yorke

Director: **Gerry O'Hara**

ELABORATE security operations are put into force when Khadi, a Middle Eastern politician, is to pay a secret visit to Britain to attend vital talks with the Foreign Office. During a full-scale rehearsal for the visit, a girl infiltrates the grounds and is seen filming the security arrangements. She is pursued by a member of the security forces and, when she opens fire on him, is shot dead. She is later found to have been Pilar Hernandez, a member of a fanatical Arab terrorist group who are Khadi's bitter enemies.

CI5 are called in to tighten up the security arrangements, and to find out how the girl learned of Khadi's visit, but the politician's own security chief, Aziz Doad, and his associate Alousha, tell Cowley that they plan to make their own enquiries. Cowley begins by interviewing British politician Roger Masterson, the man who had arranged Khadi's visit, but when Masterson explains that only he and his woman assistant, Frances Cottingham, knew of the plans, Cowley's suspicions are aroused and he asks Bodie to follow Frances' movements. Bodie follows the woman to a concert where she meets a dark-skinned young man who is evidently her lover.

Doyle meanwhile has moved into the flat immediately below the one where the terrorist girl had been living for a few days, with an air hostess named Shelley Hunter. The CI5 man befriends the girl, but she seems quite innocent of any involvement with the terrorist. One night when Shelley is in Doyle's flat, the CI5 man hears intruders in the flat above and races upstairs to investigate.

A dummy run that has been staged for the visit of a Middle Eastern official is found to have been recorded by a foreign student....Martin Shaw and Lewis Collins on location in Black Park, Fulmer, Buckinghamshire, during shooting on the story A HIDING TO NOTHING.

He finds two men searching Shelley's room and gives chase. During the rooftop battle, which follows, one of the men escapes, but the other falls from the roof to the street below and is taken to hospital badly injured. Cowley and Doyle visit him the following night and, when they discover that it was Doad who sent the men to search the flat, they decide to set a trap for the security man and his associates. Cowley tells Doad that he already has the information on where the security leak occurred - through Frances Cottingham. Frances is questioned about her association with the young man, Luis Delgado, and she explains that Luis is a struggling young musician who is trying to support himself by journalism. Under pressure from Cowley she confesses that she told Luis about Khadi's visit. So that he would have a good story to offer the press. Bodie then informs her that there is no such person as Luis Delgado and that the young man has duped her. Cowley asks her to meet Luis once more and give him false information that Khadi is to go to the Crableigh Hotel for talks; the CI5 men will then trap the terrorists in the hotel.

Frances gives the man the false information but highly distressed by the affair, she is run down by a motorist and taken to hospital. On the day of Khadi's arrival, Cowley, Alousha, Doad and Bodie wait to escort him to the Foreign Office talks, while Doyle and other CI5 men wait for any terrorist attack at the hotel. However, only Luis arrives at the hotel, and Doyle discovers he is working for Israeli Intelligence. Now convinced that Luis has no connection with the terrorists, Doyle radios Bodie with a warning to expect an attack on Khadi's convoy and sets off to help his colleague. Alousha, who is driving Khadi's car, suddenly jumps out of the limousine seconds before a terrorist rocket attack is launched at the convoy and, as Cowley seizes the wheel and accelerates the car to safety, Bodie and the other CI5 agents launch a counter-attack on the terrorists. Doyle arrives in time to help Bodie trap Alousha and his informant - Shelley, who was waiting to drive Alousha to safety.

Production Unit

Created by	Brian Clemens
Executive Producers	Albert Fennell, Brian Clemens
Music	Laurie Johnson
Producer	Raymond Menmuir
Associate Producer	Chris Burt
Script Editor	Chris Menaul
Production Manager	Ron Purdie
Production Accountant	Terry Connors
Assistant Director	David Bracknell
Location Manager	Peter Carter
Continuity	Gladys Pearce
Casting	Maggie Cartier
Art Director	William Alexander
Set Dresser	Robin Tarsnane
Stunt Arrangers	Peter Brayham, Frank Henson
Wardrobe Supervisor	Donald Mothersill
Lighting Cameraman	Dusty Miller
Camera Operator	Mike Proudfoot
Focus Puller	Robin McDonald
Make Up	Bernard Brown
Hairdresser	Paula Gillespie
Supervising Editor	John S. Smith
Editor	Alan Killick
Sound Recordist	David Crozier

Boom Operator	Mike Silverlock
Dubbing Editor	Peter Lennard
Dubbing Mixer	Hugh Strain
Music Editor	Alan Willis

An Avengers MARK 1 Production For LONDON WEEKEND TELEVISION

Lewis Collins prepares to film a car scene in Woodstock Road, North London (outside Shelley's flat) during A HIDING TO NOTHING.

Shooting / Location Schedule

Production Dates: Tuesday 22nd May to Tuesday 5th June, Thursday 12th July, 1979. Production Number: 9D11332. Locations in *italics* were originally scheduled but ultimately not used.

22 May	**Masterson's house**: Uplands House, Monroe Drive, East Sheen, London, SW14
23 May	**Mews & car park**: Hay's Mews, Farm Street / South Audley Street, Mayfair, London, W1
	Mews & subway: Pitts Head Mews (junction with Curzon Place), London, W1 / 25 Park Lane (subway), London, W1
	Cowley's park meeting: Mount Street Gardens, off South Audley Street, Mayfair, London, W1
2nd Unit	**Streets: Bodie (car chase)**: Barrington Road / Palace Road / Priory Road, Hornsey, London, N8
	Streets: (Frances run over): *Harringay West Station footbridge, Stapleton Hall Road, London, N4*
	Park Road & Lynton Road (Doyle's car) / Palace Road / The Grove (footpath), Hornsey, London, N8

24-25 May	*Int: Shelley's flat*: Flats 4-10 Enmore Court, Enmore Gardens, Sheen, London, SW14
28-29 May	*Frances' apartment*: Flat 6M, Hyde Park Mansions, Cabbell Street, Lisson Grove, London, NW1
30 May	*Suburban Hotel*: Holiday Inn, 128 King Henry's Road, Swiss Cottage, London, NW3
31 May	*Crableigh Hotel*: Burnham Beeches Hotel, Grove Road, Burnham, Buckinghamshire Warfield Hall, Forest Road, Warfield, Berkshire *Airfield*: RAF Northolt, West End Road, off Western Avenue, Ruislip, Middlesex
2nd Unit	*Festival Hall & car park*: Royal Festival Hall, South Bank, Lambeth, London, SE1 Royal Albert Hall, doors 13-14, Kensington Gore, Kensington, London, SW7 *Parking: Bodie's car*: Prince Concert Road, Kensington, London, SW7
1 June	*Ext: Shelley's flat / GPO van / Bodie's car*: 35 Woodstock Road, Finsbury Park, London, N4
4 June	*Country roads / Ambush*: Black Park, Gate 12: Peace Road, Uxbridge Road (A412), Fulmer, Buckinghamshire
5 June	*Briefing room & hospital*: St. Bernards Hospital, Windmill Lane, Southall, Middlesex *Int: Cowley's car*: Empire Way / Wembley Park Drive, Wembley, Middlesex.
2nd Unit: 12 July	*Crableigh Hotel*: Warfield Hall, Forest Road, Warfield, Berkshire *Ext: Airfield car run-by*: White Waltham Airfield, Waltham Road, White Waltham, Berkshire *Ext: Country roads - car run-bys*: Lemsford Village Road, Lemsford, Hertfordshire

CI5's Doyle (Martin Shaw) and Bodie (Lewis Collins) are on A HIDING TO NOTHING in Black Park, Fulmer, Buckinghamshire.

DEAD RECKONING
by **Philip Loraine**
© Copyright Mark 1 Productions Ltd MCMLXXIX

Stefan Batak I	Derek Godfrey
Anna Batak	Carol Royle
Stefan Batak II	Alan Tilvern
Paul	Milos Kirek
Michael	Michael Hadley
Chauffeuse	Sally Harrison
Vashunin	Gabor Vernon
Bulgarian Officer	Jeffrey Chiswick
Reporter	Walter McMonagle
Bride	Jane Sumner

Uncredited

CI5 Agent (Frontier Post)	Jimmy Muir
CI5 Agent (Frontier Post)	Paul Heasman
Russian Agent (Frontier Post)	Dave Cooper
CI5 Agent (Safe house)	Gerry Paris
CI5 Agent (Safe house)	Robert Smythe
Reporter	Ron Watkins
1st Thug	Romo Gorrara
2nd Thug	Chris Webb
Priest	Dick Sullivan
Bridegroom	Maurice Thorogood
Thug in lift	Don McClean
2nd Thug	Reg Turner
CI5 Agent (Keen's Lodge)	Ray Bunby

Director: **Denis Lewiston**

IN conditions of the greatest secrecy, a Russian spy caught by the British is exchanged for a spy called Stefan Batak who has been caught by the Russians. Batak has latterly been working in Russia as an agent for British Intelligence, but because his loyalties are suspect, MI5 wish to keep him at arm's length and CI5 are asked to handle his debriefing when he arrives secretly in London. Cowley begins the painstaking questioning of Batak, while Doyle, posing as a journalist, goes to meet the man's daughter, Anna. The girl, a music student, is very anxious to meet her father behind the Iron Curtain. It appears to Doyle that she does not know anything about her father's life and career, or that he has arrived in London. While Doyle is talking to her at her college, one of her student friends called Michael, contacts a dangerous man named Paul, and as Doyle makes his way out of the college Paul, unseen, shouts to Doyle that Anna is Batak's daughter and Batak is in the UK.

CI5 are extremely concerned that, despite all their security precautions, the fact of Batak's arrival is known. Later that day, as Doyle and Bodie drive

Batak across town to a London CI5 safe house, their way is blocked in a side street and a gunman opens fire on them. Doyle manages to save Batak from injury, but the gunman escapes. With the arrival of the police and journalists on the scene, CI5 loses all hope of keeping Batak's arrival a secret.

As the newspapers carry accounts of Batak's arrival in London, Cowley is under pressure to make a statement about him. In the meantime, Anna is taken to see her long lost father. Arrangements are made for a press conference but on the way Batak collapses and dies before Cowley's men can get him to hospital. Apart from his own men, the only person who has been near Batak since his arrival in Britain is Anna. She is amazed that the finger points to her, despite the fact that Bodie had told her about her father's career as a spy, and about his treachery and cruelty. Doyle meanwhile has noticed Michael watching the girl, and decides to follow him and film the people he meets. Michael meets with Paul, and the two men then enter a house in a London square. As Doyle leaves his car and prepares to film the proceedings in the house two men see him and attack him. He defends himself and gives them the slip.

In this scene from DEAD RECKONING Bodie (Lewis Collins) is about to exchange a Russian spy, Vashunin (Gabor Vernon), for Stefan Batak.

The film shows a brief glimpse of a man in the house - a man who resembles someone shown in a picture at Anna's flat, and Doyle tells Cowley that he suspects this man of being the real Batak. When the CI5 Chief discovers that the man they thought was Batak was poisoned with a slow-acting drug before he left Russia, he decides that the real Batak must have entered England secretly and arranged that the imposter would be taken for him in a well-publicised death. Anna, hoping to help her real father, only pretended to recognise the imposter. She has meanwhile been snatched from Bodie's guard and taken to see her real father. But CI5 are in hot pursuit and Michael and Paul warn Batak that he must make quick his escape. Anna, uncertain whether she wants to go with a man she knows to be a murderer, delays their departure. Paul persuades Michael to kill the girl, but Bodie rushes in to save her and Cowley takes Batak into custody.

In DEAD RECKONING Doyle (Martin Shaw) is forced to defend himself after he has been caught photographing a gang's headquarters.

Production Unit

Created by	Brian Clemens
Executive Producers	Albert Fennell, Brian Clemens
Music	Laurie Johnson
Producer	Raymond Menmuir
Associate Producer	Chris Burt
Script Editor	Gerry O'Hara
Production Manager	Ron Purdie
Production Accountant	Terry Connors
Assistant Director	Gordon Gilbert
Location Manager	Peter Carter
Continuity	Gladys Pearce
Casting	Maggie Cartier
Art Director	William Alexander
Set Dresser	Robin Tarsnane
Stunt Arranger	Peter Brayham
Wardrobe Supervisor	Donald Mothersill
Lighting Cameraman	Norman Langley
Camera Operator	Mike Proudfoot
Focus Puller	Robin McDonald
Make Up	Bernard Brown
Hairdresser	Paula Gillespie
Supervising Editor	John S. Smith
Sound Recordist	Chris Munro
Boom Operator	Gary Weir
Dubbing Editor	Peter Lennard

Dubbing Mixer   Hugh Strain
Music Editor   Alan Willis

An Avengers MARK 1 Production For LONDON WEEKEND TELEVISION

Shooting / Location Schedule

Production Dates: Monday 11th to Tuesday 26th June, 1979. Production Number: 9D11333

11 June	***Frontier Posts & streets***: Black Park, Peace Road, Fulmer, Buckinghamshire
12 June	***Church / Churchyard***: St. Andrews, Thornhill Square, Barnsbury, London, N1
13 June	***Keen's Lodge***: St. Hubert's House, St. Hubert's Lane, Gerrards Cross, Buckinghamshire
14-15 June	***College Of Music***: National Liberal Club, 1 Whitehall Place, Whitehall, London, SW1
18-20 June	***Safe house & streets***: Southall Gas Works, White Street, Southall, Middlesex
20 June	***Van (Bodie) & lorry stunt***: Wolseley Road (run-bys) / Birchington Road (lorry), Crouch End, London, N8
	Int: Cowley's car (route to Keen's Lodge): Wolseley Road / Shepherds Hill, Crouch End, London, N8
	Ext: Cowley's car (route to Keen's Lodge): Wolseley Road, Crouch End, London, N8
21 June	***Car stunt / ambush house***: 7 Ferme Park Road (café) / Stapleton Hall Road, Stroud Green, London, N8
22 June	***Bodie's flat***: Northway House, 1379 High Road, Whetstone, London, N20
	Int: Doyle's car (with Anna): Hendon Lane, Church End, London, N3
	Ext: Anna's flat: 5 Crescent Road, Church End, London, N3
25 June	***No.11 House & square***: St. Andrews, 8 Thornhill Square, Barnsbury, London, N1 (*original schedule as No.11 house, appears as No.8*)
	Ext: Cowley's car run-bys: Caledonian Road (near Bridgeman Road / Carnegie Street), Barnsbury, London, N1 / Pentonville Road, Islington, London, N1
	Int: Cowley's car: Thornhill Road / Offord Road / Roman Way, Barnsbury, London, N1
26 June	***Hospital / Projector room***: St. Bernards Hospital, Windmill Lane, Southall, Middlesex
2nd Unit:	
	Int: Bodie's car (ambush & radio): Elliman Avenue / Oatlands Drive, Slough, Berkshire

MIXED DOUBLES
by **Brian Clemens**
© Copyright Mark 1 Productions Ltd MCMLXXIX

Rio	Michael Coles
Macklin	Ian McCulloch
Coney	David Beames
Joe	Nickolas Grace
Serpoy	Paul Hertzberg
Callard	Bill McGuirk
Barmaid	Lesley Daine
Big Punk	Mark Wingett
Diplomat	Lindsay Campbell
President Parsali	Walter Randall
Chambermaid	Ena Cabayo
Scruffy Man	John Barrard
Plain clothes sergeant	Clifford Earl
Security Man	Charles Cork

Uncredited

Gang Member	Graham Crowther
House Security Guard	Derek Chaffer
CI5 Man	Eric Kent
Gerry (CI5 Man)	Gerry Paris
CI5 Man	Eddie Powell

Director: **Roger Tucker**

AN important Middle Eastern leader named Parsali is due to arrive in Britain for the signing of a peace treaty. CI5 are committed to protecting him and Bodie and Doyle are sent to a tough training expert named Brian Macklin so that they will be at the peak of physical fitness to safeguard Parsali. Meanwhile, a notorious assassin called Rio, who has been hired to kill Parsali, finds two hit men, Frank Coney and Joe. The location for the treaty ceremony is being kept a tight secret, but one of Parsali's aides in Britain, Achmed Serpoy, a traitor, who is working for Parsali's enemies, tells Rio where the signing will take place. Rio tells the man that the place is too well guarded for an assassination attempt. Serpoy tells Rio that a reserve meeting place has been arranged. Rio explains that he will ensure that the signing ceremony is disrupted and plans the assassination for the second location.

When the body of a woman who has accidentally discovered Rio's plans is found dead by the police, CI5 are alerted to the fact that an Arab was seen leaving the scene of the murder. A description of the man from a witness leads Cowley to suspect that the man is Rio and, assuming that the man must be in the UK to kill Parsali, he warns Bodie and Doyle that they must be extremely vigilant when they guard the visiting statesman.

In MIXED DOUBLES actor Martin Shaw had to have his hair in curlers at the start of each days filming to maintain continuity!

So that they can be familiar with the site, he drives them to the place where the treaty is to be signed. They are also shown the reserve location, which is at present only lightly guarded. Rio has already photographed the second location and has made Coney and Joe learn its ground plan thoroughly; he has also rehearsed them on how to enter the house secretly, how to hide in an attic until Parsali arrives and how to shoot the statesman and his guards during the signing ceremony. Rio has summoned Serpoy and murders him when he arrives. When Serpoy's body is found dumped in

London, it appears as though he has been tortured and Cowley assumes that the man must have given away the planned location for the signing ceremony.

As Serpoy is not supposed to know the site of the reserve location, Cowley decides the ceremony should take place at the second rendezvous. Security guards arrive at the house with security equipment but, following Rio's plans, Coney and Joe are already installed in the attic. The two men spend an anxious night preparing for their attack the next day, knowing that if they fail to follow plans exactly, they will be killed. Downstairs, Bodie and Doyle also spend a sleepless night, thinking and talking about what may happen the next day. Parsali is brought to England in a destroyer, then flown straight to the house by helicopter.

A crowd of diplomats and press men, all vetted closely by security men, gather in the house to witness the signing ceremony and, as Parsali makes a short speech, Bodie and Doyle are alert for any sign of an attack. As they walk through the house, Bodie glances to the stairs and sees Coney about to draw his gun. By chance, Bodie had met Coney a few days earlier, when Coney saved his life in a pub brawl and, thinking the man is a friend, does not immediately shoot him. Seconds later, however, Doyle throws Parsali to the ground as Joe begins shooting, injuring many of the bystanders. A bullet from Bodie fatally hits Coney, but Joe makes his escape into the grounds, pursued by Doyle. Waiting for his men in a car and seeing Doyle pursuing Joe, Rio tries to drive away but Joe shoots him, then Joe is shot dead by Doyle.

Production Unit

Created by	Brian Clemens
Executive Producers	Albert Fennell, Brian Clemens
Music	Laurie Johnson
Producer	Raymond Menmuir
Associate Producer	Chris Burt
Script Editor	Gerry O'Hara
Production Manager	Ron Purdie
Production Accountant	Terry Connors
Assistant Director	David Bracknell
Location Manager	Peter Carter
Continuity	Gladys Pearce
Casting	Maggie Cartier
Art Director	William Alexander
Set Dresser	Robin Tarsnane
Stunt Arranger	Peter Brayham
Wardrobe Supervisor	Donald Mothersill
Lighting Cameraman	Dusty Miller
Camera Operator	Mike Proudfoot
Focus Puller	Robin McDonald
Make Up	Bernard Brown
Hairdresser	Paula Gillespie
Supervising Editor	John S. Smith
Editor	Alan Killick
Sound Recordist	Chris Munro

Boom Operator	Gary Weir
Dubbing Editor	Peter Lennard
Dubbing Mixer	Hugh Strain
Music Editor	Alan Willis

An Avengers MARK 1 Production for LONDON WEEKEND TELEVISION

CI5's Doyle (Martin Shaw) and Bodie (Lewis Collins) in MIXED DOUBLES.

Shooting / Location Schedule

Production Dates: Monday 25th June to Friday 6th July; Wednesday 11th to Thursday 12th July, 1979. Production Number: 9D11334. Locations in *italics* were originally scheduled but ultimately not used.

25-26 June	**Workshop**: Southall Gas Works, Beaconsfield Road, off Randolph Road, Southall, Middlesex
27 June	**Int: Cheap hotel**: Cadby Hall, Blythe Road, Hammersmith, London, W14
28 June	**Pub**: The White Lion, White Street, Southall, Middlesex
29 June-2 July	**Warehouse 1**: Southall Gas Works, Beaconsfield Road, Southall, Middlesex
	House 1: *Southall Gas Works, Southall, Middlesex*
3-6 July	**House 2**: Warfield House, Bracknell Road, Warfield, Berkshire
	Street: Serpoy's dead body found: Brent Road, off Scotts Road, Southall, Middlesex
2nd Unit:	
11 July	**Cheap hotel**: Cadby Hall, Blythe Road, Hammersmith, London, W14
12 July	**House 1**: Brocket Hall, Marford Road, Lemsford, Hertfordshire

NEED TO KNOW

by **Brian Clemens**
from a story by **Chris Menaul**
© Copyright Mark 1 Productions Ltd MCMLXXIX

Manton	Patrick O'Connell
Drake	Norman Jones
Ryan	Karin McCarthy
Gorky	Niall Buggy
Tully	Simon Oates
Ivan	Richard Parmentier
Ambassador	David King
Pymar	Tom Georgeson
Minister	Bernard Gallagher
Choy	Chua Kahjoo
Maroff	Yuri Borienko
Sikor	Anthony Chinn
Minder	Kristopher Kum
1st Cop	Nigel Miles Thomas
2nd Cop	Mike Kemp

Uncredited

Security Guard	Trevor Wedlock
Embassy gate Guard	Les Conrad
Security Van Driver	Harry Fielder

Director: **William Brayne**

AFTER a fire at his home reveals evidence that he is selling secret information to the Chinese, Andy Drake, a senior MI5 man, is arrested by the Special Branch and, because Cowley has brought Drake into MI5, he too falls under suspicion of treachery and is taken in for questioning by two top MI5 men, Frederick Manton and John Tully. Cowley knows that as Drake is being held under normal police custody and has a solicitor to defend him, there is no chance that he will have to give full information about his activities, nor will he convince MI5 that Cowley had nothing to do with his allegiance to the Chinese. Determined that he will not spend the rest of his career under a cloud of vague suspicion and see his career terminated because of it, the CI5 Chief tells Bodie and Doyle that they must help him clear his name. Their first assignment is to go to the London Chinese quarter, and arrest a Chinese criminal named Choy. Meanwhile Gorky, a senior KGB official in London, is also interested in Drake's arrest and plans to snatch Drake from custody so that the KGB can learn about his operations with the Chinese. The man is confident that he will be able to seize Drake with the help of secret information supplied by a top Russian agent placed high in the ranks of MI5. Drake's solicitor, Sara Ryan, is aware that attempts will be made to snatch her client, and demands complete details of where he is being held.

CI5's George Cowley (Gordon Jackson) takes aim in NEED TO KNOW.

She also wants to be informed when he is to be moved from one prison or courtroom to another. Cowley tells Manton and Tully that Bodie and Doyle will snatch Drake using gas stun guns and question him so that his own reputation will be cleared; he explains that he will use Choy at the scene, so that it will be assumed that the Chinese have taken their own man away. The two MI5 men are able to give Cowley details of Drake's movements and the CI5 Chief decides to make the snatch on a lonely stretch of road near Cheltenham. Gorky receives a tip-off that Cowley is going to snatch Drake, and he decides to let CI5 make the snatch then take Drake from Cowley's men. Following Cowley's example, they too decide to use stun guns and plan to use agents who are Chinese, so that the Chinese will be blamed for the attack. So that their source inside MI5 will not be suspected of divulging secret information on Drake's whereabouts, Gorky and his men kidnap Sara Ryan and plan to kill her; if she disappears, it will be assumed that it was she who gave away the information about Drake's movements.

As the prison van carrying Drake to Cheltenham travels along the lonely stretch of road, Bodie and Doyle stage a skilful attack. They knock out Drake's guards with stun gas and are about to scramble Drake into their car when two KGB agents attack the CI5 men. Armed with a rifle in case his men require assistance, Cowley watches from a distance, but the Russians leave his men unharmed on the ground and speed off, with Drake, to a hideaway. Drake is to be interrogated by the KGB agent working for MI5. Cowley's men apologise to their boss for their failure, but Cowley tells them that their failure was anticipated and planned; he explains that Drake is not a traitor at all, but a loyal MI5 agent who has knowingly been used to trap a suspected Russian source in MI5. Drake has a directional finding aid embedded in his arm enabling CI5 to locate the gang's hideout. Sara Ryan is rescued and CI5 find the KGB plant, Manton, ready to question Drake. Manton tries to escape, but is shot by Cowley.

Production Unit

Created by	Brian Clemens
Executive Producer	Albert Fennell, Brian Clemens
Music	Laurie Johnson
Producer	Raymond Menmuir
Associate Producer	Chris Burt
Script Editor	Gerry O'Hara
Production Manager	Ron Purdie
Production Accountant	Terry Connors
Assistant Director	Gregory Dark
Location Manager	Peter Carter
Continuity	Gladys Pearce
Casting	Maggie Cartier
Art Director	William Alexander
Set Dresser	Robin Tarsnane
Stunt Arranger	Peter Brayham
Wardrobe Supervisor	Donald Mothersill
Lighting Cameraman	Norman Langley
Camera Operator	John Maskall
Focus Puller	Robin McDonald
Make Up	Bernard Brown
Hairdresser	Paula Gillespie
Supervising Editor	John S. Smith
Sound Recordist	Chris Munro
Boom Operator	Gary Weir
Dubbing Editor	Peter Lennard
Dubbing Mixer	Hugh Strain

Music Editor   Alan Willis

An Avengers MARK 1 Production For LONDON WEEKEND TELEVISION

Bodie (Lewis Collins) and Doyle (Martin Shaw) are ambushed in NEED TO KNOW.

Shooting / Location Schedule

Production Dates: Monday 9th to Friday 20th July, 1979. Production Number: 9D11335

9 July	*Int / Ext: Cowley's place*: 21 Ennismore Garden Mews, Knightsbridge, London, SW7
10 July	*Int / Ext: Bodie's flat*: 44 Lansdowne Crescent, Notting Hill, London, W11
11-12 July	*Embassy / Gorky's office*: 4 The Grove, Highgate, London, N6
	Ext: Drake's burnt-out house: 32 Milton Park, Highgate, London, N6
13 July	*Chinese Club*: The Dock, Port A Bella Dock, Ladbroke Grove, London, W10
16 July	*Safe House*: Rowley Farm, Black Park Road, Fulmer, Buckinghamshire
17-18 July	*Rapworth Hall*: Stanmore Hall, Wood Lane, Stanmore, Middlesex
	Int: Bodie's car: Wood Lane, Stanmore, Middlesex
19-20 July	*Ambush*: B3018: Binfield Road (over M4 Motorway), Berkshire
	Ambush cars: run-by: Callins Lane / The Street, Shurlock Row, Berkshire
	Court & courtyard: Windsor Police Station, St. Leonards Road, Windsor, Berkshire

Three-Week Summer Break from Monday 23rd July to Friday 10th August

THE PURGING OF C I 5
by **Stephen Lister**
© Copyright Mark 1 Productions Ltd MCMLXXIX

Phillips	Simon Rouse
Susan	Sally Harrison
Lake	Norman Gregory
Billy	Chris Fairbank
King	Ian Gelder
Matheson	Paul Antony-Barber
Williams	Ben Thomas
Pennington	James Smith
Murray	Leo Dolan
Parks	Peter Jolley
Dave	Bill Treacher
Wakeman	Martha Nairn
Catrall	Terry Yorke
1st Doctor	David Gretton
2nd Doctor	Nalini Moonasar
Uncredited	
CI5 Agent (Hospital)	Terry Creasy

Director: **Dennis Abey**

SOMEONE is out to eliminate CI5; Cowley narrowly escapes with his life when a bomb explodes in his office and Williams, a CI5 man lured to a derelict building for a meeting with an informant, Billy, is also killed when a bomb detonates in a room he is searching. Cowley receives a further anonymous telephone threat promising further attacks on CI5 men, and an urgent warning is sent out to all field operatives. Two agents named King and Matheson do not hear the warning on their car radio as they are searching a house; an informer who told them that they would find evidence that a crime had been committed there has lured them to the house. Finding nothing of interest, the two men leave. As Matheson inserts the ignition key into his car, the vehicle explodes and his is killed instantly, but King has also suffered the blast. He manages to tell Bodie and Doyle about Billy before he dies. Cowley orders his men to find Chris and Billy, the two informers who led the CI5 men to their deaths. The police, in a deserted railway siding, finds Chris's car, and the two CI5 men find Chris dead in a nearby railway carriage, with a large sum of money by his side. Chris has been killed from a distance by a rifle bullet as he collected his pay-off for betraying Williams.

Billy, the second informer, is found and questioned by Bodie and Doyle and he admits that he led Matheson and King to the house by telephoning them with a message. However, he insists that he had no idea that the information was a trap and explains that a man whom he sees occasionally, but does not know by name gave him the information. Bodie and Doyle believe Billy's story, and decide that the best way of catching the man is to let

Billy find the man himself. The informer is freed and told to contact CI5 when he sees the man again. Another bomb attempt is made, this time on Bodie's life, but the agent discovers the bomb in his home and Doyle is able to defuse it. A CI5 agent, Susan, contacts Cowley with the news that Billy has seen the man again, and the two men drive to the office where the man, Parks, has been seen. However, Susan, parked across the street from Parks' office, decides not to wait for her colleagues to arrive, and enters the building alone. She finds Parks armed, and overpowers him. When Bodie and Doyle arrive, they threaten to shoot the man in cold blood if he does not help them and the terrified Parks, blurts out that he was hired to set up the bombing of CI5 operatives by 'Wakeman'.

Agent Susan Fischer (Sally Harrison) with the CI5 team in THE PURGING OF CI5.

Cowley tells his colleagues that Wakeman once managed to infiltrate CI5, but was killed; Wakeman's associate, Philip Catrall, has arrived in the UK recently and could well be behind the bombing campaign. The CI5 team trace Catrall to a caravan, which he uses as a home. Catrall has booby-trapped the caravan to explode when the men are inside. The three men spot the bomb in time and escape, but only Cowley is declared alive, hoping it will lure Catrall into a trap to try and kill the CI5 Chief. As expected, the man arrives at the hospital to try another attempt on Cowley's life, but is captured in the act. As the CI5 team are leaving, reports are fed back by Susan that Wakeman's sister, Lisa, might be working with the criminal. A girl bystander in the hospital attempts to kill Cowley, who is thrown to safety by Phillips, and the girl is arrested outside the hospital as she tries to escape. Cowley's wrist is injured in the fall, but he is otherwise unhurt.

Production Unit

Created by	Brian Clemens
Executive Producers	Albert Fennell, Brian Clemens
Music	Laurie Johnson
Producer	Raymond Menmuir
Associate Producer	Chris Burt
Script Editor	Gerry O' Hara
Production Manager	Ron Purdie
Production Accountant	Terry Connors

On location at Southall Gas Works, Middlesex, actor Martin Shaw relaxes between takes on THE PURGING OF CI5.

Assistant Director	Gregory Dark
Location Manager	Peter Carter
Continuity	Gladys Pearce
Casting Director	Esta Charkham
Art Director	William Alexander
Set Dresser	Robin Tarsnane

Stunt Arranger	Peter Brayham
Wardrobe Supervisor	Donald Mothersill
Lighting Cameraman	Dusty Miller
Camera Operator	John Maskall
Focus Puller	Robin McDonald
Make Up	Bernard Brown
Hairdresser	Paula Gillespie
Supervising Editor	John S. Smith
Editor	Alan Killick
Sound Recordist	Chris Munro
Boom Operator	Gary Weir
Dubbing Editor	Peter Lennard
Dubbing Mixer	Hugh Strain
Music Editor	Alan Willis

An Avengers MARK 1 Production For LONDON WEEKEND TELEVISION

On location at Southall Gas Works, Middlesex for THE PURGING OF CI5: THE PROFESSIONALS: Martin Shaw, Gordon Jackson and Lewis Collins.

Shooting / Location Schedule

Production Dates: Monday 13th to Friday 24th August, 1979. Production Number: 9D11336

13 August **Railway sidings**: Thorntonfield Sidings, Warton Road, Stratford, London, E15
Manhole / street: Warton Road, Stratford, London, E15

14 August	***Ext / Int: Bodie's flat***: 44 Landsdowne Crescent, Notting Hill, London, W11
	Int: Doyle's car (streets around Bodie's flat): Ladbroke Grove, Notting Hill, London, W11
15 August	***Woods & caravan***: Southall Gas Works, Beaconsfield Road, Southall, Middlesex
16 August	***Disused House / Garage***: The Water Tower, The Straight, Southall Gas Works, Middlesex
	Fire Engine / Doyle's car: The Crescent / The Straight, Southall, Middlesex
	Int: Phone Box: South Road, Southall, Middlesex
	Doyle's car run-by (route to Bodie's flat): Randolph Road, Southall, Middlsex
17 August	***Cowley's office & records***: Cadby Hall, Blythe Road, Hammersmith, London, W14
20-21 August	***Ext: Hotel***: Lionel Mansions, Haarlem Road, Brook Green, London, W14
	Hotel roof & corridors: Cadby Hall, Blythe Road, Hammersmith, London, W14
22 August	***Flats / explosion***: 28 William Parnell House, Bagleys Lane, Sands End, London, SW6
	Office block: C.C.R Plant Offices, Fulham Gas Works, Sands End Lane, London, SW6
23-24 August	***Hospital***: Royal Free Hospital, Rosslyn Hill, Hampstead, London, NW3
	Ext: Doyle's car (route to gasworks with Parks): Fleet Road, Hampstead, London, NW3
	Ambulance run-by: 88 Fleet Road, Hampstead, London, NW3
	Streets: Police car / Ambulance (hospital route): Rosslyn Hill / Pond Street, Hampstead, London, NW3
	Int: Susan's car: Garnett Road, Hampstead, London, NW3
	Int: Doyle's car (route to flats): Upper Park Road, Hampstead, London, NW3
	Int: Doyle's car (route to gasworks with Parks): Lawn Road / Upper Park Road, Hampstead, London, NW3

FUGITIVE

(originally *The Fugitive*)
by **Gerry O'Hara**
based on a story by **Anthony Read**
© Copyright Mark 1 Productions Ltd MCMLXXIX

Werner	Michael Byrne
Karen	Vickery Turner
Christina	Brigitte Kahn
Heinrich	Andrew Seear
Klaus	Conrad Asquith
Slater	Paul Antrim
Julie	Eleanor David
Silverstein	Tony Sibbald
Receptionist	Jillian Mack
Quentin	Christopher Asante
CI5 Girl	Maureen Darbyshire
1st CI5 Sniper	Ronald Alexander
2nd CI5 Sniper	Malcolm Hughes
3rd CI5 Sniper	Pat Connell
Man at Door	Chris Hallam
Black Girl	Tania Rogers
Uncredited	
CI5 Man (Pub)	Mark Taylor
Blonde Lady in Pub	Ingrid Bradley
Delivery Driver	Reg Woods
CI5 Man (Forensic)	Ray Knight
CI5 Man (Airfield)	Harry Fielder

Director: **Denis Lewiston**

CHRISTINA Herzog, wanted by the police in Germany on charges relating to terrorist activities, escapes to England and settles down to a blameless existence working in a public library - unaware that CI5 are keeping her under surveillance and that a CI5 girl agent, Julie, works in the library with her. Julie notices that Christina's pattern of behaviour alters at about the time that a CIA agent working on an important international conference is murdered in London.

Cowley suspects that Christina or others in her German terrorist group may have been involved in the murder and he orders Bodie and Doyle to bring the girl in for questioning. The CI5 men decide not to approach Christina in the library when they see that she is talking animatedly to an American girl, Karen Vandenberg. Karen is demanding that Christina help her old friends and Christina is quarrelling with her. Bodie follows Karen as she leaves the library, but loses her in the busy London streets. Doyle follows Christina and watches as she goes to a run-down boarding house and emerges with a large holdall. He trails her to a canal and challenges her when she is about to drop the bag in. The surprised girl throws the bag into the water and runs away, firing at Doyle as she does so. Doyle quickly overpowers her and she is taken to CI5 HQ; the bag is recovered and contains arms. Cowley asks the girl closely about whether she was throwing the arms away, or leaving them in the water, carefully wrapped, to be picked up later by her associates. Christina maintains that she is trying to start a new life for herself in England and has no connection now with the terrorist group, of which she was once a leader. Cowley is unconvinced and suspects that the love affair that Christina shared with the other notorious leader of the group, Werner Dreisinger, may not be over.

Karen, meanwhile, has taken Christina's place in the affection of Werner and is waiting with the terrorists to take delivery of the arms from Christina. When the girl fails to bring the arms, another terrorist, Bruchmann, visits Christina in the library. As he approaches the girl, Bodie and Doyle attempt to arrest him, but when the man draws a gun, the CI5 men kill him. When Cowley discovers the dead man was another member of the German terrorist group, he realises that they must be in London, for some particular criminal purpose. As the murdered CIA agent was connected with the forthcoming international conference, he suspects that this may be the terrorist's target. With the group needing to buy more arms after Christina failed to deliver, Bodie and Doyle visit a dealer named Slater. Karen has been seen arranging a meet with Slater, and when she goes to the pub to take delivery of the arms, she meets Bodie instead. Bodie convinces her he is working for Slater and has the arms for her. Karen has her doubts until Doyle, arriving at the pub as Bodie and the girl are leaving, tries to arrest the girl. Bodie scrambles Karen into his car and, as Doyle races after them firing his gun, Bodie shoots at the CI5 man sending him tumbling to the ground as the two get away.

The girl takes Bodie back to the house where the terrorist group are hiding and tells her associates that Bodie saved her life and can be trusted. However, Werner, who witnessed the earlier events, realises that they were staged and Bodie is apprehended. He tells his group that the attack on the conference will have to be cancelled, but with Bodie as a hostage they may be able to exchange him for Christina. The terrorist leader telephones Cowley and arranges an exchange at a deserted airfield. Werner has strapped a bomb to Bodie and warns Cowley that it will be exploded if there is a disturbance. As Christina walks over to the terrorists, Karen is annoyed that Werner warmly welcomes her. Suddenly, smoke bombs begin to burst around the group and snipers, who have been hidden by Cowley, open fire. In the confusion, and with Doyle's help, Bodie is able to destroy the detonator around his neck. As Christina tries to run away, she is shot dead by Karen, who is then apprehended.

Production Unit

Created by	Brian Clemens
Executive Producers	Albert Fennell, Brian Clemens
Music	Laurie Johnson
Producer	Raymond Menmuir

Associate Producer	Chris Burt
Script Editor	Gerry O'Hara
Production Manager	Ron Purdie
Production Accountant	Terry Connors
Assistant Director	David Munro
Location Manager	Peter Carter
Continuity	Gladys Pearce
Casting Director	Esta Charkham
Art Director	William Alexander
Set Dresser	Robin Tarsnane
Stunt Arranger	Peter Brayham
Wardrobe Supervisor	Donald Mothersill
Lighting Cameraman	Michael Davis
Camera Operator	John Maskall
Focus Puller	Robin McDonald
Make Up	Bernard Brown
Hairdresser	Sue Love
Supervising Editor	John S. Smith
Sound Recordist	Chris Munro
Boom Operator	Gary Weir
Dubbing Editor	Peter Lennard
Dubbing Mixer	Hugh Strain
Music Editor	Alan Willis

An Avengers MARK 1 Production For LONDON WEEKEND TELEVISION

FUGITIVE: Lewis Collins in 'The Green Man' pub car park, Wembley.

Shooting / Location Schedule
Production Dates: Tuesday 28th August to Friday 7th September, Tuesday 18th to Wednesday 19th September, 1979. Production Number: 9D11337

28 August	*Library*: Polytechnic Of North London, Ladbroke House, 62-66 Highbury Grove, Highbury, London, N5
	Cowley's car: Highbury Hill, Highbury, London, N5
29 August	*Int: Office & pub*: The Green Man, Dagmar Avenue, Wembley, Middlesex
	Int: Car (Bodie & Karen): Dagmar Avenue / Park Lane, Wembley, Middlesex
	Hairdressers: Hair By Robert, 4 Court Parade, East Lane, Wembley, Middlesex
30 August	*Interrogation room & CI5 records*: Cadby Hall, Blythe Road, Hammersmith, London, W14
31 August	*Walled garden*: West London College, 50 Brook Green, Hammersmith, London, W14
3 September	*Library*: Polytechnic Of North London, Ladbroke House, 62-66 Highbury Grove, London, N5
4 September	*Hotel*: Eurocrest Hotel, Empire Suite, Empire Way, Wembley, Middlesex
	Street & tube station: Bridge Road, Wembley & Wembley Park Tube Station, Wembley, Middlesex
	Bus stop & bus run-by: 123 Wembley Park Drive, Wembley, Middlesex.
5 September	*Airfield*: Fairoaks Airport, Chertsey Road, Chobham, Surrey
6 September	*Canal & disused warehouse*: Camley Street, Kings Cross, London, NW1
	Warehouse area: 184 York Way (Fortune Of War pub), London, N7
	Christina's flat / Doyle's car: 61 Arthur Road, Holloway, London, N7
7 September	*Rooming house & garden wall / Van stunt*: Hood Court, Mayton Street / Caledonian Road (Russet Crescent Estate), Upper Holloway, London, N7
18 September	*Airfield / Warehouse area*: Alexandra Palace, Muswell Hill, London, N8
	House / Library road / flowers: 35 & 37 Loraine Road, off Holloway Road, Holloway, London, N7
	Ext: Doyle's car run-by: Holloway Road, Holloway, London, N7
	Int: Doyle's car (radio): Hornsey Road, Holloway, London, N7
19 September	*Ext / Int: Pub / Library phone box*: The Green Man, Dagmar Avenue, Wembley, Middlesex
	Hairdressers: Hair By Robert, 4 Court Parade, East Lane, Wembley, Middlesex
	Van / Phone box: First Way, Wembley, Middlesex

THE ACORN SYNDROME
by **John Kruse**
© Copyright Mark 1 Productions Ltd MCMLXXIX

Guthrie	Michael Craig
Copeland	Ronald Hines
Viv Copeland	Lynda Marchal
Lucas	Ian Redford
McCabe	Alun Lewis
Sandy Copeland	Oona Kirsch
Nancy	Kate Dorning
Inspector Grainger	John Michael McCarthy
Joe	Nigel Humphreys
Sam	Stewart Harwood
Eva	Gennie Nevinson
Coleman	Sean Chapman
Angadi	Alan Igbon
Male Hostage	Christopher Saul
Female Hostage	Jennifer Granville
Child	Becci Hunt
Langton	John Hoyce
Miss Kendall	Hilary Crane
Mrs. Forbes	Sue Nicholls
Styles	Charles Pemberton
Landlady	Patricia Marks
Uncredited	
Uniformed Policeman	Ray Knight
Uniformed Policeman	Reg Turner
Uniformed Policeman	Don Hann
Boy On Bike	Simon Tasker
1st Thug	Eddie Powell
2nd Thug	Rex Harding
CI5 Driver	Bill Hemmings
CI5 Man	Ray Bunby

Director: **Martin Campbell**

BY chance, Doyle disturbs two men, Angadi and Coleman, making a phone call from a telephone box. The men seem panic-stricken when they see the gun carried by Doyle. Coleman draws a gun, then they race off in their car and are chased and trapped by Bodie and Doyle in a residential street. The two men grab a family from a garden, rush into a house with their hostages and, after barricading themselves in, threaten to kill the family if they are attacked. The CI5 men find a phone number scribbled on a cigarette packet in the men's car and tell Cowley as he arrives on the scene, that the number may be the one the men were phoning. The number is found to be that of a company manufacturing secret weapons, and Cowley sends the two men to check the company, Apex McInross, and its managing director, Guthrie, in case there is any criminal link between the two men and the secret weapons. Guthrie explains that all his company's secrets are kept in his private office safe, the keys to which he always keeps on him, and there could be no theft of information.

Meanwhile, inside the house, now surrounded by police, Angadi and Coleman telephone their organisation to ask for help. They are told that arrangements will be made for the escape, and they will be given a signal when to leave. When the signal arrives, the two men nervously walk outside behind their hostages and wait for the expected assistance. As they edge forwards, they are both shot dead by rifle fire from a nearby block of flats. Bodie and Doyle arrive, but only manage to get the number of a car racing away with the gunmen inside it.

Cowley knows that for the men to be so summarily executed by their employers they must have been only hirelings for some particular crime, which must involve Apex McInross in some way, so full surveillance on Guthrie is arranged. While watching a video tape recording of Guthrie leaving Apex McInross with his personal assistant, Copeland, Bodie notices that Copeland borrows a key from Guthrie for a few seconds and rushes back into the office. Suspecting that the key may have been for the top secret safe, CI5 investigate and find that Copeland had ample opportunity on the occasion the tape was recorded to photocopy the secret documents relating to the defence weapons. Lucas tells Bodie and Doyle that Copeland has taken the day off to go to his daughter's school sports day. They drive to the school and discover that there is no sports day and Copeland's daughter, Sandy, has not been in for several days. Without revealing that they are CI5 agents, Bodie and Doyle visit Copeland's home, to discover that both he and his wife seem under a great deal of tension. As the agents leave the house, they see the car that raced away from the scene of the shooting earlier. They follow the car for some distance until Cowley orders them to stop.

The CI5 forensic experts search of Angadi and Coleman's own car has revealed traces of blonde hair in the boot; CI5 realise that the two men acted guiltily when accosted by chance because they had just kidnapped Sandy Copeland, taken her to their hideout and were phoning her father to tell him to hand over the secret Apex McInross papers if he wanted to see her again. An examination reveals that the car has recently been driven in a type of soil particular to one area of London, so Doyle is sent to search the area for the gang's hideout. Copeland has told no one of his daughter's kidnapping, but CI5, watching his house, see a message arrive from the kidnappers. Bodie, hidden in the boot of Copeland's car leads the CI5 team to the meeting place where he hands over copies of the secret Apex McInross papers to East German agents, but Copeland becomes distraught when, having done as the gang have asked, he still does not see Sandy. CI5 move in and capture the gang, but not before a message has gone out to kill Copeland's daughter. Doyle, meanwhile, has found the gang's hideout and races to Sandy's aid.

The daughter of a British Government engineer who is working on a defence protect is kidnapped, and the only way she will be safely returned is if he agrees to betray secrets to enemy agents. Martin Shaw as Doyle at Apex McInross in a scene from THE ACORN SYNDROME.

Production Unit

Created by	Brian Clemens
Executive Producers	Albert Fennell, Brian Clemens
Music	Laurie Johnson
Producer	Raymond Menmuir
Associate Producer	Chris Burt
Script Editor	Gerry O'Hara
Production Manager	Ron Purdie
Production Accountant	Terry Connors
Assistant Director	Gregory Dark
Location Manager	Peter Carter
Continuity	Gladys Pearce
Casting Director	Esta Charkham
Art Director	William Alexander
Set Dresser	Terry Parr
Stunt Arranger	Peter Brayham
Wardrobe Supervisor	Donald Mothersill
Lighting Cameraman	Dusty Miller
Camera Operator	John Maskall
Focus Puller	Robin McDonald
Make Up	Bernard Brown
Hairdresser	Sue Love
Supervising Editor	John S. Smith
Editor	Alan Killick
Sound Recordist	Chris Munro
Boom Operator	Gary Weir
Dubbing Editor	Peter Lennard
Dubbing Mixer	Hugh Strain
Music Editor	Alan Willis

An Avengers MARK 1 Production For LONDON WEEKEND TELEVISION

Shooting / Location Schedule

Production Dates: Monday 10th to Wednesday 26th September, 1979. Production Number: 9D11338. Locations in *italics* were originally scheduled but ultimately not used

10 September   **Farm (hostage)**: Shenleybury Farm, Black Lion Hill, Shenley, Hertfordshire

11-12 September **Copeland's villa**: The Trees, Barnham Drive, Elstree, Hertfordshire

13-14 September **Siege House**: 37 The Hoe, By The Wood, Carpenders Park, Hertfordshire

17 September   **Int: Guthrie's Office**: Second Floor, 46-48 High Street, Slough, Berkshire

                   Estate Agent's Office: Bucklands Estate Agents, 44 High Street, Slough, Berkshire

18-19 September	***Apex McInross HQ***: Combermere Barracks, St. Leonards Road, Windsor, Berkshire ***Guthrie's House***: Cranbourne Hall, Drift Road, Winkfield, Berkshire
20 September	***Desk collection***: Ossian Mews, Ossian Road, Stroud Green, London, N4 ***Streets: Car chase (desk)***: St. James's Lane / Ellington Road / Lenister Road / Linden Road, Muswell Hill, London, N10
21 September	***Phone box 1***: London Road (near Harris Lane), Shenley, Hertfordshire ***Phone box 2***: Brook Avenue, Borehamwood, Hertfordshire ***Phone box 3 / car change***: Stratfield Road, Borehamwood, Hertfordshire ***Int: Bodie's car***: Butterfly Lane / Watling Street, Elstree, Hertfordshire ***Doyle's van / country roads (Farms 1, 3)***: Buckettsland Farm, Buckettsland Lane, Well End, Shenley, Hertfordshire ***Doyle's van / country roads (Farm 2)***: Ravenscroft Farm, Mimms Lane, Rabley, Ridge, Hertfordshire
2nd Unit:	
24 September	***Studio pad / Surveillance room***: 35 Loraine Road, off Holloway Road, Holloway, London, N7 ***Int: Cowley's car***: Holloway Road (near Hornsey Street), Holloway, London, N7
25 September	***Girl's school***: All Saints Pastoral Centre, Shenley Lane, London Colney, Hertfordshire
26 September	***Copeland's villa***: The Trees, Barnham Drive, Elstree, Hertfordshire ***Water splash Road***: Black Park, Fulmer, Buckinghamshire ***Van & ambush***: *Black Park, Fulmer, Buckinghamshire* North Thames Gas Works, Uxbridge Road, Slough, Berkshire

Martin Shaw and Lewis Collins on location at Combermere Barracks, Windsor, for THE ACORN SYNDROME.

SLUSH FUND

by **Roger Marshall**
© Copyright Mark 1 Productions Ltd MCMLXXIX

Van Niekerk	Stuart Wilson
Hope	Matthew Long
Sir Kenneth	David Swift
Betty Hope	Lynda Bellingham
Geiser	Jeremy Young
Seymour	Timothy Carlton
Kookie Girl	Victoria Burgoyne
Hotel receptionist	Raymond Brody
Barman	John Eastham
Hotel Porter	Len Howe
First Youth	Mario Renzullo
2nd Youth	Ricky Wales
Reporter	Chris Sullivan
Boy On Bike	Simon Tasker
Uncredited	
Young CI5 Agent	Graham Crowther

Director: **William Brayne**

CI5 are warned that a dangerous killer named Van Niekerk is arriving in the UK, and Bodie and Doyle are sent to meet him as he travels to London. After a struggle, they overpower Van Niekerk and Bodie questions him about his reason for coming to Britain. Van Niekerk will say nothing, so Doyle assumes his identity and books into a hotel room in Van Niekerk's name, while CI5 agents wait outside to see who comes to call on him. While he waits, Doyle befriends a girl who is also staying at the hotel. A package arrives addressed to Van Niekerk and Doyle discovers that it contains a loaded gun. A second package arrives shortly afterwards, containing the name, address and photograph of Martin Hope, the man who Van Niekerk is supposed to kill. Hope, is formerly the aviation correspondent of a national newspaper and has apparently led a blameless existence and neither Doyle or Cowley can understand why any organisation should want him killed.

Bodie breaks into Hope's home, and finds a newspaper cutting about the death of Hope's brother in one of the notoriously dangerous Fohn aircraft. Manufactured in haste by a consortium of European companies, the Fohn aircraft are widely rumoured to be faulty, and fifty of them have crashed, killing their pilots. Cowley investigates Hope's background and discovers that, after his brother's death, Hope became particularly interested in the Fohn; for the last few years he has been collecting material about its defects which were covered up for the sake of the manufacturers and many international public figures who accepted large bribes to buy the aircraft. Hope has now left his newspaper job for a few months to write a book on the Fohn, and it is expected that when published, the controversial book, will ruin the reputations of many important men. Cowley is convinced therefore that the Fohn manufacturers have hired Van Niekerk to silence Hope. Cowley and Bodie go to see Van Niekerk but find that he has escaped by killing the young CI5 guard. Bodie knows that with Van Niekerk free, Doyle is in great danger, and he rushes to the hotel where his associate is staying. Van Niekerk has reached the hotel first and, finding that Doyle is impersonating him, follows the agent to an underground car park, attacks him and pushes him into the boot of a car.

Returning back to the hotel, the assassin finds the address and photograph of Hope, and is then disturbed by the girl Doyle met at the hotel. Bodie later finds her body; Van Niekerk has killed her. Meanwhile, the car in which Doyle is trapped is stolen by two youths and taken on a reckless joyride through the countryside. When the youths crash the car near a quarry, Doyle is thrown out of the boot to safety. He contacts HQ and is picked up by Bodie. They race to the newspaper building where Hope works and save the man from Van Niekerk's attempted assassination. CI5 agents have also followed the man who delivered the gun to the assassin, and Cowley tricks him into revealing that he hired Van Niekerk to kill Hope on the orders of Sir Kenneth, the boss of the company manufacturing the Fohn. Sir Kenneth refuses to admit guilt and is later found drowned in his swimming pool.

Production Unit

Created by	Brian Clemens
Executive Producers	Albert Fennell, Brian Clemens
Music	Laurie Johnson
Producer	Raymond Menmuir
Associate Producer	Chris Burt
Script Editor	Gerry O'Hara
Production Manager	Ron Purdie
Production Accountant	Terry Connors
Assistant Director	John O'Connor
Location Manager	Peter Carter
Continuity	Gladys Pearce
Casting Director	Esta Charkham
Art Director	William Alexander
Set Dresser	Robin Tarsnane
Stunt Arranger	Peter Brayham
Wardrobe Supervisor	Donald Mothersill
Lighting Cameraman	Norman Langley
Camera Operator	John Maskall
Focus Puller	Robin McDonald
Make Up	Bernard Brown
Hairdresser	Sue Love
Supervising Editor	John S. Smith
Sound Recordist	Chris Munro
Boom Operator	Gary Weir
Dubbing Editor	Peter Lennard
Dubbing Mixer	High Strain

| Music Editor | Alan Willis |

An Avengers MARK 1 Production For LONDON WEEKEND TELEVISION

Bodie (Lewis Collins) collects Doyle (Martin Shaw) after his CI5 partner has been for a rather 'uncomfortable' ride in the boot of a car in SLUSH FUND.

Shooting / Location Schedule

Production Dates: Monday 24th September to Friday 5th October, 1979. Production Number: 9D11339. Locations in *italics* were originally scheduled but ultimately not used.

24 September	**Sir Kenneth's House & pool**: Mount Fidget, Fulmer Rise Estate, Fulmer Common Road, Fulmer, Buckinghamshire
25 September	***Int: Cowley's club / coffee shop***: Inverness Court Hotel, Inverness Terrace, Bayswater, London, W2

	Cowley's car run-by: Bayswater Road, Bayswater, London, W2
26-27 September	***Safe House / Interrogation***: Stubbing House, Henley Road, near Maidenhead, Berkshire
28 September	***Empty House***: Flat 101, Bluebird Walk, Chalkhill estate, Wembley, Middlesex
30 September	***Railway station & train***: Gatwick Station, London Road, Horley, West Sussex & Redhill Station, Station Road, Redhill, Surrey
	Airfield: White Waltham Airfield, Waltham Road, White Waltham, Berkshire
1-2 October	***Hotel 1***: London Tara Hotel, Wrights Lane, London, W8
3 October	***Newspaper building***: Express Newspapers, Fleet Street, London, EC4
4-5 October	***Hope's House***: 1 Windsor Crescent, Wembley, Middlesex
	Shops: Empire Way, Wembley, Middlesex
5 October	***Quarry / run-bys / phone box***: Castle Lime Works, off Swanland Road, Potters Bar, Hertfordshire / Warrengate Lane, Potters Bar, Hertfordshire
2nd Unit	***Airport terminal (Doyle)***: Heathrow Airport, Bath Road, Hayes, Middlesex

Location manager Peter Carter secured filming in the press-room of the Daily Express newspaper in SLUSH FUND. Pictured here by one of the many printing presses are Martin Shaw and Lewis Collins.

WEEKEND IN THE COUNTRY

by **Gerry O'Hara**
© Copyright Mark 1 Productions Ltd MCMLXXIX

Case	Bryan Pringle
Mrs. Shaw	Sarah Lawson
Georgie	Brian Croucher
Judy	Louisa Rix
Vince	Ray Burdis
Liz	Jacqueline Reddin
Daniel	Marcus D'Amico
Ben	Brian Hawksley
Golf partner	Brian Coleman
Announcer	Gordon Honeycombe
Sally	Susan Wooldridge
Police driver	Barry Woolgar
Duty sergeant	Colin Rix
Inspector Cross	Tim Meats
Onlooker	Peter Hill
Receptionist	Catherine Riding
Security man	Pat Gorman
Uncredited	
Ambulance Man	Reg Turner
CI5 Agent	Stuart Myers
Police Station Officer	Derek Chafer
Lorry Driver	Tony Allen

Director: **James Allen**

BODIE and Doyle are spending a weekend leave with Doyle's girlfriend Judy Shaw and her family at their farm in the country. An attractive girl named Liz also joins them for the weekend. Doyle and Judy go on horseback to meet Liz and Bodie, and Judy's horse shies away and bolts when they come across a man in the woods. Judy is thrown to the ground and the man, Bert Case, though badly wounded, produces a gun and forces Judy and Bodie back to the farmhouse. Case has been wounded while escaping from the police after an unsuccessful robbery, and when they arrive at the farm, two other criminals who escaped with him, and are looking for a car in which to make their escape join them. The two men, Vince and Georgie, hold Judy's mother and younger brother Daniel captive while they search for transport, but they find only Mrs Shaw's old Land Rover, which is in need of repair and will not start. Vince molests Liz and is surprised by Bodie's sudden counter-attack, but the other men soon overpower the CI5 man. They are further surprised when Doyle offers to tend Case's wounds and does so with skill.

Doyle (Martin Shaw), Bodie (Lewis Collins) and their latest girlfriends (Jacqueline Reddin, pictured top left) are on a quiet WEEKEND IN THE COUNTRY when they unwittingly get caught up at a farmhouse siege in which they must try and escape from a group of gun-toting fugitives.

Later that day, a local policeman arrives at the farm to report that Judy's rider-less horse has been involved in an accident and killed. Judy, watched carefully by Georgie, takes the message and sends the policeman away. Daniel tries to escape but is recaptured by Vince. Bodie cools the situation by offering to repair Mrs. Shaw's car. Guarded by Georgie, he tackles the engine but Georgie, curious about the men's expertise with cars, first-aid and fighting, tries to get Bodie to betray his identity; Bodie laughingly says they are civil servants. Meanwhile, at CI5 HQ, Cowley, needing his men on a case, unsuccessfully tries to contact them at the farm; the gang has cut all the telephone cables. Back at the farmhouse, Vince continues his pursuit of Liz, but she succeeds in fighting him off with a kitchen knife. Both the criminals and the hostages are relieved when they hear that Bodie has managed to fix the car, and the thugs prepare to leave. Locking their prisoners in a cellar, they decide to keep Daniel with them as a hostage in case of trouble.

Bodie however has 'rigged' the car to break down and the criminals return to the farm. Still desperate to make their escape before the police move in, they decide to send Judy, guarded by Georgie, to the main road nearby. She is to stop a passing car, which they will then steal for their escape. Bodie and Doyle are now urgently needed in London and Cowley telephones the local police station to find out why he cannot contact the Shaw's farm; when he is told that Judy's horse was found injured by the roadside. Cowley decides to investigate with a CI5 girl named Sally. As they approach the farm, they see Judy signalling by the roadside. Cowley stops the car and Georgie races out with a gun, but he is soon disarmed. With the information given by Judy, Sally and Cowley approach the farm cautiously and when Bodie and Doyle spot Sally's approach through a window, they attack Case and Vince. The two men are quickly overpowered and arrested and show intense anger when they discover that their 'civil servant' captives are in fact law enforcers.

Production Unit

Created by	Brian Clemens
Executive Producers	Albert Fennell, Brian Clemens
Music	Laurie Johnson
Producer	Raymond Menmuir
Associate Producer	Chris Burt
Script Editor	Gerry O'Hara
Production Manager	Ron Purdie
Production Accountant	Terry Connors
Assistant Director	Gregory Dark
Location Manager	Peter Carter
Continuity	Gladys Pearce
Casting	Esta Charkham
Art Director	William Alexander
Set Dresser	Terry Parr
Stunt Arranger	Peter Brayham
Wardrobe Supervisor	Donald Mothersill
Lighting Cameraman	Dusty Miller
Camera Operator	John Maskall
Focus Puller	Robin McDonald
Make Up	Bernard Brown
Hairdresser	Sue Love
Supervising Editor	John S. Smith
Editor	Alan Killick
Sound Recordist	Chris Munro
Boom Operator	Gary Weir
Dubbing Editor	Peter Lennard
Dubbing Mixer	Hugh Strain
Music Editor	Alan Willis

An Avengers MARK 1 Production For LONDON WEEKEND TELEVISION

Behind-the-scenes on WEEKEND IN THE COUNTRY: Filming the sequence where Cowley (Gordon Jackson) and Sally (Susan Wooldridge) land by helicopter to meet up with Inspector Cross (Tim Meats).

Shooting / Location Schedule

Production Dates: Monday 8th to Friday 19th October, 1979. Production Number: 9D11340

8 October	**Golf Club / Police station**: North Middlesex Golf Club Friern Barnet Lane, Whetstone, London, N20
9 October	**Woods / Field / Lake**: Warfield Hall, Forest Road, Warfield, Berkshire
10-12 October	**Farmhouse**: Scotlands Farm, Forest Road, Newell Green, Warfield, Berkshire
12 October	**Country Hotel**: Burnham Beeches Hotel, Grove Road, Burnham, Buckinghamshire
2nd Unit	**Ext: CI5 office**: Slough Library (side entrance), 85 High Street, Slough, Berkshire
	Int: CI5 office: Second Floor, 46-48 High Street, Slough, Berkshire
15-18 October	**Farmhouse**: Scotlands Farm, Forest Road, Newell Green, Warfield, Berkshire
19 October	**Field / Helicopter**: Warfield Hall, Forest Road, Warfield, Berkshire
	Road & field: fight: Cabbage Hill, Forest Road, Warfield, Berkshire
	Road (Horse): Osborne Lane (junction Church Lane), Warfield, Berkshire

TAKE AWAY

by **Roger Marshall**
© Copyright Mark 1 Productions Ltd MCMLXXIX

Esther	Chai Lee
D.S Colin	John Forgeham
D.C Jack	James Marcus
Jimmy	Gary Shail
Callahan	Phil Brown
Annie	Sharon Duce
Chai Ling	Pik Sen Lim
Chi Sang	Arnold Lee
Siu Sang	Fiesta Mei Ling
Meyer	George Little
Ngan Hung	Andy Ho
Johnny Chong	Richard Rees
Boss	Ken Watson
Girl in Bed	Anna Coombs
Kidnapper 1	Vincent Wong
Kidnapper 2	Rex Wei
Girl Companion	Peta Bernard
Diter Kroll	Jon Rumney
Helmut Brenick	Gertan Klauber
Cheng	Dennis Matsuki
1st Child	Jason Forgeham
2nd Child	Jonesta Forgeham
Uncredited	
Wino	Fred Woods
Uniformed Policeman	Ray Knight
1st Thug	Chua Kah-Joo
2nd Thug	James Lye
Milkman	Alan Swaden
D. S Colin's Undercover Agent	Jimmy Muir
D. S Colin's Undercover Agent	John Cannon
CI5 Agent	Gerry Paris

Director: **Douglas Camfield**

WHEN CI5 are asked to investigate a drug smuggling operation, which is having international repercussions, Cowley suspects that an East German agent called Diter Kroll, may be masterminding the drugs trade to create hostility between the allies'. The drugs are shipped from Hong Kong to London and then by courier to Germany, where they are sold to the American forces stationed there. The trade has become so widespread, that it is causing antagonism between Britain and America. CI5 get a lead when Ngan Hung, a Chinese courier from London, is arrested by German police when he tries to hand over a parcel of drugs to his German contact. Hung is questioned, but will reveal nothing about he organisation, which sent him to make the delivery. Cowley sends a Chinese police sergeant, Esther, to question Hung's family in London. She discovers that the man's son has been murdered and his brother brutally attacked by Triad criminals in order to persuade him to act as their courier; fearing further repercussions, the family is too terrified to say more.

In order to gain information on the drugs scene, Doyle has gone undercover in Soho as a fruit seller, while Bodie has moved into a derelict building inhabited by drug addicts. A girl there died from an overdose some weeks earlier and Bodie tries to persuade her grief-stricken boyfriend, Jimmy that the best way to avenge her death is to tell the police about the drug pushers. A meeting is arranged with Cowley, but they find Jimmy dead; he has hung himself from the ceiling of his room. Bodie asks Jimmy's sister, Annie, to help him, but she too is terrified to help.

Events take a turn when a Chinese woman, Siu, is kidnapped by Chinese thugs and her husband, Chi Sang, fails to report the crime to the police, but a witness to the kidnapping does so. Esther is sent to the restaurant run by the man and his wife, and finds another woman impersonating Mrs. Sang. When Doyle suspects that Siu is being held to force Chi Sang to work for the Triad gang, Cowley orders the restaurant to be kept under close surveillance. CI5 agents are watching when Chi is picked up by the gang and taken to Heathrow to catch a plane for Hong Kong and Siu is released when the plane departs. Esther tries to persuade the woman to give evidence against her kidnappers, but she is too scared. Esther is followed back to the flat she is sharing with Doyle, and a few minutes later, two Chinese thugs arrive and attack her and Doyle. In the ensuing fight, both of the thugs are killed.

Despite giving no information about the drug pushers, Annie is attacked by the Chinese and intimidated into leaving London. Cowley places Siu and her family under CI5 protection and they are driven to a safe house. CI5 watch as Chi Sang returns to London and hands a package to another Chinese man. They follow the courier to a motel and shortly afterwards Kroll; the East German suspected by Cowley, arrives and enters the man's room. CI5 agents surround the motel and Kroll and the Chinese give up. The package from Hong Kong is found to contain a huge amount of heroin but, to Bodie and Doyle's disgust, Kroll claims diplomatic immunity and all witnesses in the case, including Chi and Siu Sang, are too terrified of Triad reprisals to give evidence to convict the Chinese criminals.

Production Unit

Created by	Brian Clemens
Executive Producers	Albert Fennell, Brian Clemens
Music	Laurie Johnson
Producer	Raymond Menmuir
Associate Producer	Chris Burt
Script Editor	Gerry O'Hara
Production Manager	Ron Purdie
Production Accountant	Terry Connors
Assistant Director	John O'Connor

Location Manager	Peter Carter
Continuity	Gladys Pearce
Casting	Esta Charkham
Art Director	William Alexander
Set Dresser	Terry Parr
Stunt Arranger	Chris Webb
Wardrobe Supervisor	Donald Mothersill
Lighting Cameraman	Norman Langley
Camera Operator	John Maskall
Focus Puller	Robin McDonald
Make Up	Bernard Brown
Hairdresser	Sue Love
Supervising Editor	John S. Smith
Sound Recordist	Chris Munro
Boom Operator	Mike Silverlock
Dubbing Editor	Peter Lennard
Dubbing Mixer	Hugh Strain
Music Editor	Alan Willis

An Avengers MARK 1 Production For LONDON WEEKEND TELEVISION

In TAKE AWAY a team of Hong Kong police join CI5 in London to help crack a local heroin supply and protection racket. It's down to agents Bodie (Lewis Collins) and Doyle (Martin Shaw) to expose a scheme to smuggle drugs to the United States by teams of Triads and European agents.

Shooting / Location Schedule

Production Dates: Friday 19th October to Friday 2nd November, 1979. Production Number: 9D11341. Locations in *italics* were originally scheduled but ultimately not used.

19 October	**Car Park / Interrogation Room**:	EMI Elstree Studios, Borehamwood, Hertfordshire
22 October	**Johnny's place**:	Sandringham Flats, Charing Cross Road, Soho, London, WC1
	Wino Street:	Ingstre Place, off Broadwick Street, Soho, London, W1

23-24 October	***Squat (house) / Int: Annie's flat***: 143 Highbury New Park, Highbury, London, N5
24 October	***Streets (where Annie is attacked)***: *232 Seven Sisters Road, London, N5 / Hornsey High Street, London, N8* Green Lanes / Statham Grove, Stoke Newington, London, N16
	Int: Mortuary: Hornsey Coroners Court, Myddelton Road, London, N8
25 October	***Motel***: The Master Brewer Motel (rooms 115, 122, 123), Western Avenue, North Hillingdon, Middlesex
2nd Unit	***Tube stations***: Ickenham station, Glebe Avenue / Heathrow Central, Heathrow Airport, Middlesex
26 October	***Soho Streets & markets***: Ingstre Place / Broadwick Street / Golden Square, Soho, London, W1 / Berwick Street Markets, Soho, London, W1
	Street: Cowley's car (Doyle picked up): Trenchard House, Broadwick Street, Soho, London, W1
	Ext: Annie's flat: Macclesfield Street, off Shaftesbury Avenue, Soho, London, W1
	Street: Soho shop: Gerrard Street (shot from Sandringham Flats), Soho, London, W1
29-30 October	***Esther's Flat***: 121 Walkinshaw Court, Elizabeth Avenue, Islington, London, N1
31 October	***Restaurant***: Happy House, 25 Broadway Parade, Tottenham Lane, Crouch End, London, N8
	House opposite restaurant: Builders opposite Happy House, Topsfield Parade, Crouch End, N8
	Int: Ngan Hung's shop: Action In Distress, 32 Topsfield Parade, Tottenham Lane, Crouch End, N8
1 November	***Int: Meyer's office***: Regency House, Peterborough Road, Harrow, Middlesex
	Int: Callahan's office: Kirkland House, 11-15 Peterborough Road, Harrow, Middlesex
	Ext: Embassy: American Embassy, 24 Grosvenor Square, London, W1
2 November	***School***: Coleridge Primary School, Crescent Road, Crouch End, London, N8
	Boarding House: Phaedra Hotel, 12 Shepherds Hill, Highgate, London, N6
	Int: Cowley's car: Stanhope Road, Crouch End, London, N6
	Railway arch (Siu Sang dumped): Northwood Road, Crouch End, London, N6

INVOLVEMENT

by **Brian Clemens**
© Copyright Mark 1 Productions Ltd MCMLXXIX

Ann	Patricia Hodge
Charles Holly	William Russell
Turner	Ray Ashcroft
Tony	Christopher Guard
Buzz	Valentine Pringle
Marli	Peter Holt
Vicar	Peter Godfrey
Secretary	Kirstie Pooley
Conroy	Peter Burton
Butler	Philip Anthony
Uncredited	
Marli's accomplice	Graham Crowther
Benny	Vic Gallucci
Driver (Café getaway)	John Cannon
Driver (Café blockade)	Cliff Diggins
CI5 Agent	Julian Hudson

Director: **Chris Burt**

BODIE and Doyle follow Conroy, a man wanted for questioning by Cowley, into a block of flats and when the man pulls a gun and aims it at Doyle, Bodie shoots Conroy dead. These events are witnessed by a tenant at the flats, Ann Holly, who watches the shooting with horror and Doyle, who finds the girl attractive, calls to see her later. He tells her about his work in CI5, but the girl finds his occupation hard to accept. Because Conroy was known to have Italian connections, Bodie and Doyle try to find a young informant on Italian crime named Benny. They finally find him lying seriously injured after a beating meant to silence him and Benny dies later in hospital. Doyle, distressed by what has happened, goes to see Ann Holly and tells her that someone he has known for a long time has been hurt and the girl is surprised to find that Doyle is not as tough as she first supposed.

To throw more light on why Benny has been killed and to track down his murderer, CI5 instigate a search for Benny's associate Tony. He is traced to a shabby tenement building and, as Bodie and Doyle go to question him, they notice Buzz, a flamboyant black criminal, leaving the building. Tony can tell them nothing about Benny's killers except that their organisation is planning to bring a huge consignment of illegal drugs to the UK soon and they might be nervous in case Benny talked. The relationship between Doyle and Ann develops and, when Bodie tells his boss that Doyle and the girl are likely to get married, Cowley decides that Bodie must check out Ann's background. Reluctantly, Bodie agrees and leaves to talk to the girl. He discovers from her that her mother is dead and she has not seen her father since she was a child and knows nothing of him. Bodie traces her father, Charles Holly, and learns that he is a wealthy company director with an interest in flying. The CI5 man later plants an automatic camera outside Charles Holly's house and when the photographs are developed, he is amazed to see that one of his callers was Buzz, the black criminal associated with Tony. When Doyle is confronted with this evidence and that Ann's father may be linked to the organisation that had Benny killed, he is furious, but is forced to admit that he met Ann in the building where Conroy ran to hide. Later, Doyle is shown an old photograph by Ann from her family album, a photograph that shows Conroy and her father together in the RAF.

INVOLVEMENT: In which Bodie shoots a suspect dead in front of a horrified witness, and Doyle falls in love! Lewis Collins pictured here during a break in filming at Cadby Hall, Hammersmith, West London.

Bodie tells Cowley that a skilled pilot in a small plane could fly into Britain low enough to avoid detection by radar. If Holly were the head of the gang, an ideal landing place would appear to be a clearing in a wood near Holly's home. On the day of the landing the CI5 agents arrest Holly, Buzz and other men as they meet the plane and take delivery of a large package of drugs. Back at CI5 HQ Holly explains that he has not seen Ann for sixteen years; Conroy ran into the flats because his sister had a place there. Doyle is relieved by the news, but Ann has overheard Doyle's rash questioning of her father. She tells Doyle that he should have had more trust in her and as he evidently cannot believe what she says, their relationship is at an end.

Production Unit

Created by	Brian Clemens
Executive Producers	Albert Fennell, Brian Clemens
Music	Laurie Johnson
Producer	Raymond Menmuir
Associate Producer	Chris Burt
Script Editor	Gerry O'Hara
Production Manager	Ron Purdie
Production Accountant	Terry Connors
Assistant Director	Gregory Dark
Location Manager	Peter Carter
Continuity	Gladys Pearce
Casting	Esta Charkham
Art Director	William Alexander
Set Dresser	Terry Parr
Stunt Arranger	Peter Brayham
Wardrobe Supervisor	Donald Mothersill
Lighting Cameraman	Dusty Miller
Camera Operator	John Maskall
Focus Puller	Robin McDonald
Make Up	Bernard Brown
Hairdresser	Sue Love
Supervising Editor	John S. Smith
Editor	Alan Killick
Sound Recordist	Chris Munro
Boom Operator	Mike Silverlock
Dubbing Editor	Peter Lennard
Dubbing Mixer	Hugh Strain
Music Editor	Alan Willis

An Avengers MARK 1 Production For LONDON WEEKEND TELEVISION

Shooting / Location Schedule

Production Dates: Monday 5th to Tuesday 20th November, 1979. Production Number: 9D11342. Locations in *italics* were originally scheduled but ultimately not used

5 November	***Ext: Church***: All Saints Church, Church Hill, Binfield, Berkshire
	Holly's place: The Priory, Church Lane, Binfield, Berkshire
6-7 November	***Doyle's place***: 62 Frithville Gardens, off Uxbridge Road, Shepherd's Bush, London, W12
7 November	***Park***: Ravenscourt Park, Paddenswick Road, Hammersmith, London, W6
8 November	***Pub***: Western Arms, 337 Kensal Road, Kensal Town, London, W10
	Int: Bodie's car (route to 'Tony' streets): Kensal Road / Golborne Road, Kensal Town, London, W10
	Streets: Bodie's car (Tony on side-street): TV Exchange, 60 Golborne Road, Kensal Town, London, W10
	Elkstone Road, London, W10
	Phone Box: Golborne Road (near Trellick Tower, Golborne Road), Kensal Town, London, W10
	Disco: The Dock, Port A Bella Dock, Ladbroke Grove, London, W10
9 November	***Luigi's bar***: Arocaria Kebab House, 48C The Broadway, Crouch End, London, N8
	Tony's place: 29 Blythe Mansions, Highcroft Road, Upper Holloway, London, N19
	Int / Ext: Bodie's car (with Tony): Tottenham Lane (near Rokesly Avenue), Crouch End, London, N8
10 November	***Woods***: Black Park, Fulmer, Buckinghamshire
12-13 November	***Streets (chase)***: Shepherd's Bush Shopping Centre, Shepherd's Bush Green, London, W12
	Streets (chase): Ravenscourt Gardens / Goldhawk Road, Hammersmith, London, W6
	Ann's apartment: Flat 35, Stamford Court, Goldhawk Road, Hammersmith, London, W6
14-16 November	***St. Patrick's Hospital***: Blythe House, Blythe Road, Hammersmith, London, W14
	CI5 HQ: Cadby Hall, Blythe Road, London, W14
19-20 November	***Café / Turner's car stunt***: Rendevous Café, Blythe Road, Hammersmith, London, W14: Originally scheduled for 13th November.
	The Café, 1-3 Tottenham Lane, Hornsey, London, N8 / Gisburn Road, Crouch End, London, N8
	Streets (car chase): *Masbro Rd / Hofland Rd / Milson Rd / Faroe Rd / garages rear of Rayburne Court, Hammersmith, London, W14: Originally scheduled for 13th November.*
	Haringey Park / Landrock Road / Bourne Road / Weston Park / Felix Avenue, Crouch End, London, N8
	Street fight with Marli: rear of Broadway Parade, Felix Avenue, Crouch End, London, N8
	Bodie's car run-by (route to streets - Tony): Weston Park (near Bourne Road), Crouch End, London, N8

Int: Bodie's car (after van chase with Marli): Tottenham Lane / Weston Park, Crouch End, London, N8
Int: Cowley's car (after Ann's apartment): Ferme Park Road, Crouch End, London, N8

Series III Production Unit: uncredited

Production Assistants	Marlene Butland, Jane Oscroft
Location Assistant	Geoff Austin
2nd Assistant Directors	Andrew Warren, Peter Cotton, Roy P. Stevens
3rd Assistant Directors	Keith Young, Jerry Daly, Waldo Rogue
Secretary to Executive Producer	Linda Matthews
Secretary to Mr. Menmuir	Antonia Deutsch
Trainee Secretary	Marilyn Smith
Unit Runner	Trevor Puckle
Clapper / Loader	Bill Malone, Simon Hume
Camera Grip	Malcolm Smith
Sound Assistants	Ian Munro, Don Hawkins
Art Dept. Assistants	Gillian Atkinson, Jamie Leonard, Terry Parr
Production Buyer	Bert Gardner
Casting Secretary	Caroline Culbertson
Publicist	Paul McNicholls
Publicist Secretary	Lucinda Pugh
Wardrobe Assistants	Susan Wain, Terry Smith
Assistant Production Accountant	Sotos Louca
Cashier	Sailianne Branson
Property Masters	Arthur Wicks, Alf Smith, Barry Arnold
Storeman / Dressing Props	Ted Stickley
Dressing Props	Darrel Patterson
Stand-By Props	Bill Stark, Peter Benson, Dennis Kirkham
Stand-By Carpenter	Gordon Moore
Stand-By Painter	Jim Ede
Stand-By Stage-Hand	Arthur Feehan
Construction Manager	Jeff Woodbridge
Special Effects	Ian Wingrove, Peter Davey, Mike Collins
Unit Nurse	Susan Michael
Gaffer	George Boner
Electrician	Arthur Whitmarsh
Generator Operator	Mike Davey
Assistant Editors	Mark Auguste, Peter Gray
Assistant Dubbing Editors	Saeed Akhtar, Brian Trenery
Dialogue Editor	Michael Crowley
Producer's Driver	Barry Myall
Unit Drivers	Ivan Ellias, Geoff Bowers, Derek Vincent, Chris Streeter
Unit Minibus Driver	Nick Perry

Wardrobe Truck Driver	Frank Barretta
Make Up Bus Driver	Michael Devetta
Construction / Props Return Driver	Dave Bruyea
Props Return Driver	Larry Williams
Catering Vehicle Driver	John Lane
Dinning Bus Driver	Fred Borg
Cameras	Joe Dunton: J D C Cameras, Wembley Park Drive, Wembley, Middlesex
Electrical	Tony Lucas: Lee Electric, Wembley Park Drive, Wembley, Middlesex
Processing Lab	Steven Barker: Rank Film Labs, Denham, Middlesex
Insurance	Ruben Sedgwick, Pinewood Studios, Buckinghamshire: Robin Hillyard, Peter Robey, David Havard
Sound Transfer	Location Sound Facilities, 57 Ramsey Road, London, W3
Unit Minibus, Construction Prop Truck / Props Return Van, Dining Bus furnished by	Dennis Ley: D & D Location, Boyers Yard, Staines Road, Feltham, Middlesex
Make Up Bus	Mike Mulally Transport, 10 Murray Road, Ottershaw, Surrey
Wardrobe Truck	Willie Fonfe: Willies Wheels, Englefield Green, Egham, Surrey
Caterers	J & J Foods, 33 Langley Park Road, Iver, Buckinghamshire: John Lane, John Engleman
Unit Doctors	Chalkhill Health Centre, Wembley Park, Middlesex: Dr. Elliott Mass, Dr. Symonds

SERIES III ACTION CARS

Bodie: **Ford Capri 3.0 S**: UOO 303T (Real index: COO 251T) - *The Madness Of Mickey Hamilton, Backtrack, Stopover, Runner, A Hiding To Nothing, Dead Reckoning, Mixed Doubles, Need To Know, Fugitive, The Acorn Syndrome, Slush Fund, Involvement.*
Morris Marina 1300 7CWT van: GLH 107N - *Servant Of Two Masters.*
Ford Cortina 2.0GL: HPU 724T - *The Acorn Syndrome*

Cowley: **Ford Granada 2.8i Ghia**: YHJ 766T (Real index: FEV 24T) - *The Madness Of Mickey Hamilton, Servant Of Two Masters, Backtrack, Stopover, Runner, A Hiding To Nothing, Dead Reckoning, Mixed Doubles, Need To Know, The Purging Of CI5, Fugitive, The Acorn Syndrome, Slush Fund, Weekend In The Country, Take Away, Involvement.*

Doyle: **Ford Escort RS 2000**: PNO 641T (Real index: PNO 672R) - *The Madness Of Mickey Hamilton, Servant Of Two Masters, Stopover, Runner, A Hiding To Nothing, The Purging Of CI5, Fugitive, The Acorn Syndrome, Involvement.*

	Ford Cortina 2.3 Ghia estate: HPU 754T - *The Acorn Syndrome*.
CI5:	**Ford Cortina 2.3 GL**: VHK 537S - *Backtrack*.
CI5:	**Ford Cortina 2.0 GL**: VHK 536S - *Servant Of Two Masters, Backtrack*.
CI5:	**Ford Cortina 1.6 GL**: VHK 534S - *Backtrack, Runner, A Hiding To Nothing*.
CI5:	**Ford Cortina 2.0 GL**: HPU 724T - *The Purging Of CI5, Fugitive, The Acorn Syndrome, Take Away, Involvement*.
CI5:	**Ford Cortina 2.0 GL**: HPU 725T - *The Purging Of CI5, Fugitive, The Acorn Syndrome, Involvement*.
Misc:	**Ford Fiesta 1.1 L van**: YPU 750S - *The Madness Of Mickey Hamilton, Runner*.
Misc:	**Ford Escort 1.1 L**: BPU 903T - *Runner, A Hiding To Nothing*.
Misc:	**Datsun 180B**: FLA 941T - *Runner* (with false index: UMD 25P in some scenes), *Take Away*.
Police:	**Rover SD1 3500**: SYY 904S - *Need To Know, The Purging Of CI5, The Acorn Syndrome, Weekend In The Country, Take Away*.
Misc:	Air Film Services (Helicopter) - *Stopover*.
Misc:	Alan Mann Helicopters - *The Acorn Syndrome*.

TRANSMISSION DATES

1: THE PURGING OF CI5
27th October 1979
2: BACKTRACK*
3rd November 1979
3: STOPOVER
10th November 1979
4: DEAD RECKONING
17th November 1979
5: THE MADNESS OF MICKEY HAMILTON*
24th November 1979
6: A HIDING TO NOTHING
1st December 1979
7: RUNNER
8th December 1979
8: SERVANT OF TWO MASTERS*
15th December 1979

* These episodes were originally planned to be filmed in the Series II block, but were completed and transmitted here as Series III.

SERIES IV

FOXHOLE ON THE ROOF

DESPITE a limited run of only eight new episodes, the televised third series had been a runaway success, so on Monday 24th March 1980, producer Ray Menmuir agreed with Michael Grade, London Weekend Television's director of programmes, to generate a further thirteen episodes. However, Grade was concerned with the growing discontent of actor Martin Shaw and asked Menmuir to consider recasting the part of Doyle.

Grade's fears were further highlighted when Martin Shaw expressed his views in the 'Daily Mail' newspaper on Monday 7th April. Predominantly concerned with the actor's appearance in the Dennis Potter play, *Cream In My Coffee* (broadcast Sunday 2nd November 1980), Shaw stated that the play was the first chance he had been given to prove his versatility since he'd become a household name as Doyle.

Martin Shaw (interviewed at the time): "I'm enjoying every minute of the play, which is more than I can say for working on *The Professionals*. It had nothing to do with the crew or the other actors, although there was some aggro between Lewis Collins, my partner in the series, and me, but that's now resolved. My complaint was with the men who ran the show. I suppose it was partly my fault. I signed a four-year contract on the verbal understanding that I'd be allowed to accept other offers of work if they didn't conflict with my commitment on *The Professionals*.

"But when it came to the point, they said 'no' and I've had to turn down several good films because of their churlish attitude. Fortunately, my track record was pretty good before *The Professionals* and the offers have kept coming in.

"These men are not creative people, they're accountants, businessmen. They don't realise how it refreshes an actor to get away from playing the same role over and over again. On *The Professionals* they have very little respect for the cast, even in little ways like providing chairs for you to sit on between takes. And it is a very exhausting series, with all those punch-ups and all the running around!

"James Bond had been very successful and rightly so, but it had its own niche, which was 'We are sexy and we are violent and we don't really mean it'. You know, all very tongue-in-cheek, and I thought its all been done before, so why bother to do it again."

Brian Clemens: "We didn't do anything tongue-in-cheek. We tried to inject humour into it, which I think is slightly different. But, I mean, they had to believe in what they were doing. If they didn't believe in the story the audience wouldn't. The comments had come at a time when it wasn't sure if we'd go to a new series, and the fact that we were kind of irritated Martin."

Martin Shaw: "It was a continual constant frustration. I mean, we had researched quite a bit, both actors, you want to research, you want to do it properly. We had been trained by the SAS. And so when you were asked to kick a door down and stand framed in the doorway with the light behind us, we'd say, 'Come on please, you're an easy target in the doorway, you'd get cut off at the knees. Can we do it properly?' 'No, no, they will never know', they said."

Following Martin Shaw's outcry in the press, Ray Menmuir duly replied to Michael Grade at LWT and on Thursday 10th April wrote the following:

Re: 'The Professionals' Series IV

This is to confirm our conversation of 24 March, 1980, that we will be producing thirteen episodes of the above for a 9.00 pm transmission slot.

I have investigated the possibility of holding a two-parter in reserve in the event of recasting the part of Doyle. This poses a number of production problems, the two major ones being a re-shoot of the main titles, and, consequently, an interruption in the flow of transmission prints. In the light of Monday's double page spread in The Mail, I am of the opinion that we should decide to re-cast, or not, at episode 4 or 5 so that the main titles and billings re-shoot can be included in the budget and the schedule. A large proportion of the main title re-shoot budget would be off-set by having a cheaper replacement and the costs we would incur in shooting on a disconsolate principal.

I should be grateful for your early decision.

The letter was also copied to the following LWT directors: John Blyton (controller of programme management); Eric Flackfield (controller of programme planning and presentation); John Davies (assistant head of drama); and Judith Thomas (head of legal services).

Michael Grade weighed up the recasting process, the budget involved in re-shooting the main title sequence, the short space of time in which these had to be completed, and decided that Martin Shaw would not be asked to leave - filming would continue as planned.

Since breaking his ankle in November 1978, Lewis Collins had kept up his parachute training with the Parachute Regiment (TAVR) and in February earned his Red Beret. Unfortunately in April, whist trying to earn his Wings he broke his other ankle. He recovered just in time to begin filming on this batch of episodes.

Meanwhile, pre-production was well underway and numerous details had to be taken care of simultaneously, from the hiring of the production crew, to selecting writers, and assigning directors. Ford Motor Company, once again, provided the transport for the new series. Bodie was given a new Strato silver Ford Capri 3.0S, OWC 827V, which bore OWC 827W as it's false index. Doyle would also get a Ford Capri 3.0S, after the Escort RS2000 had been discontinued, and with Ford no longer wishing to publicise an old model, OAR 576V, finished in Solar gold, appeared from episode 3, *Black Out*, wearing OAR 576W. The reason for its late arrival was that Ford was uncertain about which vehicle to give Mark 1. Was it essential to give two Capri's publicity? A Ford Cortina was offered and declined by producer Ray Menmuir. Cowley would be given a new Midnight blue Ford Granada 2.8i Ghia, OWC 822V, wearing OWC 822W on screen.

 Ford also loaned two Cortinas, a Venetian red 1.6LS, MHK 545V, and a Highland green 2.0GL, MHK 547V, to be used as CI5 cars or for whatever the stories called for, meaning even more publicity for Ford Motor Company. Also loaned among the batch was a Cordoba beige Ford Transit, OHJ 280V, and from Opel, two 2.0S Rekord Estate's, NKX 453V and NKX 454V. Kingsbury Motors provided the remainder of the vehicles and Alan Mann the helicopters

Unavailable to resume his position of associate producer, Chris Burt stepped aside for Roy Stevens to take over. Stevens had a wealth of experience, and since 1960 had been the associate producer on David Lean's *Ryan's Daughter*, production manager on the David Bowie film *The Man Who Fell To Earth*, and second unit director on Alistair MacLean's *Bear Island*.

Roy Stevens: "I directed the second unit, which all seemed to run smoothly. I later insisted to the production office that the headrests on the Capri's are left off on all occasions. This would stop the 'disappearing headrest' syndrome apparent on so many episodes. The reason was quite simple - the second unit shoots were normally filmed some time behind the main unit and things like the headrests were not on the continuity notes."

Ken Ryan took over from art director William Alexander. He had started on *The Professionals*, the previous year, as Alexander's assistant but left, after two episodes, to work on the movies *Bear Island* and *The Human Factor* starring Richard Attenborough. Ryan's career had started back in 1966 when he worked as an assistant on *The Trap*, which was followed with work on *Quatermass And The Pit*, *Submarine X-1*, *Ring Of Bright Water* and *The Last Shot You Hear*. Later, in 1978, he worked on the feature *Silver Bears* and the Richard O'Sullivan TV series, *Dick Turpin*. When William Alexander became unavailable for this batch, due to his commitment to the second series of *Minder*, he suggested Ken to the producers.

Ken Ryan: "*The Professionals* was a very busy, fast, and manic production to say the least! I was chiefly responsible for the art department's budget and schedule of work. The look of the sets or locations transports audiences into the world of the story, and is, therefore, a crucial factor in making the show credible. These settings are rarely left to chance; a great deal of work and imagination goes into constructing suitable backdrops to any story, and into selecting appropriate locations and sets. Filming locations may range from a Victorian room, to a late-night café, to the interior of a Police Squad room. The look of a set or location is vital, and is an essential element in making the show convincing.

"My first task on any episode would be to read the script, then assess the visual qualities that would help create the right atmosphere and bring the story to life. After preparing a careful breakdown of the script, a meeting would be arranged with the director and producer to discuss how best to shoot it, taking into careful consideration the budget set aside. During the shoot I would have to check on the construction and dressing of all the sets at each location for the following day's filming."

The Gun: *Two young boys find a gun in a garden, and a trail of murders leads Bodie and Doyle to an illegal heroin consignment being smuggled into Britain. Cowley plays a hunch and Bodie saves a school teacher from death.*

The production office issued the Unit List to relevant personnel on Thursday 12th June and the first episode, *The Gun*, by Christopher Wicking, which had been approved on 19th May, entered production on Monday 16th. Originally called *The Gun, The Horse And The Mules*, it was directed by Denis Lewiston.

When a gun is found by two school boys Bodie and Doyle find themselves on the trail of a large shipment of heroin due to arrive in England. Celia Gregory played Inger North, a teacher friend of Bodie's, in THE GUN.

Peter Carter (location manager): "We used Kienzle Data Systems in Slough as the CI5 HQ for several episodes of this batch, because the producer's were looking for a more plush office than we could get out of Cadby Hall, Hammersmith. Although gone today, Kienzle's computer offices were fairly modern at the time. They proved impractical later in the year, with traffic, or whatever, and we returned to Cadby Hall."

Denis Lewiston (director): "I wasn't that keen on doing anymore. I didn't think the scripts were that good this time round. I got the impression they were left-overs from the previous batch and I remember they had to change certain characters names, like we couldn't use Jesus for obvious reasons (the original first name of the boy Tony Domenguin).

"I basically used the show as a stepping-stone to get onto *Hill Street Blues* in America, where I made full use of my hand held work. I didn't seem to get on well with Dusty Miller, the lighting cameraman, who they'd bought in from *The Sweeney*. I think he looked upon me as just another cameraman, the same as him. The guest cast I was allowed wasn't brilliant either as you couldn't repeat actors in the same batch, so most of the ones available were not up to scratch."

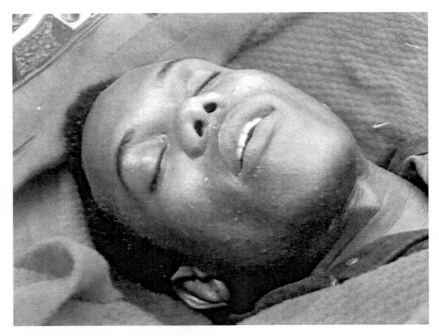

Drug addict Paul Bailey (Burt Caesar), is killed by a pusher who then hastily discards THE GUN, only for it to be found by a young boy - who then accidentally shoots his friend in the process.

Zoot Money had his own band in the 1960's called *Zoot Money's Big Roll Band* and was in Eric Burdon's *New Animals*. He made his stage debut at the National Theatre in *Line 'Em* and had parts in the films *Waterloo Bridge, Handicap,* and *Riding High*.

Zoot Money: "My character G. G Lesley (originally called Tom Dooley in early script drafts) was supposed to be the same age as me. It sounded like typecasting but it wasn't. It was the most serious role I'd ever had. I didn't sing in it - I didn't take parts where I had to sing because it was just too easy to play make-believe. I wanted to act. I played the 'thickest bloke in the nick' months earlier in the *Porridge* film. He was so thick; I didn't think he even knew he was in prison. Lewis and I were old friends from his Mojos days, I left all the rough stuff to him, but we did manage a bit of leaping around in the bar afterwards..."

Gary (Robert Gwilym) chases Tony (Barry Angel) in search of THE GUN.

Rufus Andrew (unit manager): "I joined the production as a unit manager from this episode. I remember driving from the other side of London to the first days shoot at the café on York Way, Islington. I was late and I was supposed to be the first guy there to direct the crew where to park, and set up their equipment.

"Zoot Money caused us problems also. The scenes we did with him at the hospital (Northwick Park, Harrow) did not go as planned. You see, Zoot liked his drink, and I don't think he had recovered from a drinking session the night before with Lewis Collins. Much to the crew's amusement he wasn't getting his lines right. His eyes were blood shot and he was slurring his lines. When director Denis Lewiston and Ray Menmuir saw the rushes the following day, they went mad. They were so bad, all his scenes had to be re-shot by a second unit."

The football match scenes used boys from Holloway School, Hilldrop Road, North London, who were collected at 8.00 am for a days shoot.

Peter Carter (location manager): "We'd usually get extras in, but there wasn't time to get a fleet of similar aged boys, so I was asked by the producers if I could sort it out. My old school proved very helpful, and a school competition was held to see which boys would be selected to appear on the show."

71. EXT. HOSPITAL/SIDE ENTRANCE. DAY.

Gary's car parked near laundry vans, etc.

BODIE & DOYLE leaning in from driver/passenger side.

          BODIE
Blood. Inger said she thought the boy looked unconscious as it drove off.

          DOYLE
Must've slugged him to shut him up. Do you think he took him into casualty?

They can't really believe it, but walk off to check.

Nearby we can see a dozen wheelchairs that are in the process of being repaired.

72. EXT. PARK AREA. DAY.

GARY has stolen one of the wheelchairs and is pushing DOMENGUIN - blanket-wrapped, apparently asleep - through the park, which looks quite 'natural'.

He pulls up at a bench, parks the chair, sits on the bench beside it, checking JESUS' forehead.

          GARY
You just can't be out this long ... wake up, hey ...

He shakes JESUS, the head lolls, and GARY has to catch his torso or he'll slip out of the chair.

GARY can think of nothing safe to do. Across from him is a water fountain. He walks over to get a drink.

ON JESUS -
as Gary's FOOTSTEPS move off. One of JESUS' eyes opens. He is simply doing an ace job of faking.

ON GARY -
pushing the button on the fountain. Water jets into the air, then dies to a trickle. GARY tries it again, the same thing happens. He has to keep his mouth tight over the spout and slurp.

He has enough, turns back and we turn with him - to see that the wheelchair is empty.

GARY RUNS -
looking desperately, and sees JESUS a couple of hundred yards away. He gives chase - and though he didn't have much luck the last time this happened, his determination and desperate need give him a little extra speed.

Also, JESUS is running towards a fenced-in playground area with roundabouts, etc. - and no immediately obvious way out of the park.

ON JESUS -
looking for an exit along the fence.

ON GARY -
getting closer.

ON JESUS -
stumbling a little, getting dizzy from his head wound and the sudden exertion. But he doesn't give up, starts off across the grass - but GARY is able to catch him and drag him down under a tree.

          GARY
You stupid kid. I'm trying to help you ...

JESUS is groggy, looks confused.

          JESUS
Help me?

A deleted scene from THE GUN - although scheduled it was not filmed.

7. EXT. 'UP ALLNIGHT CAFE'. DAWN.

    Garbage sacks, a few DERELICTS in doorways, maybe a
    dustcart cruising by picking up the detritus of a swinging
    night.

    PAUL pockets the blade, and hails approaching taxi.

    ACROSS THE STREET -
    a figure moves in a doorway, from where he has been
    anxiously watching and waiting.

    It's GARY. He is about to move after PAUL - but the taxi
    pulls in.

    NOW INGER APPEARS -
    at the door of the cafe.

                    INGER
            Paul. Come back. I do want to
            help...

    GARY SEES HER -
    seems to recognise her. He reaches for the gun hidden
    in his belt beneath his windcheater. Is he going to fire
    on Paul? On Inger? He is obviously confused himself.

    THE TAXI -
    pulls away with PAUL inside. INGER goes back into the
    cafe.

    GARY RUNS -
    round the corner to where his own car is parked. He gets
    in, and drives off after the taxi.
                                        END OF TEASE??

108. INT. BODIE'S CAR/TRAVELLING. DAY.

    BODIE driving. DOYLE beside him.
                    BODIE
            How have you been managing
            without your motor?

    DOYLE produces half a dozen car keys.
                    DOYLE
            It's amazing how many people
            leave the keys in their cars...

109. EXT. LONDON STREETS. DAY.

    BODIE's car drives on and is lost in the heart of the
    traffic.

                        ENDS

*Two more deleted scenes (scenes 7, and 108-109) from THE GUN - again
scripted but not filmed.*

In THE GUN Celia Gregory portrayed Inger North.

On Wednesday 25th June London Weekend Television managed to sell the first thirty-nine episodes (series 1-3) to the United States, who pre-purchased this batch, in a $1,000,000 deal. The episodes went out twice a week on cable TV in Los Angeles and Detroit. Americans at that time paid around $40 dollars to see the latest shows and films, breaking away from the American Networks, which were plagued by advertisements. LWT were particularly overjoyed after Thames TV had failed to sell *The Sweeney* to the States.

Brian Clemens: "You must remember that unless you can sell a series to America you only break even money-wise. That doesn't mean I write for the American market, but unless you have a big financial success you don't get to make another series. We couldn't get on the networks, because at the time they were going through a very anti-violence thing and they felt *The Professionals* was too tough for them. My agent, John Redway, went to America and worked out a deal with Jerry Perenchio of Embassy, a US distributor. The Americans were particularly interested in the show because they knew Gordon Jackson from *Upstairs Downstairs*. We wanted to make a major movie of *The Professionals*, which may have got us on the American network. But Martin Shaw wanted script approval and there was no way I was going to give an actor script approval."

Wild Justice: *Is Bodie cracking up? If not, why should he disobey orders and arrange a mysterious - and deadly - motorcycle race with the leader of a gang of Hell's Angels? Doyle is assigned to keep an eye on his partner - with high speed results.*

Ranald Graham's *Wild Justice* script was approved on the 28th May (The original outline was published in the October 7-13 1978 issue of TV Times as *Episode Minus One*), and began filming on Monday 30th June under the control of Dennis Abey. At this point the second unit was filming scenes missed by the first unit on *The Gun*, including the exterior of Devlin's council flat, but much of this footage was not edited into the final print.

In order to add realism to the scrambling scenes, filmed at Knowl Hill, Berkshire, Mark I hired the services of Nick Beamishe and Perry Leaske of the British Suzuki team. Suzuki themselves providing Doyle's hill bike (stunt rider Jonathan Wright riding in the race), and the 1000cc example he is seen using in the early scenes. Other riders were courtesy of Dave Martin, who also supplied the Hell's Angel's bikes, and Peter Hudson.

When Bodie challenges biker King Billy to the 'Widowmaker' it was decided that it was too dangerous for Lewis Collins to ride the motorcycle, and despite his protests, it was Jonathan Wright - with Dave Watson doubling as Ziggy Byfield's character - who performed the stunt.

Dennis Abey: "Lew just wanted to try everything that looked dangerous - he seemed to get off on it! I couldn't risk him being injured though, so I had to put my foot down and tell him he couldn't due to insurance stipulations."

Behind-the-scenes on WILD JUSTICE actor Ziggy Byfield (King Billy) receives the attention of the make-up department: Sue Black (far left) and Stella Hunter.

Colin Webb (stunt rider hired via Dave Martin): "Martin did none of his own stunts, he was not allowed to ride a bike at all, due to insurance worries, although he did have a ride around a flat field at lunchtime, albeit in one gear. He did have some action shots taken, but he was stationary! There was a stunt man on site but his Motocross talent was lacking. The person who doubled as King Billy was a British Championship Motocross racer, Dave Watson. When we were directed to follow the 'Professionals' stuntman around the track he crashed on the second corner and several of us ran over him! After that the director, Dennis Abey, abandoned the idea of the stuntman leading us and left us to our own devices as he was so impressed by the action. If I remember correctly Lewis Collins didn't go anywhere near a bike, he just swanned around with some blonde on his arm."

Production Unit notes issued at this time praised cast and crew for their outstanding efforts during the filming of the scrambling scenes:

The producer commends the unit for the outstanding rushes over the past few days'. Please provide wet weather gear, as the forecast isn't sunny. Please refrain from submitting Petty Cash Vouchers written in red; if written in red, they mean you pay us instead of us paying you!

Actress Sarah Douglas was born (15th December 1952) in Stratford-Upon-Avon and has, since her role as Dr. Kate Ross in WILD JUSTICE, made a respectable career playing villainesses in both film and television. She is best remembered for her portrayal as Ursa in the first two SUPERMAN movies.

There are references to Splodgenessabounds's hit record 'Two Pints Of Lager And A Packet Of Crisps Please', but the head biker asks for six pints of lager. The line appears to have been ad-libbed (the single only charted on the 14th June) as it did not form part of the original script.

Dennis Abey (director): "By this time both Martin and Lewis wanted out of the show and they were causing the producers lots of grief. I usually managed to keep on top of things, but even for me they were getting a bit of a handful. In the scene where Cowley goes to do up Doyle's neck-tie, we had to insert the dialogue about the suit being borrowed from Bodie. Martin said his 'character would never wear such an outfit' and refused to play the scene any other way.

For WILD JUSTICE Mark I hired the services of Nick Beamishe and Perry Leaske of the British Suzuki team. Martin Shaw joins them (top - centre).

"For the scenes we shot at Knowl Hill, we had hired a 1000cc Harley Davidson bike (from Dave Martin). When Lewis arrived on set, he told me he wanted a BMW as it would suit his image more. I told him it was too late to change it, we were hours from the studio. He then refused to do the scenes all together. I called his bluff and told him it was 11:45, nearly time for lunch, and the scene had to be shot that afternoon. If he wouldn't budge, we'd spend the rest of the day in the pub. By mid afternoon, we were still there, so I gave in and sent the unit driver to go and get the BMW. We still managed to get the scenes done - a little rushed I grant you - but we got there! Producer Ray Menmuir was extremely pleased with what we'd achieved."

"He also kept telling me to be like director Martin Campbell. I told him 'No Way' - he was too serious for my liking and I just can't work like that. I saw the show as a big laugh from start to finish. I'd made my money doing commercials and, therefore, treated the show from a humorous aspect. I wasn't afraid to speak my mind - Martin and Lew liked that!"

Location manager Peter Carter's original 'recce' shot of Warfield Hall, Berkshire; where the opening siege training scenes were filmed.

The opening sequence filmed at Warfield Hall, Berkshire, was derived from the ending of the Iranian Embassy siege, which had finished in May.

Ray Menmuir (producer): "Before the Iranian Embassy siege, there was a great deal of caution about the SAS. But from that moment attitudes began to change. There was that national boost. Before, there had been a mystery about them. Did they travel incognito? Did they speak thirty-eight languages? Suddenly, they became part of the overall 'law and order' framework of our society. I think people felt relieved, in a way. Certain things that have happened since have qualified people's attitudes to the police, for instance. Whether it is out of fear, or whatever, I don't know. While they felt secure, they could go heavy on 'the fuzz'. Things have happened since which have made them insecure. And they do want someone to help, or protect, or solve the uncomfortable problems we have.

"Initially, our freedom to tell stories about such areas was very welcome. Because the top line of fiction helped us to get into the action elements, and they were the whole basis of the show. Sitting quite back, the only thing one really asks for is invention. The beginning is not about 'what', 'who', 'where', 'can I', can't I' - it's about ideas. If you want to say something - as long as it's treated in a dramatically acceptable way. Because I didn't want arguments based on a writer's particular attitude at a particular time - you can say it, because behind the action, the human condition in some form or another has got to be illuminated.

"The more we did though, the more difficult it became. Not because it was fictional, but because, by elimination, the area to work in became restrictive. We couldn't go into police work; having done foreign diplomats, KGB, Chinese, African, English aristocrats, corruption stories and many other areas. So the framework kept narrowing."

Actors Lewis Collins and Martin Shaw relax on the set of WILD JUSTICE.

Martin Shaw on location for WILD JUSTICE. All the scrambling scenes were filmed at H F Warner Limited, Star Works, Knowl Hill, near Maidenhead, Berkshire.

In this episode, the guns used were so new even the SAS and Army hadn't been issued with them. The rifles were the Enfield XL64ES - so new at the time that they were simply known as the New Personal Weapon. The 5.56mm rifle eventually replaced the 7.62mm SLR (Self Loading Rifle) that, was standard British Infantry issue. The Enfield fires between 700 and 850 rounds per minute. It was lighter and shorter than previous issues, which made it ideal for highly mobile infantry units like the SAS or the Paras. Four of the rifles had just finished their NATO trails when they were loaned to Mark I productions personal armourers, Bapty, for use when Bodie and Doyle had to simulate the SAS siege attack, filmed at Warfield Hall, Berkshire.

Peter Brayham (stunt arranger): "If you were on a shoot and needed the guns for three or four days, you'd have a practical gun, which fired blanks and a dummy one. Overnight they'd be put in the local police station, but more often than not, the guy who'd signed them in wasn't in the next day, and that held up shooting."

Mike Collins (special effects supervisor): "Take a bullet hole in a door. A highly sophisticated detonator, which is specially designed for motion pictures, creates the effect and special effects work. It enters from the side of the door facing the gun and takes the debris from the woodwork with it. What you actually see on the screen, however, is the debris being blown out forward but it happens so fast that it looks real. The detonator is actually placed behind the door."

The motor-cycle and side platform used in WILD JUSTICE was specially constructed by William Withey at AGT Engineering, Luton, Bedfordshire.

Black Out: *A mysterious kidnapping provides Bodie and Doyle with a vital lead concerning an important diplomatic mission. But the two must race against the clock to find out how the parts of the puzzle fit together.*

Production commenced on *Black Out*, by Brian Clemens, on Monday 14th July having been approved on 12th May (with further revisions on 2nd July). The script re-uses the opening sequence of Clemens' *Danger Man* episode *The Girl In Pink Pyjamas*, and had appeared as a text-based feature called *High Noon For The Professionals* in 'TV Times' dated November 24-30 1979. Picking up the director's reins was William Brayne.

Dennis Abey and the second unit were still completing scenes from the previous episode *Wild Justice* at this stage.

In BLACK OUT CI5 discover that a possible terrorist attack is being planned, and the only clue they have in solving it is a German girl (Linda Hayden)!

It was during this series that Brian Clemens decided to expand Cowley's team by one, and introduced a new semi-regular character, CI5 agent, Murphy. Played by actor Steve Alder, the character appeared in this, his first story, and went on to appear in six other episodes.

Born in 1950 he attended Goodal Secondary School in Leyton, East London and during the late 1960's and early 1970's he lived with the model-actress Ayshea Brough, who was at the time starring in Gerry Anderson's *UFO*. Before landing the part of Murphy, he appeared in *Kiss The Girls And Make Them Cry*, a 4-part mini-series for the BBC's *Love Story* series.

Brian Clemens: "There was never any thought about the Murphy character taking over, should Lewis or Martin leave the show. I just wanted to remind London Weekend that we could have other people in it - use another guy to compliment the team. The Murphy character wasn't the one. It was never my thinking that we'd use him to replace anyone, because I think that we would have brought in perhaps somebody bigger than that, although Steve Alder was an excellent actor and wonderful in the part."

Esta Charkham (casting director): "Steve was hired because they asked me to find someone extremely good looking to keep Martin and Lewis on their toes. I'm pretty sure there was no chance that he'd been earmarked to take over."

Steve Alder (Murphy): "I was approached by the casting director to appear in the show, and during my brief interview was told I would be a line-feed: they needed the extra person in order to keep Martin and Lewis happy and share scenes. The emphasis was on Martin and in hindsight had I been a more 'well known' face I'm pretty sure I could have replaced Martin had he been forced to leave the show. I think they wanted to see how I got on with Lew, with whom I seemed to spend much more air-time with. My time on the show was very hectic, and we always seemed to be fighting the schedules to keep each show filmed in the allocated 10-day turnaround.

"I was a little disappointed that the Murphy character was not allowed to develop much more, thinking that maybe, had another series been made, that I'd get equal billing either as Martin's replacement or as a trio."

Lewis Collins on the set of BLACK OUT - with the anti-tank gun being used by a terrorist group to disrupt a diplomatic conference at Harrodene.

Bodie's new watch is a TAG Heuer Manhattan and Doyle's is also Swiss (an Orfina), while Cowley's is German, an ICW. One of the CI5 men is called O'Hara after the script editor, Gerry O'Hara. The village of Mingaye was so called after set dresser Don Mingaye, who had been one of the main art directors throughout the 1960's and 1970's with Hammer films. However, the village name caused slight confusion on the day of filming! The art department's notes depicted the road sign was to read Maidstone and Canterbury; and that Gerda's scripted line was: "Didn't you say Canterbury or Maidstone? Maidstone. Somewhere off the Maidstone road." The script was duly amended on the day to read 'Mingaye' much to the amusement of the production crew on location in Waltham St. Lawrence, Berkshire.

On Friday 18th July, while filming the concluding scenes to this story at the Hart Ward of the Royal Free Hospital in Hampstead, North West London,

Bodie had to have his arm in plaster. Therefore, the services of the hospital plasterer, Beth Morgan, were called upon to suitably dress Lewis Collins arm.

British actress Linda Hayden was born (19th January 1953) in Stanmore, Middlesex. She trained at the famous Aida Foster Stage School where she regularly attended drama, dancing and singing classes in addition to her academic schooling. Her big break came at the tender age of fifteen in the 1968 film BABY LOVE. This was a stepping-stone to later roles in British horror films (BLOOD ON SATAN'S CLAW) and sex comedies (LET'S GET LAID).

However, he found himself in the cast to no avail, as there was no time to film the scene. He had to go through the process again on Friday 25th when the scene was eventually filmed at the 'Bell And Dragon' pub, Cookham High Street, Berkshire.

On Tuesday 22nd July, the production office received the following note from *Wild Justice* director Dennis Abey:

Loved the shoot. Loved the rushes. Loved the fish. Can't wait for the rough cut.
Thanks for a great two weeks -
Luv Dennis 'A'

On the Friday 25th July associate producer Roy Stevens issued a memorandum to: Ray Menmuir, Ron Purdie (production manager), Terry Connors (accountant), Dominic Fulford (first assistant director) and David Cherrill (first assistant director), stating that the main unit were not making full use of the production office cars:

THE PROFESSIONALS IV - ACTION VEHICLES
The following vehicles are available as Action Vehicles whenever required:

Ford Granada	Cowley's car: OWC 822V
Ford Capri	Bodie's car: OWC 827V
Ford Capri	Doyle's car: OAR 821V
Ford Cortina	2.0GL Green: MHK 547V
Ford Cortina	1.6LS Red: MHK 545V
Rover	SD1 Police car: WVP 150T
Leyland	EA van: RCW 400T
Ford Transit van	Beige: OHJ 280V
2 Opel Rekords	2.0S Estate Cars: NKX 453V
	NKX 454V

RS/hep

A later edition included the correct index for Doyle's Ford Capri - OAR 576V.

It's Only A Beautiful Picture...: *What link can there be between industrial espionage and the theft of several art treasures? CI5 agents Bodie and Doyle uncover the crimes of Colonel Sangster, a criminal mastermind who leads them a merry dance before the case is over.*

It's Only A Beautiful Picture...., by Edmund Ward, was approved by Mark 1/LWT on 1st July, entering production on Monday 28th with Denis Lewiston in control.

Denis Lewiston (director): "They asked me to do another, so I did. Another awful script, which I seem to recall was extensively re-written by Gerry O'Hara, inserting huge chunks of dialogue and action."

On call for the duration of the episode were two Rotweiller dogs, supplied courtesy of animal handler Danny Graber. The unit was, not surprisingly, issued with the following note:

Important unit note: under no circumstances should members of the crew pet, feed or become familiar with the dogs on call today.

A gang is stealing and selling industrial secrets to foreign countries. In this scene from IT'S ONLY A BEAUTIFUL PICTURE... Jeremy Sangster (Moray Watson) and James Tibbs (Jonathan Newth) have got the better of Bodie (Lewis Collins).

Denis Lewiston (director): "While filming at White Waltham airfield I had trouble with Lewis Collins; I called for a shoot, but Lewis was nowhere to be seen. I found him round the back of the aircraft hangers on the phone to his girlfriend. They were arguing (reports stated that Lewis Collins had just got engaged to his then girlfriend, Marion Sheffield). I told him to get on with it and leave his personal life at home. He looked up and said, 'Sod this, and sod you', to put it mildly, and walked off the set. I contacted Ray Menmuir and told him what had happened. Somehow, he got hold of Collins and threatened him with legal action, reminding him of the ankle incident from a few years ago. He returned to the set with his tail between his legs. I later noticed that I was being treated like a leper. No one from the production crew would talk to me, as I had not only upset their friend, but got him in trouble with the producer. I vowed never to direct on the show again."

Ray Menmuir: "Working so hard, so long and under so much pressure, it's inevitable that people come under stress and that apart from unavoidable problems of technical hold-ups, there is some squabbling. Part of my job was to help soften the situation and even to cajole a little at times. The important thing was we keep the show moving and what ever the problem I faced, I had to find a solution, and quick."

Martin Shaw: "It wasn't a good day for me either. I'd hurt my back shortly after filming had begun that morning. I was slammed up against a bolt on the hanger door, which hit the base of my spine. The right side of my hip had gone into a spasm."

But he refused to mention the pain on set because it would have messed up rehearsals and affected the already tight schedule.

Away from the action every spare moment Lewis Collins had was taken up with his new 'toy', a movie camera, which he was learning to use professionally.

A sound recordist lends Lewis Collins a hand with the actor's new film camera; which he is putting into practice during filming at White Waltham Airfield, Berkshire, on the set of IT'S ONLY A BEAUTIFUL PICTURE.

Lewis Collins *(interviewed at the time)*: "In my spare time I plan to make a film about my parachute Regiment. It will take me about a year to do as I plan to shoot a lot of footage. But I have both an excellent script and cameraman to help me out. The final result should, hopefully, be more entertaining than the 'Lochs of Scotland'-type documentary they show at cinemas before the main movie."

With scenes set in an Art Gallery and a Naval club (Cowley's club), location manager Peter Carter secured the services of Celia Plunkett at the Rowan Gallery, Berkeley Square and The Naval Club, Hill Street, West London, courtesy of Commander P. E Travis. As a consequence the unit were, not surprisingly, issued with the following note:

The producers would greatly appreciate the unit offering full respect for the traditions of the locations we are filming in today, and trust that the unit will dress and behave accordingly i.e. in a subdued and conventional manner.

Meanwhile, Gordon Jackson and *Wild Justice* guest star, Marsha Fitzalan, were called for post-sync work (on *Wild Justice*) at De Lane Lea Studios, Soho, West London, as some of their dialogue was not clear enough on the original shoot.

Assistant director David Cherrill, born in 1948, was relatively new to the business, having become a first assistant on the 1978 feature *Force 10 From Navarone*.

David Cherrill: "One of the first things they warned me about was Lewis Collins. I'd only been in the industry a few years and hadn't realised the two guys, Martin and Lewis, were such a handful. I was told that Lewis would try and con me when doing any stunts and if I wasn't sure if he was allowed to do it, I had to check. Not take his word for it. They couldn't afford a repeat of the ankle incident from 1978. Before this episode, I had to contend with a mad director on *Wild Justice* - Dennis Abey! What a guy, a laugh from start to finish."

Blood Sports: *Following a political assassination, CI5 uncover an international terrorist organisation from South America and Bodie and Doyle go undercover to save the life of a foreign diplomat.*

Gerry O'Hara's *Blood Sports* script was finalised on Sunday 29th June (with further revisions implemented on 8th August), and commenced production on Monday 11th August marking the directorial debut of Phil Meheux. Following Ray Menmuir's tradition of hiring cameramen to direct, Meheux joined the team.

Phil Meheux: "I had not long finished the cinematography on the films *Scum* and *The Long Good Friday*, when I got a call from Ray saying how impressed he was with my work. He asked if I'd like to direct an episode, so I agreed - it's something I'd always fancied having a go at, and television seemed the perfect medium."

The first day's shoot called for Bodie to be involved in a cricket match; The Metropolitan Police Sports and Social club, Bushey, was utilised for this. The club supplied the cricket gear and also twenty players who appeared on screen.

Phil Meheux: "The good thing about this scene was all the cricketers, thankfully, knew exactly what they were doing, and it was a nice bit of work from location guy Peter Carter, who not only secured the location, but agreed to have members of the club in the filming - even if we had to 'wait' for some of them to turn up!"

BLOOD SPORTS.

CI5 move in to protect Anita Cabreros (Michelle Newell), the daughter of a South American President after his son - and her brother - is assassinated on the field of a polo match in the story BLOOD SPORTS.

Phil Meheux (director): "It was a long, hard, ten days work. I had terrible trouble with Martin, complaining about the slightest of things. We did a scene where they (Bodie and Doyle) are having a drink at a bar (The Dock, Ladbroke Grove, West London), and Martin decided that things were not set up correctly and the scene should be done differently. I said to him, 'it doesn't really matter; the scene is pure padding and may be cut out anyway'. I told him I was the director, not him. Lewis, on the other hand, I had a great admiration for, and when we did *Who Dares Wins*, a few years later, I said to him, his career should increase immensely now. Somehow he didn't seem that bothered if it did or not, and as we know, it didn't.

"In another scene, Martin is in the Capri having a chat with Lewis by radio (talking to Bodie about taking Anita to see a Luis Buñuel film). I seem to recall that for budgetary reasons, the only way to direct the scene was for me to have the passenger seat removed, so I could crouch down in the footwell, and prompt him his scenes. Those Capris were murder to work with. We had no duplicate vehicles, so had to wait for them to be available or get driven to the location from the studios, which usually held up filming. I wasn't that convinced that the script was up to scratch, but I have since been told it ranks among one of the show's best episodes. Ray must have liked it because he told me he'd like me to have another go in the future..."

The scenes involving Doyle meeting Anita were executed, on Thursday 14th August, at London House, (William Goodenough House), Mecklenburgh Square, West Central London. The location was visited by Mrs. Jones from the Mentally Handicapped Society who made a short 8mm film on a days filming on location with a film crew.

Phil Meheux (director): "A scene at the university book shop was not even filmed, due to Martin Shaw's constant complaining."

The story's conclusion, where Doyle confronts Lacoste, was filmed at St. Hubert's House, near Gerrards Cross, Buckinghamshire.

Rufus Andrews (unit manager): "What an odd place that was. Eerie. The owners of the house (Mr. & Mrs. Reed) were always dressed in nightgowns and bedclothes, no matter what time of the day it was. You'd look around and they were there, watching you. They followed the crew everywhere. Weird!"

Departing the production, after a disagreement with Phil Meheux, was first assistant director Dominic Fulford. His career had started back in the 1960's working on the Roger Moore series *The Saint*, *The New Avengers*, and by 1978 on features such as *Superman*.

Nick Daubeny (second assistant director): "Dom resigned. He'd had enough by this stage. Phil Meheux wanted to do things, like car stunts, without gaining permission. He asked me to go also, which I did. He'd been offered a position on the feature, *The Monster Club*."

Industry newcomer Simon Hinkly, who had just completed the Bob Hoskins film *The Long Good Friday*, took over as first assistant director for the last day of production on the episode.

Simon Hinkly: "I remember being told they'd just got rid of the first assistant, and I met the crew on the last days shoot at Windsor Great Park. I took over properly on the next episode, *Hijack*."

Gladys Pearce (continuity): "I also left at this point to do the underwater continuity on *Raise The Titanic*, which was being filmed in Malta."

Kay Mander assumed the position for the next episode, before Pat Rambaut took on the role.

Pat Rambaut (continuity): "I had been understudy to Renee Glynne on *The New Avengers* and that was hectic. After three episodes on *The Professionals*, I decided I didn't want to do it anymore. It was always rush,

rush, rush, and being in my early twenties, I was too young to get so stressed."

```
                    MARK I PRODUCTIONS LIMITED
                       "THE PROFESSIONALS"
                      CALL SHEET NO: 5

    EPISODE:  5 - "BLOOD SPORTS"       DATE:      FRIDAY,15TH.AUGUST,1980.
    DIRECTOR: PHIL MEHEUX               UNIT CALL: 7.30.AM LEAVE STUDIO
                                                   8.30.AM ON LOCATION
    SETS: (1) EXT.USED CAR LOT         SC.NOS:(1) 58.Day.
          (2) EXT.MEWS GARAGE                 (2) 59.61.63.Day.
          (3) EXT.ROOMING HOUSE               (3) 65.66.Day.
          (4) INT.ROOMING HOUSE               (4) 64.74.Day.
    LOCATIONS: (1) -   Crouch Hill Motors, Mount Pleasant Crescent, Stapleton Hill Road,N.4.
               (2) -   Ossian Mews, Ossian Road, London. N.4.
               (3)&(4) 86, Shaftesbury Road, London.N.19.

    ARTISTE              CHARACTER              MAKE-UP/HAIR           ON SET

    GORDON JACKSON       COWLEY                 From Second Unit
    MARTIN SHAW          DOYLE                  8.00.am.               8.30.am.
    LEWIS COLLINS        BODIE                  8.00.am.               8.30.am.
    HARRY TOWB           SPENCE                 7.45.am.               8.30.am.
    MIKE SAVAGE          OPERATOR               9.30.am.               10.00.am.
    STEPHEN BENT         NORMAN                 11.30.am.              12.00.noon.

    STAND-INS
    RON WATKINS for Mr.Jackson          -         -                    12.30.pm.
    BILL RISLEY for Mr.Shaw             -         -                    8.30.am.
    GERRY PARIS for Mr.Collins          -         -                    8.30.am.

    ACTION VEHICLES:  Via Production Office: Doyle's car - Capri(gold) Reg.No:
                                             CAR 576V - 8.30.am., on Location (1).
                      Via Art Dept:          Range of Second Hand cars including
                                             Jaguar to be in position on Location
                                             (1) by 8.30.am.
                                             Car being resprayed - to be on Location
                                             (2) by 9.30.am.
                      Via Kingsbury:         Norman's car - Old open top MG -
                                             12.00.noon on Location (3)
    PROPS:            As per script and to include: Sign on Jaguar(Sc.58.).
                      Sheets of newspaper, practical spray-paint gun with paint,
                      Daily Express, Doyle's RT bleeper and receiver(Scs.59-63).
                      Steel crutch and battered holdall for Norman(Scs.65,66,64.)
                      and contents of holdall which include: French, American and
                      English bank notes(Sc.74.).
    ART DEPT:         "FOR SALE" sign on Jaguar (Sc.58). Daily Express with
                      headline article on Cabreros killing(Sc.59.). Stickers and
                      flags to dress Car Lot.
    CATERING:         Tea on arrival. AM and PM breaks + lunch for 65 people.
    TRANSPORT:  (1)   UNIT CAR(Geoff) to pick-up Mr.Shaw at 7.40.am., and
                      convey to location by 8.00.am.
                (2)   UNIT CAR(Jeff) to pick-up Mr.Collins at 7.40.am., and
                      convey to location by 8.00.am.
                (3)   UNIT MINIBUS(Nick) - to leave studio at 7.30.am., and
                      be on location at 8.30.am.
```

The fifth call sheet issued for BLOOD SPORTS - a valuable insight in to a days filming on THE PROFESSIONALS: it is a document issued to the cast and crew of a production, informing them where and when they should report for a particular day of shooting. Call sheets also include other useful information such as contact information, the schedule for the day, which scenes and script pages are being shot, and the address of the shoot location.

Doyle (Martin Shaw), Cowley (Gordon Jackson) and Bodie (Lewis Collins) - no ordinary round of golf for THE PROFESSIONALS in the story BLOOD SPORTS.

Cast by director Phil Meheux in a minor role was a little known Irish actor, Pierce Brosnan, who would go onto a leading role in the American mini-series, *The Mannions*.

Esta Charkham (casting director): "He'd taken *The Professionals* part in order to pay the fare to fly to the United States to appear in it. Later he would star in *Remington Steele* before becoming James Bond in *Goldeneye*."

On Saturday 16th August, the second unit completed scenes for *It's Only A Beautiful Picture...*, which they had missed on Thursday 31st July. They ranged from establishing shots of Leicester Square to a Capri run-by on Fulham's Imperial Road.

A map of Burnham Beeches, Buckinghamshire, issued to the production team for a days filming (Tuesday 12th August 1980) on BLOOD SPORTS.

Hijack: *An East European official uses a swoop on the London Bullion Market to escape from behind the Iron Curtain - but he hasn't reckoned with CI5's involvement. Doyle prevents a murder attempt and Cowley derives great satisfaction from denting the man's plans.*

From Tuesday 26th August Martin Campbell directed the Roger Marshall script *Hijack*, which had been finalised on the 8th July (with further revisions added on 19th August).

On 19th August, a memorandum was issued to all production staff from producer Raymond Menmuir over concerns regarding the use of the Czech Embassy in the script:

Owing to advice just received from the Legal Department, we have to delete all references to the Czech Embassy, etc. and replace as indicated in the attached (referring to the amended pages of the script issued with this statement*). I apologise for this additional marking up of scripts, but think this method easier than issuing twenty odd new pages.*

In HIJACK, Rachel Davies played Deborah, Doyle's girlfriend, while British actor Stephen Yardley was Roy Swetman. Born (24th March 1942) in Ferrensby, North Yorkshire, he was raised in Essex and attended Brentwood public school. He made early TV appearances through the 1960's in series like DANGER MAN and had an extended run in Z CARS in 1967.

When broadcast, on the 30th November, rescheduled from the 16th November, this episode achieved 17.6 million viewers, and number three in the weekly ratings chart.

53. EXT. WATES ESTATE. DAY.

FORENSICS are working on garage where driver and guards were stashed.

UNIFORMED POLICE are doing house-to-house inquiries - talking to HOUSE OWNERS either side (did they see anything suspicious? Anything at all, etc.).

Ice cream truck - with Pied Piper message - passes through FRAME.

PAN with it to opposite side of street ... DOYLE and BODIE are sitting in their car.

54. INT. CI5 CAR. DAY.

DOYLE and BODIE - eating ice cream cones - watch activity across street.

> DOYLE
> ... out of the whole of London ...

> BODIE
> Not to mention the Home Counties.

> DOYLE
> Very true ... they choose a garage ...

> BODIE
> An <u>unlocked</u> garage.

> DOYLE
> Also true ... where the owners <u>happen</u> to be away, bucket-and-spading.

> BODIE
> Lucky, wouldn't you say.

> DOYLE
> (cryptic)
> Would I!

> BODIE
> So, what we saying - one of the rip-off gang lives round here?

> DOYLE
> (looking round)
> Why not? Suburbia - mortgage-land ... working wives ... Dalmation dogs ... probably has the next locker to you at the Golf Club.

> BODIE
> Or he knows Mister or Missus Holiday-Maker.

THEIR P.O.V. - HOUSE.

The WIFE - in brief shorts and sun top - comes out of house to do some tidying up in garden - cutting dead roses, etc.

> BODIE'S VOICE
> Wouldn't mind being tied-up in her garage.

RESUME SCENE.

As before.

> DOYLE
> Yeah. Do a bit in my garden any day.

> BODIE
> You don't have a garden.

> DOYLE
> (as if he'd forgotten)
> Don't I?

> BODIE
> NO!

DOYLE flicks his fingers: foiled again.

> DOYLE
> Suppose I could always buy a window box.

A deleted scene from THE PROFESSIONALS script HIJACK. Oddly this sequence was scheduled but never filmed.

By the time of the film diary's assembly, locations had still not been finalised for the vast majority of the scenes, which would need to be filmed for this instalment. Eventually, and with little time to spare, some scenes were filmed amid a car breaker's yard in South Wimbledon, London.

Rufus Andrews (unit manager): "Out of shot, one of the guys had to drive through the gates. Instead, he ended up hitting a railway sleeper and damaged the car. Shooting was held up while the car was fixed."

Jill Baker, who played Amanda, was required to spend part of her location time mounted on horseback. Jill wasn't comfortable with horses and this was confirmed during filming on 29th August at Black Park, Fulmer, Buckinghamshire, when the sequence with Martin Shaw and James Snell, who was portraying the hit man sent to kill her, was rehearsed just prior to filming. Jill's fears were further highlighted when James Snell was required to fire his weapon while she was mounted on horseback. Concerned that the noise made by the rifle might frighten her steed, she was assured that the horse had been trained not to react and all would be fine throughout filming. But when the time came, the horse promptly panicked and bolted!

Terry Yorke (stunt arranger): "We had to do a stunt in Black Park, involving Martin Shaw in the Capri and guest star, Jill Baker, on horseback. She was the target of an assassin and Martin had to block the horse, and her, from the gunshot, with his car. We had one problem. Jill couldn't ride. I taught her the basics in half a day! Just enough time to get things set up, and the filming done on time. I must say, that she did it very well."

Martin Campbell (director): "All of the action in James Bond (*Goldeneye*) I can attribute back to *The Professionals*. Everything I learnt in *The Professionals* is up there on screen in Bond. And it does seem incredible to me now that some of the stunts they pulled they did themselves; Martin Shaw was always doing his own stunts and did it very well, as did Lewis."

One of the tasks faced by location manager Peter Carter was to find a suitable location to portray the Embassy featured in the story. One of the locations he scouted was Peacock House, Kensington, West London. An ornate blue and green glazed-brick tiled mansion, this Grade I listed mansion was designed by architect Halsey Ricardo and built in 1906 for Ernest Debenham of the supermarket store of the same name. After an initial recce director Martin Campbell agreed the property contained the necessary appearance needed for the story. The script required that CI5 agent Murphy would follow Merhart by motorcycle as he left the Embassy. On the 3rd September, after filming a take of Murphy riding the motorbike, actor Steve Alder, began to turn the vehicle when it skidded on a patch of dry mud, causing it to fall on top of him, resulting in a bruised left knee and right shin. The injury was only superficial and filming continued.

Steve Alder (Murphy): "The bike I was riding actually fell down on top of me and hurt my ankle - I seem to recall that they had fitted the brakes on it incorrectly or something like that - I was a little bruised and they insisted we continued with the shot or we'd end up losing a half days shoot. That's how we used to work on the show - never mind the actors, let's just get the scene in the can; and Martin was always going on about that too. With Lew, the more dangerous it was, the better; he loved taking risks when they let him."

Silver bullion is being shipped into Britain via the Iron Curtain, only for it to be hijacked by one of the group's own officials. Martin Shaw takes a break in filming HIJACK for this publicity shot.

Director Martin Campbell cast Dave King (born 23rd June 1929), the blues singer turned comedian, as Harry Walter.

Dave King: "It was a very fast set to work on, and the director (Martin Campbell) was very military in his style, he'd say 'camera here...on the double....lights over there.....come on, come on!' His eagerness to get shots in the can and impress the producers came to a slight halt when we did the scenes on the dual carriageway near Pinewood Studios. This scene where the lorry is hijacked was filmed at a busy point of the day, and whereas local residents were well aware of the filming, the passing motorists in the busy road were not. We'd start a take, and cars would slow down and see what was going on, which didn't flow with the scene very well, especially when they started waving at the film crew. I remember one guy in a lorry saw Lewis Collins, and shouted out, 'Hey, Bodie! Give us a hand-brake turn mate!' Lew always loved the attention, but Martin usually shrugged his shoulders and wanted to get on with the scene in question."

With production on *Hijack* complete, the 'Daily Express', dated Saturday 6th September, printed that both Martin Shaw and Lewis Collins were finding the show a chore and that it was becoming stale.

Lewis Collins: "Both Martin and I felt there were severe limitations in the characters by this stage, and it was restricting not being able to tackle other offers that had come in, due to our commitment to the series."

ITV launched the new series on the 7th September beginning with the previous year's *The Acorn Syndrome*, which together with seven other episodes, was not shown due to the ITV dispute. In order to get the programmes broadcast the planning department paid no attention to continuity and would inter-mix episodes from the present fourth series, as and when, they became available (a total of fifteen episodes would be shown). The reason was simple: *The Professionals* was up against the BBC's *Shoestring*, starring Trevor Eve. Bodie and Doyle were not scheduled to grace the screens until December, but when LWT's director of programmes, Michael Grade, was made aware that the second *Shoestring* series was going ahead from the 5th October, *The Professionals* was deliberately brought forward.

You'll Be All Right: *Notorious villain Jack Stone seeks the services of Bodie and Doyle when his family become the pawns in a long-standing vendetta. Someone is putting the frighteners on his wife and kids - but why?*

Production commenced on Gerry O'Hara's *You'll Be All Right*, on Monday 8th September (the second draft of the script was approved on the 12th August), with newcomer to the show, John Crome picking up the director's reins. Crome went on to direct 'The Who' in their 1981 music video *You Better You Bet*.

Stock footage of the Isle of Wight (the Needles at Alum Bay and Parkhurst Prison) is used for establishing shots of the prisons.

John Crome (director): "This was my first drama. I had done commercials and documentaries. I was selected as I'd done several commercials using child actors and this story had a fair percentage of children in it. In pre-production talks Ray Menmuir told me that my method of directing should be in a similar vein to Martin Campbell. The other odd stipulation was that I was told to keep Martin and Lewis away from each other. By this time the scripts had made allocations to keep them apart. As I discovered they never seemed to be on set at the same time for long anyway; cars would pick them up and whisk them away to nightclubs, pubs, or whatever.

"Next was to cast the children, which we did at the Anna Scher Theatre School in Islington, London (which has produced such talent as Tim Roth and Kathy Burke). The boy, Jason Savage, impressed me when I asked him, 'So what do you hate the most?' he looked up, glared and said, 'People like you, asking me questions like this!'"

78. INT. SMALL SUPERMARKET. DAY.

CHRISSIE is pushing a trolley with a few items in it. She reaches the check-out, starts putting the goods on the counter. The CASHIER begins ringing up the prices.

CHRISSIE is puzzled when she finds a give-away pamphlet amongst the goods in the trolley. She turns it over. There is a written note on the other side.

INSERT: The note reads:

'Did he get the message?'

CHRISSIE reacts with horror, she turns around, looks down the two narrow avenues of goods. There is an anti-theft mirror suspended on one of the corridors - five or six shoppers are going about their business.

The CASHIER rings up the total.

> CASHIER
> (a sari-wrapped
> Indian girl)
> Three pounds, seventy-five, madam.

CHRISSIE searches distractedly for her money.

A short deleted scene from the original YOU'LL BE ALL RIGHT script.

"We stayed close to Lee Studios, Wembley, for much of the night shooting, using the stream, at the back of the house, simply because it was there. We also had an amusing night shoot with one of the Lee Lighting guys. He was an Essex gypsy lad, who was lifting some of the lights into position. As we were about to start shooting, we heard a Police car heading our way. The guy dropped the equipment, expensive stuff at that, and jumped over a wall into some bushes. He told me he'd done it just for a laugh, but I think there was more to it than that! The Police car just carried on going.

"When Lewis jumps through the fence in the final part, I thought it would be different to see that, instead of having him coming over the top, round the side or whatever. In the end, poor old Lewis charged through it with some force. Watch it and you'll see what I mean. I also decided that on the basic car run-bys, I didn't want panning shots from cameras set up on pavements. So we did the run-bys from moving vehicles using cameras positioned inside them, filming through back windows, etc. Again, I just wanted to be different from the norm.

Lewis Collins and Martin Shaw on the set of YOU'LL BE ALL RIGHT.

Actor Steve Alder was CI5 agent Murphy in YOU'LL BE ALL RIGHT.

"Much of the best camera work was lit by Norman Langley; Dusty Miller was the credited cameraman but there was always a lot of switching due to scheduling difficulties. The scheduling problems were mainly due to the night shooting, and the fact that Martin and Lewis refused to spend more than one minute on set than they needed to be. That is why they had cars standing by to take them home between scenes (this was a standard actors contract clause). What it meant was we had to get the most out of the blocks of scenes with each actor so that we didn't lose them too often. Added to that, was the fact that at that time they were barely talking to each other - I can only speculate why?"

The scene involving Chrissie crashing the car underwent a number of changes from what was initially planned in both the script and the filming schedule. The sequence was originally scripted thus:

Ext: Streets & shop front
Chrissie ran the car up onto the pavement, avoiding a shopkeeper and plunging head on into the wide, plate-glass window of an antique shop.
Ext: Street & Bodie's flat
Bodie was jogging round the block, just after six in the morning, and was just passing his car when Control made contact with him about the crash.
COWLEY: *She's smashed the car. Eastern Way. The police are there now.*
BODIE: *Oh God. How are they?*
COWLEY: *Bruised, but alive. 45's on his way.*

Producer Ray Menmuir decided the stunt would be too costly to mount, and the script was duly amended; the car hits a mobile snack bar at the entrance to a park cycleway.

Rufus Andrews (unit manager): "We'd been given a Morris Minor to be used by the Stone family. However, director John Crome decided it looked too new and shiny, so I volunteered to drive it around and bash it up a little. I drove it to Camden Lock and scraped it along a wall. Only 'minor' damage I might add."

In YOU'LL BE ALL RIGHT, casting director Esta Charkham choose Geraldine Sherman (pictured above) to play Chrissie Stone, opposite British actor Derrick O'Connor as Jack Stone, who was one of the brothers in the Euston drama FOX. Geraldine, born (20th October 1944) in Hampton Court, Surrey, took the part when she visited London with her husband, Jamie (Oscar Hammerstein's son), who was, at the time, directing OKLAHOMA in Britain.

Kickback: *Bodie's loyalty to C15 is placed on the line when a ghost from his SAS past reenters his life. Lured into joining a gang of ruthless terrorists in the role of a hired assassin, he finds his allegiances tested to the full.*

On Monday 22nd September *Kickback*, by Stephen Lister, saw another new director join the show. Ian Sharp (born in Clitheroe, Lancashire on 13th November, 1946) worked at the BBC making documentaries first for the General Features Department and then for Music and Arts, notably *Arena* and *Omnibus*. In 1978 the BBC gave him three months sabbatical to make a movie called *The Music Machine*, and it was this experience that fired his ambition to turn to film drama. His first break came in 1980 on the *Minder* episode *All Mod Cons*.

Gerry O'Hara (script editor): "I encouraged Stephen Lister to produce another script and he did this, which I was very proud of. It had Bodie and an SAS colleague going undercover to prevent a killing, by faking it. It was the first episode directed by Ian Sharp. I was astonished by his cleverness as a director. There's a battle between a car and a helicopter which I thought was brilliantly done, knowing how incredibly difficult it was to do dangerous work like that within our schedules."

Ian Sharp (director): "Getting that done wasn't easy as producer Ray Menmuir was a hard man; if you didn't turn up with the goods you were out so *The Professionals* was a very hard training ground for me. When we had the pre-production meeting you had to say what you wanted and give a reason why you wanted it. So if you wanted a dolly or crane, or use a helicopter for a gun fight like in *Kickback*, then you had to explain why you wanted it, and you had better use it otherwise you were on the carpet the next morning, and we'd start shooting the next day very early. It was a good training ground and very disciplined, and I've never regretted it."

The sequence involving the helicopter was slightly amended when in the script, the car, driven by stuntman Marc Boyle, meets up with a tractor in a narrow country lane and crashes in a nearby field. However, in the finished product the car overturns in a field after hitting a tractor/plough while being pursued by the helicopter.

Prop man Barry Arnold added the padding to the anti-roll bars, which were fixed to form a protective shell around the car's interior. And Marc was also kitted out in padded gear before getting in. The windscreen had a hole knocked into it so that it would shatter spectacularly. A specially angled ramp was set up and camouflaged. All Marc had to do was to get his speed up to 50mph and, because it was tilted to just the right angle, it would roll the vehicle over. The stunt suitably impressed the producers that Ian Sharp became the show's resident second unit director.

Peter Brayham (stunt arranger): "When we roll a car it doesn't just happen, we have to make sure that the speed, weight distribution, timing, everything, is absolutely right. It takes at least four days preparation and three or four cameras, if I could get them, to film it. I once turned over an eight-seater 1936 Buick limousine, when I was told it couldn't be done."

Jo Hidderley (camera clapper/loader): "I was nearly knocked unconscious by the helicopter. We had set up the camera to focus on the helicopter, which wasn't really that far off the ground. As I had to get the clapperboard in front of the lens, and also out of shot, my back was to the helicopter. As it approached I felt the gush of wind from the blades overhead and it was enough to make me think, 'Shit, that was close!' After the take I was told that the helicopter's skids had been only a few inches from the top of my head."

Ted Hawes (stills photographer): "I remember the photo-shoot that was called upon that day. It had been arranged that we'd do a stills session with Lewis Collins running up and then dangling from one of the helicopter skids, despite the fact that in the episode Lewis' scenes were actually shot with him in the helicopter. I'm pretty sure the producers decided that the original idea of having him chasing the car while holding onto the outside of the helicopter was deemed way too dangerous. However, we still managed to get our stills session as the helicopter wasn't that far from the ground. Not to be outdone, and to highlight the rivalry between the two stars, Martin Shaw decided he would also have a go, despite his character not even appearing in the scene."

In KICKBACK Bodie (Lewis Collins) and Keller, an old acquaintance from his days in the SAS, go undercover in order to trap a would-be assassin.

Producer Ray Menmuir had to hire or approve the appointment of every single person involved in the production.

Ray Menmuir: "You sometimes have a nose for talent. Sometimes you know the work a person has done and you know their reputation. Sometimes, they are newcomers (referring to Ian Sharp), but something tells you that they have the talent to do the job. It's instinctive. That's what makes a producer or a director. Once I'd given them the job to do, I had to let them get on with it, their way. No two people think alike and there were times when you wanted to suggest what you yourself would do. You just had to bite your tongue and hope they'd deliver what was expected from them.

"What we couldn't control was what I call the 'organic influence'. It's an organic thing that develops as it goes along. Each actor responds in different ways to different things and as a producer you watch it happen. If you see things happen which you like, then you make sure that you develop it. Personally, I don't talk about these unconscious reactions to anyone - the fewer people who know about them the better otherwise it becomes a conscious effort on behalf of the actors and could be spoiled. Suffice to say that Lewis and Martin responded in different ways in different situations and I hope I helped to bring out the best in them!"

During Cowley and Nairn's 'park' meeting the two actors (Gordon Jackson and James Faulkner) nearly bumped into a children's climbing frame as unit manager Rufus Andrews explains:

Rufus Andrews (unit manager): "What looked like a simple scene to shoot turned out a bit of a headache; the two actors were so engrossed in getting their lines right, after numerous takes, that they almost walked straight into the climbing frame. We'd had constant interruptions during the day as Kensington Gardens was crawling with kids. And they just were not listening to us to get out of shot."

CI5's Bodie (Lewis Collins) on location 'underwater' in KICKBACK.

An incident occurred while filming the sequences at Myddelton Square, Finsbury, North London that members of the production crew would not forget!

Rufus Andrews (unit manager): "I nearly got punched by one of the residents there. Mike Collins, the special effects guy, had rigged up that a red door, on one of the houses, had to be propelled through the air to simulate the house being blown up. As ever, he broke every rule in the book, and went mad with the explosive. The door hurtled past the crew and ended up half way across the road. One of the residents emerged from the cloud of smoke and threatened to 'knock my block off'. He hadn't been told of the filming, or the explosion, and due to the deafening noise, his budgie had a heart attack and died! With this, the fire brigade and police turned up, as another resident had called them thinking the street was on fire. They had been informed of what was happening and calmed the situation down."

Ian Sharp (director): "My favourite quote was to Mike Collins (or Dr. Death as he was affectionately known) immediately after the massive explosion; when we had all got over the devastation caused by his over-enthusiasm, Lewis Collins turned to him and in his best Michael Caine accent said, 'You were only supposed to blow the bloody door off!' "

Malcolm Smith, who was in charge of the camera grips (handles, rails, etc), recalled an amusing incident during filming on location in West London.

Malcolm Smith: "We were filming at Cadby Hall, Hammersmith. The scene involved a stunt where Martin Shaw is hanging out of a speeding yellow van. As the van drove off, Martin was supposed to be holding onto the back doors, but he couldn't keep his grip and fell out. That caused a few laughs amongst the camera crew, and we had to set up the shot again."

Location manager Peter Carter had arranged with Keith Sargent, of the Islington Borough Council Press & Publicity office, North London, that a car stunt could be safely staged at the Royal Agricultural Hall, Liverpool Road, Islington, which had laid derelict since the early 1970's.

Chris Streeter (transportation co-ordinator): "During the car chase, filmed inside the derelict building, the Capri was scratched quite badly and the front panel creased. The scene was shot while the Lord Mayor of London (Sir Peter Gadsden) was paying us a visit and I seem to recall it took us a few weeks before we could fix the Capri. When we did, we couldn't match the paint, and even Martin Shaw commented about the different shade. We took great pride in looking after the cars loaned to us by Ford. The others, from Kingsbury Motors or 99 Cars, we hammered to death."

Discovered In A Graveyard: *The victim of a terrorist bullet, Doyle lies close to death, a deep-seated despair depriving him of the will to live. Together with other CI5 agents, Bodie tracks down the girl responsible - but arrives too late to save her life.*

Monday 6th October saw director Anthony Simmons taking control of *Discovered In A Graveyard*. Writer Christopher Wicking submitted a story, which Mark 1 had approved on 12th September (with further revisions on 24th September).

Doyle has a framed epitaph/poem on his bedroom wall, 'Discovered In A Graveyard - Baltimore 1692', which reads:

Go placidly amid the noise and haste...and remember what peace there may be in silence. Do not distress yourself with imaginings; many fears are born of fatigue and loneliness. You are a child of the universe, no less than the trees and the stars. Be at peace with God, whatever you conceive Him to be; in the noisy confusion of life, keep peace with your soul. With all it's shame, and drudgery, and broken dreams, it is still a beautiful world.

The poem was in reality called 'Desiderata' and written by Max Ehrmann in 1927. Despite the implication the title is Latin for 'Things To Be Desired' and not 'Discovered In A Graveyard'.

When Bodie calls in the licence number of Mayli's yellow Citroen 2CV, he rather oddly quotes an old RAF version of the phonetic alphabet: 'George William Leonard 656 Jane' rather than the usual 'Golf Whiskey Lima...Juliet'.

There's also a sequence of Doyle shopping accompanied by Mozart's Piano Concerto No.21 (the 'Elvira Madigan'), which was inserted at the request of Martin Shaw; Mozart being one of his favourite composers.

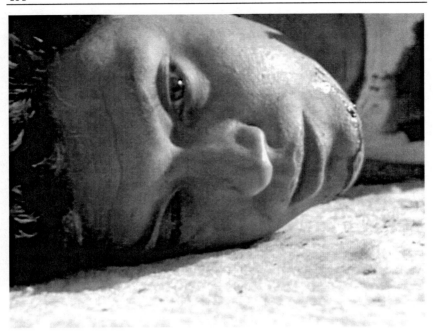

Whilst investigating a bombing plot Doyle (Martin Shaw) is shot and left for dead in his flat. A scene from DISCOVERED IN A GRAVEYARD.

Christopher Wicking (writer): "I actually got away with a sort of miniature *A Matter Of Life And Death* in this one, where Doyle gets shot and spends most of the show in a coma, while we go into fantasy sequences in his subconscious mind as he tries to rationalise his life, which seems mainly to consist of killing people, and decides whether or not to die. I say 'got away with', but this is unfair, Ray (Menmuir) and Gerry (O'Hara) were both excited by the idea, and the challenge involved in pulling it off. Director, Tony Simmons laboured long and lovingly over it. I was pleased to write something 'personal' while seeing how far the series framework could be stretched."

Lighting cameraman Norman Langley remembered vividly how much extra effort went into the filming of this episode:

Norman Langley (lighting cameraman): "Anthony Simmons and I spent the first week of the two weeks' preparation time out of the studio wandering around London, looking at the locations and discussing the script. The script was different to the normal run of *The Professionals* so we had to come up with something. Tony on that first week was very shell-shocked because he had just lost a big movie he was directing, after a disagreement with the director of photography. This show had to be very good to get his confidence back. After many stops for coffee and the odd drink at lunchtime and lots of soul searching on his part we came up with a plan. The visuals were mainly my ideas and he let me have a free hand."

In DISCOVERED IN A GRAVEYARD Doyle is shot and as the hospital fights to save his life, Bodie (Lewis Collins) goes on a chase to find his partner's assailant.

Anthony Simmons (director): "I had just left the set of the movie *Green Ice* for which I'd been doing pre-production work for over twelve months. I was left with little alternative but to hand the movie over to another director, and headed off to Florida for a short break to try and cool off. This is when I received the call from Gerry O'Hara saying he needed help with a script that he really wanted to do. On seeing the script I was immediately impressed with the quality of the writing but Gerry and myself decided to change quite a few scenes before we were happy with the final draft for filming. We added more to the 'fantasy-dream' sequences, making these much longer and more prominent. It isn't that evident on playback, but all these scenes were slightly slowed down to fewer frames than normal and under-exposed to give them a more dark and gloomy feel. Due to the ever so slight slowing down of the frames we had to overlay the voice track again which meant post production on this episode ran a little longer than normal. This wasn't a problem because Ray Menmuir, on top of the usual ten days of filming, allowed us a little extra time to get this show right both in pre- and post production.

"Martin Shaw spent much of his shooting time in a hospital bed, and kept telling everyone he was 'having a well-deserved rest!' He seemed to take the episode full on, and never failed to put in that little extra effort to get all his death-bed scenes right, agreeing to have his chest hair shaven to add that extra reality to the end result. Playing the character of Mayli, was Megami Shimanuki - in her first major acting role. Her fresh face was a welcome addition, even though her English may not have been the best. She never failed to impress, and was always willing to go that extra mile to get things right."

The conclusion to the story was originally scripted with a much longer tag scene set in the hospital, but was ultimately trimmed from the shooting schedule for timing reasons.

Int: Hospital

Bodie visits Doyle at the hospital. Bodie brings Doyle a bunch of grapes.
BODIE: *How are you, Raymond?*
DOYLE: *Punctured.*

Mayli Kuolos (Megumi Shimanuki) in DISCOVERED IN A GRAVEYARD.

BODIE: *Do you like grapes?*
DOYLE: *Love 'em.*
BODIE: (eats a grape) *Me too.*
DOYLE: *Cowley told me about the girl.*
BODIE: *A pretty pair of almond eyes. She asked after you, just at the end*
DOYLE: *How touching. How did you find out about her?*
BODIE: (grins) *You told me.*
DOYLE: *I did?*
BODIE: *Sort of. Whatever was going on in that head of yours, it was certainly dramatic.*

DOYLE: *Like a bad dream. The shooting, her face, her eyes, the feeling of being dead. A vivid, very bad dream. A death dream, I suppose.*
BODIE: *But you didn't die. I wouldn't let you.*
DOYLE: *I suppose I was technically dead when they were operating. From what Siegel tells me.*
BODIE: *Yeah, okay. In that sense I suppose you did 'die'. For a few minutes.*
DOYLE: (grins) *Well there you go. And I can tell you this. Having done it once, it won't be so bad the next time...*

DISCOVERED IN A GRAVEYARD: Doyle (Martin Shaw) is gunned down.

Mike Collins (special effects supervisor): "The explosion of the van in the opening sequences was no trick. We really did blow it up. We need to know where the camera crew can be placed safely without being hit by debris, which in this case was behind the wall. We use what's called 'ringers' for vehicles that need to be totally destroyed. We find an identical van or car to the one being driven; usually, it's a written off vehicle from a breakers yard and rig that up. We filmed the stunt in the car park of a sports centre (Sobell Sports Centre, Holloway, North London) as we couldn't get permission to do an explosion anywhere near the hotels."

Meanwhile, Lewis Collins had been asked to try out a new, very fast and very expensive Porsche for ATV's *Motor Show '80* programme broadcast on Wednesday 15th October.

Lewis Collins: "We went down to a track near Lichfield, Staffordshire. I couldn't believe it; the track is a figure-of-eight and so small it's like driving round the block. I'm told they have racing down there but you'd have to be crazy to try your hand at it. I had never driven a car like that before. I told the film crew, who were in a helicopter as well as on the ground, I'd take it round and see how it held the road but they, of course, said they were running out of time, they only had a few hundred feet of film left and would I get a move on? So I said, 'O.K, I'll give it a whirly first time round'. I managed to spin straight off the track. And they left it in the programme just to show that Lewis Collins can make mistakes - but even the best professional drivers can do that."

An explosive start to DISCOVERED IN A GRAVEYARD after the van being followed by Bodie and Doyle bursts into flames behind a West End Hotel in London. More tricks from the bag of 'Dr. Death', Mike Collins - the special effects supervisor.

Foxhole On The Roof: *Roddy Barker and his henchman Stacey combine to make life difficult for Cowley's team. Armed with an arsenal of weapons, they build a rooftop fortress and place a nearby hospital under siege.*

Foxhole On The Roof, scripted by Brian Clemens (with some uncredited help from Dennis Spooner), began filming on Monday 20th October, under the control of director Bill Brayne.

Roddy Barker (Stanley Meadows) is released from prison and visits his old friend Jack Cobber (Ron Pember) to reveal his latest plan. However, Cobber isn't prepared to go along with his old colleague, leaving Barker to set up a FOXHOLE ON THE ROOF of a derelict warehouse near the River Thames; here he shows CI5 what can be done if his demands are not met....

This episode, when broadcast on the 7th November 1982 (as the opener to the televised fifth series), achieved 13.7 million viewers (in the new slot of 9:15 on Sunday nights), and fourth place in the weekly ratings chart.

Brian Clemens (creator and co-executive producer): "We had to bring in steeplejacks and mountaineers to show us how to tackle the chimney climb, involving Lewis Collins and Steve Alder. The two actors had to be coached in sophisticated mountaineering techniques, though we did use stand-ins for the long shots. But Lewis and Steve took it in their stride."

The scene showed the two men climbing the chimney and the tense moment when Murphy is shot and hangs limp from his climbing harness. But climbing up a real factory chimney was one stunt that needed the real experts,

the professional stunt men, and brought in were two professionals who were highly trained climbers.

The chimney utilised for the action was further along Rotherhithe Street, South East London (at Lavender Dock, by the 'Dock pump house'), from where the bulk of the 'foxhole' sequences were shot at Chambers Wharf Cold Storage depot - which at the time was being used by Courage breweries.

After serving a 25-year prison term a recently released criminal puts a hospital under siege from a fortified foxhole on top of a nearby building. Bodie (Lewis Collins) scales a nearby chimney in order to gain a vantage point in FOXHOLE ON THE ROOF.

Bill Brayne (director): "*Foxhole on the Roof* was our most expensive episode. It was about an idea, which could have originated in the 1930's or 1950's - someone climbs a factory chimney. In the UK in the 1980's there were few, which were not all demolished in the phase of modernising from the 1960's. We needed to find a very long one, and we needed a decent climber too. Stuntmen are specialists and in fact there are not many jobs where one must climb a chimney. Then we finally found this mountain climber who worked in a sports business. He said 'Yes, no problem. I needn't see it'. Of course I said, 'I would like you to handle it once at least'. In the event these chimney scenes took ages to set up and when the climber arrived he needed six hours to reach the top. They were very complex scenes to complete for a TV film at the time."

The long shots were taken of the two climbers kitted out as Bodie and Murphy. For them it was just another day's work, but there was one moment when all didn't go as planned. The Murphy stand-in got quite a shock when he acted out the scene where Murphy is wounded and topples from the top of the chimney. He unexpectedly ended up hanging virtually upside-down from the harness - an angle he hadn't anticipated!

Gerry O'Hara (script editor): "When the guy on the chimney does what looks like a 20 foot fall; I still think is one of the most frightening pieces of film I've ever seen."

The close-up shots of Lewis Collins and actor Steve Alder were mocked up, not back the film studio, but in the grounds of the Chambers Wharf Cold Storage warehouse. The chimney top was cleverly reconstructed, standing around 35-feet high, with the camera crew using a scaffolding rosta to get their shots.

Steve Alder (Murphy): "I particularly recall filming this episode which we did down by Chambers Wharf where my character was up the chimney with Bodie. I spent most of it hanging upside down! We filmed that quite late in the year and it was very cold and wet - mind you, we weren't really up there; they had constructed a mock-up of the top part of the chimney on the ground, and both mine and Lew's scenes were filmed from the ground looking up. I wanted to climb the chimney for real, as I was a keen climber, but they (the production company) wouldn't allow it, as I wouldn't be covered by the insurance. I remember seeing the episode for the first time on the TV, and thought how convincing it looked. Actors were never asked to see the rushes, or even the completed show, so I had to wait to see that on the box, some time later."

The scene, where Roddy dashes across the rooftop and grabs the ladder to soar away into the sky, required quite a bit of meticulous preparation by the crew. Stuntman Del Baker needed a protective harness - and a wig! Hairdresser, Sue Love, fitted the grey false hair in place. It had to be stuck with double-sided tape and glue in order for it not to fly off with the first gust of wind.

Gerry O'Hara: "That was some heavy stuff. We'd actually got him (Del Baker) dangling on a rope off a helicopter flying across the Thames past Tower Bridge and the Houses Of Parliament. It was quite a dangerous stunt, but the guys always liked taking risks in the name of authenticity."

CI5's Ray Doyle (Martin Shaw) in a scene from FOXHOLE ON THE ROOF.

Roddy Barker's target was a hospital, and production manager Ron Purdie recalled that the reason the school was chosen to act as a hospital was that it was a half-term holiday, so making it easy to shoot the relevant scenes.

The contemporary setting of *The Professionals* ensured that make-up and hair dressing requirements were small-scale in terms of a drama series. Only on the days when large numbers of extras were needed was additional help required. The various injury effects and make-up transitions required were frequently complicated by the need to create and develop them out of narrative order. The need to maintain continuity in a schedule often shot out of sequence is a crucial feature of the work in both make-up and costume. To help ensure absolute continuity, both departments, as usual, compiled continuity books noting all the relevant visual details and containing Polaroid photographs of the actors at the end of each sequence shot.

Make up girl Sue Black spent years as a beautician in D. H Evans store in London's Oxford Street, before a newspaper advertisement for trainees for the BBC make up department sent her into the film industry, working on programmes like *Pebble Mill* and *The Benny Hill Show*.

Sue Black: "I used to hang around for hours on end, sometimes in the freezing cold and rain, usually not needed at all, but I had to be always waiting around for a director's call. You have to be a different sort of person to someone who clings to a staff job. It was not knowing where you were going to be, and what you were going to be called upon to do, that was the exciting thing about the series. For instance, the smell from Chambers Wharf was awful.

"I used Max Factor Pan-stick a lot because it was light in texture but covered well. Martin and Lewis' only problem was they had heavy beard lines, especially at the end of the day, but we had electric razors on hand. Gordon was never a problem. He liked to look natural and healthy. He was a perfect gentleman and even used to bring us cups of tea.

"I would also be responsible for simulating scratches, bruises, black eyes, bullet wounds and all manor of physical injuries. Martin used to like his neck massaging in the morning and as I was a fully trained masseuse, I did that too. We had a great nicknames for Ray Menmuir, by changing his surname we called him 'Ray Manure', and as he only had four fingers on one hand we used to say he'd got 'his hand caught in the till'. The stunt boys used to go around saying, ' be careful or he'll give you a bunch of fours!'

"I was promised a ride in the helicopter by the pilot, Captain Alan Davies, but in the end I wasn't allowed, as I wasn't insured by the production company. That upset me a bit, because I was really looking forward to that as I'd never been up in a helicopter before."

Rufus Andrews (unit manager): "Things didn't always run smoothly on this one. One day we turned up at the Chambers Wharf warehouse and we'd been locked out and the brewery press office wouldn't let us have the keys as, apparently, the producers hadn't paid for filming on that day. It was, of course, a mix up, and they did eventually let us in."

Jo Hidderley (camera clapper/loader): "I remember the huge array of fans that had followed Martin Shaw and Lewis Collins to the Chambers Wharf location. They were forever chasing the guys around, looking for autographs and glimpses of them in action. I was in the camera car one day, when a couple of kids asked me to get Martin's autograph. Kids would usually knock on the window and pose the request. I eventually just used to get some scraps of paper from the floor and write the names out myself. The kids used to go off 'happy as Larry'. I swear they weren't all there, because some of them had even witnessed me doing it!"

The Ojuka Situation: *President Ojuka, the deposed head of the African State of Betan, is in London seeking Britain's help to regain his position. Agents Bodie and Doyle are assigned to guard him - but treachery follows their every step.*

The Ojuka Situation, penned by David Humphries, who had submitted stories for *Target*, *Minder* and *Shoestring* and scripted the films *The Stud* and *Quadrophenia*, entered production on Monday 2nd November (less than a week after being approved), under the control of director Christopher King.

Christopher King: "The great skill in putting those two boys together was that in Lewis Collins you had a personality actor and then you had Martin, who had come out of the RSC playing gritty roles.

"There was something really magical that happened on screen because they fired off each other in such a brilliant way. You'd see Martin working to find the reality in a scene and Lewis, because he was the personality actor, could take a scene just by lifting an eyebrow."

Initial proceedings took place on location at Haileybury Junior School, Imperial Road, Windsor, Berkshire, where the crew spent two days filming. First assistant director Gregory Dark, who'd previously worked on LWT's *Dick Turpin* TV series, and the feature *Carry On Emmanuelle*, recalled the shoot:

Gregory Dark (first assistant director): "Along the front of the school was a long wall and while filming was taking place the kids all lined up behind it. They looked like birds perching on a telegraph line!

"While escorting Ojuka to the hotel, where the conference is taking place, a dramatic car chase ensues and this was filmed in the glorious countryside at Burnham Beeches, Buckinghamshire. We filmed that very late in the day and we were losing daylight hours, so we rushed it. On screen, you'll see that the Capri crashes and gets damaged. Well, it did for real! We'd rigged up a kind of ramp, but Lewis missed it and buckled the front suspension and the front of the car; it had to be towed away as it was no longer driveable."

When an assassination attempt is made on a deposed African dictator Cowley (Gordon Jackson) and Bodie (Lewis Collins) become involved in THE OJUKA SITUATION.

After our trio escape from the woods they seek refuge at the nearest hotel, in reality the Burnham Beeches Hotel. The script originally had the hotel in Reigate, but it's mentioned on screen as The Beeches, near Slough, an ad-libbed line from Lewis Collins.

American actor Clarke Peters guest starred as Colonel Ojuka and shared some amusing moments on set with Lewis Collins. Between filming scenes in the stories conclusion at Leys Farm, Burnham, Buckinghamshire, a piece of rope became the source of enjoyment. The rope was one of the props for the show and it gave Peters a chance to prove that Paul Daniels was not the only star with magic hands, when with one hand he flicked the rope and - hey presto - it tied itself into a knot. It left Collins fascinated!

Charles Dance and Clarke Peters guest starred in THE OJUKA SITUATION. Charles was born (10th October 1946) in Redditch, Worcestershire, and studied graphic design at art school in Leicester. He was coached in acting by two retired RADA actors, which led to work at the Royal Shakespeare Company. American actor Clarke was born (7th April, 1952) in New York City, USA, and grew up in Englewood, New Jersey. He moved to London in the 1970's and one of his first acting roles was in THE PROFESSIONALS.

What you didn't get to see on screen were the unusual audience that watched the filming at the farmhouse and proved a headache for the sound crew. A whole flock of birds nesting in a nearby ivy spent much of the time chirping and chattering incessantly.

David Crozier (sound recordist): "The sound was recorded live and not post-synchronised - added on afterwards in a special studio, so the birds caused us problems. We had to wait for the little blighters to stop."

Crozier operated a special trolley, which served as a mobile sound unit. It was an invention, which grew out of the series, and the problems faced by the sound team. The main problem was that filming moved from one location to another very frequently, sometimes four times in one day. He needed equipment, therefore, that could be packed up quickly and moved on and which could be ready to go again in record time. Bit, by bit, more refinements were added to the trolley and it even had a large striped fishing umbrella for work on rainy days.

The machine, which recorded the sound, was a NAGRA tape recorder using 1/4-inch tape and by means of a mixer panel, it could take up to seven different microphones at once. What it recorded was later linked to the film, which had been shot by a special crystal pulse recorded on a special sound track running down the centre of the tape. The track was then used by the transfer machine back at the laboratories to transfer accurately the sound onto the 16mm separate magnetic track used in editing.

David Crozier: "It was just like a domestic tape recorder, but upgraded. It would work in any temperature and still be reliable. It even used to run in the rain safely and could be used in conditions of high vibration like in the back of a car going at speed. Another problem we had were the sensitive microphones would pick up any sounds, like the birds for instance, but even aeroplanes and dogs barking used to get picked up. I was also responsible for recording Bodie and Doyle's 'walkie-talkie' voice and the crew would also communicate by radio. These were constantly on the blink and needed lots of attention."

The Sound Department was also responsible for hiding away tiny radio microphones, hence no wires, on the actors so that they couldn't be seen by the viewers.

Don Hawkins (maintenance engineer and third sound man): "Even that required lots of skill, for if they were placed against prickly or abrasive clothing, the rubbing sound as it chafed against the microphone would be picked up on the tape. And every time the actor changed costumes, we'd have to check the microphones again. It became very interesting when it came to women. We had to be clever at finding places to put them. They needed to be two to three inches from the mouth so if they were wearing a deep neckline, it could be tucked into the collar. We even used the bra to hide them, but it was all done as tactfully as possible."

Operation Susie: *Two teenage overseas students are found to be drug traffickers. But why does somebody in high places want them dealt with quietly? Cowley and his team discover the answer - and Bodie and Doyle find themselves hunted men.*

Ranald Graham's *Operation Susie* began filming on Monday 17th November, under the control of Ian Sharp, in a plot involving the death of two drug-dealing student revolutionaries, drawing CI5 into a deadly game to protect the third.

On Monday 10th November, one week before filming on *Operation Susie* was due to begin, director Ian Sharp and key members of his production team embarked on a recce of the chosen locations. At this stage, all the sites had been decided upon with the exception of the scenes centred on the hotel streets. These scenes were mainly composed of car run-bys and a few subtle stunts.

Rufus Andrews (unit manager): "We had to do a car stunt with Doyle's gold Capri near Queensway/Inverness Place in Bayswater, London. I told Peter Carter, our location guy, it would be difficult to do it here. It was just too busy. For budgetary reasons, it was too late to change it, and it was very hairy watching Martin do the skid. Lewis and he were always competing against each other, placing bets on who could do the best car stunts.

"We also had problems at St. Bernard's Hospital, near Southall. At the time it was a lunatic asylum; the inmates were forever walking into shot and interrupting the filming. Quite frightening really."

Martin Shaw, Gordon Jackson, and Lewis Collins during a break in filming OPERATION SUSIE.

Martin Shaw and Lewis Collins were also still causing problems, both claiming they were feeling trapped and wanting to quit the show. Creator and co-executive producer, Brian Clemens, issued the following harsh words in a press statement:

Brian Clemens (Mark 1 Productions press statement: November 17th 1980): "I'm sorry to hear from time to time that the boys don't want to do any more programmes. I can accept that screaming around corners in a car on two wheels can get boring after a while, but I am also aware of a lack of loyalty in our profession at the moment. I think it's a young man's malaise. I know that Gordon Jackson is professional enough to continue as long as London Weekend want to go on screening the show. Stars who quit television at their peak all too often find themselves on the road to obscurity - what has Farrah Fawcett achieved since she left *Charlie's Angels*? We finish making the current series just before Christmas and if LWT want another one I think Lewis Collins will find he hasn't got much say in the matter. But if they don't, then I hope he'll go out and get a proper job!"

The original script had a much longer sequence involving Bodie and Doyle at the Magistrates Court and was scripted as follows.

Ext: Magistrates Court: Doyle's car
Bodie and Doyle empty their pockets of ID and Bodie puts them in the glove-box.
BODIE: *Park back down the road a way. We'll pick up a car from that row by the houses.*
DOYLE: *Are we doing this because we love him, or our jobs?*

BODIE: (grins and shakes his head) *What's the matter? Looking for some extra motivation?*
DOYLE: *We can't all be Hamlet.*
BODIE: *Rescuing a damsel in distress, and she's certainly in distress.*
DOYLE: *Aren't you supposed to be in love with the woman?*
BODIE: *Work on it.*
DOYLE: *Aren't damsels supposed to be young, innocent, and vulnerable?*
BODIE: *She's young. But you can't have everything. Besides, we're no knights on white chargers.*
DOYLE: *Peasants with a smoke bomb.*
BODIE: *What a good idea.*
Bodie opens the boot of the car and Doyle finds a small. Silver canister.
DOYLE: *Visibility's good.*
BODIE: *Got this funny feeling there's afternoon fog due.*
DOYLE: *It's chance. We'd have to move fast.*
BODIE: *But if Cowley's right, they'll be making a strike at her as she leaves court*
DOYLE: (looks at his watch) *Talking of which.* (Looks at the parked cars) *Ford Cortina?*
BODIE: *Don't like the steering. How about a Rover 2000?*
DOYLE: *I'm not travelling in anything that looks so much like a Citroen. Had a Citroen once. Nearly killed me in repair bills. What about...?*
BODIE: *What about something foreign?*
DOYLE: *Why not?*

The script fell foul of story editor Gerry O'Hara's scissors once more and the original closing tag scene was dropped:

<u>Ext: Old South Bank Rail terminal</u>
Diana Molner's body is put in the ambulance.
COWLEY: *I'm sorry this had to happen.*
DOYLE: *Me too. She was a nice kid.*
COWLEY: *They're all nice kids to start with. But Diana Molner and her brother did not die in vain.*
BODIE: *How's that, Sir?*
COWLEY: *There's been a coup in Escondia. Reports are just coming in. General Olivares has been replaced.*
DOYLE: *So...so her father was behind her all the time?*
COWLEY: *Unlikely. I should imagine the cocaine racket, to get money for guns, was a crackpot scheme of their own. They hatched it up after Diana met Philip Latimer, the chemist.*
DOYLE: *Crackpot. Yet it might have worked.*
BODIE: *Except for Northcott.*
COWLEY: *Northcott's intervention may well have forced General Molner to play his hand.*
DOYLE: *Apart from perverting our foreign policy, what was Northcott getting out of it?*
COWLEY: *It's a little bit early to say.*
BODIE: *A China pig in Switzerland, with a slot in its back?*
COWLEY: *We'll find out.*
Cowley walks away to his car.

DOYLE: *Sir? Just one more thing.*
BODIE: *Two things.*
DOYLE: *His job...And mine...*
COWLEY: (picks up the car R/T) *Alpha One to Control. Operation Susie is closed, as of now.* Agents Three-Seven and Four-Five are fully reinstated as CI5 operatives (Cowley drives off).
DOYLE: *Did he thank us?*
BODIE: *Does he ever?*

Des Glass (Islington resident): "When I was a lad growing up in Islington, North London, *The Professionals* crew were regular visitors to these parts. So I have been lucky enough to meet all three of the regulars and get their autographs, myself and my friends were, and still are, huge fans of the show so when I saw them in town again we would rather naughtily bunk off school to watch them filming.

"There was one rather amusing incident that almost destroyed our faith in the tough men of CI5 at our tender age: In the forecourt of the old Royal Free Hospital, which was the Magistrates courthouse in *Operation Susie*, when we were stood next to the Gold Capri with autograph books, Lewis and Martin were sat in the car having a coffee; as we all gave them our books to sign, Lewis spilt some of his coffee on his sleeve, then from his other sleeve he pulled a tissue to mop up the slight spillage.....and it was Pink! The hardest man on television had a pink tissue secreted up his sleeve! It was very funny at the time.

"They all seemed personable and willing to sign autographs for the many kids that gathered around the Capris, but Gordon was definitely an old school gentleman, patiently talking to the kids and their parents and making sure that every autograph book and scrap of paper was signed. What a guy."

Stunt arranger Peter Brayham recalled how he put the Wham! Bang! Wallop! into the programmes.

Peter Brayham: "First thing I did was to read the script and find out about the story and the characters involved. I had to put together a fight sequence that suited the story and fit it in with the background of the characters. Doyle was a karate expert so I included karate moves for him. Bodie was ex-SAS. In fact, as the series progressed, both Martin and Lewis became so good at the fight sequences that I talked to them as though they were stuntmen. It was easy for them to copy people because they were trained to act, but my job was to show them how to act the part, not with words, but physically. Each fight was a sequence of choreographed moves, in the same way as a dance routine. We practiced it very slowly at first and if I saw that an actor has a particular weakness - say he's not too good with his left or with his legs - then I'd take out any moves involving them. It's far better to watch fifteen moves - or numbers as we call them - expertly done than to watch fifty, which are not."

The Untouchables: *When Bodie loses heavily at poker and a foreign diplomat buys his marker, things look desperate for Cowley's department. As Bodie sinks lower and lower into a bottomless pit of treachery, Cowley plays his trump card.*

The Untouchables, by Brian Clemens, began filming on Monday 1st December, under the control of director William Brayne.

Martin Shaw, Gordon Jackson, and Lewis Collins share a drink during THE UNTOUCHABLES.

The scenes involving Bodie preparing for his date with Claire Terringham were scripted somewhat differently to what was actually filmed; the following sequence was dropped altogether due to timing reasons:

Int: Bodie's flat

Bodie is preparing for his date with Claire Terringham.
Doyle watches him...
DOYLE: (looking at Bodie) *Dog.*
BODIE: *Handsome dog.*
DOYLE: *You're so vain sometimes it makes me sick.*
BODIE: *It's the details that win hearts. This is a double assignment - one for Cowley - and one strictly personal.*
DOYLE: *She'll laugh in your face.*
BODIE: *I'll turn the other cheek.*
DOYLE: *She'll think you're jumped up.*
BODIE: *She'll get a new meaning of the word 'jump'*
DOYLE: *Terringham's daughter? What a score.*
BODIE: *Ring up a girl, or two. You can use this place. Ring up the redhead, Chrissie whatsername...*
DOYLE: *Pearson? She's into Buddhists.*
BODIE: *Well, that blonde the, Sue Barker. Touch of class...*
DOYLE: *Likes rugby players.*
BODIE: (sighs) *There's a can of beer in the fridge. Have fun.*

DOYLE: *Terringham's daughter...*
BODIE: *Good things always come to the deserving. And the aristocracy deserve me...lucky girl...lucky, lucky girl...*
DOYLE: *If her father's a 'Sir' does that make her an 'Honourable' - or a 'Lady'? Or what?*
BODIE: *A dame. And I know about dames.*
The door bell rings
BODIE: *That'll be her now. Come to whisk me away in her limousine by Mister Rolls and Mister Royce.*
DOYLE: *She'll see through you in an instant. Boy doing a man's job.*

Another scene, also scheduled to be filmed in Bodie's flat, was dropped for similar reasons:

Int: Bodie's flat
Bodie has returned from the Hi-Fi shop with his equipment.
BODIE: *Damn, Damn, Damn.*
DOYLE: *Problems?*
BODIE: *I know Cowley. He won't wear it. I know he won't.*
DOYLE: *Won't wear what?*
BODIE: *I can hear him now. He'll spout some crud about 'should have known better Bodie'. He'll deny my expenses for sure.*
DOYLE: *Bodie - what the hell are you talking about?*
BODIE: *My Hi-Fi. I went and bought it back.*
DOYLE: *So I see. What about it?*
BODIE: *Scratched! And the bugger charged me forty quid more than he gave me for it. Forty quid! 'Market's going up', he said. 'Funny,' I said, when I sold it to you the market was going down.' 'Must be the weather,' he said. Forty quid!*
DOYLE: *Well. Forty quid. Man's got to make a living.*
BODIE: *Damn thing's broken too. My tweeter's gone for a Burton!*
DOYLE: *Sounds painful. But cheer up. Cowley might meet the cost if we pull this one off today. Five hours and three minutes from now.*

On the 8th December the script required sequences to be filmed at J & N Wade on Finchley Road, Golders Green, North West London, which was acting as Taylor's office. A few simple scenes were called for between Doyle and Taylor, but Martin Shaw just couldn't get the easiest of things right!

Doreen Soan (continuity): "While opening a can of lager, for some obscure reason only known to the crew, the beverage exploded all over the place - someone playing a practical joke! Then, someone positioned one of the desk lights very close to the edge of the table - and on queue Martin knocked it clean off. Third time lucky and the scenes were in the can."

The sequences filmed at Wildwood Road, Hampstead Heath, North West London, where Rahad superbly, and conveniently, saves Anna on her runaway horse, required the use of a tracking vehicle; which, with a camera crew inside, would follow the horses as they galloped through the wood. A Citroen 2CV was used for this; supplied by first assistant director Simon Hinkly. The cars had a fold-back canvas roof and very soft suspension making it an ideal choice.

Simon Hinkly: "These cars were extensively used in the film industry at the time because the camera and its operator could easily be mounted in them."

The horse-riding scenes were considered too dangerous for actor Keith Washington and actress Marilyn Galsworthy so stunt doubles, Terry Yorke and Tracey Eddon, doubled for Rahad and Anna.

Bodie (Lewis Collins) and Doyle (Martin Shaw) have fallen out!. But all is not what it seems in this scene from THE UNTOUCHABLES.

Stephen Snow: "I recall the scenes we did on Tuesday 9th December, because it was the day after John Lennon was shot. I was a guest at the filming and was with Lewis when the news about John Lennon was announced. He was a friend of Lennon through his dad Bill Collins who was in the music business and managed a band called 'Badfinger' (Lewis Collins would often help out backstage in the early Seventies, when the band was touring). Lew was quite upset about the incident.

"The scenes in the car park at the Manor Cottage pub in Finchley, North London, by the entrance to the St Marylebone cemetery on the junction with East End Road, took about two hours to get right. Martin was approaching the pub from the Finchley end, in other words coming across the traffic. They didn't want Martin to be seen waiting in the queue to get across the road, so the crew were continually trying to stop the traffic to give him a clean sweep into the pub car park. But because they were filming in rush-hour traffic and it was very dark, the cars refused to stop and give Martin a clean pass. Like I say, after around two hours of trying, they eventually got the scenes in the can.

"They had similar problems outside the club on Chalk Farm Parade, when Lew had to get out of the car and enter the club. It took about three hours, because the pavement there is quite narrow, and it became impossible for the camera crew to set themselves up with the curious onlookers that has gathered to watch the filming. Also bear in mind that just along from the club was Chalk Farm tube station, which is quite busy at that time of the night. Once inside the production encountered further problems and the scene that took around twenty takes was with Lew and Nero at the bar, where Lew says 'you win some and lose some', and for some reason they both got the giggles.

In THE UNTOUCHABLES Bodie (Lewis Collins) is offered the opportunity to clear up all his gambling debts by a foreign diplomat - who in exchange wants to have some vital secrets from CI5.

"The filming with John Junkin was always on a closed set as the area was always very small inside the house and they were all done on the same shoot I think. Mind you Lewis nearly failed to turn up after lunch. 'The Flask' pub was just up the road, and after Lew had had his share of drinks, he was nearly run over by a passing motorist walking back to the set."

On the set of THE UNTOUCHABLES Martin Shaw finds himself grounded!

The shooting of *The Professionals* involved a large number of people and required a large-scale technical back up in the engineering and craft areas. To enable the director to concentrate on the artistic aspects of the production, the organisation and co-ordination of actors and crew was largely delegated to the lighting cameraman and his team.

John Maskall (camera operator): "It was the final episode after a long hard slog and I'd worked on the last two series, almost non-stop. I had to work very closely with Bill Brayne, the director. You sometimes have to coax the actors into the best position for the camera but most of the time, you have to use your skill to adjust them. What ever happens you have to make sure that you don't inhibit them. It all comes down to teamwork though. It's not all down to one person. The whole thing about *The Professionals* was that you'd got a bloody good writer, bloody good actors and it was sorted in that way. The production team come together in terms of the director, myself, even the assistant and the grips. Everybody is working towards a set end and that produces a style in the end, it really does! I mean I produced the camera operation side - just remember it's derelict London, the locations you're using and remember the style is because of those locations. If you're filming in Oxford say, it will be totally different. Just one person deciding doesn't make the style: the style evolves under the director's eyes and supervision.

"The cameras used were German 16mm Arriflex 16SR's. 16mm has an economical advantage, but the lens gives a greater depth of field and the cameras were lighter and easier to use in small rooms and in the back of cars. We used two types, one which was 'blimped', or padded to cut down as much noise as possible, and up to three standard cameras for the action sequences when there was money in the budget to do so."

Stunt arranger Peter Brayham (left) on the set of THE UNTOUCHABLES with actors Lewis Collins and Martin Shaw.

The crew used an average of eight rolls of film a day, which only a total of five and a half rolls are needed to make a 52-minute episode. It took 400-feet of film for ten minutes viewing with the unit only completing around five minutes of filmed footage each day.

Chris Sargent (focus puller): "I was responsible for the equipment, making sure that everything was where it was supposed to be and all cleaned and ready for use. Then, during rehearsal, I had to work out what the focus needed to be depending on what was going to be happening on the eventual shot. I got told what the exposure was and I had to make sure the right filter was on. And make sure there wasn't any hair in the gate - in other words that there were no 'foreign bodies,' which would appear on the final print."

Dusty Miller, whose vast experience had included *The Sweeney*, *Van Der Valk* and the features *Get Carter* and *Pulp*, was the lighting cameraman.

Dusty Miller: "I create the mood for the scene to be shot. I have to know the limitations of the lighting equipment used and to balance that against the daylight available. Coloured gels or smoke can be used to simulate a late nightclub scene where a room is full of cigarette smoke. Very rarely is anything discussed in terms of style or anything else on the shoot. It's basically up to me to sort out what it ought to look like. Such informality is not really leaving everything to chance since directors take for granted the high degree of standardisation in approach that exists within the various craft areas across television. This is encouraged by the way operators first train as assistants and serve long apprenticeships before they move up the ladder; a process that tends to perpetuate naturalistic approaches to production."

Peter Hall was the camera grip, whose special responsibilities were for the bits and pieces like the handles, dollies (which the camera sits on) and rails, which were used for the camera to 'track' along whilst it was in action.

Not one to rest on his laurels with the production having only just finished, Monday 15th December saw Lewis Collins preparing to walk from London to Liverpool! Following the A41 from The Holiday Inn, Marble Arch, with boxer John Conteh, he embarked on a nine-day 243-mile walk raising money for the charity PHAB (the Physically Handicapped and Able Bodied). On Friday 19th the BBC's consumer programme *Pebble Mill At One* dedicated an 8-minute segment to the two stars who talked in depth to Marian Foster about the walk. The march hit the headlines on Saturday 27th when, nearing the end of the walk, Conteh went on a drunken rampage after a drinking session with his colleagues leading to headlines like: 'Conteh floored by a fairy'! However, Collins played no part in the brawl and later continued the walk. The following month Lewis Collins made a guest appearance on the Saturday morning children's show, *Tiswas*.

Lewis Collins and ex-boxer John Conteh set off on their charity walk from London to Liverpool to raise money for the charity PHAB.

SERIES IV EPISODE GUIDE

Martin Shaw and Lewis Collins joke around during WILD JUSTICE.

THE GUN

(originally *The Gun, The Horse and The Mules*)
by **Christopher Wicking**
© Copyright Mark 1 Productions Ltd MCMLXXX

Inger	Celia Gregory
Gary	Robert Gwilym
Tony	Barry Angel
Franco	Peter Kelly
G. G. Lesley	Zoot Money
Jerry Lee	David John
Wendell	Nigel Pegram
Patricia Buchanan	Sylvestra Le Touzel
Dr. Schulman	Martin Milman
Paul	Burt Caesar
Devlin	Joss Buckley
Café Manager	Ray Marioni
Claudine	Francesca Whitburn
Mrs. Bergen	Prudence Rennick
Vicar	Michael F. Kenny
Plain clothes man	Tony Wredden
CI5 man	David Vann
Uncredited	
Café customer	Michael Praed
Guard	Eric French
Workmate	Nick Wilkinson
Police Driver	Tim Douglas
Mrs. Devlin	Tina Martin
Taxi Driver	Paul Calley
Franco's Bodyguard (Mac)	Steve Emerson
Nick	Greg Powell
CI5 Man	Peter Roy
CI5 Man	Dennis Plenty
CI5 Man	Jerry Baker
Prokopp	Richard Atherton

Director: **Denis Lewiston**

BODIE receives a telephone call from a girlfriend named Inger North. She is a teacher in an international school in London, and asks Bodie to meet her because she is with a former pupil at a café. Paul Bailey, is a heroin addict and is giving her information about a large shipment of drugs, a 'horse', which is expected to arrive in the UK later that week. Paul panics when he realises that Inger has telephoned CI5, and flees when Bodie and Doyle arrive. The drug smuggling organization, supplying Paul already suspect that he is a risk to them and arranged for a man named Gary Benesch to murder him.

The next morning, Paul is found dead near the houseboat where he lived with his girlfriend Patricia Buchanan. Patricia, the daughter of an important industrialist, is also a former pupil of the school and a heroin addict. Benesch reports to his boss, Franco, that he has murdered Paul, and Franco tells him to hide the gun. However, when Benesch hears police sirens nearby, he becomes worried and tosses the gun over the garden wall of a house belonging to the pop singer, G. G Lesley. Lesley is away and the gun is found in the garden by his schoolboy son Jerry Lee and Jerry's friend, Tony Domenguin. The boys play with the gun and when Benesch returns to retrieve it, he finds Jerry Lee lying wounded and Tony holding the gun. Benesch tries to take the gun from the boy, but Tony runs away.

He telephones for an ambulance to help his friend, and then tries desperately to find a safe place for the gun. A pupil at the international school, he is expected to play in a football match later that day. Benesch goes to the school to find the boy and waits by the football ground for an opportunity to grab him. CI5 are also at the school to question the headmaster about possible links between his pupils and drug smuggling.

Doyle goes to question Patricia in hospital, where she has just given birth to a baby and, after he has questioned her, her father complains strongly about her harassment by CI5. Jerry Lee has now been taken to hospital, and the police are told that the same gun that was used to murder Paul Bailey shot him. CI5 first suspect that Jerry Lee's father may be involved in drug smuggling, and his son was shot as some kind of revenge, but further police enquiries reveal that another schoolboy was seen running away from the shooting, and Cowley sends Bodie and Doyle back to the school to find Tony. When they arrive, they are told that Tony is missing; Benesch has abducted the boy and knocked him unconscious.

Benesch befriends the boy, hoping he will be able to tell him where the gun is. Franco, meanwhile, worried about the man's incompetence arrives and takes them both to Franco's home, where they are locked in a cellar. The car used for the kidnapping has been linked to Benesch, and Bodie and Doyle go to the man's flat and find a message left by Tony, mentioning the name 'Franco', which he has overheard. CI5 trace Franco's house, where he and his gang are arrested. Tony is found safe, but on discovering where the gun is hidden, Benesch has fled to the hall where a school play is planned. Inger North is at the school and finds the gun among some toy ones in a box. Only her quick thinking saves her from being murdered by Benesch, when she aims the gun at him and shoots him. Cowley suspects that parents at the school may be involved in the drug smuggling. If their children were threatened, they were almost sure to co-operate with the drugs gang.

Production Unit

Created by	Brian Clemens
Executive Producers	Albert Fennell, Brian Clemens
Music	Laurie Johnson
Producer	Raymond Menmuir
Associate Producer	Roy Stevens
Script Editor	Gerry O'Hara

Production Accountant	Terry Connors
Assistant Director	Dominic Fulford
Location Manager	Peter Carter
Continuity	Gladys Pearce
Casting	Esta Charkham
Art Director	Ken Ryan
Set Dresser	Don Mingaye
Stunt Arranger	Del Baker
Wardrobe Supervisor	Donald Mothersill
Lighting Cameraman	Dusty Miller
Camera Operator	John Maskall
Focus Puller	Chris Sargent
Make Up	Sue Black
Hairdresser	Sue Love
Lighting by	Lee Electric
Supervising Editor	John S. Smith
Sound Recordist	David Crozier
Boom Operator	Mike Silverlock
Dubbing Editor	Peter Lennard
Dubbing Mixer	Hugh Strain
Music Editor	Alan Willis

An Avengers MARK 1 Production For LONDON WEEKEND TELEVISION

Shooting / Location Schedule

Production Dates: Monday 16th to Monday 30th June, 1980. Production Number: 9D10070

16 June	***Ext / Int: Café***: Olde Canal Snack Bar, 130-132 York Way, King's Cross, London, N1 ***Street (Paul flees café perused by Gary)***: York Way estate, Treaty Road, King's Cross, London, N1 ***Street (Paul escapes from Gary)***: Copenhagen Primary School, Treaty Road, Kings Cross, N1
17 June	***Franco's house***: 13 Park Place Villas, off Maida Avenue, Maida Vale, London, W2
18 June	***CI5 Computer room***: Kienzle Data Systems, 224 Bath Road, Slough, Berkshire
19 June	***Hospital wards***: Northwick Park Hospital, Watford Road, Harrow, Middlesex
20 June	***Airport Arrivals lounge***: TWA, 380 Kensington High Street, Kensington, London, W14
23 June	***Int / Ext: Lesley's house / Inger's house***: Chestnuts, 350 Jersey Road, Osterley, Middlesex ***Int / Ext: Gary's car***: Jersey Road, Osterley, Middlesex
2nd Unit	***Aces High Casino / Car park***: Eurocrest Hotel, Empire Way, Wembley, Middlesex

	Warehouse Complex (Devlin's work place): Royal Free Hospital, Fleet Road, Hampstead, London, NW3
	Int: Bodie's car (route to playing fields): Constantine Road / Agincourt Road, Hampstead, London, NW3
	Int: Bodie's car (radio from Cowley): South End Road, Hampstead, London, NW3
24 June	***Playing Fields (Football pitch)***: Hampstead Heath Extension, Wildwood Road, Hampstead, London, NW11
	Street (CI5 agent 6.8 picks up wrong driver): Middleway, Hampstead Garden Suburb, London, NW11
	Int: Bodie's car (with Inge): Wildwood Road, Hampstead, London, NW11
25 June	***The Lincoln School & play***: Henrietta Barnet School, Central Square, Hampstead, London, NW11
26 June	***Houseboat / River***: 'Calliach', Thistleworth Marine, Railshead Road, Isleworth, Middlesex
	Streets: Gary chases Tony: Richmond Lock, Ranelagh Drive, Richmond, Surrey
	Int: Bodie's car (call from Inger - route to café): Netheravon Road / Beverley Road / Airedale Avenue, Chiswick, London, W4
	Int: Bodie's car (Bodie and Doyle discuss Lesley - route to CI5 HQ): Beverley Road / Netheravon Road / Chiswick High Road, Chiswick, London, W4
27 June	***Play Hall***: Hampstead Garden Suburb Church Hall, 11 Northway, London, NW11
	Franco's house: 13 Park Place Villas, off Maida Avenue, Maida Vale, London, W2
	Int / Ext: Franco's car: Maida Avenue, Paddington, London, W2
	Bodie's & Cowley's car run-bys (route to Franco's house): Southway / Central Square, Hampstead Garden Suburb, London, NW11
2nd Unit:	
30 June	***Second Hospital***: Northwick Park Hospital, Watford Road, Harrow, Middlesex
	Streets (Tony flees with gun) / phone box: Wembley Park Tube station, Bridge Road, Wembley, Middlesex
	Ext: Gary's flat: 71 Dagmar Avenue, Wembley, Middlesex
	Ext: Devlin's council flat: 65 Chalkhill Road, Wembley, Middlesex: *Original schedule - scene not filmed*
	Police car run-by: Dagmar Avenue, Wembley, Middlesex
	Airport (Prokopp followed by CI5): Heathrow Airport, Approach road only, Hayes, Middlesex

WILD JUSTICE

by **Ranald Graham**
© Copyright Mark 1 Productions Ltd MCMLXXX

Jack Craine	Larry Lamb
Dr. Kate Ross	Sarah Douglas
Sally	Jenny Twigge
King Billy	Ziggy Byfield
Jennifer Black	Marsha Fitzalan
Cheryl	Frances Low
D.C.I. Botham	Paul Humpoletz
Shusai	Robert Lee
Dr. Philip Hedley	Llewellyn Rees
Rose	Jack McKenzie
Mediator	Robert Ashby
Bike Kid	Richard Huw
Terrorist	Brian Attree
Desk Sergeant	Kenneth Hadley
Race Official	Tommy Wright
Uncredited	
Girl Hostage	Tracey Eden
Billy's Gang	Nick Gillard
Billy's Gang	Gareth Milne
Billy's Gang	David Holland
Billy's Gang	Jim Dowdall
Billy's Gang	Graham Crowther
Pub Customer	John Carney
Dave	Derek Moss
Uniformed Policeman	Les Conrad

Director: **Dennis Abey**

JACK CRAINE, the man responsible for keeping all CI5 agents at a peak of fitness and competence, is dismayed to find that Bodie is falling behind the other agents in every kind of training and test programme. Bodie has a medical and is found perfectly healthy. Craine tells Cowley that Bodie should either be rested or his training doubled to stimulate further effort. Cowley decides on the latter course of action and insists that even the mental agility tests set for CI5 agents by psychologist Dr. Kate Ross have to be completed faster than usual. Cowley talks to Doyle and to Bodie's present girlfriend, Jennifer, but neither can produce any reason for Bodie's sudden lack of competence; however Jennifer is puzzled that Bodie seems to like taking her to a shabby pub where Hell's Angels congregate. One evening, Bodie tries to start a fight with the leader of the Hell's Angels, King Billy, but Jennifer intervenes. Afterwards, in a fit of temper and frustration, Bodie punches his fist into the side of his car, and then seems more relaxed and happy.

Why is Bodie falling behind in training and obsessed with a motorcycle gang? It's up to Doyle to find out. Martin Shaw prepares to film a scene at Warfield Hall, Berkshire, in WILD JUSTICE.

Bodie's performance in training sessions suddenly improves and Craine reports to Cowley that he is quite pleased with the agent. Dr. Ross, however, reports that Bodie's test results for her are disturbing; she recommends that the agent should be taken off any assignments for the time being. Cowley is not unduly worried, but she later she explains that because of some unknown recent trauma, Bodie has been suffering from recurring bouts of elation and depression, which have now reached a point where the agent has probably got a death wish.

Bodie has invited Doyle to bring his motorbike to a race meeting attended by large numbers of Hell's Angels including King Billy, who has always won in the past. Though annoyed by the dangerous riding habits of the gang, Doyle manages to win the race, but to his amazement, Bodie isn't content with this victory over King Billy and flaunts Doyle's triumph laughingly in front of the whole gang. When this reckless behaviour fails to produce any reaction from King Billy, Bodie challenges the Hell's Angel leader to race up a nearby cliff-face called the Widowmaker.

Cowley discovers that a Hell's Angels gang leader was suspected of the murder of Williams, a man from Bodie's old SAS platoon. The only witness to the death, Williams' girlfriend Cheryl, has dared not testify for fear of reprisals from the gang. When he discovers that Bodie may seek out revenge he proceeds to the motorbike race, only to be told by Doyle, who is unaware of Bodie's intentions, that he has challenged a gang of Hell's Angels to some rather unsavoury antics. Cowley tells Doyle the truth behind Bodie's death wish and the men race to the scene. King Billy and four members of his gang attack Bodie. Doyle rushes to Bodie's aid and, after being beaten off by Bodie puts the other gang members out of action. Bodie, meanwhile, has put a stranglehold on King Billy and is only stopped as Cowley threatens to shoot him. Cheryl agrees to identify the gang in court, so Bodie releases the man into Cowley's custody.

Production Unit

Created by	Brian Clemens
Executive Producers	Albert Fennell, Brian Clemens
Music	Laurie Johnson
Producer	Raymond Menmuir
Associate Producer	Roy Stevens
Script Editor	Gerry O'Hara
Production Manager	Ron Purdie
Production Accountant	Terry Connors
Assistant Director	David Cherrill
Location Manager	Peter Carter
Continuity	Gladys Pearce
Casting	Esta Charkham
Art Director	Ken Ryan
Set Dresser	Ted Western
Stunt Arranger	Paul Weston
Wardrobe Supervisor	Donald Mothersill
Special Effects	Mike Collins

Lighting Cameraman	Norman Langley
Camera Operator	John Maskall
Focus Puller	Chris Sargent
Make Up	Sue Black
Hairdresser	Sue Love
Lighting by	Lee Electric
Supervising Editor	John S. Smith
Editor	Alan Killick
Sound Recordist	David Crozier
Boom Operator	Mike Silverlock
Dubbing Editor	Peter Lennard
Dubbing Mixer	Trevor Pyke
Music Editor	Alan Willis

An Avengers MARK 1 Production For LONDON WEEKEND TELEVISION

Shooting / Location Schedule

Production Dates: Monday 30th June to Monday 14th July, 1980. Production Number: 9D10071

30 June	***Restaurant***: The House On The Bridge, High Street, Eton, Berkshire
	Street: Cowley meets Jennifer: Thames Street, Windsor, Berkshire
	Int: Doyle's flat / CI5 office: Warfield Hall, Forest Road, Warfield, Berkshire
1 July	***Country Roads***: Warren Row (junction with Lutmans Haven), Knowl Hill, Berkshire
	Scramble Hotel / Pub: Seven Stars Pub, Bath Road, Knowl Hill, Berkshire
	Scramble track: H. F Warner Limited, Star Works, Knowl Hill, Berkshire
	CI5 training area (weather cover): Warfield Hall, Forest Road, Warfield, Berkshire
2-4 July	***Scramble track***: H. F Warner Limited, Star Works, Bath Road, Knowl Hill, Berkshire
4-9 July	***Martial Arts Gym / CI5 Centre / Rooftops***: Warfield Hall, Forest Road, Warfield, Berkshire
10 July	***Pub***: Chequered Flag pub, 86 East Lane, Wembley, Middlesex
	Ext: Doyle's flat: East Lane, Wembley, Middlesex
	Ext: Martial Arts Gym / Cowley's car: Greens Court, 143 East Lane & East Lane, Wembley, Middlesex
2nd Unit:	
14 July	***Martial Arts Gym & Roadside (Bodie's car)***: Warfield Hall, Forest Road, Warfield, Berkshire
	CI5 Lab inserts & Computer keys: Kienzle Data Systems, 224 Bath Road, Slough, Berkshire

Is Bodie cracking up? If not, why has he picked a fight with a group of Hell's Angels? Lewis Collins poses for the stills cameraman during filming of the siege training sequences shot at Warfield Hall, Berkshire, for WILD JUSTICE.

BLACK OUT

by **Brian Clemens**
© Copyright Mark 1 Productions Ltd MCMLXXX

Stuart	Ben Cross
Gerda	Linda Hayden
Murphy	Steve Alder
Mr. Parker	Sylvester Morand
Mrs. Parker	Jill Martin
Henry	Timothy Stark
Humber	John Arnatt
Dr. Marsand	Gareth Armstrong
P.C Fenton	Kevin Quarmby
Betty Fenton	Amanda Leigh
Bank Manager	Derek Ensor
Minter	John Cording
Doctor	Louis Mahoney
Nurse	Fionn O'Farrell
Rector	Cyril Conway
Corrigan	Paul Gale
Barmaid	Julia Blalock

Uncredited

Vicar	Evan Ross
Ambulanceman	Len Gilbey
Ambulanceman	Ken Netsall
1st Gunner	Rex Harding
2nd Gunner	Nick Hobbs
Driver	Val Musetti
African VIP	Jules Walter
VIP's Aide	Louis St. Just
1st Man	Gerry Crampton
2nd Man	Ken Barker
CI5 Marksman (Milk Float)	Ray Knight
CI5 Marksman (Milk Float)	Bill Hemmings
CI5 Man (John)	Jimmy Muir
CI5 Man	Bill Burns
Businessman	Alan Cope

Director: **William Brayne**

A SCANTILY-CLAD, pretty girl rushes into a London church and collapses before the astonished vicar and curate. She is examined by a doctor and found to be suffering from concussion and amnesia following a severe blow to the head. Speaking in German, she talks confusedly about Harrodene and, because Harrodene helicopter base is to be the venue for important diplomatic talks, CI5 are called in to see the girl. Cowley orders

Bodie and Doyle to accompany the girl and the doctor in the ambulance that is to take the girl to hospital. On the way, the ambulance's path is blocked by one car while men firing machine guns from another car attack the ambulance and the doctor is killed. Doyle leaps from the vehicle, firing at the attackers and the men are also killed when their car crashes. The blocking car drives hurriedly away but there are no survivors left at the scene to explain this attack on the girl, but Cowley decides that she must know something about the talks at Harrodene for such an attempt to be made on her life.

The CI5 team find themselves driving around the countryside and London to find a gang of villains who plan to assassinate a lobby of international diplomats with a powerful anti-tank gun. Their only clue to solving the case is a young girl - but she has amnesia! Lewis Collins takes a break from driving in BLACK OUT.

The German girl, Gerda Helm - by now speaking English - can remember nothing, but there is evidence that she came from Kent and Cowley tells the men to drive her around the area, in the hope that some familiar sight there may spark off her memory. The girl soon begins to recognise landmarks in Kent and directs the agents to a large country house. As they approach the house, the girl becomes further agitated by some unpleasant memory. In a downstairs room, Bodie and Doyle find a man lying dead and signs of a recent struggle. Upstairs they find a child's nursery full of trampled toys. The girl hazily recalls that she looked after a little boy named Henry, but there is no sign of the boy or his parents.

As the girl's memory returns, she tells the men that her name is Gerda Helm and that she is a German au pair working as a nurse maid to Henry's parents, John and Melissa Parker. The day before, while Mr. Parker was away on a holiday, armed men broke into the house and seized her, Mrs. Parker and Henry; the dead man at the house was a gardener who tried to fight off the intruders. They were taken to a hideout in London and held prisoner. She had been struck on the head and was severely concussed, but remembered the kidnappers talking about Harrodene. She escaped by jumping out of a window and ran to the church. CI5 find out that John Parker is a director of a bank, but they can find no possible connection between the family and the Harrodene talks. While Cowley and Bodie go to check the security arrangements at Harrodene, Doyle and a CI5 agent named Stuart, are sent to search for possible kidnap hideouts near the church where Gerda first appeared. The following morning, the two men notice a house with a boarded-up window and, suspecting that this may be the window from which the girl made her escape, they raid the house and shoot a man dead. Mrs. Parker and her son Henry are found safe in an upstairs room.

Mrs. Parker has no idea why she and her son were kidnapped, but is able to tell Cowley that her husband was visiting a friend in East Anglia, Sam Goodmead. When Goodmead is found murdered, CI5 realise that Mr. Parker may have been kidnapped too; an wrapper for some large ammunition is been found at the house and Cowley is worried that the gun may be used on the VIP meeting at Harrodene later that day. He orders Bodie and Doyle to widen their search around the helicopter base for possible firing points, but there is a town nearby and Bodie despairs as he tries to search all the buildings in the area. Noticing a branch of the bank of which Mr. Parker is a director, Bodie impulsively goes into the building and is told by the bank staff that Mr. Parker has been busy for some time in his office on the top floor with some unknown visitors. Ignoring the shouts of the bank staff, Bodie races up to Parker's office, bursts into the room and spots an anti-tank gun positioned to fire at the helicopter base. He immediately comes under attack, but manages to deflect the gun from its target and the gang is rounded up when Cowley's reinforcements arrive and overpower the criminals. Parker, lying bound on the floor, tries to stop Bodie until he is told that his wife and son are safe at CI5 headquarters.

The old cricket ground at Southall Gas Works, Middlesex, was utilised for this explosive set-up from BLACK OUT.

Production Unit

Created by	Brian Clemens
Executive Producers	Albert Fennell, Brian Clemens
Music	Laurie Johnson
Producer	Raymond Menmuir
Associate Producer	Roy Stevens
Script Editor	Gerry O'Hara
Production Manager	Ron Purdie
Production Accountant	Terry Connors
Location Manager	Peter Carter
Continuity	Gladys Pearce
Casting	Esta Charkham
Art Director	Ken Ryan
Set Dresser	Don Mingaye
Stunt Arranger	Paul Weston
Wardrobe Supervisor	Donald Mothersill
Lighting Cameraman	Dusty Miller
Camera Operator	John Maskall
Focus Puller	Chris Sargent
Make Up	Sue Black
Hairdresser	Sue Love
Lighting by	Lee Electric
Supervising Editor	John S. Smith
Sound Recordist	David Crozier
Boom Operator	Mike Silverlock
Dubbing Editor	Peter Lennard
Dubbing Mixer	Hugh Strain
Music Editor	Alan Willis

An Avengers MARK 1 Production For LONDON WEEKEND TELEVISION

Shooting / Location Schedule

Production Dates: Monday 14th to Friday 25th July; Wednesday 30th July, 1980. Production Number: 9D10072

14 July	***Embankment café***: Queens Walk, Jubilee Walk, under Hungerford Bridge, Lambeth, London, SE1
	Doyle's car: Pier (Doyle meets Stuart): Lambeth Pier, Lambeth Palace Road, London, SE1
	Streets: Kidnap house (Doyle's car): 134 Downham Road, Islington, London, N1
15 July	***Kidnap house***: 134 Downham Road, Islington, London, N1
16 July	***Church***: Ealing Parish Church, St. Mary's Road, Ealing, London, W5
	Ext: Bodie's car: Ranelagh Road / St. Mary's Road / Church Gardens, Ealing, London, W5
	Ambulance run-by: Church Gardens / Church Place, Ealing, London, W5

17 July	***Ambulance & explosion***: 'old' cricket ground, The Straight, Southall Gas Works, Middlesex
	St. Ann's Village: Bodie's car: The Bell Pub, The Street & Halls Lane, Waltham St. Lawrence, Berkshire
	St. Ann's village: Bodie's car run-by: Smewins Farm Barn (Waltham Barn), Smewins Road, off Broadmoor Lane, White Waltham, Berkshire
	St. Ann's Village: Ice cream van: Shurlock Row Garage, Broadmoor Lane (B3024), Waltham St Lawrence, Berkshire
	St. Ann's Village: swings: Waltham Road / Butchers Lane, White Waltham, Berkshire
	St. Ann's Village: Bodie's car run-by: church: Church Hill, off Waltham Road, White Waltham, Berkshire
18 July	***Hospital ward & corridors / Ext: Ambulance***: Royal Free Hospital, Rosslyn Hill, Hampstead, London, NW3
21 July	***Parker's house***: The Old Place, Boveney Road, Boveney, near Dorney, Berkshire
22 July	***Chopper base / Town skyline / Int: Club hut (Bodie & Cowley)***: Blackamore Lane (field behind Police Station), Maidenhead, Berkshire / Ray's Social Club, Blackamore Lane, Maidenhead, Berkshire
23 July	***Int: Bank top floor & private suite***: Scandia Steel Ltd, 11th Floor, Berkshire House, Queen Street, Maidenhead, Berkshire
	Int: Bank lift & counter area: South Of England Building Society, King Street, Maidenhead, Berkshire
	Ext: Town (stand-by set): Fleming House, King Street, Maidenhead, Berkshire
24 July	***Town / Car park / Bank roof***: Top Floor, Multi Storey Car Park, Broadway, Maidenhead, Berkshire
	Bodie: High Street: Barclays Bank, 92 High Street, Maidenhead, Berkshire
25 July	***Pub: 'Tag' scenes***: Bell & Dragon, High Street, Cookham, near Maidenhead, Berkshire
	Police house: 2 South Field Close, Dorney, near Windsor, Berkshire
	Sam's yard & hut: ICI Sailing Club, Amerden Lane, off Bath Road, Maidenhead, Berkshire
2nd Unit:	
30 July	***Bodie's car / Pub yard / Skittle alley / Pub front***: Stonor Arms, (B480), Stonor, near Henley-on Thames, Oxon
	Ext: Hospital car park (Bodie's car): Eurocrest Hotel, Shoppenhangers Road, Maidenhead, Berkshire
	Streets: Bodie's car: St. Mark's Road, off Bath Road, near Windsor Castle Pub, Maidenhead, Berkshire
	Doyle's car: Kidnap house run-bys: Gordon Road / College Glen (junction with Belmont Vale) / Raymond Road, Maidenhead, Berkshire

IT'S ONLY A BEAUTIFUL PICTURE...

by **Edmund Ward**
© Copyright Mark 1 Productions Ltd MCMLXXX

Colonel Jeremy Sangster	Moray Watson
James Tibbs	Jonathan Newth
Sarah Gresham	Prunella Gee
Sam Armitage	Neil McCarthy
Snapper Ullmann	Anthony May
Ralston	Antony Carrick
Galbraith	Dennis Burgess
Betty Marlow	Jo Rowbottom
Gillespie	William Moore
Ebert	Andrew Hilton
Perce Wilmot	Peter Rutherford
Works Manager	James House
George Gorton	Roger Martin
Miss Piper	Charmian May
Supervisor	Stephen Churchett
Smithson	Hugh Morton
CI5 Receptionist	Noreen Leighton
Uncredited	
Security Guard	Derek Chafer
Street Photographer	Ron Watkins
Foreman	Stephen Wade
Driver	John Cannon
Crane	Brunco McLoughlin
Driver's Mate	Vic Galluci
Uniformed Policeman	Peter Roy
Uniformed Policeman	Reg Turner
Uniformed Policeman	Douglas Stark

Director: **Denis Lewiston**

THE crimes of a country squire named Colonel Jeremy Sangster come to the attention of CI5. Sangster runs a sophisticated and efficient thieving operation from his large country house; he employs a young ex-Army officer, James Tibbs, to investigate possible thefts in advance and then his estate workers help Tibbs to carry out the robberies. Cowley's attention is aroused when Tibbs takes photographs of a secret blast furnace process and sells them to an East German diplomat. A civil servant called Henry Galbraith explains to Cowley that the thieves must be stopped before other vital industrial secrets are lost to overseas rivals; he is particularly anxious about an oil-drilling process called Strayton Four. Cowley instructs Doyle and Bodie to start their investigations into the gang by trying to track down the expert photographer who has been used in the thefts. After a long search, Bodie and Doyle discover his name is Snapper Ullmann, but although Ullmann is frightened by the arrival of the CI5 men and gives them all the help he can, he only knows part of the telephone number of the HQ of the thieves.

Various industrial secrets and highly-valuable art treasures are being stolen and sold by a gang who are using the blind routine of Customs to their full advantage. Doyle (Martin Shaw) leaps into action in a scene from IT'S ONLY A BEAUTIFUL PICTURE...

CI5 discover that of the few telephone numbers, which fit with the digits given by Ullmann, the only likely base for the thieves is the home of Colonel Sangster; his import/export business, run from a local airfield, also provides the perfect cover for exporting stolen goods. Sangster however is a respected leader of his local community and Cowley realises that it will be difficult to conduct a close investigation into his affairs. He therefore arranges for Doyle to join the local rural police force to find out what he can about Sangster and for Bodie to spend time in the area, posing as a sugar beet machinery salesman. Bodie meets Tibbs and Sangster's gamekeeper, Sam Armitage, who has with him a vicious dog. The photographer Ullmann has been found dead in his studio; at the time a man with a dog was seen leaving the area and Bodie is in no doubt that the gamekeeper was the murderer. It is obvious to CI5 that Sangster has the perfect set-up for a thieving operation, but they still lack proof to convict him. To tempt Sangster into action, Cowley asks for the top-secret Strayton Four machine to be used as bait.

With great reluctance, Galbraith signs over all responsibility for the machine to Cowley. The fact that the machine is to be moved from one site to another is given publicity in the press and CI5 are confident that Sangster won't resist the challenge to steal it in transit. As suspected the man steals the Strayton Four machine and arrives at his airfield, where Bodie and Doyle are waiting, to be flown by Tibbs to the wealthy South American purchaser. The CI5 team put an end to Sangster's plans and Cowley hands back the responsibility for the machine to a relieved Galbraith.

Production Unit

Created by	Brian Clemens
Executive Producers	Albert Fennell, Brian Clemens
Music	Laurie Johnson
Producer	Raymond Menmuir
Associate Producer	Roy Stevens
Script Editor	Gerry O' Hara
Production Manager	Ron Purdie
Production Accountant	Terry Connors
Assistant Director	David Cherrill
Location Manager	Peter Carter
Continuity	Gladys Pearce
Casting	Esta Charkham
Art Director	Ken Ryan
Set Dresser	Don Mingaye
Stunt Arranger	Terry Yorke
Wardrobe Supervisor	Donald Mothersill
Special Effects	Mike Collins
Lighting Cameraman	Norman Langley
Camera Operator	John Maskall
Focus Puller	Chris Sargent
Make Up	Sue Black
Hairdresser	Sue Love
Lighting by	Lee Electric
Supervising Editor	John S. Smith
Editor	Alan Killick
Sound Recordist	David Crozier
Boom Operator	Mike Silverlock
Dubbing Editor	Peter Lennard
Dubbing Mixer	Hugh Strain
Music Editor	Alan Willis

An Avengers MARK 1 Production For LONDON WEEKEND TELEVISION

What link can there be between industrial espionage and the theft of several art treasures? CI5 agent Doyle (Martin Shaw) uncovers the crimes of Colonel Sangster, a criminal who leads him a merry dance before the case is over in IT'S ONLY A BEAUTIFUL PICTURE...

CI5 go undercover in order to crack a sophisticated and efficient gang of art thieves. Martin Shaw, Gordon Jackson, and Lewis Collins pose for a publicity shot on the set of IT'S ONLY A BEAUTIFUL PICTURE...

Shooting / Location Schedule

Production Dates: Monday 28th July to Friday 8th August; Saturday 16th August, 1980. Production Number: 9D10073

28 July	***Ullmann's photographic studio***: O'Mahoney Studio, 40 Fulham Palace Road, Hammersmith, London, W6
29 July	***Int / Ext: Sangsters Arms country pub & garden***: The Three Horseshoes, Back Lane, Letchmore Heath, Elstree, Hertfordshire
	Ext: Village pond: The Green, Letchmore Heath, Elstree, Hertfordshire
30 July	***Lab gardens***: Napier Terrace, off Upper Street, Islington, London, N1
	Galbraith's office: The Mayor's Office, Islington Town Hall, Upper Street, Islington, London, N1
	Staircase (weather cover): Islington Town Hall, Upper Street, Islington, London, N1
31 July	***Int / Ext: Sangster's house drawing room (safe) / Conservatory (weather cover)***: Leggatts Park, Great North Road, Potters Bar, Hertfordshire
2nd Unit	***Ext: Battersea helicopter & Heliport***: Westland Heliport, Lombard Road, Battersea, London, SW11
	Int: Galbraith's car & run-bys: Lombard Road / Vicarage Crescent, Battersea, London, SW11

1 August	***Motorway service station***: Elf Petrol Filling Station, Talgarth Road, Hammersmith, London, W14 ***Int: Doyle's car (route to service station)***: Townmead Road / Bagley's Lane, Sands End, Fulham, London, SW6 ***Art Gallery***: Rowan Gallery, 31a Bruton Place, Berkeley Square, Mayfair, London, W1 ***Cowley's club***: The Naval Club, 38 Hill Street, Mayfair, London, W1
4-6 August	***Forest track / Airfield / Packing Shed***: Fairey Hangers, White Waltham Airfield, Waltham Road, Berkshire
7 August	***Blast Furnace***: Bon Accord Foundry, 797 Weston Road, Slough, Berkshire ***CI5 HQ / Draughting room (safe) & corridor***: Kienzle Data Systems, 224 Bath Road, Slough, Berkshire
8 August	***Gillespie's office / Police Station***: T.A Centre, Elmgrove Road, Harrow, Middlesex ***Int: Ralston's car***: Elmgrove Road, Harrow, Middlesex
2nd Unit	***Country Pub***: The Three Horseshoes, Letchmore Heath, Elstree, Hertfordshire ***Country lane lay-by (van ambush)***: off Church Lane, Aldenham, Hertfordshire
2nd Unit: 16 August	***Transport Bay / Oil Refinery loading bay***: DRG Sellotape Products, Elstree Way, Borehamwood, Hertfordshire ***Motorway run-by (Sangster's car)***: A1 Barnet By-Pass, Borehamwood, Hertfordshire ***London streets: with Cowley***: Waterloo Place, corner of Pall Mall, by Crimea Guards Memorial, London, SW1 ***London street: photographer - Trafalgar Square***: Trafalgar Square, Westminster, London, WC2 ***London street: Capri parked***: Leicester Square, junction St. Martins Street, London, WC2 ***London street: Soho / strip clubs***: Walkers Court / Brewer Street / Rupert Street, Soho, Westminster, London, W1 ***POV London car shot - on move***: Marble Arch, Mayfair, London, W1 ***Galbraith's car driving over Thames***: Lambeth Bridge, Lambeth, London, SE1 ***Industrial road run-by***: Imperial Road / Townmead Road, Fulham, London, SW6

BLOOD SPORTS

by **Gerry O'Hara**
© Copyright Mark 1 Productions Ltd MCMLXXX

Rene Lacoste	Yves Beneyton
Anita Cabreros	Michelle Newell
Captain Hidalgo	Michael Griffiths
Harry Spence	Harry Towb
Killer	Oliver Smith
Helen Tippett	Elizabeth Spender
Lonnie	Ruby Wax
Killer's Girl	Sue Robinson
Norman	Stephen Bent
Radio Man	Pierce Brosnan
Sir Basil Benton	Leonard Trolley
Spray Operator	Mike Savage
Mrs. Davis	Prim Cotton
Jaime 'Francesco' Cabreros	Johnathon Morris
CI5 Man 9.3	Rory McCallum
CI5 Man 9.4	Ben Roberts
Team Manager	Terry Yorke
Police Driver	Jim Barclay
CI5 Chauffeur	Jon Cartwright
Golf Partner	Jonathan Milton
CI5 Butler	Gerald Martin
West Indian	Peter Francis
Uncredited	
Uniformed Policeman	Pat Gorman
Uniformed Policeman	Douglas Stark
Anita's Driver	Mike Rickleby
Taxi Driver	Chris Houlton
Fiesta Car Driver	Jimmy Muir
Despatch Rider	John Delaney
Horse Rider	Don McClean
Horse Rider	Bill Hemmings
Party Guest	Mark Taylor

Director: **Phil Meheux**

JAIME 'Francesco' Cabreros, the son of a South American President, is shot dead while playing polo in England. In the confusion following his death, the killer is able to drive away unnoticed. Because of the political implications of the shooting, CI5 are called in, and Bodie and Doyle arrive at the polo field to find Jaime's stepsister Anita distraught with grief at his sudden death; she is certain that her father's political opponents killed Jaime.

In BLOOD SPORTS, the polo-playing son of a South American President is assassinated. Doyle (Martin Shaw) is drafted in to protect the victim's stepsister, Anita Cabreros, played by British actress Michelle Newell. Probably best known for her role in the BBC mini-series THE CLEOPATRAS.

Witnesses remember a fast sports car pulling away just after the shooting and this car is later found parked at a motorway services car park. The CI5 men find that the car has been booby-trapped, but they manage to defuse the bomb safely and a careful examination reveals fingerprints of a specialist mechanic with a police record, Norman. When Norman is warned that CI5 want to speak to him, he leaves his home hurriedly, but before Bodie and Doyle manage to catch up with him, he is shot dead by a van-driver at a set of traffic lights.

A representative of Jaime's father, Señor Raoul Hidalgo, comes to the UK to check on CI5's investigations into the boy's death. Hidalgo tells Cowley about the Cabreros family and about the stepsister Anita. Because Anita's loyalties are suspect and because she might be in danger, Cowley decides to have her watched. Doyle is sent to get to know her, and he meets her after lectures at London University, where she is studying. Bodie meanwhile is sent to plant listening devices in her flat and to arrange for her telephone calls to be monitored. Doyle enjoys Anita's company and finds her attractive, but Bodie tells him that she already has a boyfriend, a Frenchman. When the Frenchman leaves Anita's flat, CI5 agents follow, and lose, him.

When Anita discovers that CI5 have bugged her flat, she becomes very angry. Cowley points out that she might be in danger from Jaime's killers and that her French boyfriend, whom she knows as Pepe Fierro, is in fact, a known terrorist called Rene Lacoste. It is likely that Rene only befriended her in order to make plans for Jaime's murder. She agrees to help the CI5 men. Cowley asks Señor Hidalgo and the girl if they would be prepared to risk their lives to draw the killers into the open; they are both obvious targets for assassination by the President's enemies. Later, Señor Hidalgo sets off to play golf, while Anita is sent to stay at an English country house with friends. The golf game is a ploy and CI5 men are positioned around the course waiting for the killers to strike. At the same time, Doyle is alerted that Lacoste has been seen approaching the house where Anita is staying and he races off. Meanwhile Bodie spots someone take aim at Hidalgo and he and the CI5 team prevent the assassination, while Doyle arrives in time to overpower Lacoste and save Anita's life.

Production Unit

Created by	Brian Clemens
Executive Producers	Albert Fennell, Brian Clemens
Music	Laurie Johnson
Producer	Raymond Menmuir
Associate Producer	Roy Stevens
Script Editor	Gerry O'Hara
Production Manager	Ron Purdie
Production Accountant	Terry Connors
Assistant Director	Dominic Fulford
Location Manager	Peter Carter
Continuity	Gladys Pearce
Casting	Esta Charkham
Art Director	Ken Ryan

Set Dresser	Don Mingaye
Stunt Arranger	Terry Yorke
Wardrobe Supervisor	Donald Mothersill
Special Effects	Mike Collins
Lighting Cameraman	Dusty Miller
Camera Operator	John Maskall
Focus Puller	Chris Sargent
Make Up	Sue Black
Hairdresser	Sue Love
Lighting by	Lee Electric
Supervising Editor	John S. Smith
Sound Recordist	David Crozier
Boom Operator	John Cook
Dubbing Editor	Peter Lennard
Dubbing Mixer	Hugh Strain
Music Editor	Alan Willis

An Avengers MARK 1 Production For LONDON WEEKEND TELEVISION

Shooting / Location Schedule

Production Dates: Monday 11th to Friday 22nd August, 1980. Production Number: 9D10074. Locations in *italics* were originally scheduled but ultimately not used

11 August	**Cricket ground**: Metropolitan Police Sports and Social Club, Aldenham Road, Bushey, Hertfordshire
	(*Motorway*) *Service area car park*: Thatched Barn Hotel, Rowley Lane, Borehamwood, Hertfordshire
12 August	**Golf Course, house-overlooking course**: Burnham Beeches Golf Club, Green Lane, Burnham, Buckinghamshire
2nd Unit	**Golf Club road: horse pass**: Pumpkin Hill, near Victoria Drive path, Burnham Beeches, Buckinghamshire
	Golf Club road: Doyle's car stunt: Green Lane / Park Lane, Burnham Beeches, Burnham, Buckinghamshire
	Golf Club road: Car run-bys: Green Lane / Grove Road, Burnham Beeches, Burnham, Buckinghamshire
13 August	**Golf Club**: Burnham Beeches Golf Club, Green Lane, Burnham, Buckinghamshire
	Ext / Int: Sir Basil's House: St. Hubert's House, St. Hubert's Lane, Gerrard's Cross, Buckinghamshire
14 August	**Int: Bodie's car (University route)**: Old Oak Lane / Victoria Road, North Acton, London, NW10
	London University: London House, Overseas Graduates, Mecklenburgh Square, St.Pancras, London, WC1
	Ext: Bodie's car (University): Guilford Street / Doughty Street, Mecklenburgh Square, London, WC1
	Ext: Doyle's car / Book shop: London House - as above: *Original schedule only - scene not filmed.*

15 August		*Used Car forecourt*: Crouch Hill Motors, Mount Pleasant Crescent, Stapleton Hall Road, London, N14
		Mews car repair garage, spray yard: Ossian Mews, Ossian Road, Stroud Green, London, N4
		Rooming house: 86 Shaftesbury Road, Upper Holloway, London, N19
2nd Unit		*Patio / Park / Party / Window*: Brent Town Hall, Forty Lane, Wembley, Middlesex
		Ext: Cowley's car (radio - cricket match): Wembley Park Drive, near Elmside Road, Wembley, Middlesex
		Int: Cowley's car (radio - cricket match): Empire Way, Wembley, Middlesex
		Int: Cowley's car (radio - spray yard): North Circular Road (near Randall Avenue), Neasden, London, NW2
		Roads around golf course: Burnham Beeches Golf Course, Green Lane, Burnham, Buckinghamshire
18 August		*Int: Anita's flat*: Lochbie Mansions, 10 Warltersville Road, Crouch Hill, Hornsey Rise, London, N4
19 August		*Ext: Anita's flat*: Granville Court, 48 Mountview Road, Stroud Green, London, N4
		Hillside Mansions, Jacksons Lane, Highgate, London, N6
		Int: Radio truck: Warltersville Road, Crouch Hill, Hornsey Rise, London, N4
		Int: Anita's flat: Lochbie Mansions, 10 Warltersville Road Crouch Hill, Hornsey Rise, London, N4
20 August		*Funeral Parlour*: Saville & Son, 569 High Road, Wembley, Middlesex
		Hotel suite: Eurocrest Hotel, Empire Way, Wembley, Middlesex
		Bistro & bar: The Dock, Port A Bella Dock, Ladbroke Grove near Kensal Road / Narrow Boat Pub, London, W10
21 August		*Norman's car / Doyle's car / traffic lights*: The Broadway Clock Tower, Crouch Hall Road, Hornsey, London, N8
		Tube / Taxi / Bus stop: Chalk Farm station, Chalk Farm Road, Camden, London, NW1
		Int: Doyle's car: Chalk Farm Road, Camden, London, NW1
		Ext: Doyle's car (skid in road): Adelaide Road (near Beaumont Walk), Camden, London, NW3
		Doyle's car: Suburban roads (factory): Braybrook Street / Osmund Street / Mellitus Street, East Acton, London, W12
22 August		*Polo Ground*: Guards Club, Smiths Lawn, Windsor Great Park, Windsor, Berkshire
2nd Unit:		
		Doyle's car run-by (traffic lights): Tubbs Road / Station Road, Harlesden, London, NW10
		Ext: Doyle's car in traffic: Notting Hill Gate (near Pembridge Gardens), Notting Hill, London, W11

HIJACK

by **Roger Marshall**
© Copyright Mark 1 Productions Ltd MCMLXXX

Harry Walter	Dave King
Amanda	Jill Baker
Josef Merhart	Dennis Lill
Deborah	Rachel Davies
Swetman	Stephen Yardley
Sir Alan Sternfield	Richard Murdoch
Ambassador	Robert Rietty
Ross	Mark Eden
Murphy	Steve Alder
Dusty	Anthony Douse
Wally	Patrick Durkin
Amanda's mother	Jill Dixon
Sergeant	Lloyd McGuire
Chief Inspector	Nicholas Donnelly
Hitman	James Snell
Receptionist	Charles Baillie
Taxi driver	Maurice Lane
Room service waiter	Vic Tablian
Boy	Gora Dasgupta
Waiter	Verne Morgan
CI5 Man	Michael Worsley
Uncredited	
Hijacker	Manny Michaels
Hijacker	Mike Varey
Lorry Security Man	Mike Stevens
Lorry Security Man	Lou Hooper

Director: **Martin Campbell**

DOYLE'S girlfriend Deborah shares a flat with a Ministry of Defence secretary called Amanda, and during a visit there, Doyle is surprised to see Amanda meet with a businessman of a doubtful repute, Harry Walter and East European Embassy official, Josef Merhart. The official is very anxious to make some money and escape from his dreary life behind the Iron Curtain and has asked Amanda to introduce him to Walter. Merhart tells Walter that his government regularly moves huge amounts of silver from England to East Europe and back as part of speculative buying and selling on the London bullion market. The silver is moved from London to Tilbury in a lorry with one driver and an escort of two men following behind in a car, unarmed: each load of bullion is worth around four million pounds. The two men decide to steal a load, and they plan to hijack the lorry when it makes its next trip. Walter's assistant, Roy Swetman, wants a driver named Dusty Rhodes to be used on the robbery and uses Walter's money to bring Dusty, who is on remand, out on bail.

The planned robbery has to be postponed for one day so that Dusty can be bailed and Merhart has to postpone the shipment of silver for one day. Doyle meanwhile has made enquiries about Merhart and arranged for Amanda's telephone to be tapped, but CI5's attentions are fully occupied by an investigation of a suspected terrorist hideout in London. This investigation ends when Doyle and Bodie break into the hideout and find an Arab girl suspect dead in her bath, with a suitcase of bomb-making equipment in her room. The following Tuesday the lorry carrying the silver is flagged down by one of Walter's men dressed in police uniform. The driver stops and both he and the escort drivers are seized. Dusty Rhodes then drives the lorry away.

Because of its diplomatic aspects, CI5 are asked to investigate the robbery and Cowley tells the ambassador in London that, for the robbery to be so perfectly timed there must have been a security leak from the embassy staff. Cowley learns from Doyle that Merhart has been seen at Amanda's. Cowley has the embassy official put under surveillance. The hijacked lorry driver and the escort are found locked in a garage and Bodie is told that the day of the shipment was changed at the last minute. CI5 pinpoint that it was Merhart who arranged for the last-minute alteration to the date of the silver transfer. Amanda, meanwhile, reading a newspaper report of the robbery, begins to suspect that this was the reason that Merhart wanted to meet Walter and she tells Walter that she is very frightened - especially as Deborah's boyfriend, Doyle, has been asking questions. Walter tells her to go to her mother's in the country, but no sooner does she leave, he arranges for her to be killed. Wanting to talk to Amanda about her role in the robbery, Doyle finds out where the girl is and arrives in time to prevent the murder attempt.

Merhart discovers that his telephone is bugged and drives to where the silver has been hidden, intending to flee with as much of the bullion as he can carry. Cowley and CI5 have followed him and arrive in time to arrest him. Knowing that his countrymen will almost certainly shoot the man, Cowley sends Merhart back to the embassy.

Amanda, meanwhile, is hidden in a hotel with Bodie and Doyle. Not realising that it was Walter who had arranged her death she rings him from the hotel and Walter immediately orders Swetman to go and silence her. Bodie and Doyle stop the assassin. Cowley, however, has insufficient evidence to convict Walter, but takes great pride in telling him all the stolen silver has been safely returned.

Production Unit

Created by	Brian Clemens
Executive Producers	Albert Fennell, Brian Clemens
Music	Laurie Johnson
Producer	Raymond Menmuir
Script Editor	Gerry O'Hara
Production Manager	Ron Purdie
Production Accountant	Terry Connors
Assistant Director	Simon Hinkly

Location Manager	Peter Carter
Continuity	Kay Mander
Casting	Esta Charkham
Art Director	Ken Ryan
Set Dresser	Don Mingaye
Stunt Arranger	Terry Yorke
Wardrobe Supervisor	Donald Mothersill
Special Effects	Mike Collins
Lighting Cameraman	Norman Langley
Camera Operator	John Maskall
Focus Puller	Chris Sargent
Make Up	Sue Black
Hairdresser	Sue Love
Lighting by	Lee Electric
Editor	Alan Killick
Sound Recordist	David Crozier
Boom Operator	Mike Silverlock
Dubbing Editor	Peter Lennard
Dubbing Mixer	Hugh Strain
Music Editor	Alan Willis
Post Production Supervisor	John S. Smith

An Avengers MARK 1 Production For LONDON WEEKEND TELEVISION

Off-duty CI5 agent Ray Doyle (Martin Shaw) shares a tender moment with his girlfriend, Deborah (Rachel Davies) in HIJACK.

An East European official uses a swoop on the London Bullion market to escape behind the Iron Curtain, but he hasn't reckoned on CI5's intervention. In one of her first roles was British actress Jill Baker (as Amanda), pictured above on the set of HIJACK with Lewis Collins.

Shooting / Location Schedule

Production Dates: Tuesday 26th August to Friday 5th September, Wednesday 17th September, 1980. Production Number: 9D10075

26-28 August	***Amanda's Town flat***: Cavendish House, Wellington Road, St. John's Wood, London, NW8 ***Surveillance house***: 134 Downham Road, Islington, London, N1
29 August	***Main Road 1 (Harry & Swetman at roadside)***: Coronation Avenue / Uxbridge Road (A412), George Green, Berkshire ***Main Road 2 (Lorry hijack & lay-by)***: Uxbridge Road (A412), junction Billet Lane, Iver Heath, Buckinghamshire ***Wates Estate: Suburban house & garage***: The Larches, Pinewood Green, Iver Heath, Buckinghamshire
2nd Unit	***Game Keeper's cottage / Horse stunt***: Black Park Cottage, Black Park, Queen's Drive, Fulmer, Buckinghamshire
1 September	***Scrap Metal yard***: P. Atkinson Limited, 169 Boundary Road, South Wimbledon, London, SW19 ***Harry's office Car park (roof top)***: The Tower car park, Christchurch Road, Collier's Wood, London, SW19 ***High Rise Council block: Dusty's flat***: Copeland House, Garratt Lane, Tooting, London, SW17 ***Street: Taxi rank***: Hazelhurst Road (outside Colnbrook Court), Tooting, London, SW17
2 September	***Int: Indian Restaurant***: Curry House, Wembley Park Drive, Wembley, Middlesex ***Ext: Football stadium***: Wembley Stadium, Empire Way, Wembley, Middlesex
3 September	***Embassy***: Peacock House, 8 Addison Road, Holland Park, Kensington, London, W14 ***Hotel & Restaurant***: Hendon Hall Hotel, Ashley Lane, Hendon, London, NW4
4 September	***Int: Police station interview room***: 54-56 Wharf Road, Islington, London, N1 ***Canal Wharf & barge***: City Road Basin, off Wharf Road, Islington, London, N1 ***Ext / Int: Cowley's car (roadside)***: Noel Road, Islington, London, N1
5 September	***Hotel Hardy***: Phaedra Hotel, 12 Shepherds Hill, Highgate, London, N6
17 September	***Int / Ext: Cowley's car (run-by & radio-phone)***: Joel Street (near Argyle House), Northwood Hills, Middlesex

YOU'LL BE ALL RIGHT

by **Gerry O'Hara**
© Copyright Mark 1 Productions Ltd MCMLXXX

Jack Stone	Derrick O'Connor
Chrissie Stone	Geraldine Sherman
Linda Stone	Melissa Wilks
Nick Stone	Jason Savage
Len Hatch	Derek Francis
Roz Hatch	Janet Davies
Liz Spalding	Hazel McBride
Murphy	Steve Alder
Ned Turner	Malcolm Storry
Barney Moss	Don Hawkins
Anne	Sally Faulkner
Mrs. Johnson	Shirley Dixon
Billiard player	Freddie Boardley
Gardener	Arthur Whybrow
Rod	Stephen MacKenna
Pearson	Richard Albrecht
Lou	Grant-Ashley Warnock
CI5 mechanic	Graeme Eton
Labourer	James Butchart
Pat Weaver	Tex Fuller
Schoolgirls	Kellie Byrne, Joanne Bell
Uncredited	
Teacher	Mike Mungarvan
Teacher	Charlie Gray
Ambulanceman	Len Gilbey
Uniformed Policeman	Alan Troy

Director: **John Crome**

THE notorious Maiden Lane robbery has been the subject of two books and a serialisation in the Sunday newspaper. Most of the thieves who took part in the robbery are in jail, but one of them, Colin Roberts, died in a car blaze shortly afterwards. Only one of the ringleaders, Jack Stone, has never been caught, despite a prolonged and intensive police search. Doyle is astonished one early morning to receive a telephone call from Stone, explaining that he is living with his family in a London suburb and is prepared to give himself up to CI5 on certain conditions. Bodie and Doyle secretly head for Stone's home, where he has been hiding in a small attic. He tells the CI5 men that some enemy from his past has discovered where he is living and has sent several notes to his family threatening to punish him. His children's pet dog and cat have also been killed.

Stone promises that he will give himself up, if Bodie and Doyle will first eliminate this danger to his family. Cowley agrees to the deal and reminds his men that Stone's wife Chrissie is the daughter of the retired criminal Len Hatch. The men assume that someone who was disappointed about their share of the proceeds from the Maiden Lane robbery may bear a grudge against Stone, who was reputed to have taken a large amount of money for himself. Stone assures them that the robbery did not make him rich. Protection is arranged for Stone's children; a CI5 agent, Liz Spalding, guards eleven-year-old Linda, while Bodie guards the seven-year-old boy, Nick. However, Bodie misses Nick as he leaves school one day and the boy is walking home with a school friend when a large Mercedes car drives straight at them. Bodie is just in time to swoop the boys out of danger and the car accelerates away.

Bodie (Lewis Collins) attempts to cut off Pat Weaver's escape route through the Stone's garden in this scene from YOU'LL BE ALL RIGHT. The Stone's house was an empty property in Brook Avenue, Wembley, Middlesex - location manager Peter Carter had gained permission for its use from the local estate agent. It was especially chosen due to its close proximity to Lee Studios (the unit base), which was a necessary requirement due to the excessive amount of night shooting needed for this episode.

CI5 agents are keeping a watchful eye on the Stone's, but Chrissie finds a threatening letter in her shopping. The realisation that the enemy is so close to her terrifies her and she decides to take her children to stay with her father, Len Hatch. Chrissie drives away from her house early one morning. The CI5 man watching the house is drowsy after a night on duty and is too late to stop the car speeding off. Chrissie spots someone following her, and panic-stricken, she crashes her car. She is slightly hurt in the accident, but the children are uninjured.

While visiting Len Hatch, Cowley sees some of the Hatch family photographs, including some of the wedding of Colin Roberts, who was Len's nephew. Mrs. Hatch tells him that Colin's wife, Peggy, was so distressed by her husband's death in the car blaze, that she killed herself. Cowley also notices pictures of Peggy's father, Pat Weaver, himself a petty criminal and wonders if Weaver might bear a grudge against Stone, the man who escaped from a tragedy that killed his son and, indirectly, Peggy. Weaver is known to have an allotment near the Stone's home and might by chance have seen Stone there. Bodie and Doyle trace Weaver's present address and find the rat poison, which was used to kill the Stone's pets.

CI5 agents are sent to guard the Stone's premises, while Liz, the CI5 girl, stays with the family inside. One night, when Stone slips out for a stroll, the CI5 men notice Weaver creep into the house and after a dash through the Stone's garden, Bodie shoots him. Though Cowley is worried that, now that CI5 have dealt with the danger to his family, Stone may disappear again but true to his word, Stone gives himself up to Bodie and Doyle.

Production Unit

Created by	Brian Clemens
Executive Producers	Albert Fennell, Brian Clemens
Music	Laurie Johnson
Producer	Raymond Menmuir
Script Editor	Gerry O'Hara
Production Manager	Ron Purdie
Production Accountant	Terry Connors
Assistant Director	Gregory Dark
Location Manager	Peter Carter
Continuity	Pat Rambaut
Casting	Esta Charkham
Art Director	Ken Ryan
Set Dresser	Don Mingaye
Stunt Arranger	Peter Brayham
Wardrobe Supervisor	Donald Mothersill
Special Effects	Mike Collins
Lighting Cameraman	Dusty Miller
Camera Operator	John Maskall
Focus Puller	Chris Sargent
Make Up	Sue Black
Hairdresser	Sue Love
Lighting by	Lee Electric
Editor	Bob Dearberg GBFE
Sound Recordist	David Crozier
Boom Operator	Mike Silverlock
Dubbing Editor	Peter Lennard
Dubbing Mixer	Hugh Strain
Music Editor	Alan Willis
Post Production Supervisor	John S. Smith

An Avengers MARK 1 Production For LONDON WEEKEND TELEVISION

Shooting / Location Schedule

Production Dates: Monday 8th to Friday 19th September, 1980. Production Number: 9D10076

8 September	***Int: CI5 Computer room***: Kienzle Data Systems, 224 Bath Road, Slough, Berkshire
	Service station (CI5 Garage): 175 Bath Road, Slough, Berkshire
	Streets: Doyle's car run-by (roundabout): Farnham Road / Northborough Road, Manor Park, Slough, Berkshire
	Int: Doyle's car & run-by: Long Furlong Drive (near Kennedy Park), Britwell, Slough, Berkshire
9-12 September	***Stone's house / stream / Doyle's place***: 21 Brook Avenue, Wembley, Middlesex
15 September	***St. Margaret's school / St. Luke's school***: Rokesly Junior Schools, Rokesly Avenue / Elmfield Avenue, Crouch End, London, N8
	Streets near school: Nick and Lou walk home: Rokesly Avenue / Tottenham Lane / Ferme Park Road, Crouch End, London, N8
	Third street: Mercedes car / box stunt: Bourne Road / Haringey Park, Hornsey Vale, London, N8
	Liz Spalding's flat: Dale Court, Park Road, Crouch End, London, N8
16 September	***Streets / lock-ups / car chase run-bys***: Alexandra Park Road (near Alexandra Avenue), Wood Green, London, N22
	Mobile snack-bar stunt (cycleway): Alexandra Park, off Bedford Road, Muswell Hill, London, N22
17-18 September	***Len Hatch's house***: Dutch Lodge, 33 Astons Road, Moor Park, Northwood, Hertfordshire
	Prison 1 / Prison 2: T. A Centre, Elmgrove Road, Harrow, Middlesex
19 September	***Billiard Hall***: Hope & Anchor, Tottenham Lane, Hornsey, London, N8
	Bookmakers shop: A. R Dennis Bookmakers, 167 Priory Road, Hornsey, London, N8
	Allotments: Alexandra Palace Way, Muswell Hill, London, N22
	High Rise Block (Weaver's girlfriends flat): Ilex House, Crouch Hill, Stroud Green, London, N4
2nd Unit:	
	Third street: Mercedes car / box stunt: Bourne Road / Haringey Park, Hornsey Vale, London, N8
	Streets: Bodie's car run-by: Park Lane / Dagmar Avenue, Wembley, Middlesex
	St. Paul's Cathedral (Memorial service): St. Paul's Cathedral, St. Paul's Churchyard, London, EC4

KICKBACK

by **Stephen Lister**
© Copyright Mark 1 Productions Ltd MCMLXXX

Jimmy Keller	Norman Eshley
Sheila Kaufmann	Meg Davies
Benedek	Peter Whitman
Major Nairn	James Faulkner
Travaioli	Hal Galili
Murphy	Steve Alder
Spelman	Ben Howard
Russell (James) Sutherland	Job Stewart
Simms	Christopher Mitchell
Richardson	Roy Purcell
Donatti	Marc Boyle
Valerii	Val Musetti
Price	Ian Fairbairn
Uncredited	
Yacht Security Guard	Andrew Andreas
Sutherland's Driver	Ronnie Watkins

Director: **Ian Sharp**

BODIE and Doyle are sent to arrest a group of Italian terrorists meeting in London, but to his surprise, Bodie finds that one of the terrorists, Jimmy Keller, is a friend who served with him in the SAS and once saved his life. Cowley meets Major Nairn, the head of SAS and learns that Keller has been working undercover with the terrorist organisation for two years and is now one of their most trusted members. Cowley is anxious because a photograph of a leading public figure, Alexander Richardson, has been found in the terrorists' hideout. One of the arrested terrorists, Carl Spelman, has confessed that Richardson is to be murdered by contract to earn money for the organisation. Keller tells Bodie and Doyle that he is supposed to organise the Richardson killing, so Bodie is 'recruited' as the assassin and the terrorists too accept him. Bodie however soon becomes suspicious of Keller's true allegiances when Keller takes him to a country farmhouse and introduces him to his girlfriend, a wanted German terrorist named Sheila Kaufmann.

Cowley tricks Spelman into leading CI5 to the people who are paying the terrorists to murder Richardson and the SAS man takes him to the office of Mr. Price. Cowley learns from Price that it is the industrialist, James (Russell) Sutherland, who is paying for Richardson's assassination. Richardson is to be killed because he is on the verge of revealing Sutherland's business swindles during an official inquiry. Richardson is warned that an assassination attempt is to be made on his life, but Cowley asks if the man will allow the attempt to go ahead; Richardson will be protected from harm by a bullet-proof vest and because Cowley's man on the inside, Bodie, is to be the hit man. By tapping Sutherland's telephone, Cowley learns that Sutherland is to meet the leader of the terrorists, Renato Travaioli, and pay him £500,000 for Richardson's murder. When Sutherland hears that Richardson has been assassinated, he sets off to pay the terrorist leader - he does not know that Richardson is unhurt. Leaving the scene of the shooting with Keller, Bodie is stunned when his friend suddenly stops the car, hits him on the back of the head, and throws his body onto the pavement.

Cowley and the squad watch the meeting between Sutherland and Travaioli, and the handover of the money is photographed for use as evidence. Sutherland is arrested, but the terrorist leader drives to a safe house with the money, only to be met by Keller, who subdues the man, steals the money and leaves the body in gas-filled room set to explode. Having recovered from his earlier injury, Bodie heads for the farmhouse and intercepts Donatti, a terrorist who has suspected a double-cross, before Sheila can be harmed. Bodie forces her to reveal that Keller had planned to steal the money and Bodie goes to Keller's hideout, a London warehouse, to confront his friend. As Bodie arrives, terrorists, who have realised what Keller's intentions are, and are planning to kill him, surround him and Keller. After a gunfight, the terrorists are killed and Keller is taken into custody, after being wounded taking a bullet intended for Bodie.

Production Unit

Created by	Brian Clemens
Executive Producers	Albert Fennell, Brian Clemens
Music	Laurie Johnson
Producer	Raymond Menmuir
Script Editor	Gerry O'Hara
Production Manager	Ron Purdie
Production Accountant	Terry Connors
Assistant Director	Simon Hinkly
Location Manager	Peter Carter
Continuity	Pat Rambaut
Casting	Esta Charkham
Art Director	Ken Ryan
Set Dresser	Don Mingaye
Stunt Arranger	Peter Brayham
Wardrobe Supervisor	Donald Mothersill
Special Effects	Mike Collins
Lighting Cameraman	Dusty Miller
Camera Operator	John Maskall
Focus Puller	Chris Sargent
Make Up	Sue Black
Hairdresser	Sue Love
Lighting by	Lee Electric
Editor	Alan Killick
Sound Recordist	David Crozier
Boom Operators	Mike Silverlock, John Samworth
Dubbing Editor	Peter Lennard
Dubbing Mixer	Hugh Strain

Music Editor Alan Willis
Post Production Supervisor John S. Smith

An Avengers MARK 1 Production For LONDON WEEKEND TELEVISION

Martin Shaw poses for the stills cameraman on the set of KICKBACK.

Shooting / Location Schedule

Production Dates: Monday 22nd September to Friday 3rd October, 1980.
Production Number: 9D10077

22 September	**Marina (boat yard)**: Harleyford Marine, Harleyford Estate, Marlow, Buckinghamshire
23-24 September	**Int: Bodie's car (route to Keller's warehouse)**: Queen Caroline Street / Talgarth Road / Shepherd's Bush Road, Hammersmith, London, W14
	Int / Ext: Keller's warehouse / Price's office: Cadby Hall (Block Y), Blythe Road, Hammersmith, London, W14

	CI5 HQ Interrogation room: Spelman escapes: Cadby Hall, Blythe Road, Hammersmith, London, W14
	Int: CI5 car (with Spelman): Sinclair Road / Maclise Road, Hammersmith, London, W14
	Ext: CI5 car (with Spelman): Addison Gardens / Elsham Road / Sinclair Road / Hofland Road, Hammersmith, London, W14
	Park: Cowley & Nairn: Kensington Gardens, Kensington Road, London, SW7
25 September	***Int: Cowley's car***: 78 Liverpool Road (past Northern Auto Repair), Islington, London, N1
	Int / Ext: Radio van / Warehouse: Royal Agricultural Hall, Liverpool Road, Islington, London, N1
	Warehouse streets & stunt: Barford Road / Liverpool Road, Islington, London, N1
	Street (Sutherland's car & CI5 cars): Cloudesley Street, Islington, London, N1
25-29 September	***Motorway bridge (Keller meets Benedek)***: Littlefield Green (B3024) (over M4 Motorway), White Waltham, Berkshire
	Int / Ext: Keller's car: Crockford Bridge, Shurlock Road / Callins Lane, Waltham St. Lawrence, Berkshire
	Benedek's caravan: Pool Lane, off Broadmore Lane, Waltham St. Lawrence, Berkshire
	Airfield: White Waltham Airfield, Waltham Road, White Waltham, Berkshire
	Keller's farmhouse: Halls Farm, Halls Lane, Waltham St. Lawrence, Berkshire
30 September	***Richardson's place***: 4 The Grove, Highgate, London, N6
	Car run-by (Richardson on route): Highgate West Hill / South Grove, Highgate, London, N6
	CI5 Safe house & garage: 70 Coolhurst Road (garage) / Wolseley Road (Cowley's car), Crouch End, London, N8
1 October	***Park: Richardson's assassination***: Finsbury Park, Hornsey Gate, Endymion Road, Finsbury Park, London, N4
2 October	***Traviolli's house & explosion***: 15 Myddelton Square, Finsbury, London, N1
	Alleyway: Keller & Bodie: Chadwell Street, Finsbury, London, N1
3 October	***Sutherland House***: The Tower, 125 High Street, Collier's Wood, London, SW19
	Int: Sutherland's car: Upper Tooting Road / Tooting High Street, London, SW17

DISCOVERED IN A GRAVEYARD

by **Christopher Wicking**
© Copyright Mark 1 Productions Ltd MCMLXXX

Dr. Siegel	Derek Waring
Hogan	Philip Latham
Mayli Kuolo	Megumi Shimanuki
Colonel Lin Foh	Vincent Wong
Malone	Richard Moore
Coroner	Owen Holder
Murphy	Steve Alder
Editor	David Yip
Caretaker	Rayner Bourton
Rita	Julie Sullivan
Nurse Hale	Toni Kanal
Blonde	Linda Lou Allen
Desk Clerk	Michael Maynard
Old lady	Betty Lawrence
German lady	Elisabeth Choice
CI5 man	Brian Abbott
Embassy man	Rex Wei
Service waiter	Peter Polycarpou
Nurse	Heather Emmanuelle
Ambulance man	Gary Taylor
Uncredited	
Uniformed Policeman (Court)	Pat Gorman
Plain clothes Policeman (Court)	Mike Reynell
Uniformed Policeman	Jimmy Muir
Second Embassy Man	Richard Lee

Director: **Anthony Simmons**

BODIE and Doyle are pursuing two suspected terrorists through the London streets. The terrorists drive their van into a car park underneath a West End hotel and, while trying to escape from the CI5 men, crash the van. As the van crashes, a bomb they are carrying in it explodes and both men are killed. Staying at the hotel is Colonel Lin Foh, the hated leader of a foreign power who has been deposed by a revolution and has come to Britain for medical treatment. Assuming that the bomb was intended for him, he asks Cowley for full police protection. Cowley tells him that the British do not want foreign quarrels settled on the London streets and orders him to leave Britain as soon as possible. After the inquests on the dead terrorists, Bodie and Doyle leave the coroner's court and a small Citroen follows Doyle home. The driver watches Doyle enter his flat and later, finding Doyle unarmed, shoots the CI5 man at point blank range. Bodie finds his partner lying seriously injured and races to summon medical help. At the hospital, Cowley refuses to allow Bodie to wait while doctors struggle to save Doyle's life and Bodie is sent to his colleague's flat to search for clues about the identity of Doyle's attacker. Bodie finds that bullets embedded in the wall of the flat are of the same type as those used in a recent terrorist murder in Amsterdam.

Cowley is certain that the attack on Doyle is linked to the two dead terrorists and Bodie tries to recall the exact events leading up to the explosion; he remembers that, when they were following the two terrorists, they watched one of the men meet the other in a shop. In a shop next door, Doyle had met a girl who sold him a jewelled ring and, later on in the chase after the terrorist van, Doyle mentioned seeing the girl again. As Doyle hovers between life and death in a hospital bed, Cowley worries that the CI5 man may not make the necessary mental effort to survive. However, though racked by violent dreams, Doyle recovers consciousness, long enough to give some information on his attacker; Bodie sees Doyle's fingers forming the shape of a ring.

Bodie finds the ring and traces it back to the girl; Mayli Koulos, the daughter of a journalist who died in one of Colonel Lin Foh's prisons. Assuming that Mayli is in league with the terrorists who tried to plant the bomb at the hotel, Cowley talks to the British Government official, Peter Hogan, about the case. To his horror, Cowley learns that Hogan was informed by Mayli's embassy why the girl was in London. Hogan explains that he did not inform Cowley of the girl's intentions, because the British Government had not yet decided what its attitude should be to Foh's enemies. Astounded by Hogan's admission, Cowley threatens to give the newspapers the full scandalous story that Doyle's life is in the balance because of 'diplomatic niceties', and Bodie is sent to protect Lin Foh from any further attempts on his life. When Bodie finds Mayli's room, Mayli has already killed her prey and escapes from Bodie at the same time. Wounded in the battle, she gains access to the safety of her own embassy. However, when they find that she is dying from her injuries, the embassy staff put her outside so that her martyrdom in pursuit of her country's enemy will be made public. Bodie calls an ambulance for her and she is taken to hospital. Doyle recovers from his wounds and leaves the hospital some weeks later.

Production Unit

Created by	Brian Clemens
Executive Producers	Albert Fennell, Brian Clemens
Music	Laurie Johnson
Producer	Raymond Menmuir
Script Editor	Gerry O'Hara
Production Manager	Ron Purdie
Production Accountant	Terry Connors
Assistant Director	Gregory Dark
Location Manager	Peter Carter
Continuity	Pat Rambaut
Casting	Esta Charkham

Art Director	Ken Ryan
Set Dresser	Don Mingaye
Stunt Arranger	Peter Brayham
Wardrobe Supervisor	Donald Mothersill
Special Effects	Mike Collins
Lighting Cameraman	Norman Langley
Camera Operator	John Maskall
Focus Puller	Chris Sargent
Make Up	Sue Black
Hairdresser	Sue Love
Lighting by	Lee Electric
Editor	Bob Dearberg
Sound Recordist	David Crozier
Boom Operator	John Samworth
Dubbing Editor	Peter Lennard
Dubbing Mixer	Hugh Strain
Music Editor	Alan Willis
Post Production Supervisor	John S. Smith

An Avengers MARK 1 Production For LONDON WEEKEND TELEVISION

Whilst investigating a bombing plot Doyle is shot and left for dead in his flat, and as the hospital fights to save his life, he seems unable to decide whether he wants to live or die...meanwhile, both Cowley (Gordon Jackson) and Bodie (Lewis Collins) make an all out effort to find the girl who shot him in DISCOVERED IN A GRAVEYARD.

Shooting / Location Schedule

Production Dates: Monday 6th to Friday 17th October, Wednesday 5th November, 1980. Production Number: 9D10079

6 October	***West End Hotel (underground car park)***: NCP, Lowndes Square, (Sheraton Park Tower Hotel), Knightsbridge, London, SW1
7 October	***Doyle's flat***: Oakwood Court, Kensington, London, W14
	CI5 phone room: Cadby Hall, Blythe Road, Hammersmith, London, W14
8 October	***Int / Ext: Hogan's office***: Islington Town Hall, Upper Street / Richmond Grove, Islington, London, N1
	Int: Cowley's car: Northchurch Road, Islington, London, N1
9-10 October	***Int / Ext: Hospital***: Royal Free Hospital, Rosslyn Hill, Hampstead, London, NW3
	Street: Paper shop & Bodie's car: 92 Haverstock Hill Steele's Road (Bodie's car), Belsize Park, London, NW3
13 October	***Mayli's Bric-A-Brac shop***: Commercial Place (Camden Lock Place), Camden, London, NW1
	Int: Bodie's car (with Cowley): Chalk Farm Road, Camden, London, NW1
	Streets: Doyle (shopping): Chalk Farm Road, Camden, London, NW1
	Bodie's car & van: Malden Road (near Rhyl Street), Kentish Town, London, NW5
	Int / Ext: Charlie's rooming house: 54 Malden Road, Kentish Town, NW5
	Int / Ext: Launderette: Coin Op, 6 Malden Road, Kentish Town, London, NW5
	Ext: Hotel street / Bodie's car & van: Adelaide Road / Holiday Inn, 128 King Henry's Road, Swiss Cottage, London, NW3
14-15 October	***Palace Hotel & car park / CI5 computer room***: Heathrow Airport Hotel, Bath Road, Hayes, Middlesex
	Int: Bodie's car (Palace Hotel): Bath Road, Harlington, Middlesex
16 October	***Graveyard / Cemetery (all fantasy)***: Dissenters' Chapel, Kensal Green Cemetery, Harrow Road, London, W10
	Coroner's court & outside: St. Pancras Coroners Court, Camley Street, St. Pancras, London, NW1
17 October	***Embassy / Phone box 1 & 2***: 12 Park Place Villas, Maida Vale, London, W2
2nd Unit:	***Hospital: Doyle's room***: Northwick Park Hospital, Watford Road, Harrow, Middlesex
	Van explosion: Sobell Sports Centre car park, Hornsey Road, Holloway, London, N7
5 November	***Ext: Bodie's car 'night' run-by (Embassy route)***: Cabbell Street, Lisson Grove, London, NW1

FOXHOLE ON THE ROOF

by **Brian Clemens**
© Copyright Mark 1 Productions Ltd MCMLXXX

Roddy Barker	Stanley Meadows
Paul Stacey	Karl Howman
Jack Cobber	Ron Pember
Murphy	Steve Alder
Inspector Newton	Robert Putt
Sergeant Wood	C. J. Allen
Dunston	Roderic Leigh
Maisie	Barbara Keogh
Doctor	Richard Simpson
Nurse	Lorrain Grey
Tessa	Kim Goody
Bob	Alan Polonsky
Merton	Peter John
Bob's girl	Sarah Kenyon
Bud	Peter Joyce
Patients	Peggy Bullock, Jean Campbell-Dallas
Uncredited	
Party Guest	Alan Swaden
Party Guest	Bill Burns
RAF Security Guard	Chris Webb
CI5 Marksman	Terry Plummer
CI5 Marksman	Bill Hemmings
CI5 Marksman	Dave Church
Uniformed Policeman	Dennis Plenty

Director: **William Brayne**

INSTEAD of celebrating his freedom from prison after serving a 25-year prison sentence for violent crime, Roddy Barker puts into execution criminal plans that he has made during his term in jail. He and one of his two accomplices, Paul Stacey, take a selection of powerful stolen weapons to the roof of a high warehouse in London and settle down in a foxhole they have built there. Their arrival is seen by a squatter who, after watching them unload their weapons and close an impenetrable steel door on the stairs, calls the police and CI5.

When the Squad arrives, the only evidence found to confirm the man's story is an ammunition clip dropped by Stacey as he made his way to the roof. Cowley is puzzled why the gunmen have taken his unusual action until, a short while later; they begin to blast off machine-gun fire at the windows of a nearby hospital ward full of post-operative patients. No one in the ward is killed, but when the doctors and nurses rush to help the patients who have been injured, they are driven back by further shots from the men. There are no high vantage points nearby from which CI5 can fire at the gunmen, but Bodie and fellow CI5 agent, Murphy start scaling a tall industrial chimney, which overlooks the warehouse roof. Cowley calls for a police helicopter, but as the pilot flies low over the warehouse, Stacey, wearing a blonde wig and dressed as a woman, walks out of the foxhole with his hands up and word 'hostage' pinned to his back. In response to this new threat, Cowley orders the helicopter to leave. He also sends Doyle to find out what he can about the identities of the men in the foxhole above them.

The criminals inform Cowley that until £500,000 is brought to them and arrangements are made for their safe getaway, they will not allow anyone to go to the assistance of the hospital patients. Doyle, meanwhile, has found that the ammunition clip found on the stairs contains the fingerprints of Paul Stacey, a well-known criminal. He visit's Stacey's home and persuades Stacey's girlfriend, Tessa, to tell him what she knows. She tells him that her boyfriend is involved in a daring crime and that the name Thomas Dunston was mentioned. Doyle discovers that Dunston was once in the air force, and as the weapons were stolen from a nearby air force base, he immediately connects the man to the robbery and heads for his house.

At the warehouse, the ransom money has arrived and is hoisted up to the building's roof. While Barker and his 'hostage' are out of the foxhole, Murphy and Bodie, who are hanging from the top of the chimney that they have scaled, attempt to shoot Barker, but the shot misses and Barker retaliates and wounds Murphy. At the moment a car is brought to the building, a helicopter bearing police colours approaches the warehouse roof again. Cowley is unable to make contact and realises that the helicopter belongs to the criminals and is approaching to whisk them away. However, as Barker pushes his 'hostage' up the rope ladder, Bodie, seeing that the 'hostage' is really a man, fires at Stacey and the criminal falls back onto the roof. Barker grabs the ladder and shouts at Dunston in the helicopter to fly him away, but Doyle is sitting beside the pilot with a gun at his head. Barker, not wishing to return to prison, leaps off the rope ladder and is instantly killed on the ground far below.

Production Unit

Created by	Brian Clemens
Executive Producers	Albert Fennell, Brian Clemens
Music	Laurie Johnson
Producer	Raymond Menmuir
Script Editor	Gerry O'Hara
Production Manager	Ron Purdie
Production Accountant	Terry Connors
Assistant Director	Simon Hinkly
Location Manager	Stuart Freeman
Continuity	Doreen Soan
Casting	Esta Charkham
Art Director	Ken Ryan

A post-operative ward in a hospital is held to ransom by a newly-released convict. CI5 agents Bodie (Lewis Collins) and Murphy (Steve Alder) hatch a plan to bring him down before he takes a fatal shot at the hospital, but in scaling a chimney things go horribly wrong for the two agents when Murphy is shot and left dangling...

Set Dresser	Terry Parr
Stunt Arranger	Peter Brayham
Wardrobe Supervisor	Donald Mothersill
Special Effects	Mike Collins
Lighting Cameraman	Dusty Miller
Camera Operator	John Maskall
Focus Puller	Chris Sargent
Make Up	Sue Black
Hairdresser	Sue Love
Lighting by	Lee Electric
Editor	Alan Killick
Sound Recordist	David Crozier
Boom Operator	John Samworth
Dubbing Editor	Peter Lennard
Dubbing Mixer	Trevor Pyke
Music Editor	Alan Willis
Post Production Supervisor	John S. Smith

An Avengers MARK 1 Production For LONDON WEEKEND TELEVISION

Shooting / Location Schedule

Production Dates: Monday 20th to Friday 31st October, Friday 7th November, Monday 1st December, 1980. Production Number: 9D10078

20 October	***Jack Cobber's flat***: Hurley House, Cotton Gardens Estate, Kennington Lane, Lambeth, London, SE11
21-30 October	***Warehouse & rooftop***: Chambers Wharf Cold Storage, Chambers Street, Bermondsey, London, SE16 ***Newton & CI5's temporary base***: Old Mill Car Valet, 33 Bermondsey Wall West, Bermondsey, London, SE16 ***Forensic Laboratory / RAF Records / Hospital***: St. Joseph's School, George Row, Bermondsey, London, SE16 ***Chimney***: Lavender Dock (entrance next to Lavender Dock Pump House), Rotherhithe Street, Rotherhithe, London, SE16
31 October	***Stacey's home / Dunston's country home***: Larkenshaw Farm, Stonehill Road, Chobham, Surrey ***RAF Pirbright***: Ministry of Defence Navy Records, Chobham Business Centre, 319 Chertsey Road, Chobham, Surrey
7 Nov	***CI5 HQ Computer room***: Cadby Hall, Blythe Road, Hammersmith, London, W14
1 December	***Ext: Newspaper shop (Doyle's car)***: 162 Thornbury Road, Osterley, Middlesex ***Int: Doyle's car (on route to RAF records)***: Jersey Road / Alderney Avenue, Osterley, Middlesex

THE OJUKA SITUATION
by **David Humphries**
© Copyright Mark 1 Productions Ltd MCMLXXX

President Ojuka	Clarke Peters
Katunda	Shope Shodeinde
Avery	Geoffrey Palmer
Murphy	Steve Alder
Headmaster	John Horsley
Parker	Charles Dance
Faroud	Al Matthews
Salesman	Harry Fowler
Major Danby	Robert Swann
Inspector	Colin McCormack
Doctor	Michael Bertenshaw
Hotel receptionist	Jane West
2nd Doctor	Derek Smith
CI5 girl	Emma Relph
Detective	Bruce Alexander
Felix Ojuka	Paul Medford
Uncredited	
Ojuka's Bodyguard	Richard Sheekey
1st Assassin	Dinny Powell
2nd Assassin	David Holland
Uniformed Policeman	Peter Roy
Uniformed Policeman	Pat Gorman
Uniformed Policeman	Tony O'Leary
CI5 Man	Gus Roy
Thug 1 (Driver)	Romo Garrara
Thug 2 (Passenger)	Reg Turner
CI5 Man	Ray Knight
Limousine Driver	Eddie Powell
Gunman (Woods)	Gregg Powell
Parker's Aide	Peter Brace
Parker's Aide	Dave Griffiths

Director: **Christopher King**

COLONEL Hakim Ojuka, the head of the African state of Betan until his enemies deposed him, hopes to regain power in Betan with the help of the British. He is in Britain for an international conference at which his future will be discussed. Ojuka and his wife, Katunda, are under the protection of the British Army and an army security officer is with them when they go to visit their son, Felix, at a school in the country. As they leave the school three armed men attack them. Ojuka, who is armed, shoots back at their attackers, as does the security officer and although Ojuka is unscathed, three of the gunmen and the security officer are killed. CI5 are given the job of protecting the visiting African, and Bodie and Doyle are assigned to get him safely to the conference. Before they leave, however, Cowley insists that Ojuka hands over his firearm. Cowley then makes enquiries from the Home Office as to why Ojuka, a man known to have many enemies in Britain, was allowed to risk his life by visiting his son.

That night at the safe house where the two CI5 agents are guarding Ojuka, three men try to break in and kill the African. Bodie and Doyle are able to kill all three before they reach their target. This new incident makes Cowley decide that it is too risky for Ojuka to remain in London and he orders his colleagues to take the man to the country hotel where the conference is to be held; Ojuka's wife, Katunda, is to remain at the safe house.

During their journey, Bodie and Doyle realise that a car is tailing them. The car gains on them and the men inside begin to fire at the CI5 car, forcing it off the road. Armed men approach Ojuka from the car. Before they can reach him, Doyle fires and kills the men. This third attack convinces the CI5 men that Ojuka's enemies are being tipped off about his whereabouts and they decide that the only way to ensure his safety is for them to abandon all CI5 plans and take Ojuka to a quiet hotel of their choosing.

Special Effects supervisor Mike Collins, on the set of THE OJUKA SITUATION. Mike Collins macabre nickname, 'Doctor Death' was given to him by actress, Joanna Lumley when she was asked about explosions in THE NEW AVENGERS series, which he had set up. She told Michael Parkinson on his chat show: "My friend Doctor Death looks after those for me!"

In a dramatic conclusion to THE OJUKA SITUATION, Bodie (Lewis Collins) catches up with Avery (Geoffrey Palmer) and Katunda (Shope Shodeinde).

They find a hotel in Slough and then contact Cowley to report this latest incident. Cowley has discovered that the senior Home Office official who gave permission for Ojuka's visit to his son's school, also has substantial business interests in Africa; he might therefore be involved with Ojuka's enemies and be passing on information to the gang to protect his business interests. Cowley explains this to Bodie over the radio and tells him that the Home Office official, John Avery, has a large house near to the conference hotel; this may be the base used by the gang who are trying to kill Ojuka. Bodie is ordered to check on Avery's home and keep watch, while Doyle guards Ojuka at the Slough hotel.

Without Doyle's knowledge or permission, Ojuka telephones his wife to tell her that he is safe. Katunda, however, secretly hates her husband for crimes he committed against her people in Africa; it is she who has been betraying him to his enemies since they arrived in England. She tells the leader of the gang, Faroud, that her husband is at the Slough hotel. Faroud arranges for a hired killer named Parker and two henchmen to free Katunda from the CI5 safe house, then take her to her husband. When Doyle opens the door to Katunda, Parker's men overwhelm him and the both he and Ojuka are taken prisoner. They are taken to Avery's home, where Faroud tells Ojuka that he will be taken home to Betan and publicly executed for his crimes. Bodie sees Avery arrive in a helicopter and realises that Ojuka is to be flown out of the country and Doyle will probably be killed. With this in mind, he ignores Cowley's orders not to intervene and rushes in to help his colleague. Cowley arrives and Katunda and Avery are handed over into police custody. Safe at last, Ojuka sets off for the conference with Cowley as his escort.

Production Unit

Created by	Brian Clemens
Executive Producers	Albert Fennell, Brian Clemens
Music	Laurie Johnson
Producer	Raymond Menmuir
Script Editor	Gerry O'Hara
Production Manager	Ron Purdie
Production Accountant	Terry Connors
Assistant Director	Gregory Dark
Location Manager	Peter Carter
Continuity	Doreen Soan
Casting	Esta Charkham
Art Director	Ken Ryan
Set Dresser	Richard Rooker
Stunt Arranger	Peter Brayham
Wardrobe Supervisor	Donald Mothersill
Special Effects	Mike Collins
Lighting Cameraman	Michael Davis
Camera Operator	John Maskall
Focus Puller	Chris Sargent
Make Up	Sue Black
Hairdresser	Sue Love
Lighting by	Lee Electric
Editor	Bob Dearberg
Sound Recordist	David Crozier
Boom Operator	John Samworth
Dubbing Editor	Peter Lennard
Dubbing Mixer	Hugh Strain
Music Editor	Alan Willis
Post Production Supervisor	John S. Smith

An Avengers MARK 1 Production For LONDON WEEKEND TELEVISION

A sacked former African Head attempts to get reinstated in office using the help of the British Government, but the plan is sidetracked by one particular civil servant who now wants him dead. Bodie (Lewis Collins) and Doyle (Martin Shaw) in scenes from THE OJUKA SITUATION.

Shooting / Location Schedule

Production Dates: Monday 3rd to Friday 14th November, 1980. Production Number: 9D10081

3-4 November	***Int / Ext: Public School***: Haileybury Junior School, Clewer Manor, Imperial Road, Windsor, Berkshire
5 November	***Mansion Block - Safe House One***: 6 Cabbell Street (from Old Marylebone Road), Lisson Grove, London, NW1
6-7 November	***Int / Ext: CI5 HQ / Coroners / Police Station***: Cadby Hall, Blythe Road & Brook Green (Block A), Hammersmith, London, W14
10-11 November	***Bodie's car & ambush***: Hawthorn Lane / Lord Mayor's Drive / Halse Drive / Dukes Drive / McAuliffe Drive, Burnhan Beeches, Buckinghamshire
	Int / Ext: Beeches Hotel / Pub bar (Parker): Burnham Beeches Hotel, Grove Road, Burnham, Buckinghamshire
12-13 November	***Avery's country home / Faroud's house***: Leys Farm, Thompkins Lane, East Burnham, Buckinghamshire
	Country road (Parker's car): Hawthorn Lane, Burnham Beeches, East Burnham, Buckinghamshire
	Int: Parker's car: Farnham Lane, East Burnham, Buckinghamshire
	Int: Cowley's car (on route to Avery's home): Church Lane, Stoke Green, Wexham, Buckinghamshire
14 November	***Int / Ext: Ministry Buildings - Avery's office***: Islington Town Hall, Upper Street / Richmond Grove, Islington, London, N1

OPERATION SUSIE
by **Ranald Graham**
© Copyright Mark 1 Productions Ltd MCMLXXX

Diana Molner	Alice Krige
Rudiger Molner	Ewan Stewart
Northcott	Harold Innocent
Jane	Maggie Henderson
Somerfield	John Line
MacLean	Donald McKillop
Torres	Alexander Davion
Smith	George Raistrick
Deville	Robert McBain
Powell	Andrew MacLachlan
Philip Latimer	Robert Morgan
Harris	P. H. Moriarty
Dodds	Geoffrey Freshwater
D.I. Harrington	Bernard Finch
Student	Colm Daly
Dr. Roberts	Jim Wiggins
Receptionist	Jackie Downey
Driver	Roger Owen
1st Ambulance man	Barry Copping
Uncredited	
Northcott's Heavy	Joey Bartlet
Court Security Agent	Walter Henry
Court Solicitor	Lionel De Clerc

Director: **Ian Sharp**

TWO South American students, Diana Molner and her teenage brother Rudi, together with Philip Latimer, a chemist, are involved in 'cocaine trafficking' in London. Three armed men named Charlie Powell, Joe Smith and Dan Harris interrupt their operations, and when Rudi tries to drive the men away at gunpoint, an innocent bystander, Pamela, is shot dead in the crossfire. Latimer is also wounded in the ensuing fight.

By the time CI5 arrive to investigate the shooing, Diana and Rudi have managed to drag Latimer to their car and have driven him to a hospital for treatment. Smith and Harris meanwhile receive orders that, as Diana and her brother are witnesses to the dead girl's murder; they must be found and silenced. Harris discovers the students as they leave the wounded Latimer in a hospital casualty ward. He tries to kill Molner but, although Rudi is wounded in the attempt, he manages to shoot Harris dead. Rudi then hijacks a car from the hospital car park and drives his sister to safety. When Bodie and Doyle arrive at the hospital and find Harris's body, they are concerned that the man is carrying an official walkie-talkie and may be a Secret Service agent.

Cowley finds further evidence to support this theory, when the registration number of the Molner's abandoned car leads him to Diana Molner's records. To his surprise, he finds that these are being held in confidence by the Foreign Office.

Meanwhile, Raoul Northcott, the man behind the assassination attempts on the Molner's lives and head of the Foreign Office's 'dirty tricks' department MI11, is annoyed when his men report that CI5 are also trying to find the students. He nevertheless instructs his men to continue their search, follow the CI5 men until the Molners are found, and kill them. Meanwhile, Latimer dies of gunshot wounds.

Having taken refuge in a hotel, the Molners force a doctor to tend to Rudi's wounds and then leave for a new hideaway. Bodie and Doyle have in the meantime, rigged up a loudspeaker to their car calling for the Molners to give themselves up into CI5 care for their own protection. Diana telephones Cowley, but when the ambulance arrives, Northcott's men open fire on the CI5 agents and Rudi is killed. Cowley learns that Diana is the daughter of a left-wing general in the South American state of Escandiaz. Other details on the Molner family are being held by the Foreign Office and Cowley suspicious that its head, Northcott, may be involved in the recent killings investigates the matter further. His suspicions are confirmed when the MI11 man arrives at the CI5 safe house where Diana is being kept and introduces Cowley to an Escondiaz Embassy official named Eduardo Torres. The man insists that Diana has diplomatic immunity and must be handed over to him immediately.

Cowley discovers from a personal contact, that the Escondiaz ruling right-wing junta support their country's economy by selling cocaine; Diana and Rudi, who oppose the junta, have been selling artificial cocaine in London to undermine the junta's market. Northcott must have been instructed to put a stop to the Molners' activities. Cowley, fearing for Diana's life, orders Bodie and Doyle to take the girl to a secret hiding place to protect her. However, a CI5 lawyer tells Cowley that he must co-operate with Northcott and tell him where Diana can be found. Cowley then discovers from a trade unionist leader who supports the left wing in Escondiaz that Diana's father, General Molner, with the support of the British Prime Minister, is leading a coup against the ruling junta. To confirm his suspicions about Northcott, Cowley visits the Foreign Office official and arrests him for treason demanding that he stops his agents from attacking Diana and his men. The agents are already involved in a pitched battle with Bodie and Doyle, and by the time Northcott's order to cease firing arrives, Diana Molner has been killed.

Production Unit

Created by	Brian Clemens
Executive Producers	Albert Fennell, Brian Clemens
Music	Laurie Johnson
Producer	Raymond Menmuir
Script Editor	Gerry O'Hara
Production Manager	Ron Purdie
Production Accountant	Terry Connors

Assistant Director	Simon Hinkly
Location Manager	Peter Carter
Continuity	Doreen Soan
Casting	Esta Charkham
Art Director	Ken Ryan
Set Dresser	Don Mingaye
Wardrobe Supervisor	Donald Mothersill
Special Effects	Mike Collins
Lighting Cameraman	Dusty Miller
Camera Operator	John Maskall
Focus Puller	Chris Sargent
Make Up	Sue Black
Hairdresser	Sue Love
Lighting by	Lee Electric
Editor	Bob Dearberg
Sound Recordist	David Crozier
Boom Operator	John Samworth
Dubbing Editor	Peter Lennard
Dubbing Mixer	Hugh Strain
Music Editor	Alan Willis
Post Production Supervisor	John S. Smith

An Avengers MARK 1 Production For LONDON WEEKEND TELEVISION

Bodie (Lewis Collins) and Doyle (Martin Shaw) in OPERATION SUSIE.

Shooting / Location Schedule
Production Dates: Monday 17th to Friday 28th November, 1980. Production Number: 9D10080

17 November	**Philip Latimer's place**: 18 Shepherds Hill, Crouch End, London, N6
18 November	**Streets (Common meeting: Northcott & Smith)**: High Road / Duckett's Common, Willoughby Road, Hornsey, London, N8

	Shops (Chemist) / Ext: Rudi's van: Petter Chemist, 47 The Broadway, Crouch End, London, N8
	Int: Rudi's van: Tottenham Lane (near Nelson Road), Crouch End, London, N8
	Street: Diana & Rudi pull up to tend to Philip: Avenue Road / Crescent Road, Crouch End, London, N8
	Walkway: Northcott & Smith: Parkland Walk, Crouch End Hill, Crouch End, London, N8
19 November	***CI5 HQ & Forensic laboratory / College***: West London College & Cadby Hall, Brook Green, Hammersmith, London, W14
20 November	***Hospital***: St. Bernards Hospital, Uxbridge Road, Southall, Middlesex
21 November	***Streets: Range Rover drops off Rudi & Diana***: Inverness Place / Inverness Terrace, Bayswater, London, W2
	Streets: Doyle's car followed by Smith's car: Queensway / Inverness Place, Bayswater, London, W2
	Streets: Doyle's car / Smith's car skid (parked cars): Inverness Place, Bayswater, London, W2
	B&B Streets: Doyle's car with Bodie on megaphone: Queensborough Terrace, Bayswater, London, W2
	Hotel: Rudi calls doctor, then flags down taxi: Baron Hotel, 1 Queensborough Terrace, Bayswater, London, W2
	Streets: Doyle's car / Smith's car, re: Diana spotted again: Queensborough Terrace, Bayswater, London, W2
	Streets: Doyle's car / Smith's car stunts, re: Diana seen: Inverness Place, Bayswater, London, W2
24 November	***Streets: Doyle's car turns in road re: sighting***: Shepherds Hill (Stanhope Road junction), Crouch End, London, N6
	Street: taxi drops Diana & Rudi off: Archway Road, Crouch End, London, N6
	Hotel: Diana & Rudi take refuge: Phaedra Hotel, 12 Shepherds Hill, Highgate, London, N6
25 November	***CI5 safe house***: Leggatts Park, Great North Road, Potter Bar, Hertfordshire
26 November	***Int: Northcott's office***: Islington Town Hall, Upper Street / Richmond Grove, Islington, London, N1
	Int: Café: Tiffin Bar, 265 Upper Street, Islington, London, N1
	Int: Cowley's car (orders to get Diana): 265 Upper Street, Islington, London, N1
	Street: Cowley's meeting with Alex MacLean: Milner Place, Islington, London, N1
27-28 November	***Magistrate's Court***: Royal Free Hospital, Liverpool Road, Islington, London, N1
28 November	***Old South Bank Terminal***: South Lambeth Freight Yard, Nine Elms Lane, South Lambeth, London, SW8

THE UNTOUCHABLES
by **Brian Clemens**
© Copyright Mark 1 Productions Ltd MCMLXXX

Rahad	Keith Washington
Anna	Marilyn Galsworthy
Sir John Terringham	Robert Flemyng
Hollis	John Junkin
Nero	Joe Marcell
Hart	Nick Brimble
Clare Terringham	Lucy Hornak
Taylor	John Francis
Fisk	Andrew Sargent
George	Andy Pantelidou
Al	Ramsay Williams
Gregory	Brogden Miller
Tina	Vicki Michelle
TV Commentator	Clive Panto
Anna Jones	Linda Spurrier
Blonde	Imogen Bickford-Smith
Lucho	Terry Paris
Kaffir	Neville Rofaila
Uncredited	
Embassy Officer	Derek Chafer
Smart Man	Keith Bell
Girl	Susie Silvie
Club customer	John Cannon
Uniformed Policeman	Reg Turner

Director: **William Brayne**

TEFALI Rahad, the cultural attaché to an Arab embassy in London, is also a skilled and ruthless killer. Because they have no hard evidence against him, the British authorities cannot expel Rahad from Britain for fear of causing a rift between Britain and his country. The Special Branch has tried to have the man followed in the hope of collecting evidence about him, but Rahad complains and the surveillance is stopped. Believing that CI5 have a better chance of trapping Rahad, Cowley sends Bodie to a gambling club whose owner is in touch with a criminal called Johnny Hollis, one of Rahad's friends.

Bodie builds up a picture of himself at the club as a man on a moderate salary who is desperate to gamble and win large sums of money so that he can afford to keep up with his wealthy girlfriend, Clare Terringham. Believing that Bodie is vulnerable to exploitation, the club owner tells Hollis to order his henchman, Martin Hart, to keep an eye on Bodie. Knowing that he is being followed, Bodie sells his expensive hi-fi equipment and goes to Clare's home. The butler turns him away and Bodie angrily leaves. Seeing Doyle meet Bodie outside the house, Hart follows Doyle and asks him about Bodie.

CI5 are assigned to frame an Arab Diplomat - who is a ruthless killer, that can't be touched by British law. Lewis Collins prepares for shooting on THE UNTOUCHABLES.

Doyle tells him that he has unsuccessfully tried to get Bodie to abandon his gambling because his job with CI5 could be in jeopardy. Hollis is delighted to learn that Bodie works for CI5 and decides that under financial pressure, Bodie might be persuaded to pass on CI5 secrets. Bodie asks Hart to find him a really profitable gambling game and Hart promises to fix a game up with Hollis. Alone and unarmed, Bodie goes to Hollis' luxury home, where a few wealthy men, including Rahad, are gathered to play cards. As the game progresses, Bodie asks Hollis for more and more credit and by the end of the evening he is hopelessly in debt. Hollis tells him that in return for information on CI5, he might be prepared to overlook Bodie's debts. Bodie feigns shock at this development, but promises to think about the offer.

Meanwhile, Doyle has found an attractive blonde prostitute, Anna, of the type favoured by Rahad and Cowley has arranged for Rahad to meet the girl. Anna is with Rahad when he receives an urgent summons to meet someone. She later tells Doyle that she only understood two words of the Arabic instructions given to Rahad; the words 'Faisid', and 'morning'. Faisid is the name of a prominent Arab politician in London, and the CI5 man is instantly alert to a possible assassination attempt on Emura Faisid's life by Rahad. Cowley and Doyle keep a careful watch on Faisid's home and see him safely back from a mid-morning stroll. As he arrives at his front door, a bomb concealed in a bulky newspaper in his letterbox explodes and Faisid is killed.

A short while later, Rahad sees Doyle searching his car; Doyle flees the scene, but Anna tells the Arab that Doyle works for CI5. Rahad asks Hollis to find out why he is being watched by CI5 agents. Bodie is brought to Rahad and he tells the Arab that Anna is the daughter of the famous anti-Muslim, anti-Arab leader Dame Sara Jones. After a demonstration outside Rahad's embassy in a few days' time, Anna will then make a public announcement in front of the television cameras about her affair with Rahad. The Arab suggests a plan where thugs will infiltrate the demonstration and that Anna is 'accidentally' killed in the struggle. Bodie agrees to arrange this, but only if Rahad himself withdraws the Swiss francs necessary to finance the operation. Rahad obliges and is tricked into handing over the money to Harry Taylor, the leader of the thugs who has secretly been hired by Doyle for the occasion. That night, watching the television coverage in Hollis' flat, Rahad is surprised to see that the thugs are protecting Anna and that the Anna at the demonstration is not the Anna he has been having an affair with. CI5 burst into the room and show Rahad photographs taken of him handing over the money to Taylor - the man who protected his country's enemy, Anna Jones. Rahad will be recalled by his country and almost certainly be executed for his 'crimes'.

Production Unit

Created by	Brian Clemens
Executive Producers	Albert Fennell, Brian Clemens
Music	Laurie Johnson
Producer	Raymond Menmuir
Script Editor	Gerry O'Hara
Production Manager	Ron Purdie
Production Accountant	Terry Connors
Assistant Director	Simon Hinkly
Location Manager	Peter Carter
Continuity	Doreen Soan
Casting	Esta Charkham
Art Director	Ken Ryan

Bodie and Doyle are assigned to frame an Arab Diplomat - who is a ruthless killer, but can't be touched by British law. Playing Anna, the 'attractive blonde' prostitute in THE UNTOUCHABLES was British actress Marilyn Galsworthy who acted for fifteen years in the famous classical theatre group - the Royal Shakespeare Company, appearing opposite Patrick Stewart and Alfred Molina.

Set Dresser	Don Mingaye
Stunt Arranger	Peter Brayham
Wardrobe Supervisor	Donald Mothersill
Special Effects	Mike Collins
Lighting Cameraman	Dusty Miller
Camera Operator	John Maskall
Focus Puller	Chris Sargent
Make Up	Sue Black
Hairdresser	Sue Love
Lighting by	Lee Electric
Editor	Alan Killick
Sound Recordist	David Crozier
Boom Operator	John Samworth
Dubbing Editor	Peter Lennard
Dubbing Mixer	Hugh Strain
Music Editor	Alan Willis
Post Production Supervisor	John S. Smith

An Avengers MARK 1 Production For LONDON WEEKEND TELEVISION

Lewis Collins and Martin Shaw on location at the Royal Agricultural Hall, Islington, North London, as Bodie and Doyle in THE UNTOUCHABLES.

Shooting / Location Schedule

Production Dates: Monday 1st to Friday 12th December, 1980. Production Number: 9D10082

1-2 December	***Rahad's Embassy***: Chestnuts, 350 Jersey Road, Osterley, Middlesex
	Doyle arrests blonde prostitute leaving embassy: Jersey Road / Wood Lane, Osterley, Middlesex
3-5 December	***Ext: Pub car park meeting (Doyle & Cowley)***: The Manor Cottage Tavern, 57 East End Road, East Finchley, London, N2
	Int: Doyle's car (with Taylor): East End Road, East Finchley Road, London, N2 / Finchley Road, Golders Green, London, NW11
	Hollis' house: 22 West Hill Park, Merton Lane, Highgate, London, N6
8 December	***Taylor's office***: J & N Wade Limited, 1071 Finchley Road, Golders Green, London, NW11
	Ext: Woods (Rahad meets Taylor): Hampstead Heath: Wildwood Road / Hampstead Way, London, NW11
	Anna & Rahad: horses: Hampstead Heath: Wildwood Road / Hampstead Way, London, NW11
9 December	***Int: Car (Bodie & Claire)***: Adelaide Road, Chalk Farm, London, NW3
	Club & bar: New Eton Inn Club, Chalk Farm Parade, Adelaide Road, London, NW3
	Hi-Fi Shop: Parkview Electronics, 5 Malden Road, Kentish Town, London, NW5
	Bodie's house: 26 South Villas, off Camden Square, Camden Town, London, NW1
	Doyle's car / Bodie's car (Hi-Fi shop route): South Villas / Camden Park Road / Torriano Avenue / Leighton Road, Camden Town, London, NW1
2nd Unit	***Faisid's house & explosion***: 28 Hamilton Terrace, St. Johns Wood, London, NW3
	Faisid's Mosque: London Central Mosque, 146 Park Road, St. John's Wood, London, NW1
	Street: Railway arch (Doyle, Fitz & Taylor): Prowse Place, Camden Town, London, NW1
10 December	***Sir John's / Claire's house***: 53 Avenue Road, St. John's Wood, London, NW3
	Hotel Street (Doyle meets George): Holiday Inn, 128 King Henry's Road, Swiss Cottage, London, NW3
	Restaurant & street: Julius's, 39 Upper Street, Islington, London, N1
	Warehouse & gun fight: Royal Agricultural Hall, Liverpool Road, Islington, London, N1

11 December	***Doyle's house***: House 1, 94 Woodland Gardens, Muswell Hill, London, N10
12 December	***Ahmed's flat***: 63-84 Oakwood Court, Kensington, London, W14
	Ext: Ahmed's flat (Fire escape): rear of Oakwood Court, Oakwood Lane, Kensington, London, W14

Series IV Production Unit: uncredited

Production Assistant	Jane Oscroft
Unit Manager	Rufus Andrews
Assistant Location	Geoff Austin
2nd *Assistant Director*	Nick Daubeny, Melvin Lind
3rd *Assistant Director*	Simon Manley, Chris Thompson
Secretary to Mr. Fennell	Linda Matthews
Secretary to Mr. Menmuir	Hilary Pearson
Trainee Secretary	Julie Humphreys
Unit Runner	Kenneth Shane
Clapper / Loader	Jo Hidderley
Camera Grip	Malcolm Smith, Peter Hall
Sound Assistant	Don Hawkins
Art Department Assistant	Gillian Atkinson
Production Buyer	Dennis Griffin
Art Department Trainee	Tracy Lee
Casting Secretary	Anne Henderson
Wardrobe Assistant	Vicki Scott, Gary Wells
Unit Publicist	Paul McNicholls
Publicity Secretary	Lucinda Pugh
Assistant Accountant	Margaret Woods, John Bigland
Cashier	Robert Campbell
Property Master	Robin Monk, Barry Arnold, Brian Wells
Dressing Props	Ted Western
Storeman / Dressing Props	Gerry Bourke
Stand-by Props	Micky Matthews, Terry Greenwood, Barry Arnold, Stephen Wheeler
Carpenter	Gordon Moore
Painter	Jim Ede, Frank Adam
Stagehand	Arthur Feehan
Unit Nurse	Susan Michael
Gaffer	George Boner
Electricians	Arthur Whitmarsh, Tom Casey, Charles Davies
Stills Photographer	Doug Webb, Ted Hawes
Special Effects Assistant	Mark Meddings
Dialogue Editor	Mark Auguste, Harriet Burke, Stefan Henrix
Assistant Dubbing Editor	Shirley Shaw
Assistant Music Editor	Brian Trenery
Producers Driver	Barry Myall
Transport Co-Ordinator	Chris Streeter

Unit Drivers	Jim Magill, Geoff Bowers, Jeffrey Rolfe
Unit Mini Bus Driver	Nick Perry
Make Up Bus Driver	Mike Mulally
Wardrobe Truck Driver	Tony Wise
Construction / Prop Driver	Dave Bruyea
Props Return Van Driver	Mark Daubney
Catering Vehicle Driver	John Lane
Dining Bus Driver	Fred Borg
Camera	J D C Cameras, Wembley Park Drive, Wembley, Middlesex
Laboratories	Rank Labs Ltd, Denham, Middlesex
Insurance	Ruben Sedgwick Insurance, Pinewood Studios, Iver Heath, Buckinghamshire
Sound Transfer	Location Sound Facilities, 57 Ramsay Road, London, W3
Unit Minibus, Construction / Prop Truck, Prop Return Van, Dining Bus by	D & D Location, Boyers Yard, Staines Road, Feltham, Middlesex
Make Up Bus	Mike Mulally Transport, 10 Murray Road, Ottershaw, Surrey
Wardrobe Truck	Willies Wheels, 13 Lodge Close, Englefield Green, Egham, Surrey
Caterers	J & J Foods, 33 Langley Park Road, Iver, Buckinghamshire
Doctors	Chalkhill Heath Centre, Wembley, Middlesex: Dr. Elliott Mass, Dr. Symonds, Dr. Levere
Film Studios	Lee International, Wembley, Middlesex
2nd Unit Directors	Roy Stevens, Ian Sharp
2nd Unit Assistant Directors	Dominic Fulford, David Cherrill, Simon Hinkly, Gregory Dark, Richard Holt
2nd Unit 2nd Assistant Directors	Nigel Goldsack, Andrew Warren, Jerry Daly, Melvin Lind
2nd Unit 3rd Assistant Directors	Fraser Copp, Jerry Daly, Keith Young, Anthony Aherne
2nd Unit Continuity	Pat Rambaut, Majorie Lavelly, Georgina Hamilton
2nd Unit Lighting Cameramen	Norman Langley, Dusty Miller, Michael Davis
2nd Unit Camera Operator	John Boulter, Malcolm Vinson, Mike Proudfoot
2nd Unit Camera Grip	John Brady
2nd Unit Camera Focus	David Litchfield
2nd Unit Clapper / Loader	Ian Foster, Garry Dawes, Joe Hidderley, Nigel Seal
2nd Unit Boom Operator	Charles McFadden, John Stevenson, David Inner, Robin Maddison, Peter Istead, Gary Weir
2nd Unit Sound Mixer	Geoff Hawkins, Chris Munro, Ron Barron

2*nd* Unit Make Up	Sue Black, Bernard Brown, Derry Hawes, Stella Hunter, Sylvia James
2*nd* Unit Hairdressers	Sue Love, Betty Sheriff, Celia Mitchell
2*nd* Unit Wardrobe	Don Mothersill, Gary Wells
2*nd* Unit Wardrobe Assistant	Vicki Scott
2*nd* Unit Stand-by Props	Micky Mathews, Terry Greenwood, Gerry Bourke, Steve Wheeler
2*nd* Unit Electrician	Arthur Whitmarsh

SERIES IV ACTION CARS

Bodie: **Ford Capri 3.0 S**: OWC 827W (Real index: OWC 827V) - *The Gun, Wild Justice, Black Out, Blood Sports, Hijack, You'll Be All Right, Kickback, Discovered In A Graveyard, The Ojuka Situation, The Untouchables.*
Opel Rekord 2.0 S Estate: NKX 454V - *It's Only A Beautiful Picture...*

Cowley: **Ford Granada 2.8i Ghia**: OWC 822W (Real index: OWC 822V) - *The Gun, Wild Justice, Black Out, It's Only A Beautiful Picture..., Blood Sports, Hijack, You'll Be All Right, Kickback, Discovered In A Graveyard, Foxhole On The Roof, The Ojuka Situation, Operation Susie, The Untouchables.*

Doyle: **Ford Cortina 2.0 GL**: MHK 547V - *The Gun.*
Ford Capri 3.0 S: OAR 576W (Real index: OAR 576V) - *Black Out, It's Only A Beautiful Picture..., Blood Sports, Hijack, You'll Be All Right, Kickback, Discovered In A Graveyard, Foxhole On The Roof, Operation Susie, The Untouchables.*
Suzuki LJ 80 Jeep: GGN 810T - *Wild Justice.*

CI5 car: **Ford Cortina 2.0 GL**: MHK 547V - *Wild Justice, Black Out, It's Only A Beautiful Picture...,Blood Sports, Hijack, Foxhole On The Roof.*

Misc: *Operation Susie, The Untouchables* (with false index: NLC 88V).

CI5 car: **Ford Cortina 1.6 LS**: MHK 545V - *The Gun, Hijack, Kickback, Foxhole On The Roof.*

Misc: *Black Out, Blood Sports, Operation Susie.*

Police: **Rover SD1 2600**: WVP 150T - *The Gun, Wild Justice, It's Only A Beautiful Picture..., Foxhole On The Roof, Operation Susie.*

Police: **Rover SD1 3500**: DUC 204V (Real index: SYY 904S) - *Hijack, Foxhole On The Roof, Operation Susie.*

Misc: **Datsun 180B**: FLA 941T - *The Ojuka Situation.*

Misc: **Ford Transit**: OHJ 280V - *It's Only A Beautiful Picture..., Foxhole On The Roof.*

Misc: **Opel Rekord 2.0 S estate**: SOO 636T (Real index: NKX 454V) - *Hijack, Discovered In A Graveyard.*

Misc: Alan Mann Helicopters - *Kickback, Foxhole On The Roof.*

TRANSMISSION DATES

1: THE ACORN SYNDROME*
7th September 1980
2: WILD JUSTICE
14th September 1980
3: FUGITIVE*
21st September 1980
4: INVOLVEMENT*
28th September 1980
5: NEED TO KNOW*
5th October 1980
6: TAKE AWAY*
12th October 1980
7: BLACK OUT
19th October 1980
8: BLOOD SPORTS*
26th October 1980
9: SLUSH FUND*
2nd November 1980
10: THE GUN
9th November 1980
11: HIJACK
16th November 1980: *Postponed: Not Broadcast*
11: HIJACK
30th November 1980
12: MIXED DOUBLES*
7th December 1980
13: WEEKEND IN THE COUNTRY*
14th December 1980
14: KICKBACK
20th December 1980
15: IT'S ONLY A BEAUTIFUL PICTURE...
27th December 1980

* These episodes were filmed as Series III, but transmitted here as Series IV.

SERIES V

NO STONE

PRE-PRODUCTION on the final batch of episodes began in January, when it was decided that LWT needed five more episodes to go with the un-broadcast episodes from series four, to make up a programme run consisting of eleven episodes. The stars' contracts would expire at the end of May and, therefore, production would begin as soon as possible.

On Friday 13th March, Lewis Collins was arrested for firing a loaded weapon, a 12-bore shotgun, in his home. Two female members of the charity Action, with whom Collins had a close working relationship, had called at his home in Park Avenue, North Finchley, London. After an argument he went inside and fired a shotgun into the lounge wall. The two women had approached him for an interview and an argument broke out over the funds raised during the previous years charity walk with John Conteh. The police were called; by 3 am he was arrested and spent the rest of the night in Golders Green police station. The police took his shotgun, and other weapons found in his home, and charged him with possessing a shotgun with intent to endanger life. He was bailed to appear at Hendon Magistrates Court in North London on 30th March.

Lewis Collins pictured above on Friday 13th March, after he was charged with discharging a firearm with intent to endanger life. He was bailed to appear at Hendon Magistrates Court, North London, on 30th March.

In April the show received two awards; 'The Most Compulsive Male Characters On TV', in a TV Times Top Ten Awards poll, and The Television And Radio Industries Club, voted it the 'ITV Programme Of The Year'.

Not returning to the production, due to his commitment to the third *Minder* series, was location manager Peter Carter. Industry newcomer, David Barron, who received help from assistant director, Bill Westley and film director Tony Simmons' son, Matthew, filled his position.

Matthew Simmons (location assistant): "My main task was to manage the location once it had been found - with me doing this it meant that David (Barron) could solely concentrate on finding the areas to film in. Once the ideal location was agreed I could begin negotiations over contracts and fees for the site, and make all the necessary arrangements for filming to take place, including co-ordinating parking facilities, available power sources, catering requirements, and permissions from the relevant authorities. I was also responsible for ensuring that everyone in the cast and crew knew how to get to the filming location, and made sure that unit direction signs were clearly visible along the major routes. During filming the health and safety of everyone also fell on my shoulders. After the shoot, I had to make sure that the location was securely locked, and satisfactorily cleaned, before returning it to its owners. Any damage would be reported to the production office and, if necessary, insurance proceedings instigated."

David Barron (location manager): "My main role was to identify and find ideal locations based on the script I had been given, but I would also be involved in negotiating with each of the location's owners a number of issues, such as the cost and terms of the hire, crew and vehicle access, parking, noise reduction, and what official permits were required. It was early days for me in the industry and I can't say that I enjoyed my time on the programme. It was very hectic, and in order to stop people moaning about repeated use of certain areas, I found locations that hadn't been used before, like Luton Airport or North Mymms Park."

Ray Menmuir: "For this run of episodes I ordered two silver Ford Capri's. After the early series we were able to assure Ford of another series and I was able to advise production dates; they would run the cars off the assembly line for us, but we had difficulty in arriving at the same arrangements as we had in previous years due to the restricted number of episodes. I recall there was a lot of uncertainty surrounding the date of the last run and they could not get two silver cars from stock so we had to be content with the change of colour. They were marvellous screen cars and very popular. They kept on going. We had no trouble with them whatsoever over the course of the show."

Barry Reynolds (Ford Press Office): "We just didn't have two silver cars to give them. The 3.0S was to be discontinued and replaced by the 2.8 Injection, so we had no need to keep the former on the books."

Bodie got the Strato silver 3.0S, VHK 12W, while Doyle drove the Tibetan gold 3.0S, VHK 11W. Cowley remained with a Midnight blue Ford Granada 2.8i Ghia, UJN 696W. All vehicles wore their correct indexes, as, with production at an end, there was no real need to hide their true identities.

Cry Wolf: *Is Susan Grant crying wolf? The police are convinced she is - Cowley is not so sure. What part does Henry Laughlin play in the scenario? Bodie and Doyle are sent to find out.*

The first episode before the cameras, on Monday 16th March, was *Cry Wolf*, scripted by Paul Wheeler (received at LWT on the 17th February), and directed by Phil Meheux.

Born on the 23rd May 1934, in Kingston, Jamaica, Wheeler found he was getting a better income from his TV plays than his salary from the foreign office, under MI6. One of his first scripts was for the Hammer series, *Journey To The Unknown* in 1968, followed with submissions to *Poldark*, *Danger UXB*, *Minder* and *Tenko*. Along the way he scripted the movies *Puppet On A Chain* (1970), *Caravan To Vaccares* (1974) and *Swashbuckler* (1976).

When Susan Grant contacts the police, saying she is being stalked and is in fear of her life, they think she is making the whole story up! Sheila Ruskin guest starred (far right) as the young girl in CRY WOLF.

Phil Meheux (director): "We cast Alan MacNaughtan and not only was Martin Shaw telling me what to do, but Alan was at it too. He was writing his own dialogue and acting out his own scenes!"

Occasionally casting director Esta Charkham liked to play tricks on the stars, for instance, when she hired Gordon Jackson's wife, Rona Anderson, to appear without telling him.

Esta Charkham: "I just knew that Rona was perfect for the part so I discussed it with Phil Meheux, the director, and then offered it to her without telling Gordon a thing about it. I believed it was the first time they had played together, but later found out they had both been in *The Prime Of Miss Jean Brodie* (1968). She was a well known West End actress and fitted the part of a mother of a girl who had the frighteners put on her by an old friend of Cowley."

Gordon Jackson (commented at the time): "We just don't see eye to eye over acting. She went to drama school - I didn't. So we have totally different viewpoints."

When her daughter Susan begins to get threatening phone calls in CRY WOLF, Mrs. Grant enlists the help of George Cowley, an old friend of the family. Rona Anderson played Mrs. Grant, pictured here with her real-life husband, Gordon Jackson. Born (3rd August 1926) in Edinburgh, Scotland she appeared in the acclaimed movies THE PRIME OF MISS JEAN BRODIE as the Chemistry teacher, Miss Lockhart; as Alice, Scrooge's fiancée, in SCROOGE; and in the television series BACHELOR FATHER.

MARK I PRODUCTIONS LIMITED   "THE PROFESSIONALS" - SERIES V

EPISODE 1 - "CRY WOLF"   SECOND UNIT

            LOCATION MOVEMENT ORDER FOR THURSDAY, 9TH APRIL 1981

SET: (1) INT.FLAT NEXT DOOR
                (2) INT.LIFT

LOCATION: 1   FLAT 104
                    BLOCK 4
                    NAPIER COURT
                    NAPIER AVENUE
                    LONDON
                    S.W.6

                    Contact: HEAD PORTER - MR THOMAS (FLAT 27 - FOR KEY)
                              PUTNEY   736 1337

SET: (3) EXT.FIRE ESCAPE

LOCATION: 2   CADBY HALL
                    BLYTHE ROAD
                    HAMMERSMITH
                    LONDON W14

                    Contact: MR IVOR SEARY   603 2040

ROUTE   Leave Studio and turn left down Empire Way and Harrow Road.
TO   Turn left towards Central London, continue on Harrow Road
LOCATION 1   through Harlesdon to right turn into Scrubs Lane. Continue
                down Scrubs Lane under A40 and into Wood Lane to Shepherds
                Bush Green. Follow one-way system round green then take left
                turn Shepherds Bush Road to Hammersmith Broadway.

                Take third exit off Broadway (Fulham Palace Road) and continue
                to left turn into New Kings Road, then take first right, Hurlingham
                Road (under railway bridge) and first right again - Edenhurst
                Avenue. Ranelagh Court at junction of Edenhurst Avenue and
                Ranelagh Gardens.

ROUTE
TO
LOCATION 2   From Napier Avenue return to New Kings Road and turn right.
                Continue to Munster Road and turn left. At Fulham Road turn
                left again and continue to right turn into Fulham Palace Road
                to Hammersmith Broadway and take 6th exit Hammersmith Road.
                Continue to left turn (at Lyons Supermarket) into Blythe Road.
                Cadby Hall entrance on left after approximately 150 yards.

PARKING: Unit Vehicles to park at bottom left hand side - Z Block.
                NO Parking on right of yellow lines by No. 2 Despatch.

                Private Cars to park in NCP Car Park (Olympia) 100 yards
                past Cadby Hall.

                                                    David Barron
                                                    LOCATION MANAGER

The 'second unit' movement order for CRY WOLF prepared by location manager David Barron for filming on Thursday 9th April.

The charity office scenes were filmed at Globe House, Yiewsley, Middlesex. Harry Devine, a young police constable at the time had to have a few words with the two stars. When Martin and Lewis arrived on set, Harry recalls having to advise them they were driving the wrong way down this one-way street!

Guido Reidy (sound assistant): "In one scene, Lewis has to reverse down the narrow drive outside the offices, after a Vauxhall has blocked him in. As he did so, he went straight into the front of the car (VW Golf) belonging to our third assistant director, Chris Brock. It was only a slight tap, but Brockey did well out of it, as, I think, his girlfriend worked for a car body shop at the time. You'll see the damage on the front wing of the Capri on screen. They (the producers) weren't happy about that! We also did some night filming in Fulham, when Lewis had to jump between two high-rise flats. He didn't want a 'stand-in', so he did it himself and banged his knee on the way across during the rehearsals. The injury needed quite a bit of attention and in the end the stunt guy completed the scene."

A Man Called Quinn*: Unaware that he is being controlled by the enemy, ex-CI5 agent Quinn sets out to kill his ex-superiors. Cowley, Bodie and Doyle find themselves playing a deadly game of cat and mouse - with Cowley as Quinn's target.*

A Man Called Quinn, was approved on 13th March, and entered production on Monday 30th under the guidance of director Horace Ové. Born in Trinidad in 1939, Ove had written, and directed, the movie *Pressure* for the BFI in 1976. Tony Barwick's script bore an uncanny resemblance to his 1971 episode of the ITC series *The Protectors*, entitled *The First Circle*. He had worked almost exclusively with Gerry Anderson on shows such as *Captain Scarlet And The Mysterons*, *Joe 90*, *Thunderbirds*, *The Secret Service*, and *UFO*

In A MAN CALLED QUINN Jack Canon is portrayed by Linal Haft, who became well known for his British Telecom TV adverts with Maureen Lipman.

Lewis Collins was absent on the first day of production of A MAN CALLED QUINN as he was appearing at Hendon Magistrates Court, North London, charged with possessing a shotgun with intent to endanger life. The case was adjourned until 11th May.

    A scene planned but ultimately removed from the shooting schedule involved Cowley visiting Quinn's ex-wife, Teresa, at a bookshop she ran:
Int: Bookshop
Cowley enters Teresa Quinn's bookshop.
TERESA: *Can I help you?*
COWLEY: *Do you have a copy of 'My University' by Kim Philby?*
TERESA: *I don't think we* (looks up) - *George Cowley.*

COWLEY: *Have I changed that much?*
TERESA: *No. No you haven't. If anything, you look trimmer.*
COWLEY: *Two piece suits and obligatory callisthenics. You look well - Teresa.*
TERESA: *I look the way I deserve; black coffee, white wine and an addiction to milk chocolate to get me through the long afternoons. The book trade isn't exactly booming.*
COWLEY: *So I'm told.*
TERESA: *If there's one product a country can't afford to let go down the drain, that product is the book; all right! With a capital bloody B! No price is too expensive to pay for a book. Because the alternative means prices don't mean anything anymore.*
COWLEY: *Quinn's on the loose.*
TERESA: *From Repton? How could he get out of there?*
COWLEY: *I think we all thought he was finished - broken - he'd become a fixture. Quiet, docile, harmless...Do you still go to see him?*
TERESA: *George, I - look. I know it's a platitude; but life goes on. It became pointless. Heart-breaking. He won't last five minutes.*
COWLEY: *The sooner he's back, the better for him.*
TERESA: *The better for you mean! He'd be impressed - if he had a mind that is - to know that you, George Cowley, Alpha himself, has stirred himself to come looking. I didn't know you came out from behind your computers, your memory banks, your technology, to show a human face. It must be important!*
COWLEY: *They broke him. Not us. We want him back.*
TERESA: *Yes, yes. You'll have him back if he comes to me.*
COWLEY: *The doctor who looked after him was strangled...*
TERESA: *Oh, God. Get out, George. I know how to dial nine- nine- nine.*

The removal of this scene may have been largely due to the fact that the rough cut of this episode ran to nearly 90 minutes.

John S. Smith (supervising editor): "Ray Menmuir had brought in newcomer Horace Ove to direct the episode, but Horace was a slow and plodding director and literally filmed everything he could see - every shot to him was like a Rembrandt, he didn't want anything edited out. In the cutting rooms he caused havoc, and eventually went to Menmuir and complained that we were taking out the best shots. Ray sat him down and told him we were shooting a single 52-minute programme, and not a two-parter. We had to trim it down. To say Horace was not pleased is an understatement."

Chris Brock (third assistant director): "In the final scenes, we were filming at Chalgrove airfield in Oxfordshire. Guest star Steven Berkoff was worse than a kid with a new toy. He'd been rigged up with a blood bag by Arthur Beavis' special effects guys, but refused to leave it alone. He kept touching it and it burst. It took Arthur ages to set it up again.

"We also did a 'car run-by' filmed on the A412, just outside Slough. We'd turned into the industrial estate, just off the dual carriageway, and Martin and Lewis were resting in the Capri. By this time, they were huge stars and were constantly mobbed wherever they went, and that day was no exception. A crowd had gathered and one of the kids went up to the window of the car, tapping gently on it for Martin to open it. When he opened it, the kid asked, 'Which one are you, Bodie or Doyle?' The answer was 'Doyle'.

With that, the kid raised his fist and punched Martin in the face and made quick his getaway. We were in fits of laughter for ages. He was only a young lad, so Martin saw the funny side of it also."

Dacre Holloway: "Part of this episode was filmed at Queen Elizabeth Barracks Church Crookham, just outside Fleet in Hampshire. The exact scenes I can't remember but there was one filmed in an ammunition bunker as well as outside where they threw a grenade from behind a sandbagged bunker. There was also a chase scene through the barrack blocks and they did the final scene showing one of the three stars driving off in a Land Rover? I was the driver of this vehicle as well as the Land Rover in the background to the earlier explosive scene.

"QEB was the home to the UK based Gurkha Battalion at the time. I was their Education Officer and liaison officer for the filming. It took place over two days separated by a week or so as they were a bit slow on day one and ran out of actor time as they were needed early the next day and it was cheaper to come back later than keep them on for a bit longer."

Gary Weir (boom operator): "Filming was also called for in some disused houses. In a room, not being used for the shoot, sound recordist David Crozier, spotted a lime green antique wardrobe, and after filming, decided he would take it home and strip it. He was experienced with antiques and realised the wardrobe was worth some money. He loaded the wardrobe in his car that evening; transporting it back to his home, where he locked the antique in his garage. Some days later, it was decided that some scenes had to be reshot in the house; but the hierarchy were paying a visit that day, and realised the wardrobe they had paid for, and put in the house, had gone. 'What's happened to the wardrobe?' said producer Ray Menmuir. David held his hands up and returned the half stripped item back where he found it."

Guido Reidy (sound assistant): "It was called 'bottorsniking'. David told me that he, and another boom guy/sound assistant, had started doing it years back. You basically took anything that looked valuable from skips or derelict houses. It was all done in good fun, and sometimes there was a race between the sound and camera crew to get to the items first. Mind you, David used to have some great sayings, he'd look up and, for no apparent reason say, 'ten pigs, dear heart', or 'absolutely'.

"We had assistant director Gino Marotta (*Sir Francis Drake, UFO, The Prisoner, Return Of The Saint*) on this one. What a grouch! We were filming near Primrose Hill/Fellows Road, rigging up Bodie's car. He always thought we had too many people on the sound crew. He'd look up and say, 'How come - Man on the moon - three on sound'. He assumed the sound could be added on later and we were taking too long. He would always be rushing us along."

Gino Marotta: "There was good reason to keep the crew disciplined. As the first assistant I was responsible for making sure every aspect of the shoot remained on schedule. My job started well in pre-production of any said episode, where I would have to break down the script into a shot-by-shot storyboard and work with the director and production manager to establish the shooting order, and how long each scene would take to film. I then drew up the overall shooting schedule and daily call sheets. During production I would have to report back to the production office and provide information as to what had been filmed so there was little time for relaxation and waiting around for simple procedures to be performed."

Lawson's Last Stand: *Lieutenant Colonel Peter Lawson vanishes from an army hospital. He is in possession of valuable NATO secrets and may have been abducted by the Russians. Bodie and Doyle are sent to find him - with explosive results.*

Lawson's Last Stand commenced on Monday 13th April, with Ranald Graham's script having been approved on the 27th March. Ian Sharp directed his third episode.

The original story had Len 'Nobby' Clarke running a café, not a forge - this was changed at short notice, when a suitable café could not be found in the rural location required in the script.

CI5's Bodie (Lewis Collins) and Doyle (Martin Shaw) report back to Cowley on Lawson's latest movements in LAWSON'S LAST STAND. But has Lawson really gone 'bananas'?

This episode had an extra ingredient of realism added, due to the use of real military equipment, and real life commandos. On location with the crew at Battersea Park, South West London, between the 23rd and 24th April, were the actual serving members of the 42 Royal Marines Logistics Regiment from Plymouth. They were wearing NBC suits, designed for use in Nuclear, Bacterial and Chemical warfare. Also seen was an up-to-date fire engine; a stretched Land Rover, it had a long wheel-base, which had been developed for fire fighting by the Royal Air Force.

Martin Shaw: LAWSON'S LAST STAND.

Martin Shaw poses for a publicity shot during the filming of LAWSON'S LAST STAND.

An armoured reconnaissance vehicle called 'The Fox' brings back memories for Lewis Collins.

Lewis Collins: "I had to throw a grenade into the tank and it exploded. Then the tank was hosed down with fire fighting foam. We had not realised there was a driver standing at its side. He emerged, covered in foam, and not at all amused."

There is a continuity error in the final scene when the tank is being doused down; a soldier runs on and falls flat on his backside!

Les Martin: "I was an extra on the episode. At the time I was with the Territorial Army (C Squadron, Royal Yeomanry) and we were asked to supply a vehicle for filming. We spent all day filming in Battersea Park. My brother (Keith Martin) was the driver of 'The Fox' and I was the commander. I remember the filming well: we had about five takes when Martin Shaw jumped on the back of the vehicle, but he kept missing his foot-hold and falling. On the one they kept in, it was me that fell over at the end of the shot and fell on my backside! We were also in the respirators in the reflection of the mirror device, at the same time standing at the back of the 4-tonner lorry and we also ran in at the end. But the best bit was after filming when we drove back to the studios and had a good drink in the bar (not the driver), then on the way back, all the fuses blew on the vehicle (no lights), and we had a police escort from one side of London to our base in Croydon. It was great fun and whenever I see *The Professionals*, I think of the day we filmed and the fact they used about ten seconds of our contribution. Great memories."

The dramatic conclusion to LAWSON'S LAST STAND was filmed in Battersea Park, South West London.

Third assistant director Chris Brock recalled filming amid a Royal Artillery Depot at Victoria Barracks, Windsor, Berkshire.

Chris Brock: "The soldiers were taking 'pot-shots' at us through the windows. We spent quite some time filming there as the director, Ian Sharp, wanted the Horseguards soldiers to be in shot when they were on parade - so we had to rehearse without them and go for a 'take' at exactly the right time."

No Stone: *What is the connection between Jimmy Kilpin, a terrorist group, and the death of a Judge, a Clerk of Court and a QC? Cowley and his team must put the jigsaw together to prevent further explosive deaths.*

Roger Marshall's *No Stone* script was at LWT's office on 29th April, but had already entered production on Monday 27th, under the control of associate producer Chris Burt.

Sound recordist David Crozier hides behind his trolley of gadgets in NO STONE.

Martin Shaw and Lewis Collins got to handle some very special weaponry, Steyr-AUG assault rifles. Made from very light yet extraordinary strong plastic, they can fire 750 rounds a minute and were so new at the time, that the S.A.S were still testing them for possible use. The rifles were made available thanks to Jim Shortt - a close friend of Collins. As Director of Training for The Combat Training Team, Shortt was responsible for training Regular & Reserve NATO forces in Combat. He was also contracted to train specialist units in both anti-terrorist and counter-terrorist skills, including training units of the United States Army and Air Force in 1980.

Jim Shortt: "I was on set for the day at Homerton, East London, and responsible for the use of the Steyr-AUG rifles there. One of the show's directors visited us at RAF (USAF) Alconbury in October 1980 when we were training USAF Police SWAT teams. They liked the AUG's we were using and borrowed them for the show."

8th *May 1981: Trainee Shelia Barratt holds the NO STONE clapperboard.*

A lengthy scene involving Cowley and Ulrike's mother was cut from the shooting schedule:

Int: Mrs. Wynant's Kensington Hotel
Cowley meets with Mrs. Wynant in the Hotel lounge.
MRS. WYNANT: *Neither my husband nor I has heard from Judy.*
COWLEY: *What about her trust fund? Money left by her uncle.*
MRS. WYNANT: *Not a penny of it's been touched!*
COWLEY: *Mrs. Wynant. Two of my men are dead. A third is seriously injured...*
MRS. WYNANT: *I'm sorry. Obviously I'm sorry. I don't accept it had anything to do with Judy.*
COWLEY: *You see, Mrs. Wynant. She is with this group. Probably in command of it.*
MRS. WYNANT: *Judy back in England? I don't believe you. You're - you're trying to frighten me.*
COWLEY: *Why, what reason? Mrs. Wynant, your daughter is in danger. Serious danger. Best thing that could happen is for her to be arrested.*
MRS. WYNANT: *That's your version, Mr. Cowley.*

COWLEY: *What's yours? (pause) Where'd she learn German?*
MRS. WYNANT: *We had German au pairs...housekeepers. We had to have au pairs! Bill's work took him aboard - My god! You people - social critics, marriage counsellors. Is there nothing you can't do?*
COWLEY: *So, she gets away - this time. Even get out of the country. How will it end? How can it end? That bedroom you're keeping aired, the wardrobe of clothes - she won't be coming home. It's not going to happen.*
MRS. WYNANT: *You sound so sure.*
COWLEY: *She's a murderess. She's even changed her name, you know that? Not Judy Wynant any more.*
MRS. WYNANT: *I don't know much about terrorists. But I know that much! Reject your family, change your name. So easy to reject things today.*
COWLEY: *We did it.*
MRS. WYNANT: *Rubbish.*
COWLEY: *Of course we did.*
MRS. WYNANT: *I adored my parents.*
COWLEY: *Your parents were probably, what? - staunch, small town conservative? I know mine were. You rebelled against them, them and their clichés. You flirted with Leftism, a parlour pink liberal. I was. This mess is nothing like that, Mrs. Wynant. This is not a phase, this is not a pose. This is anarchy - nihilism - wholesale murder!*
MRS. WYNANT: *I can't help you. I'm sorry.*
COWLEY: *I don't need your help. It is your daughter who wants it!*

Martin Shaw as Doyle and Lewis Collins as Bodie on the set of NO STONE.

George Johnson: "In *No Stone*, the reversing/parking car which causes the car bomb to go off (injuring the court officials) was actually filmed in

Northampton Square; home of The City University London. The 'bombed' building is diagonally across from the University library. I know this, as I was studying Chemistry at City University at that time (Chemistry is no longer taught here), and was in the crowd watching the scene where the Capri comes screeching round the corner to the scene with the blown out window where the ambulance and Cowley are. It took half a day just to set up and film this bit (everyone was watching from the University Library windows - not much work that day!), and I seem to recall that it was done in about four takes."

On the set of NO STONE at Eastern Hospital, Homerton, East London: Peter Hall (camera grips), Mike Tomlin (camera operator) and Chris Burt (director).

A remote control bomb disposal robot, called the Hunter, makes its debut tackling a car bomb in the story's conclusion. Brilliant yellow and almost silent, the machine, if it can't solve a problem with mechanical 'grapplers and disrupters,' tends to dispose of it with the sawn-off shotgun mounted under its video camera. It's said to be more advanced than the 'Wheelbarrow' robot used in Northern Ireland.

As an expensive star, and with the bomb set to go off, the Hunter was withdrawn from the danger area and stuntman, Frank Henson, took over as the bomb-disposal guinea pig, dressed in a protective suit with armoured plates in the trousers and a torso shield.

Terry Frost (bomb disposal man): "You see, nothing will save you if you're on top of a bomb when it goes off. The force alone will scatter your body parts for quite a distance. All that protective clothing can do is save looking for the pieces."

Guido Reidy (sound assistant): "The remote control motorised robot (the Hunter) being used to disarm the bomb in the car, kept stopping and going in all sorts of directions. Just as well we were on a film shoot - and not in a real situation! I also remember that day because, Ron Purdie, the production manager, whom we'd nicknamed the 'Silver Fox', due to his grey hair, went through our cash sheets with a red pen, saying, 'not paying that, or that, or that!' "

When the bomb finally exploded *(pictured above)*, Arthur Beavis and his special effects team had to make the blast look spectacular. Genuine explosions are not usually photogenic, so they packed the car with black powder and petrol to give maximum effect.

Behind-the-scenes with camera clapper/loader Nigel Seal on location at Eastern Hospital, Homerton, East London, for the episode NO STONE.

Nigel Seal (camera clapper/loader): "...which may sound like a pretty unimportant job, but without the clapperboard, the guys who handled the processing of the film back at the laboratories wouldn't have been able to do their jobs. It's the clap sound made by the clapperboard that is used to synchronise, or put together, the film action and the sound that goes with it. I also had to phone the lab each day to get a report on the film that had been rushed in the day before. I also kept the magazines loaded with one roll of film at a time and kept a written record of everything that was shot."

Spy Probe: *Bodie and Doyle infiltrate an organisation which is hiring killers. Their victims - nobodies. Why? Cowley orders them to find the link, but is there someone in the background hindering their progress.*

The final episode, *Spy Probe*, by Tony Barwick, was approved by LWT on 30th April and shooting started on Monday 11th May, with director Dennis Abey in control. However, Lewis Collins was absent from the first day's filming because he was appearing at Hendon Magistrates Court regarding his gun charge. The charge of possessing a shotgun with intent to endanger life and threatening to kill one of the charity workers was dropped and he was fined £300 for attacking the women.

Martin Shaw and Lewis Collins on the set of SPY PROBE, the final episode in production.

When writer Tony Barwick submitted the 'second draft' of the script to the production office on 30th April (which had two different working titles, *Spy Trap* and *Spy Chase*), the ending was clear, Bodie and Doyle survive. But did producer Ray Menmuir change that last scene?

DOYLE: *He's going to ram us!*
A flare gun is fired. The flare lands in the cockpit and explodes. Clouds of black smoke spew out of the launch. Will the two boats still collide?

Ray Menmuir: "I'm not sure where that idea came from; there may have been talks about it by the unit publicist, Paul McNicholls, but it was purely for the press."

The firearm used by Doyle is a Smith & Wesson model 29, as used by Clint Eastwood in the *Dirty Harry* movies. A six-shot revolver generating enough power to blast a round through two bodies, producing a huge recoil and near-deafening noise. Bodie gets the use of a Walther PPK; it was originally made as a Police Pistol (Polizei Pistole Kriminal - PPK). The gun was favoured by many armed agencies, including German officers and the Gestapo in World War II. The East German SSD and the West German BND, also used it; the gun eventually suffered metal fatigue, causing stoppages.

In SPY PROBE an organisation, which hires killers to assassinate virtual nobodies on sight, is infiltrated by CI5's Ray Doyle (Martin Shaw).

Dennis Abey (director): "I enjoyed the pre-production talks. It was at this stage that I could have my say on what could be changed from Tony's script. When Gerry O'Hara handed me the script for my approval, I opened it, looked for a few minutes, stood up and threw it out the window, claiming it was rubbish. He knew I was joking, opened his desk drawer and said, 'Don't worry, I've got another one here'. I'd become predictable, what a shame. Then I said to Menmuir, 'How many explosions can I have then?' He, too, knew me by now and told me I was allowed only one, but as many as I wanted off camera! I insisted on doing the 'fun' stuff rather than let the second unit take care of it. I mean, what's the point in directing if I couldn't do the car chases or explosions. I told Menmuir I could do the second unit stuff in half the time normally allocated to them.

"In the opening scenes by the canal at Brentford, I made Martin carry the camera on his chest, making him point it up to his face. The picture broke up, but I still think the shot looked effective in the rushes the following day. That'll teach him to keep asking for close ups. The two guys were still going on about who had the most screen time.

"I then decided we could have some fun with the two Capris almost colliding in the street in Fulham (Doneraile Street). It was unscripted and purely done to see if I could get away with it, which I did. More car chasing was to be had at the Master Brewer Motel, when I got one of the cars to nearly hit a milk float, simply because I'd seen one, or shall we say, nearly hit one, earlier that morning on my way to the location. Luckily we managed to get one to use in the filming and put my idea in to practice."

Doyle's Ford Capri arrives on location for SPY PROBE at the Master Brewer Motel, Middlesex.

The car stunt at the Motel was as a result of director Dennis Abey's forward thinking? In the sequence a milk float is used to add 'spice' to the chase when it is seen avoiding the speeding cars - but the idea was only concocted that very morning?

Camera assistant and clapper/loader Nigel Seal carries the equipment into the Motel.

Joking around on the set of SPY PROBE, camera operator Mike Tomlin and stunt driver Graham Crowther (who doubled for Martin Shaw - Doyle). Clapper/loader Nigel Seal pops into shot at the far right of the picture.

In the script the characters of Ferris and Twig used a disused warehouse as an office/hideout. This was realised in Albions Yard, near Kings Cross train station, London, but it wasn't an easy days shoot for the Mark I production team:

Matthew Simmons (location assistant): "This was, and still is, a busy part of London, but the yard was chosen because it was walled off from the surrounding traffic. The mannequins seen, and used in the story, were not props but came with the location, and I believe remained there for an episode of *Minder* a few years later. What should have therefore been quite an easy and quiet shoot turned out not to be by far! The unit next door was a car body repair shop, and they were using various air-powered tools to remove a front wing of a car. That was fine during rehearsals but during a take it was producing problems for the sound guys because the noise from the grinding and air-compressor was pretty loud. We had to keep going next door and asking them to stop working during the take. Thing is, they didn't realise we had quite a few takes to do, so they'd stop for a few minutes then start again. In the end I think they got annoyed with us and carried on regardless, which caused us to stay on longer than we had been scheduled for."

While filming in Fulham, South West London, Martin Shaw's character (Doyle) had to stop an assassin by opening his car door (Ford Capri, VHK 11W) into the path of the man.

Frank Watts (lighting cameraman): "Martin actually opened the car door so hard onto the guy's knee that he dented the Capri's door. The poor guy was in pain for ages. We did it on the second take."

Dennis Abey: "I did re-write the ending just for a laugh and nearly got it on film. When the policeman pulls in Bodie and Doyle's dinghy, he looks in the boat, turns to Cowley and says, 'It's empty, Sir'. Cowley then looks up and says, 'Thank God for that, I couldn't stand those two anyway!' The boys liked that one. Filming the scenes at Victoria Deep Water Terminal was a hairy experience, we were so close to the water and I spent a lot of the time with the camera crew in the 'tracking' dinghy."

Lewis Collins: "Martin was driving the motorboat and I was on the side, firing at the baddies. We were whizzing along when he turned a corner and I fell overboard. The trouble was that my foot caught under the seat. I hit the water at about 45-knots and was dragged along underwater. Martin was looking the other way and the crew on the other boat were screaming at him. He thought they were waving him along and carried on. It was only about 30-seconds but I thought I was finished. When I got out I said to Martin, 'Listen, mate, I know it's the last episode, but I'd like to come out of it alive.'"

Gavin Bouquet (assistant art director): "Filming at Victoria Deep Water terminal was very frightening; just one slip and you were in the water! We were that close. It was one of those days when it was sunny, then cloudy, and then drizzling; I think you get the picture. We had terrible trouble with the continuity involved in the two stars hair? Martin's hair would start out curly and when it drizzled, it became damp, and would straighten up. Lewis, on the other hand, would start out straight and as it became wet would go wavy. When we did the boat scenes the situation got worse. Director Dennis Abey was having kittens! Using a garden spray squirter, filled with water, we would spray their hair. Martin and Lewis had great fun spraying each other in all the wrong places!"

Martin Shaw and Lewis Collins clown around while filming SPY PROBE.

Guido Reidy (sound assistant): "David Crozier was on the old 'bottorsniking' at Cadby Hall in Hammersmith. We were doing the interrogation scenes and in the forecourt was a skip full of old tiles. We loaded the lot into boom operator, Gary Weir's Ford Capri. The rear end of his car was almost touching the floor. He drove it like that for several miles! How the police never stopped him was beyond me! David was very pleased with his find!"

A repeat of this episode on Friday 28th August 1987, five years after the series ended, achieved 10.1 million viewers and seventh place in the weekly ratings chart.

Production on *The Professionals* ceased on Friday 22nd May.

Gerry O'Hara (script editor): "I should think I talked to fifty or sixty writers over the four years I worked on the show. Deciding on stories was the most fatiguing part of the whole thing. The ones who couldn't get it on were the ones who always lapsed into static situations, with dialogue coming through in chunks of paragraphs. We were basically an action show, we had to have momentum, and that required short speeches and often-throwaway speeches, which still gave enough information. This became the biggest difficulty, and it increased with the number of shows we did. Writers, hundreds of miles apart, were running into each other, writing the same dialogue and situations.

"Also, because we set out to make the show move, the action content had to be given its head. You plant action or intrigue in the teaser; then you work to the first commercial break and have to bring up the action line, and again at the end of the second act and very much so at the end of the third. To make the 52-minute running time, you have to slot in an interesting story with interesting dialogue, and it would be very high content to have 20-minutes of action and 32-minutes of dialogue. We keep our pauses as short as we dare, we rarely let our actors stand still and we did create fluidity.

"The most vexing thing though is that sometimes the most mundane storyline seemed to give the impetus for a go-ahead just because it contained the right elements; you can see the action would be there and that the three leads would be well exercised."

Brian Clemens (creator and co-executive producer): "We had a lot of fun doing it. Although it was criticised, I still feel that we never exploited violence for it's own sake. The success of portraying violence on the screen depends on how it is done and I think we managed to hit the right formula. Because the programmes were extremely fast moving, we had to push existing camera techniques to the very limit. It wasn't only Martin or Lewis who had to be pretty fit, the technical boys responsible for capturing everything for the series had to be pretty quick off the mark as well. I would like to have carried on being involved in *The Professionals* for a long time, but the production costs, especially when you had as much action as we did, plus all the equipment, such as helicopters, were on the increase. The amount of money needed to do the last batch would have provided a budget for a feature film at the time."

Martin Shaw: "Both Lewis and myself were exhausted! I mean real, total exhaustion, both mental and physical. We worked flat out for 12-to-15 hours a day, five days a week, hurling ourselves all over the place. I had to snatch every possible moment of sleep I could, even if it was only ten minutes in the back of a car. There was no time for a social life. You had to keep your body in peak condition to stand any chance of getting through a series like that in one piece."

Spokesman (LWT press office): "It had been incredibly popular around the world, with some fifty countries taking it, but it was not just the cost which brought the series to a halt. There has to be an end to everything, even the successful shows."

When the media reported that filming of *The Professionals* had finished in May, lots of fans got hold of the wrong end of the stick and thought no more episodes were to be shown. What the media had failed to realise was that with few exceptions, all television programmes produced at the time were made in batches of thirteen, and the first four series had followed this trend. The last six of those, which were filmed late in 1980, plus the five new episodes constituted this final series.

Therefore, what the media actually meant was that the contracts with actors, Lewis Collins, Martin Shaw and Gordon Jackson were at an end, and with Collins and Shaw more adamant than ever that they would not be staying with the series, no new contracts were to be signed. LWT, aware of the show's growing popularity, transmitted a series of eleven repeats, billed as a 'new series' from Sunday 13th September at 9.00 pm, keeping the eleven new episodes 'in the can' until autumn 1982, when these were screened from Sunday 7th November.

Martin Shaw: "I don't want to knock *The Professionals* too much because it did me a lot of good and made me a great many friends. But after four years of it, I was getting pretty desperate to find something else to do. I am very inventive and like to think about a character I'm playing. But with Doyle, the only thing that really worked was to play him as 'Mister Super Cool' and try and be myself in front of a camera. I was worried about being typecast. I became a bit apprehensive about the future. What I gambled on was all my previous credits on television and in stage plays to see me through."

The programme became popular in Australia, New Zealand, parts of the USA, Nigeria and Austria to name but a few. In Germany, devastated fans bombarded the TV stations with protests and petitions when they heard that *Die Profis* was to disappear from their lives forever because the TV moguls felt that the episodes so far unseen by the Germans were 'too English', or 'too violent'.

And so the series came to an end...............

****

In April 1988, a plan by the ITV Network to repeat episodes of *The Professionals* was overturned by Martin Shaw. He had objected to repeats because he was a 'serious actor' and could stop the show going out because Equity, his union, demanded that its members have the right to veto repeats if it is more than five years since the programme was first shown.

Shaw's original contract, a standard Equity agreement, allowed LWT to repeat the series a maximum of three times within five years of first transmission. Trouble began when programme controllers at ITV decided to include one of the series in the networks summer schedules, which began on the 26th June and finished around September time. Because of Equity's insistence on the five-year rule, which ran out at the end of 1987, it meant re-negotiating with the actors involved.

Ann Hutton (Martin Shaw's agent: 1988): "Mr. Shaw does not want them shown. It is an old series now. He does not look like that anymore and feels the image it gives of him is wrong and out of date."

Payment was arranged for the four episodes shown without Union agreement in January and February, with the seven planned being returned to the archive. However, it wasn't Martin Shaw who was the only party affected. Under Equity rules, the stars were due 150% of their original fee if the programme was shown within two years, rising to 200% after five years. An unhappy Gordon Jackson stood to loose more than £50,000. His wage had been £3,700 per episode, Collins, £2,400 and Shaw £2,200, and actor Steve Alder, who played Murphy in seven episodes, would have got around £200 per repeat. Tim Johnson, Equity's film organiser, who had been involved in the discussions with LWT, claimed that around 500 actors might have been entitled to repeat fees.

Lewis Collins (interviewed at the time): "It's not just for myself that I'm angry. Martin didn't even approach me, and that upset me. But there are a lot of stuntmen, for instance, who have retired or been injured who could do with a spot of extra cash. I don't want to bring the violins out, but the boys who have gone out of the game were looking forward to a little Christmas box and they're the ones who will suffer.

"I'm a serious actor, too. We're all serious actors. That doesn't mean that we should deprive the public of enjoying something good we've done in the past, whatever we look like on screen."

Peter Brayham (stunt arranger, interviewed at the time): "Shaw and Collins were different animals. There was always great competition between them. But as far as I'm concerned, Lew is tops. He really is one of the most physical actors I know. He moves instinctively, and the only problem I used to have was to stop him killing himself! He'd always want to do his own stunts. As for Martin, if Lew would do it, so would he. I always had to step in to stop them because it was too dangerous. But now if I saw Martin I'd tell him, 'You are being selfish. So pull yourself together'. I'm very angry with him. I think about the guys who did so much for the series, and aren't going to be able to earn much anymore. It wouldn't do Martin any harm for people to see him as he was then, and to be honest I think he did some better performances in *The Professionals* than anything else!"

In October 1991, Martin Shaw had a change of heart after being touched by the plight of Gordon Jackson's widow. Rona Anderson was unwell and struggling to make ends meet. He hoped that the reruns would bring a £40,000 windfall for Mrs. Jackson, after her 66-year old husband had died from cancer in January 1990.

Brian Clemens (interviewed at the time): "I'm very pleased that Martin changed his mind. When I heard about Gordon's widow I thought it was a very noble gesture on his part."

Martin Shaw admits that the experience of playing Doyle has left him feeling uneasy about meeting some of his admirers.

Martin Shaw: "Fan worship makes me feel very uncomfortable. I don't even like giving autographs. I think it demeans both the person asking for it and the person giving it. People come up to me all the time and say, 'You're my youth, man!' That's sweet because it's not obsessive, that's real. In the same way that people collect 1970's Corgi and Dinky toys, I remind them of what it was like to be young."

Martin's fame in *The Professionals* brought him some unwelcome attention too, including an obsessive female who found out where he lived, went to the post office and had all his post redirected to her house for a year.

"So, for 12 months, everything that was supposed to be delivered to me was sent to this woman. She would open all my letters, read them and then deliver them by hand to my door the following day! If she thought there was a letter I shouldn't see, she destroyed it. She just wanted to know everything about me, so she borrowed my letters for 24 hours!"

During the weekend of 1st March 1997, it was revealed that Lewis Collins was in negotiations with David Wickes Television (DWTV) in a revival of *The Professionals*, which would see him commanding the elite unit. But that's another story………..

Always time for a bite to eat....Gordon Jackson and Donald Mothersill (wardrobe supervisor) enjoy a spot of lunch while taking a break in filming SPY PROBE.

SERIES V EPISODE GUIDE

Last minute adjustments for actor Lewis Collins on the set of NO STONE.

CRY WOLF

by **Paul Wheeler**
© Copyright Mark 1 Productions Ltd MCMLXXXI

Susan Grant	Sheila Ruskin
Laughlin	Alan MacNaughtan
Mrs. Grant	Rona Anderson
Bauer	David Neal
Miller	Ian Bartholomew
Neville Grant	Simon Templeman
Smith	Timothy Block
Joan	Zoe Gonord
Mason	Barrie Cookson
Sergeant Watson	Ian Blair
Superintendent	Rex Robinson
Doctor	Vass Anderson
Old lady	Aimee Delamain
Sergeant	Duncan Miller
P.C.	Rob Heyland
Night porter	Arthur Nightingale
Uncredited	
Car Park Thug	David Holland
Car Park Thug	Graham Crowther
Uniformed Policeman	Peter Roy
Uniformed Policeman	Tony O'Leary

Director: **Phil Meheux**

SUSAN Grant was adopted as a child when both her parents were presumed dead. She now lives in London and works in a charity office. When she realises that she is being followed and someone tries to unnerve her with a series of anonymous telephone calls and eerie sound effects, she becomes frightened and tells the local police. The police however believe that she is simply imagining this persecution. Her adoptive mother, Mrs. Grant, gets in touch with George Cowley, who is an old friend of the family. Cowley promises to find out who is bothering Susan and sends Bodie to strike up an acquaintance with her. Bodie takes the girl out to supper and, after talking to her at some length, reaches the conclusion that the events she describes are real. Next day as Susan leaves work, Bodie follows her in his car. A man called Miller pretends to stall his car in front of Bodie and blocks his path. Unaware of this incident, Susan goes shopping. A man named Smith follows her around the supermarket and, when she reaches home, she is horrified to find that a hideous black plastic spider has been pushed into her grocery bag.

As Bodie examines this latest attempt to scare Susan, Henry Laughlin, a man of around fifty, who works with Susan and lives near her, arrives and is disconcerted to find Bodie in the flat. CI5 check up on Laughlin and discover that he is an ex-revolutionary who has dedicated his life to rallying support for political prisoners throughout the world.

Meanwhile, Bodie discovers that Susan's phone has been tampered with. That afternoon Bodie sees Susan meet a young man. The couple has a bitter argument and the man walks away in anger. CI5 records show that this man is Susan's feckless brother Neville; he has been losing large sums of money and is constantly trying to get Mrs. Grant and Susan to lend him more. That night, Bodie spends the night at Susan's flat and finds the device, which creates the eerie sound effects. In the middle of the night, Smith bursts into the flat with a gun and grabs Susan; holding the girl as a shield, he aims the gun at Bodie. Susan breaks free and Bodie is able to shoot the intruder dead. Concerned for the girl's safety, Bodie suggests that Susan should leave London for a while and accompanies her to Mrs Grant's country cottage. A man called Bauer watches their departure; who is responsible for the attacks on Susan's life. Annoyed that CI5 have interfered and that Smith has failed in his murder attempt, Bauer sends Miller to kill Bodie and Susan.

Miller breaks into the cottage and attempts to chloroform Susan, but Bodie is prepared for the intruder and overpowers him. Miller divulges nothing and is taken away into police custody. Pretending to be his lawyer, Bauer visits Miller in his cell and kills him. Mrs. Grant receives a visit from Laughlin and he tells her that he knows who has been persecuting Susan and has taken steps to stop it. He sends his solicitor, Mason, to hand Bauer a package, but Doyle, who has been watching Laughlin and Mason, follows the solicitor to the meeting place and seizes the package. The package is found to contain tapes, which give evidence of torture of political prisoners in South America. Furious that he has lost the package and suspecting that Laughlin has set up with CI5, Bauer telephones Laughlin and tells him that, because of his foolish behaviour, Susan will now suffer. Bauer kidnaps Susan and takes her at gunpoint, in Bodie's car, to a remote aerodrome. Doyle, however, following a tracking device in Bodie's car, arrives in time to stop Bauer flying out of the country with the girl.

Cowley tells Susan that Laughlin is her real father. Presumed dead when she was still a young child, he had in fact been held prisoner. By the time he was released, Susan had been adopted by the Grants. Laughlin felt he could not disturb this arrangement but, when he assembled the evidence against the American torturers and refused to hand it over to those people that it incriminated, Bauer, who knew about Susan's adoption, threatened her life unless Laughlin handed him the evidence. Laughlin resisted for as long as he could but frightened for his daughter's safety, asked Mason to hand Bauer the evidence.

Production Unit

Created by	Brian Clemens
Executive Producers	Albert Fennell, Brian Clemens
Music	Laurie Johnson
Producer	Raymond Menmuir
Associate Producer	Chris Burt
Script Editor	Gerry O'Hara

Production Manager	Ron Purdie
Production Accountant	Terry Connors
Assistant Director	Bill Westley
Location Manager	David Barron
Continuity	Doreen Soan
Casting	Esta Charkham
Art Director	Allan Cameron
Set Dresser	Peter Russell
Stunt Arranger	Peter Brayham
Wardrobe Supervisor	Donald Mothersill
Special Effects	Mike Collins
Lighting Cameraman	Frank Watts
Camera Operator	Malcolm Vinson
Focus Puller	Mike Tomlin
Make Up	Alan Boyle
Hairdresser	Jan Dorman
Lighting by	Lee Electric
Supervising Editor	John S. Smith
Sound Recordist	David Crozier
Boom Operator	Gary Weir
Dubbing Editor	Peter Lennard
Dubbing Mixer	Trevor Pyke
Music Editor	Alan Willis

An Avengers MARK 1 Production For LONDON WEEKEND TELEVISION

In CRY WOLF the plane with which Bauer has planned his escape crashes....

Shooting / Location Schedule

Production Dates: Monday 16th to Friday 27th March; Thursday 9th April; Thursday 16th April, 1981. Production Number: 9D10200

16-17 March **Susan's flat / lifts / car park**: Napier Court, Edenhurst Avenue / Napier Avenue, Fulham, London, SW6
Henry Laughlin's flat: Hurlingham Court, Ranelagh Gardens, Fulham, London, SW6

8 March	*Police Station*: Wealdstone Police Station, 78 High Street, Wealdstone, Middlesex
19-20 March	*Associated Charities (Susan's office)*: Globe House, Bentinck Road, Yiewsley, Middlesex
	Street: Postbox: 74 High Street, Yiewsley, Middlsex
	Int / Ext: Bodie's car (kidnap run): Station Road / High Street / Falling Lane, Yiewsley, Middlesex & High Road, Cowley, Middlesex
	Int / Ext: Doyle's car (kidnap run): The Avenue / Southfield Road, Bedford Park, London, W4
23 March	*The 'Chinese Garden' Restaurant*: Copperfield Restaurant, 14 The Parade, Watford, Hertfordshire
	Alleyway and fight: Wells Yard, Wellstones, Watford, Hertfordshire
24 March	*Food Store*: Europa Stores, 194 Kensington High Street, Kensington, London, W14
	CI5 HQ / Mason's office / Morgue / Interrogation: Cadby Hall, Blythe Road, Hammersmith, London, W14
	Park: Bauer & Mason: Ravenscourt Park, Hammersmith, London, W6
25-26 March	*Mrs. Grant's country house / Bauer's House*: Sarratt Mill House, New Road, Church End, Sarratt, Hertfordshire
27 March	*Airfield*: Chalgrove Airfield, Cuxham Road, Chalgrove, Oxfordshire
	Country lane: Doyle's car (Airfield route): Warpsgrove Lane, Chalgrove, Oxfordshire
2nd Unit:	
9 April	*Susan's flat*: Napier Court, Edenhurst Avenue / Napier Avenue, Fulham, London, SW6
16 April	*Int: Susan's car*: 105-109 Shenley Road, Borehamwood, Hertfordshire
	Streets: Bodie's car & Susan's car: Shenley Road, Borehamwood, Hertfordshire

Susan Grant (Sheila Ruskin) is unaware of the truth behind work colleague Henry Laughlin (Alan MacNaughtan). But what secret does he really hold in CRY WOLF?

A MAN CALLED QUINN

by **Tony Barwick**
© Copyright Mark 1 Productions Ltd MCMLXXXI

Quinn	Del Henney
Krasnov	Steven Berkoff
Granger	Bernard Archard
Howard	Peter Howell
Jack Canon	Linal Haft
Harris	Johnny Shannon
2nd Interrogator	Christopher Ettridge
Landlady	Margo Cunningham
Doctor	Christopher Scoular
Male Nurse	Malcolm Mudie
Policeman	Peter Woodward
Johnson	John Owens
Uncredited	
Clinic Male Nurse	Dennis Plenty
Uniformed Policeman	Derek Moss
Gunman	Terry Plummer
Gunman	Romo Garrara
Gunman	Cliff Diggins

Director: **Horace Ové**

QUINN, an ex-Secret Service agent, now a patient in a mental home, is normally quiet and docile with the doctors and staff of the establishment. One day, as he is sitting waiting for an injection from Dr. Grey, Quinn looks up to see not the doctor, but the KGB agent Krasnov. Quinn's disturbed mind suddenly reverts back to the time when he was a prisoner of the KGB. He dives out of the window and races across the asylum grounds to escape; the staff who pursue him he sees as Russian guards with dogs, and he desperately fights them off. Clear of the asylum, Quinn finds a large house nearby and breaks in. He has found some money and changed his clothes from a wardrobe as the house owner and a friend return home. As the two men accost the intruder, Quinn suddenly sees them as more Russian guards and violently attacks them, before making good his escape.

Cowley is notified of Quinn's escape and he orders Bodie and Doyle to search for the man while he himself goes to see the doctors who were treating Quinn; they tell him that, although Quinn has partially recovered from his long ordeal at the hands of the KGB, a sudden shock could bring back all his past experiences. Quinn meanwhile has booked into a bed-sitter and tries to get some rest. As he sleeps, he relives again the time when the KGB tortured him for the names of the British Secret Service chief. When he wakes, he finds the names of the men, 'Granger, Howard, Leniston and Morris' scrawled on the walls of his bedroom. Assuming that he has written the names in his sleep, the sight of them sets off an idea in his confused mind.

He leaves his bed-sitting-room and goes to a secluded spot in the country where he uncovers a rifle buried in the ground. Staff at the asylum are now shocked when they find the real Dr. Grey has been shot and his body dumped in the establishment grounds.

In A MAN CALLED QUINN, an ex-spy escapes from a secure hospital and begins a campaign of murder against his former colleagues.....which includes George Cowley (Gordon Jackson)!

Cowley fears that Quinn might be trying to seek out those who sent him on his missions. Leniston himself has recently died of natural causes, but Cowley goes to warn Granger of the danger. However, as the two are talking Granger is shot dead and a second shot narrowly misses Cowley's head. Quinn's whereabouts is located, but he gives Bodie and Doyle the slip. The two CI5 agents then go to guard the second name on the list, a Bomb Squad officer named Howard. He is saved and reveals that 'Morris', the fourth name on the list, was the nickname of Cowley, their own chief. Worried that Cowley may be in danger, Cowley is escorted to a safe house. However, the CI5 Chief's location is discovered, and it is only down to his men's quick thinking that he is saved when an explosion destroys his office.

The next day, Cowley gives his agents the slip, but Bodie has secretly placed a bugging device on Cowley's clothing and the two men follow their boss as he goes to meet Quinn at a remote cottage. Cowley has discovered that the bullet fired at him during his meeting with Granger is of a different calibre to the one that killed Granger; there were two gunmen at the spot. Cowley believes that a third party is supervising Quinn's killing campaign and that it was planned when Quinn was in the hands of the KGB. It would have been easy for the Russians to implant a programme in Quinn's mind to kill his secret service chiefs with one of their agents triggering the plan during the last few days. Quinn immediately names Yuri Krasnov and a meeting takes place at a deserted airfield. When Krasnov shows, he is bewildered that, instead of killing Cowley, he sides with the enemy and opens fire on him. Bodie and Doyle arrive in time to battle, and kill, Krasnov's Russian agents, but Quinn leaps in to a car, and as his mind veers to the past, he thinks that he is in a small plane and flying out for his next mission. Quinn is killed when he crashes the car at the airfield boundary.

Can Quinn's (Del Henney) target really be George Cowley, the head of CI5 (Gordon Jackson)?

Production Unit

Created by	Brian Clemens
Executive Producers	Albert Fennell, Brian Clemens
Music	Laurie Johnson
Producer	Raymond Menmuir
Associate Producer	Chris Burt

Script Editor	Gerry O'Hara
Production Manager	Ron Purdie
Production Accountant	Terry Connors
Assistant Director	Gino Marotta
Location Manager	David Barron
Continuity	Doreen Soan
Casting	Esta Charkham
Art Director	Allan Cameron
Set Dresser	Peter Russell
Stunt Arranger	Peter Brayham
Wardrobe Supervisor	Donald Mothersill
Special Effects	Arthur Beavis
Lighting Cameraman	Barry Noakes
Camera Operator	Malcolm Vinson
Focus Puller	Mike Tomlin
Make Up	Alan Boyle
Hairdresser	Jan Dorman
Lighting by	Lee Electric
Editor	Brian Freemantle
Sound Recordist	David Crozier
Boom Operator	Gary Weir
Dubbing Editor	Peter Lennard
Dubbing Mixer	Trevor Pyke
Music Editor	Alan Willis

An Avengers MARK 1 Production For LONDON WEEKEND TELEVISION

A former colleague of Cowley's goes on the run when he believes that the KGB have drugged him. However, A MAN CALLED QUINN, reaches the end of the road in the explosive conclusion to this story.....

Shooting / Location Schedule
Production Dates: Monday 30th March to Friday 10th April, 1981. Production Number: 9D10201

30 March	***Repton Clinic***: St. Huberts House, St. Huberts Lane, Gerrards Cross, Buckinghamshire ***Army Camp***: Queen Elizabeth II Gurkha Barracks, Aldershot Road, Church Crookham, Hampshire
31 March	***Car run-bys: Bodie & police / Int: Bodie's car***: Bishops Bridge Road / Harrow Road / Warwick Avenue / Bloomfield Road, Paddington, London, W9 ***Street: Bodie's car***: Randolph Avenue, Maida Vale, London, W9 ***Park***: Primrose Hill Park, Primrose Hill Road, London, NW3 ***Johnson's Garage***: D. E Fisher Motor Crash Repairs, 265-269 Finchley Road, West Hampstead, London, NW3
1 April	***Jack Canon's house / Int / Ext: Cowley's car***: Little Heath, 46 Sheen Common Drive, East Sheen, Richmond, Surrey
2 April	***Bodie's car run-bys (route to Rooming house)***: Latimer Road, North Kensington, London, W10 ***Rooming house (Quinn)***: 2 Bracewell Road, North Kensington, London, W10
3 April	***Woods / Country cottage***: Black Park Cottage, Black Park, Queens Drive, Fulmer, Buckinghamshire
6 April	***Granger's country home***: Magna Carta House, Magna Carta Lane, off Staines Road, Wraysbury, Berkshire ***Int: Cowley's car (route to Granger's house)***: Staines Road, Wraysbury, Berkshire
7 April	***Car chase: Bodie & Quinn***: Great Church Lane / Colet Gardens (Church 1 - aerial); Hofland Road / Masbro Road / Fielding Road, Hammersmith, London, W14 (church 2) ***Cars: Truck stunt***: Cadby Hall 'forecourt', Blythe Road, Hammersmith, London, W14 ***Streets: escort to safe house***: Hammersmith Road, Hammersmith, London, W14 ***Street: Bodie / Doyle pick up Cowley***: Augustine Road, Hammersmith, London, W14 ***Bodie's car run-by: Cowley shopping***: Lakeside Road / Richmond Way (chemist), Hammersmith, London, W14 ***Int: Safe house***: Cadby Hall, Blythe Road, Hammersmith, London, W14
8 April	***Army Camp***: Queen Elizabeth II Gurkha Barracks, Aldershot Road, Church Crookham, Hampshire
9 April	***Int: Bodie's car (Doyle on radio)***: The Frithe (near Berry Field), Slough, Berkshire ***Bodie's car run-by***: Uxbridge Road (A412), Slough, Berkshire ***Ext: Safehouse***: Canal Works, Bentinck Road, Yiewsley, Middlesex
10 April	***Airfield***: Chalgrove Airfield, Cuxham Road, Chalgrove, Oxfordshire

LAWSON'S LAST STAND
by **Ranald Graham**
© Copyright Mark 1 Productions Ltd MCMLXXXI

Lt. Colonel Peter Lawson	Michael Culver
Tug Willis	John Hallam
Len Clarke	Michael Angelis
Brigadier Tennant	Donald Pickering
Lavinia Lawson	Helen Cherry
Dr. Lowe	Stephen Greif
Doreen	Eve Bland
Professor	Allan Mitchell
Army Major	Prentis Hancock
Lt. Colonel Tony Manning	Doyne Byrd
Police Chief	Roger Nott
Army guard	Tim Swinton
Senior guard	Robert Cavendish
Guard	Brian Binns
Pedestrian	Max Harvey
Uncredited	
Security Man	Vic Gallucci
Marston Dale Manager	Bill Burns
Policeman	Ray Knight
Javelin Man	Bill Hemmings

Director: **Ian Sharp**

AN army brigadier approaches CI5 to ask for help in finding a young Lieutenant-Colonel, Peter Lawson, who has vanished from the army hospital where he was undergoing a mental check-up. The brigadier explains that, though Lawson has had a brilliant army career thus far, he committed a series of disastrous and astonishing mistakes on a recent NATO exercise in Europe and has been brought back to the British hospital to have his mental condition investigated. He is also in possession of valuable NATO secrets and may have been abducted by the Russians. Bodie and Doyle are sent to find Lawson and Cowley discovers from Lawson's mother that he has recently been wanting the address of one of his most devoted army corporals, now a civilian, called Len 'Nobby' Clarke. Bodie and Doyle find that Len is away from home with Lawson; together with another ex-soldier called Tug Willis, Len is practicing drills under Lawson's directions.

The CI5 men report to Cowley that they have found Lawson and that, although his behaviour is eccentric, he has obviously not been abducted and is doing no harm. However, Lawson is drilling Len and Tug as part of a careful plan which he has worked out with the thoroughness of an army manoeuvre and which he is single-mindedly determined to carry out because of a personal obsession. Len and Tug have been persuaded to help him, partly by

Lawson's appeal to their army instincts to obey an officer and partly by promising them a large financial reward for their loyal service. As the first part of his plan, Lawson takes Len and Tug on a bank hold-up. They steal a large amount of money and shoot a bank employee who tries to raise the alarm.

Lieutenant Colonel Peter Lawson (Michael Culver) vanishes from a Military hospital. He is in possession of valuable NATO secrets and may be abducted by the Russians. In this scene Bodie (Lewis Collins) attempts to put a stop to LAWSON'S LAST STAND.

Film footage taken at the bank during the robbery shows that the robbers were Lawson, Nobby and Tug. The bank employee has been seriously injured during the raid, and Bodie and Doyle feel guilty that they assumed Lawson's intensive training of his men to be harmless. Using money from the bank raid, Lawson purchases equipment and transport for his men and, wearing army uniforms, they go to an army barracks. Lawson reports at the gatehouse that he has come to visit a friend stationed there. They are admitted to the barracks and Lawson's friend welcomes them warmly. At the first opportunity, Lawson knocks his friend unconscious and helps Nobby and Tug to steal a large quantity of powerful weapons from the arms store. The theft is reported to CI5 and Cowley becomes concerned about the plan in Lawson's deranged mind, which requires such enormous firepower.

Lawson puts all-important military and civil installations on full alert in case of an attack and Cowley anxiously awaits developments. Doyle learns from the Brigadier that Lawson suffered a great 'defeat' in the recent NATO exercise because, theoretically, nerve gas was used against his men and they were all 'killed'. Realising that Lawson may be harbouring an obsession against nerve gas, Bodie and Doyle race to the nearest chemical warfare research establishment. By the time they arrive, Lawson has already launched an attack on the place and stolen two canisters of the most deadly nerve gas in the world. Nobby is accidentally killed by Tug during the attack, but Lawson assures Tug that their operation is of such importance to Britain's future that Nobby has not died in vain.

Tug, acting on Lawson's orders, ensures that a note containing Lawson's demands reaches the authorities; it explains that Lawson is balanced precariously in a park in a crowded part of London, with the nerve gas attached to a hand-grenade. If Lawson is alarmed or disturbed in any way, he will drop the pin of the hand-grenade and the canister will explode. Lawson demands that all three chemical warfare establishments in Britain must be destroyed and their destruction shown on the portable television set he has with him. Meanwhile, CI5 and the army have arrived on the scene and Bodie has spotted a blind spot where Lawson will be unable to see him. He manages a sprint at Lawson at the same time as Doyle races towards him in an armoured tank. Bodie grabs the hand-grenade and canister and hurtles them into the tank where they explode harmlessly in the cabin of the armoured tank.

Production Unit

Created by	Brian Clemens
Executive Producers	Albert Fennell, Brian Clemens
Music	Laurie Johnson
Producer	Raymond Menmuir
Associate Producer	Chris Burt
Script Editor	Gerry O'Hara
Production Manager	Ron Purdie
Production Accountant	Terry Connors
Assistant Director	Bill Westley
Location Manager	David Barron
Continuity	Doreen Soan
Casting	Esta Charkham
Art Director	Allan Cameron
Set Dresser	Peter Russell
Stunt Arranger	Peter Brayham
Wardrobe Supervisor	Donald Mothersill
Special Effects	Arthur Beavis
Lighting Cameraman	Frank Watts
Camera Operator	Malcolm Vinson
Focus Puller	Mike Tomlin
Make Up	Alan Boyle
Hairdresser	Jan Dorman
Lighting by	Lee Electric
Supervising Editor	John S. Smith
Sound Recordist	David Crozier
Boom Operator	Gary Weir
Dubbing Editor	Peter Lennard

Dubbing Mixer	Hugh Strain
Music Editor	Alan Willis

An Avengers Mark 1 Production For LONDON WEEKEND TELEVISION

Shooting / Location Schedule

Production Dates: Monday 13th to Friday 24th April, 1981. Production Number: 9D10202

13 April	**Military Hospital**: Aldenham House, Haberdashers Askes' School, Butterfly Lane, Elstree, Hertfordshire
14 April	**Len's forge / ford / Int: Bodie's car**: Batford Forge, off Lower Luton Road (Crabtree Lane ford), Batford, near Harpenden, Hertfordshire
	Country road (Lawson): Sauncey Woods, Batford, near Harpenden, Hertfordshire
15 April	**Waste ground (Quarry)**: Cripps Farm Landfill site, Springwell Lane, Rickmansworth, Hertfordshire
16 April	**Lawson's camp / Len's grave**: Aldenham Park, Tykes Water Lake Bridge, Elstree, Aldenham
	Caravan Site (Tug's home): Radnor Hall, Allum Lane, Elstree, Hertfordshire
	Int: Pub: Wagon & Horses, Watling Street, Elstree, Hertfordshire
17 April	**Regimental Barracks (Tennant & Manning)**: Victoria Barracks, Victoria Street, Windsor, Berkshire
	Lavina Lawson's house: North Mymms Park House, Tollgate Road, Welham Green, Hertfordshire
20 April	**Int: Bank**: Barclays Bank, 375 Regents Park Road, Finchley, London, N3
	Restaurant / Street (Cowley meets Tennant): 119 Ballards Lane / Cornwall Avenue, Finchley, London, N3
	Ext: Cowley's car (radio): Cornwall Avenue, Finchley, London, N3
21 April	**Marston Dale**: Fulmer Grange, Framewood Road Fulmer, Buckinghamshire
22 April	**CI5 HQ / Projection room**: 151 Wembley Park Drive, Wembley, Middlesex
23-24 April	**London park**: Battersea Park, Queenstown Road, Battersea, London, SW11
	Street: Whitehall (Tug hands over parcel to policeman): Whitehall, Westminster, London, SW11

NO STONE

by **Roger Marshall**

© Copyright Mark 1 Productions Ltd MCMLXXXI

Ulrike	Sarah Neville
Jimmy Kilpin	John Wheatley
Hockley	Philip York
Ross Kilpin	Godfrey James
Tessa Kilpin	Briony McRoberts
Cook	Philip Martin Brown
June Cook	Chrissie Cotterill
Prison officer	Brian Miller
Tree	Simon Dutton
Wilfred Robard	Seymour Green
Clerk	Milton Johns
Allison	Brian Southwood
Joe	Mark Drewry
Jones	Nicholas Owen
Terrorist / Foreman	James Simmons
Terrorists	Michael Praed, William McBain
Policeman	Jonty Miller
Plainclothes man	Earl Robinson
Jackie	Maria Harper
Uncredited	
Prison Security	Jimmy Muir
Prison Security	Vic Gallucci
Policeman	Derek Moss
Policeman	Brendan Flannigan
Policeman	Ray Knight
CI5 Man	Ron Watkins
Burger Van Owner	Pat Gorman
Burger Van Customer	Andy Barrett
Bomb Squad Man	Frank Henson

Director: **Chris Burt**

IN the hope of reducing his own sentence for his part in terrorist crimes, Jimmy Kilpin, a young man on trial, is giving the authorities information about the terrorist gang. His counsel, Tim Hockley, tells him in confidence that unless he produces more information, he will still receive a prison sentence. Terrified of being locked away and attacked by other prisoners for his treachery, Kilpin tells Hockley about a large cache of arms hidden by the terrorists in the countryside. Hockley advises him to tell this to the authorities, but then secretly contacts the leader of the terrorists and tells them what Kilpin has proposed. When Kilpin is taken from prison to unearth the buried weapons, he is given a CI5 escort. They reach the remote spot and the

CI5 men start digging. Suddenly the terrorist gang hiding in the trees attacks them. The men open fire on the CI5 men with automatic weapons, seize Kilpin and make quick their getaway.

In NO STONE Martin Shaw and Lewis Collins got to handle some very special weaponry, Steyr-AUG assault rifles.

One of the men killed in the ambush, Cook, is a close friend of Ray Doyle's and two of the other CI5 men are badly wounded. Cowley is appalled when he receives word that his men have been attacked, and orders Bodie and Doyle to leave no stone unturned to find the men who murdered Cook. Doyle however must first break the news of his friend's death to his wife, who is expecting their second child in a few weeks. Cowley meanwhile talks to Kilpin's father. He is extremely wealthy and hopes to trace his son's whereabouts by offering a large reward.

Suspecting that Kilpin's counsellor, Hockley, must have played some part in communicating between Kilpin and the gang, Bodie and Doyle face the man with their suspicions. Hockley, however, easily evades the two agents' questions. One of the wounded CI5 men recovers consciousness to identify the leader of the gang as an English girl, Judy Wynant, now calling herself Ulrike Herzl. The following day, the newspapers receive a tape-recording from Ulrike in which she declares that she is waging war on a UK legal system, which, she says, suppresses the poor and favours the rich. Ulrike and her gang hold Kilpin to 'trial' at their hideout and, declared guilty of treachery; Kilpin is hanged. Hockley leaves pictures of the hanging in a public telephone box for the authorities to find, but CI5 have been following the man and he is photographed delivering the terrorist's pictures. Ulrike and her gang leave their hideout and shortly afterwards a bomb explodes outside eminent legal chambers.

A second bomb is discovered in a car parked outside the Royal Courts of Justice in London, and Bodie and Doyle confront Hockley with the evidence tying him to the terrorists. He informs them that the gang will almost certainly be leaving the country by plane. Cowley and his squad race to the airport and bring in the gang for questioning. They are aware that a third bomb has been planted somewhere and they trick Ulrike into giving away that it has been placed outside a magistrate's court.

At the scene, a bomb disposal officer locates the bomb and defuses it. However, as they leave the area, Cowley and his men are shocked to see an enormous explosion kill the officer. Ulrike has tricked them and said nothing about a second bomb being planted.

Production Unit

Created by	Brian Clemens
Executive Producers	Albert Fennell, Brian Clemens
Music	Laurie Johnson
Producer	Raymond Menmuir
Associate Producer	Chris Burt
Script Editor	Gerry O'Hara
Production Manager	Ron Purdie
Production Accountant	Terry Connors
Assistant Director	Gino Marotta
Location Manager	David Barron
Continuity	Doreen Soan
Casting	Esta Charkham
Art Director	Allan Cameron
Set Dresser	Peter Russell
Wardrobe Supervisor	Donald Mothersill
Special Effects	Arthur Beavis
Lighting Cameraman	Barry Noakes
Camera Operator	Malcolm Vinson
Focus Puller	Mike Tomlin
Make Up	Alan Boyle
Hairdresser	Jan Dorman
Lighting by	Lee Electric
Editor	Brian Freemantle
Sound Recordist	David Crozier
Boom Operator	Gary Weir
Dubbing Editor	Peter Lennard
Dubbing Mixer	Hugh Strain
Music Editor	Alan Willis

An Avengers MARK 1 Production For LONDON WEEKEND TELEVISION

Martin Shaw and Lewis Collins pictured during filming of NO STONE.

Actors Martin Shaw and Lewis Collins with Steyr-AUG assault rifles.

Shooting / Location Schedule

Production Dates: Monday 27th April to Friday 8th May, 1981. Production Number: 9D10203

27-28 April	*Int / Ext: Prison*: Victoria Barracks, Sheet Street, Windsor, Berkshire
	Ulrike's camp / caravan / phone box / tunnel: Green West Road, Jordans, Buckinghamshire & Farm Lane, Jordans, Buckinghamshire
29 April	*Ross Kilpins house*: Chantry, Barnet Lane, Deacons Hill, Elstree, Hertfordshire
	Motorway: van / car run-bys: A1M Barnet By-Pass, near Cecil Road, South Mimms, Hertfordshire
30 April	*Arms dump*: Cripps Farm Landfill site, Springwell Lane, Rickmansworth, Hertfordshire
	Helicopter POV (arms dump route): Stockers Lake, Rickmansworth, Hertfordshire
1 May	*Phone Box*: Penfold Street, Lisson Grove, London, NW8
	Ext: Hockley's flat / Street: Doyle's car: Blair Court, 2 Boundary Road, St. Johns Wood, London, NW8
	Int: Hockley's flat: Lord's View, off St. Johns Wood Road, St. Johns Wood, London, NW8
4 May	*Surveillance house*: 129 Brackenbury Road, Hammersmith, London, W6
	Surveillance house street: Bodie's car: Aldensley Road, Hammersmith, London, W6
	'Target' house: 102 Brackenbury Road, Hammersmith, London, W6
	Hospital (Allison) / CI5 HQ / Coroners: Cadby Hall, Blythe Road, Hammersmith, London, W14
5 May	*Cook's house*: 33 Peter Avenue, Willesden Green, London, NW10
6 May	*Phone box & police car*: Temple Place (near Temple Tube Station), Westminster, London, WC2
	Int: Hospital canteen: Tessa Kilpin's workplace: City University, 10 Northampton Square (Ashby Street), Finsbury, London, EC1
	Bomb 1: Legal Chambers (explosion) / Cowley's ca run-bys: 22 Northampton Square, Finsbury, London, EC1
	Bomb 2: Cortina: Royal Courts Of Justice, Carey Street, Westminster, London, WC2
7 May	*Airport*: Luton Airport, Airport Way, Luton, Bedfordshire
8 May	*Bomb 3: Government offices / Cowley's car*: Eastern Hospital, Homerton Row, London, E9
	Burger Van (Bodie & Doyle meet Cowley): Homerton Row, Homerton, London, E9
2nd Unit:	*Int: Bodie's car (radio)*: Bloomfield Road, Little Venice, London, W9
	Int: Hockley's flat: Lord's View, off St. Johns Wood Road, London, NW8

SPY PROBE

(originally *Spy Trap* & *Spy Chase*)
by **Tony Barwick**
© Copyright Mark 1 Productions Ltd MCMLXXXI

Dawson	Paul Daneman
Minister	Graham Crowden
Miss Walsh	Joyce Grant
Williams	Patrick Ryecart
Ferris	Barry Stanton
Twig	Nick Stringer
The Voice of Kovac	Raymond Brody
Flynn	John Hart Dyke
Mitchell	Christopher Banks
Lewis	Patrick Brock
Man	Jim Dowdall
CI5 Man	John Ashbury
CI5 Girl	Susan Worth
Uncredited	
CI5 Man	Ray Knight
CI5 Man	Dennis Plenty
Car Driver	Peter Brayham
Milk Man	David Holland

Director: **Dennis Abey**

DOYLE, is undercover and infiltrates an organisation that is hiring killers. He is contacted by a man called Ferris and is taken to a disused factory where a violent man named Twig tries out his combat skills. The men decide that Doyle is competent, but Kovac, the organisation's director, suspects that Doyle may be an infiltrator. Bodie meanwhile, also working undercover on the case and already hired by the organisation, has been hired to kill another 'target' with Williams, another hired assassin. They are instructed to kill Miss Walsh, who used to work for the Secret Service. When outside the woman's home, Williams shows his reluctance to carry out the killing. Bodie leaves him in the car, and pretends to kill Miss Walsh; shots are heard and the next day the obituary column carries word of the woman's 'death'. Knowing that Miss Walsh has valuable experience in dealing with secret organisations, Cowley visits the woman and asks her to help CI5 on the case. Later, when Cowley is called to meet the new acting Head of MI6, Nigel Dawson, Cowley tells him and his minister that he is seriously concerned about security leaks in the British Secret Service. Dawson reassures the minister that all spies have been eradicated. Cowley decides that Bodie and Doyle should continue to work for the organisation in the hope of uncovering the man behind it; none of the CI5 men realise that Ferris and Twig are under orders to eliminate their employees once they have completed their allocated tasks.

British actor Nick Stringer played Twig in SPY PROBE. Born (10th August 1948) in Torquay, Devon, he has appeared in numerous well-known television shows, including PRESS GANG, THE BILL and BUTTERFLIES.

Miss Walsh arrives at CI5 headquarters and begins to search through the files of all the ex-secret service personnel. She later confides to Cowley, that those who have died in unusual circumstances and might have been murdered were only junior ex-employees. Kovac contacts Ferris and Twig and tells them that Doyle is definitely an undercover agent and orders his men to kill him. Bodie and Williams are given the task of killing Doyle. As they take him away to a quiet wood to eliminate him, Williams is forced to reveal that he, too, is working undercover and is employed by MI6. Cowley is furious about MI6's involvement, but is told by the Minister, that both departments must work together.

Ordered to speed up the killings, Ferris and Twig are given a list of fourteen junior secret service employees to be shot. Cowley decides that Williams should remain in CI5 custody, while his men are given the task of preventing the killings. They are, however, unable to prevent Twig shooting the last name on the list, a man called Mitchell.

Twig is shot as he tries to escape and Ferris is arrested and taken to CI5 HQ. He takes the squad to Kovac's motel, but Kovac escapes by car. Chased by the CI5 agents, and rather than face capture, he swallows a suicide pill. Cowley recognises the man as a top KGB official and asks Miss Walsh why the Russians should send a top agent to organize the killing of junior MI6 personnel. She explains that, although each of the men know very little secret information, their combined knowledge could have revealed the identity of a Russian spy. This man must be Dawson. Cowley has Williams released and when the man reports to Dawson that Kovac is being interrogated by CI5, Dawson, fearing that Kovac may incriminate him, tries to leave the country,

Bodie and Doyle give chase as the man tries to escape by boat up the Thames. In the ensuing battle, Dawson's boat crashes and the spy is killed.

Doyle (Martin Shaw) and Bodie (Lewis Collins) are in deadly pursuit of Nigel Dawson who tries to escape the CI5 agents by boat - in SPY PROBE.

Production Unit

Created by	Brian Clemens
Executive Producers	Albert Fennell, Brian Clemens
Music	Laurie Johnson
Producer	Raymond Menmuir
Associate Producer	Chris Burt
Script Editor	Gerry O'Hara
Production Manager	Ron Purdie
Production Accountant	Terry Connors
Assistant Director	Bill Westley
Location Manager	David Barron
Continuity	Doreen Soan
Casting	Esta Charkham
Art Director	Allan Cameron
Set Dresser	Peter Russell
Stunt Arranger	Peter Brayham
Wardrobe Supervisor	Donald Mothersill
Special Effects	Arthur Beavis
Lighting Cameraman	Frank Watts
Camera Operator	Malcolm Vinson
Focus Puller	Mike Tomlin
Make Up	Alan Boyle

Hairdresser	Jan Dorman
Lighting by	Lee Electric
Supervising Editor	John S. Smith
Sound Recordist	David Crozier
Boom Operator	Gary Weir
Dubbing Editor	Peter Lennard
Dubbing Mixer	Hugh Strain
Music Editor	Alan Willis

An Avengers MARK 1 Production For LONDON WEEKEND TELEVISION

Joining Martin Shaw and the cast of SPY PROBE was British actor Barry Stanton as Ferris.

Shooting / Location Schedule

Production Dates: Monday 11th to Friday 22nd May, 1981. Production Number: 9D10204

11 May	***Docks / Canal***: Brentford Dock, off Dock Road / Catherine Wheel Road, Brentford, Middlesex ***Street: Canal phone box***: Brent Way, Brentford, Middlesex ***Int: Ferris' car (traffic lights)***: Half Acre, Brentford, Middlesex ***Fullers Boat yard***: Thames Lock Wharf, Dock Road, Brentford, Middlesex ***Foot bridge (Ferris & Twig kill assassin)***: Brent Road, off Half Acre, Brentford, Middlesex
12 May	***Ferris' & Twig's warehouse (mannequins)***: Albion Yard, Balfe Street, Kings Cross, London, N1
13 May	***Streets: Ferris & Twig collect Doyle***: Shepherd's Bush Road (near Brook Green), Hammersmith, London, W6 (car interior 1) / Hammersmith Road (car interior 2) / Blythe Road / Masbro Road, Hammersmith, London, W14 ***Int: Cowley's car / Ext: Dawson's office***: Brook Green (Cadby Hall), Hammersmith, London, W14

	Int: House (Bodie & Williams collect bag): Walpole Court, Springvale Estate, Blythe Road, Hammersmith, London, W14
	Int: Car (Bodie & Williams): Hammersmith Grove, Hammersmith, London, W6
	Streets (Ferris & Doyle): Stonor Road / Avonmore Road, Hammersmith, London, W14
	CI5 Mobile snack bar: Avonmore Trading Estate, Avonmore Road, Hammersmith, London, W14
	Canal footpath (Bodie & Williams): Bloomfield Road / Westbourne Terrace, Little Venice, London, W9
	Left Luggage office: Paddington train station, Eastbourne Terrace, London, W2
14 May	*Kovac's motel room*: Master Brewer Motel, Western Avenue, North Hillingdon, Middlesex
15 May	*Miss Walsh's house / Woods (with Williams)*: Leys Farm, Thompkins Lane, East Burnham, Buckinghamshire
18-19 May	*Car chase (with Kovac)*: Inglethorpe Street / Woodlawn Road / Stevenage Road, Fulham, London, SW6
	House: target no: 4: 42 Stevenage Road, Fulham, London, SW6
	Streets: Wilson's house wall: target no: 8: Stevenage Road, Fulham, London, SW6
	Mitchell's house: 38 Doneraile Street, Fulham, London, SW6
2nd Unit	*Billiard room / Minister's office / Tea Room*: National Liberal Club, 1 Whitehall Place, London, SW1
	Whitehall Car run-by: Whitehall, Westminster, London, SW1
	Squash courts / Changing rooms: The Queen Mother's Sports Centre, 223 Vauxhall Bridge Road, London, SW1
20-21 May	*CI5 HQ / Dawson's office*: Cadby Hall, Blythe Road, Hammersmith, London, W14
22 May	*Int: Car (Ferris & Twig collect envelopes)*: Naval Row / Blackwall Way, near East India Dock, London, E14
	Water Terminal Dock: Victoria Deep Water Terminal, Riverside Walk, East Greenwich, London, SE10

Series V Production Unit: uncredited

Production Assistant	Jane Oscroft
Assistant Location	Matthew Simmons
2nd Assistant Director	Gerry Toomey
3rd Assistant Director	Chris Brock
Secretary to Mr. Fennell	Linda Pearson
Secretary to Mr. Menmuir	Hilary Pearson
Secretary to Mr. O'Hara	June Rose
Trainee Secretary	Tina Windmill
Unit Runner	Kenneth Shane

Clapper / Loader	Nigel Seal
Camera Grip	Peter Hall
Sound Assistant	Guido Reidy, Ian Munro
Assistant Art Department	Gavin Bocquet
Production Buyer	Ron Baker
Casting Secretary	Anne Henderson
Wardrobe Assistant	Tony Allen
Unit Publicist	Paul McNicolls
Publicity Secretary	Fiona Searson
Assistant Production Accountant	John Bigland
Cashier	Pat Gallen
Property Master	John Allenby
Dressing Props	Edward Allenby
Storeman	Keith Vowles
Stand-by Chargehand Props	Michael Pugh
Stand-by Props	Roy Cannon
Carpenter	Howard Harrison
Painter	Jack Newman
Stagehand	David Rutter
Unit Nurse	Susan Michael
Gaffer	Laurie Shane
Electricians	Steve Blake, Jim Smart, Michael Davey
Assistant Editor	Roy Lafberry
Producers Driver	Barry Myall
Transport Co Ordinator	Chris Streeter
Unit Drivers	Geoff Bowers, Jim Magill, John Collins
Unit Minibus Driver	Robert Beherns: D & D Location
Make Up Bus Driver	Frank Barretta: Willie's Wheels, Trailer & Caravan Centre, Station Road, Egham, Surrey
Construction / Prop Truck Driver	William Horsnell
Props Return Driver	Tom Brown-Innes: D & D Location
Catering Driver	John Squires
Dining Bus Driver	Fred Borg
Camera	J D C Cameras, Wembley Park Drive, Wembley, Middlesex
Lee Electrical: Contact	Tony Lucas
Film Labs	Rank Film Labs, Denham, Middlesex: Steve Barker
Insurance	Ruben Sedgwick Insurance, Pinewood Studios, Iver Heath, Buckinghamshire
Caterers	J & J Foods, Lamgley Park Road, Iver, Buckinghamshire
Dubbing	Trevor Pyke Sound, 142 Wardour Street. London, W1
2nd *Unit* 2nd *Assistant Director*	Micky Murray, Terry Pearce
2nd *Unit* 3rd *Assistant Director*	Jerry Daly
2nd *Unit Continuity*	Majorie Lavelly
2nd *Unit Camera Operator*	John Boulter

2nd Unit Camera Focus	David Litchfield
2nd Unit Clapper/Loader	Simon Hume
2nd Unit Sound Mixer	Geoff Hawkins, Chris Munro
2nd Unit Boom Operator	Ken Nightingall
2nd Unit Make Up	Peter Robb King
2nd Unit Hairdresser	Mark Nelson
2nd Unit Wardrobe Assistant	Tony Allen

SERIES V ACTION CARS

Bodie: **Ford Capri 3.0 S**: VHK 12W - *Cry Wolf, A Man Called Quinn, Lawson's Last Stand, No Stone, Spy Probe.*

Cowley: **Ford Granada 2.8i Ghia**: UJN 696W - *A Man Called Quinn, Lawson's Last Stand, No Stone, Spy Probe.*

Doyle: **Ford Capri 3.0 S**: VHK 11W - *Cry Wolf, No Stone, Spy Probe.*

Police: **Rover SD1 3500**: SYY 904S - *Lawson's Last Stand.*

TRANSMISSION DATES

1: FOXHOLE ON THE ROOF*
7th November 1982
2: OPERATION SUSIE*
14th November 1982
3: YOU'LL BE ALL RIGHT*
21st November 1982
4: LAWSON'S LAST STAND
28th November 1982
5: DISCOVERED IN A GRAVEYARD*
5th December 1982
6: SPY PROBE
12th December 1982
7: CRY WOLF
9th January 1983
8: THE UNTOUCHABLES*
16th January 1983
9: THE OJUKA SITUATION*
23rd January 1983
10: A MAN CALLED QUINN
30th January 1983
11: NO STONE
6th February 1983

*These episodes were filmed as Series IV, but transmitted here as Series V.

THE ACTORS

LEWIS COLLINS: Ex-SAS Sergeant and mercenary William Andrew Philip Bodie was played by Lewis Collins, who was born on the 27th May 1946, and lived in Birkenhead, Merseyside, where his father, Bill, worked as a shipwright. Lewis' schooldays were spent at Bidston Primary and later Grange School and he went on to develop an interest in guns while helping out on his aunt's farm in Shropshire. Aged twelve he joined the Liverpool Central Rifle Club at Mason Street Barracks to take part in .22 calibre league matches and .303 service, rifle shooting on the Army's Altcar Rifle Ranges near Liverpool. Lewis won various trophies such as the cup for the County of Lancashire, competing against both soldiers and civilians. He scored an impressive 586 points out of 600!

"The ranges were fun; we didn't just shoot with rifles. We got a go at everything, machine-guns, mortar bombs, once I even fired a rocket launcher at a target. The problem with being kids was we didn't always take things too seriously, and when paratroopers were dropping on top of us and black-faced commandos were running around us we'd join in. We'd crawl along the tunnels emerging to find ourselves under live fire from the ranges! Also on the nearby rough tracks I learnt how to ride motorcycles."

When he was thirteen, Lewis learned how to play the drums and, together with his piano playing father, they would do turns at various clubs over the next three years. As a youngster Collins also had an interest in contemporary music and joined a rock and roll band called 'The Renegades' and within a couple of years they were playing the famous Cavern Club, sometimes appearing on the same bill as 'The Beatles'.

Too young to become a professional musician, when he left school at fifteen, and after he saw a demonstration at Blackpool Tower of Ladies' hairdressing by Europe's top stylists, he became a ladies hairstylist at Andre Bernard's salon in Liverpool. Here he met Paul McCartney's brother, Mike, who got Lewis into acting by doing sketches for his group 'The Scaffold'. Lewis recalled quite a big career mistake he made at this time:

"The Beatles were looking for a new drummer to replace Pete Best - whom I looked remarkably like. Mike suggested that I go and audition. I said, 'Me? I'm on nearly forty quid a week as a hairdresser'. In the end, 'The Beatles' took on Ringo."

After three years in hairdressing, Lewis moved on, learning to play the bass guitar and turning pro and joining his first professional band, 'The Georgians', after seeing the job advertised in a local paper. His return to show business was in June 1964, when he was offered his first professional gig at the Star Club, Hamburg.

'The Eyes' were a hard-hitting Liverpool rock band, and the club was a musical sausage factory of non-stop cabaret, the working hours were prodigious.

"I still remember vividly the agony, despite the pills, of playing with blistered fingers. I learned a lot in Hamburg...six months put ten years on me. On top of that trouble followed us around and I was knifed in the face and had to fight my way out of trouble."

An offer to join 'The Mojos' brought Lewis and fellow musician, Ainsley Dunbar, back to Liverpool to team up with his already successful band having scored a top-ten hit, in March 1964, with *Everything's Alright*. New Years Eve 1964/5 was their first gig after only three days preparation.

"I can remember one disastrous night when we were gigging around England. We were driving from Penzance through some beautiful countryside in the early hours of the morning when suddenly the wheel fell off the van and we saw it overtake and disappear down the lane! We ended up in a ditch and spent the rest of the night at a 45-degree angle waiting for daylight when we could find the wheel nuts and repair the wheel. Luckily we all saw the funny side and kept awake by telling each other jokes!"

'The Mojos' managed another couple of minor hits, though in September 1966 they split-up, after which Lewis spent eight months playing with the 'Rob Storme Group' (five part harmony *Beach Boys* style) before a six month stint back with the reformed *Mojos*, which later became 'Skool', and another six months run of one-nighters.

"A very good band on stage, but we had a 'problem or two' and no hit records and it deteriorated into a backing group for Paul and Barry Ryan. I vowed that this was my last shot at big time pop, and if this group did not make it I'd quit the game."

When 'Skool' finally folded in the summer of 1967, it was time to sit down and review his situation for the second time.

"It was a stormy year for me, Christine (a girl he almost married) broke off our relationship and moved to Switzerland and shortly after this my mother died, I didn't know where I was going or what I wanted to do."

Turning his hand to various occupations, Lewis became a lorry driver, sales assistant, waiter, and a door-to-door salesman of soft drinks, but unsettled in these jobs in the Spring of 1968, he enrolled in the London Academy of Music and Dramatic Art (LAMDA) for three years. At twenty-two he had his first big Shakespearian role as Romeo to actress Susan Blake's Juliet.

After a brief spell in New York he returned to Britain to join Chesterfield Repertory Company for forty-two weeks as an actor, assistant stage manager, which meant when you never had a part in the production you had to help with all the back-stage jobs.

"It was gruelling, but well worth it. I got my Equity card and learnt the ropes."

Here, in August 1971, he played his first line on stage: "Halt! Who goes there?" in Strindberg's *A Dance Of Death*. He managed to get it wrong as: 'Who goes there? Halt!'

"God I was so frightened. I was so good! Every five minutes I'd walk past the window and back, as a sentry. All my relatives were sitting there going, 'Oh, he's a lad!' "

Actor Lewis Collins enjoys a game of tennis in early Spring 1978.

In the coming months, he appeared as a policeman in *Love On The Dole* and, in early November, had a part in the Dylan Thomas play *Under Milk Wood*.

He moved to the Glasgow Citizens' Theatre for twelve months, playing the pick of classical roles, and by the age of twenty-five, he was playing *Tamburlaine The Great* at the Edinburgh Festival, claiming to have learnt his lines in just three days.

"I had to, it was going on in five days. It's a helluva part, not many people have ever played it. When Albert Finney did it at the National Theatre in 1976 that was the third time it had been performed in full in London. It was a challenge for me to get as far with it as we could. But the best work I've ever done (in November 1972) was in a Glasgow studio, The Close Theatre, which has since burnt down, a modern interpretation of *The Marat/Sade*. Or to be precise, *The Persecution and Assassination of Marat as Performed by the Inmates of the Asylum of Charenton Under The Direction of the Marquis De Sade...!* I played De Sade and it was the most involved thing I've ever done."

He also toured with the Prospect Theatre playing Macheath in *The Threepenny Opera*. At the Citizens Theatre in December he played Gloucester in *Lear*. During the Christmas period, into the New Year of 1973, he portrayed Van Helsing in *Dracula* and, by March, he was playing the Provost in *The Government Inspector*, and Ulysses in *Troilus And Cressida*.

During his year in Scotland, he found another side to his life as a teacher, giving drama lessons to deaf children. This snowballed into a trip to Canada where he held lectures and workshops for Indian children on their reservation, and was later to tour America and its universities in the same capacity.

Back in Britain, in September, he appeared at London's Royal Court Theatre in the premier of David Story's *The Farm*, directed by Lindsay Anderson, which later transferred to the Mayfair Theatre. A varied career followed including various TV series like the *Z Cars* episode *Waste* (25th February 1974) where he portrayed a retarded Liverpool lad. In *Warship* (*Away Seaboat's Captain*) he played Leading Seaman Steele, followed by a policeman role, PC Henry Williams, in *Crown Court* (*Arson*) on the 4th May. Plus appearances in the afternoon soaps *Marked Personal* and *Rooms*, where he was locked up in a cellar. Back in the theatre he appeared (Birmingham Repertory), as The Count in *Blues Whites and Reds*.

In late 1974 he played Bobby, the lead in the television play *They Disappear When You Lie Down*, which won him the role of Gavin in the sit-com *The Cuckoo Waltz*, that ran for three years between 1975 and 1977. A part he claimed he didn't enjoy: "Gavin was so painfully shallow."

Between series he tried his hand at directing and acting in lunch-time theatre at The Open Space and Maximist Actor's Arena (*Double Double* in 1975) in the West End. He took the solo lead, Leonard Brazil, in the play *City Sugar* at the Arts Theatre in Cambridge. At Leicester Square Theatre he played Simon Gasgoine in *The Real Inspector Hound*.

His only film credit was as a rugby playing extra in *Confessions Of A Driving Instructor*:

"You won't see me though, I'm just in a rugby pack with a beard on. I was on and off just like that. I was out of work for about six months after *Cuckoo Waltz* so I was glad of a quick fifty quid. After the success of the *Cuckoo Waltz*, it became apparent that I might stand a chance of achieving popularity. I realised that it was now vital that I made a name for myself. So the more I did, the more chance I stood of hitting the big-time."

Back on television he appeared in the *Friendly Encounter* episode of the series *Village Hall*. By chance, he was cast by director Ernest Day to co-star alongside Martin Shaw in *The New Avengers* episode *Obsession*; Collins' performance would eventually lead to him being cast in *The Professionals*.

He was offered a world tour with Derek Jacobi and Timothy West but turned it down in order to play Bodie.

Lewis Collins training with Territorial Paras in 1980 - on the set of WILD JUSTICE.

Everyone from Joe Public to Princess Margaret loved *The Professionals* and the admiration for Lewis grew because he literally took his work home with him!

A year after joining the series, he joined the Territorial Paras and by February 1980 he'd proved himself mean enough to win a coveted Red Beret from the regiment. Later, rumours abounded that he'd tried to join the Territorial SAS, but was apparently rejected on the grounds that he was a celebrity.

Immediately after *The Professionals* Lewis was cast in the action movie *Who Dares Wins* (aka *The Final Option*), which was inspired by the Iranian Embassy siege in London during May 1980 and focused on the dramatic rescue staged by Britain's elite special force, the SAS (Special Air Service). Although successful in Britain, the film failed to impress and a sequel, set during the Falklands war, was shelved. Months were spent training with ex-SAS officers, romping through the Brecon Beacons in preparation for the part. It was all a bit unnecessary as Lewis points out:

"I'm ashamed to watch it, you can't take it seriously. It's a joke...some officers of the SAS watched it and just laughed."

A third bid to gain international stardom came in 1982 when auditions were being held to replace Roger Moore as James Bond. The media were quick to lend Lewis support and were fully expecting him to take on the 007 role. But it was not to be, producer Cubby Broccoli turned Lewis down after an apparently 'difficult' interview.

Lewis' press statement issued in August noted:

"It would be nice to get back to the original Bond, not the character created by Sean Connery, but the one from the books. He's not over-handsome, over-tall. He's about my age and has got my attitudes. I was in Cubby's office for five minutes, but it was really over for me in seconds. I have heard since that he doesn't like me. That's unfair. He's expecting another Sean Connery to walk through the door and there are few of them around. I think he's really shut the door on me. He found me too aggressive. I knew it all, that kind of attitude. Two or three years ago that would be the case, purely because I was nervous and defensive. I felt they were playing the producer bit with fat cigars. When someone walks into their office for the most popular film job in the world, a little actor is bound to put on a few airs. If Cubby couldn't see I was being self-protective I don't have faith in his judgement."

In December 1982 Lewis found himself the target of the *This Is Your Life* show. The programme opens with a car, driven by stuntman Peter Brayham, screeching to a halt by the kerb just as Lewis steps out of a nightclub. Gordon Jackson jumps out of the car and shouts, 'Bodie', in true Cowley style. Martin Shaw didn't actually appear in the studio, but recorded a sequence from Dartmoor where he was filming for *The Hound Of The Baskervilles.*

By the mid-1980's Lewis found himself in low-budget films such as *Codename:Wildgeese, Commando Leopard* and *The Commander,* struggling to hit the big-time that was expected of him. Guest slots followed in *Robin Of Sherwood* (*The Sheriff Of Nottingham*), the American film *Misfits* (aka *Carley's Web*) and the German series *Blaues Blut* (aka *Blue Blood*) (*Bounty*). In 1988 he was cast as a Victorian police sergeant in the mini-series *Jack The Ripper.*

Moving to Los Angeles by the early 1990's he studied film direction and settled there permanently following his marriage, in 1992, to a young 24-year-old blonde school teacher called Michelle Larrett. They have three sons, Oliver, Elliot and Cameron. Since then he has been sporadic in his work choices with turns as a guest presenter (*The ITV awards* in 1999), radio feature (*Confessions* in 1997), theatre (*Dangerous Corner* in 1999) and most recently popping up in *The Bill* in 2002.

Actor Lewis Collins weight-training at his home in Golders Green, North London, in early 1978.

MARTIN SHAW: Martin Shaw who was born on the 21st January 1945 in Birmingham and went on to attend Ryland Road School and then Great Barr comprehensive portrayed Ex-Metropolitan Police Force officer, Ray Doyle. One of Shaw's teachers, Tom Knowles, encouraged Martin's aspirations to be an actor by having him join the Pied Piper Company, which was really nothing more than a group of street performers. Upon leaving school his first job was in a sales office and later he studied electroplating at night classes before being accepted into the London Academy of Music and Dramatic Art (LAMDA), where he became a pupil for three years.

"They gave me everything I needed to know. I developed a real 'gut' feeling for acting there. I was taught to be a chameleon, to change both the body and the mind according to the part."

He was then lucky enough, in 1965, to go straight into acting work being appointed the assistant stage manager at Hornchurch Repertory Company, where his first role was in the Dorothy L. Sayers pot-boiler crime drama *Busman's Honeymoon*. He played a Scottish-Jewish moneylender called McBride. Followed by roles in *Oh, What A Lovely War!*, *Celebration*, *The Knack*, *Macbeth*, *Misalliance*, *Tom Jones*, *The Anniversary*, *Lock Up Your Daughters* and *A Winter's Tale*. From there he went to the Bristol Old Vic, where he spent a year playing the part of Joey in Harold Pinter's play *The Homecoming*. Followed by *Message From The Grass* and *Celebration*, before a stint at the Palace Theatre, Watford in *The Indians Want The Bronx*. By 1967, Martin was starting to obtain television work such as the one-off play *Love On The Dole*, as an Irish revolutionary called O'Leary for Granada TV, which led to Granada's *Summer Playhouse* (*Travelling Light*), *Son Of The City*, and the part of the hippie student Robert Croft in *Coronation Street*.

Martin Shaw during a break in filming THE PROFESSIONALS story A HIDING TO NOTHING.

He continued his television work with appearances in the *Strictly Private And Confidential* episode of *Public Eye*, followed with *The System* (*Them Down There*), *City '68*, and an LWT play called *Another Part Of The Forest*. In October 1968, he went on to appear at the Royal Court Theatre playing Cliff Lewis in *Look Back In Anger* with Jane Asher, followed, in October 1969, with the part of Paul in *The Contractor*. Meanwhile, his roles in television continued, including *Fraud Squad* (*All Claims Paid For*), *Two Feet On The Ground*, and the *Strange Report* episode, *Report 7931 SNIPER: When Is Your Cousin Not?*

In February 1970, he went into the West End proper playing opposite John Gielgud at The Lyric Theatre, London, in *The Battle Of The Shrivings*, followed by *Hobson's Choice* and from the 14th September *Cancer*. In a change of direction he then took on the role of drunken Welshman, Dr. Huw Evans in the first thirteen episodes of the hospital sit-com *Doctor In The House*. With the arrival of the seventies Martin became more established on TV, taking the part of Horatio in ATV's version of *Hamlet*, alongside Sir John Gielgud, Michael Redgrave, Margaret Leighton and Richard Chamberlain.

Breaking into film, he was cast as Banquo, a leading part in Roman Polanski's 1971, often violent interpretation of *Macbeth*.

"An amazing film. I don't understand why it didn't do well. I thought it was spectacularly good. I learned a lot from it."

But this failed to promote him to movie actor status and Shaw's career continued mainly in TV and theatre with guest-star work, in April 1972, in *A Place In The Sun* (*Achilles Heel*).

"It was a TV play about soccer. I trained hard for that, felt at the peak of my whole life when we started filming with Fulham FC. I went out on the park with a couple of Fulham apprentices, doing an exercise known as 'Triangles', where you keep running all the time. After three minutes, I was nearly sick, literally. I was heaving with fatigue. And those guys carried on for four hours! It's quite inconceivable what they can do."

The LWT series *Villains* followed, where his character was called Monty, and in late 1973 he played Frank Tully in the thirteen part series *Helen: A Woman Of Today*. He joined the National Theatre Company and took parts in the play's *Saturday Night, Sunday Morning* and *The Bacchae*. In March 1974, he starred opposite Claire Bloom in *A Street Car Named Desire* at the Piccadilly Theatre.

"Initially, I turned it down...because of Marlon Brando's classic film version. I thought it was out of my range. But the director was amazing, an American called Ed Sherrin; an unforgettable character. He was an American-Pole, like Kowalski, which helped me, being English and comparatively weedy, to build the role. I started off shouting a lot, and Ed says, 'No, no, you're a king around here; kings don't need to shout, kings just speak quietly. People shout'. That's one of the best things he said to me. I used to drive round Piccadilly Circus just staring at my name in big neon lights! But it was also a bit scary because I thought, 'Now that I've gained this sort of stature, I'll have to make sure I deserve it.' "

Then Martin did two instalments of *Play Of The Month* (*Electra* and *Love's Labour's Lost*) in consecutive years. The fantasy film *The Golden Voyage Of Sinbad* was released in 1974 complete with, what was then considered to be, state of the art special effects and Shaw's third movie *Operation Daybreak* was made two years later.

"I spent three winter months in Prague on that. I always saw it as dark and depressing, black and eerie, but returning there on Boxing Day, after the Christmas break on the film, the city was empty and I was stunned by how beautiful it was. The atmosphere had changed. A couple of days later, it was the same old Prague. People had forgotten their jollity and gone back to the daily grind of having to find twelve American dollars to buy a razor-blade!"

Martin Shaw during THE PROFESSIONALS story DEAD RECKONING.

Martin Shaw relaxes after production on THE PROFESSIONALS has ceased.

In 1975 the drama-documentary series *The Explorers* saw him playing a leading role, as Robert Burke, in the episode *Burke And Willis*. This was followed by appearances in the *Z Cars* spin off series, *Barlow* (*Asylum*) and *On The Move*. In May1976, he starred in *Miss Julie* by Strindberg, at the Greenwich theatre, followed in October by *Teeth 'n' Smiles* at Wyndhams Theatre opposite Helen Mirren. At the Bristol Old Vic, he played Daniel de Bosola in *The Duchess Of Malfi*.

Meanwhile, back on television he made appearances in *Spice Island Farewell*, *Beasts* (*Buddyboy*) and *Sutherland's Law* (*Blind Jump*). All this led to him appearing as Larry Doomer in the *Obsession* episode of *The New Avengers*, which in turn led to *The Professionals*. Prior to his engagement on the show he still managed to appear in *The Duchess Of Duke Street (Family Matters)*, *Play Of The Week* (*Exiles*), the anthology series *Jubilee (Our Kid)* and the *Z Cars* episode *Domestic*, where he played Graham Moffat.

The Professionals ran until 1983 during which time Martin also played Jack Butcher in the TV film *Cream in My Coffee* (1980); Sir Henry Baskerville in *The Hound of the Baskervilles* (1983); and Archibald Carlyle in *East Lynne* (1983).

In 1981 Martin returned to the stage playing Vernon in the Neil Simon/Marvin Hamlish show *They're Playing Our Song* at the Shaftesbury Theatre. His partner in this was Gemma Craven. In 1983 he appeared at the Apollo Theatre in *The Country Girl*; and in 1985 he played The King in Alan Bleasdale's *Are You Lonesome Tonight?* at The Phoenix, where he portrayed Elvis Presley's final twenty-four hours in August 1977. Other stage roles include *The Big Knife* (Albery Theatre, 1986); *Other People's Money* (Lyric Theatre, 1990); *Betrayal* (Almeida Theatre, 1991); *Sienna Red* (Liverpool and Birmingham, 1992) with Francesca Annis; Lord Goring in Oscar Wilde's *An Ideal Husband* (Globe Theatre, 1992); *Rough Justice* (Apollo Theatre, 1994). He then went on to play Lord Goring in *An Ideal Husband* again on Broadway in 1995 and returned to the West End in a hugely successful revival of the play at The Haymarket Theatre and The Old Vic in 1996 and 1997. For this role he was nominated for an Olivier Award and a Tony and received the New York Drama Desk Critic's Award. Since then he has appeared at the Theatre Royal, Windsor in *Vertigo* (1998).

During the 1980's Martin's television appearances included *The Last Place on Earth* playing Robert Falcon Scott (1985); Roskov in *Intrigue* (1988); and Suleyman in *The Most Dangerous Man in the World* (1988). His films included *Facelift* (1984); *Ladder of Swords* (1988); and *Cassidy* (1989). In 1990 Martin played Ian McBride in *Who Bombed Birmingham* with Ciarán Hinds and Roger Allam; and followed this in 1991 with *For The Greater Good* playing MP Peter Balliol. In 1992 he played Chief Superintendant Mike Barclay in *Black and Blue*.

Never one to take the obvious role, he even refused the lead in the American TV series *The Equalizer* returning to high-profile television roles in the 1990's. In 1993 Martin took over from Tim Pigott-Smith in the TV series *The Chief* playing Chief Constable Alan Cade, this was followed in 1996 by his role as Cecil Rhodes in the BBC's mini-series *Rhodes*, alongside Neil Pearson. Martin's son Joe played the young Cecil in the first series. In 1998 he travelled to Prague to film the TV series *The Scarlet Pimpernel* in which he played the role of secret policeman Chauvelin alongside Richard E. Grant who played Sir Percy Blakeney.

Martin has also enjoyed success in the medical drama *Always and Everyone* that started in 1999, playing Consultant Surgeon Robert Kingsford.

In 2001 Martin returned to our screens in a new BBC drama *Judge John Deed* in which he played the part of a judge who involves himself in the cases he tries. It was written by Gordon Frank Newman who also wrote another drama, which Martin appeared in, *Black and Blue* (1992), which delves into the hitherto emotion-free world of the High Court judge. Martin plays a crusading barrister turned maverick judge who, to the annoyance of the Lord Chancellor's department, loses none of his liberal zeal when he dons the red robes. The cast also included Jenny Seagrove, Christopher Cazenove and Donald Sinden. When offered the lead role, Martin jumped at the chance, as he was impressed by Deed's fearsome intellect and emotional sensitivity. He's also become the new Adam Dalgliesh, starring in P D James' *Death In Holy Orders* in 2003 and *The Murder Room* in 2005.

In 2006 he narrated and appeared in a DVD chronicling the *Merlins over Malta* project, which featured the return of a World War II Supermarine Spitfire and Hawker Hurricane from Britain to Malta for the first time in 50-years.

In December 2006, he presented the six part 'Discovery Channel Real Time' TV series *Martin Shaw: Aviators*, which followed the two-year restoration of his Boeing Stearman bi-plane after it was crashed by another pilot at Old Buckenham airfield in Norfolk. He fulfilled a lifetime ambition to take the controls of a Spitfire owned by Maurice Bayliss, and screamed down the runway at Cranfield in an English Electric Lightning owned by Russell Carpenter. It was not allowed to take off, but did reach 150 mph in three seconds. Martin also compared notes with Ken Wallis, the nonagenarian builder and developer of the modern autogyro.

After the sixth series of *Judge John Deed* had been filmed, Martin appeared in the series *Apparitions* broadcast by the BBC in 2008 and in the police drama *Inspector George Gently*, he appeared in the title role.

Most recently, he appeared as Sir Charles Cartwright in a 2009 adaptation of Agatha Christie's *Three Act Tragedy*.

Martin has also narrated many audio-books including Tolkien's *The Hobbit* and *The Silmarillion, Gulliver's Travels* and Emily Bronte's *Wuthering Heights*.

Martin has been married three times; his first wife was Jill Allen who is the mother of his two sons and one daughter. They married at twenty-three and divorced in 1982. He then married Maggie Mansfield, an alternative therapist. His third wife was Vicki Kimm whom he met when she interviewed him on Pebble Mill at One. He lives, with his present partner, Karen da Silva, in a beautiful Quaker house in a Norfolk village, once owned by an ancestor of Abraham Lincoln, and owns a crofter's cottage in Scotland.

Of his three children; Joe has turned his attention mostly to television and films in the popular ITV drama *Bad Girls* and film *Shoreditch*; and both Sophie and Luke have turned their attention to the stage. Sophie appeared in *Top Girls*, which ran at the Aldwych Theatre and the Yvonne Arnaud Theatre, Guildford, and Luke appeared at The Mill at Sonning in *Relatively Speaking*, by Alan Ayckbourn, in February 2002.

GORDON JACKSON: The head of CI5 and ex-Secret Service operative George Cowley was brought to life by veteran Scottish actor Gordon

(Cameron) Jackson, who was born in Glasgow on the 19th December 1923, the youngest of five children. He attended Hillhead High School and encouraged by his English teacher, a keen amateur actor himself, Jackson did radio plays for the BBC drama department in his home city and also a stint in *Children's Hour*. A London film combine were searching for an authentic Scots lad to play a shop floor type in the 1941 Tommy Trinder comedy *The Foreman Went To France* and checking the BBC's files sent for seventeen year old Jackson. By now Gordon was serving an apprenticeship with Rolls Royce and after the film returned to the drawing office. A year later, and the same film company sent for him again for *Millions Like Us*.

Gordon Jackson during a break in filming THE PROFESSIONALS original Title sequence in September 1977.

"My employers proved very understanding at the time. They allowed me time off to pursue the offer. Then, gradually, this became such an occurrence that a firm decision had to be made between a career in engineering, or as an actor."

His time was now spent between Glasgow, doing repertory theatre, and London, where he was under contract to the impeccable Ealing Studios, where they were making propaganda films during the war. He also joined the never-ending run of the stage farce, *Seagulls Over Sorrento*, with Cockney clown Ronald Shiner.

Gordon Jackson as George Cowley - head of CI5 in THE PROFESSIONALS.

Up to becoming involved with *The Professionals*, Gordon had appeared in over sixty films. These included; *Tunes Of Glory*, with the acting knights, Alec Guiness and John Mills; *The Prime Of Miss Jean Brodie*, with Maggie Smith and *The Night Of The Generals*, with Peter O'Toole and Omar Sharif. Hollywood's huge *Mutiny On The Bounty*, with Marlon Brando; *Those Magnificent Men In Their Flying Machines*; *The Ipcress File* with Michael Caine and *The Medusa Touch* with Richard Burton. In *Floodtide*, he met a lovely young actress from Edinburgh called Rona Anderson, who was playing the boss's daughter and he, the brilliant young ship designer. She became his wife two years later in 1951.

On stage he appeared in *Macbeth*, *Hamlet*, *Hedda Gabler*, and the Chichester Festival productions of *Twelfth Night* and *Noah* (he was also in the last filmed *Hamlet*, the version according to director Tony Richardson and Scots actor Nicol Williamson).

Television work included *Mystery And Imagination*, *Theatre 625*, *The Avengers* and *Budgie*, but he really came to the public's attention in 1971 when he took on the role of Hudson, the butler, in *Upstairs Downstairs*, which ran for five series until the end of 1975. Proving popular almost everywhere, particularly in the USA, he was awarded the 'British Actor Of The Year' in 1974 and, a year later, a 'Supporting Actor' Emmy for his role.

Jackson would take part in Gene Roddenberry's pilot, *Spectre*, filmed at EMI Elstree Studios and the adaptation of Alistair Maclean's *The Golden Rendezvous*, before being offered the part of Cowley.

Shortly after completion of *The Professionals*, Gordon appeared in the Australian mini-series *A Town Called Alice*, where he won Australia's Logie award for his role. He went on to take a few small TV and film projects, including appearances in *Hart to Hart*, *Campion* and *Shaka Zulu*, and the films *The Shooting Party* and *The Whistle Blower*. From 1985 to 1986, Jackson narrated two afternoon cookery shows in New Zealand called *Fresh and Fancy Fare* and its successor *Country Fare*. His last role before his death was in *Effie's Burning*, and this was broadcast after his death.

In 1989, he was diagnosed with bone cancer. He died the following year (14th January 1990), aged 66, in London and was cremated at Golders Green Crematorium, North London.

MERCHANDISE

AS with many other television series of the time, *The Professionals* spawned numerous merchandising tie-ins.

TOYS / GAMES

The Professionals Crimebuster Kit
(*model no: 2290. Thomas Salter Toys*. 1979)
The kit contained: a pistol with removable silencer, telescopic sight, gun magazine and shoulder support, shoulder gun holster, 126 'real' camera, secret radio transmitter, a code watch and CI5 ID cards with wallet. The box artwork actually included a specially commissioned photograph of the two stars modelling the toys, taken on the set of *Hunter/Hunted* in 1978.
A 'cut-down' version called the **Action Pack** (*model no: 2213*) was also issued containing the gun, identity card, belt, shoulder holster, and a bonus item in the form of a set of rub-down transfers.

The Professionals CI5 Ford Capri Set
Corgi Toys had originally planned to release the Mk.II Capri in 1979 and it featured in the catalogue the same year. To be released as C342 and C343, the white model measured 124mm and was on a 1/36 scale. It was never released.
Model no: 342 (1980)
Contained within the display box was a silver Ford Capri (scale: 1/36) with opening boot and bonnet, and plastic figurines of Cowley, Bodie and Doyle. There were nine design variations (differing grilles, bumpers and interiors). Deleted in 1982.
Model no: 64 (1980)
The same company issued a miniature set (scale: 1/64), which contained just the silver Capri. There were five design variations. Deleted in 1984.
Model set: 2536 (1980)
This set contained the silver Capri (model 64) and a Rover SD1 Police car in a 'Corgi Junior Twin Pack'. The cars were individually numbered 64B and 64C respectively and were only available until 1981.
The retailer shop display stand for the above items included a specially commissioned photographic session undertaken on the set of *Stopover* on the 26th April 1979.
Model no: 57401 (1999)
A re-issue of the 1/36 scale model. Complete with figurines of Bodie and Doyle.

The Professionals Electric Slot Road Racing Game
(*Ideal Toys*. 1982)
The idea was a variation on the Scalextric racing sets. It included 21-feet of track, a silver Capri, hand controls, trestle supports and a security van.

The Professionals Jigsaw Puzzles
(*Stafford Pemberton*. 1979)
Four 250-piece 17x12-inch different items were issued, with No.1 photographed by the Earl Of Lichfield.
No:1 Cowley, Bodie & Doyle (studio session from series 1)
No:2 Doyle (*Hunter/Hunted*)
No:3 Bodie (*In The Public Interest*)
No:4 Bodie & Doyle (*Man Without A Past*)

In 2004, *Ravensburger* produced a 1000-piece jigsaw puzzle depicting 'Classic TV Of The Seventies' featuring a shot taken from *Hunter/Hunted*.

The Professionals Poster Art Kit
Contained a double-sided 22x14-inch poster and came complete with a set of coloured felt-tipped pens

The Professionals T-Shirt's
Brockum International Ltd (1979)
The company released both a long-sleeved T-Shirt and standard short-sleeved item; endorsed by LWT featuring a montage of photographs of Bodie and Doyle with *The Professionals* logo.
Video Gems (1993)
Launched by the company to promote the release of their videos, the item bore a back-and-white still from *The Purging Of CI5*. Initially planned as 'give-aways' on promotional releases, the company only produced a limited run, before the item was withdrawn due to copyright infringements.
Fastroute (1997)
The first T-Shirt contained the original 'typewriter' CI5 logo, with the second one displaying the later version. Initially a giant-sized poster of the later logo was issued, but due to lack of demand, a limited production run resulted.
Distribution Network Company (1999)
This company produced two items, one bearing the familiar CI5 logo and another depicting a shot of Bodie from *Killer With A Long Arm*.
Granada Commercial Ventures (2003)
The company issued a design depicting Bodie's Capri (UOO 303T) and the silhouette logo, to several high-street stores including Virgin (Fruit Of The Loom) and Asda's clothing brand George.

The Professionals Automatic Pistol
(*Lone Star Products*. 1979)
The company issued four different sets of toy guns. Aimed at 5-10 year olds, the guns had a silencer and holsters. Set 1183 was the small boxed version of Bodie's Browning, 1184 was a carded Browning with shoulder holster, 1185 was a carded gun (Doyle's P38) with extension rifle and silencer, and 1186 was a big boxed version containing the Browning and shoulder holster. All but 1185 had a magazine in the butt of the pistols that came out to put caps in. Each box had a photo taken on the set of *In The Public Interest* and *Stopover*.

PUBLICATIONS

Sphere Books Ltd issued fifteen paperback novels, during the course of the show. 'Ghost-author' Ken Blake adapted each from the original series scripts.

1: **Where The Jungle Ends** (1978)
Episodes featured: *Old Dog With New Tricks, Long Shot, Where The Jungle Ends, Killer With A Long Arm*
2: **Long Shot** (1978)
Episodes featured: *Heroes, Private Madness, Public Danger, The Female Factor, Everest Was Also Conquered.* n.b: *Long Shot* is not included!
3: **Stake Out** (1978)
Episodes featured: *Stake Out, When The Heat Cools Off, Close Quarters*
4: **Hunter/Hunted** (1978)
Episodes featured: *First Night, Hunter/Hunted, The Rack*
5: **Blind Run** (1979)
Episodes featured: *Blind Run, Man Without A Past, In The Public Interest*
6: **Fall Girl** (1979)
Episodes featured: *Fall Girl, Not A Very Civil Civil Servant, A Stirring Of Dust*
7: **A Hiding To Nothing** (1980)
Episodes featured: *Stopover, Runner, A Hiding To Nothing*
8: **Dead Reckoning** (1980)
Episodes featured: *Dead Reckoning, Mixed Doubles, Need To Know*
9: **No Stone** (1981)
Episodes featured: *A Man Called Quinn, No Stone*
10: **Cry Wolf** (1981)
Episodes featured: *Lawson's Last Stand, Cry Wolf*
11: **Spy Probe** (1981)
Episodes featured: *Spy Probe, The Madness Of Mickey Hamilton*
12: **Foxhole** (1982)
Episodes featured: *Foxhole On The Roof, The Ojuka Situation*
13: **The Untouchables** (1982)
Episode featured: *The Untouchables*
14: **Operation Susie** (1982)
Episode featured: *Operation Susie*
15: **You'll Be All Right** (1982)
Episodes featured: *You'll Be All Right, Discovered In A Graveyard*

Seven hardback versions were also released, numbers 1-6 and 15. 1, 2, 5, 6 and 15 were published by *Severn House Books* and adapted by Kenneth Bulmer, while 3 and 4 were issued by *Barker Books* and written by Ken Blake. All adaptations were identical to the paperback versions but the in-house 'phantom' author was renamed for contractual reasons.

Annuals
Between 1978 and 1984 various companies produced seven annuals. They all contained a fair share of articles and hundreds of photographs (The dates

listed are not necessarily the ones printed on the front cover; annuals usually stated the year following publication).

1: published by *Brown Watson* © 1978
2: published by *Grandreams Ltd* © 1979
3: published by *Grandreams Ltd* © 1980
4: published by *Stafford Pemberton* © 1981
5: published by *Stafford Pemberton* © 1982
6: published by *Purnell* / produced *Stafford Pemberton* © 1983
7: published by *Purnell* © 1984

Other annuals also devoted space to *The Professionals*, including *FAB 208, Diana, Eagle, Photo Love, My Guy, Jackie, Oh Boy!* and *TV Detectives.*

Magazines
A number of companies produced magazines/poster magazines devoted to *The Professionals*. All contained hundreds of privately commissioned photographs and interesting articles.

April 1978:	**Super Agent No 1 The Professionals** (published by *Danacell Ltd*)
April 1978:	**FAB 208: Tribute To The Professionals** (published by *IPC Magazines*)
May 1978:	**Super Agent No 2 The Professionals** (published by *Danacell Ltd*)
October 1978:	**FAB 208: A Close Up On The Professionals** (published by *IPC Magazines*)
November 1978:	**Shaw and Collins Are The Professionals** (published by *Danacell Ltd*)
December 1979:	**The Professionals No 1** (magazine) (published by *Walton Press*)
January 1980:	**The Professionals No 2** (magazine) (published by *Walton Press*)
November 1980:	**The Professionals Vol 2 No 1** (published by *Multi Language Publications*)
December 1980:	**The Professionals Vol 2 No 2** (published by *Multi Language Publications*)
January 1981:	**The Professionals Vol 2 No 3** (published by *Multi Language Publications*)
February 1981:	**The Professionals Vol 2 No 4** (published by *Multi Language Publications*)
September 1981:	**The Professionals Vol 3 No 1** (published by *Colonna Press Ltd*)
October 1981:	**The Professionals Vol 3 No 2** (published by *Colonna Press Ltd*)
November 1981:	**The Professionals Vol 3 No 3** (published by *Colonna Press Ltd*)

December 1981:   **The Professionals Vol 3 No 4**
                (published by *Colonna Press Ltd*)
February 1982: **The Professionals Postamag No 1**
                (published by *Colonna Press Ltd*)
March 1982:   **The Professionals Postamag No 2**
                (published by *Colonna Press Ltd*)
November 1982: **TV Super Hits No 4 The Professionals** (postamag)
                (published by *Walkerprint Ltd*)

Who's Who Among The TV Super Sleuths
(*TV Times* Extra. November 1979)
Three features represented *The Professionals*, including an unused Brian Clemens script in which Bodie and Doyle meet for the first time! The story was called *Operation Impossible*

The Complete Professionals
(published by *Macdonald Queen Anne Press*. 1986)
Written by Dave Rogers, this book contained a wealth of photographs and a complete run down on each episode.

Shut It!
(published by *Virgin Books*. 1999)
The book claimed to be 'A Fan's Guide To 70's Cops On The Box' and was split between *The Sweeney* and *The Professionals*. Written by Martin Day and Keith Topping, it offered a tongue-in-cheek insight into both shows.

Other publications also devoted space to *The Professionals* during the course of the show, including *TV Times, Look In, FAB 208, Oh Boy, My Guy, Woman's Realm, Woman's Weekly, Photoplay, Crime Busters, TV Detectives Special, Jackie, The Biker, Blue Jeans, Video Times, Mad, Tops, Patches, Weekend, Titbits, Mates, The Television Crimebusters Omnibus, Suzy,* and *Eagle.*

MISCELLANEOUS PUBLICATIONS

London Weekend Television Fan Club
London Weekend Television began an official fan club based on the series. Headed by Maureen Street, it offered news and information about the show via various newsletters. New members received a Fan Club CI5 Kit containing two large 24x17-inch posters, two colour A4 photos, four badges, four stickers, membership certificate, membership card, bookmark, secret CI5 code card, CI5 carrier bag, and an autographed photo-card. Set up in late 1978, six newsletters were issued: Winter 1978, January 1979, April 1979, Summer 1979 and Winter 1979. The fan club then folded as there was uncertainty regarding the comeback of the series, but members were promised a further newsletter should the series return in 1980.

Professionabelia
To fill the void left by the demise of the LWT fan club, in early 1981, Paula Baldwin, the editor of *The Professionals* magazines, together with photographer Ted Hawes, set up *Professionabelia*. Licensed by LWT they offered fans the opportunity to purchase all the available merchandise (annuals, paperbacks, etc) as well as eight exclusive photographs, a set of foto-stickers and a selection of different key rings. The company folded in late 1983.

The Professionals Colouring Book
(published by *Stafford Pemberton*. 1982)
Two Colouring/Activity books were issued by the company and were mainly drawings copied from photographs.

The Professionals Posters
(published by *Scandecor*. 1978-1981)
Ref: 1058. 1978: Measuring 27x39-inches this poster featured a shot of Martin Shaw and Lewis Collins taken on the set of *Man Without A Past*.
Ref: 2220. 1981: Measuring 27x39-inches this poster featured a shot of Martin Shaw and Lewis Collins during a 1978 studio photo session.

Golden Wonder Crisps cards
(*Golden Wonder*. 1979)
Inside special packets of crisps two cards depicted the stars of the show. They were part of a set of 24 cards titled 'All Stars' and Martin Shaw featured on number 17 and Lewis Collins on number 23.

Postcard Sets
(*London Postcard Company*. 1999)
Two sets were produced containing nine 6 x 4 inch cards. Set 1: GA 2251-GA 2259. Set 2: GA2260-GA GA2268. The company also issued four different bookmarks to accompany on-line orders. Later, a newly produced 'pack' GA15084 was issued containing nine cards. Another set depicted *The New Professionals*, DWT4501-DWT 4509.

(*Strictly Ink Trading Cards*. 2005/2006)
In July 2005 *Strictly Ink Trading Cards* announced a set of cards destined for release at the end on 2005. However, December actually only saw a limited edition preview set of 10 cards. 999 numbered sets were issued at this time, before the full 50 card boxed set, limited to 1999, was due to be released in early 2009.

VIDEOS / DVD

Eight first series episodes were released by *Guild Home Video* from 1981:
1: *The Female Factor, Where The Jungle Ends*
2: *Close Quarters, Heroes*
3: *Old Dog With New Tricks, When The Heat Cools Off*

4: *Killer With A Long Arm, Everest Was Also Conquered*
In the USA, *Transworld Entertainment* issued two videotapes in 1985:
Vol 1: 30001: *The Female Factor, Where The Jungle Ends*
Vol 2: 30002: *Operation Susie, Heroes*

In 1987 *Highlight Video* in Germany issued seven different videos under the German title, *Die Profis*. The episodes were ones that broadcaster ZDF deemed either too violent or not suitable for the German market. They were dubbed in German and used a collective title for each cassette - the English translation is in brackets:
1: 7003: Die Erpressung (The Execution): *Foxhole On The Roof / The Acorn Syndrome* (February 1987)
2: 7004: Die Verfolgung (The Chase): *Where The Jungle Ends / Close Quarters* (March 1987)
3: 7005: Streng Geheim (Top Secret): *Blind Run / Fugitive* (April 1987)
4: 7006: Der Auftrag (The Job): *Mixed Doubles / No Stone* (May 1987)
5: 7007: Im Untergrund (Underground): *The Untouchables / Long Shot* (June 1987)
6: 7008: Doppeltes Spiel (Double Cross): *Kickback / In The Public Interest* (July 1987)
7: 7009: Das Drogensyndikat (Drugs Syndicate): *The Gun / Old Dog With New Tricks* (August 1987)

Video Collection International Ltd issued the next batch of videos in 1988 / 1989:
1: VC 3242: *Klansmen, Stake Out* (1988)
2: VC 3249: *A Man Called Quinn, No Stone* (1988)
3: VC 3303: *Hunter/Hunted, Private Madness, Public Danger* (1989)

From 1992, British company *Sound Image Group* issued the following on their *Video Gems* (later to be renamed *TV Gems*)label:
1: R1505: *Old Dog With New Tricks, The Rack* (1992)
2: R1506: *A Hiding To Nothing, Runner* (1992)
3: R1538: *Foxhole On The Roof, Operation Susie* (1992)
4: R1543: *The Purging Of C 1 5, The Female Factor* (1992)
5: R1550: *Wild Justice, Involvement* (1993)
6: R1604: *Backtrack, Mixed Doubles.* A *W. H Smith* exclusive (WH1604) also contained *The Rack, Old Dog With New Tricks* (1993)
7: R1613: *Discovered In A Graveyard, The Ojuka Situation* (1993)
8: R1622: *Private Madness, Public Danger, Killer With A Long Arm* (1993)
9: R1659: *Heroes, Where The Jungle Ends* (1993)
10: R1661: *Close Quarters, Everest Was Also Conquered.* A Woolworth's exclusive (WR1661) also contained *Klansmen* (1993)
11: R1663: *Stake Out, When The Heat Cools Off* (1993)
12: R1670: *Long Shot, Look After Annie* (1993)
13: R1685: *Hunter/Hunted, First Night* (1993)
14: R1713: *In The Public Interest, Man Without A Past* (1993)
15: R1719: *Rogue, Blind Run* (1994)

16: *A Stirring Of Dust, Not A Very Civil Civil Servant* (not released)
A box set (R1718) containing seven episodes was also released.

In 1995 *Pyramid Home Entertainment,* under license from *SIG Video Gems,* released a limited run of budget tapes containing one episode per tape:
1: PY2021: *Foxhole On The Roof*
2: PY2022: *Operation Susie*
3: PY2023: *The Purging Of C I 5*
4: PY2024: *The Female Factor*
5: PY2025: *Involvement*
6: PY2026: *Wild Justice*

In 1997 *Contender Entertainment Limited,* under the *Kult TV* label, acquired the rights to the series and proceeded to release all 57 episodes:
Issue 1:
Vol: 1: KLT 1000: *When The Heat Cools Off, The Female Factor*
Vol 2: KLT 10002: *Old Dog With New Tricks, Klansmen*
Vol 3: KLT 10003: *Heroes, Dead Reckoning*
Vol 4: KLT 10004: *Close Quarters, Man Without A Past*
Vol 5: KLT 10005: *Hunter/Hunted, Stake Out*
Vol 6: KLT 10006: *The Rack, The Female Factor*
Vol 7: KLT 10007: *The Madness Of Mickey Hamilton, Rogue*
Vol 8: KLT 10008: *Everest Was Also Conquered, Blind Run*
Each video had the London Postcard Company's set of postcards numbers 1-8. Volume 1 contained a promo music CD. Volume 5 contained a cut version of *Hunter/Hunted.* Also released as two box sets of four tapes.
Issue 2:
Vol 1: KLT 10009: *Private Madness, Public Danger, First Night, A Stirring Of Dust*
Vol 2: KLT 10010: *Where The Jungle Ends, In The Public Interest, Not A Very Civil Civil Servant*
Vol 3: KLT 10011: *Killer With A Long Arm, Servant Of Two Masters, A Hiding To Nothing*
Vol 4: KLT 10012: *Look After Annie, Backtrack, Stopover*
Vol 5: KLT 10013: *The Purging Of C I 5, Hijack, Blood Sports*
Vol 6: KLT 10014: *Wild Justice, Need To Know, You'll Be All Right*
Vol 7: KLT 10015: *Runner, Mixed Doubles, Kickback*
Vol 8: KLT 10016: *The Untouchables, Involvement, Take Away*
Also released as two box sets of four tapes.
Issue 3:
Vol 1: KLT 10018: *Discovered In A Graveyard, Long Shot, The Gun, Fugitive*
Vol 2: KLT 10019: *The Ojuka Situation, Black Out, Cry Wolf, No Stone*
Vol 3: KLT 10020: *Foxhole On The Roof, The Acorn Syndrome, Lawson's Last Stand, Hunter/Hunted*
Vol 4: KLT 10021: *Operation Susie, Slush Fund, A Man Called Quinn*
Vol 5: KLT 10022: *Weekend In The Country, It's Only A Beautiful Picture..., Spy Probe*

In 2002 the same company then proceeded to release four box sets on DVD (1: 10th June, 2: 5th August, 3: 9th September and 4: 30th December). Box set 1 included a free car sticker and a *W. H Smith* exclusive contained four postcards (GA2251, GA2254, GA2254 and GA2259) from the set issued by the *London Postcard Company*. Box set 2 contained two postcards (GA2253 and GA2256) from the same company's set of cards (initially through *MVC* stores only). Box set 3 was offered in *W H Smith* with two specially commissioned postcards. All the box sets contained an exclusively produced booklet.

An exclusive deal was struck up with *Britannia Music & Video Club*, for sixteen split discs in newly designed separate cases. However, Volume 3, despite being correct on the sleeve and the disc cover (*Close Quarters, Look After Annie, When The Heat Cools Off* and *Stake Out*) actually played the episodes from Volume 2 (*Heroes, Private Madness, Public Danger, The Female Factor* and *Everest Was Also Conquered*). Volume 4 displayed the correct front cover of *Klansmen* and *Rogue*, but the back sleeve displayed the title *Close Quarters* with the *Klansmen* synopsis. The error was further compounded when the disc actually played the stories *Stopover* and *Runner*. Both volumes were also issued in their correct form.

In October 2004 *Marks & Spencer*, in conjunction with *Contender*, produced an exclusive two-disc set containing the first eight episodes.

In recognition of the shows success on DVD, *Contender* proceeded to re-issue the four box sets in a redesigned package in 2005. Set 1 was released on 26th September, and was followed by Set 2 on 24th October, Set 3 on 26th December, and Set 4 on 13th February 2006.
(T21-7527-4095D).

Australian Reel Entertainment released the following 'unofficial' single episode videos:

1: *Close Quarters*	100496
2: *Everest Was Also Conquered*	100497
3: *When The Heat Cools Off*	100498
4: *Long Shot*	100499
5: *Look After Annie*	100500
6: *First Night*	100501
7: *Rogue*	100502
8: *Backtrack*	100503
9: *A Hiding To Nothing*	100504
10: *Involvement*	100505

In Japan, *Suncrown* released seven first series videos, complete with Japanese subtitles and the original opening title sequence:
Vol 1: 74CH-4009: *Private Madness, Public Danger*
Vol 2: 74CH-4010: *Killer With A Long Arm*
Vol 3: 48CH-3096: *Old Dog With New Tricks, The Female Factor*

Vol 4: 48CH-3097: *Heroes, Where The Jungle Ends*
Vol 5: 48CH-3142: *Look After Annie, Everest Was Also Conquered*
Vol 6: 48CH-3143: *Close Quarters, Long Shot*
Vol 7: 48CH-3148: *When The Heat Cools Off, Stake Out*

Stingray DVD in Japan released a compilation box set on November 11th 2005. Disc 1: *Blind Run, The Purging Of CI5*. Disc 2: *Mixed Doubles, Servant Of Two Masters, Kickback*. Disc 3: *Foxhole On The Roof, The Untouchables, Private Madness, Public Danger*. Disc 4: *Heroes, Close Quarters, Cry Wolf*.
Special Features included the opening title sequence (assault-course version); a rare Japanese preview (10 episodes); DVD Advert (60 seconds) and the Commercial break sign. A 16-page booklet was also included.

Ultimate DVD Magazine also carried a free promo DVD containing the episode *Where The Jungle Ends*. It was produced in conjunction with Contender Entertainment to promote their DVD releases.

RECORDS

TV Themes
(*Weekend Records*. DJM 22081. 1978)
Contains a version of the theme by the Laurie Holloway orchestra. The middle section uses the incidental music that accompanies the car chase from *Hunter/Hunted*.

Music From The Avengers, The New Avengers, The Professionals
(*Unicorn-Kanchana*. KPM 7009. 1980)
Composed by Laurie Johnson, this album contains the main title themes from all three series, plus twelve other pieces of incidental music from the series. A 7" single version was released in a full colour sleeve
(*Unicorn-Kanchana CI5*. 1980)
The same album was released in the US as Original Television Scores: *The Avengers, The New Avengers, The Professionals*
(*Starlog / Varese Sarabande*. ASV 95003)
A CD version of the album was due for release in 1988 (*Varese Sarabande*. VCD 47270), but due to contractual problems the project was shelved.

Out Of The Box / Pacific Strip
(*Polydor*. POSP 356. 1981)
Performed by The Wright Orchestra, this single contains a burst of the theme in a medley that includes *The New Avengers, Hart To Hart* and *CHiPs*.

Lewis Collins:
When You Come Home Again / Take It Out On Time.
(*Sour Grape*. SG111. 1982)
The single was released on 24th September 1982. Poor distribution and sales shelved the scheduled follow-up record and album.

Martin Shaw:
Cross My Heart And Hope To Die / I'll Come Alone
(*Nouveau Music*. NMS 4. 1984)
Both songs were written by Shirlie Roden and produced by Jon Miller. Published by D'Arc Music. Recorded at Redan Studios. The single included a free poster.

A Is For Action
(*Music For Pleasure / EMI*. LP: MFP 5705-1; Cassette: 41 5705-4. 1985)
Performed by The Power Pack Orchestra

ITV Themes
(*Pickwick International*. LP:SHM3247; CD:PWKS 516; Cassette: HSC 3247. 1988)
Performed by Stanley Black and the London Symphony Orchestra.

Favourite TV Themes
(*Music Club*. MCCD 069. 1992)
Performed by The South Bank Studio Orchestra. It does contain the middle sequence that is on the original sheet score for the TV theme, instantly recognisable as the car chase incidental music from *Hunter/Hunted*.

The Rose And The Gun
(*Fly Records / Unicorn-Kanchana*. FLY CD103. 1992).
A new version of the theme (later heard on the Nissan TV ad) recorded by the London Studio Symphony Orchestra.

Best Of The TV Detectives
(*Soundtrack Music Records*. 7243 8 3149827. 1994)
A version of the theme by Chris Cozens.

The A To Z Of British TV Themes: Volume 1
(*Play It Again*. PLAY 010. 1996)
Despite claiming to have 'original versions', this theme is the same version as used on Favourite TV Themes by the South Bank Studio Orchestra.

This Is The Return Of Cult Fiction
(*Circa Records Ltd - Virgin Records Ltd*. VTCD 112 7243 8 421662 7. 1996)
Features the version of the theme from The Rose And The Gun.

Laurie Johnson's Big Band: Volume 2
(*Horatio Nelson Records*. CDSIV 6160. 1996)
A newly recorded version arranged by Laurie Johnson.

Theme From The Professionals
(*Virgin*. VSCDT 1643. 1997)
Mix's from Blue Boy, Galdez Ambrose, and Alexia, who performs a version with lyrics.

Cult TV Themes From The Seventies
(*Future Legend Records Ltd.* FLEG 8 CD. 1997)
Performed by a little-known band called Earthling Scum.

The Professional - The Best Of Laurie Johnson
(*Redial-Polygram.* CD 557 210-2. 2001)
A compilation from the composer's history in music.